Ian Watson is a veteran SF author. He co-edited *Changes: Stories of Metamorphosis* with Michael Bishop, and *Afterlives: Stories about Life after Death* with Pamela Sargent.

Ian Whates is a rising SF author who founded NewCon Press in 2006 to publish the original anthologies *TimePieces*, *disLOCATIONS* and, more recently, the all-women anthology *Myth-Understandings*, and also *Celebration*, a collection to commemorate the 50th anniversary of the British Science Fiction Association, of which he is Development Director as well as editor of its on-line news and reviews magazine *Matrix*.

Also available

The Mammoth Book of 20th Century Science Fiction
The Mammoth Book of Best British Mysteries
The Mammoth Book of Best Horror Comics
The Mammoth Book of Best of Best New SF
The Mammoth Book of Best New Manga 3
The Mammoth Book of Best New SF 22
The Mammoth Book of Best War Comics
The Mammoth Book of Bikers
The Mammoth Book of Boys' Own Stuff
The Mammoth Book of Brain Workouts
The Mammoth Book of Celebrity Murders
The Mammoth Book of Comic Fantasy
The Mammoth Book of Comic Quotes
The Mammoth Book of Cover-Ups
The Mammoth Book of CSI
The Mammoth Book of the Deep
The Mammoth Book of Dickensian Whodunnits
The Mammoth Book of Dirty, Sick, X-Rated & Politically Incorrect Jokes
The Mammoth Book of Egyptian Whodunnits
The Mammoth Book of Extreme Fantasy
The Mammoth Book of Funniest Cartoons of All Time
The Mammoth Book of Hard Men
The Mammoth Book of Historical Whodunnits
The Mammoth Book of Illustrated True Crime
The Mammoth Book of Inside the Elite Forces
The Mammoth Book of Jack the Ripper
The Mammoth Book of Jacobean Whodunnits
The Mammoth Book of Killers at Large
The Mammoth Book of King Arthur
The Mammoth Book of Maneaters
The Mammoth Book of Modern Battles
The Mammoth Book of Modern Ghost Stories
The Mammoth Book of Monsters
The Mammoth Book of Mountain Disasters
The Mammoth Book of New Terror
The Mammoth Book of On the Edge
The Mammoth Book of On the Road
The Mammoth Book of Pirates
The Mammoth Book of Poker
The Mammoth Book of Prophecies
The Mammoth Book of Roaring Twenties Whodunnits
The Mammoth Book of Sex, Drugs and Rock 'N' Roll
The Mammoth Book of Short Spy Novels
The Mammoth Book of Sorcerers' Tales
The Mammoth Book of The Beatles
The Mammoth Book of The Mafia
The Mammoth Book of True Crime
The Mammoth Book of True War Stories
The Mammoth Book of Unsolved Crimes
The Mammoth Book of Vampire Romance
The Mammoth Book of Vintage Whodunnits

THE MAMMOTH BOOK OF

ALTERNATE HISTORIES

Edited by
IAN WATSON and IAN WHATES

ROBINSON

RUNNING PRESS
PHILADELPHIA · LONDON

Constable & Robinson Ltd
3 The Lanchesters
162 Fulham Palace Road
London W6 9ER
www.constablerobinson.com

First published in the UK by Robinson,
an imprint of Constable & Robinson, 2010

A copy of the British Library Cataloguing in Publication Data
is available from the British Library

UK ISBN 978-1-84529-779-4

1 3 5 7 9 10 8 6 4 2

First published in the United States in 2010 by
Running Press Book Publishers.

9 8 7 6 5 4 3 2 1

Digit on the right indicates the number of this printing

US Library of Congress number: 2009929931
US ISBN 978-0-7624-3842-6

Running Press Book Publishers
2300 Chestnut Street
Philadelphia, PA 19103-4371

Visit us on the web!
www.runningpress.com

Printed and bound in the EU

Contents

Acknowledgments

Introduction

"There is an infinitude of Pasts, all equally valid," wrote André Maurois, the French novelist and biographer. "At each and every instant of Time, however brief you suppose it, the line of events forks like the stem of a tree putting forth twin branches." This is quoted in *Virtual History: Alternatives and Counterfactuals*, edited by historian and political commentator Niall Ferguson. These days alternative history is almost respectable amongst historians, leading to such other recent well-received volumes of essays as Robert Cowley's *What If? Military Historians Imagine What Might Have Been* or Andrew Roberts' *What Might Have Been: Leading Historians on Twelve "What Ifs" of History*. Some other historians frown at counterfactuality; although, if the "Many Worlds" interpretation of Quantum Physics is correct, all possible alternatives might indeed occur in a branching multiverse. What's more, was our own world's history in any sense inevitable, or even highly plausible, simply because it actually happened? Who, for instance, in 1975 might have imagined that a few years later a female British prime minister would be sending a nuclear-armed armada all the way to the South Atlantic in a quarrel about some remote islands full of sheep? Who could have supposed that British counter-terrorism laws, provoked by planes flying into the World Trade Center, would be used for the first time bizarrely to seize the assets of a mild-mannered Icelandic bank, on account of mortgages stupidly sold to poor house buyers in the United States?

Essays about What Might Have Been are already fascinating, but it has long been a delight of science fiction writers to put flesh upon the bones. Consequently, here you'll find what might have happened if the Roman Empire had never declined and fallen; how Islam might have triumphed much more widely; how the Native American Indians might have repelled the European invasion; how the other Indians, of India, might have forged an empire in place of the British Empire; how the civilized Chinese might already have been ensconced in California when the uncouth Europeans first arrived there; how the Pope might *really* have offended King Alfred of the burnt cakes; and much much more that has surely happened else-where (or elsewhen) in alternity, even if it didn't happen quite that way in our version of reality. You'll find award-winning classics of the sub-genre nestling alongside equally worthy nuggets that might previously have escaped your notice and more recent gems, including three splendid, brand-new stories by special invitees James Morrow, Stephen Baxter and Ken MacLeod. These feature the alternative truth about the *Titanic*, the trial for heresy of Darwin's bones along with one of his descendants, and a near-future Scotland that begins as far south as London.

                                        Ian Watson and Ian Whates

The Raft of the Titanic

James Morrow

15 April 1912
Lat. 40°25′ N, Long. 51°18′ W

The sea is calm tonight. Where does that come from? Some Oxbridge swot's poem, I think, one of those cryptic things I had to read in tenth form – but the title hasn't stayed with me, and neither has the scribbler's name. If you want a solid education in English letters, arrange to get born elsewhere than Walton-on-the-Hill. "The sea is calm tonight." I must ask our onboard *littérateur*, Mr Futrelle of Massachusetts. He will know.

We should have been picked up – what? – fourteen hours ago. Certainly no more than sixteen. Our Marconi men, Phillips and Bride, assure me that Captain Rostron of the *Carpathia* acknowledged the *Titanic*'s CQD promptly, adding, "We are coming as quickly as possible and expect to be there within four hours." Since the Ship of Dreams sailed into the Valley of Death, sometime around 2.20 this morning, we have drifted perhaps fifteen miles to the south-west. Surely Rostron can infer our present position. So where the bloody hell is he?

Now darkness is upon us once again. The mercury is falling. I scan the encircling horizon for the *Carpathia*'s lights, but I see only a cold black sky sown with a million apathetic stars. In a minute I shall order Mr Lightoller to launch the last of our distress rockets, even as I ask Reverend Bateman to send up his next emergency prayer.

For better or worse, Captain Smith insisted on doing the honourable thing and going down with his ship. (That is, he insisted on doing the honourable thing and shooting himself, thereby guaranteeing that his remains would go down with his ship.) His gesture has left me *en passant* in command of the present contraption. I suppose I should be grateful. At long last I have a ship of my own, if you can call this jerry-built, jury-rigged raft a ship. Have the other castaways accepted me as their guardian and keeper? I can't say for sure. Shortly after dawn tomorrow, I shall address the entire company, clarifying that I am legally in charge and have a scheme for our deliverance, though that second assertion will require of the truth a certain elasticity, as a scheme for our deliverance has not yet visited my imagination.

I count it a bloody miracle that we got so many souls safely off the foundering liner. The Lord and all His angels were surely watching over us. So far we have accumulated only nineteen corpses: a dozen deaths during the transfer operation – shock, heart attacks, misadventure – and then another seven, shortly after sunrise, from hypothermia and exposure. Grim statistics, to be sure, but far better than the thousand or so fatalities that would have occurred had we not embraced Mr Andrews' audacious plan.

Foremost amongst my immediate obligations is to start keeping a record of our tribulations. So here I sit, pen in one hand, electric torch in the other. By maintaining a sort of captain's log, I might actually start to feel like a captain, though at the moment I feel like plain old Henry Tingle Wilde, the Scouser who never got out of Liverpool. The sea is calm tonight.

16 April 1912
Lat. 39°19′ N, Long. 51°40′ W

When I told the assembled company that, by every known maritime code, I am well and truly the supreme commander of this vessel, a strident voice rose in protest: Vasil Plotcharsky from steerage, who called me "a bourgeois lackey in thrall to that imperialist monstrosity known as White Star Line." (I'll have to keep an eye on Plotcharsky. I wonder how many other Bolsheviks the *Titanic* carried?) But on the whole my speech was well received. Hearing that I'd christened our raft the *Ada*, "after my late wife, who died tragically two years ago", my audience responded with respectful silence, then Father Byles piped up and said, so all could hear, "Right now that dear woman is looking down from heaven, exhorting us not to lose faith."

My policy concerning the nineteen bodies in the stern proved more controversial. A contingent of first-cabin survivors led by Colonel Astor insisted that we give them "an immediate Christian burial at sea", whereupon my first officer explained to the aristocrats that the corpses may ultimately have "their part to play in this drama". Mr Lightoller's prediction occasioned horrified gasps and indignant snorts, but nobody moved to push these frigid assets overboard.

This afternoon I ordered a complete inventory, a good way to keep our company busy. Before floating away from the disaster site, we salvaged about a third of the buoyant containers Mr Latimer's stewards had tossed into the sea: wine casks, beer barrels, cheese crates, bread boxes, foot-lockers, duffel bags, toilet kits. Had there been a moon on Sunday night, we might have recovered this jetsam *in toto*. Of course, had there been a moon, we might not have hit the iceberg in the first place.

The tally is heartening. Assuming that frugality rules aboard the *Ada* – and it will, so help me God – she probably has enough food and water to sustain her population, all 2,187 of us, for at least ten days. We have two functioning compasses, three brass sextants, four thermometers, one barometer, one anemometer, fishing tackle, sewing supplies, baling wire, and twenty tarpaulins, not to mention the wood-fuelled Franklin stove Mr Lightoller managed to knock together from odd bits of metal.

Yesterday's attempt to rig a sail was a fiasco, but this afternoon we had better luck, improvising a gracefully curving thirty-foot mast from the banister of the grand staircase, then fitting it with a patchwork of velvet curtains, throw rugs, signal flags, men's dinner jackets, and ladies' skirts. My mind is clear, my strategy is certain, my course is set. We shall tack towards warmer waters, lest we lose more souls to the demonic cold. If I never see another ice floe or North Atlantic growler in my life, it will be too soon.

18 April 1912
Lat. 37°11′ N, Long. 52°11′ W

Whilst everything is still vivid in my mind, I must set down the story of how the *Ada* came into being, starting with the collision. I felt the tremor about 11.40 p.m., and by midnight Mr Lightoller was in my cabin, telling me that the berg had sliced through at least five adjacent watertight compartments, possibly six. To the best of his knowledge, the ship was in the last extremity, fated to go down at the head in a matter of hours.

After assigning Mr Moody to the bridge – one might as well put a sixth officer in charge, since the worst had already happened – Captain Smith sent word that the rest of us should gather post-haste in the chartroom. By the time I arrived, at perhaps five minutes past midnight, Mr Andrews, who'd designed the *Titanic*, was already seated at the table, along with Mr Bell, the chief engineer, Mr Hutchinson, the ship's carpenter, and Dr O'Loughlin, our surgeon. Taking my place beside Mr Murdoch, who had not yet reconciled himself to the fact that my last-minute posting as chief officer had bumped him down to first mate, I immediately apprehended that the ship was lost, so palpable was Captain Smith's anxiety.

"Even as we speak, Phillips and Bride are on the job in the wireless shack, trying to raise the *Californian*, which can't be more than an hour away," the Old Man said. "I am sorry to report that her Marconi operator has evidently shut off his rig for the night. However, we have every reason to believe that

Captain Rostron of the *Carpathia* will be here within four hours. If this were the tropics, we would simply put the entire company in life-belts, lower them over the side, and let them bob about waiting to be rescued. But this is the North Atlantic, and the water is twenty-eight degrees Fahrenheit."

"After a brief interval in that ghastly gazpacho, the average mortal will succumb to hypothermia," said Mr Murdoch, who liked to lord it over us Scousers with fancy words such as *succumb* and *gazpacho*. "Am I correct, Dr O'Loughlin?"

"A castaway who remains motionless in the water risks dying immediately of cardiac arrest," the surgeon replied, nodding. "Alas, even the most robust athlete won't generate enough body heat to prevent his core temperature from plunging. Keep swimming, and you might last twenty minutes, probably no more than thirty."

"Now I shall tell you the good news," the Old Man said. "Mr Andrews has a plan, bold but feasible. Listen closely. Time is of the essence. The *Titanic* has at best one hundred and fifty minutes to live."

"The solution to this crisis is not to fill the life-boats to capacity and send them off in hopes of encountering the *Carpathia*, for that would leave over a thousand people stranded on a sinking ship," Mr Andrews insisted. "The solution, rather, is to keep every last soul out of the water until Captain Rostron arrives."

"Mr Andrews has stated the central truth of our predicament," Captain Smith said. "On this terrible night our enemy is not the ocean depths, for owing to the life-belts no one – or almost no one – will drown. Nor is the local fauna our enemy, for sharks and rays rarely visit the middle of the North Atlantic in early spring. No, our enemy tonight is the temperature of the water, pure and simple, full stop."

"And how do you propose to obviate that implacable fact?" Mr Murdoch inquired. The next time he used the word *obviate*, I intended to sock him in the chops.

"We're going to build an immense platform," said Mr Andrews, unfurling a sheet of drafting paper on which he'd hastily sketched an object labelled *Raft of the Titanic*. He secured the blueprint with ashtrays and, leaning across the table, squeezed the chief engineer's knotted shoulder. "I designed it in collaboration with the estimable Mr Bell" – he flashed our carpenter an amiable wink – "and the capable Mr Hutchinson."

"Instead of loading anyone into our fourteen standard thirty-foot life-boats, we shall set aside one dozen, leave their tarps in place, and treat them as pontoons," Mr Bell said. "From an engineering perspective, this is a viable scheme, for each life-boat is outfitted with copper buoyancy tanks."

Mr Andrews set his open palms atop the blueprint, his eyes dancing with a peculiar fusion of desperation and ecstasy. "We shall deploy the twelve pontoons in a three-by-four grid, each linked to its neighbours via horizontal stanchions spliced together from available wood. Our masts are useless – mostly steel – but we're hauling tons of oak, teak, mahogany and spruce."

"With any luck, we can affix a twenty-five-foot stanchion between the stern of pontoon A and the bow of pontoon B," Mr Hutchinson said, "another such bridge between the amidships oarlock of A and the amidships oarlock of E, another between the stern of B and the bow of C, and so on."

"Next we'll cover the entire matrix with jettisoned lumber, securing the planks with nails and rope," Mr Bell said. "The resulting raft will measure roughly one hundred feet by two hundred, which technically allows each of our two thousand plus souls almost nine square feet, though in reality everyone will have to share accommodations with foodstuffs, water casks, and survival gear, not to mention the dogs."

"As you've doubtless noticed," Mr Andrews said, "at this moment the North Atlantic is smooth as glass, a circumstance that contributed to our predicament – no wave broke against the iceberg, so the lookouts spotted the bloody thing too late. I am proposing that we now turn this same placid sea to our advantage. My machine could never be assembled in high swells, but tonight we're working under conditions only slightly less ideal than those that obtain back at the Harland and Wolff shipyard."

Captain Smith's moustache and beard parted company, a

great gulping inhalation, whereupon he delivered what was surely the most momentous speech of his career.

"Step one is for Mr Wilde and Mr Lightoller to muster the deck crew and have them launch all fourteen standard life-boats – forget the collapsibles and the cutters – each craft to be rowed by two able-bodied seamen assisted where feasible by a quartermaster, boatswain, lookout, or master-at-arms. Through this operation we get our twelve pontoons in the water, along with two roving assembly craft. The AB's will forthwith moor the pontoons to the *Titanic*'s hull using davit ropes, keeping the lines in place until the raft is finished or the ship sinks, whichever comes first. Understood?"

I nodded in assent, as did Mr Lightoller, even though I'd never heard a more demented idea in my life. Next the Old Man waved a scrap of paper at Mr Murdoch, the overeducated genius whose navigational brilliance had torn a three-hundred-foot gash in our hull.

"A list from Purser McElroy identifying twenty carpenters, joiners, fitters, bricklayers, and blacksmiths – nine from the second-cabin decks, eleven from steerage," Captain Smith explained. "Your job is to muster these skilled workers on the boat deck, each man equipped with a mallet and nails from either his own baggage or Mr Hutchinson's shop. For those who don't speak English, get Father Montvila and Father Peruschitz to act as interpreters. Lower the workers to the construction site using the electric cranes. Mr Andrews and Mr Hutchinson will be building the machine on the leeward side."

The Old Man rose and, shuffling to the far end of the table, rested an avuncular hand on his third officer's epaulet.

"Mr Pitman, I am charging you with provisioning the raft. You will work with Mr Latimer in organizing his three hundred stewards into a special detail. Have them scour the ship for every commodity a man might need were he to find himself stranded in the middle of the North Atlantic: water, wine, beer, cheese, meat, bread, coal, tools, sextants, compasses, small arms. The stewards will load these items into buoyant coffers, setting them afloat near the construction site for later retrieval."

Captain Smith continued to circumnavigate the table, pausing to clasp the shoulders of his fourth and fifth officers.

"Mr Boxhall and Mr Lowe, you will organize two teams of second-cabin volunteers, supplying each man with an appropriate wrecking or cutting implement. There are at least twenty emergency fire-axes mounted in the companionways. You should also grab all the saws and sledges from the shop, plus hatchets, knives and cleavers from the galleys. Team A, under Mr Boxhall, will chop down every last column, pillar, post and beam for the stanchions, tossing them to the construction crew, along with every bit of rope they can find, yards and yards of it, wire rope, Manila hemp, clothesline, whatever you can steal from the winches, cranes, ladders, bells, laundry rooms and children's swings. Meanwhile, Team B, commanded by Mr Lowe, will lay hold of twenty thousand square feet of planking for the platform of the raft. Towards this end, Mr Lowe's volunteers will pillage the promenade decks, dismantle the grand staircase, ravage the panels, and gather together every last door, table and piano lid on board."

Captain Smith resumed his circuit, stopping behind the chief engineer.

"Mr Bell, your assignment is at once the simplest and the most difficult. For as long as humanly possible, you will keep the steam flowing and the turbines spinning, so our crew and passengers will enjoy heat and electricity whilst assembling Mr Andrews's ark. Any questions, gentlemen?"

We had dozens of questions, of course, such as, "Have you taken leave of your senses, Captain?" and "Why the bloody hell did you drive us through an ice-field at twenty-two knots?" and "What makes you imagine we can build this preposterous device in only two hours?" But these mysteries were irrelevant to the present crisis, so we kept silent, fired off crisp salutes and set about our duties.

19 April 1912
Lat. 36°18′ N, Long. 52°48′ W

Still no sign of the *Carpathia*, but the mast holds true, the spar remains strong and the sail stays fat. Somehow, through no particular virtue of my own, I've managed to get us out of iceberg country. The mercury hovers a full five degrees above freezing.

Yesterday Colonel Astor and Mr Guggenheim convinced Mr Andrews to relocate the Franklin stove from amidships to the forward section. Right now our first-cabin castaways are toasty enough, though by this time tomorrow our coal supply will be exhausted. That said, I'm reasonably confident we'll see no more deaths from hypothermia, not even in steerage. Optimism prevails aboard the *Ada*. A cautious optimism, to be sure, optimism guarded by Cerberus himself and a cherub with a flaming sword, but optimism all the same.

I was right about Mr Futrelle knowing the source of "The sea is calm tonight." It's from "Dover Beach" by Matthew Arnold. Futrelle has the whole thing memorized. Lord, what a depressing poem. "For the world, which seems to lie before us like a land of dreams, so various, so beautiful, so new, hath really neither joy, nor love, nor light, nor certitude, nor peace, nor help for pain." Tomorrow I may issue an order banning public poetry recitations aboard the *Ada*.

When the great ship *Titanic* went down, the world was neither various and beautiful, nor joyless and violent, but merely very busy. By forty minutes after midnight, against all odds, the twelve pontoons were in the water and lashed to the davits. Mr Boxhall's second-cabin volunteers forthwith delivered the first load of stanchions, even as Mr Lowe's group supplied the initial batch of decking material. For the next eighty minutes, the frigid air rang with the din of pounding hammers, the clang of furious axes, the whine of frantic saws and the squeal of ropes locking planks to pontoons, the whole mad chorus interspersed with the rhythmic thumps of lumber being lowered to the construction team, the steady splash, splash, splash of provisions going into the sea, and shouts affirming the logic of our labours: "Stay out of the drink!" "Only the cold can kill us!" "Twenty-eight degrees!" "*Carpathia* is on the way!" It was all very British, though occasionally the Americans pitched in, and the emigrants proved reasonably diligent as well. I must admit, I can't imagine any but the English-speaking races constructing and equipping the *Ada* so efficiently. Possibly the Germans, an admirable people, though I fear their war-mongering Kaiser.

By 2.00 a.m. Captain Smith had successfully shot himself, three-fifths of the platform was nailed down, and the *Titanic*'s bridge lay beneath thirty feet of icy water. The stricken liner listed horribly, nearly forty degrees, stern in the air, her triple screws, glazed with ice, lying naked against the vault of heaven. For my command post I'd selected the mesh of guylines securing the dummy funnel, a vantage from which I now beheld a great mass of humanity jammed together on the boat deck: aristocrats, second-cabin passengers, emigrants, officers, engineers, trimmers, stokers, greasers, stewards, stewardesses, musicians, barbers, chefs, cooks, bakers, waiters and scullions, the majority dressed in lifebelts and the warmest clothing they could find. Each frightened man, woman and child held onto the rails and davits for dear life. The sea spilled over the tilted gunwales and rushed across the canted boards.

"The raft!" I screamed from my lofty promontory. "Hurry! Swim!" Soon the other officers – Murdoch, Lightoller, Pitman, Boxhall, Lowe, Moody – took up the cry. "The raft! Hurry! Swim!" "The raft! Hurry! Swim!" "The raft! Hurry! Swim!"

And so they swam for it, or, rather, they splashed, thrashed, pounded, wheeled, kicked and paddled for it. Even the hundreds who spoke no English understood what was required. Heaven be praised, within twelve minutes our entire company managed to migrate from the flooded deck of the *Titanic* to the sanctuary of Mr Andrews's machine. Our stalwart ABs pulled scores of women and children from the water, plus many elderly castaways, along with Colonel Astor's Airedale, Mr Harper's Pekingese, Mr Daniel's French bulldog and six other canines. I was the last to come aboard. Glancing around, I saw to my great distress that a dozen lifebelted bodies were not moving, the majority doubtless heart-attack victims, though perhaps a few people had got crushed against the davits or trampled under-foot.

The survivors instinctively sorted themselves by station, with the emigrants gathering at the stern, the second-cabin castaways settling amidships, and our first-cabin passengers assuming their rightful places forward. After cutting the mooring lines, the ABs took up the lifeboat oars and began to stroke furiously. By the grace of Dame Fortune and the hand of Divine Providence, the *Ada* rode free of the wreck, so that when the great steamer finally snapped, breaking in two abaft the engine room, and began her vertical voyage to the bottom, we observed the whole appalling spectacle from a safe distance.

22 April 1912
Lat. 33°42′ N, Long. 53°11′ W

We've been at sea a full week now. No *Carpathia* on the horizon yet, no *Californian*, no *Olympia*, no *Baltic*. Our communal mood is grim but not despondent. Mr Hartley's little band helps. I've forbidden them to play hymns, airs, ballads or any other wistful tunes. "It's waltzes and rags or nothing," I tell him. Thanks to Wallace Hartley's strings and Scott Joplin's syncopations, we may survive this ordeal.

Although no one is hungry at the moment, I worry about our eventual nutritional needs. The supplies of beef, poultry and cheese hurled overboard by the stewards will soon be exhausted, and thus far our efforts to harvest the sea have come to nothing. The spectre of thirst likewise looms. True, we still have six wine-casks in the first-cabin section, plus four amid-ships and three in steerage, and we've also deployed scores of pots, pans, pails, kettles, washtubs and tierces all over the platform. But what if the rains come too late?

Our sail is unwieldy, the wind contrary, the current fickle, and yet we're managing, slowly, ever so slowly, to beat our way towards the thirtieth parallel. The climate has grown bearable – perhaps forty-five degrees by day, forty by night – but it's still too cold, especially for the children and the elderly. Mr Lightoller's Franklin stove has proven a boon for those of us in the bow, and our second-cabin passengers have managed to build and sustain a small fire amidships, but our emigrants enjoy no such comforts. They huddle miserably aft, warming each other as best they can. We must get farther south. My kingdom for a horse latitude.

The meat in steerage has thawed, though it evidently remains fresh, an effect of the cold air and the omnipresent brine. I shall soon be obligated to issue a difficult order. "Our choices are clear," I'll tell the *Ada*'s company, "fortitude or refinement, nourishment or nicety, survival or finesse – and in each instance I've opted for the former." Messrs Lightoller, Pitman, Boxhall, Lowe and Moody share my sentiments. The only dissenter is Murdoch. My chief officer is useless to me. I would rather be sharing the bridge with our Bolshevik, Plotcharsky, than that fusty Scotsman.

In my opinion an intraspecies diet need not automatically entail depravity. Ethical difficulties arise only when such cuisine is practiced in bad faith. During my one and only visit to the Louvre, I became transfixed by Théodore Géricault's *Scène de naufrage* "Scene of a Shipwreck", that gruesome panorama of life aboard the notorious raft by which the refugees from the stranded freighter *Medusa* sought to save themselves. As Monsieur Géricault so vividly reveals, the players in that disaster were, almost to a man, paragons of bad faith. They ignored their leaders with insouciance, betrayed their fellows with relish and ate one another with alacrity. I am resolved that no such chaos will descend upon the *Ada*. We are not orgiasts. We are not beasts. We are not French.

4 May 1912
Lat. 29°55´ N, Long. 54°12´ W

At last, after nineteen days afloat, the *Ada* has crossed the thirtieth parallel. We are underfed and dehydrated but in generally good spirits. Most of the raft's company has settled into a routine, passing their hours fishing, stargazing, card-playing, cataloguing provisions, bartering for beer and cigars, playing with the dogs, minding the children, teaching each other their native languages, repairing the hastily assembled platform and siphoning seawater from the pontoons (to stabilize the raft, not to drink, God knows). Each morning Dr O'Loughlin brings me a report. Our infirmary – the area directly above pontoon K – is presently full: five cases of chronic *mal de mer*, three of frostbite, two of flux, and four "fevers of unknown origin".

Because the *Ada* remains so difficult to navigate, even with our newly installed wheelhouse and rudder, it would be foolish to try tacking towards the North American mainland in hopes of hitting some hospitable Florida beach. We cannot risk getting caught in the Gulf Stream and dragged back north into frigid waters. Instead we shall latch onto every southerly breeze that comes our way, eventually reaching the Lesser Antilles or, failing that, the coast of Brazil.

As darkness settled over the North Atlantic, we came upon a great mass of flotsam and jetsam from an anonymous wreck: a poaching schooner, most likely, looking for whales and seals but instead running afoul of a storm. We recovered no bodies – lifebelts have never been popular amongst such scallywags – but we salvaged plenty of timber, some medical supplies, and a copy of the *New York Post* for 17 April, stuffed securely into the pocket of a drifting macintosh. At first light I shall peruse the paper in hopes of learning how the outside world reacted to the loss of the *Titanic*.

The dry wood is a godsend. Thanks to this resource, I expect to encounter only a modicum of hostility whilst making my case next week for what might be called the *Medusa* initiative for avoiding famine. "Only a degenerate savage would consume the raw flesh of his own kind," I'll tell our assembled company. "Thanks to the Franklin stove and its ample supply of fuel, however, we can prepare our meals via broiling, roasting, braising, and other such civilized techniques."

5 May 1912
Lat. 28°10′ N, Long. 54°40′ W

I am still reeling from the *New York Post*'s coverage of the 15 April tragedy. Upon reaching the disaster site, Captain Roston of the *Carpathia* and Captain Lord of the *Californian* scanned the whole area with great diligence, finding no survivors or dead bodies, merely a few deck chairs and other debris. By the following morning they'd concluded that the mighty liner had gone down with all souls, and so they called off the search.

The *Ada*'s company greeted the news of their ostensible extinction with a broad spectrum of responses. Frustration was the principal emotion. I also witnessed despair, grief, bitterness, outrage, amusement, hysterical laughter, fatalistic resignation, and even – if I read correctly the countenances of certain first-cabin and amidships voyagers – fascination with the possibility that, should we in fact bump into one of the Lesser Antilles, a man might simply slip away, start his life anew, and allow his family and friends to count him amongst those who'd died of exposure on day one.

If the *Post* report may be believed, our would-be rescuers initially thought it odd that Captain Smith had neglected to order his passengers and crew into lifebelts. Rostron and Lord speculated that, once the *Titanic*'s entire company realized their situation was hopeless, with the Grim Reaper making ready to trawl for their souls within a mere two hours, a tragic consensus had emerged. As Stanley Lord put it, "I can hear the oath now, ringing down the *Titanic*'s companionways. 'The time has come for us to embrace our wives, kiss our children, pet our dogs, praise the Almighty, break out the wine and stop trying to defy a Divine Will far greater than our own.' "

Thus have we become a raft of the living dead, crewed by phantoms and populated by shades. Mr Futrelle thought immediately of Samuel Taylor Coleridge's "The Rime of the Ancient Mariner". He muttered a stanza in which the cadaverous crew, their souls having been claimed by the skull-faced, dice-addicted master of a ghost ship (its hull suggestive of

an immense ribcage), return to life under the impetus of
angelic spirits: "They groaned, they stirred, they all uprose, nor
spake nor moved their eyes. It had been strange, even in a
dream, to have seen those dead men rise." And when we all
come marching home to Liverpool, Southampton, Queens-
town, Belfast, Cherbourg, New York, Philadelphia and Boston
– that too will be awfully strange.

9 May 1912
Lat. 27°14′ N, Long. 55°21′ W

This morning the Good Lord sent us potable water, gallons of
it, splashing into our cisterns like honey from heaven. If we
cleave to our usual draconian rationing, we shall not have to
take up the Ancient Mariner's despairing chant – "Water, water
everywhere, nor any drop to drink" – for at least two months.
Surely we shall encounter more rain by then.

Predictably enough, my directive concerning the steerage
meat occasioned a lively conversation aboard the *Ada*. A dozen
first-cabin voyagers were so scandalized that they began
questioning my sanity, and for a brief but harrowing interval it
looked as if I might have a mutiny on my hands. But in time
more rational heads prevailed, as the pragmatic majority
apprehended both the utilitarian and the sacramental dimensions of such a menu.

Reverend Bateman, God bless him, volunteered to oversee
the rite – the deboning, the roasting, the thanksgiving, the
consecration – a procedure in which he was assisted by his
Catholic confrères, Father Byles and Father Peruschitz. Not
one word was spoken during the consumption phase, but I
sensed that everyone was happy not only to have finally received
a substantive meal but also to have set a difficult precedent and
emerged from the experience spiritually unscathed.

14 May 1912
Lat. 27°41´ N, Long. 54°29´ W

Another wreck, another set of medical supplies, another trove
of cooking fuel – plus two more legible newspapers. As it
happened, the *Philadelphia Bulletin* for 22 April and the *New
York Times* for 29 April carried stories about the dozens of religious services held earlier in the month all over America and the
United Kingdom honouring the *Titanic*'s noble dead. I
explained to our first-cabin and second-cabin passengers that I
would allow each man to read about his funeral, but he must
take care not to get the pages wet.

Needless to say, our most illustrious voyagers were accorded
lavish tributes. The managers of the Waldorf-Astoria, St Regis,
and Knickerbocker hotels in Manhattan observed a moment of
silence for Colonel John Jacob Astor. (Nothing was said about
his scandalously pregnant child bride, the former Madeleine
Force.) The rectors of St Paul's church in Elkins Park,
Pennsylvania, commissioned three Tiffany windows in memory
of the dearly departed Widener family, George, Eleanor and
Harry. Senator Guggenheim of Colorado graced the *Con-
gressional Record* with a eulogy for his brother, Benjamin, the
mining and smelting tycoon. President Taft decreed an official
Day of Prayer at the White House for his military adviser,
Major Butt. For a full week all the passenger trains running
between Philadelphia and New York wore black bunting in
honour of John Thayer, Second Vice-President of the
Pennsylvania Railroad. During this same interval the flags of all
White Star Line steamers departing Southampton flew at half-
mast in memory of the company's president, J. Bruce Ismay,
even as the directors of Macy's Department Store in Herald
Square imported a Wurlitzer and arranged for the organist to
play each day a different requiem for their late employer, Isidor
Straus. The Denver Women's Club successfully petitioned the
City Council to declare a Day of Mourning for Margaret
Brown, who'd done so much to improve the lot of uneducated
women and destitute children throughout the state.

On the whole, our spectral community took heart in their

epitaphs, and I believe I know why. Now that our deaths have been duly marked and lamented, the bereaved back home can begin, however haltingly, to get on with the business of existence. Yes, throughout April the mourning families knew only raw grief, but in recent weeks they have surely entered upon wistful remembrance and the bittersweet rewards of daily life, wisely heeding our Lord's words from the Gospel of Matthew, "Let the dead bury their dead."

18 June 1912
Lat. 25°31′ N, Long. 53°33′ W

To reward our steerage passengers for accepting the *Medusa* initiative with such élan, I made no move to stop them when, shortly after sunrise, they killed and ate Mr Ismay. I could see their point of view. By all accounts, from the moment we left Cherbourg Ismay had kept pressing the captain for more steam, so that we might arrive in New York on Tuesday night rather than Wednesday morning. Evidently Ismay wanted to set a record, whereby the crossing-time for the maiden voyage of the *Titanic* would beat that of her sister ship, the *Olympic*. Also, nobody really liked the man.

I also went along with the strangling and devouring of Mr Murdoch. There was nothing personal or vindictive in my decision. I would have acquiesced even if we didn't detest each other. Had Murdoch not issued such a boneheaded command at 11.40 p.m. on the night of 14 April, we wouldn't be in this mess. "Hard a-starboard!" he ordered. So far, so good. If he'd left it at that, we would've steamed past the iceberg with several feet to spare. But instead he added, "Full astern." What the bloody hell was Murdoch trying to do? Back up the ship like a bloody motorcar? All he accomplished was to severely compromise the rudder, and so the colossus slit us like a hot knife cutting lard.

When it came to Mr Andrews, however, I drew the line. Yes, before the *Titanic* sailed he should have protested the paucity of lifeboats. And, yes, when designing her he should have run the bulkheads clear to the brink, so that in the event of rupture the watertight compartments would not systematically feed one another with ton after ton of brine. But even in his wildest fancies, Mr. Andrews could not have imagined a three-hundred-foot gash in his creation's hull.

"Let him amongst you who has designed a more unsinkable ship than RMS *Titanic* cast the first stone," I told the mob. Slowly, reluctantly, they backed away. Today I have made an eternal friend in Thomas Andrews.

5 December 1912
Lat. 20°16′ N, Long. 52°40′ W

Looking through my journal, I am chagrined to discover that the entries appear at such erratic intervals. What can I say? Writing does not come easily for me, and I am forever solving problems more pressing than keeping this tub's log up to date.

Since getting below the Tropic of Cancer, we have endured one episode of becalming after another. Naturally Mr Futrelle supplied me with an appropriate stanza from Coleridge. "Down dropt the breeze, the sails dropt down – 'twas sad as sad could be, and we did only speak to break silence of the sea." And yet we are much more than the poet's painted ship upon a painted ocean. The *Ada* abides. Life goes on.

In August, young Mrs Astor gave birth to her baby, faithfully attended by Dr Alice Leader, the only female physician on board. (Mother and child are both thriving.) September's highlights included a spellbinding public recitation by Mr Futrelle of his latest Thinking Machine detective story, which he will commit to paper when we reach dry land. (The plot is so devilishly clever that I dare not reveal any particulars.) Last month our resident theatre company staged a production of *The Tempest*, directed by Margaret Brown and featuring our fetching movie-serial actress Dorothy Gibson as Miranda. (The shipwreck scene provoked unhappy memories, but otherwise we were enchanted.) And, of course, each dawn brings a plethora of birthdays to celebrate. Mr Futrelle informs me of the counterintuitive fact that, out of any group of twenty-three persons, the chances are better than fifty-fifty that two will share a birthday. I couldn't follow his logic, but I'm not about to question it.

On the romantic front, I've been pleased to observe that our young wireless operator, Harold Bride, has set his cap for a twenty-one-year-old Irish emigrant named Katie Mullen. (Though Mr Bride has not been pleased to observe me observing him.) In June, Mr and Mrs Strauss marked their forty-first wedding anniversary. (Mr Lightoller arranged a candlelit dinner for them above pontoon F.) In July, Mr Guggenheim and his mistress, Mme Léotine Aubert, finally got married, Rabbi Minkoff officiating. (They passed their honeymoon in the gazebo above pontoon D.) Sad to say, last month Mr and Mrs Widener decided to get divorced, despite the protests of Father Byles and Father Montvila. The Wideners insist their decision has nothing to do with the stress of the sinking, and everything to do with their disagreements over women's suffrage. I personally don't understand why the gentler sex wishes to sully its sensibility with politics, but if ladies really want the vote, I say give it them.

7 July 1913
Lat. 9°19′ N, Long. 44°42′ W

For reasons that defy my powers of analysis, a steady cheerfulness obtains aboard the *Ada*. Despite our isolation, or perhaps because of it, we've become quite attached to our crowded little hamlet. Notwithstanding the occasional doldrums, literal and figurative, our peripatetic tropical isle remains a remarkably congenial place.

I am aided immeasurably by the incompetence of captains who came before me. Thanks to the superfluity of wrecks, and our skill in plundering the flotsam and jetsam, we are blessed with a continual supply of fresh meat, good ale, novel toys for the children, *au courant* fashions for the first-cabin women, lumber for new architectural projects, rigging to improve our manoeuvrability, firearms to discourage pirates, and lambskin sheaths to curb our population. Drop by the *Ada* on any given Saturday night, and you will witness dance marathons, bridge tournaments, poker games, lotto contests, sing-a-longs, and amorous encounters of every variety, sometimes across class lines. We are a merry raft.

Even our library is flourishing. This last circumstance has proved especially heartening to young Harry Widener, our resident bibliophile, who needs bucking up after his parents' divorce. Jane Austen is continually in circulation, likewise Charles Dickens, Anthony Trollope, Conan Doyle, and an epic Polish novel, at once reverent and earthy, called *Quo Vadis*. We also have *The Oxford Book of English Verse*, compiled in 1900 by Arthur Quiller-Couch, so now I need no longer pester Mr Futrelle when I wish to ornament my log with epigraphs.

At least ten weeks have passed since anybody has asked when we're going to reach the Lesser Antilles. How might I account for this cavalier attitude to our rescue? I suspect that the phenomenon traces in part to the special editions of the *New York Herald-Tribune* and the *Manchester Guardian* that we salvaged last May. In both cases, the theme of the issue was "The *Titanic* Catastrophe: One Year Later". Evidently the outside world has managed to extract a profound moral lesson from the tragedy. Man, our beneficiaries have learned, is a flawed, fallible and naked creature. Our pride is nothing of which to be proud. For all our technological ingenuity, we are not gods or even demiurges. If a person wishes to be happy, he would do better planting his garden than polishing his gaskets, better cultivating his soul than multiplying his possessions.

Given the ethos that now obtains throughout North America, Europe and the British Empire, how can we blithely go waltzing home? How dare we disillusion Western civilization by returning from the dead? I've consulted with representatives from steerage, amidships and the aristocracy, and they've all ratified my conclusion. Showing up now would amount to saying, "Sorry, friends and neighbours, but you've been living in a Rousseauesque fantasy, for the *Titanic*'s resourceful company defeated Nature after all. Once again human cleverness has triumphed over cosmic indifference, so let's put aside all this sentimental talk of hubris and continue to fill the planet to bursting with our contrivances and toys."

To be sure, we also have certain personal – you might even say selfish – reasons to keep the *Ada* as our address. Colonel Astor, Mr Widener and Mr Guggenheim note, with great exasperation, that according to our salvaged newspapers the American Treasury Department intends to levy a severe tax on people at their level of income. (Ironically, these revenues will be due each year on the day the *Titanic* went down.) Reverend Bateman and Father Byles aver that their castaway flocks have proven a hundred times more attentive to the Christian message than were their congregations on dry land. At least half our married men, regardless of class, confess that they've grown weary of their wives back home, and many have started courting the nubile colleens from steerage. Surprisingly, some of our unescorted married women admit to analogous sentiments. Consider the case of Margaret Brown, our Denver suffragette and rabble-rouser, who avers that her marriage to J. J. Brown lost its magic many years ago, hence her proclivity for throwing herself at me in a most shocking and, I must say, exciting manner.

And, of course, we continue to expand our material amenities. Last week we put in a squash court. This morning Mr Andrews showed me his plans for a Turkish bath. Tomorrow my officers and I shall consider whether to allocate our canvas reserves to a canopy for the emigrants, analogous to the protection enjoyed by our second-cabin and forward residents. All in all, it would appear that, as captain of this community, I am obligated to defer our deliverance indefinitely, an attitude with which the vivacious Mrs Brown heartily agrees.

11 December 1913
Lat. 10°17′ S, Long. 32°52′ W

Looking back on Vasil Plotcharsky's attempt to foment a socialist revolution aboard the *Ada*, I would say that it was all for the best. Just as I suspected, the man is besotted with Trotsky. At first he confined his political activities to organizing marches, rallies and strikes amongst the steerage passengers and former *Titanic* victualling staff, his aim being to protest what he called "the tyrannical regime of Czar Henry Wilde and his decadent courtiers". Alas, it wasn't long before Mr Plotcharsky and his followers broke into the arms locker and equipped themselves with pistols, whereupon they started advocating the violent overthrow of my regime.

But for the intervention of our resident logic *meister*, Mr Futrelle, who can be as quick as his fictional Thinking Machine, Plotcharsky's exhortations might have led to bloodshed. Instead, Futrelle explained to the Trotskyites that, per Karl Marx's momentous revelation, the land of collectivist milk and classless honey is destined to rise only from the rubble of the Western imperialist democracies. The Workers' Paradise cannot be successfully organized within feudal societies such as contemporary Russia or, for that matter, the good ship *Ada*. In due time, with scientific inevitability, the world's capitalist economies will yield to the iron imperatives of history, but for now even the most ardent Bolshevik must practise forbearance.

Mr Plotcharsky listened attentively, spent the following day in a brown study, and cancelled the revolution. To tell you the truth, I don't think his heart was in it.

Of course, not all of Vasil Plotcharsky's partisans were happy with this turn of events, and one of them – a Southampton butcher named Charles Barrow – argued that we should forthwith institute a democracy aboard the *Ada*, as an essential first step towards a socialist utopia. Initially I resisted Mr Barrow's argument, whereupon he introduced his cleaver into the conversation, and I assured him that I would not stand in the way of progress.

And so a bright new day has dawned aboard the *Ada*. Mr Andrews' astounding machine is now considerably more than a raft, and I am now considerably less than her captain. On 13 October, by a nearly unanimous vote, Mr Plotcharsky and Colonel Astor abstaining, we became the People's Republic of Adaland. Our constitutional convention, drawing representatives from the aristocracy, the second-cabin precincts and steerage, dragged on for two weeks. George Widener, John Thayer and Sir Cosmo Duff-Gordon were scandalized by the resulting document, mostly because it forbade the establishment of a state church, instituted a unitary Parliament oblivious to class distinctions, and – owing to the tireless efforts of Margaret Brown and her sorority of suffragettes – enfranchised every adult female citizen. I keep trying to convince Widener, Thayer and Duff-Gordon that certain concessions to modernity are better than the Bolshevik alternative.

On 13 November I was elected the first Prime Minister of Adaland in a landslide, thereby vindicating the platform of my Egalitarian Party and giving pause to Father Peruschitz's Catholic Workers Party, Sir Cosmo's Christian Entrepreneurs Party, Thomas Andrews's Technotopia Party and Vasil Plotcharsky's Communist Party. Two days after my triumph at the polls, I asked Maggie Brown to marry me. She'd done a splendid job as my campaign manager, attracting over eighty per cent of the female vote to our cause, and I knew she would make an excellent wife as well.

17 April 1914
Lat. 13°15′ N, Long. 29°11′ W

The week began with an extraordinary stroke of luck. Shortly after noon, poking through the wreck of a frigate called the *Ganymede*, we happened upon a wireless set, plus a petrol engine to supply it with power. In short order John Phillips and Harold Bride got the rig working. "Once again I have the ears of an angel," enthused a beaming Phillips. "I can tell you all the gossip of a troubled and tumultuous world."

Woodrow Wilson has been elected the 28th President of the United States. The Second Balkans War has ended with a peace treaty between Serbia and Turkey. Mahatma Gandhi, leader of the Indian Passive Resistance Movement, has been arrested. Pope Pius X has died, succeeded by Cardinal della Chiesa as Pope Benedict XV. Ernest Shackleton is headed for the

Antarctic. The feisty suffragette Emmeline Pankhurst
languishes in prison after attempting to blow up Lloyd George.
Nickelodeon audiences have fallen in love with a character
called the Little Tramp. A great canal through the Isthmus of
Panama is about to open. The second anniversary of the *Titanic*
disaster occasioned sermons, speeches, editorials and religious
observances throughout the Western world.

Good Lord, has it been two years already? It seems only
yesterday that I watched Mr Andrews unfurl his blueprint in the
chartroom. So much has happened since then: the launching of
the *Ada*, the consumption of Ismay and Murdoch, the reports
of our collective demise, our decision to remain waterborne for
the nonce, the birth of this republic – not to mention my
marriage to the redoubtable Maggie.

Adaland continues to ply the Atlantic in a loop bounded on
the north by the Tropic of Cancer and on the south by the
Tropic of Capricorn. We last crossed the equator in late
February. Mrs Wilde marked the event by organizing an elaborate masquerade ball reminiscent of the fabled Brazilian
Carnaval. The affair was a huge success, and we shall probably
do the same thing three months hence when we hit the line
again.

At least once a week we find ourselves within hailing distance
of yet another pesky freighter or presumptuous steamer. By
paddling furiously and hoisting all sails – our spars now collec-
tively carry ten thousand square feet – we always manage to
outrun the intruder. In theory, thanks to our wireless rig, we
have endured the last of these nerve-wracking chases, for
Phillips and Bride can now sound the alarm well before we
become objects of unwanted charity.

2 September 1914
Lat. 25°48′ S, Long. 33°16′ W

Against the dictates of reason, in defiance of all decency, with
contempt for every Christian virtue, the world has gone to war.

According to our wireless intercepts, the Western Front stretches a staggering four hundred and seventy-five miles across northern France, the Boche on one side, the Allies on the other, both armies dug in and defending themselves with machine guns. In my mind's eye I see the intervening terrain: a no-man's-land presided over by Death, now on holiday from Coleridge's skeletal ship and reigning over a kingdom of muck, blood, bone, mustard gas and barbed wire, whilst Life-in-Death combs her yellow locks, paints her ruby lips, and sports with the boys in the trenches. Between 4 August and 29 August, Phillips informs me, 260,000 French soldiers died the most wretched, agonizing and pointless deaths imaginable.

"I was under the impression that, since the *Titanic* allegedly went down two years ago, self-delusion had lost favour in Europe," Mrs Wilde remarked. "How does one account for this madness?"

"I can't explain it," I replied. "But I would say we now have more reason than ever to remain aboard the *Ada*."

Although the preponderance of the butchery is occurring thousands of miles to the northeast, the British and Germans have succeeded in creating a nautical war zone here in the tropics. Mr Phillips has inferred that a swift and deadly armoured fleet, under the command of Admiral Craddock aboard HMS *Good Hope*, has been prowling these waters looking for two German cruisers, the *Dresden*, last seen off the Brazilian state of Pernambuco, and the *Karlsruhe*, recently spotted near Curaçao, one of the Lesser Antilles. If he can't catch either of these big fish, Craddock will settle for one of the Q ships – merchant vessels retrofitted with cannons and pom-poms – that the Germans have deployed in their efforts to destroy British commercial shipping around Cape Horn. In particular Craddock hopes to sink the *Cap Trafalgar*, code name *Hilfskreuzer B*, and the *Kronprinz Wilhelm*, named for the Kaiser himself.

We are monitoring the Marconi traffic around the clock, eavesdropping on Craddock's relentless patriotism. Two hours ago Mr Bride brought me a report indicating that the *Kronprinz Wilhelm* is being pursued by HMS *Carmania*, one of the British Q ships that recently joined Craddock's cruiser squadron. Bride

warns me that the coming fight could occur near our present
location, about two hundred miles south of the Brazilian island
of Trindade (not to be confused with the West Indies island of
Trinidad). We would be well advised to sail far away from here,
though in which direction God only knows.

14 September 1914
Lat. 22°15′ S, Long. 29°52′ W

A dizzyingly eventful day. Approaching Trindade, we were
abruptly caught up in the Great War, bystanders to a furious
engagement between the *Carmania* and the *Kronprinz Wilhelm*.
There is blood on our decks tonight. Bullets and shells have
shredded our sails. From our infirmary rise the moans and
gasps of a hundred wounded German and British evacuees.

I had never witnessed a battle before, and neither had any
other Adaland citizens except Major Butt and Colonel Weir,
who'd seen action in the Philippines during the Spanish-
American War. "Dover Beach" came instantly to mind. The
darkling plain, the confused alarms, the ignorant armies
clashing by night, or, in this case, at noon.

For two full hours the armed freighters pounded each other
with their 4.1-inch guns, whilst their respective supply vessels –
each combatant boasted a retinue of three colliers – maintained
a wary distance, waiting to fish the dead and wounded from the
sea. On board the *Ada*, the children cried in terror, the adults
bemoaned the folly of it all, and the dogs ran in mad circles
trying to escape the terrible noise. With each passing minute the
gap separating the *Carmania* and the *Kronprinz Wilhelm*
narrowed, until the two freighters were only yards apart, their
sailors lining the rails and exchanging rifle shots, a tactic
curiously reminiscent of Napoleonic-era fighting, quite unlike
the massed machine-gun fire now fashionable on the Western
Front.

At first I thought the *Carmania* had got the worst of it. Fires
raged along her decks, her bridge lay flattened by artillery shells,
her engines had ceased to function, and she'd started to lower

away. But then I realized the *Wilhelm* was fatally injured, her hull listing severely, her crew launching life-boats, her colliers drawing nearer the fray, looking for survivors. Evidently some shells had hit the *Wilhelm* below her waterline, rupturing several compartments. A North Atlantic iceberg could not have sealed her doom more emphatically.

Owing to the relentless explosions, the proliferating fires, the rain of bullets, and the general chaos, nearly three hundred sailors – perhaps three dozen from the *Carmania*, the rest from the *Wilhelm* – were now in the water, some dead, some wounded, most merely dazed. Fully half the castaways swam for the colliers and lifeboats of their respective nationalities, but the others took a profound and understandable interest in the *Ada*. And so it happened that our little republic suddenly found itself in need of an immigration policy.

Unlike the *Titanic*, the *Wilhelm* did not break in two. She simply lurched crazily to port, then slowly but inexorably disappeared. Throughout the sinking I consulted with the leaders of Parliament, and we soon reached a decision that, ten hours later, I am still willing to call enlightened. We would rescue anyone, British or German, who could climb aboard on his own hook, provided he agreed to renounce his nationality, embrace the founding documents of Adaland, and forswear any notion of bringing the Great War to our waterborne, sovereign, neutral country. As it happened, every sailor to whom we proposed these terms gave his immediate assent, though doubtless many prospective citizens were simply telling us what they knew we wanted to hear.

Being ill-equipped to deal with the severely maimed, we had to leave them to the colliers, even those unfortunates who desperately wanted to join us. I shall not soon forget the bobbing casualties of the Battle of Trindade. Even Major Butt and Colonel Weir had never seen such carnage. A boy – and they were all boys – with his lower jaw blasted away. Another boy with both hands burned off. An English lad whose severed legs floated alongside him like jettisoned oars. A German sailor whose sprung intestines encircled his midriff like some grisly life-preserver. The pen trembles in my hand. I can write no more.

29 October 1914
Lat. 10°35′ S, Long. 38°11′ W

Every day, fair or foul, the Great War chews up and spits out another ten thousand mothers' sons, sometimes many more. Were the *Ada*'s scores of able-bodied Englishmen, Irishmen, Welshmen and Scotsmen to sail home now and repatriate themselves, the majority would probably wind up in the trenches. The beast needs feeding. As for those hundreds of young men who boarded the *Titanic* intending to settle in New York or Boston or perhaps even the Great Plains, they too are vulnerable, since it's doubtless only a matter of months before President Wilson consigns several million Yanks to the Western Front.

And so it happens that a consensus concerning the present cataclysm has emerged amongst our population. I suspect we would have come to this view even without our experience of naval warfare. In any event, the Great War is not for us. We sincerely hope that the participating nations extract from the slaughter whatever their hearts desire: honour, glory, adventure, relief from ennui. But I think we'll sit this one out.

Yesterday I held an emergency meeting with my capable Deputy Prime Minister, Mr Futrelle, my level-headed Minister of State, Mr Andrews, and my astute Minister of War, Major Butt. After deciding that the South Atlantic is entirely the wrong place for us to be, we set a north-westerly course, destination Central America. I can't imagine how we're going to get through the canal. Mrs Wilde assures me we'll think of something. Lord, how I adore my wife. In January we're expecting our first child. This happy phenomenon, I must confess, caught us completely by surprise, as Mrs Wilde is forty-six years old. Evidently our baby was meant to be.

15 November 1914
Lat. 7°10′ N, Long. 79°15′ W

Mirabile dictu – we've done it! Thanks to Mrs Astor's diamond tiara, Mrs Guggenheim's ruby necklace, and a dozen other such gewgaws, we managed to bribe, barter and wheedle our way from one side of the Isthmus of Panama to the other. Being a mere 110 feet side to side, the lock chambers barely accommodated our machine, but we nevertheless squeaked through.

The *Ada* is heading south-southwest, bound for the Galápagos Islands and the rolling blue sea beyond. I haven't the remotest notion where we might end up, luscious Tahiti perhaps, or historic Pitcairn Island, or Pago Pago, or Samoa, and right now I don't particularly care. What matters is that we are rid of both the Belle Époque and the darkling plain. Bring on the South Pacific, typhoons and all.

Night falls over the Gulf of Panama. By the gleam of my electric torch I am reading the *Oxford Book of English Verse*. Three stanzas by George Peele seem relevant to our situation. In the presence of Queen Elizabeth, an ancient warrior doffs his helmet, which "now shall make a hive for bees". No longer able to fight, he proposes to serve Her Majesty in a different way. "Goddess, allow this aged man his right to be your beadsman now, that was your knight." The poem is called "Farewell to Arms", a sentiment to which we Battle of Trindade veterans respond with enthusiastic sympathy, though not for any reasons Mr Peele would recognize. Farewell, ignorant armies. Auf Wiedersehen, dreadful *Kronprinz Wilhelm*. Adieu, fatuous *Good Hope*. Hail and farewell.

I am master of a wondrous raft, and soon I shall be a father as well. Over two thousand pilgrims are in my keeping, and at present every soul is safe. Strange stars glitter in a stranger sky. Colonel Astor's Airedale and Mr Harper's Pekingese howl at the bright gibbous moon. The sea is calm tonight, and I am a very lucky man.

Sidewinders

Ken MacLeod

1. The Trafalgar Gate

I bought a kilo of oranges in Soho – Covent Garden would have none at this time of year – and walked down Whitcomb Street and around the corner on Pall Mall to the Square. The Gate faced me, a concrete henge straddling the entrance to Duncannon Street. There wasn't much of a queue, just a line four abreast filling the pavement along the front of the National Gallery and St Martin's in the Fields. I passed the two hours it took me to get to the front reading the latest Amis *fils* in paperback. I turned the last page and chucked the Penguin to a hurrying, threadbare art student seconds before I'd have had to relinquish the book to the security bin.

"Papers, please."

I resisted the temptation to monkey the guard's cockney. String bag slung on the thumb, rope of my duffel bag clutched in the fingers of one hand, I passed the documents over with the other, for a frowning moment of scrutiny. Then the guard waved me on to the Customs table. Wanded, searched, duffel bag contents spread out and thrust back in any old how. Passport scanned and stamped. One orange taken "for random inspection". I've paid worse tolls. As long as the stack of Marie Thérèse thalers and the small change in my boot-heels made it through, I was good to go any-where.

I walked under the arch and into Scotland.

*   *   *

They don't like you to call it Scotland, of course. Officially, East London is the capital of the GBR (which – the tired joke notwithstanding – doesn't actually stand for "Gordon Brown's Republic" but is the full name of the state, derived from the standard ISO abbreviation for "Great Britain" and accepted as its legal designation at the exhausted end of the 1978 UN Security Council session that imposed the settlement, ending the bloody civil war that followed the Colonels' Coup of '73). But it's mostly Scottish accents you hear on the streets, along with Asian and African and Islingtonian – the few thousand white working-class Londoners who stayed in the East are in high demand as faces and voices for the regime: actors, diplomats, border guards. North Britain (another name they don't like) speaks to the world in a cockney accent.

I walked up Duncannon Street, avoiding eye contact with anyone in a plastic fake-leather jacket. The bank is still called the Royal Bank and the currency is still called the pound. Come to think of it, the Party is still called Labour. Zigzagging the Strand and Kingsway, I was 100 metres from Holborn when I noticed I was being followed. Usual stuff – corner of the eye, shop-window reflection, tail still there after I'd dashed across the four lanes (GBR traffic's mercifully two-stroke, and sparse) and walked on. Worse, when I checked again in a parked wing-mirror the guy vanished in plain sight. (In *my* plain sight, that is. No one else noticed.)

Another sidewinder, then. One who knew I was on to him. Shit. Jack Straw's boys (and girls) I could dodge with my eyes shut. This was different.

There's a procedure for everything. For this situation, SOP is to take a long step sideways – chances are, the sidewinder who's spotted you spotting him has just hopped into an adjacent probability (like, one where you took a different route) and is sprinting ahead to hop back further up the road (following *his* SOP, natch). But he'd know that, so if he knew I was a sidewinder . . . but I had no evidence of that, yet. Either way, the trick was to take a bigger or a smaller jump than he'd expect, but one that would still keep me on track to catch an Edinburgh train at King's Cross.

I turned sharp left onto High Holborn and walked briskly towards the border. Long before I'd reached Princes Circus, I was the only person on the street. There isn't a wall between East and West London – they've learned that much – but planning blight, student hostels and regular patrols fill the function almost as well. From a sidewinder's angle, though, the good thing about the band of run-down property east of Charing Cross Road is that it's a debatable land, a place where the probabilities are manifold, and therefore a prime locale for long sideways steps.

I clambered over concrete rubble, waded through fireweed, crunched broken panes, and stood still and did that thing in my head.

2. That thing in my head

You do it too.

Those times when you *know* you left the front-door keys on the kitchen table, not beside the phone, and there's no one else around who *could* have moved them? Big secret: it wasn't the little people messing with your head. That street entrance or shop front you've never noticed before, though you must have driven past it a hundred times? Shock revelation: you're not living *The Truman Show*, and nobody's shifting the scenery.

You're shifting, *in* the scenery: sideslipping between entire universes whose only difference may be where you left the keys last night, or how a town plan turned out thirty years ago, or a planning permission last month, or . . .

You're doing it all the time, unconsciously. Sidewinders do it consciously. Don't ask me how, or how many of us there are. You don't want to know. Most of us, by a sort of natural selection, end up in the probability where they're happy, or at least content. A small minority are intrinsically malcontent, or seduced by the possibilities, or both.

Some of that minority get recruited. You don't want to know about that, either. Let's just say there are two sides. Well, there are an infinity of sides, but they collapse, on inspection, to two: the Improvers, and the Conservers.

The Improvers want to put "wrong" histories "back on track"; the Conservers want all possible histories to unfold unhindered. This conflict has, I'm told, been going on for some time. I suspect it's waged from great shining bastions of widely separated probability where civilization is vastly more advanced than it is anywhere we can reach, each of them perhaps far outside the human branch of history altogether. The best-laid plans of Miocene men, or of the wily descendants of dinosaurs on an Earth the asteroid missed . . .

That's the sort of question we sidewinders argue amongst ourselves. For you, for now – all you need to know is, I'm an Improver.

And right now I was on the run from a Conserver.

3. Tairlidhe is my darlin', the young chevalier

I stepped out of the bank doorway I found myself in, nodded to the footman, and caught a tram. Tall buildings, fat with sandstone and gross with gilt, filled the view from the top-deck window. The streets buzzed with electric velocipedes and reeked with ethanol-fuelled cars. The pavements were more crowded than those of the world I'd come from, and the crowds whiter. Here and there a Mahometan, a Hindoo or a Jew walked, distinct in their costume and dignity. Blacks and Chinese were more common and less noticeable, porters and street-merchants for the most part. Slavery was abolished in 1836, after the Virginia Insurrection made it too expensive; the Opium Wars were never fought.

Discreetly, I unscrewed a boot-heel and thumb-nailed out a 1997 shilling with the head of Charles X. The conductor grumbled, but gave me a fistful of nickel in change that weighed down my jacket pocket as I jumped off. King's Cross is in the same place, with the same name – it's one of those sites that's a converse to the debatable lands: a place implacable, straddling probabilities like railway lines. The statue in the front is of Luipoldt II.

I plunged to the ticket office through the foetid cloud of pomade and pipe-smoke and bought a single to Edinburgh. Display-boards clattered with flip-plates of digits and destinations. An express at twelve of the clock, platform three. I bought a newspaper and a packed lunch, and took my seat. The train – French-fangled, electric – glided out as all the church-bells of London pealed noon, flashed through the villages north of London – Camden, Islington, Newington – at an accelerating clip that reached 150 miles an hour as we passed Barnet. Too fast to read the sign, but I knew the town. There's always, for me, a frisson at Barnet – it's where the last battle of the Second Restoration was fought, when the Bonny Prince and his men routed the Hornsey militia and found London defenceless before them.

The endless fields of England rolled by, the spring ploughing well under way, sometimes with one man behind a horse, sometimes with a great modern contraption from the Massey manufactories, drawn by a phalanx of Clydesdales. I leaned on the table, munched bread and cheese and sipped stout, and worried idly about my soft spot for this probability. How does one weigh the absence of total war and totalitarian revolution, against the continuance of Caliph and Romanoff and Manchu, and Voltaire at Ferney broken on the wheel?

I was in the non-smoking carriage, with the ladies, which didn't bother me at all. My clothes, while unfashionable, raised no more than a momentary eyebrow. A bum-freezer here is a pea-jacket there, and Levi makes denim jeans across a surprising range of probabilities.

Across the table – not Pullman, but the idea is obvious enough – sat a young lady, bowed over a thick book. Black brows knitted under her bonnet, lips moving as she read, her thin face pallid, her gown frayed at the cuffs. She glanced up as I turned a rustling page of *The Times*, and I smiled politely and looked back at the science page. Antarctic continent found – Spanish claim disputed. The young woman sighed. I looked up again.

"A heroine in jeopardy, milady?" I asked.

She shot me an indignant glance.

"I am not reading a *novel*," she said. "I study zoology."

"Ah," I said. "Your pardon. An admirable pursuit."

"But it is so hard!" she cried. "All those lists!"

"The Latin names," I murmured, nodding sagely, "of the great Linnaeus? They can indeed be a trial – "

She shook her head. "It is not that. So many disconnected facts to commit to memory!" Then she frowned. "I cannot place your accent, sir."

"New Scotland," I said, with a self-deprecating smile. "Hence the barbaric twang."

She took this bold-faced lie without demur. I told another.

"My name," I said, "is Steve Jones."

"And mine," she said, "is Mary Ann Dykes."

"At your service, miss."

"Thank you. Delighted to make your acquaintance."

I gave my occupation, disingenuously, as commercial traveller in oranges. She gave hers as confidential servant.

"And why, if I may make so bold, are you studying zoology?"

"I am an orphan, sir," she said. "I say this not to elicit sympathy, but to explain. I go to seek a post as a governess, in the Scottish capital. The mistress of the house has ambitions for her sons to be physicians, and I have been told that comparative anatomy is – but no!" She smiled suddenly. "That is true, but merely my excuse. The subject intrigues me."

"As I said, an admirable pursuit."

"But most taxing. Before my father passed away, he taught me the rudiments of mathematics, and of Newton. Would that zoology had its Newton!"

"I know little of that science," I mused aloud, "but I have sometimes thought that, just as our poor will multiply to the limits of their wages, or of the poor-rates, the entire brute creation must perforce indulge in an even more wanton and thoughtless reproduction of their kind . . ."

Mary Ann didn't blush. This history had no Victoria. She frowned.

"Yes?" she said. "Your drift, sir?"

"Yet as we see," I went on, "the world is not over-run with" – I glanced out of the window – "rabbits, let us say, or nettles. All that are born do not survive, and those who do must, on average, have some perhaps slight advantage which – so to speak – *selects* them for survival over their less fit brethren. If we dare to imagine this process repeated, generation after genera-tion, over many ages and revolutions of the Earth . . . but I fear I am rushing too far, in too speculative a direction."

"No!" she said. She clutched my wrist, then withdrew her too-hasty hand. This time, she did blush. "Please, do go on."

I did. By the time we reached the southern shore of the Firth of Forth, her textbook was covered with delighted scribbles linking facts at last, and her face with astonished smiles and happy frowns at the results.

I was about to part with her, at the station – which is called simply Edinburgh Central, Walter Scott in this world having remained an advocate at the Bar – smug in my Improving zeal, when she caught my elbow.

"Mr Jones," she said, "may I presume upon our acquaintance to ask you to escort me to my destination? It is in the West Port, and – " She looked away.

"And the Grassmarket is notorious for footpads, and you cannot afford a cab? Don't worry, Miss Dykes. I can't afford one either. Let us walk together."

I carried her luggage. It was pathetically light.

"Mr Jones," she enquired anxiously as we emerged from the rear of the station on to Market Street and caught our first stag-nant whiff of the Nor Loch, "I see you carry no weapon."

"I need none," I assured her. "I am an adept in the martial arts of the East."

She laughed. "Ancient arts are no match for a good pistol, sir, but I still trust in your protection."

Across the Royal Mile, down St Mary's Street into the Cowgate, then along beneath the North Bridge and Charles IV

Bridge towards the Grassmarket. High, dank walls like cliff-faces dripped. Opium dens wafted their dark allure. Gypsy fiddles enlivened the air around hostelries. Homeward cars and velocipedes splashed through the noxious puddles. After the Cowgate, the Grassmarket was respectability itself, even with its tinker stalls, beggar families, skulking footpads, stilt-walking clowns, and carousing students of medicine, divinity and law. The flag of the Three Kingdoms, aflutter in the evening breeze, could be glimpsed over the Castle which, like its Rock, straddles history sturdy and aloof with only its flags changing, above the Grassmarket's seething pool of probabilities.

Out of that seething pool stepped my pursuer. Two metres in front of us, and no one in between. If I hadn't recognized his face, the levelled thing in his hand would have identified him surely enough. In this world, it might have seemed no more than a glittering toy, but Mary Ann divined its sinister import in an instant. Or perhaps she just reacted to my start. She clutched my upper arm with both hands. From the point of view of one about to draw on the martial arts of the East, this was not a welcome move, however pleasing it might have been under other circumstances.

After a split second of bafflement, I realized that my pursuer must have stayed in the GBR, guessed – or been leaked – my destination and blithely taken the faster train of that more advanced world, then sidestepped to this world of Tairlidhe's victory to await me. How he'd found out that this was the world to which I'd fled to evade him, I didn't care to guess. Infiltration and defection are permanent possibilities, across all probabilities.

I had no choice. I sidestepped, back to the GBR. I may have hoped my pursuer wouldn't expect that, but in all honesty it was a reflex.

I had never before sidestepped with someone holding on to me. I was almost as surprised as Mary Ann to find us still together, in a different Grassmarket.

"What is this?" she cried, gazing around bewildered at the suddenly airier, cleaner, brighter and even noisier space of the plaza. She let go off me, and took a swift pace or two back and looked at me with suspicion and dread. "What arts of the East have you used, Mr Jones? Sorcery? Illusion?"

"Not these, I fear," I said. "This is real. It is a different reality than that to which you are accustomed – one in which history took a different turn, centuries ago."

She seemed to grasp the concept at once.

"Are there many such?"

"An infinite number," I told her.

"But how marvellous! And yet how obvious, that the Creator's infinity should be reflected in His creations!"

"That's one way of looking at it," I allowed.

Mary Ann looked around again, more calmly now, though I could see her quivering.

"I see this is a history in which the Covenanters' memory is honoured," she said. She pointed to one of a trio of statues. "I recognize that visage, of Richard Cameron. But who are the others?"

"They will mean nothing to you," I said.

"I want to see them, all the same."

She was intrigued by the pedestrian crossing, and impressed by the vehicles, tinny and two-stroke though they were. I nudged her to stop her staring at women with bare heads and short skirts. We stopped beneath the statues.

The stern man in the homburg, with upraised, didactic, forefinger:

"John Maclean," she read from the plinth. "A preacher, was he?"

"In a manner of speaking," I said. "And in his manner of public speech, by all accounts."

The man in the short coat, with glasses and pipe – and, Scotland being Scotland in all manifestations, with a traffic cone on his head:

"And 'Harold Wilson, martyr of British democracy'?" She recoiled almost, frowning. "A *democrat*? A radical?"

"Not precisely," I said, looking around distractedly. "It would take too long to explain. That man who confronted us – he may catch up at any moment. I must go."

"What about me, Mr Jones?" Mary Ann said.

"I'm sorry," I said, still looking about. "I can't take you with me. It's far too dangerous. You'll be safe here for now." My gaze alighted on a tall concrete building, from which hung a banner with a jowly, frowning, face and the letters "GB". I pointed.

"Remove your bonnet," I said. "It's not customary here. Your dress will pass. Go to that building, ask for the Women's Institute, and say that you have just arrived from London, penniless. Say nothing of where you really come from, lest you be consigned to a lunatic asylum. You will be made welcome, and given employment. Learn what you can in this world, and as soon as possible I'll take you back to yours."

"But – "

Out of the corner of my eye, I saw my pursuer emerge from the pub called The Last Drop, and peer around.

"Goodbye, Miss Dykes," I said.

I handed her the oranges – they were for here, after all, where they were scarce – and sidestepped as far as I'd ever dared in a single jump.

4. Storm Constantinople!

And fell briefly into a world of Latin buzz and blazing neon, of fairy lights suspended on nothing above a grassy park, on which robe-clad dark-skinned people strolled beneath a Rock with no Castle, and with an evening sky alight with the artificial constellations of celestial cities in orbit overhead. I sprinted across the sward, towards where the King's Stables Road wouldn't be. I'd never been in this probability, but I recognized it by report: this is the one where Spartacus won, slavery fell, capitalism rose, and the Romans reached the Moon in about 500 (Not) AD and Alpha Centauri a century or two later . . .

I leaped a stream that in most other worlds had long since been a sewer, sidestepped in mid-air, in a familiar but much less hopeful direction, and came down with a skid and a thud on dust and ash. I stumbled, flailing, and trod on a circle of glowing embers which I as quickly jumped out of, scattering more ash.

"Oi!" someone shouted. It must have been his fire.

"Sorry!" over my shoulder. Then I ran without looking back. Around me the early evening was lit only by scattered small fires, some of them behind the window-spaces of what buildings remained standing. Grass and weeds poked through the crazed tarmac under my feet. A few metres in front of me, a random leaf of grass or scrap of paper caught fire. I threw myself forward, hitting the ground with a pain I wouldn't feel for minutes. I side-stepped into an adjacent probability, as one might roll on the ground, got up and ran on.

The Improver base in this Edinburgh lies beneath where a multi-storey park had been, close to the unaltered Castle Rock. I reached the door – saw a red bead on the wall – flinched aside – keyed the code in the lock – dived through.

I stood up in low fluorescent lighting, pale corridors. I suspected my pursuer would be after me. I rang the alarm. Two guards were ready for him when he slipped into our space from a probability where the car park's floors hadn't pancaked in the blast from Rosyth. His capture took only a moment: a hiss of gas, a thrown net, the laser pistol knocked from his fingers.

The guards tied him in the net to a chair. I tried to interrogate him, before the effects of the gas wore off and he gathered his wits enough to sidestep.

"Why are you after me?"

His head jerked, his eyes rolled, his tongue lolled. "Isn't it obvious? You were on a mission to undermine the GBR!"

"What's that to you?" I said. "To Conservers, that regime must be an abomination anyway – radical, revolutionary even – isn't that everything you're against?"

"No, no." He struggled to focus his eyes and control his drool. "It's a rare marvel. A socialist state that works, that has survived the fall of Communism, because of the computerized planning developed at Strathclyde from the ideas of Kantorovich and Neurath. You have no idea, do you, where that might lead? Nor do we, but we want to find out."

"Well," I said, "sorry about that, old boy, very interesting no doubt, but I'm fucked if my relatives will suffer in this Caledonian Cuba a second longer than they have to."

He inhaled snot. "Fuck you."

I could see I wouldn't get much more out of him, so I whiled the minutes before he recovered enough to slip away by taunting him with what I'd done on the train. He looked at me with horror and loathing.

"You introduced *Darwin* to that world?"

"Who?" I said. "Wallace's theory of natural selection – that's what I outlined."

He thrashed in the net. "Whoever. You know what you may have done, if that young woman should be the one who convinces that world that evolution happened? Some day, perhaps many years hence, in some backwater of an Eastern empire, a young man – an Orthodox seminarian in Georgia, perhaps – will read her work, lose his faith, and go on to lead a bloody revolution – "

" – which will happen anyway, in one or other of these shit-holes," I said. "We're working on that problem."

"I wish you luck," he said drily. He was coming to, now, almost ready to vanish before our eyes.

"And what about this world?" I demanded. "This post-atomic horror? Would you have us leave it too?"

"Yes," he said. "To see what comes of it. Let it be."

And he went. The net slumped to the chair. I looked at the guards, shrugged.

"*C'est la vie*," one of them said. "Come on, you need a coffee. And some bandages."

I followed them to the first-aid station, then to the canteen. As I sipped hot black coffee, I found myself gazing idly at the room's walls, which were papered with old newspaper and magazine pages, saved from ruins. A particularly striking front page of the *Daily Mirror*, from May 1968, showed four long-haired young people in white T-shirts with a big black cross, which in a colour picture would have been red. The caption identified the youths as Andreas Baader, Ulrike Meinhof, Bernadette Devlin and Danny Cohn-Bendit. They stood on a platform in front of a huge crowd, the wind blowing in their hair, AK-47s in their uplifted hands, and behind them the skyline of Istanbul. The city in whose streets they would, a few hours later, fall to a hail of machine-gun bullets – along with a shocking proportion of the youthful crowd.

What good could come, I thought, of probability as crazy as this? One in which Pope Paul VI had responded to the Israeli victory in the Six-Day War of 1967 by claiming Palestine again for the Church, and urged the youth of Europe on a crusade to win it back? A crusade that had ended with an assault on Istanbul, a city too stubborn to let the human tide through? And where the massacre had sparked an international incident that had escalated to an all-out thermonuclear exchange?

While worlds like that – and worse – exist, I remain an Improver.

I caught up with Mary Ann Dykes a few weeks later, on another of my jaunts to the Republic. I'd made my dead-letter drops for the dissidents, I had a spare few hours, and I sought her out. I found her working in a women's refugee centre, giving, as she put it, something back for the help she'd been given. Her hair was trimmed, her skirt short, her cheeks pink, her habits unladylike. I spoke to her outside, as she took a cigarette break on the street. She'd applied for a place at Glasgow, to study zoology.

"I can take you back," I told her. "Back to your own world, where the knowledge you've picked up can make you famous, and rich."

She sucked hard on her cigarette and looked at me as if I were crazy. She waved a hand at the street, all ruts and litter and Party posters flapping in the breeze and GB's face and Straw's surveillance cameras everywhere.

"Why?" she demanded. "I like it here."

There's pleasing some people, that's the trouble.

The Wandering Christian

Eugene Byrne & Kim Newman

"I'm dying," said the madman next to him.

"So," Absalom grunted, feeling the arrowhead shift against his ribs, "there's a lot of that about."

"No," said the madman, eyes like candle flames, "I'm really dying."

Absalom coughed, bringing up blood. The arrow had dimpled one of his lungs, and he was slowly drowning, he supposed, his blood filling up his lungs. He knew more about doctoring than the barber-surgeons who occasionally came round to see what they could do for the wounded. As a soldier, he was more than familiar with the many ways a man could die.

He tried to remember whether he had seen the madman before, up on the walls of Rome, maybe defending one of the gates. Now, he was bearded and scrawny, his hands pressed on the yellow rag he held to his liver, trying to keep his insides in. His armour and weapons were long gone, passed on to a healthier defender.

"It's the end of time," he said. "What date is it?"

"The second day of Tammuz."

"No," the madman coughed, "the year? I've forgotten."

Absalom knew his One True Testament. "It's 4759," he said. "4759 years since the creation of the world. It's not the end of time at all. The Messiah has not come."

The madman grimaced, painfully. Absalom realized he really

was mad. Twenty-two years of soldiering, and he would die a forgotten hero with only a lunatic for company.

"Even if Rome falls, it will not be the end of time. The Chosen People will endure."

The madman began to choke, and Absalom thought he was about to pass away, but his coughs changed, turned to bitter laughter. He was beyond pain, beyond everything.

"The Chosen People," he said, "the Chosen People . . ."

Outside the walls, the Persians were gathered, half-heartedly building their earthen ramps to the edge of the city, barely bothering to launch attacks with their huge wooden siege-towers any more. They were catapulting rocks and corpses into the city, and firing rains of arrows, but mainly they waited for starvation and disease to do their job for them. At first, Shah Yzdkrt, known as Yzdkrt the Flayer, had decreed that all Gentiles would be allowed to pass unharmed through the besieging ranks and, after paying a small tribute, be allowed on their way. But the rumour was that those citizens foolhardy enough to believe him had been meekly led to a glade on the Tevere and slaughtered, their bodies dumped into the river in an attempt to poison the city's water supply. Two months ago, rabbi Judah, a good and humble merchant well known for his charitable works, was sent out to parley with the Persians, taking with him gifts for Yzdkrt and a message of peace from the Emperor. Yzdkrt had him slowly stripped of his skin, and his hide was stretched out on the ground before the main gate as a reminder to the besieged Romans of the fate the Shah had set aside for them all.

Governor David Cohen was ruthlessly enforcing siege regulations on the populace, military and civilian. Soldiers were on half-rations, all others on quarter-rations. Absalom heard that anyone who used water for washing was being put to death. Certainly, no one had offered to clean his wounds, with the result that even if he didn't drown he'd be eaten up by the mange spreading from the cuts on his body. The wounded were being stacked up in the catacombs, out of sight, but it was impossible to silence their screams. When he had been on patrol up above, everyone had been spooked by the groans coming from under the earth. Now he was with the groaners, and he thought he had a foretaste of Hell. There were a few lamps, but it was mainly gloomy, and some straw had been spread to lie on, but it was filthy with blood and shit. Latrines had been dug, but most of the wounded were unable to get to them without help, and there was no one to help. The tunnels were trickling with sewage.

A few of the more zealous or compassionate rabbis left their other trades or duties and ventured into the catacombs to comfort the dying. Absalom could always hear the low mumble of the kaddish under the screaming.

Rumours were the only entertainment the dying had. Absalom received the rumours from Isaac bar-Samuel to his left and passed them on to the madman as they came his way. It was rumoured that Governor Cohen was expecting an army of relief directly from the North, led by the Emperor in person; that the plague raging in the city had spread to the Persians, and that Yzdkrt himself had succumbed; that the men of Rome, no matter how young or old, were used up, and that the women were being impressed to bear arms against the Zoroastrian unbeliever. The madman took it all lightly, laughing as the yellow stain spread up his side.

The rats would have been a problem, only Governor Cohen had organized gangs of children to hunt them for food. The shochets were setting aside the dictates of kashrut and learning to make do with rodent meat. In the catacombs, where any animal that got within reach of a man deserved the swift death it inevitably got, even the niceties of butchering were being ignored. Raw ratmeat was tough, but chewing something helped lessen the pain.

A new rumour came down from Isaac. Above, it was noon-time, but the sky was dark. The sun had been blotted out, and a peculiar sign was visible in the sky, an upright cross, like the skeleton of a kite, stood out in fire against the black. The rabbis and scholars were arguing its significance, and no one could tell whether the sign was meant for the Chosen People inside the walls or the infidel beyond.

Absalom told the madman, and, for the first time, got a reaction out of him.

"It has come. It is time. One thousand years."

"What's the babbling idiot talking about?" Isaac asked.

Absalom shrugged, feeling a stabbing under his arm as his broken bones shifted.

"I don't know. He's mad."

There was a lot of that about too.

"No," the madman said, "listen . . ."

It was quieter than usual. The dying were calming down.

A rabbi scuttled around the corner, bent over by the low roof. He was hardly more than a boy, his beard still thin and wispy. His robes were full of tears, each rip a ritual sign of grief for a dying man he had attended. All the rabbis in the city were looking like beggars these days.

"Hear me," the madman said, "hear my confession . . ."

"What, what," said the rabbi, "confession, what's this, what's this?"

"Is it true about the sky?" Absalom asked.

"Yes," said the rabbi, "a rain of blood has fallen, and a lamb with a glowing heart has been seen in the clouds. Most significant."

"Of course, of course," said the madman. "He has returned. It was prophesied."

"I don't know what you're talking about," said the rabbi, "I know all the prophecies by heart, and this is without precedent."

"Hear me out."

There was something about the man that persuaded the rabbi. Absalom was interested too, and Isaac. A few of the others, dim shapes in the dark, pulled themselves nearer. The madman seemed to glow. His pain was forgotten, and he let the rag fall away from his festering wound. It was a bad one. Absalom could see into the man's entrails, and could tell they were not healthy. It must have been a sword stroke at one of the gate skirmishes that had done for him. But the madman did not feel the hurt any more. He sat up, and, as he spoke, his eyes glowed brighter . . .

*　*　*

My name is Joseph. I was born in Judaea a thousand years ago. No, I'm not mad. Well, maybe I am. A thousand years, a thousand deaths, would send anyone mad. Whatever, I'm a thousand years old.

When I was born, Judaea was ruled by the old Roman Empire. Romans were accustomed to being welcomed, or at least tolerated, as wise and beneficent rulers throughout their imperial domain. But they could never persuade the Judaeans to accept their rule and there was always a revolt going against them. The biggest of these, led by Judas of Galilee, was against a poll tax the Romans imposed. It was suppressed with efficient brutality. But the Romans never broke the spirit of the Jewish people, the Chosen People . . .

In a shithole called Nazareth, there grew up a humble carpenter. We were born in the same year, so we're the same age. He was Yeshua bar-Joseph; called, in the Romanized form, Jesus, son of Joseph. About the age of thirty, He decided to quit His trade and become a travelling preacher. He pulled in the crowds wherever He went. He also gathered a small band of dedicated followers, hangers-on who believed all He said and talked Him up with the rabble, and bully boys who kept Him out of trouble with the priests and the occupation goons. As Yeshua's reputation spread, so did the stories about Him, stories of miracles that He performed – walking on water, raising the dead, curing the sick, the crippled, the blind, the leprous . . . Back then, the cure for anything was a miracle. He could also turn water into wine, which made him very, very popular.

His disciples decided that Yeshua was the promised one, the Redeemer, the Messiah of the Jews. Others said He was the son of God. Yeshua the Nazarene, son of Joseph became known as Yeshua the Anointed One. In later years He would be called by the Greek word meaning the anointed one, Christos.

As I said, this was a bad time for Judaea politically; the Messiah, if Yeshua was He – something He never denied – was expected to rescue the country from the Romans.

He also annoyed the priests by saying the Law was only a starting point for moral improvement. His love of ordinary people no matter how much they had sinned and no matter how vile their status, annoyed the clergy even more. The ordinary people, understandably, loved Him. He mixed with harlots and tax-collectors and Samaritans. The scum of the earth. If you want to get a sect together, that's a good way to start. People who've been pissed on all their lives love being told they're something special. Rich people already know they're special.

It wasn't long before everyone in power wanted Yeshua dead. The Romans thought He might be a dangerous revolutionary. The Pharisees disagreed with His preaching. The Sadducees, who were rich and who wanted to placate the Romans and not disturb the status quo, regarded Him as a distasteful upstart with some funny ideas about people being resurrected after death. The Zealots, real diehards who wanted to remove the Romans by force, wanted to use Him as a figurehead for a revolt, even though He had renounced the use of violence. His ideas were peace, love, justice and prayer and He preached that the kingdom of God was coming, though He never said when it would arrive. If you want to know what happens to people who preach peace, love and justice, go ask Rabbi Judah.

After three years preaching on the road, Yeshua visited Jerusalem for the first time. Although He was just a hick from up-country Galilee coming to the political and religious centre of Judaea for the first time, He got a spectacular welcome. The mob turned out to see Him arrive. He came riding in on a donkey as if to say "look, I'm no better than any of the rest of you". And everyone was expecting Him to do great things. They threw palms to the ground in front of Him and lined the streets, asking him to do magic tricks. A cousin of mine, Jacob the wine merchant, turned up with a cartload of waterbags, and tried to get Him to turn them into wine, and he got beaten up by Peter bar-Jonah, who was Yeshua's strongarm man. That was one of the first things that put me off this so-called Anointed One.

His entry into Jerusalem raised everyone's expectations. And what's more, He had walked into the arms of the Romans and the priests. They would have no trouble getting their hands on Him now.

Everyone waited a few days to see what would happen. In the end, the priests decided to remove Him. One of Yeshua's close friends, Judas, was a Zealot. He wanted Yeshua to raise the people against the Romans, but when it became clear Yeshua would do no such thing, Judas tried to force His hand. He thought that if he led the priests to Yeshua, his friend would be forced to run from them and led the revolt, or that the people would be so outraged by the sight of Yeshua being put on trial for sedition or blasphemy that they would spontaneously rise up. Judas went to the priests and told them he could set Yeshua up for a nice quiet arrest. The priests agreed, and Judas led an armed posse of temple guards to Yeshua. But Yeshua, instead of making a hasty escape, went along meekly. Judas started to realize he'd made a big mistake, and emptied a few wineskins in misery.

The next day, Yeshua was taken before the Council of the Sanhedrin, who drew up a series of charges against Him. They wanted Yeshua safely dead, but they couldn't condemn Him to death themselves. They had to make a case that would convince the Romans to execute Him.

The priests, you understand, were not all evil men. Many of them were worried that the Nazarene would lead the whole of Judaea into confrontation with the Romans. This provincial troublemaker might have plunged the whole country into war, and that would have been bad for business for everybody. The high-priest, Caiaphas, told the other council members it was their duty to condemn this one man in order that the rest of the nation should not suffer.

Many members of the council wanted to hang a blasphemy charge on Yeshua, but Caiaphas persuaded them to ignore that, and use the charge that would frighten the Roman authorities most. So they alleged unfairly that He had been inciting revolt against Roman rule. A few days before, Yeshua had thrown a fit in the Temple, and kicked some money-changers out of the Court of the Gentiles, so the small business lobby was against Him. A couple of money-changers were prepared to allege that He was shouting "death to Caesar" as he roughed them up.

So the Sanhedrin handed Yeshua over to the Romans.

The procurator of Judaea at this time was Pontius Pilate. He

was an arrogant, insensitive blockhead. He enjoyed antag-
onizing the Jews, not that that was difficult. I don't even think
he always did it deliberately. He was just too stupid to understand all our little sensitivities.

So here he was, confronted with this guy the priests and a lot
of the mob wanted put to death. Nobody in the crowd seemed
to be a friend of the Nazarene any more. Perhaps everyone was
disappointed He hadn't challenged the Romans after all.

Pilate was a Roman; he respected due process of law. And the
Nazarene had committed no crime he could see. But he was in
a difficult position; much as he enjoyed lording it over his
subjects, he didn't want to start a riot, and the mob wanted
Yeshua dead. So you'd think he would have no problem just
killing the Nazarene quickly, and getting back to the baths or
eating grapes or whatever it is that Roman governors did all day.
Maybe he was just suspicious and didn't want to do anything
until he fully understood what was going on. That would have
been a problem, because no one understood what was going on.

Then Pilate's wife interfered. She was Claudia Procula, a
granddaughter of the Emperor Augustus, which gives you some
idea of how well-connected the procurator was back in Rome.
Just as he was sitting in judgment on Yeshua, he got a message
from Claudia, claiming that she had just had the worst nightmare ever, and all on account of the Nazarene. In the dream,
she foresaw all kinds of terrible things if her husband executed
the man. So now Pilate was having real trouble making his mind
up, which for him was pretty unusual.

What concluded the argument for Pilate was politics back
home. This was the time of the Emperor Tiberius. Tiberius was
cracked. He had retired to the island of Capri, surrounding
himself with astrologers and quacks. And, if you believe the
gossips, a small army of young people to cater to his increasingly
bizarre sexual tastes. For a while, the Empire was effectively run
by his guard commander, Sejanus, who, given a free hand, set
about clearing the way for himself to succeed Tiberius. Every
potential rival, including members of the imperial family, was
murdered or executed on trumped-up charges. Sejanus' plan
worked well enough until the Emperor's sister-in-law managed

to get to Capri and tell Tiberius what his Praetorian favourite was really getting up to. So Sejanus was toppled, and there was the usual bloodbath in which all his associates, including his children, were slaughtered. Pontius Pilate, a self-seeking dickhead, had been a supporter of Sejanus. Now, a year or two after the fall of Sejanus, Pilate's loyalty to Caesar is questionable as far as Caesar is concerned.

Caiaphas knew this, and he whispered to Pilate that Yeshua was setting Himself up as King of Judaea. He added that Pilate could be no friend of Caesar's if he did not execute the Nazarene. The last thing Pilate needed was a letter from Rome telling him to come home with his will written out in triplicate. He gave his permission for the Nazarene to be put to death. As was the usual practice, Yeshua was taken out and executed at once.

I know, my friends, that we live in a barbaric age in which the days of the great Roman Empire are sometimes looked on fondly, but the way they killed Christos was atrocious. Believe me, Absalom, an arrow in the lungs is a luxurious hot bath next to crucifixion.

That was what the Romans did to Him. It was reserved for those they despised the most. It's the worst possible way I've ever come across for a man to die. No Roman noble or citizen could be crucified because it was considered a form of death unfair for free men. It was for slaves, thieves, bandits and – of course – for those who rebelled against Rome.

It all started with a thrashing. The soldiers trussed you up and flogged you. They used a long whip with pieces of bone or metal studded in the end. The thong wrapped itself right around the body, tearing off flesh as it went. After three times thirteen lashes – sometimes more – there was more skin hanging off your back and chest than was left hanging on.

Having softened you up like this, they made you lift a heavy wooden beam and stagger off to the place of execution. In Jerusalem at this time, it was a small hill outside the city walls called Golgotha, the Place of Skulls.

Here there was a vertical wooden post six or seven feet high. When you got there, you were invited to drop the beam you'd been carrying. Then the soldiers knocked you over and lay the back of your neck in the middle of the beam. Then they stretched out one of your arms along the beam. A couple of the men held the arm down while another one took one of those big, long four-sided nails and hammered it through your wrist into the wood below.

Having nails through the wrist is extremely painful. Believe me, I know.

After they'd done this with the other arm, the whole execution squad lent a hand to lift up the crossbeam with you hanging from it, yelling your lungs out in agony, or maybe just biting your tongue, determined not to give those filthy bastards any pleasure by letting on you were suffering.

But then you found it very difficult not to yell out when they actually lifted you off the ground.

There was a hole in the middle of the beam roughly under your head. This they slotted into the vertical piece already wedged in the ground.

Now they bent your knees upward until the sole of one foot was pressed flat against the vertical piece. Well fuck my old sandals if they didn't then produce another one of those big nails.

A nail through the foot is more – much more – painful than a nail through the wrist. They hammered it through one foot, and when the point came through the sole of that foot, they hammered it through the other foot and into the wood.

Then they would leave you alone. Some would watch, maybe they would take bets with one another on how long you'd live. After a while, it got boring, and they'd post a guard and go off to get drunk or screw a hog or whatever it was that legionaries did in their time off.

About now, you'd wish that you were back in the barracks being flogged. If, by any strange mischance, you had not gone out of your mind, you might have time to wish they had flogged you harder because the flogging weakened you. And the weaker you were, the sooner you died. And death was the only thing you desired. Death was the only thing left.

You didn't bleed much, but the pain was indescribable. The weight of your body hanging from your wrists pulled your chest upwards as though you'd taken the biggest, deepest breath ever. But you couldn't breathe out. To breathe out, you'd have to push upwards with your legs. Pushing up with your legs was indescribably painful because of that bloody nail running through your feet.

At the same time, there was even more pain coming from cramps in your hands, along your arms and shoulders and chest.

You were in all this pain, and you could hardly breathe. If you were really lucky, you'd bleed, or more likely suffocate, to death in perhaps five hours. If you weren't lucky, it could take days.

And those clever, cunning, oh-so-bloody civilized Romans could vary it. They could hammer a piece of wood into the vertical piece, like a little seat under your arse. That meant it was slightly easier to breathe because you didn't have to push on your legs so much, so you hung there for longer. Or they could tie your arms to the cross-piece as well as nailing them there. That had the same effect. Maybe the sons of bitches used both methods. I've seen poor bastards spend nearly a week dying that way. If the Romans liked you – or your relatives bribed them – they could break your legs. That way, you couldn't push yourself up to breathe even if you wanted to, so you suffocated fairly quickly.

So don't talk to me about the old Roman civilization. I know they had central heating and straight roads and the greatest army the world has ever known, but at the back of all that they were the biggest shits in creation. Look, if some barbarian king back in the Dark Ages wanted you dead, what did he do? Cut off your head, or bludgeon your brains out, or drown you, or throw you off a high rock. All pretty quick. The Romans, being three times as clever and ten times as organized as any barbarian were a hundred times more savage in their methods of murdering people.

And that's what they did to Yeshua Christos.

Pilate, being Pilate, got his revenge on the priests for blackmailing him. Whenever someone was crucified, the law said that you had to have a plaque on the top saying what crime the victim was condemned for. Pilate ordered that the inscription read

"Yeshua of Nazareth, King of the Jews", and had it written in Latin, Greek and Hebrew to make sure everyone got the message. This was hung around Yeshua's neck when He was on his way to the execution and then it was nailed to the top of the cross.

So how do I know all these things? Well, first, I was there when He was crucified. Secondly, I've been crucified myself. Lots of times. They say you have no memory for pain. That's crap. I shiver every time I pass a carpenter's shop or hear someone hammering. And I'm immortal. Or I was until today.

A thousand years ago, my name was Cartaphilus. I was a good, law-biding, unimaginative orthodox Jew. And I worked as doorkeeper to Pontius Pilate. He needed doorkeepers because most people who came to visit a Roman governor were either too important to touch a door themselves or too busy crawling and begging to bother with one. The first time I met Yeshua of Nazareth was as he was being led out to be executed. He had just been scourged. The soldiers had put this crown of thorns on Him. They wanted to have their part in annoying the priests as well and were playing up to Pilate's crack about Yeshua being King of the Jews. Yeshua was being led out, struggling under the weight of the cross-piece of the crucifixion-frame.

Now at that time most of what I knew about Him was rumour – that and what my cousin Jacob the wine-merchant said when he dropped in to have his head bandaged. Some people were claiming Yeshua was the Messiah, the king of the Jews. But the high priest Caiaphas had wanted Him condemned to death. Being a good Jew, I figured that anything Caiaphas said must be kosher. If the high priest wanted the Nazarene killed, then he had his good, religious, reasons. So, what can I say? I was an idiot.

The Nazarene was trying to get through the door. I spat on Him. He fell down under the weight of the wooden beam. I put my foot on His back, where He had been whipped and the flesh was hanging off him. I pushed with my foot and told Him to get up and get a move on.

Someone had told me He sacrificed and ate small children. And, back then, I was callous.

He cried out. Then He got up, picked up the beam with some effort and he looked at me. He said, "I am going quickly to my death. But you will wait a long time for death. You will be waiting until I return."

I didn't know what to make of this. I didn't think much about it. A couple of soldiers hit Him with the flats of their swords and off He went to Golgotha.

His words didn't sink in at first, then a strange panic overtook me. I realized He'd put some kind of curse on me. Even if He was a blasphemer, He was still some kind of holy man. I was very troubled. An hour and a half after He had spoken to me, I quit my doorkeeper's job forever.

I ran to Golgotha. He was nailed to his cross in between two Zealots. He was still alive, but quiet, not struggling and groaning as much as the other two. There weren't many other people around, just some ghouls. His disciples had all deserted him. Whether Yeshua was the son of God or not, no man would want to be associated with Him and run the risk winding up nailed to the next-cross-but-one.

There were a few women around. Friends and relatives. And the execution squad was there, playing dice for his possessions. But there was a strange thing, a Roman officer – I don't know if he was in charge of the execution squad – was pacing up and down, looking at the dying man and muttering to himself.

The Centurion looked at me and beckoned me over. In those days, you did everything in your power to avoid those people. They brutalized their own soldiers enough, and they could be lethal to ordinary civilians, especially in a country they could barely control. I was terrified as I walked over to him. But all he did was grab me by the shoulders, look straight into my eyes and say, "Truly, this man was the son of God." All he wanted was someone to listen.

The son of God! Only afterwards did I realize what a queer thing this was for a Roman to be saying. Romans believed in lots of gods. The only people around who believed in one god were we Jews. Maybe the Centurion was Jewish. I don't know.

The son of God!

If the Centurion was right, then I was condemned forever.

I lost my reason. I walked to the foot of the cross and begged the Nazarene to forgive me. But it was too late. He was in too much pain to take any notice.

Then I went over to the women, who were all crying and pulling at their hair and I joined them. One of the whores had seen me kicking Him. They didn't want to know me. I can't blame them for that.

I was too troubled and too ashamed to seek out the Nazarene's friends. Not that he had many at this stage. His male followers were in hiding. Even good old Peter, who was no slouch when it came to beating the crap out of money-changers and wine-merchants, was at this moment loudly claiming he had never heard of Yeshua and didn't like him anyway. As for Judas the Zealot, he hanged himself because his plan had gone wrong. I regretted that. In the next few years, he would have been company.

I began to wander. I left my wife and my family and walked first north, towards Galilee. I don't know why. An evil spirit within me told me that I must wander the face of the world until He should return.

The nights were always the worst. As evening drew in and the shadows lengthened, my own shadow would become that of Yeshua struggling under the weight of that wooden beam.

Years later, I heard what happened. The Romans liked to leave corpses hanging to rot as an example to any other would-be offenders. But the Jewish law would not permit bodies to be exposed in this way on the Sabbath, and the day after Yeshua's execution was the Sabbath. Joseph, a man from a place called Arimathea, a rich and influential Jew who was friendly both with Yeshua's family and with Pilate, approached the governor. After the Romans had checked that Yeshua was dead, Joseph got permission to take the body down and he buried It in the tomb he had bought for himself.

A few days later, Yeshua of Nazareth rose from the dead. He visited his frightened followers who took strength from seeing Him again. Some time after that He ascended to Heaven to take his place at the right hand of the Lord.

Don't be so shocked, rabbi. Just because it isn't in your One True Testament doesn't mean it didn't happen.

Yeshua's followers now dispersed throughout the Empire and beyond, spreading the story of how He had come to save man from his sins. Some of them began their work right there in Jerusalem, but they were driven out by the authorities. One of them, a man named Stephen, was stoned to death for blasphemy.

At first, followers of Christos and those they baptized into their faith seemed to be forming a new sect of Judaism, but soon it became clear that there were important differences. One of the others, Philip, met an Ethiopian on the road from Jerusalem to Gaza. The Ethiopian was an important court official in the service of the queen of his country. He was a eunuch. As you know, a man who is not whole may not become a Jew. The eunuch asked Philip, "Is there anything to prevent me being baptized?" And Philip answered, "Nothing."

From now on, said the Christians, there would be no distinction between Jews and Gentiles, slaves and freedmen, men and women. The Ethiopian returned to Nubia and told his fellow citizens the good news.

The number of Christians multiplied rapidly. The faith was taken by the missionaries into Africa and Syria, to Mesopotamia and even as far as India. Syria, with its great cities of Antioch, Damascus and Edessa, became a great centre of the Christian religion.

Don't be ashamed that you've not heard of Christianity. It was a long time ago.

What of me?

My travels took me to Rome where I found a thriving community of believers in the Christian sect. I joined them, and learned more of Yeshua's teachings. I was baptized into their faith, meaning they dunked me in water in a ceremony similar to that of immersion in the mikveh. I changed my name to Joseph in honour of Joseph of Arimathea.

By now, I was almost a hundred years old, though I looked no older than the day on which I had abused our Saviour. My new faith brought me peace of a sort, for Yeshua Christos taught that the most loathsome of sins would be forgiven by the Lord His

Father. I had spat on Him and kicked Him, and while I dared not admit this to my comrades I could hope that when He returned I would be forgiven. In those days we all believed His return was imminent. This is what we told one another, and it is what we preached to any who were willing to listen, and many who did not wish to hear. We were a nuisance to some, offensive to others. Some of our number, including Peter the thug, were executed by the authorities. My cousin Jacob the wine-merchant, whose fault all this was, prospered and lived to be one hundred and fifteen, at which age he was still fathering children.

We were unsure of our relationship with the orthodox Jews. Most of us considered ourselves a Jewish sect. Others, generally the hotheads, thought we should be completely separate. There were many Jews in Rome and we debated with them whether or not Yeshua had been the Messiah. We believed so, but they did not. On many occasions we fought openly in the streets. We gradually came to realize there was no reconciliation between us.

There was a great fire that wrecked the city centre. The Emperor Nero's new palace was badly damaged. Nero was spendthrift and unpredictable and unpopular, and the rumour went about the market that he had started the fire deliberately. Another story had it that he had done nothing to quench the fires, and had played a lyre and recited his poems as the city burned, for he considered himself a great artist. Having been burned alive and having heard Nero recite in public, I can honestly say I preferred the former experience.

Nero, probably at the suggestion of one of his toadies, wanted to blame the fire on the Jews. The Jews were unpopular in Rome for while their religion was tolerated, they did not worship the Roman Gods. Nero's wife Poppaea discouraged him from persecuting the Jews. She was not Jewish herself, but was sympathetic to them. She said that Nero should instead blame the Christians. Nero readily agreed. We were to be used in the manner of a scapegoat.

Nero, by the way, also ordered the death of the aged Pontius Pilate. I don't know why. Pilate was in Gaul at that time, and the story goes that he was staked out, cut open in a few places and eaten alive by worms. Perhaps this was just wishful thinking on our part.

Nero ordered his brutish Praetorian prefect Tigellinus to do his dirty work. The soldiers came for us and, after trials of sorts in which they seemed more interested in our "hatred of humanity" than our alleged arson, we were despatched in all manner of ways. Not by crucifixion, but by the sword, or by being sewn into the skins of wild animals and being attacked and eaten by dogs in the circus. That was a good one – it hurt like a bastard. At first, our persecution was popular. People disliked us for our disdain for their gods, and for preaching our own faith so aggressively. Then Nero's excesses turned many to pity, while others were inspired by the way in which we died for our faith. This happened particularly after Nero ordered that Christians be tied to crosses that were set in tubs of oil. This was at night and we were then set ablaze and used like oversized torches to light an avenue through the Emperor's gardens, along which His Talentless Majesty proceeded in his chariot.

I was one of those Christians.

I've said much about suffering already, so I shall spare you a detailed description of what it is to be set in oil and pitch and burned alive. In spite of all the pain and the terror which I and my brothers and sisters experienced, I am proud to say that we all went to our deaths without show of fear and with great joy, for would we not soon be reunited with our Saviour?

But imagine my surprise when, after experiencing considerable physical agony and apparently dying, I woke up the next day as though nothing had happened. In Judaea.

That's a bloody long way from Rome.

Now I began to fully understand the meaning of Yeshua's curse upon me. To atone for my great sin I would have to wander the world of men until His return. This was the first occasion on which I had died and now I found I had not been granted the release of death but had remained among men. My soul was chained to the earth in the same body and my martyrdom in the Emperor's gardens had not taken.

Whenever I died subsequently, I would not know what happened to my corpse, but I always awoke in the same body –

or a similar one – in some new and frequently distant land.

Waking from the dead this first time in Judaea, I soon discovered what my purpose was to be.

I entered Jerusalem and, without bothering to seek out others among the Christian community, I begged food and drink and preached the good news of Christos in public. Within three days the Sanhedrin had me stoned to death as a blasphemer. Again, I did not truly die. I woke up in a different place, Corinth. Again I preached the message of Christos and again, though it took me a few years this time, I was martyred.

At around the same time as the last great Jewish rebellion against Rome, which as you know resulted in the destruction of the Temple and the sack of Jerusalem, I became a professional martyr. At the same time as the Romans were causing the Jews to disperse throughout the world, I, too, travelled, seeking out death. The Voice of the Lord told me that in this way I was doing penance for my sin, that the example shown to others by martyrs would win people over to our Church.

For almost three hundred years after the death of Yeshua, a great many of his followers died martyrs' deaths. Martyrdom was an idea we borrowed from the Jews and turned into a fine art, my friends. Martyrdom, we told ourselves, was a second baptism and a highway to heaven, which indeed it was – for everyone except me. Every time a crowd lynched me, or a magistrate ordered me be burned, beheaded or savaged by animals, I awoke in a new place and sought out the Christian community and joined it, or simply preached the gospels in the nearest town square.

The persecutions were more intense at some times than at others. When they did occur, they were for a number of reasons.

In the early days, for instance, we would always hold our meetings before dawn. This went against the spirit of the Twelve Tables, which were at the centre of Roman law and which forbade nightly meetings. So the Romans got suspicious of us, thinking we were conspiring, or committing shameful acts. We would sing or chant, exchange oaths not to commit crimes and we would have a meal in common. This led us to be suspected of magic.

They despised us, too, for the simplicity of our faith. Sophisticated patricians looked down on us because we avoided demonstrative argument, preferring to talk about Yeshua's miracles and re-tell parables they thought were childish. They called us "Galileans" and mocked our faith as a religion for slaves.

Before too long, they also came to despise many of us for the way in which we sought out martyrdom. The Emperor Marcus Aurelius, a snobbish old dilettante who fancied himself as a philosopher, said he hated the vulgar and undignified way in which we went to our deaths. Tell me, what were we supposed to do? If wild dogs had chewed his balls off in the circus, I'm sure he would have been really fucking dignified about it.

But I think what annoyed educated pagans most was our certainty that there was only one true God. The Romans tolerated all religions, even the Jews, on the principle that each man should worship in the way he sees most fitting. Now we came along and preached the absolute truth in the face of their ancient deities – gods that had, after all, brought Rome great prosperity and success. And now we working-class upstarts came along saying everyone else was wrong and that we had a monopoly of truth.

All manner of wild rumours circulated about us. They said we worshipped the head of an ass. They said that we met every week to sacrifice and then eat a baby. You can imagine how I felt when I first heard that old chestnut. I couldn't bring myself to sneer at those stupid enough to believe it. After all, I am cursed not only with longevity but with a perfect memory. Now you know why I wasn't too impressed yesterday when Isaac told us the rumour that old Yzdkrt out there dines on babies every Sabbath. Mind you, with him it just might be true.

The Romans also accused us of incest, perhaps from our habit of calling one another "brother" and "sister". They said that we worshipped the genitals of our priests. More damaging were the stories of sexual licence because, I regret, some of these were true.

We were scattered throughout the Empire. Congregations developed with little contact with one another, and there was no unifying authority to establish the detail of our rites and beliefs. Mainly this made little difference and most Christians lived – or tried to live – good and pious lives. But there were heresies in a few places; some, for example, debated whether Christos had been god or man – He was obviously both – and other points of belief. The worst heresy I ever witnessed was that of the Phibionites.

They lived in Alexandria, and I landed among them the day after I'd had my head cut off in Philadelphia. The sect had been founded by a man named Nicholas of Antioch and their rites took the idea of heavenly love to obscene extremes. They held their wives in common and would, in a travesty of our communion ceremony, smear semen and menstrual blood on their hands offering these as the "body and blood" of our Redeemer. If any woman among them became pregnant as a result of one of their orgies, they would abort her and eat the foetus mixed with honey and pepper.

It became clear to me that these were not wicked or licentious people. They had just been led tragically astray by Satan, and they sincerely believed that in offering up what they called "the essence of man" in sacrifice, they were honouring the Lord.

I poisoned them all and prayed for the salvation of their souls. Mine too.

What else was I to do? Had I reported them to the authorities, I would only have been handing them a great propaganda opportunity. They would simply have said, "Look, this is how all Christians behave."

I tried in all things to emulate the example of Yeshua, as I had heard from those who knew him and as I read in our sacred books, the Gospels. Though we needed leaders, though we had our elders and priests and bishops, I never sought a position of prominence in the Church because I, who had kicked our Saviour, was never worthy of it. I wanted to be the humblest member of each congregation I joined. At other times, I lived the life of a beggar, travelling the roads and preaching in every town I came to.

I would sometimes go for years on end without being martyred, no matter how much I sought it. At other times, I could be killed ten times in a month. If you are tempted to say that being killed was no penance for me because I would always wake up again, you are mistaken. Almost every time I and my brethren were arrested we suffered torture or humiliation. Death itself was frequently agonising. Though I am still not worthy of God's mercy for abusing his only-begotten son, I have suffered a great deal of physical pain.

I have been beheaded, starved to death, flayed alive, strangled, hanged, crucified, burned, gored by bulls, bitten by dogs, clawed by leopards, crushed by bears. And that's not counting plague, poison, accident, lightning-bolts, murder, drowning and bad falls.

Frequently, martyrdom was a public spectacle in the local arena, paid for by some fat local worthy to earn popularity by pandering to the blood-lusts of the mob. Carthage was the worst. Once, a Christian woman named Perpetua and her servant-girl Felicitas were sent into the arena to face wild animals. One was just a frail girl, barely out of childhood. The other had given birth a day or two before. Both were half-naked. I watched as the crowd roared its disapproval at this sickening spectacle and offered thanks to the Lord. But it turned out that all they wanted was for the women to be clothed more modestly. When they came back, fully covered, a few minutes later, the good people of Carthage cheered and applauded and sat back to enjoy the show, their sense of decency fully intact. Comrades, the greatest burden I carry is that of my sin, but the second hardest thing for me after that is to follow Yeshua's edict to love all men.

Meanwhile, events in the Roman Empire continued their course, often affecting us. We were never great in number, but by the second century after Yeshua's death, we had a terrible reputation. At the beginning of the reign of Emperor Marcus Aurelius, for instance, there was a great plague. Nero, had he known it, had set a vogue, and the Christians were blamed in many places for this pestilence. By now, there was a popular expression, "the rains fail because of the Christians".

Marcus Aurelius was succeeded by his ridiculous, hedonistic son Commodus. He was besotted by every vice imaginable and, rather than govern, gave himself up to pleasure. He abandoned his father's war with the German tribes, which endangered the security of the borders. He began to believe he was Hercules and became fond of wrestling. When people could take no more of this behaviour, they had him strangled in his sleep by Narcissus, who was a real wrestler. From the point of view of the Romans, Commodus' lack of interest in military matters was a disaster. It was scarcely any better for we Christians, for while the Romans occasionally wished us extinct, the Empire provided something approaching peace and prosperity. The alternatives were much worse, for now barbarians of numerous races and savage beliefs were crowding in on the frontiers.

After Commodus, the next hundred years were like the end of the world. A succession of weak Emperors, always looking behind their backs for treachery, vied for the imperial purple. Usually they were second-rate soldiers. In a period of fifty years, there were twenty-one Emperors. Only two of them, my friends, died of old age. It's hard to remember the names of any of them, apart from Elagabalus and Valerian. Elagabalus was insane, dominated by his mother and was given to suffocating dinner-guests under rose petals. That one sounds interesting. Valerian was captured by the Persians and flayed alive by King Shapur who had his skin dried and salted and kept on display as a trophy. Yzdkrt outside probably regards Shapur as a hero. People from that part of the world always were keen on skinning people. I don't know why. Anyway, for a Roman Emperor to be captured and to suffer such a humiliating death was terrible. Nobody could feel safe any more.

I saw none of these things; most Christians eschewed service in the army. Yet on my martyrdom-induced travels, I could tell that the framework of the Empire was rotting. If there were any blessing hidden in this chaos it was that our Church gained more converts. We were always the first to help people in distress with money and labour, and we offered people a vision of hope in a troubled time. People began to respect and even like us. And with the officials distracted by other troubles, we could practise our religion openly in many places.

For all practical purposes, the Empire collapsed. But people clung on to the idea of Empire. Many, many, places that I visited at this time were untouched by war and prospered. Others were less lucky. Even the fortunate regions did not know when the army of one imperial contender or another would march through like a locust swarm and just requisition what it wanted. Much worse, in the frontier regions, there was the ever-present fear that barbarians, who were jealous of Roman prosperity and eager for human and material plunder, would sweep across the river or the ramparts, killing, burning, and raping everything in their path. I saw it happen often enough. I tell you, you haven't known real discomfort until you've been buggered by a Visigoth.

At the end of the third century after Christos' birth, the Emperor Diocletian restored some order. The government had been organized so that four men ruled together; one in the east, one in the west and their two named successors. Diocletian, Emperor of the East, happened to be the strongest among his own tetrarchy. Need I add that Diocletian was an enthusiastic persecutor of Christians? His persecution had two causes. First, there was an occasion on which the entrails of sacrificial animals looked particularly unpromising and the pagan priests, reaching for the usual excuse, blamed the Christians for it. Second, he consulted the oracle of Apollo at Didyma, who told him that his ability to give advice was being hampered by the Christians. It got to the point where if a man's wife didn't want sex of an evening, she said the Christians had given her a headache. Diocletian passed an edict of persecution, ordering our churches destroyed, our services banned and our scriptures burned. This was in the eastern half of the Empire, and the persecution was ferocious. I got to be burned along with a pile of Gospels in the market place at Caesaraea. The western half of the Empire was relatively unaffected.

Diocletian's sidekick and supposed successor, the Caesar Maximin, was really keen on carrying out his master's edict in the provinces he controlled. He ordered that food on sale in the markets be sprinkled with libations or blood from pagan offerings. Checks on Christians were to be carried out at city gates or public baths. He put about scandalous libels about Christos. Guess what? Christos was supposed to eat babies! Big fucking surprise! Prostitutes were tortured into confessing that they had taken part in Christian orgies and our bishops were ordered into new jobs as shit-shovellers in the imperial stables. However, Maximin's campaign was not a brilliant success. He had to offer tax-breaks to get city authorities to bother persecuting us. There were a very large number of martyrdoms, it is true, and lots of Christians paid bribes or offered sacrifices before a statue of the Emperor in order to save themselves. But most ordinary pagans weren't too bothered about hounding us. Everyone knew by now the stories about child-sacrifice and incest and conspiracy were nonsense – well, most of them did. In many places, Christians had shown more compassion and charity than the rest of the community put together, especially in times of crisis. And there had been plenty of those recently. So what Diocletian and Maximin had hoped would be a killer blow to the Church, at least in the East, was nothing of the sort.

We had our own problems. I've already mentioned how disunified we were. We were now arguing among ourselves on various fine points of belief, and even the persecutions were causing bitter argument. Some said those who had not had the courage to face martyrdom and who had sacrificed to the Emperor to save their lives should not be readmitted to the Church. Others pointed out the all-encompassing love of God which welcomes all repentant sinners. It was a bad time for us.

But now, something completely unexpected happened. Diocletian abdicated and the strong man among the tetrarchy turned out to be a man named Constantine. Some years previously, he had been at the head of troops in the north of Britain – a cold, miserable, wet, piss-sodden island that I don't recommend you ever visit. At the same time, I wound up there after being martyred at Edessa under Diocletian's persecution. I had surrendered myself to the pagan soldiers, who told me to look to my safety and hide myself. They took a great deal of persuasion before they would imprison and kill me. In Britain, I had barely got my mouth open and the name of Yeshua out when I was thrown into a pit full of hungry wolves.

Constantine, on the death of his father, was proclaimed tetrarch by his troops, an event I did not witness directly. The other tetrarchs, however, had fallen to fighting among themselves, while Constantine bided his time. For five years, he trained his army and put it about that he was descended from one of the great imperial houses. Then he did something wonderful.

He announced his conversion to Christianity.

It seems he had been impressed by the fortitude, not to say guts, of a Christian missionary he had seen being thrown into a pit full of wolves at York. A year later, he had seen a Christian preaching in Gaul who was the dead image of the first man. That was one of the few times I ever encountered someone from an earlier life in a later one and, typically, I can't remember seeing the future Emperor at either occasion. The wolves, in the first place, and the jeering crowd, in the second, distracted me. Still, that's the nearest I've come to influencing the course of history.

I joined Constantine's army as an infantryman. After all, I had never been martyred in battle before.

There were a few other Christians in the army. Christians had regarded it as forbidden to serve in the imperial forces, but many had done so since soldiering, like being a blacksmith or tailor is a trade and a man cannot be prevented from practising his trade. I knew it was my duty to lend my strength, such as it was, to a Christian commander who might become a Christian Emperor.

Constantine's army was, for the main part, a pagan force, with lots of thick provincials, particularly Germans, and almost no real Romans. The soldiers worshipped German tribal deities, the orthodox Roman gods, or were followers of Mithras. None were upset by Constantine's conversion. The Romans regarded a man's religion as his own business, and it was almost traditional for an Emperor or would-be Emperor to favour a particular cult. So nobody was uncomfortable with the idea of a Christian leader and my comrades-in-arms and I got along well enough once they had beaten me up and twisted my arm until I promised to stop trying to convert them.

Constantine bided his time until at last he broke with the tetrarchy and marched across the Alps to invade Italy. His aim was to overthrow the tetrarch Maxentius, whose base was at Rome.

While Constantine was a Christian, many of his officers consulted soothsayers and astrologers. Not one of them said that the omens for Constantine's success were good. Some predicted outright disaster. There was a Jew, Benjamin, in our platoon, and he went around for days shaking his head and waving his hands whenever anyone asked him how he expected us to do in the war.

We marched into Italy, fought a series of skirmishes and small battles and on each occasion we thrashed that bastard Maxentius. With the remains of his army, Maxentius retreated to Rome and barricaded himself in the city to pass his days and nights furiously sacrificing to his pagan gods and casting spells against Constantine.

Now we reached the outskirts of Rome, expecting that we would have to settle down to a long siege. As you know, this isn't an easy city to take by force and it was no different back then, seven hundred years ago.

But on the day we arrived there was a strange sign in the noonday sun. Not all the soldiers could see it, but many did. It was the sign of the cross, symbol of the love of Christos, set into the middle of the sun's orb.

Does that sound familiar?

Beneath it there appeared a legend in Latin writing. I explained to those of my fellow-soldiers around me – they could not read – that it said, "by this sign, conquer".

A message from God! Or so we thought.

Everyone who saw the sign understood it to mean that Christianity was about to win us the war. In camp that night, we talked of nothing else, and the other soldiers were at last interested in hearing what I had to tell them about Christos. Benjamin converted on the spot since, as a Jew, he had a head start on Yeshua's teachings, which extended the One True Testament.

Constantine, who had also seen everything, now gave orders that a special banner be made bearing the sign of the cross to be carried at the head of the army. He further ordered that we soldiers paint the sign of the cross on our shields, for had it not said in the sky that we would conquer by that sign? This was an order I complied with joyfully, though many of the other soldiers grumbled because they had already painted the images or symbols of their pagan gods, or the thunderbolts of Zeus, on their shields.

The following day dawned and, before Constantine could set about investing the city properly, Maxentius emerged from the gates to offer us pitched battle.

This looked really promising, because there were 40,000 trained fighting men in our army, while Maxentius could barely muster half that number, and many of them were reluctant conscripts. Even without the sign of the cross in the sky we would have been confident of winning.

The two armies faced one another on a plain to the north of the city crossed by the Tevere. We grunts guessed that Constantine's strategy would be to overwhelm the enemy's flanks, try to surround him, then squeeze Maxentius like an orange in his fist. We were looking forward to the squeezing.

This is indeed how the battle began, with cavalry and infantry at either side advancing first. But then the enemy's heavy cataphract cavalry came charging at our centre, which is where I was posted. This should not have panicked us; we should have set our spears in the ground and presented the enemy with a bristling wall of sharp steel. But something went wrong. In a moment in which the course of history can be made by the irrational behaviour of a few people, somebody panicked and ran. That started everybody off.

Benjamin got about ten yards before some horseman got his lance through him.

Constantine, mounted on his horse behind us, with a man bearing the banner of the cross next to him, tried to rally the troops, but now a rout set in. Men dropped their cross-painted shields and threw down their weapons to make a quicker getaway. It was madness, as even an imbecile would have known had he not been seized by blind terror. For in running away and refusing to form a wall against the enemy, they simply made it easier for the cavalry to come among them and cut them down like ripe corn.

Constantine tried to close the gap in his line, calling for men to either side to move in and repel the cavalry, but it was too late. Maxentius, seizing his chance, was following up his attack with infantry who were now rushing across to split our army in two. Then the cataphracts reached Constantine himself and overwhelmed him and captured his banner. I heard cheering in the distance and saw the top of the banner above the fighting as it was carried towards Maxentius' lines. I knew we were lost. Moments later, I was beheaded – I think – by a single sword-stroke from behind and died again. What we had thought was a sign from God had been a cruel deception by Satan.

So, in my lives, I've been at two sieges of Rome and, each time, I've been with the losing side.

The death of Constantine robbed the Empire of a strong and able ruler who could have restored it to stability and then to glory. His defeat also completely discredited our Church. Maxentius, believing all his sacrifices to the pagan gods had brought him success, ensured his victory, and then deliberately spared the lives of as many of Constantine's soldiers as possible. This was his way of making sure that the story of the Christian God's false promise to Constantine would be spread widely.

Now the persecutions more or less stopped, but the death of Constantine had a powerful effect. The Romans, who judged a deity by its effectiveness, merely laughed at us where they had once hated us. While this was happening, we had become busily caught up in bitter theological arguments among ourselves.

Maxentius was overthrown within a few years by another little general and the Empire, beset on all sides by barbarians, lapsed into painful decline. Some of the barbarians were placated with lands, others with positions of high office, but anyone could see that the Roman Peace had become a hollow joke. The Empire was formally split into Eastern and Western kingdoms a hundred years later.

The Eastern and Western kingdoms fragmented in religion just as they did politically. Many worshipped the old Roman gods, others turned to the ancient Greek ones. The Persian religion of Zoroaster became popular in the Eastern kingdom and was adopted by King Justinian and Queen Eudoxia. Among the common people of the countryside there were spirits older than antiquity to be propitiated at set times of the year. The barbarians, meanwhile, brought in their childish, idiotic cults. In the West, rulers and soldiers remained loyal to Mithras.

The Western kingdom collapsed completely five hundred years ago, and its place was taken by barbarian fiefdoms whose rulers constantly warred with one another while retaining varying amounts of old Roman customs and laws. The Eastern kingdom prospered after a fashion, and the military successes of King Justinian and then King Belisarius kept the barbarians at bay.

I was rarely martyred for my faith now, and for over three hundred years I wandered the world, preaching the Gospels. I gained few converts. Most people thought I was a crank to be either pitied or kicked out of town by the nightwatchmen. I travelled as far as India, but the Indians, too, have their ancient gods and would not listen to me.

There were still many Christian communities left in the world, but they were increasingly to be found in isolated places, among more simple, credulous people. It was a very depressing time. At first, people would tell jokes about Constantine's defeat and how stupid and cowardly Christians were. They would say our churches were built of reeds because Mithras-worshippers didn't like pulling down stone buildings. Or they would ask how many Christians it takes to hammer in a nail, and answer none, because the nail usually hammers them. After a while, even the jokes stopped as more and more people just forgot all about the Christians. I think I preferred it when they were still telling jokes about us. Oh, here's another one – why do Christians wear big crosses on their tunics? No? It's to make it easier for the archers.

I drifted towards the country that in the time of the Empire had been known as Gaul and part of which was now the kingdom of the Franks. I reverted to my old trade of doorkeeper and found employment at the court of King Charles, son of

King Pepin the Short, just after his accession. I had not intended to stay, but I became aware that this was a place in which interesting things were happening.

Charles was everything you would expect a great king to be – a brave and resourceful soldier and a great athlete. He was over six feet tall and very handsome. People always remarked on his keen and expressive eyes, though I never saw anything special in them myself. Charles was also, as kings at that time went, very learned. He could speak Latin and Greek, though he could not, at first, read or write. That's the credit side of his account.

He had a terrible secret, however. Early in his reign, his power went to his head in a strange way. A king can have any woman – or for that matter, any man or boy – he wants. The woman Charles wanted when he was a young man was his sister Iolande. I saw it myself. The worst-kept secret on earth was the fact that the Frankish king was sneaking into the chamber of his sister in his big, cold castle at Aachen every night.

What do you do if you see something like that? You can keep your peace, which is what most people did. You can plot to overthrow the king for his shocking, unnatural vice. But in the court of King Charles of the Franks, nobody dared to do that. In any case, morals had sunk to such a low ebb that few were as shocked by this as you might imagine. The third thing is you can plot to lure him away from his vice. That is what a group of courtiers and soldiers, led by Duke Bohemond of Rennes resolved to do.

There was a Jewish banker in town, Abraham of Milan, who occasionally did business with the royal treasury. His daughter was rumoured to be amazingly beautiful, though I have to say that in Aachen in the Dark Ages, that wasn't too difficult. Having both eyes, a nose, and half your teeth would make a Cleopatra of you. Bohemond, who had been one of Pepin the Short's most loyal servants, was disgusted by Charles' incest and determined to lure the king from the bed of his sister. Anything was worth a try, so he and his cronies threatened to kill Abraham and all his family if they didn't get a look at the girl. I was the one who got to take this message to the old banker.

Abraham immediately agreed to help out, and emphasized how delighted he would be to allow a dozen heavily armed knights into his house to check out his daughter.

The girl's name was Deborah, and the rumours about her were not wrong. Bohemond and his friends turned up and found she had the most beautiful, unblemished complexion you ever saw, blooming like the skin of a healthy baby. Her hair was long and very dark, but not as dark and deep as her eyes. She was fifteen years old and shapely. Every man in that room would gladly have hacked off his right arm with an axe to possess the beautiful Deborah.

Deborah, being a good girl, did as her father commanded and took her clothes off and submitted to inspection. Duke Bohemond, who normally delegated everything, took it on himself to ensure that the girl was in good health all over and was indeed a virgin.

Having been passed fit, she was brought to court at once, masquerading as a servant to Bohemond's wife. Charles noticed her quickly and, better than we dared hope, went wild for her. But Deborah said that there was no way he could have her unless he married her. And there was no way he could marry her unless he became a Jew.

This she said to him for two years. Every spring, Charles quit his freezing castle to go to war against someone. Each autumn he returned to find Deborah grown more beautiful. And more devious. Deborah would only see the king in the presence of chaperones. "Convert, marry me and I'm all yours," she kept saying.

This was a problem for Charles. Like all the Frankish nobility, he had been a worshipper of Mithras all his life. He feared a terrible vengeance would be exacted on him if he renounced his fealty now. But, at the end of the second winter, after giving the fair Deborah fabulous gifts, after elevating her father to the position of Royal Treasurer, after giving offices and honours to both the able and the worthless hangers-on in her family and still being unable to get beneath the girl's velvet skirts, he gave in.

The King's coarse English wool drawers were bursting. His

balls were swollen to the size of two men's heads, his prick was hard enough to poleaxe the bullocks whose blood he once bathed in. "Yes, my love," he said, steam rising from his breeches, "I will become a Jew."

Do I sound bitter? No wonder. Deborah and her husband destroyed the one true faith. Because of them I am the last Christian on the face of the earth.

Charles submitted to a Beth Din, in which the dayanim quickly agreed to consider him for conversion. They were pious men I do not deny, but they were also in fear for their lives. They also had to consider the safety of the large number of Jews in town who had been attracted by stories of all the well-paid jobs to be had at Charles' court. But the dayanim could not, in all decency, allow Charles' conversion right away. They told him, as was the tradition, to start living as a Jew, they gave him instruction in the Jewish faith. That spring, he left to campaign against the Avars of the east, with a group of Jewish teachers in his baggage-train. And no pigs.

While Charles was off fighting, Duke Bohemond had Iolande ambushed while she was out riding. A couple of heavies jumped her in a quiet corner of a forest and broke her neck, making it look like she had a riding accident. Then the assassins themselves were killed, just to make sure nobody told tales. I should know, I held their horses, and had my throat cut.

That spring and summer, Charles, King of the Franks, learned to read Latin and Hebrew, captured territories the size of Italy, won three major battles and enslaved 150,000 Avar men and women. The news of his sister's death did not bother him. He returned to Aachen convinced he was ready to become a Jew. And who were the dayanim to argue with him?

The person I felt sorry for was the poor fuck who had to circumcize him. He was the most powerful ruler the West had seen in centuries, he had just slaughtered thousands of people, and the only thing he wanted in the world was to get on with his wedding. Someone had to hold a razor to the prick of this lust-bothered tyrant. I often think about the mohel. I don't know what his name was. I should have taken his place. One little slip of the knife and I could have changed the course of history. But having been killed – again – I was still in the process of walking back from Mongolia.

Back in Aachen, everything went smoothly. Charles was dipped into the mikveh, which wasn't such a bad idea because he never washed much, and emerged a fully fledged Jew. I'm not joking when I say the wedding ceremony began before he was dry and before the scab had fallen from his dick.

Even now, Deborah connived to deprive the king of his conjugal rights. For, as he discovered on retiring, it was her time of the month. She could not, she swore, have foretold this. Her menses were irregular, she said. Deborah was, he had to understand now that he was Jewish, in a state of niddah while her period lasted and for seven days afterwards.

You could go up to the royal bedchamber and see the marks the king's teeth made on the bedpost that first night.

I suppose it made his joy all the more profound when eventually she did let him into her bed. No one saw either of them for a fortnight.

Over the next few years, Charles destroyed the Lombards and took northern Italy. He stormed through the Pyrenees mountain range and defeated the Visigoths and the Sueves, taking the whole of Spain. He moved north and defeated the Saxons and made them his subjects, he took Bavaria and thrust east to push the Avars further back. He was stupendously successful, and even if you want to be mean-spirited about it and point out that there was no serious opposition to him in a lot of the lands he conquered, he alone controlled an area that was now bigger than the old Western Empire. And all the while Deborah was driving him on.

Deborah wanted to start a great dynasty, and for this she had to make something that would last. Charles could hold his Empire together for as long as he lived, which was good enough for him, but was not good enough for Deborah. She soon won him over to her way of seeing things, especially when she started bearing his children.

First, she persuaded him to capture Rome, which was no difficult feat since this place was at that stage owned by some petty princeling who was easily knocked aside. Then in a great ceremony at Hanukkah, Charles was crowned a second time. His title was to be Carolus Maximus, Charles the Great, and he was declared Roman Emperor. This gave people great hopes that the new Empire would revive the peace and prosperity of the old one. Charles moved his capital to Rome from Aachen. In a very real sense, that's why we're here now.

Moving the capital to Rome was useful for me. It meant I didn't have to walk so far to get back to where all the action was.

Deborah, meanwhile, found time to have Duke Bohemond of Rennes strangled on manufactured charges of disloyalty, for she never forgot the humiliation he inflicted on her and her father. She never forgot how cold his fingers were. For my part, I'll never forget the look on his face the night before his execution when I visited him in prison. He thought he'd had my throat cut.

To cement his vast imperial domain together, Deborah decided Charles needed a new class of bureaucrats and officials. Magistrates, tax-gatherers, prison governors, administrators and so forth. She decided that for maximum efficiency these people had to be career professionals, not temporary political appointments. They had to be literate. Aside from a few isolated Christian and pagan monks and scholars, the only literate people existing in anything approaching numbers were Jews. Over a period of years, lots of Jews became imperial officials.

Deborah's plan went further than this. She realized that the ability to read and write confers power, especially back then when perhaps one man in a thousand was literate. Deborah was also mindful of the history of her people; of the suffering and persecution they had endured. She was now able to stop this happening again by putting the Jews in a position of power. Under the Edict of Milan, Charles the Great decreed that only Jews should be allowed to learn and practise the secrets of reading and writing.

It became the law that non-Jews could not own books. The few Christian communities that were left in Charles' Empire had their scriptures confiscated. This, for us, was disastrous, for we knew that over the generations we would have no way of passing on the knowledge that God had given to us.

Meanwhile, Charles' rule had brought stability, and people began to take peace for granted. Ambitious young men wanted to get on in the world by working for the imperial bureaucracy. To do this, they had to be Jews and they had to learn to read and write. Many, many people began to convert to Judaism. Ambitious parents would send their sons to Jewish schools. At the same time, the prevalence of Judaism at the court, and the large numbers of wise Jewish elders coming to Rome made people realize what a beautiful and ancient religion it is by comparison with the crude superstitions practised by most. Fashionable and sophisticated people flocked to convert.

In a couple of generations, virtually the whole of the official and aristocratic classes and very many townsfolk had become Jews, while out in the countryside the peasants continued to worship their ancient sprites and will-o'-the-wisps.

In his later years, Charles became very fat, and died one Passover of a surfeit of salt beef. He was succeeded by his eldest son David. David followed the policies of his parents – his mother was still alive looking over his shoulder throughout his reign – and embarked on further conquests. He took Britain and Ireland, for all the good those miserable places would do him. And since he claimed to be ruler of a revived Roman Empire, logic dictated that he retake Greece, Turkey, Egypt, Judaea and those other parts of the old Eastern Empire. He made war on the Byzantine rulers with some success, but never got close to his great ambition of recapturing Judaea, and with it Jerusalem.

David had no sons. He was succeeded by his daughter Ruth, whose first act was to have her grandmother Deborah exiled to Aachen to stop her giving advice all the time. Deborah passed her few remaining years in that old cold castle where it had all started, attended by a few loyal friends. Rumour had it that she kidnapped and ate babies to try and recover her youth and beauty. You can believe that if you want.

Ruth's pagan general Roland led the armies of the Empire against the now-rotten Kingdom of the East and conquered it whole in ten years. Ruth did not marry, and there is no truth in the story that she and Roland were lovers. Roland brought back the Queen of the East, the cruel and vicious Irene to Rome bound in silken cords. Irene was dangerous, even in captivity. Had she not overthrown her own son and put out his eyes with copper needles? There was no telling what a woman like that might get up to. It was the prevailing fashion at Ruth's court for young men to wear their hair long and compose love-poems and gushingly express their chaste romantic attachment to their queen. It didn't take a wise elder to predict that it would only be a matter of time before a cabal among them transferred their affections to the fair queen of the East. In truth, Irene was sixty years old and never had been any kind of beauty. She manipulated these young idiots into conspiring to free her, raise an army and recapture her lost realm. Most of these pomaded fools wouldn't have known one end of a spear from another, and in any case not one of them could keep a secret. It was enough for Ruth to have Irene's head cut off and sentence her conspirators to work in the royal stables for the rest of their lives where I doubt they ever had the leisure to write poetry about glanders and horse turds.

With the conquest of the Eastern kingdom, the Empire was now whole again and Ruth entered Jerusalem in triumph, accompanied by Roland and the greatest army the world had seen for centuries. I was with them that day, an ordinary infantry soldier once more. I was still there a few weeks later, searching unsuccessfully for any remaining Christian community, when they were discussing rebuilding the Temple and moving the capital of the Empire to Jerusalem, for by now almost everyone of influence, however slight, had joined or been born into, the ranks of the Chosen People.

I was still there when the dreadful plague broke out among the army and the host of officials and religious people who had accompanied Ruth on her triumphal entry. It was suicidal to take so many people into such a small city and cram them all together. Any fool could have seen that it would cause illness, but I suppose it was all forgotten in the excitement. I myself died of it before it struck down both Ruth and her Mithras-worshipping general.

Ruth was succeeded by her cousin Solomon, son of David's younger brother. There were others with claims to the throne, but Solomon wisely judged that Rome was still the centre of government and immediately went there and declared himself Emperor before anyone else could. He then followed tradition and slaughtered all the other members of his family who could compete with him. Solomon declared his intention of keeping the capital in Rome until Jerusalem was plague-free.

Of course, when the plague had cleared from Jerusalem, the Saracens, an energetic people fired by the new religion of Mohammed, attacked out of the east and took the city for their own. The Empire had recaptured Jerusalem for less than three years. Men said this was God's punishment for their pride and arrogance.

Perhaps Solomon was mindful of this, or maybe he was just plain idle. Whatever the case, he made no attempt to retake Jerusalem and settled into a life of lethargy and vice, trying to outdo the splendour of his ancient namesake. Solomon the Magnificent, as he was called, imported every conceivable luxury into Rome from the East and made of it a city of unrivalled glory. With peace on most frontiers it was a golden age, in which building and the arts flourished. Solomon himself in later years became more introverted and cranky, for his insatiable appetites left him tortured with the strangury.

Solomon's long reign ended with the succession of his grandson Saul, a young man who rejected the ease of the court and who dreamed of military glory. This was just as well, because there were now predators massing on every frontier who wanted a piece of the Empire. The Saracens soon got the better of us in a great sea battle near Rhodes that left them with unrivalled control of the Mediterranean sea; their allies, the Barbary Pirates, now made life hell for merchant seamen. The Saracens had long since taken Egypt and the north coast of Africa and now they moved into Spain where Saul came to meet them with a huge army. But the army, like everything else, had grown soft under Solomon and was defeated in the battle of Salamanca. Saul himself was captured by Saladin, who treated him with hospitality and respect before releasing him. Saul died soon afterwards of shame and a broken heart. He was thirty-two years old.

Saul had been keen to enforce religious orthodoxy. That sort of thing made life difficult for a person like me who would go around saying the Jews were all wrong and that Yeshua Christos had been the Messiah. Now the religious toleration of earlier years came to an end. One of the artists that Saul patronized, Elihu the Engineer, invented a machine specially to deal with blasphemers. It was like a mill-wheel the paddles of which fired rocks in the blasphemer's general direction. To me fell the honour of being the first person to be killed by Elihu's stoning engine for saying that this man nobody had heard of had been the Messiah.

I avoided Rome, preferring to stick to less technologically advanced regions. I preached in the countryside, but a faith without books has no future. I lived among dwindling Christian communities in remote places. Then I went and lived in the lands of the Saracens for many years. Strange to relate, I was always treated with courtesy there, for the Saracens are tolerant of all religions and treat madmen with kindness. I won no converts.

Saul's place was taken by his uncle Gideon, our present ruler. He is a learned man, but I don't think he's a big enough bastard to save the Empire. It's been ten years since the Persians and the Saracens joined forces. Now they act like a pair of vultures, picking at the carcase of the Roman Empire. It is an apocalyptic struggle between Jews, Mohammedans and Zoroastrians.

There are no Christians left. The last of them I found in a monastery out on the far west coast of Ireland. These few old men had managed to keep their sacred scriptures hidden from the imperial authorities, but no one could read them except me. I begged them to break their vows of chastity and try to re-establish the seed of our faith, but they refused, saying I was mad and a heretic. By the time I found them they were in any case too old to be capable of marrying, even if we had found women of child-bearing age willing to have them. I know what you're thinking. The answer is that I found out a long time back that I was incapable of fathering children, for Yeshua's curse had also deprived me of that particular joy. And it's been a good few hundred years since I last derived even a passing pleasure in lying with women – or anything else for that matter.

I buried the last of the Irish monks three years ago, put the scriptures in my sack, took up my staff and started wandering once more, returning as always to Rome.

Now it is a millennium since the birth of Christos, the Persians are hammering at the gates of the eternal city and there is another sign in the sky.

The same sign, perhaps. This time, it should be correctly interpreted. I feel at last that my wanderings are over. Yeshua has returned, to gather up the faithful to himself while the unrighteous shall be cast down.

But where are the faithful?

*   *   *

The light in Joseph's eyes dimmed.

"He's dead," Absalom said.

The rabbi began to mumble.

"Really dead."

"A madman," someone spat. Isaac had died during the story.

Absalom wondered about Joseph's tale. If it were a fanciful lie, he had taken extraordinary care over it.

"Rabbi," he asked, "was what he said . . . ?"

"Nonsense," the rabbi said, "he was maddened, reciting an old folk tale . . ."

"This Yeshua Bar-Joseph, the Christos . . ."

"I have never heard of him."

"The sign?"

The rabbi was angry, almost afraid. He didn't answer.

Absalom hawked and spat blood.

The ground seemed to be shaking.

Around Joseph's neck were two symbols, a cross and a fish. Absalom reached out to touch them.

The dead man's body rippled like water, and dissolved into the ground.

Astonished, Absalom turned. The rabbi was gone. There had been no witnesses.

Joseph's cross was left.

Obviously, the Christos had not returned. The portent in the sky had been wrong again.

Absalom picked up the cross, and held it tight in one hand. He held it until he died.

Hush My Mouth

Suzette Haden Elgin

First time ever I saw a Silent, I was no more than a tiny child; I might have been five years old. And it meant nothing to me. It was just a woman, and not a very pretty one to look at, with her head shaved. I remember her skull; it had a lumpy look to it that bothered me. I had never before seen a bald woman, nor very many bald men. I wasn't eager to see this one, either, because my sisters had been pushing me on the swing that hung from our black walnut tree, and I had complained bitterly at being made to leave that and go look at this woman passing by.

But my father paid no mind to my fuss, hauling me up onto his shoulder and almost running out to the edge of the street, the other children hurrying along behind us. He stopped at the curb and he shook me a little bit to be sure he had my attention, and he said to me, "Now you *remember* that, boy! You put it away in your heart, and you remember it, that there was a morning a Silent walked by your house so close you could've touched her if you'd had a mind to!" The woman turned to look at us as she passed, and her smile was the only thing about her not black as the inside of our water well, and Daddy squeezed my thighs where he had me braced on his shoulder and added, "And you remember she *smiled* at you, child! See you remember that, forevermore!" And I have remembered it, as he told me to do, all these years.

She smiled at Matthias Darrow, too, him standing down on

the corner of our street with his father and his grandmother and his two big brothers. I suppose his mother was busy with her everlasting tending of the sick and with someone she couldn't leave, even for this occasion. Matthias was there, and all my other friends and their parents, lining both sides of the street to watch a Silent go by on her way to somewhere. I don't know where she could have been going; nobody told me to concern myself with that. But we all stood and watched her walk to the end of the street, tall and straight and stake-thin in her long black dress. We watched her turn the corner and go on down the side street. Not until she was out of sight did anybody move to leave the curbs and go back to what they had been doing. I remember there was a little bit of a breeze, and it stirred the branches of the pink mimosa and spread their perfume all around; I remember that smell, mimosa and hot dust and the several smells of sluggish summer river, mixed. I can smell it now, as strong as I smelled it that day.

And I remember Matthias, watching the Silent and shouting out, "Morning, ma'am!" as she went by, and his father clapping a swift hand over his mouth and bending down to tell him that he'd appreciate it if he'd behave like he had good sense, whether he did or not. And Matthias, looking up over Mr Darrow's huge hand with eyes wide and round and scared, wondering what he'd done.

Matthias broke this morning. I heard it happen. The Lord God help me, please, I'll hear it forever, the sound of his head – the sound his head made as he smashed it against the wall of his room. Bare flesh, not a strand of hair to cushion it, smacking against white-washed brick. Seven blows, it took. Seven times, that sound. That unspeakable sound.

How could a human being have the strength to take his life by battering his own head against a wall? Will you tell me that? How could he stay couscious long enough to get to the fatal blow that ended it? And to do it silently! How in the name of God could you do that and *stay silent*?

Matthias did. I could not have done it, but he did. I swear to you, as I shall swear to the judges that come to question me. I will close my eyes three times, signifying NO, when they ask me if Matthias Darrow cried out at the last. His family has no shame coming, for he died without so much as a gasp. And the town we came from, he and I, all those people who were so blazing proud to have *two* of us choose to be Silents, there's no shame coming to them, either. We took our vows together, Matthias and I, both of us just seventeen; and now he is gone.

We were expecting that he would do something. All of us had seen it coming. He had taken to chewing at his lips, so that they were always cracked and bloody. His fingers were forever twitching; he'd notice, and he'd shove them out of sight into the pockets of his robe. We watched him day by day as the tension drew his skin tight to his skull, till the bones strained to shove through the flesh and the whole head gleamed like polished ebony. When he started wearing the leather gag even in the daytime, that foul gag that stands witness to our frailty and guards us from the word spoken in sleep, we knew that he was going to break. If there had been anything we could have done to help him, we would have done it, but there was nothing to do. When the lust for language consumes a man, you can only watch him burn and dedicate your prayers to him.

We were on our guard on his behalf; we were not just praying. We had taken to being wary around him. When we walked along the balconies of the shelterhouse, one of us would walk at his side next the rail, and two others ahead and behind him, so that he could not throw himself into the courtyard. The elders had begun tasting his food and drink at the table openly, so that if he were so mad as to poison either he would have to take one of them with him into death. We watched what he picked up and what he put down; we went with him when he walked out of the building. At least one of us stayed close by no matter what he was engaged in; we were watchful of our brother. Except in the privacy of his room, where we could not follow.

I am sure I'm not the only one who wishes we had been more careless. If Matthias had been able to slip poison into his soup in the dining room, it would have been easier for him, and I would not now be hearing in my soul the wet thud of his skull against brick.

Still. It must be noted that Matthias Darrow *did not give in*. For his family there will not be the shame of a failed Silent with broken vows, sent home from the shelterhouse in disgrace. He spared them that. He spared all his vast family, spared them the scandal that shames the line down to the cousins many times removed, that is the end of respect and the beginning of a courteous pity that is like a stone hung round the neck. Matthias saw to it that his people did not have that shame to endure. The Lord God help me be as brave if I come to such a pass. The Lord God grant I never come to such a pass, and let my never-ending silent dialogue with my own foolish self be my worst failing.

All of this, we will be reminded, was born of the sin of pride, beside which murder and debauchery are no more than childish foibles. First the white man's pride; and that not being foul enough, the black man's pride to cap it off. Pride, that is not called the worst of all the sins for idle reasons. When the preacher comes this Sunday, that will be his sermon, and his text will be "Pride goeth before a fall". There is no room in this house where that text is not burned into a beam or painted over a window. Because of what pride has brought us to.

If the Union Army had let us serve with them in the Civil War, the North would have won; no one disputes that. President Lincoln himself said it was so – they would have won! But they wouldn't allow it. Not them. No black man was going to put on the uniform of a Union soldier, or ride a horse of the Union Cavalry, or march in the least last straggling row of the Union infantry. They were told we'd serve in our own clothes, or serve naked, if they felt that would be sufficient to keep us from being mistaken for their comrades at arms. But they were stiff-necked; it made no difference. No black – Negroes, they called us then – no Negro was going to be able to say he had served in the Union Army. We were not fit even to die beside them; that was their position on the matter, and they would not budge from it.

You'd have thought the Confederates would have had better sense. White and black, we'd played together as children and suckled at the same black breasts as infants and gotten blind drunk together as young men. But the Confederate Army followed the Yankees' lead, bound they'd outdo them. If a Negro was not good enough to soldier for the *Union*, well then bygod he was twice that not good enough to soldier for the South! Damn fools they were, too, for we would have fought to the death beside them and no quarter given, after the way the Union spurned us.

Abraham Lincoln, standing there for all to hear in Washington, and then the words spread across the newspapers for all to read, he said: "We shall not send our women into battle; we shall not send our children. And we shall surely not send our Negroes, who are as children, to shed their blood in a war they are not even able to understand." He said that, and we heard it, and I suppose it was nothing we hadn't heard before. But somehow his saying it made it official. He made it the official public policy of the Disunited States of America, that the blacks had not even the wisdom of children. After that, we would willingly have fought for the South, even if it meant fighting beside a man who'd ordered us whipped by the cruellest black driver in the worst slave state there ever was.

They wouldn't have it. And later, when it got to be obvious that the war could not be won without us, they still would not, for neither side was willing to be the first to say, "Well, we were wrong; I guess the blood of a black man is good enough to spill for this country."

Pride! Thus it was that nobody won that awful war, that dragged on eight terrible years. Oh, the South claimed the victory, in the strict sense of the word; there being so many blacks at home to see to the work of the plantations and the farms and the Southern towns, the South lasted longer. It was the North that first proposed to stop fighting. But there was no victory. The time came when there was nobody left with the will to fight any more, that's all. They just laid down their weapons and went home. What was left of them. To what was left of home.

They didn't last very long. Smallpox and cholera took most of them that didn't die of their battle wounds. A handful came stumbling back to the burned-out ruins that had been the glorious South; and they were ruins, themselves.

We had been prepared to kill every last one of them; with our bare hands if need be. My grandfather swears to that, and I believe him. We had been ready to kill them all. We were four million strong; even half-starved we had more strength than those ragtag men that lived through the Civil War to come home. Our women were ready, and our children, too, to do whatsoever had to be done.

But when it came right down to it we had to kill very few of them. The young men, and the older ones that had gone in when the young men were mostly dead and maimed, they brought their diseases home with them. And they went to sleep and eat with their wives and their children and their old people. The sicknesses went through those families like wildfire through a piney woods.

In another time, we would have nursed them. Some of them would have lived, and many of us would have died, and when it was over we would have been as mixed up as ever. But not this time. They hadn't considered us fit to die with them in their filthy war; we were not willing to die with them in their filthy peace. We lifted no hand either to help or to harm them, we simply waited. And when it was over we rounded up the pitiful remnant that did not die, man or woman or child, and we sent them with all courtesy into the North, out of New Africa for ever, beyond the walls at the border.

They went docilely enough. As for the occasional damn Yankee fool that decided he'd ride South and see about bringing New Africa back into the United States, we tried to reason with him. And if he would not be reasonable we took him into our courts and tried him swiftly and carried out the sentence with sufficient dispatch to discourage others from any such hopeless lost notion.

So. There we were. A sovereign nation. Mexico to the south of us, the United States to the north of us, and the oceans at either side. All the land there for our taking, much of it burned over and scorched black and covered with destruction, but no damage done that we weren't capable of setting to rights. We made the land clean again, and we cleared away the gutted buildings and put up new ones; we laid out farms and streets and set ourselves to live a decent life for the first time since we were torn out of the breast of Africa and flung like cattle onto this land.

We should have been all right. We had everything we wanted, and that one most precious thing of all – we were free. Free! The work of our hands was there to do, and the tools to do it with, and its fruits were for the first time to be *ours*. Hallelujah, it was the Promised Land; praise be to God, it was Eden . . .

And why, then, do we find ourselves, all these years later, with the work only half done, and half our strength and passions still devoted to squabbling? And the North once again eyeing our borders, thinking the time will come when we'll be ripe for conquering?

Pride again. We will be reminded, come Sunday. Pride! We who thought ourselves so fine, watching the white man both Northern and Southern destroy himself and all his kin and all his substance for pride. More fools we, because we were just as human when the time came to test us.

We'd never given the problem any thought, my grandfather says. There'd been no time to think about it, and no reason. Scattered as we were, subjugated as we were, the matter of language had not come up; under the lash, any word will do to scream with.

But we'd brought many dozens of languages with us from Africa, each one of them the language of a proud people with a proud heritage. And when it came time to choose one, to decide which one we would speak now in this New Africa, there was no question in anybody's mind. The only possible choice for the New African tongue was whatsoever language *he* spoke. "Why, *my* language, obviously!" And so said they all.

Bitter. Bitter, the fruit of pride, and harsh in the mouth. Oh God in Heaven, be you black or white or the colour of mimosa flowers, it was bitter! That it should come to this . . . our children free to go to school and learn, finally, and every forty or so in a different school learning a different language. You talk of segregation! And in our legislature, and in our churches and our colleges and our publishing houses and all our daily business of life, it is no African language we speak. Pride will not let us choose one. Only in the white man's hated English are we able to govern this land, the very name of which is a white man's name, because our pride would not and will not let us agree on a name in one of our own tongues.

And so there are Silents.

Sworn to use *no* language. Not spoken; not written; not language of the hands. Only that irreducible minimum of all signs that must be used if we are to survive. Four signs a day, we are allowed, if by no other means can we make our brother or our sister understand that the building is on fire or the piece of meat on the table is unsafe to eat or a baby is about to be born. And not even those four, unless we are forced to them.

Before we come into the shelterhouse, before we make our vows, those who serve as liaison between the Silents and the world explain this to us; they make it very certain that we understand, before they let us come.

We will be silent. That is the vow we take. Until death; or until our people can lay aside the pride that destroys them and choose a language that is not a white man's language. Whichever comes first.

Matthias Darrow, the Lord God have mercy on his soul, could not wait any longer.

A Letter From the Pope

Harry Harrison and Tom Shippey

In the year 865, according to the Anglo-Saxon Chronicle, a "great army" of the Vikings landed in England, led in legend and probably in fact by the sons of Ragnar Hairy-Breeks. In the following years this army wiped out the rival dynasties of Northumbria, killed Edmund, King of East Anglia, and drove Burgred, King of Mercia, overseas, replacing him with a puppet ruler. By 878 all the kingdoms of the English had been conquered – except for Wessex. In Wessex, Alfred, the last of five brothers, continued to fight.

But then the Vikings turned their full effort on him. At Twelfth Night 878, when all Christians were still getting over Christmas and when campaigning was normally out of the question, they made a surprise attack on Wessex, establishing a base at Chippenham, and according to the Chronicle again driving many Englishmen overseas and compelling others to submit. Alfred was forced to go into hiding and conduct a guerrilla campaign "with a small force, through the woods and the fastnesses of the fens". It was at this time that – so the story goes – he was reduced to sheltering in a peasant's hut where, immersed in his problems, he burned the good wife's cakes and was violently rebuked for it.

Yet Alfred managed somehow to stay alive, keep on fighting, and arrange for the army of Wessex to be gathered under the Vikings' noses. He then, quite against the odds, defeated the "great army" decisively, and finally made a masterstroke of statesmanship. He treated the Viking king Guthrum with great forbearance, converted him to Christianity, and became his godfather. This set up a reasonable relationship between English and Vikings, gave Wessex security, and became the basis for the later reconquest of all England by Alfred's son, grandson and later descendants (of whom Queen Elizabeth II is one).

Many historians have noted that if Alfred had not held on in the winter of early 878, England would have become a Viking state, and the international language of the world would presumably now be a form of Danish. Yet another possibility.

By 878 Alfred and Wessex stood for Christianity, and the Vikings for paganism. The later reconquest of England was for Christ as well as for the Wessex kings, and monastic chroniclers were liable to see Alfred as an early crusader. But we know, from his own words, that by 878 Alfred was already deeply dissatisfied with the ineptitude of his churchmen. We also know that about the same time Ethelred, Archbishop of Canterbury, had written to the pope to protest about Alfred's extortions – which were very likely only a demand for further contributions to resist the pagan assaults. Pope John responded by sending Alfred a letter of severe reproof – at exactly the moment when Alfred was "journeying in difficulties through the woods and fens". This letter never arrived. No doubt the letter carrier could not find the king, or thought the whole situation far too dangerous even to try.

But what would have happened if the letter had been received? Would it have been the last straw for a king already isolated, almost without support from his own subjects and his own Church? A king also with clear precedent for simply retiring to safety? Or would Alfred (as he so often did in reality) have thought of another bold, imaginative and unprecedented step to take?

This story explores that last possibility.

Alfred, Guthrum, Ethelnoth, Odda, Ubbi, Bishop Ceolred, the archbishop of Canterbury, as well as the pope, are all historical characters. The pope's letter is based on examples of his known correspondence.

A dark figure moved under the trees ahead, barely visible through the heavy mist, and King Alfred raised his sword. Behind him the last army of England – all eighteen of them – stirred with unease, weapons ready as well.

"Easy," Alfred said, lowering his sword and leaning on it

wearily. "It is one of the peasants from the village." He looked down at the man who was now kneeling before him, gaping up at the gold torque and bracelets that marked the king.

"How many are there?"

"Tw—twelve, lord King," the peasant stammered.

"In the church?"

"Yes, lord King."

The Vikings were conquerors, not raiders. Guthrum's men always quartered themselves in the timber churches, leaving the peasant huts and the larger thanes' dwellings undamaged – as long as there was no resistance. They meant to take the country over, not destroy it. The mist was rising and the lightless village was visible below.

"What are they doing now?"

As if in reply the church door swung open, a square of red light against the blackness, and struggling figures passed across it before it slammed shut again. A female shriek hung in the air, then was drowned out by a roar of welcome.

Edbert, the king's chaplain, stirred with anger. He was lean, just string and bones, all the fat squeezed out by the passion of his faith. His voice, loud and resonant, had been formed by that same faith. "They are devils, heathen devils! Even in God's own house they practise their beastly lusts. Surely He shall strike them in the middle of their sin, and they shall be carried to the houses of lamentation where the worm—"

"Enough, Edbert."

Alfred knew that his chaplain was vehement against the heathens, striking out strongly enough with his heavy mace, for all his leanness and apparent reluctance to shed blood against the canons of the Church. But talk of miracles could only anger men who had wished for divine assistance many times – so far without reward. He turned back to the peasant. "You're sure there are twelve?"

"Yes, lord King."

The odds were not good. He needed a two-to-one advantage to guarantee victory. And Godrich was still coughing, near dead with cold. He was one of the eleven king's companions who had right of precedence in every battle. But not this time. A sound reason must be concocted for leaving him behind.

"I have a most important duty for you, Godrich. If the attack should fail we will need the horses. Take them all down the track. Guard them with your life. Take Edi to help you. All others follow me."

Alfred put his hand on the kneeling peasant's shoulder.

"How will we know the door is unbarred?"

"My wife, lord King . . ."

"She is in there with the Vikings?"

"Aye, lord King."

"You have a knife in your belt? Follow, then. I grant you the throats of the wounded, to cut."

The men surged forward across the meadow, grimly eager now to end the waiting, to strike at least one nest of their enemies from the board.

This night-time raid was a pale shadow of past encounters. Nine times now Alfred had led whole armies, real armies, thousands of men, against the drawn-up line of the enemy. With the war horns bellowing, the men drumming their spears against the hollow shields, the champions in the front rank throwing up their gold-hilted swords and catching them as they called on their ancestors to witness their deeds. And always, always the Viking line had stood watching, unafraid. The horses' heads on poles grinning over their array, the terrible Raven banner of the sons of Ragnar spreading its wings in triumph.

How bold the attack; how bad the defeat. Only once, at Ashdown, had Alfred made the enemy fall back.

So there would be no triumph in this night encounter, no glory. But when this band of plunderers vanished, the rest of the invaders would know there was one Saxon king still left in England.

As they pushed through the gap in the thorn hedge and strode into the miserable cluster of wattle-and-daub huts, Alfred jerked his shield down so he could seize the handgrip, and cleared the sax knife in its sheath. In pitched battle he carried long sword and iron-mounted spear, but for these scrimmages

among the houses the men of Wessex had gone back to the
weapons of their ancestors, the Saxons. The men of the sax:
short, pointed, single-edged cleavers. He strode quickly so that
the hurrying companions could not squeeze past him. Where
was the Viking sentry? When they had reached the last patch of
shadow before the churchyard the men stopped at his signal and
pushed forward the peasant guide. Alfred looked at him once,
and nodded.

"Call now to your woman."

The peasant drew in his breath, shivering with fear, then ran
forward five paces into the little open square before the church.
He halted and at the top of his voice uttered the long, wailing
ululation of the wolf, the wild wolf of the English forests.

Instantly a harsh voice roared out from the church's tiny
belfry, little more than a platform above the roof. A javelin
streaked down at the howling man, but he had already leapt
aside. There was a scrape of metal as the Saxons drew their
weapons. The door swung suddenly outwards; Alfred held his
shield in front of him and charged for the center of the door.

Figures pushed furiously in front of him, Tobba on the left,
Wighard, captain of the king's guard, on the right. As he burst
into the room men were already down, bare-skinned bearded
figures rolling in blood. A naked, screeching woman ran across
his path, and behind her he saw a Viking jumping for the ax that
leaned against the wall. Alfred hurled himself forward and as
the Viking turned back he drove the sax in under his chin. When
he spun round, shield raised in automatic defence, he realized
the skirmish was already over. The English had fanned out in
one furious sweep and driven from wall to wall, cutting every
Viking down, stabbing savagely at the fallen; no veteran of the
Athelney winter thought for an instant of honor, or display. A
Viking with his back turned was all they wanted to see.

Even as relief flooded into him Alfred remembered that there
was one task left undone. Where was that Viking sentry? He had
been on the belfry, awake and armed. He had had no time to
come down and fall in the slaughter. Behind the altar there was
a staircase leading up, little more than a ladder. Alfred called
out in warning to the milling Englishmen and sprang towards it

with his shield high. He was too late. Elfstan, his old companion, stared at his king without comprehension, threw up his arms, and fell forward. The javelin was bedded deep in his spine.

Slowly, deliberately, an armed Viking stepped down the ladder. He was the biggest man Alfred had ever seen, taller even than himself. His biceps swelled above gleaming bracelets, the rivets of his mail shirt straining to contain the bulk inside. Round his neck and waist shone the loot of a plundered continent. Without haste the Viking threw aside his shield and tossed a great poleax from one hand to the other.

His eyes met the king's. He nodded, and pointed the spiked head of the ax at the planked floor.

"Kom. Thou. *Konungrinn*. De king."

The fight's already won, thought Alfred. *Lose my life now? Insane. But can I turn aside from a challenge? I should have the churls with their bows to shoot him down. That is all that any pirate deserves from England.*

The Viking was already halfway down the stair, moving as fast as a cat, not stopping to whirl up the ax but stabbing straight forward with the point. Reflex hurled Alfred's shield up to push the blow aside. But behind it came two hundred and eighty pounds of driving weight. The attacker fought for a neck-break hold, snatching at the sax in Alfred's hand. For a moment all the king could do was struggle to get free. Then he was hurled aside. As he hit the wall there was a clang of metal, a moan. He saw Wighard falling back, his useless right arm trying to cover the rent in his armor.

Tobba stepped forward, his fist a short flashing arc which ended at the Viking's temple. As the giant staggered back towards him Alfred stepped forward and drove his sax with all his strength deep into the enemy's back, twisted furiously, withdrew as the man fell.

Tobba grinned at him and displayed his right fist. Five metal rings encircled the thumb and fingers.

"I 'ad the metalsmith mek it for me," he said.

Alfred stared round the room, trying to take stock. Already the place was crowded, the men of the village pushing in, calling to each other – and to their women, now struggling into their clothes. They gaped down at the gashed and bloody corpses while a furtive figure was already rummaging beneath discarded armor for the loot all plunderers carried with them. Wulfhun saw this and knocked man aside. Wighard was down, obviously on the point of death. The Viking's ax had almost severed his arm and driven far too deep between neck and shoulder. Edbert, again priest not warrior, was bent over him, fussing with a phial, frowning at the mortally wounded man's words. As Alfred watched, the dying man fixed his eyes on his king, spoke haltingly to the chaplain, and then fell back, choking.

The pirate at his feet was moving too, saying something. Alfred's lifted hand stayed the eager peasant who rushed forward with his knife raised.

"What?" he said.

The pirate spoke again, in the kind of pidgin used by the invaders' captive women and slaves.

"Good stroke were that. I fought in front for fifteen years. Never saw stroke like him."

He fumbled for something round his neck, a charm pendant beneath the massive golden neck ring, concern coming into his eyes till his hand closed over it. He sighed, raised himself.

"But now I go!" he called. "I go. To Thruthvangar!"

Alfred nodded, and the peasant sprang forward.

Three days later the king sat on the camp stool which was all that Athelney could offer for a throne, waiting for the councillors to come to the meeting he had called, still tossing the Viking's mysterious pendant meditatively from hand to hand.

There was no doubt what it was. When he had first pulled it out and shown it to the others, Edbert had said straight away, with a look of horror: "It is the *pudendum hominis*! It is a sign of the beastly lusts of the devil's children, abandoned to original sin! It is the pillar which the heathen worship, so boldly destroyed by our countryman the worthy Boniface in Detmar! It is—"

"It's a prick," said Tobba, putting the matter more simply.

It was a token, the king thought now, closing his fist angrily on it. A token for all the difficulties he continued to face.

He had had two dozen companions when they all set out from Athelney. But as they made their long, circuitous ride across Somerset, first one man had dropped out with horse trouble and then another. In darkness they simply faded away into the dusk; they had had their fill of the endless, losing battles. Noblemen, king's companions, men whose fathers and grandfathers had fought for Christ and Wessex. They would go home quietly to their estates, sit and watch, perhaps send discreet emissaries to the Viking king at Chippenham. Sooner or later one of them would betray the secret of the camp at Athelney, and then Alfred too would wake one night, as he had woken so many Viking stragglers, with shrieks around him and a knife already in his throat.

It would be sooner if they heard he had begun to refuse battle with the heathen. Small as the action had been, that night raid had been important. Eighteen men could still make a difference. But why had those eighteen stayed with him? The companions, no doubt, because they still felt it their duty. The churls, maybe, because they thought the heathens had come to take their land. But how long would either motivation last against continuous defeat and fear of death? Deep in his bones Alfred knew that there was only one man in his army, only one man in Athelney, who genuinely and without pretence had no fear of any Viking who ever breathed, and that was the grim and silent churl Tobba. No one knew where he came from. He had simply appeared in the camp one dawn, with a Viking ax in his hand and two mail shirts over his gigantic shoulder, saying nothing about where he had got them, or how he had slipped through the sentries round the marsh. He was just there. To kill the invaders. If only the king could find a thousand subjects like him.

Alfred opened his fist and the golden token swung before his eyes, a shining symbol of all that troubled him. First and foremost, he simply could not beat the Vikings in the open field. During the battle-winter eight years before, he and his brother King Ethelred had led the men of Wessex to fight the Vikings' Great Army nine times. Eight times they had been beaten.

The ninth time was at Ashdown . . . Well, he had gained great credit there, and still had some of it left. While his brother had dallied at the pre-battle mass, Alfred had seen that the Vikings were beginning to move down the hill. When Ethelred refused to curtail the mass and leave early, Alfred had stridden forward on his own, and had led the men of Wessex up the hill himself, charging in the front like a wild boar, or so the poets said. Just that one time his fury and frustration had inspired the men so that in the end the Vikings had yielded, retreated to leave a field full of dead, two heathen kings and five jarls among them. They had been back again two weeks later, as ready to fight as ever.

In some ways that day's battle had resembled the little skirmish so recently fought. Total surprise, with the fight as good as won even as it began. But though the skirmish had been won, there had still been one Viking left, ready to fight on. He had cost Alfred two good men and had come within a hair of ending the campaign forever by killing the last of all the English kings still prepared to resist.

He had died well too. Better than his victim Wighard, Alfred was forced to admit. Very, very reluctantly Edbert had been compelled to reveal what the last words of the king's captain were. He had died saying: "God should have spared me this." How many years in purgatory that would cost him, Edbert had lamented, how little the faith of these degenerate times . . . Well, the dying Viking had had faith. Faith in something. Maybe that was what made them fight so with such resolution.

It was the English who were not fighting well. That was Alfred's second problem, and he knew exactly what caused it. They expected to lose. Soon after every battle began the first of the wounded would be begging their friends not to leave them on the field to be dispatched when the English withdrew – as everyone knew they would. And their friends were only too ready to help them back to their ponies. Sometimes those who assisted returned to the front, sometimes they didn't. It was surprising in a way that so many men were still prepared to obey their king's call, to turn out and fight for their lands and their right not to obey foreigners.

But the thanes were beginning to hope that when the end finally came they could make a deal with the invaders, keep their lands, maybe pay higher taxes, bow to foreign kings. They could do what the men of the north, and of the Mark, had done. Five years before Burgred, king of the Mark, had given up, collected his treasury and the crown jewels, and slipped away to Rome. The pony-loads of gold and silver he had taken with him would buy him a handsome estate in the sun for the rest of his life. Alfred knew that some of his followers were already wondering whether it would not be a good plan to depose their king, the last stubborn atheling of the house of Cerdic, and replace him with someone more biddable. There was little chance for him to forget Burgred's treachery. Far too often Alfred's wife Ealhswith reminded him of her kinsman, the former king of the Mark.

She had a son and daughter to think of. But he had a kingdom – reason enough for him to battle on. As for the rest of the English, if they fought badly it was not due to any lack of skill or want of age. It was because they had plenty to lose and almost nothing to gain. Nor had he anything to offer the loyal. No land. It had been twenty years since his pious father had given a whole tenth of all his land in all the kingdom to the Church. Land that ordinarily would have gone to supporting warriors, pensioning off the injured, making the old companions ready and eager to breed sons and send them into service in their turn. Alfred had none now to give.

He hadn't been able to beat the Vikings when he had an army – and now it was impossible to raise one. The Vikings had all but caught him in bed three months before, when every Christian in Wessex was sleeping off the Christmas festivities. He had barely escaped them, fleeing like a thief into the night. Now the Viking king sat in Chippenham and sent his messengers along the high roads. The true king must skulk in the marsh and hope that in the end news of his continued resistance would somehow seep out.

And that took him to the third of his problems. He couldn't beat the Vikings because his men would not support him. He couldn't get his men to support him because their rewards had gone to the Church. And the Church . . .

The sound of challenges from outside told him that his councillors had arrived and were about to be shown in. Swiftly Alfred gave the pendant – prick, pudendum or holy sign, whatever it was – one last look and then stuffed it into his belt-bag and forgot about it. He touched the cross that hung from a silver chain about his neck. The cross of the true Christ. Might His power still be with him. The canvas screen of his shelter was pulled aside.

He looked glumly at the seven men who came in, as they slowly and with inappropriate courtesy found places among the motley assortment of seats he could provide. Only one councillor had an unquestioned right to be there. At least two of the others he could much better have spared. But they were all he had to work with.

"I will say who is present, for those who have not met before," he began. "First, all should know Alderman Ethelnoth." The rest nodded politely to the red-faced heavy man who sat nearest to the king: the only shire-leader still to be in the field, still fighting from a bivouac like Alfred's own.

"Next, we have a spokesman from Alderman Odda." Odda was the shire-leader of Devon. "Wihtbord, what know you of the enemy?"

The young, scarred man spoke briefly and without shyness. "I have heard that Ubbi is in Bristol fitting out a fleet. He has the Raven banner with him. My master, Odda, has called out the shire levy, a thousand men at a time. He is watching the coast."

This was news – and bad news. Ubbi was one of the dreaded sons of Ragnar. Two of the others were gone. Halfdan had retired to the north, Sigurd Snake-eye was thought to be ravaging in Ireland. And – thank God – no one had heard of Ivar the Boneless for some time. Bad news. Alfred had hoped that he would only have to deal with the relatively weaker King Guthrum. But with Ubbi outfitting a fleet, the Ragnarssons still presented a great danger.

"Representing both Dorset and Hampshire we have Osbert." Glum silence greeted this remark. The presence of Osbert reminded them that the true aldermen of these two shires could not or would not come. Everyone knew that the alderman of

Hampshire had fled overseas, while the alderman of Dorset had cravenly submitted to the Viking Guthrum, so could not be trusted with knowledge of his king's whereabouts.

Almost with relief Alfred turned to the three churchmen present.

"Bishop Daniel is here in his own right, to speak for the Church—"

"And also for my lord the archbishop of Canterbury."

" – and I have further invited Bishop Ceolred to join us, for wisdom and his experience."

Eyes turned curiously to the old man, evidently in very poor health, who sat nearest the door. He was in fact the bishop of Leicester, far beyond the borders of Wessex. But Leicester was now a Viking town, and the bishop had fled to what he thought was safety with the king of Wessex. Perhaps he regretted it now. Still, Alfred thought, he might at least get some sense through to this overbearing idiot Daniel and his lord of Canterbury.

"Finally Edbert my chaplain is here to make note of all decisions reached. And Wulfsige is present as captain of my guard."

Alfred looked around at his handful of followers and kept a stern face so his black depression would not show. "Nobles, I have to tell you this. There will be a battle. I am calling the muster of Wessex for Ascension Day. It will be at Edgebright's Stone, east of Selwood. Every man of Wessex must be there or forfeit all land-right and kin-right forever."

There were slow nods. Every Christian knew when Easter was, if he knew nothing else. It had been ten days ago. In thirty more days would be Ascension. Everyone knew Edgebright's Stone. And it was far enough away from the Viking center at Chippenham to make a muster possible.

"Bishop Daniel, I rely on you to pass this message to every priest in your diocese and in the archdiocese of your lord, so that they can tell every Christian in every parish."

"How am I to do that, my lord? I have no hundreds of horsemen."

"Write, then. Make a hundred writs. Send riders on circuits."

Edbert coughed apologetically. "Lord king, not all priests

may be able to read. True they are pious men, worthy men, but —"

"They read and write quick enough when it comes to snatching land by charter!" Wulfsige's snarl was echoed by all the laymen.

Alfred silenced them with a sharp motion. 'Send the messages, Bishop Daniel. Another day we will take up the question of whether priests who cannot read should be priests or not. The day of the muster is fixed, and I will be there, even if none of the rest of Wessex follows me. But I trust my subjects' loyalty. We will have an army to fight the heathens. What I need to know is, how can I be sure of victory – this time?"

There was a long silence, while most of the men present stared at the floor. Alderman Ethelnoth slowly shook his head from side to side. No one could doubt his courage, but he had been at a lot of lost battles too. Only Daniel the bishop kept his head firmly erect. Finally, and with an impatient frown, he spoke.

"It is not for a servant of the Lord to give advice on secular matters – while laymen sit silent. But is it not clear that the issue of all battles is in the hands of God? If we do our part, he will do his, and will succor us as he did Moses and the Israelites from Pharoah, or the people of Bethulia from the Assyrians. Let us have faith, and make the muster, trusting not in the feeble strength of mortal men."

"We've had faith many times before," remarked Ethelnoth. "It's done us no good any time. Except at Ashdown. And it wouldn't have done then if the king had waited for the end of mass."

"Then that victory is the result of sin!" The bishop sat up straighter on his canvas stool and glared round him. "It is the sins of this country which have exposed us to what we now suffer! I had not thought to speak of this, but you force it on me. The sin is in this very room!"

"Who do you mean?" asked Wulfsige.

"I mean the highest. I mean the king. Deny it, lord, if you dare. But have you not again and again imposed on the rights of my true lord the archbishop? Have you not burdened his minsters with calls for tribute, for bridge money and fort money? And when the abbots, as was right and proper, refused to consent to these demands, relying on the charters given to their ancestors for ever, have you not given the land to others, and sent your officers to seize church property by violence? Where are your endowments to the Church? And how have you tried to expiate the wrong your brother did, marrying his father's widow in defiance of the laws of the Church and the word of the Holy Father himself? And what of the noble abbot Wulfred—"

"Enough, enough," Alfred broke in. "As for my brother's incest, that is between him and God. You anger me greatly with these charges. There have been no seizures by violence, except where my officers have been attacked. Wulfred brought his own troubles on himself. And as for the fort tax and the bridge tax, lord bishop, the money is to fight the heathens! Is that not a suitable object for the wealth of the Church? I know the charters except Church lands from such tolls, but they were drawn up before ever a heathen pirate set foot in England. Is it not better to give the money to me than to be pillaged by Guthrum?"

"Secular matters are not my concern," Daniel muttered.

"Is that so? Then why should my men protect you from the Vikings?"

"Because it is your duty to keep safe the kingdom committed to you by the Lord – if you wish afterwards to receive the life of the eternal kingdom."

"And what is your duty?"

"My duty is to see that the rights of the Church are not diminished or infringed in any way, no matter what Herod or Pilate—"

"Lords, lords!" It was Bishop Ceolred who broke in, his voice so frail and weak that all stared at him with alarm. "I beg you, lord Bishop. Think only what may come. You have not seen a Viking sack – I have. After that horror there are no rights for the Church, or for any of God's poor. They killed my confessor with ox bones. That dear brave man, he changed robes with me, died in my place. And me they sent out as you see now." He laid a thumbless, swollen hand on his lap. "They said I would write no more lying papers. I beg you, lords, come to an agreement."

"I cannot give away my lord archbishop's rights," said Daniel.

For some time Alfred had been aware of growing commotion in the camp outside. It did not sound alarmed – rather more joyful and excited. The canvas screen was lifted, and the massive figure of Tobba appeared in the gap, the gold ring glinting round his neck, given by the king as his personal share of the spoil three days before.

"It's an errand rider, lord. From Rome. From the pope."

"A sign!" cried Edbert. "A token from God. Even as the dove returned to Noah with olive in its beak, so peace has come to our dissensions."

The young man who entered seemed no dove. His olive skin was drawn with fatigue, his well-cut garments dusty and stained from the road. He stared around him with incomprehension, looking at the roughly dressed men, the rude quarters.

"Your pardon, gentlemen, lords? I am looking, seeking the king of English. Alfredo, king of English. One of great trust, told me here to seek . . ."

His befuddlement was obvious. Alfred controlled his anger and spoke quietly. "I am he."

The young man looked about rather obviously for a clean patch of earth to kneel on, found only mud, and with a suppressed sigh knelt and handed over a document. It was a vellum roll, a heavy wax seal dangling from it.

As Alfred unscrolled it gold leaf glinted between the carefully scribed rows of purple ink. The king held it for a moment, not knowing what to think. Could this be his salvation! He remembered the marble buildings and great power. He had been to Rome himself, twice, had viewed the grandeur of the Holy See. But that had been many years ago, before his life shut down to a blur of rain and blood, days in the saddle, nights planning and conferring. Now the Holy See had come to him.

He passed the document to Edbert. "Read it to us all."

Edbert handled the document reverently, and spoke in a hushed voice. "It is written in Latin, my lord. Illuminated by scribes – and signed by His Holiness himself. It says . . . it says . . . 'To Alfred, king of the English. Know, lord King, that we have heard of your travels . . .' no, that is trials '. . . and as you, being placed in the life of this world, daily sustain certain hardships, so in like measure do we, and we not only weep for our own – but also sorrow with you, *condolens*, having sympathy' – no, no – 'suffering alas, jointly with you.'"

Osbert muttered angrily. "Are there Vikings in Rome too?" He turned away from Bishop Daniel's furious glare. Edbert read on.

"'But for all our joint sufferings, we exhort and warn you, King, that you should not do as a foolish worldling would do, and think only of the troubles of this present time. Remember that the blessed God will not suffer you to be tempted or, or *probare*, to prove.' No – 'will not suffer you to be tempted or tried above that of which you are able, but will give you the strength to bear any of the trials which in His wisdom He has set upon you. Above all you should strive with willing heart to protect the priests, the men, and the women of the Church.'"

"That's exactly what we are all doing," grunted Ethelnoth.

"'But know, O King, that we have heard from our most reverend and holy brother, the archbishop of the race of the English who takes his See in Canterbury, that in your folly you have oppressed upon his rights and privileges as a father of those committed to his care. Now, of all sins, the sin of *avaritia*, of greed is most foul and repellent among the rulers and protectors of the Christian peoples, most abominable and dangerous to the soul. We do most solemnly therefore advise, exhort, and command by this letter from our apostolic dignity that you do now cease and desist from all oppressions against the Church, and do restore to its rulers all those privileges and rights especially in the matter of peaceful and untroubled and taxless possession of the Church's lands, which were granted to them by your ancestors, as we have heard the most godly kings of the English race, and even by your contemporaries, such as the most pious and worthy gentleman . . .' The scribe has written the name Bulcredo, my lord, but he must mean—"

"He means that runaway bastard Burgred," snarled the scarred man, Wihtbord.

"Indeed that must be it. '. . . Burgred, who now lives with us in our Holy See, in peace and in honor. So we exhort you to show honor to your priests, bishops, and archbishop, as you wish to have our friendship in this life and salvation in the life to come.'"

"It is the truth, God's truth!" Daniel cried aloud. "Spoken from the throne of God on earth. Just what I said before the message came. If we fulfil our spiritual duties, our temporal difficulties will disappear. Listen to His Holiness, my king. Restore the rights of the Church. When you do this the Vikings will be destroyed and dispersed by hand of God."

Anger clouded Alfred's face – but before he could speak Edbert hurried on.

"There's another paragraph . . ." He looked up from the paper to his master with a face of woe.

"What does it say?"

"Well, it says, it says – 'We have heard with great displeasure that our previous orders have not been obeyed. That in spite of the opinion of the apostolic See, the clerics of England have not yet unitarily given up the lay habit, and do not clothe themselves in tunics after the Roman fashion, reaching chastely to the ankle.' And then he says, well he goes on, that if this vile habit is given up and we all dress as he does, then God will love us and our afflictions will vanish like snow."

A bark of laughter came from the red-faced Ethelnoth. "So that's what's been causing our troubles! If the priestlings all hide their knees Guthrum will be terrified and run right back to Denmark!" He spat, forcefully, on the puddled floor. The pope's messenger drew back, not following the quick talk – but knowing that something was very wrong.

"You have no awareness of spirituality, lord Alderman," said Daniel, the archbishop of Canterbury's representative, pulling on his riding gloves with an air of finality, eyeing both his own long robe and Edbert's short-cut tunic and breeches. "We were asking for a message to guide us, and one has come. We must take the advice and the instruction of our father in God. I regard that as settled. There is one other matter, lord King, trivial in itself, but which I see as a trial of your good intentions and sincerity. That man, that man who came in with the message, with the gold ring round his neck. He is a runaway slave from one of my own manors. I recognize him. I must have him back."

"Tobba?" barked Wulfsige. "You can't have him. He may be a churl, he may even have been a slave, but he's accepted now. He's accepted by the companions. The king gave him that gold ring himself."

"Enough of this," Alfred said wearily. "I'll buy him from you."

"That will not do. I must have him back in person. We have had too many runaways recently—"

"I know that – and I know that they're running to the Vikings," shouted Alfred, goaded at last out of politeness. "But this man ran to his king, to fight the invaders of England. You can't—"

"I must have him back," ground on Daniel. "I shall make an example of him. The law says that if a slave cannot make restitution to his master then he shall pay for it with his hide. And he cannot make restitution to the Church for his own worth—"

"He has a gold ring worth ten slaves!"

"But since that is his possession, and he is my possession, it is my possession too. And he has also committed sacrilege, in removing himself from the ownership of the Church."

"So what are you going to do?"

"The penalty for church-breach is flaying, and I shall flay him. Not fatally. My men are most expert. But all who see his back in future will know that the arm of the Church is long. He must be delivered to my tent before sunrise. And mark this, King." Daniel turned back from the door. "If you persist in holding him, and in your other errors, there will be no passing of your messages. You will come to Edgebright's Stone, and find it as bare of men as a nunnery's privy!"

He turned and swept through the makeshift door. In the silence that followed all eyes were on Alfred. He avoided their gaze, rose and took up his long sword and strode from the room, his face set and unreadable. Wulfsige scrambled to his feet too late to bar the way.

"Where are you going?" called Edbert after him.

"Lord King, let me come with you," Wulfsige bellowed. "Guards!"

Behind, in the shelter, Osbert muttered to Ethelnoth and the others, "What's he doing? Will he do what that bastard Burgred did? Is this the end? If so, it's time we all made our peace with Guthrum—"

"I can't say," said the alderman. "But if that fool of a bishop, and of a pope, make him give up between them, then that is the end of England, now and forever."

Alfred strode through the encampment, none daring to obstruct or challenge him, and out into the wet, dripping forest and marshland along the line of the flooded river Tone. But he was not walking completely at random. The thought had been growing on him for weeks that there might come a time when he had to be away from men, from the crowds of faces looking to him for advice and orders, even from the silent pressure of his disapproving wife and coughing, fearful children at her skirts.

He knew now where he was going. To the charcoal burners. They had huts scattered all through the forests, coming out only when they needed to sell their wares, and then returning immediately to the thickets. Even in peacetime kings' officers did not bother them much. People said that they carried out strange rituals and spoke an ancient tongue among themselves. Alfred had been careful to mark one encampment down when he stumbled on it in the course of one of the hunting expeditions he and his men carried out for food, before they had begun simply to levy toll on the peasants round about. He headed straight for it through the winter dusk.

It was dark by the time he reached the first of the huts. The large man in the doorway looked at him with grave suspicion and lifted his ax.

"I wish to stay here. I will pay for my lodging."

He was taken in without fuss, or indeed recognition, when he showed them that he had both silver pennies and a long sword at his side to resist secret murder. The man looked oddly enough at the king's-head pennies when they were offered, as if wondering how long they would be tender. But the silver was good, and that was enough. No doubt they thought he was another runaway thane, deserting his allegiance, but not yet ready to go home or to approach the Vikings' court and sue for amnesty.

On the evening of the next day, the king sat in warm, homely darkness, lit only by the glow of red coals. He was alone in the hut, while the few men and women of the camp busied themselves with the complex operations of their trade. The wife had slung a griddle over the low fire and put raw griddle cakes on it, telling him in her thick accent to watch them and turn them as they cooked. He sat, listening to the crackle of the fire and smelling the pleasant mix of smoke and warm bread. For the first time for many months, the king was at peace. It was a moment taken out of time, a moment when all the pressures outside balanced each other and canceled out.

Whatever happened now, Alfred thought comfortably and lazily, would be decisive. Should he fight? Should he give up and go to Rome? He no longer knew the answers. There was a numbness within where before a fire had burned. He looked up but felt no surprise when the door scraped quietly, and through it came the massive head and shoulders of the grim churl Tobba. He was no longer wearing his gold ring, but trailed his Viking ax at his side. Stooping beneath the low roof, he came over to the fire and sat down on his haunches opposite the king. For a while neither man spoke.

"How did you find me?" asked Alfred at last.

"Asked around. Got a lot of friends in these woods. Quiet people. Don't talk much unless you knows 'em."

They sat a while longer. Absently, Tobba reached out and began to turn the cakes in his thick fingers, dropping them back on to the hot plate with faint hisses of steam.

"Got some news for you," he offered.

"What?"

"Messenger come in from Alderman Odda the morning after you left. Ubbi Ragnarsson attacked. Took his fleet down channel, landed, chased off Odda and his levy. Reckoned they was only peasants, since they only 'ad clubs and pitchforks. Chased 'em into a hill forest by the beach, bottled 'em up, reckoned that was it. That was a mistake. Come midnight, pouring rain, Odda bust out with all his men. Clubs and pitchforks they do all right in the dark. Killed Ubbi, lot of his men, took the Raven banner."

Alfred felt a reluctant stir of interest, an emotion that penetrated the numbness that possessed him. But he still did not speak, only sighed as he stared into the fire. Tobba tried to catch his interest.

"The Raven banner, you know, it really does flap its wings when the Vikings are going to win, and droops them when they're going to lose." He grinned. "Messenger said there were some kind of arrangement on the back so you could control it. Odda's sending it to you. Token of respect. Maybe you can use it in the next battle."

"If there is a next battle." The words spoken with great reluctance.

"I got an idea about that." Tobba turned a few more cakes, as if suddenly embarrassed. "If you don't mind hearing one from a churl, that is, well, really, a slave . . ."

Alfred shook his head glumly. "You will be no slave, Tobba. If I leave, you come with me. I can do at least that. I will not hand you back to Daniel and his torturers."

"No, lord, I think you should hand me over – or the messengers won't go out and there will be no army for you. But that will only be the start of it. I escaped before – can do it again. And there is something then that I could do . . ."

For several minutes the churl spoke on, low-voiced, clumsy, not used to ordering his thoughts and speaking in this manner. But he would not be stopped. Finally the two men sat other, both in different ways awed by what they had come to.

"I think it could work," said Alfred. "But you know what he's going to do to you before you escape?"

"Won't be much worse than what I've had to put up with all my life."

Alfred paused one more moment. "You know, Tobba, you could just run to the Vikings. If you took them my head they'd make you a jarl in any county you wanted. Why are you on my side?"

Tobba hung his head. "To tell . . . words, they don't come

easy. I been, my whole life, a slave, but my father, you know, he wasn't, and maybe my kids won't be, if I ever have any." His voice dropped to a mutter. "I don't see why they should grow up talking Danish. My dad didn't, nor my grandad. That's all I care about."

The door scraped again, and the burner's woman looked in, face sharp with suspicion. "'Ave you two forgotten them cakes? If you've burned them there'll be no dinner for none of us!"

Tobba looked up, grinning. "No fear of that, missis. You got two good cooks 'ere. We been cooking up a storm. 'Ere—" He scooped a cake deftly off the plate and popped it hot and whole into his cavernous mouth. "Done to a turn," he announced, blowing crumbs. "I reckon them's the best bloody cakes ever been baked in England."

It was a reluctant army that gathered at Edgebright's Stone. A smaller army than Alfred had ever led before. Before it grew even smaller word arrived that the Vikings were gathering their own at Eddington. Alfred was determined to attack before the odds became even worse.

The Vikings had left their camp in the forest soon after dawn and were drawn up in the fields close by. Their berserkers, the fiercest fighters of all, were shouting curses at the enemy as they worked themselves into a rage of battle madness. But the English soldiers stood firm despite the steady rain that soaked their chain mail, and dripped from their helmets' rims. They stirred and gripped their weapons when the wail of the lurhorns was carried by the damp air.

"They attack," said Wulfsige, standing at his king's right hand.

"Stand firm!" Alfred shouted above the thunder of running feet, the first crash of metal against metal as the lines met.

The English fought well, hacking at the linden shields of their enemies, holding their own. Men were wounded, dropped to their knees, fought on stabbing upwards under the pirates' guards. While, from behind the fighting ranks, half-armed churls staggered up with the biggest boulders they could lift, and lobbed them over their companions to crash down on the attackers. There were cries of pain and rage as the stones dislodged helmets, broke collarbones, and fell to the ground to perhaps provide a tripping block for a straining foot.

Alfred stabbed out with his sword and felt it sink deep. But at the same time he saw that his lines were being forced back in the center. "Now!" he called out to Wulfsige. "Give them the signal."

The enemy front rank shuddered and almost fell back when willing hands lifted the captured Raven banner high beside the Golden Wagon of Wessex. Now there was no flapping of jet wings to urge on the Vikings. Instead the Raven's head was down, the wings drooped in death, stitched red drops of blood dripping down from each eye.

But the line held, fought back, pushed forward once again. While to their rear the berserkers gathered, foaming with rage and chewing the edges of their shields with passion. When they attacked together none could stand before them.

At this moment Alfred saw what his opponents could not see yet and he shouted aloud. Behind the enemy, bursting out from between the trees, came a motley, skin-draped horde. They were waving clubs, crude logs of firewood, tent poles, iron pokers, tools, and weapons of any kind. They fell on the Viking rear like a great crashing wave, striking down and destroying.

For the first and only time in his life Alfred saw a heathen berserker's expression change from inhuman fury to amazement and then to plain uncomplicated fear.

Within a minute the battle was over as the Vikings, attacked from back and front, broke lines, tried to flee, and were struck down. Alfred had to force his way through his own men and their dancing half-human helpers to throw a shield over Guthrum as he was driven to the ground, to save his life and accept his surrender.

That night was a night of feasting. Magnanimous in victory, Alfred sat the defeated Viking king Guthrum at his side. He was silent for the most part, drinking deeply and heavily of the mead and ale.

"We had you beaten, you know," Guthrum finally growled. They were at that stage of the banquet when the politenesses have all been said, and men are free to talk openly. The kings' neighbors on either side, Ethelnoth, Bishop Ceolred, Alderman Odda, and a Viking jarl, had ceased to listen to their leaders and were talking among selves.

Alfred leaned over the table and hooked away the Viking's wine cup.

"If you'd like me to stop feasting and carry on fighting, that's all right by me. Let's see, you must have three- or fourscore men of your army still alive. And as soon as the others know it's safe to surrender they will all come in. When would you like to begin this battle?"

"All right, all right." Guthrum retrieved his wine cup, grinning sourly. He had been in England thirteen years and had long since dispensed with interpreters. "You won, fair enough. I'm just saying that in the battle, in the real battle, we had you beat. Your centre caving in. I could see you standing in the middle, trying to rally them. When your line broke I was going to send a hundred berserkers right down the middle, to get you. I reckoned we'd let you get away once too often already."

"Maybe." After the total victory Alfred could afford to be generous. But in spite of his experiences of losing battles, he thought this time Guthrum was wrong. It was true that the Viking hard core of veteran professionals had forced his men back in the center, but the English thanes had been standing well, with none of the dribble to the rear he had come to expect. Though their line was bent, they were still holding together.

Not that it mattered anyway who would have won. He still remembered and savored the moment when the ragged, badly armed men had fallen on the Viking rear.

"How did you get them to do it?" asked Guthrum, his voice low and confidential.

"It was a simple idea brought to me by a simple man. Your warriors are lazy. Every one of them has to have at least one English slave to cook for him and clean his gear, if not another to cut fodder for the ponies and help to look after the loot. You've had no trouble getting servants, because they have plenty to run away from. All I did was to get a message to them – a message from someone they could see was one of their own and not interested in lying to them. It was his idea to rally them. It was I who told him how it could be done."

"I know the one who did this, who came just a few days ago. They called me over to look at his back when he came in. Very skilful job. Everyone was talking about it. Even startled me. But what message could he bring that could unite these creatures?"

"A promise – my promise. I gave my word that every runaway slave in your camp would be pardoned, would have his freedom, and would receive two oxgangs of land in exchange for every Viking head."

"An oxgang? Why that must be one, or more, of what we call acres. Yes, I suppose a man could live on that. I can see the wisdom of this promise. But where did you get the land from?" He lowered his voice again, looking around out of the corners of his eyes. "Or was it just a lie? All know that you have no land or treasure. You have nothing left to give. Certainly not enough for all who fought today. What are you going to need? Four thousand acres? If you're going to promise them land in my kingdom, I can guarantee they'll have to fight for every inch of it."

Alfred frowned grimly. "I am taking it from Church estates. I have no other choice. I cannot go on doing battle with both Vikings and Church. So I defeat one – and beg mercy from the other. I firmly believe that the land granted by my ancestors was necessarily provisional, and that I have the right to reclaim it. I am breaking up several estates of the Church, and will grant them to these my new tenants. I may have to levy extra taxes to set them up with stock and gear – but at least I can count on future loyalty."

"From the slaves, perhaps. What of your bishops and priests? What of the pope? He will put your whole country under the ban."

Guthrum was well informed for a heathen and a pirate, thought Alfred. But perhaps now was the time to make the proposal.

"I mean to talk to you about that. I think I will have less trouble from the pope if I can explain to him that by taking a little land from a few minsters I have gained for Christ a whole new nation. And, you know, we cannot go on living on the same island and sharing no belief at all. This time I have sworn oaths on holy relics and you on the arm-ring of Thor, but why should we not all in future swear on the same things?

"This is my offer. I want you and your men to be baptized. If you agree I myself will be your sponsor, and your godfather. Godfathers are sworn to support their spiritual children if they come into conflict later on." Alfred eyed Guthrum steadily as he said the last words. Guthrum, he knew, would have difficulty establishing himself after this shattering defeat. He would need allies.

The Viking only laughed. He reached across the table and suddenly tapped the thong wrapped around Alfred's right wrist, touching the Viking pendant he had taken to wearing.

"Why are you wearing this, King? I know where you got it from. As soon as Rani disappeared I knew you had something to do with it. No one else could have bested him. Now let me make you an offer in return. Already you have made bitter enemies in the Church. The black robes will never forgive you now, no matter what you do. They are arrogant always and think only they have wisdom, only they can say where a man will go once he is dead. But we know better! No man, and no god, holds all the truth. I say, let the gods contest with each other and see who keeps his worshippers best. Let all men choose freely – between gods who reward the brave and the daring, and this god of the weak and timid. Let them choose between priests who ask for nothing – and priests who send innocent children to hell forever if their fathers cannot pay for baptism. Choose between gods who punish sinners, and a god who says all are sinners, so there is no reward for virtue."

He dropped his voice suddenly, in what had become an attentive silence. "Between a god who asks for tithes on the unborn calf, and our way, which is free. I make you a counter-proposal, King Alfred, king of the English. Leave your Church be. But let our priests talk freely and go where they will. And we will do the same for your priests. And then let every man and every woman believe what they will, and pay what they will. If the Christians' God is all-powerful, as they say, he will win the contest. If he is not . . ."

Guthrum shrugged. Alfred looked round at his nearest councillors, all of them staring at Guthrum with consideration in their eyes.

"If Bishop Daniel were here he would damn us all to hell for listening," remarked Ethelnoth, draining his wine cup.

"But Daniel has gone to Canterbury to whine and complain to the archbishop," observed Odda.

"It is our own doing," quavered Bishop Ceolred. "Did I not beg Daniel to show moderation? But he had no wisdom. You all know that I have lost from the Vikings as much as any and I have been a faithful follower of the Lord Jesus all my life. Yet, I say to you, maybe no man has the right to forbid another his share of the wisdom in the world. After all that we have suffered . . . who can forbid the king his will in this matter?"

"There is one thing that troubles me," said Alfred. Once more he had the heathen pendant in his hand, and was swinging it thoughtfully. "When our two armies met, mine fought for Christ and yours for the old gods. Yet mine won. Does that not show that Christ and his father are the stronger?"

Guthrum laughed explosively. "Is that what you thought all the times you lost? No." He pulled suddenly at the pendant he wore round his own neck, undid the fastening, and handed it across the table to the king. "What that victory shows is that you are a true leader. Put down Rani's pendant and take mine. He worshipped Freyr, a good god for a warrior and stallion, like Rani was. May he live in Thruthvangar, in the plains of pleasure, forever. But for kings like you and me, the true god is Odin, the father of the slain, the god of justice, the god who can say two meanings at once. Here, take this."

Again he held forward the silver medal. On it was Gungnir, the sacred spear of Odin. Alfred reached out and touched it, pushed it about on the table – then touched his chest.

"No. It is the cross of the Christ that I wear here. I have always sworn it."

"Wear it still," Guthrum said. "Wear them both until you decide."

All movement round the tables stilled, the very cupbearers and carvers stopping in their tracks to gape at the king. Alfred's eyes, sweeping along the row of faces turned to his, fell suddenly on the anguished gaze of his chaplain Edbert.

In that moment he knew the future. If men were given the free choice Guthrum offered, then all the passion, the faith, the loyalty of Edbert and his like would be of no avail. The bitter, grasping selfishness of the archbishops, the popes, the Daniels, would cancel it every time. With his mind's eye he saw the great minsters deserted, their stone carted away to use in barns and walls. He saw armies gathering on the white cliffs of England, armies of Saxons and Vikings united under the banners of Odin and Thor, ready to spread their faith to the Franks and the southerners. He saw the White Christ himself, a baby, crying forsaken on the last untended altar of Rome.

If he wavered now, Christianity would not stand.

In the tense silence Tobba leaned forward from his place behind King Alfred's chair.

He took the chain in his hand and clasped it round his master's neck. There was the tiniest sound in the silent room as metal touched metal.

Or was it the loudest sound any of them had ever heard?

Such a Deal

Esther M. Friesner

Hisdai ibn Ezra, noted merchant of Granada (retired), did his best to conceal his amusement when his servant entered and announced, "There – there is a vis – a visitor to see you, *sidi*. A – Castilian, he said to tell you."

How you twist your face and stammer Mahmoud, the old Jew thought. *You are jumpy as a flea-ridden monkey. This unexpected guest of mine has you at a loss, I see. Well, you are young yet, and it is no common thing for foreigners to frequent this house since I left the trader's calling. I still recall what a hubbub we had when the Genoese navigator first arrived, and that was supposed to be a secret visit. Lord of Hosts, whatever has become of that one? And of Daud . . .*

He banished the thought, dreading the despair it must bring him. Better to study Mahmoud's confusion and hold back laughter instead of tears.

Mahmoud was obviously waiting for his master to summon guards, or send word to Sultan Muhammad's palace of the infidel interloper's presence. When Hisdai did neither – only turning another leaf in his *Maimonides* – the servant seemed to jig out of his skin.

The old Jew swallowed a chuckle. *You look as if you could do with a little reading from the "Guide for the Perplexed" yourself, boy. You did not expect this, did you? One of those cause-mad Christians in the house of a Jew who lives quite comfortably under the reign of an Islamic lord? Least of all when the armies of Ferdinand and Isabella are camped before our walls, laying siege to Granada. No, you have every right to wear that astonished expression. If only it were not so comical!*

He sighed and set aside his book. "Are there any refreshments in this house worthy of so exalted a caller, Mahmoud? A little spiced wine? A handful of dates not too wizened? Some other delicacies that Cook may have secreted away from happier times, may the Lord bless him for the prudent ant he so wisely emulates?"

Mahmoud knit his brows, his bewilderment mounting visibly. "Come, lad!" Hisdai said, trying to hearten his servant into action. "There is no mystery here. For me to expect Cook to have secret stores of exotic titbits despite the passage of nearly a year and a half since the Christians have come before our gates – that is just my knowing Cook's character."

"Oh, it is not that, *sidi*; it is only . . ." Mahmoud paused, his tongue caught in a snare set by his discretion.

"Only what?" Hisdai ibn Ezra could not restrain a mildly cynical smile. "Fear nothing; I have heard all the whispering my servants do about me for more years than you have been alive." He stroked his silvery beard. "They call me master-merchant to my face, but behind my back I vow that more than one idle tongue wags that I have trafficked less with human clientele and more with *djinn* and *Iblis*. Is this not so?"

Very reluctantly Mahmoud nodded. Hisdai laughed. "Therefore, why stand amazed at our unheralded visitor? Give thanks that he merely comes from our enemies' ranks and not from the fiery Pit itself!"

Mahmoud made it his business to say, "O *sidi*, I do not believe the tales. How can I, who behold you daily, give credence to such lies?"

Hisdai lifted one grey and shaggy brow. "Are you quite certain they *are* lies, Mahmoud?"

Like most new servants, Mahmoud took everything his master said at face value. "They must be lies, O *sidi*. For one thing, you do not even look like a wizard."

The boy spoke truth, and Hisdai ibn Ezra knew it. If he flattered himself that he resembled the dark magicians of legend, any good mirror would disabuse him at once. He knew himself to be a small, crinkle-faced cricket-chirp of a man. White hairs – sparse beneath his turban, lush upon his chin – held constant argument with brown eyes of a youthful sparkle. Long hours of study of the driest and most petrified of scholarly subjects, which drifted off into longer hours of heavy-headed sleep, painted him old. Then he would wake and speak with such lively insight and interest of current affairs near and far that he left younger men panting to follow the lightning path of his wit and insight.

True that Paradox had long made her scruffy nest beneath the roof of the one-time merchant prince, but for a Castilian to come a-calling in these times – ! That was too much for even the most seasoned of servants to bear without dashing away at once to auction off the news to his comrades' eager ears.

Now that Mahmoud's initial startlement had faded, Hisdai could see that he was avid to have his duty done and be whisking this tale with him to the kitchens, and so the old Jew gently urged him on his way, saying, "Go now, haste. It does not do to keep demons *or* Castilians waiting."

Mahmoud departed. He returned not much later, followed by a gentleman whose decidedly simple European clothes were in startling contrast to the splendour of Hisdai ibn Ezra's flowing Moorish robes.

"Pelayo Fernández de Santa Fe, O *sidi*," Mahmoud announced, bowing. Hisdai recognized that the lad was a skilled enough servitor to lower his eyes to the very stones while still observing absolutely everything around him. This time, as others, that talent would provide Mahmoud with a most instructive spectacle.

Then Hisdai ibn Ezra gazed from the clothes before him to the face above and turned to a lump of ice as solid as any to be found on the summit of snow-capped Mulhacén. He felt the colour ebb from his face like a fleeing tide, felt for the first time the palsy of age cause his outstretched hands to tremble. The old man's breath rushed into his lungs with an audible rasping, a sound too near the final deathbed croak for any servant who valued his pay to remain unmoved.

Yet when Mahmoud rushed forward, a wail of paid loyalty on

his lips, the strength gushed back into Hisdai's body. He stood straight as a poplar and sharply motioned Mahmoud away. "Unworthy servant, where are your manners? Our honoured guest will think himself to be still among his own barbarous people. Go, fetch scented water and soft towels! Bread and salt! My finest wine! Why are you gawking? You'll gape less when one of King Ferdinand's men drives a pike through your gizzard. Go, I say!"

Mahmoud did not wait for further instructions. He had more than enough meat for meditation, and the other servants would treat him royally for it. Any diversion not connected with the infernal siege was worth its weight in gold, especially to folk who lacked anything more precious than copper.

Hisdai ibn Ezra watched Mahmoud scamper off, listening until he judged his servant's pattering footsteps had retreated a sufficient distance for his liking. Then and only then did he turn to give his visitor a proper welcome.

"You *idiot!*" He snatched the man's hat from his hands and flung it out the window into the courtyard below.

The visitor flew after his hat, but wisely halted his own flight short of the abyss. Leaning over the tiled sill, he remarked, "I see that you've kept the false awning in place down there. I thought that since you retired, you wouldn't need to maintain such emergency measures in case of dissatisfied royal customers."

"I may not deal with Sultan Muhammad any more, nor need to provide for the possibility of – ahem! – expeditious departures, but only a fool dreams any peace is permanent," Hisdai growled. "Most definitely not in these times."

His guest was unmoved by the old man's peevishness. He was still admiring Hisdai's escape stratagem, with which he seemed to be disconcertingly familiar. "To be able to jump from this height and land safely – ! Ah, one day I must try it, just to see how it feels. Unfortunately my hat missed the awning and the cushions under it and landed right in the fishpond. Was that necessary? I was rather attached to that hat."

"Would that your brain were as attached to the inside of your skull. Do you realize what you risked, coming here in the teeth of the siege like this?"

"Unless I misremember," Hisdai's guest drawled, "it was not ten months ago that I found you entertaining a certain Genoese in this very room. When I asked you how Master Columbus had managed to breach the siege, you only smiled and said, 'I have my ways. One key opens many gates, if that key be made of gold.'" He winked at Hisdai. "For once, I recalled your wisdom and used it well, particularly now that I have more of your precious keys than any locksmith."

"What is this blather of keys?" Hisdai snorted. "When Mahmoud informed me that there was a Castilian come calling – all Christians are Castilians to him – I expected to greet a common seaman bringing word from the admiral. That Genoese is no fool. He has more sense than to venture his neck for nothing!"

The young man murmured into his beard, "There you speak a greater truth than you know."

His words went unheard. As suddenly as it had erupted, Hisdai's burst of sour temper vanished altogether. He rushed to fling the silken wings of his sleeves around the "Castilian".

'Ah, Daud! Daud, my son, it is *I* who am the fool! If you are back, what else matters? My Daud – shall I call you by that abominable Castilian name you bestowed upon yourself?"

Daud pretended to take umbrage. "I thought it a very good alias, and most handy for getting past the more officious of the Catholic Monarchs' sentries. Stop a man named for Don Pelayo, he who began the reconquest of this land from the Moors? Most ill-omened at this juncture." He shook his head solemnly. "Now that Ferdinand and Isabella are about to retake the last Iberian foothold of our Moorish rulers, that would be most ill-omened indeed."

Hisdai heamed over his son's resourcefulness. "Still the clever rogue, my pride! Blessed be the lord, the God of Israel, for bringing me to this season. My heart, my child, I never thought to see your face again."

The young man laughed out of a face that was a less-wrinkled version of his sire's. His beard was somewhat shorter, the hair on his head summer midnight to Hisdai's winter dawn, but the eyes held the same fire.

"Indeed, my father, there were moments in the voyage when I myself questioned whether the next face I saw would be yours or Elijah's!" He sighed. "May Heaven witness, our valiant admiral suffered celestial visions enough for us all. There must be truth in what they say, that madness is but a divinely given spark of genius that burns with the most peculiar flame. That man has a sufficiency of such embers to burn all *al-Andalus* to ashes." Laughter departed his lips as he added, "As he may yet do."

"What is this you say, my son?" Hisdai clapped his hands to his eldest's shoulders. "Do you mean that the voyage was – a failure? The homeland we seek, the refuge for our people once these accursed Catholic Monarchs destroy Granada, is only another of the admiral's insane fancies?"

Daud's travel-tattered moustache twisted itself into a wry expression. "O my father if I hear *you* call the admiral mad, you'll have me thinking there's some truth to Mother's allegations. Why else would you commend me to a madman's care?"

Hisdai waved off his son's words impatiently. "Your mother, foremost of my wives, is a virtuous woman. As such, her price is above rubies, even if her love of gossip is beneath contempt. You are my heir, Daud! Would I entrust a diamond of untold price to a lunatic? But if the diamond is yet rough, I would select with utmost care the jeweller into whose hands I place it for proper cutting, polishing, setting, until the every refinement of his art had perfected it as it deserves to be."

"In other words, you sent me to fall off the edge of the earth for my own good," Daud concluded.

"Also to get you away from that Egyptian dancing-girl your worthless friend Barak spends all his money on," Hisdai grumbled under his breath.

Daud heard, and did his best not to choke on laughter. "Fear not, O my father! We encountered no such temptresses in the court of the Great Khan. As is well known, the almighty monarch of Cathay surrounds himself exclusively with the fairest daughters of Israel, the flowers of Judaea, the untouched virgins of Jerusalem-in-exile, the—"

"Is it so much for an old man to want his son wed to a nice Jewish girl?" Hisdai sulked into his beard.

"Ah, Father, you would not be satisfied until I wed a veritable princess!"

"And is that such a bad ambition?" Hisdai demanded.

"Not at all, not at all." Daud gazed at his father with real affection. "So it was my taste for forbidden delights that counted as one more rough spot for your Genoese jeweller to strike off? And here I thought it was the dream of establishing a new homeland for our people that drove you to pour my patrimony into those three rachitic ships you bought him."

Hisdai ibn Ezra was in no joking mood. "Daud, I see that at least one of my dreams has been in vain. You return as much the mocker as you departed."

"Oh no, my father." Daud dropped all pretence of jest. "Believe me, I return to your house a changed man. If I banter with you now, it is only to keep my heart from crumbling beneath the full weight of what I have to tell you."

Fear and consternation showed themselves boldly in the old Jew's eyes. "What news, then? Tell me! Not that the voyage failed, no, or else you could not be here, solid flesh beneath my hands. What then? The Great Khan denied our petition, rejected my gifts? Once there were many Jews in Cathay, respected, honoured, permitted to dwell in peace, to follow the ways of our fathers. Did you remind the Great Khan of the prosperity we brought the land?"

Daud nodded. "I tried. Our translator did, at any rate. Moshe ibn Ahijah is a wonderful scholar. No one was more surprised than he when the Great Khan did not know Hebrew, Arabic, Aramaic, Castilian, Greek, or Latin."

"But surely you managed to communicate? By signs? By a show of gifts? In my day, when I accompanied the caravans, I always managed to make my intents clear—"

"We, too, managed. The gifts you sent to the Great Khan," Daud replied, "were very eloquent. Entertaining, I should say. They made him laugh."

"Laugh! At masterpieces of the goldsmith's art? Gems that were the finest I could call in from our people here in *al-Andalus*, in Castilla, in France, in Italy, even across the water in *Mamlakah al-Maghribiyah*—!" Hisdai began to pace the room.

"When word first reached me of this man Columbus, I thought it to be the answer to my wildest prayers. Any half-educated man knows that the ancients proved the world to be round – that much of the Genoese's fancies needed no confirmation – but to apply that knowledge to the establishment of a westerly trade route—!" He smacked a fist into his palm. "That was the prize I desired. A way for us, for all Jews, to reach the haven of the East safely, there to live unmolested by the periodic excesses of zeal that afflict our Christian neighbours. Once there, we would prosper as never before."

"So you said, my father." Daud remained glum.

"So I said, and so it would be! The East has ever favoured us, and with new trade routes opened we would thrive. Oh, Daud, you will never know how fervently I thanked the Lord when those purblind Catholic Monarchs rejected Columbus's plan and sent him packing! You cannot begin to imagine all I did, or how speedily, to bring him here so that I might finance his scheme, and our future!"

"I recall it well. I did not spend *all* my time mooning over Barak's dancing-girl."

In his distracted state Hisdai disregarded Daud's mordant comments. "My son, the treasure I sent with you was to be the ransom of the Jews, our payment for refuge in the lands of the distant East once that vainglorious Genoese proved a safe sea route there possible. And you say the Great Khan *laughed*?"

In silence Daud reached into the large leather pouch at his side. His fist emerged overflowing with the glitter of pure gold and priceless jewels. Chains and pendants, adornments for ears, breast, wrist, and ankle, gorgeous enhancements for body parts beyond the old man's imagining all spilled over the blue-and-green carpet.

While Hisdai gaped, Daud simply plunged his hand back into the pouch and followed the first handful of gold with a second, then a third, then a fourth, each scattered with the disinterested prodigality of a rich man tossing crumbs to the birds.

"You see now why he laughed? Because next to the treasure hoard the Great Khan already commands, our gifts were regarded as no better than the pinched clay figurine one of his children might make him for a present: charming, but hardly to be taken seriously. What you behold is merely my share of the first gift the Great Khan made to us. The *first*, mark me. It was a reward."

"A – reward?" Hisdai managed to wrench his gaze away from the heap of wealth strewn so casually at his feet. "What for?"

"For making the admiral shut up about Christ." Daud shrugged. "His harangues were putting the Great Khan's priests off their stride, and they had such a lot of people to – to serve that day." An unpleasant memory appeared to grip him. Fine sweat stood out on his forehead.

"Christ?" Hisdai echoed, overlooking his son's discomfort. "But I thought he was over all that."

"My father, one does not *get over* one's faith as one does a fever," Daud commented tartly.

"Bah! Christianity was never truly the admiral's faith. It was a – a convenience, the path that seemed to him smoothest for getting on in the world, particularly as he desired royal backing for this unheard-of voyage of his." Hisdai spoke as one who knows such things too surely to debate them.

"You may be right," Daud admitted. "In all our time on board the *Tziporah*, I often thought that the admiral gave his prayers to God but his worship to himself."

"Of course I am right!" Hisdai snapped. "Christian just for show he was, and to gain the ear of the powerful. Much good it did him! He had so many royal doors slammed in his face that he had the arms of Castilla, León, y Aragón impressed on his forehead."

He began to pace the floor; kicking aside the golden baubles. "He came to me fresh from long and profitless waiting upon Ferdinand and Isabella. In my presence he no longer needed to play the pious Catholic. He told me that his own folk back in Genoa were our kindred – as if I had not already secured that knowledge before sending for him! – exiles from the Christian kingdoms of Spain. I did not have to tell him what our fate would be if Granada falls. Ah, my son, if you could have but heard how wistfully he spoke of the faith of his ancestors!"

"Was this before or after you offered him the money for his expedition?" Daud's question was dust-dry.

"Now you say he preached Christ in the Great Khan's court?" Hisdai ibn Ezra wrung his hands. 'Alas, what was he thinking of?"

"Probably the same thing he is acting on even now." Without warning, Daud seized Hisdai by the shoulders, fixing him with a terrible, burning glance. "Father; cease your wailing and pay heed. Your Genoese friend may be a visionary, but he could give the Evil One lessons in opportunism. Christopher Columbus has returned with two of your three ships intact. The *Tziporah* he ran aground off the coast of Cathay before we began our homeward sail. The *Bat-sheba* we brought safely to harbour in Tangier, where its – ah – cargo is presently being sent after me by our family connections in *Mamlakah al-Maghribiyah*, and as for the third—"

"Cargo?" Hisdai interrupted, the keen professional interest of a seasoned merchant lighting up his eyes.

"*Listen* to me, I said!" Daud came dangerously close to shaking his father soundly. "As for the *third* ship, the *Hadassah ha-Malkah*, as soon as we came within sight of Tangier, your precious admiral ordered it to veer away north. Yes – do not stare – I said north; north to the ports of the Catholic Monarchs! North with a hold filled with the later gifts of the Great Khan, beside which what you see upon the carpet here is nothing. And even now, as we speak he has gone to present himself before Ferdinand and Isabella at their battle camp at Santa Fe. Don't you see? Now he has proof that will command the attention of royalty in a manner they cannot ignore. The paltry gold of Granada's Jews was insufficient to buy us refuge from the Castilian troops, or safety for the last city where our Moorish masters allowed us to follow our faith in peace. The endless gold of Cathay *will* buy your pet Genoese what he has always hungered for – a noble title, royal patronage, and his place as the honoured favorite of our enemies!" His face was a mask of scorn as he added, "Once a snob, always a snob."

"But we must stop him!" Hisdai grabbed his son's arms in a grip that was the equal of the younger man's.

"Do you think we did not try, O my father? Too late. By the time we realized what he was about, he had gained too much time. After the wreck of the *Tziporah*, he made certain to crew the *Hadassah ha-Malkah* with men who would go along with his treachery."

"Impossible." Hisdai shook his head like one suddenly weary. "Everyone aboard those ships was of our own people. They knew our great purpose! How could they—?"

"Present promises of a greater share in a hold full of treasure weighs more with some men than dreams of a distant Jewish homeland," Daud said with neither pride nor shame.

Hisdai slumped in his son's grasp. "Even so. How can I blame them? The siege has lasted almost a year and a half. Granada is all that remains to our sultan." With faltering steps he turned from Daud and went to the window. "In the streets he is no longer called Abu Abd Allah Muhammad, but *al-zogoybi*, and in truth he is a poor devil. He will go down, and we shall fall with him. The taking of Granada is the death of our people's last truly safe haven. In the dark times to come many will fancy gold a better rock to cling to than Torah."

So rapt was Hisdai by his burden of hopelessness, he hardly noticed that when his son's shadow crept up behind him, a second shadow – then a third, then a fourth – glided silently into the room and joined it. He only half-heard Daud say, "O my father, you are wise to have kept faith."

"Faith?" Hisdai's laugh was brittle and hollow. He continued to gaze up at the steel-bright sky above Granada. "Of what use is faith? I have squandered our wealth to back the vision of a renegade! We need soldiers, Daud – not scholars, not vision-aries – and soldiers will not fight for faith alone."

"Yet I hear these Catholic Monarchs call this battle for Granada a new Crusade."

"That shows all you know of Crusades, my son. If Granada were a poor mud-hut village, these Catholic Monarchs and their minions would not care if we worshipped the birds of the air or the snakes that crawl over the face of the earth, but because we have wealth—"

"Father," Daud cautioned. "Father, it would be wiser not to speak with mockery of snakes and birds."

"I mean no scorn. Who am I to mock the Lord's creation?" Hisdai leaned heavily against the side of the window. "I am just a poor man who put his faith in dreams. Dreams fly. Only death is certain."

Then Hisdai ibn Ezra turned from the window and in that instant beheld a sight that convinced him that madness, too, is one of life's little certainties. "Blessed Lord," he murmured, and took one backward step that came near to toppling him out the window.

Daud sprang forward and seized Hisdai by the arm. "Have a care, O my father. It is not courtesy to leave your faithful so precipitously."

"Faithful?" Hisdai quavered.

"Well, so he has assured me. Although officially he is a priest of Huitzilopochtli, he has confided in me that his heart" – for some reason, Daud swallowed hard – "his heart is devoted to the worship of Quetzalcoatl, the Plumed Serpent – Uh . . . would you mind if he touched your beard? It would be an honour, and he has promised us so much—"

Giddy with trying to make sense of the gibberish Daud was spouting, Hisdai found himself face to face with a man unlike any he had ever encountered, even in the years of his widest mercantile wanderings. Straight black hair; deep copper skin marked with tattoos and other scars, wide nose ornamented with plugs of gold and jade, the apparition regarded him with an unreadable expression.

"He wants to . . . touch my beard?" Hisdai could not tear his eyes away. From the gilded and gemmed sandals on this creature's feet to the exquisite feathered mantle on his shoulders to the gorgeously plumed headdress crowning all, one thing about the new caller was certain: not even Mahmoud would mistake him or the two burly fellows accompanying him for Castilians.

As if to confirm this, Mahmoud chose that moment to enter with the refreshments, a dish that was tribute to both Cook's frugality and his creativity. "Remember to tell *ya-sidi* Hisdai that the meat is for the Castilian only," he mumbled to himself, so intent on keeping the heavy tray level that at first he did not really notice the extra people now gathered in the room. "Remember to tell him, or Cook will have my head. Master is – *was* – so fond of Rover."

This apposite consumer warning now went flying out of Mahmoud's skull as he looked up from his burden and actually *saw* his master's additional guests. One wore what looked like a leopard's pelt, the head a fanged helmet, the other was sheathed in feathered armour with an eagle's beak overshadowing his keen eyes. Both were heavily armed with eccentric weapons that looked nonetheless mortally effective for all their strangeness.

Mahmoud screamed, dropped the canine *khua-khus,* and ran. The eagle-helmed warrior threw what looked like a primitive axe, which nailed the fleeing servant's sleeve to the doorpost.

Before Mahmoud could wrench free, he was laid hold of by both bizarrely armoured men and thrust to the floor at Hisdai's feet, as if for the older man's approval.

Daud stepped in at once. "O my father," he said smoothly, "may it please you to welcome the beloved nephew of the Great Khan Ahuitzotl, the Lord Moctezuma?"

Without word or hint of their intentions, the three copper-skinned strangers fell to the carpet alongside Mahmoud and assumed positions of the utmost humble submission. Hisdai opened and closed his mouth, wet his lips numerous times, nibbled the ends of his snowy moustache, and in general made every visual preamble to speech without actually managing to utter an intelligible word. He looked as if he did not know whether to object to the display of obeisance at his feet, to demand an explanation, to offer the abused Mahmoud a raise in salary, or just to go to the window, leap for the padded awning below, and make a break for it. There was also the chance that he might miss the awning, but at the moment that did not seem like such a bad alternative to the irrationality besetting him. At the end of his reason, he searched his son's face and ultimately managed to choke out a hoarse yet eloquent plea:

"*Nu?*"

Daud looked sheepish. 'Ah, yes, there was one small matter I forgot to mention about my new friend, O my father."

He reached once more into his pouch and pulled out a rolled parchment on which was a meticulously copied drawing of a venerable-looking gentleman – bearded, fair-skinned – whose preferred mode of transport was obviously a raft made out of live snakes. "I made the drawing myself, copying it from one of Lord Ahuitzotl's holiest manuscripts," he said, showing it to Hisdai. "This is Quetzalcoatl, the Plumed Serpent, the god who departed, sailing away to the East, but whose return has been foretold. Specifically foretold. Promised, I should say, for a few years from now. Of course, as I told Lord Moctezuma, who are we to quibble if a god shows up for his appointments a trifle early?"

He tilted the page so that the light might fall on it from a better angle, and hopefully prompted his father, "You *do* see the resemblance?"

Hisdai's reaction to this unsought Annunciation would remain one of Time's unfinished mysteries. From somewhere beyond the walls a long, blood-chilling ululation shivered the air and tore all attention from every matter save itself. It was a scream beautiful in its ghastly perfection. Not even the most ignorant of hearers could command a sound that horripilating with the muezzin's common cry; not unless the muezzin had suddenly been seized with the urge to boil himself alive slowly, in a vat of vengeance-minded lobsters.

At the fearful outcry the primal instincts of every man in that small room asserted themselves. Mahmoud tendered his resignation and bolted. Hisdai clutched his grown son protectively to him as if Daud were still a child. Moctezuma and his entourage calmly lifted their heads and smiled: quaint, nostalgic smiles such as other folk might wear on hearing a dear, old, familiar cradle-tune.

"Oh, good," said Daud. The model of unflappability, he disengaged himself from his father's arms and brought a stub of charcoal and a much-folded document out his shirt bosom. The blood of generations of steel-nerved merchant princes never flowed more coolly through his veins as he consulted the parchment, checked off an item, and remarked to all concerned, "I see the rest of the cargo has arrived."

On the battleground before Granada the troops of the Catholic Monarchs knew that already.

In spite of Hisdai's protests that he had no place on the field of combat, his son, Daud, and his newfound retainers insisted that he accompany them to the city gate to view the proceedings. Shock did little to diffuse Hisdai's innate stubbornness, and he put teeth in his refusal by making that long-contemplated leap out the window.

To no avail. There were more of the eagle-helmed Cathayans in the patio below, the translator Moshe ibn Ahijah with them. They simply waited until he stopped bouncing, then (with ibn Ahijah's able intervention) hailed him as Lord Quetzalcoatl, All-Powerful Sovereign, Saviour-Whose-Coming-Was-Foretold-For-A-Few-Years-Later-Than-This-But-Who's-Counting?, and hauled him off to see how well his loyal people served him.

So it was that Hisdai ibn Ezra came to witness the end of the siege of Granada and the grim finale to all the Catholic Monarch's dreams of finishing the Reconquest. Instead the Reconquest finished them. As he stood upon the battlements of the city, Hisdai beheld a vast force of Cathayans sweep through the Christian ranks with astonishing zeal and ferocity.

"Incredible," he remarked to Daud. "And yet they make such delicate porcelains."

"I just hope Lord Tizoc and those jaguar knights of his find you a throne quickly," Daud replied, not really listening. "This is going to be over sooner than I thought."

"And why should I need a throne?" Hisdai inquired.

"Why, to receive the captives!"

"Captives?" The old Jew made a deprecating sound.

Twenty minutes later he was making it out of the other side of his mouth as he gazed down at his noble prisoners and felt distinctly uncomfortable. It was not the fault of his seat – the throne was the best Lord Tizoc's men could transport from the great Alhambra palace on such short notice – but of Hisdai ibn Ezra's new position. During his previous interviews with royalty, he had been firmly entrenched on the giving end of any and all obeisances, grovels, and general gestures of submission. This was different, and would take some getting used to.

Not all of the captives were making the transition any easier for the former merchant. Queen Isabella of Castilla y León was the only woman who could kneel in the dirt at the foot of a god's throne and still make it look as if everyone present had come to pay homage to her. Her husband and consort, Ferdinand of Aragón, crouched beside her, eyes hermetically shut, whimpering, any pretence of royal pride long since abandoned. Unlike his mate, he had been in the thick of the last battle and seen too many sights that properly belonged in a sinner's nightmare of hell.

Ferdinand and Isabella were not alone. Sultan Muhammad and his mother were with them, the regal quartet linked at the necks with a single rope whose end was fast in the hand of Moctezuma's finest jaguar warrior.

Off to one side Christopher Columbus crouched within a ring of eagle knights – the "cargo" of that ship he had abandoned because he thought a shipment of gold had the greater worth than a shipment of heathen ambassadors. The error of his commercial instincts had just been proven beyond doubt on the battlefield.

Using care, so as not to upset the towering headdress his new subjects had insisted he wear, Lord Hisdai ibn Ezra y Quetzalcoatl beckoned Daud nearer. "This is wrong," he whispered.

"Try it for a time; you may like it," Daud suggested.

"But this is blasphemy!" Hisdai maintained, pounding on the arm of his throne. *"Thou shalt have no other gods before me,* says the Lord!"

"Well, *you* have no other gods before Him, do you, Father? And if your new subjects choose to worship a Jew, they won't be the first. Given time, they might even convert entirely. If Judaism is good enough for your Lord Quetzalcoatl, I will tell them, it should be good enough for you! It won't take long. Moshe ibn Ahijah only had to explain to them about horses *once* when we reached Tangier, and you saw how well they handled the Castilian cavalry."

"Yes, but to *eat* the poor beasts afterwards—!"

"Well, they do have their little ways . . ."

Hisdai considered this. Unfortunately his meditations were interrupted by Queen Isabella, who decided to make her royal displeasure known by spitting at his feet and calling him a name that showed her deep ignorance of Jewish family life. Two of the jaguar warriors sprang forward to treat her sacrilege by a method whose directness would have warmed the figurative heart of the Inquisition. Only a horrified shout from Hisdai made them lower their obsidian-toothed warclubs, still sticky with assorted bits of skullbone and brain-matter collected in the course of the recent fray.

Moctezuma himself came before his chosen Lord, bowing low. "O august Lord Quetzalcoatl, mighty Plumed Serpent, bringer of the arts of peace, what is your will that we do with the graceless devils who dared attack your chosen stronghold and those who so poorly defended it until now?" His bastard blend of Hebrew, Arabic, Aramaic, Castilian, Greek, and Latin was really quite good for one who had only picked up snatches of the tongues on board a sailing vessel.

"He means the kings," Daud whispered. "Both Catholic and Moorish. And Granada."

"I know who and what he means," Hisdai snapped back, sotto voce. "I still don't know why he has to mean me, with all those barbarous names. What have I to do with the kings anyway?"

"Well, you'll have to do *something* with them. Your new subjects expect – they expect . . ." Daud hesitated. Having witnessed the aftermath of more than one battle while visiting the Great Khan Ahuitzotl's court, he knew just what these people expected and how touchy they would be if they didn't get it. On the other hand, there was no way short of a new Creation that his father would consent to what Lord Moctezuma had in mind, even in the name of religious freedom.

Daud was pondering this dilemma when he heard his father exclaim, "Stop pestering me, Moctezuma! I tell you I don't know *what* I want done with them! Can't it wait?"

"Puissant lord, it cannot. If we do not feed the sun—"

"What? Feed what? Daud, you speak this man's tongue better than he speaks ours, see if you can understand him. What is he trying to say?"

Daud smiled as a second, figurative sun shed the lovely rays of revelation within his mind. "Never mind, Father," he said. "I'll take care of everything. You go ahead to the palace. You know they cannot start the banquet without you."

Reluctant as he was to leave loose ends behind him, Hisdai was still too flummoxed to do other than comply with his son's suggestion. Flanked by jaguar warriors and preceded by eagle knights, he allowed himself to be led up to the splendours of the Alhambra, where the promised victory feast awaited. Word of the bizarre conquest had spread rapidly through the Jewish population of Granada, and mad celebration followed. With the help of Moshe ibn Ahijah's linguistically talented family, Jews, Cathayans, and the always pragmatic Moors had cooperated to lay on a wondrous repast in very little time. Cook was in his glory. There was not an empty goblet nor an occupied kennel left in all the city.

Hisdai had barely taken his place in the feasting hall when Daud returned and whispered something in his ear.

"A job?" Hisdai echoed. "That renegade Genoese betrays us and you give him a job?"

"Why not?" Daud made a lazy, beckoning gesture, and one of Moctezuma's doe-eyed waiting-women hastened to fetch a tray of chilled melon slices. As part of the Great Khan's favourite nephew's entourage, these select highborn ladies had been definitely off limits for the course of the voyage. Now, however, they were just another gift to Lord Quetzalcoatl's household. "You didn't want to be bothered."

Hisdai lowered his eyes. "I feared having my enemies in my power. Nothing reduces a man to his animal nature faster than the opportunity for exacting unlimited revenge."

"Most admirable. Which was precisely why I sent Christopher Columbus to deliver your will to our – I mean, your new subjects."

"My will? How, when I never stated it?"

"Not precisely, perhaps, but I assumed you wished the captives be shown mercy."

"True."

"You just couldn't trust yourself to say as much with Isabella addressing you so – unwisely."

"And shall I trust the Genoese to do as much? The Catholic Monarchs scorned him once. Has he the strength of character to resist paying them back now?"

"Perhaps not." Daud ogled the waiting-woman, and she returned a look of most exquisite promise. "Which was why I told him Moctezuma has already been advised that the fate of one captive is the fate of all."

Hisdai relaxed visibly. "My son, you are wise. But – you did tell him to request compassionate treatment? You are certain? Does Columbus know enough of the Cathayan tongue to make himself understood beyond doubt?"

Daud sighed. "Alas, no. Christopher Columbus is a man of vision, not linguistics. Which was why I took the precaution of having Moshe ibn Ahijah translate the *exact* words our once-admiral should relay to Lord Moctezuma."

The waiting-woman knelt beside him with seductive grace, offering her tray and more besides for Daud's inspection. Rumour had it that she and the others were ranked as princesses in their own land. Idly Daud wondered whether – the lady's eventual conversion permitting – such a match would satisfy Hisdai. So caught up was he in these pleasant musings that he did not hear his father's next question.

"Daud! Daud, wake up. I asked you something."

"Hmm? And what was that, O my fondle – father?"

"What he *said*. What you told the Genoese to *say*."

"Oh, that. I kept it simple. I told him to say—"

From somewhere outside a loud cheer from many throats assaulted heaven, loud enough certainly to cover the lesser cry of one man surprised by the religious practices of another.

" – have a heart."

Ink From the New Moon

A. A. Attanasio

Here, at the farthest extreme of my journey, in the islands along the eastern shores of the Sandalwood Territories, with all of heaven and earth separating us – here, at long last, I have found enough strength to pen these words to you. Months of writing official reports, of recording endless observations of bamboo drill-derricks and cobblestone canals irrigating horizons of plowed fields, of interviewing sooty laborers in industrial barns and refineries roaring with steam engines and dazzling cauldrons of molten metal, of scrutinizing prisoners toiling in salt-canyons, of listening to schoolchildren sing hymns in class-rooms on tree-crowned hilltops and in cities agleam with gold-spired pavilions and towers of lacquered wood – all these tedious annotations had quite drained me of the sort of words one writes to one's wife. But, finally, I feel again the place where the world is breathing inside me.

Forgive my long silence, Heart Wing. I would have written sooner had not my journey across the Sandalwood Territories of Dawn been an experience for me blacker than ink can show. Being so far from the homeland, so far from you, has dulled the heat of my life. Darkness occupies me. Yet, this unremitting gloom brings with it a peculiar knowledge and wisdom all its own – the treasure that the snake guards – the so-called poison cure. Such is the blood's surprise, my precious one, that even in the serpent's grip of dire sorrow, I should find a clarity greater than any since my failures took me from you.

You, of course, will only remember me as you left me – a sour little man for whom being Third Assistant Secretarial Scribe at the Imperial Library served more as punishment than privilege; the husband whittled away by shame and envy, whom you dutifully bid farewell from our farm's moon gate on the avenue of chestnuts. All so long ago, it seems. What a humiliation that the only way I could support you was to leave you. And for such an ignoble task – to examine the social structure of rebel provinces that have repudiated our finest traditions. I was so embittered that for most of my journey I referred to the region as the Sandalwood Territories of the Dawn, as if their secession from the Kingdom had happened only in their minds, two hundred years of independence from us an illusion before the forty-five centuries of our written history. Even their name for themselves seemed sheer arrogance: the Unified Sandalwood Autocracies. As if there could be any true autocracy but the Emperor's. Still, the Imperial Court had selected me to regard them as if they possessed authenticity, and I had to humble myself or face the ignominy of losing even this menial job.

I never said any of this to you then. I could barely admit it to myself. Yet, I need to say it clearly now – all of it, the obvious and the obscure – to make sense of my life and yours. Yes, I do admit, I was ashamed, most especially in your eyes. Only you, Heart Wing, know me for who I truly am – a storyteller hooked on the bridebait of words, writing by the lamp of lightning. Even so, my books, those poor, defenseless books, written in the lyrical style of a far-gone time! – well, as you know too well, we reaped no livelihood from those printed pages. My only success as a writer was that my stories won you for me. After our blunderful attempt to farm the Western Provinces, to live the lives of field-and-stream poets – a defiance of destiny and station that cost us your health and the life of our one child – after that, all my pride indeed soured to cynicism and self-pity. I felt obliged to accept the Imperial post, because there seemed no other recourse.

From that day, eighteen moons ago, until now, the shadow of

night has covered me. I was not there to console you in your grief when our second child fell from your womb before he was strong enough to carry his own breath. By then, the big ship had already taken me to the Isles of the Palm Grove Vow in the middle of the World Sea. There, I sat surrounded by tedious tomes of Imperial chronicles about the Sandalwood Territories, while you suffered alone.

Like you, I never had a taste for the dry magisterial prose of diplomacy and the bitter punctuations of war that is history. What did it matter to me that five centuries ago, during the beginning of our modern era in the Sung Dynasty, the Buddhists, persecuted for adhering to a faith of foreign origin, set sail from the Middle Kingdom and, instead of being devoured by seven hundred dragons or plunging into the Maelstrom of the Great Inane, crossed nine thousand *li* of ocean and discovered a chain of tropical islands populated by Stone Age barbarians? Of what consequence was it to me that these islands, rich in palm, hardwoods, and the fragrant sandalwood beloved of furniture makers, soon attracted merchants and the Emperor's soldiers? And that, once again, the Buddhists felt compelled to flee, swearing their famous Palm Grove Vow to sail east until they either faced death together or found a land of their own? And that, after crossing another seven thousand *li* of ocean, they arrived at the vast Land of Dawn, from whose easternmost extreme I am writing to you?

Surely, you are pursing your lips now with impatience, wondering why I burden you with so much bothersome history, you, a musician's daughter, who always preferred the beauty of song to the tedium of facts. Stay with me yet, Heart Wing. My discovery, the hard-won clarity gained through my poison cure, will mean less to you without some sharing of what I have learned of this land's history.

We know from our school days that the merchants eventually followed the Buddhists to the Land of Dawn, where the gentle monks had already converted many of the aboriginal tribes. Typical of the Buddhists, they did not war with the merchants but retreated further east, spreading their doctrine among the tribes and gradually opening the frontier to other settlers. Over time, as the Imperialists established cities and trade routes, the monks began preaching the foolishness of obeisance to a Kingdom far across the World Sea. "Here and now!" the monks chanted, the land of our ancestors being too far away and too entrenched in the veil of illusion to be taken seriously any more. Though the Buddhists themselves never raised a weapon against the Emperor, the merchants and farmers eagerly fought for them, revolting against Imperialist taxation. And out of the Sandalwood Territories of the Dawn, the settlers founded their own country: the Unified Sandalwood Autocracies.

There are numerous kingdoms here in the USA, each governed by an autocrat elected by the landowners of that kingdom. These separate kingdoms are, in turn, loosely governed by an overlord whom the autocrats and the landowners elect from among themselves to serve for an interval of no more than fifty moons. It is an alien system that the denizens here call Power of the People, and it is fraught with strife, as the conservative Confucians, liberal Buddhists, and radical Taoist-aboriginals continually struggle for dominance. Here, the Mandate of Heaven is not so much granted by celestial authority as taken by wiles, wealth, or force, grasped and clawed for.

I will not trouble you with this nation's paradoxical politics: its abhorrence of monarchs, yet its glorification of leaders; its insistence on separation of government and religion, yet its reliance on oaths, prayers, and moralizing; its passionate patriotism, yet fervent espousal of individual endeavor. There are no slaves here as at home, and so there is no dignity for the upper classes, or even for the lower classes, for all are slaves to money. The commonest street sweeper can invest his meager earnings to form his own road-maintenance company and after years of slavery to his enterprise become as wealthy as nobility. And, likewise, the rich can squander their resources and, without the protection of servants or class privilege, become street beggars. And not just men but women as well, who possess the same rights as men. Amitabha! This land has lost entirely the sequence of divine order that regulates our serene sovereignty. And though there are those who profit by this increase of social and economic mobility, it is by and large a country mad with, and subverted by, its own countless ambitions. In many ways, it is, I think, the Middle Kingdom turned upside down.

The rocky west coast, rife with numerous large cities, is the industrial spine of this nation, as is the east coast in our land. On the seaboard, as in our kingdom, refineries, paper mills, textile factories, and shipbuilding yards abound. Inland are the lush agricultural valleys – and then the mountains and beyond them the desert – just as in our country. Where to the north in our homeland the Great Wall marches across mountains for over four thousand *li*, shutting out the Mongol hordes, here an equally colossal wall crosses the desert to the south, fending off ferocious tribes of Aztecatl.

Heart Wing, there is even a village on the eastern prairie, beyond the mountains and the red sandstone arches of the desert, that looks very much like the village on the Yellow River where we had our ruinous farm. There, in a bee-filled orchard just like the cherry grove where we buried our daughter, my memory fetched back to when I held her bird-light body in my arms for the last time. I wept. I wanted to write to you then, but there were irrigation networks to catalog and, on the horizons of amber wheat and millet, highways to map hundreds of *li* long, where land boats fly faster than horses, their colorful sails fat with wind.

Beyond the plains lies the Evil East, which is what the Dawn Settlers call their frontier, because said hinterland is dense with ancient forests no ax has ever touched. Dawn legends claim that the hungry souls of the unhappy dead wander those dense woods. Also, tribes of hostile aboriginals who have fled the settled autocracies of the west shun the Doctrine of the Buddha and the Ethics of Confucius and reign there, as anarchic and wild as any Taoist could imagine.

When our delegation leader sought volunteers to continue the survey into that wilderness, I was among those who offered to go. I am sorry, Heart Wing, that my love for you was not enough to overcome my shame at the failures that led to our child's death and that took me from you. Wild in my grief, I sought likeness in that primeval forest. I had hoped it would kill me and end my suffering.

It did not. I had somehow imagined or hoped that there might well be ghosts in the Evil East, or at least cannibalistic savages to whom I would be prey, but there were neither. So, I survived despite myself, saddened to think that all our chances bleed from us, like wounds that never heal.

The immense expanse of forest – poignantly beautiful even in its darkest vales and fog-hung fens – turned out to be haunted only with the natural dangers of serpents, bears, and wolves. As for the tribes, when they realized that we had come merely to observe and not to cut their trees or encroach on their land, they greeted us cordially enough, for barbarians. To win their hospitality, we traded toys – bamboo dragonflies, kites and fire-crackers. I knew a simple joy with them, forgetting briefly the handful of chances that had already bled from me with my hope of fading from this world.

On the east coast, Buddhist missions and trading posts over-look the Storm Sea. By the time we emerged from the wild-woods, a message for me from the west had already arrived at one of the posts by the river routes that the fur traders use. I recognized your father's calligraphy and knew before I read it – that you had left us to join the ancestors.

When the news came, I tried to throw myself from the monastery wall into the sea, but my companions stopped me. I could not hear beyond my heart. We who had once lived as one doubled being had become mysteries again to each other. I shall know no greater enigma.

For days, I despaired. My failures had lost all my cherished chances, as a writer and a farmer, as a father and, now, as your mate. With that letter, I became older than the slowest river.

It is likely I would have stayed at the monastery and accepted monkhood had not news come announcing the arrival of strangers from across the Storm Sea. Numb, indifferent, I sailed south with the delegation's other volunteers. Autumn had returned to the forest. Disheveled oaks and maples mottled the undulant shores. As we ventured farther south, hoar frost gradually thinned from the air, and stupendous domes of cumulus rose from the horizon. Shaggy cypress and palm trees tilted above dunes.

Like a roving, masterless dog, I followed the others from one mission to the next among lovely, verdant islands. Hunger abandoned me, and I ate only when my companions pressed food on me, not tasting it. In the silence and fire of night, while the others slept, my life seemed an endless web of lies I had spun and you a bird I had caught and crippled. In the mirrors of the sea, I saw faces. Mostly they were your face. And always when I saw you, you smiled at me with an untellable love. I grieved that I had ever left you.

The morning we found the boats that had crossed the Storm Sea, I greeted the strangers morosely. These were stout men with florid faces, thick beards, and big noses. Their ships – clumsy, worm-riddled boxes lacking watertight compartments – featured ludicrous cloth sails set squarely, leaving them at the mercy of the winds. At first, they attempted to impress us with their cheap merchandise, mostly painted tinware and clay pots filled with sour wine. I do not blame them for underestimating our sophistication, because, not wishing to slight the aboriginals, we had approached in a local raft with the tribal leaders of that island.

Soon, however, beckoned by a blue smoke flare, our own ship rounded the headland. The sight of her sleek hull and orange sails with bamboo battens trimmed precisely for maximum speed rocked loose the foreigners' arrogant jaws – for our ship, with her thwartwise staggered masts fore and aft, approached *into* the wind. The Big Noses had never seen the likes of it.

Ostensibly to salute us, though I am sure with the intent of displaying their might, the Big Noses fired their bulky cannon. The three awkward ships, entirely lacking lee-boards, keeled drastically. Our vessel replied with a volley of Bees' Nest rockets that splashed overhead in a fiery exhibit while our ship sailed figure-eights among the foreigners' box-boats.

At that, the Big Noses became effusively deferential. The captain, a tall, beardless man with red hair and ghostly pale flesh, removed his hat, bowed, and presented us with one of his treasures, a pathetically crude book printed on coarse paper with a gold-leaf cross pressed into the animal-hide binding. Our leader accepted it graciously.

Fortunately, the Big Noses had on board a man who spoke Chaldean and some Arabic, and two of the linguists in our delegation could understand him slightly. He told us that the captain's name was Christ-Bearer the Colonizer and that they had come seeking the Emperor of the Middle Kingdom in the hope of opening trade with him. They actually believed that they had traveled twenty-five thousand *li* to the west, in the spice islands south of the Middle Kingdom! Their ignorance fairly astounded us.

Upon learning their precise location, the Colonizer appeared dismayed and retreated to his cabin. From his second in command, we eventually learned that the Colonizer had expected honor and wealth from his enterprise. Both would be greatly diminished now that it was evident he had discovered neither a route to the world's wealthiest kingdom nor a new world to be colonized by the Big Noses.

Among our delegation, much debate flurried about the implications of the Colonizer's first name – Christ-Bearer. For some centuries, Christ-Bearers have straggled into the Middle Kingdom, though the government always confined them to select districts of coastal cities. Their gruesome religion, in which the faithful symbolically consume the flesh and blood of their maimed and tortured god, disgusted our Emperor, and their proselytizing zeal rightly concerned him. But here, in the USA, with the Dawn-Settlers' tolerance of diverse views, what consequences will ensue when the Christ-Bearers establish their missions?

I did not care. Let fat-hearted men scheme and plot in faraway temples and kingdoms. Heart Wing! I will never see the jewel of your face again. That thought – that truth – lies before me now, an unexplored wilderness I will spend the rest of my life crossing. But on the day when I first saw the Big Noses, I had not yet grasped this truth. I still believed death was a doorway. I thought perhaps your ghost would cross back and succor my mourning. I had seen your face in the mirrors of the sea, a distraught girl both filled and exhausted with love. I had seen that, and I thought I could cross the threshold of this life and find you again, join with you again, united among the ancestors. I thought that.

For several more days, I walked about in a daze, looking for your ghost, contemplating ways to die. I even prepared a sturdy noose from a silk sash and, one moon-long evening, wandered into the forest to hang myself. As I meandered through the dark avenues of a cypress dell seeking the appropriate bough from which to stretch my shameless neck, I heard voices. Three paces away, on the far side of a bracken screen, the Big Noses whispered hotly. I dared to peek and spied them hurrying among the trees, crouched over, sabers and guns in hand and awkwardly hauling a longboat among them.

The evil I had wished upon myself had led me to a greater evil – and, without forethought, I followed the Big Noses. They swiftly made their way to the cove, where the Imperial ship had moored. I knew then their intent. The entire delegation, along with most of the crew, had gone ashore to the mission, to interview the aboriginals who had first encountered the Big Noses. While they drafted a report for the Emperor and the local authorities about the arrival of the Christ-Bearer in the USA, the Big Noses had hatched a nefarious plan and would meet little resistance in pirating our ship.

Clouds walked casually away from the moon, and the mission with its serpent pillars and curved roof shone gem-bright high on the bluff – too far away for me to race there in time or even for my cries to reach. Instead, I ducked among dunes and scurried through switching salt grass to the water's edge even as the Big Noses pushed their longboat into the slick water and piled in. With a few hardy oar-strokes, they reached the Imperial ship and began clambering aboard unseen by the watch, who probably lolled in the hold sampling the rice wine.

I stood staring at the ship perched atop the watery moon, knowing what I had to do but hardly believing I had such strength. I, who had iron enough in my blood to strangle my own life, wavered at the thought of defying other men, even the primitive Big Noses. Truly, what a coward I am! I stood rooted as a pine and would have watched the pirates sail our ship away, watched it depart into the dark like a happy cloud scudding under the moon – except that a scream and a splash jolted me.

The Big Noses had thrown the watch overboard. I saw him swimming hard for shore and imagined I beheld fear in his face. His craven face galled me! The watch, flailing strenuously to save his own miserable life, would make no effort to stop the barbarians from stealing the life of his own people! For I knew that we would lose nothing less if the Big Noses stole our ship and learned to build vessels that could challenge the USA and even the Middle Kingdom.

I dove into the glossed water and thrashed towards the ship. I am a weak swimmer, as you know, but there was not far to go, and the noise of the watch beating frantically to shore muted my advance. With moorings cut, the ship listed under the offshore breeze. The Big Noses, accustomed to climbing along yardarms to adjust their sails, struggled with the unfamiliar windlasses and halyards that control from the deck the ribbed sails of our ship, and so I had time to clutch onto the hull before the sails unfurled.

After climbing the bulwark, I slipped and fell to the deck right at the feet of the tall, ghost-faced captain! We stared at each other with moonbright eyes for a startled moment, and I swear I saw avidity in his features as malefic as a temple demon's. I bolted upright even as he shouted. Blessedly, the entire crew was busy trying to control the strange new ship, and I eluded the grasp of the Colonizer and darted across the deck to the gangway.

Death had been my intent from the first. When I plunged into the hold and collapsed among coils of hempen rope, I had but one thought: to reach the weapons bin and ignite the powder. I blundered in the dark, slammed into a bulkhead, tripped over bales of sorghum, and reached the weapons bin in gasping disarray. Shouts boomed from the gangway, and the hulking shapes of the Big Noses filled the narrow corridor.

Wildly, I grasped for the flintstriker I knew lay somewhere near the bin. Or did it? Perhaps that was too dangerous a tool to keep near the powder. The Big Noses closed in, and I desperately bounded atop the bin and shoved open the hatch there.

Moonlight gushed over me, and I confronted the horrid faces of the barbarians rushing towards me – and there, at my elbow, a sheaf of matches.

I seized the fire-sticks and rattled them at the Big Noses, but this did not thwart them. The oafs had no idea what these were! Those brutes dragged me down, barking furiously. I gaped about in the moonglow, spotted a flintstriker hanging from a beam. Kicking like a madman, I twisted free just long enough to snatch the flintstriker. Alas, I had inspired their fury, and heavy blows knocked me to the planks.

Stunned, I barely had the strength to squeeze the lever of the flintstriker. My feeble effort elicited only the tiniest spark, though that proved sufficient to ignite a match. The sulfurous flare startled my assailants, and they fell back. Immediately, I lurched about and held high the burning pine stick while gesturing at the powder kegs behind me. The Big Noses pulled away.

With my free hand, I grabbed a bamboo tube I recognized as a Beard-the-Moon rocket. I lit the fuse and pointed it at the open hatch. In a radiant whoosh, sparks and flames sprayed into the night. The cries of the Big Noses sounded from the deck, and the men who had seized me fled. A laugh actually tore through me as I fired two more Beard-the-Moon rockets. I was going to die, and now death seemed a fate worthy of laughter.

Perhaps the longtime company of Buddhists and Taoists had affected me after all, for I had no desire to kill the Big Noses. I waited long enough for them to throw themselves into the sea before I ignited the fuses on several heaven-shaking Thunderclap bombs. My last thought, while waiting for the explosion to hurl me into the Great Inane, focused on you, Heart Wing. Once I had committed myself to using death as a doorway, your ghost had actually come back for me, to lead me to the ancestors in a way that would serve the Kingdom. I thanked you, and the Thunderclap bombs exploded.

Yet, I did not die – at least, not in an obvious way. Later, when I could think clearly again, I realized that your ghost had not yet done with me. Who else but you could have placed me just where I stood so that my body hurtled straight upward through the open hatch and into the lustrous night? I remember none of that; however, the watch, who had made it to shore, claims that when the Imperial ship burst into a fireball, he witnessed me flying, silhouetted against the moon.

He found me unconscious in the shallows, unscathed except for singed beard and eyebrows and clothes torn. Like a meteor, I had fallen back to earth, back to life. I had fallen the way stars fall, from the remote darkness where they have shivered in the cold down into the warm, close darkness of earthly life. That night, I fell from the gloom of my solitary grief into the dark of terrestrial life, where we all suffer together in our unknowing.

Slapped alert by the watch, I sat up in the moon-dappled shallows and experienced my forty summers fall away into emptiness. The ship was gone – just as you are gone, Heart Wing, and our daughter gone into that emptiness the Buddhists call *sunyata*, which is really the void of our unknowing, the mystery that bears everything that lives and dies.

How foolish to say all this to *you*, who dwells now in the heart of this emptiness. But I, I have been ignorant, asleep. I needed reminding that time and the things of falling shall not fall into darkness but into a new freedom we cannot name and so call emptiness. All of reality floats in that vacancy, like the spheres in the void of space, like these words floating in the emptiness of the page. Words try to capture reality, yet what they actually capture are only more words and deeper doubts. Mystery is the pre-eminent condition of human being – and so, it is also our freedom to be exactly who we are, free to choose the words our doubts require.

No one in the delegation understood this when I returned to the mission to account for myself. Grateful as they were for my stopping the theft of the Imperial ship, they believed the explosion had addled me. I think the monks knew what I meant, but these monks belong to the "just so" sect of Ch'an Buddhism, so they would be the last to let on.

Be that as it may, I sat there quite agog and amazed, awakened to the knowledge that the freedom to be who I am means, quite simply, that I am alone – without you. For now, it is meant that this is so. For reasons I will never truly understand, death is denied me. So, what am I to do with this life, then, and this loneliness? This freedom to *be*, this freedom whose chances bleed from us, creates new imperatives. In the place of my failure and shame waits a gaping emptiness wanting to be filled with what I might yet be.

As I meditated on this, the delegation wrote an official missive admonishing the Big Noses for their attempted thievery and threatening to report them to the Emperor. The Big Noses, all of whom had escaped the explosion and fled to their ship, replied with a terse letter of halfhearted apology. With no other Imperial vessel anywhere in the vicinity and none of the Autocracies' forces nearby, our host, the monastery's abbot, urged us to accept the apology.

The delegation decided, in an effort to both placate and hurry the Colonizer on his way, to load his ships with all the porcelain in the mission, several remarkable landscape paintings, a jade statue of Kwan Yin, goddess of serenity, as well as bales of crops the Big Noses had never before seen, notably tobacco, peanuts, and potatoes. By then, inspired by my lack of family and career, I had decided to take the poison cure required by my sorrow: I have, dear wife, forsaken my return to the Middle Kingdom to go with the Colonizer on his return voyage across the Storm Sea to his homeland.

Do you chastise me for being so foolish? Indeed, the decision weighed heavily, as I had hoped to return to our homeland and administer the rites myself at your gravesite. But if what I have learned of the emptiness is true, then you are no more there than here. The path of the Way is a roadlessness without departure or arrival. I have decided, Heart Wing, to follow that path, to fit the unaccomplished parts of my life to the future and embrace the unknown.

The delegation strove in vain to dissuade me. They fear that I have gone truly mad. But I do not care at all. I know you would understand, Heart Wing, you whom I first won with the bride-bait of stories written by the lamp of lightning. So, as absurd as this may be, I sit here now, writing to you on the quarterdeck of a leaky vessel named *Santa Maria*.

I can tell from the way he looks at me that the Colonizer is still angry that I deprived him of his booty, and I know he has only taken me on board with the expectation of getting useful information from me. However, for now, our ignorance of each other's language offers me a chance to win the Big Noses' respect by my deeds – and to watch and learn about these barbarians.

In time, I will understand their language. I will inform their monarch of the wonders of the Middle Kingdom, of the achievements of the Unified Sandalwood Autocracies, of the glory of our people. And I will write again from the far side of the world, from so far east it is the west, where sun and moon meet. And from there, I will send back to the Kingdom and the USA stories everyone will read, stories of another world, written in ink from the new moon.

Dispatches From the Revolution

Pat Cadigan

Dylan was coming to Chicago.

The summer air, already electric with the violence of the war, the assassination attempts successful and unsuccessful, the anti-war riots, became super-charged with the rumor. Feeling was running high, any feeling about anything, real high, way up high, eight miles high and rising brothers and sisters. And to top it all off, there was a madman in the White House.

Johnson, pull out like your father should have! The graffito of choice for anyone even semi-literate; spray paint sales must have been phenomenal that summer. The old bastard with a face like the dogs he lifted up by their ears would not give it up, step aside, and graciously bow to the inevitable. He wuz the Prezident, the gaw-damned Prezident, hear that, muh fellow Amurricans? *Dump Johnson, my ass, don't even think about it boys, the one we ought to dump is that candy-assed Humphrey. Gaw-damned embarrassment is what* he *is.*

And the President's crazy, that's what he *is,* went the whispers all around Capitol Hill, radiating outward until they became shouts. *Madman in the White House – the crazy way with LBJ!* If you couldn't tell he was deranged by the way he was stepping up the bombing and the number of troops in Viet Nam, his conviction that he could actually stand against Bobby Kennedy clinched it. Robert F. Kennedy, sainted brother to martyred Jack, canonized in his own lifetime by an assassination attempt. Made by the only man in America who was obviously crazier than LBJ, frothed-up Arab with a name like automatic weapons fire, Sirhan Sirhan, ka-boom, ka-boom. The Golden Kennedy had actually *assisted* in the crazed gunman's capture, shoulder to shoulder with security guards and Secret Service as they all wrestled him to the floor. Pity about the busboy taking that bullet right in the eye, but the Kennedys had given him a positively lovely funeral with RFK himself doing the eulogy. And, needless to say, the family would never want for anything again in this life.

But Johnson the Madman was going to run! Without a doubt, he was a dangerous psychotic. Madman in the White House – damned straight you didn't need a Weatherman to know which way the wind blew.

Nonetheless, there *was* one – after all, hadn't Dylan said the answer was blowin' in the wind? And if he was coming to Chicago to support the brothers and sisters, that *proved* the wind was about to blow gale force. Storm coming, batten down the hatches, fasten your seatbelts, and grab yourself a helmet, or steal a hardhat from some redneck construction worker.

Veterans of the Civil Rights Movement already had their riot gear. Seven years after the first freedom ride stalled out in Birmingham, the feelings of humiliation and defeat at having to let the Justice Department scoop them up and spirit them away to New Orleans for their own protection had been renewed in the violent death of the man who had preached victory through non-violence. He'd had a dream; the wake-up call had come as a gunshot. Dreaming was for when you were asleep. Now it was time to be wide awake in America.

Annie Phillips
"There were plenty of us already wide awake in America by *that* late date. I'd been to Chicago back in '66, two years to the month in Marquette Park. If I was never awake any other day in my life before April '68, I was awake *that* day. Surrounded by a thousand of the meanest white people in America waving those Confederate flags and those swastikas, screaming at us. And then they let fly with rocks and bricks and bottles, and I saw when Dr King took one in the head. I'd thought he was gonna

die that day and all the rest of us with him. Well, he didn't and we didn't, but it was a near thing. After, the buses were pulling away and they were chasing us and I looked back at those faces and I thought, 'There's no hope. There's really no hope.'

"When Daley got the court order against large groups marching in the city, I breathed a sigh of relief, I can tell you. I felt like that man had saved my life. And then Dr King says, okay, we'll march in Cicero, it's a suburb, the order doesn't cover Cicero. *Cicero*. I didn't want to do it, I knew they'd kill us, shoot us, burn us, tear us up with their bare hands and teeth. Some of us were ready to meet them head-on. I truly believe that Martin Luther King would have died that day if Daley hadn't wised up in a hurry and said he'd go for the meeting at the Palmer House.

"Summit Agreement, yeah. Sell-Out Agreement, we called it, a lot of us. I think even Dr King knew it. And so a whole bunch of us marched in Cicero anyway. I wasn't there, but I know what happened, just like everybody else. Two hundred dead, most of them black, property damage in the millions, though I can't say I could ever find it in me to grieve for property damage over people damage. Even though I wasn't there, something of me died that day in Cicero and was reborn in anger. By '68, I had a good-sized bone to pick with good old Chi-town, old Daley-ville. I don't regret what I did. All I regret is that the bomb didn't get Daley. It had his name on it, I put it there myself, on the side of the pipe. 'Richard Daley's ticket to hell, coach class.'

"Looking back on it, I think I might have had better luck as a sniper."

Excerpt from an interview conducted covertly at Sybil Brand, published in The Whole Samizdat Catalog, *1972?, exact date unknown*

Veterans of the Free Speech Movement at Berkeley also knew what they were up against. Reagan's tear-gas campaign against campus protestors drew praise from a surprising number of people who felt the Great Society was seriously threatened by the disorder promoted by campus dissidents. The suggestion that the excessive force used by the police caused more problems rather than solving any was rejected by the Reagan administration and its growing blue-collar following alike.

By the time Reagan assumed the governorship, he had already made up his mind to challenge Nixon in '68. But what he needed for a serious bid was the southern vote, which was divided between Kennedy and Wallace. Cleverly, the ex-movie actor managed to suggest strong parallels between campus unrest and racial unrest, implying that both groups were seeking the violent overthrow and destruction of the government of the United States. Some of the more radical rhetoric that came out of both the student left and the civil rights movement, and the fact that the student anti-war movement aligned itself with the civil rights moment only seemed to validate Reagan's position.

That the southern vote would be divided between two individuals as disparate as Robert F. Kennedy and George C. Wallace seems bizarre to us in the present. But both men appealed to the working class, who felt left out of the American Dream. Despite the inevitable trouble that Wallace's appearances resulted in, his message did reach the audience for which it was intended – the common man who had little to show for years, sometimes decades of hard work beyond a small piece of property and a paycheck taxed to the breaking point, and, as far as the common man could tell, to someone else's benefit. Wallace understood that the common man felt pushed around by the government and exploited this feeling. In a quieter era, he would have come off as a bigoted buffoon; but in a time when blacks and students were demonstrating, rioting, and spouting unthinkable statements against the government, the war, and the system in general, Wallace seemed to be one of the few, if not the only political leader who had the energy to meet this new threat to the American way of life and wrestle it into submission.

Some people began to wonder if McCarthy hadn't been right about Communist infiltration and subversion after all . . . and that wasn't Eugene McCarthy they were wondering about. By the time of the Chicago Democratic Convention, Eugene

McCarthy had all but disappeared, his student supporters a liability rather than an asset. They undermined his credibility; worse, they could not vote for him since the voting age at that time was a flat twenty-one for everyone . . .

Carl Shipley

"I hadn't been around Berkeley long when the Free Speech Movement started. Like, the university, Towle, Kerr, all of them were so out-to-lunch on what was happening with us. They thought they were dealing with Beaver Cleaver and his Little League team, I guess. And with us, it was, 'Guess what, Mr Man, the neighborhood's changing, it ain't Beaver Cleaver any more, it's Eldridge Cleaver and Wally just got a notice to report for his physical and maybe he doesn't want to go get his ass shot off in southeast Asia and maybe we've had enough of this mid-American conservative bullshit.' That's why they wanted to shut down Bancroft Strip. That was the first place I went to see when I got there and it was just like everybody said, all these different causes and stuff, the Young Republicans hanging in right along with the vegetarians and the feminists and people fund-raising for candidates and I don't know what-all.

"So we all said fuck this shit, you ain't closing us down, we're closing you down. And we did, we closed the university down. We had the power and we kept it – and then in comes Ronald Reagan two years later in '66 and he says, Relax, Mr and Mrs America, the cavalry's here. I know you're worried about the Beave, but I've got the solution.

"He sure did. By spring 1968, a lot of campus radio stations all over California were off the air and the campus newspapers were a joke. No funding, see. And by then, everyone was too sick of the smell of tear gas to fight real hard. That was Reagan's whole thing – sit-ins and take-overs weren't covered by the right of free assembly, they were criminal acts. Unless you had to be in a building for a class, you were trespassing. I got about a mile of trespassing convictions on my rap sheet and so do a lot of other people. And Mr and Mrs America, they were real impressed the way Reagan came down on the troublemakers.

"Sure were a *lot* of troublemakers. Too many to keep track of.

That's what happened to me, you know. Got lost in the court system. The next thing I knew, it was 1970, and nobody remembered my name except the guards. And they could remember my number a lot easier. Still can.

"The thing is, I *never* burned my draft card. That was a frame-up. I wouldn't have burned it. I was ready to go to Canada, but I intended to keep my draft card. As a reminder, you know. And not even my parents believed me. By then, I'd been into so much radical shit, they figured everything the pigs said about me was true.

"But the fact is, everything I owned was in the building when it burned. So of course my draft card burned up with it! But I never set that fire. My court-appointed lawyer – this is me, laughing bitterly – said if I told my 'crazy story' about seeing off-duty cops with gasoline cans running from the scene just before the explosion, the judge would tack an extra five years on my sentence for perjury. I should have believed him, because it was the only time anyone told me the truth."

Interview conducted at Attica, published in Orphans of the Great Society, *Fuck The System Press, 197? (circulated illegally in photocopy)*

Some say, even today, that Reagan wouldn't have taken such an extremist path if Wallace hadn't been such a strong contender. Nixon's mistake was in dismissing Wallace's strong showing, choosing to narrow his focus to the competition within his own party for the nomination. This made him look dinky, as if he didn't care as much about being president as he did about being the Republican candidate for President. That would show those damned reporters that they couldn't kick around Dick Nixon, uh-huh. Even if he lost, they'd have to take him seriously; if he actually won, they'd have to take him even more seriously. Which made him look not only dinky, but like a whiner – the kind of weak sister who, for example, might stand up in front of a television camera and rant about cocker spaniel puppies and good Republican cloth coats, instead of telling the American people that rioting, looting, and draft-card burning would no longer

be tolerated. Even Ike's coat-tails were enough to repair
Nixon's image and Ike himself was comatose or nearly so at
Walter Reed after a series of heart attacks.

The Republican National Convention was notable for three
things: Rockefeller's last minute declaration of candidacy,
which further diluted Nixon's support, the luxuriousness of the
accommodations and facilities, and its complete removal from
the rioting that had broken out in Miami proper, where an
allegedly minor racial incident escalated into a full-scale battle.
The convention center was in Miami Beach, far from the
madding Miami crowd, a self-contained playground for the
rich. You couldn't smell the tear gas from Miami Beach, and
the wind direction was such that you couldn't hear the sirens
that screamed all night long . . .

"Carole Feeney" [this subject is still a fugitive]
"I told everybody it was the goddam fatcat Republicans that we
ought to go after, not the Democrats. But Johnson the Madman
was running and everyone really thought that he was going to
get the nomination. I said they were crazy, Kennedy had it in
the bag. But Johnson really had them all running scared. I tried
talking to some of the people in the Mobe. Half of them didn't
want to go to either convention and the other half were trying to
buy *guns* to take to Chicago! Off the pigs, they kept saying. Off
the pigs. Jesus, I thought, the only pig that was going to get offed
was Pigasus – the real pig that the Yippies were going to
announce as the candidate from the Youth International Party.
That was cute. I mean, really, it was. I said, let's go ahead and
do that somewhere in California, film it and send the film to a
TV station and let them run it on the news. Uh-uh, nothing
doing. Lincoln Park or bust. Yeah, right – Lincoln Park *and*
bust. Busted heads, busted bodies, busted and thrown in
jail.

"So I wasn't going to go. Then I found out what Davis was
doing. I couldn't believe it – Davis Trainor had been in on
everything practically from the beginning. He was real good-
looking and real popular, he had this real goofy sense of humor
and he always seemed to come up with good ideas for guerrilla

action. He actually did all the set-up work on the pirate radio station we ran out of Oakland and he worked out our escape routes. Not one of us got caught in the KCUF caper. We called it our Fuck-You caper, of course.

"Then I'm doing the laundry and I find it – his COIN-TELPRO ID – stuffed into that little bitty pocket in his jeans. You know, it's like a little secret pocket right above the regular pocket on the right. The one thing I always hate about the movement was that it was as sexist as the Establishment. If you were a woman, you always got stuck doing all the cooking and the cleaning and the laundry and stuff. Unless you were a movement queen like Dohrn. Then you didn't have to do anything except make speeches and get laid if you wanted. Oh, they threw us a sop by letting us set up our own feminist actions and stuff, but we all knew it was a sop. We kept telling each other that after we changed things, it would be different and for now, we'd watch and listen and learn. Besides, everyone knew that the Establishment wouldn't take women as seriously as they would men. I wonder now how much any of us believed that – that it would really be different, that we could change things at all.

"Anyway, I went straight to the Mobe with my discovery, but it was too late – Davis discovered his pants were missing and he'd already split. I really didn't want to go to Chicago after that, but the alternative seemed to be either stay home and wait to get busted, or go to Chicago and get busted in action. I was still enough of an idealist that they talked me into Chicago. If I was going to get busted, I might as well be accomplishing something, and, anyway, after the revolution, I'd be a National Heroine, and not a political prisoner.

"So, the revolution's come and gone and here I am. Still working for the movement – the feminist movement, that is. What little I *can* do, referring women with unwanted pregnancies to safe abortionists. Yes, there *are* some. Not all of us were polysci majors – some of us were pre-med, some of us went to nursing school. It costs a goddam fortune but *I'm* not getting rich on it. It's for the risk, you know. I could get life as an accessory, and there was a woman in Missouri who *did* get death for doing what I'm doing.

"Nobody in my family knows, of course. Especially not my husband. If *he* knew, he'd probably kill me himself. Odd as it sounds, I don't hate him . . . not when I think what good cover he is, and what the alternative would be if I didn't have such good cover . . ."

Part of a transcript labelled "Carole Feeney" obtained in a 1989 raid on a motel said to be part of a network of underground "safe houses" for tax protestors, leftist terrorists, and other subversives; no other illegal literature recovered.

The source of the DYLAN IS COMING! rumor never was pinpointed. Some say it sprang into being all on its own and stayed alive because so many people wanted it to be true. And for all anyone knows, perhaps it actually was true, for a little while anyway; perhaps Dylan simply changed his mind. The more cynical suggested that the rumor had been planted by infiltrators like the notorious Davis Trainor, whose face became so well known thanks to the Mobe's mock wanted poster that he had to have extensive plastic surgery, a total of a dozen operations in all. The poster was done well enough that it passed as legitimate and was often allowed to hang undisturbed in post offices, libraries, and other public places, side by side with the FBI's posters of dissidents and activists. One poster was found in a Minneapolis library as late as 1975; the head librarian was taken into custody, questioned, and released. But it is no coincidence that the library was audited for objectionable material soon after that and has been subject to surprise spot checks for the last fifteen years, in spite of the fact that it has always showed 100 per cent compliance with government standards for reading matter. The price of a tyrant's victory is eternal vigilance.

This was once considered to be the price of victory. Nothing buys what it used to.

Steve D'Alessandro
"By Sunday, when Dylan didn't show, people were starting to get angry. I kept saying, well, hey, Allen Ginsburg showed. Allen Ginsburg! Man, he was like . . . *God* to me. He was doing

his best, going around rapping with people, trying to get everybody calmed down and focused, you know. A whole bunch of us got in a circle around him and we were chanting *Om, Om.* I was getting a really good vibe and then some asshole throws a bottle at him and yells, *Oh, shut up, you fag!*

"I went crazy. Sure, I was in the closet then because the movement was not as enlightened as some of us wished it were. The FBI was doing this thing where it was going around trying to discredit a lot of people by accusing them of being queer, and everybody caught homophobia like it was the measles. I ain't no fairy, no sir, not me, I fucked a hundred chicks this week and my dick's dragging on the ground so don't you call *me* no fag! It still stings, even when I compare it to how things are now. But then, I don't expect any kind of enlightened feeling in a society where I have to take hormone treatments so I won't get a hard-on when I see another guy.

"Anyway, I found the scumbag that did it and I punched him out. I gave *him* a limp wrist. I gave him *two* of them. And I know I had a lot of support – I mean, a lot of straights admired Ginsburg, too, even if he was gay, just on the basis of *Howl*, but later, a bunch of Abbie's friends blamed me for creating the disturbance that gave the police the excuse they needed to wade in and start busting heads.

"Sometimes I'm afraid maybe they were right. But Annie Phillips told me it was just a coincidence. About me, I mean. She said they came in because they saw a black guy kissing a white girl. I guess nobody'll ever really know for sure because the black guy died of his injuries and the white girl never came forward.

"I prefer to think that's what made Annie and her crowd go ahead with the bomb at the convention center. I don't like to think that Annie really wanted to blow anybody up. It was kind of weird how I knew Annie. Well, not weird, really. I probably owed Annie my life, or damn near, and so did a certain man of African-American descent. We were lucky it was her that walked in on us that day. She was enlightened, or at least tolerant, and we could trust her not to say anything. I didn't think she liked white people too much, but I'd heard she'd been with Martin Luther King a couple of years before on those marches and I couldn't blame her. Anyway, she couldn't give me away without giving away the brother, but to this day I believe it really didn't matter to her – homosexuality, that is. Maybe because the Establishment hated us worse than they hated blacks.

"Anyway, I wasn't intending to be in the crowd that crashed the gate at the convention center on Wednesday. Nomination day. We'd been fighting in the streets since Monday and Daley's stormtroopers were beating the shit out of us. Late Tuesday night, the National Guard arrived. That's when we knew it was war.

"On Wednesday, we got hemmed in in Grant Park. People were pouring in by then, and nobody had expected that. It was like everyone was standing up to be counted because Dylan hadn't, or something. Anyway, there were maybe ten to twelve thousand of us at the band shell in the park, singing, listening to speeches, and then two kids went up a flagpole and lowered the flag to half mast. The cops went crazy – they came in swinging wild and they didn't care who they hit or where they hit them. I was scared out of my mind. I saw those cops close up and they looked as mad as Johnson was supposed to be. On the spot, I became a believer like I'd never been before – Madman in the White House and Madman Daley and his Madman cops. It was all true, I thought while I curled up on the ground with my hands over my head and prayed some kill-crazy pig wouldn't decide to pound my ass to jelly.

"Somebody pulled me up and yelled that we were supposed to all go to in front of the Hilton. I ran like hell all the way to the railroad tracks along with everybody else and that was where the Guard caught us with the tear gas. Man, I thought I was going to die of tear-gas suffocation if I didn't get trampled by the people I was with. Everyone was running around like crazy. I don't know how we ever got out of there but somebody found a way onto Michigan and Avenue and somehow we all followed. And the Guard followed after us. Somebody said later they weren't supposed to, but they did. And they weren't carrying pop-guns.

"Well, we ran smack into Ralph Abernathy and his Poor People's Campaign mule train and that was more confusion. Then the Guard waded in and a lot of Poor People went to the hospital that night (it was after seven by then). I'll never forget that, or the sight of all those TV cameras and the bright lights shining in our eyes. We were all staggering around when a fresh busload of riot cops arrived, and that's another sight I'll never forget – two dozen beefy bruisers in riot gear shooting out of that bus like they were being shot from cannons and landing on all of us with both feet and their billyclubs. I lost my front teeth and I was so freaked I didn't even feel it until the next day.

"I was freaked, but I was also furious. We were all furious. It was like, Johnson would send us to Viet Nam to be killed or he'd let us be killed by Daley's madmen cops on the Chicago streets, it didn't matter to him. I think a lot of us expected the convention to adjourn in protest at our treatment. At least that Bobby Kennedy would speak out in protest against the brutality. The name Kennedy *meant* human rights, after all. Nobody knew that Kennedy had been removed from the convention center under heavy guard because they were all convinced that someone would make another attempt on his life. I heard that later, before they clamped down on all the information. He was about to get the fucking *nomination* and he was on his way back to his hotel. They said Madman Johnson was more like Mad-Dog Johnson over that, but who the fuck knows?

"George McGovern was at the podium when we busted in. I hadn't really been intending to be in that group that busted in, but I was carried along and when I saw we were going to crash the amphitheatre, I thought, what the fuck.

"I almost got crushed against the doors before they gave and I barely missed falling on my face and getting run over by six thousand screaming demonstrators. And the first person I saw was Annie Phillips.

"I thought I was in a Fellini film. She was dressed in this godawful *maid's* uniform with a handkerchief around her head mashing down her Afro, but I knew it was her. We looked right into each other's eyes as I went by, still more carried along with the crowd than running on my own and she put both hands over her mouth in horror. That was the last time I saw her until she was on TV.

"I just managed to get out of the way and stay to the back of the amphitheatre itself. I just wanted to catch my breath and try to think how I was going to get out of all this shit without getting my head split open by a crazy Guardsman or a cop. I was still there when the bomb went off down front.

"The sound was so loud I thought my ears were bleeding. Automatically, I dropped to the floor and covered my head. There was a little debris, not much, where I was. When I finally dared to look, what I saw didn't make any sense. I still can't tell you exactly what I saw. I blocked it out. But sometimes, I think I dream it. I dream that I saw Johnson's head sitting on a Texas flagpole. I'm pretty sure that's just my imagination because in the dream he's got this vaguely surprised-annoyed expression on his saggy old face, like he's saying, *What the fuck is goin' on here?*

Anyway, the next thing I knew, I was out on the street again, and somebody was crying about how they were bombing us now along with the Viet Namese. Which was about the time the Guard opened fire, thinking we were bombing them, I guess.

"I was lucky. I took a bullet in my thigh and it put me out of the action. Just a flesh wound, really. It bled pretty impressively for a while and then quit. By then, I was so out of my head I can't even tell you where I staggered off to. The people who found me in their front yard the next morning took care of me and got me to a hospital. It was a five-hour wait in the emergency room. That was where I was when I heard about Kennedy."

Part of the data recovered from a disk taken in a raid on an illegal software laboratory, March 1981

Jack Kennedy had died in the middle of a Dallas street, his head blown off in front of thousands of spectators and his horrified wife. Bobby Kennedy had narrowly missed meeting his end during a moment of triumph in a Los Angeles hotel. Ultimately, that seemed to have been only a brief reprieve before fate caught up with him . . .

Jasmine Chang

"Everyone heard the explosion but nobody knew whether it was something the demonstrators had done or if the National Guard had rolled in a tank or if the world had come to an end. I ran down to the lobby with just about everyone else on the staff and a good many of the hotel guests, trying to see what was happening outside without having to go out in it. Nobody wanted to go outside. That night, the manager on duty had told us that anyone who wanted could stay over if we didn't mind roughing it in the meeting rooms. I made myself a sleeping bag out of spare linens under a heavy table in one of the smaller ones. The night before, the cops had cracked one of the dining room windows with a demonstrator's head. I wasn't about to risk my neck going out in that frenzy.

"Well, after the explosion, we heard the rifle fire. Then the street in front of the hotel, already crowded, was *packed* all of a sudden. Wall-to-wall cops and demonstrators, and the cops were swinging at anything they could reach. They were *scything* their way through the crowd, you see – they were mowing people down to make paths so they could walk. It was one of the worst things I've ever seen. For a while, it was *the* worst. I wish it could have stayed that way.

"The lobby was filling up, too, but nobody really noticed because we were all watching that sickening scene outside. The whole world was watching, they said. I saw a camera crew and all I could think was their equipment was going to get smashed to bits.

"I don't know when Kennedy came down to the lobby. I don't know why the Secret Service didn't stop him, I don't know what he thought he could do. He must have been watching from his window. Maybe he thought he could actually address the crowd – as if anyone could have heard him. Anyway, he was there in the lobby and none of us really noticed him.

"The demonstrator who forced his way into the revolving door – he was just a kid, he looked about fifteen years old to me. Scared out of his mind. The revolving door was supposed to be locked but when I saw that kid's face, I was glad it wasn't.

"Then the cops tried to force their way in after him but they got stuck, there was a billyclub jammed in the door or something. And the kid was babbling about how they'd blown up Kennedy at the convention. 'They threw a bomb and killed Kennedy! They blew him up with Johnson and McGovern!' he was yelling over and over. And Bobby Kennedy himself rushed over to the kid. I'm pretty sure that was the first any of us really noticed him, when it registered. I remember, I felt shocked and surprised and numb all at once, seeing Kennedy right *there*, right in the middle of a lobby. Like he was *anybody*. And nobody else moved, we all just stood there and stared like dummies.

"And Kennedy was trying to tell the kid who he was, that he wasn't dead and what bomb and all that. The kid got even more hysterical, and Kennedy was shaking him, trying to get something coherent out of him, we're all standing there watching and finally the cops manage to get through the revolving door.

"They must have thought the kid was attacking Kennedy. That's all I can figure. Even if that's not how they looked. The cops. They looked . . . *weird*. Like they didn't know what they were doing, or they did know but they'd forgotten why they were supposed to do it. I don't know. I don't *know*. But it was so weird, because they all looked exactly alike to me right at that moment, even though when I looked at them again after, they weren't anything alike, even in their uniforms. But they looked like identical dolls then, or puppets, because they moved all at once together. Like a kick-line of chorus girls, you know? Except that it wasn't their legs that came up but their arms.

"I know that when they raised their guns, they were looking at the kid, and I thought, 'No, wait!' I tried to move towards them, I was reaching out and they fired.

"It was like another bomb had gone off. For a moment, I thought another one *had* gone off, just a split second before they were going to fire. Then John Kennedy – I mean, Bobby, *Bobby* Kennedy – that's a Freudian slip, isn't it? – he did this clumsy whirl around and it looked like he was turning around in anger, like people do sometimes, you know? Like he was going, 'Dammit, I'm leaving!' And then he went down, and it was so awful because – well, this is going to sound really strange, I guess, but . . . well . . . when you see people get shot on a TV show, it's like choreographed or something, they do these kind of graceful falls. Kennedy was . . . they'd robbed him of his dignity. That's the only way I can think to put it. They shot him and humiliated him all at once, he looked clumsy and awkward and helpless.

"And I was outraged at that. I know it must sound weird, a man got shot, *killed*, and I'm talking about how he looked undignified. But that's what taking someone's life is – taking their humanity, making them a thing. And I was outraged. I wanted to grab one of those cops' guns and make *them* into *things*. Not just because it was Bobby Kennedy, it could have been anyone on that floor at that moment, the kid, the manager, my supervisor – and I hated my supervisor's guts.

"Right then, I understood what the demonstrations were about, and I was against the war. Up until then, I'd been kind of for it – not really *for* it, more like, 'I hate war, but you're supposed to serve your country.' But right then, I understood how horrifying it must be to be told to make somebody into a thing, or be told you have to go out and risk being made into a thing. To kill, to be killed.

"All that went through my mind in a split second and then I started screaming. Then I heard this . . . *noise* . . . under my screams. I heard this weird groan. It was Kennedy. They say he was dead by then and it must have been the air going out of his lungs past his vocal cords that made the sound. Awful. Just awful. I ran and pulled the fire alarm. It was the only thing I could think to do. And this other chambermaid, Lucy Anderson, she started pounding on the front windows and screaming, 'Stop! Stop! They killed Kennedy! They killed Kennedy!' Probably no one could hear her but even if anyone had, it wouldn't have mattered, because most of the people out there thought Kennedy was already dead in the explosion.

"It wasn't the Fire Department that used the hoses on those people. The cops commandeered the fire trucks and did that. And we were stuck in that hotel for another whole day and night. Even after they cleared the streets, they wouldn't let any of us go anywhere. Like house arrest.

"The questioning was awful. Nobody mistreated me or hit me or anything like that, it was just that they kept *at* me. I had to tell what I saw over and over and over and over until I thought they were either trying to drive me out of my mind so I wouldn't be able to testify against those cops, or trying to find some way to make it seem like *I* was really the one who'd done it.

"By the time they told me I could leave the hotel, I was mad at the world, I can tell you. Especially since that Secret Service agent or whoever he was told me I'd be a lot happier if I moved out of Chicago and started over somewhere else. He really screwed that one up, and it was lucky for me he did. I left, and I was far, far away when the shit really hit the fan. I started over, all right – I got a new name and a new identity. Everybody else who was in that lobby – Lucy Anderson, the manager, the other staff and guests – they all disappeared. The last anyone saw of them, the Secret Service was taking them away. The cops vanished, too, but I have a feeling they didn't vanish to quite the same thing as the others.

"And the kid killed himself. *They* said. Right. Sure. I bet he couldn't survive the interrogation.

"Of course, all that was a long time ago. Hard to imagine now how things were then. I was only twenty, then. I was working days and taking college courses at night. I wanted to be a teacher. Now I'm in my early forties, and sometimes I think I dreamed it all. I dreamed that I lived in a country where people *voted* their leaders into office, where you just had to be old enough and not a convicted felon and you could vote. Instead of having to take those psychological tests and wait for the investigators to give you a voting clearance. It *is* like a dream, isn't it? Imagining that there was a time in this country when you could *be* anything you wanted to be, a teacher, a doctor, a banker, a scientist. I was going to be a teacher. I was going to be a history teacher, but those are mostly white people. My family's been in this country forever, but because I'm Oriental, I've got conditional citizenship now . . . and I was *born* here! I suppose I shouldn't complain. If anyone found out I saw Kennedy get it, I'd probably be unconditionally dead. Because *everyone knows* that the rumor that Kennedy was shot by some cops with a bad aim in a hotel lobby is just another stupid lie, like the second gunman in Dallas in 1963. *Everyone knows* Kennedy died in the explosion at the convention center. That's the official version of how he died and it's the official version, government certified, that's the truth.

"Where I live, they have routine segregation, so I can't use any of the whites' facilities. I've thought about applying to move to one of the larger cities where there's elective segregation and nothing's officially 'white only', but I hear the waiting lists are years long. And somebody told me that everything is really just as segregated as here, they're just not as open and honest about it. So maybe I'd really be no better off . . .

"But I wish that I could have become a teacher – any kind of teacher – instead of a cook. I can't even become a chef because that's another men-only field. I don't *want* to be a chef necessarily, because I really don't like to cook and I'm not very good at it. But it was all I could get. The list of available careers for non-whites gets smaller all the time.

"Sometimes, I think it actually wasn't meant to be this bad. Sometimes I think that nobody really wanted the military to take over the government for real, I think it was just panic about so many of the Democratic candidates dying along with the President in that blast and the rioting that wouldn't stop and all that. It did seem as if the country was completely falling apart and somebody had to do something fast and decisive. Well, sure somebody should have. Somebody should have figured out who was the President with Madman Johnson and Humpty Humphrey and all those Senators dead – there had to be *somebody* left, right? All of Congress wasn't there. I mean, if I'd known, if a lot of us had known how things were going to come out, I think we'd have just let Ronald Reagan be President for four years, run him against Wallace or something and kept free elections, instead of postponing the elections and then having them abolished.

"People panicked. That's what it all came down to, I think.

They were panicking in the streets, they were panicking in the
government, and they were panicking in their homes. Our own
panic brought us down."

*Undated typescript found in a locker in the downtown San Diego
bus terminal, 9 April 1993*

Our own panic brought us down. For many who were eyewitness
to certain events of 1968, this would seem to be a fitting coda, if
coda is the word, for the ensuing twenty-five years . . .

Oh, hell, I don't know why I'm bothering to try to sum this
up. How do you sum up a piece of history gone wrong? How do
you sum up all of a country that believes it was saved from chaos
and destruction? And who am I asking anyway? I'm out of the
country now, another wetback who finally made it across the
border to freedom. There was a time when wetbacks went north
to freedom but I'm pretty sure nobody would remember that
now. Mexico is sad and dusty and ancient, the people poor and
suspicious of Anglos, though I'm so brown now that I can pass
convincingly as long as I don't try to speak the language – my
accent is still atrocious.

But the freedom here – nothing like what we used to have but
the constraints are far fewer. You don't need to apply for a
travel permit in-country, you just *go* from place to place. Of
course, it's not really that hard to get a travel permit in the US,
they give them out routinely. But I'm of that generation that
remembers when it was different, and it galls me that I would
have to apply for one at all if I wanted to go from, say, Newark,
to, say, Cape May. I've deliberately chosen two cities I've never
been to, just in case these papers fall into the wrong hands. God
knows enough of my papers have been lost over the years.
Sometimes I think it's a miracle I haven't been caught.

It's a hell of a life when you're risking prosecution and
imprisonment just for trying to put together a true account of
something that happened two and a half decades ago.

Why I bothered – well, there are a lot of reasons. Because I've
learned to love truth. And because I want to atone for what I did to
"Carole Feeney" and the others. I'm still amazed that she didn't
recognize me, but I guess twenty years is a long time after all.

I really thought I was doing the right thing at the time. I thought infiltrating the leftist groups was all right if it was just to make sure that nobody was stockpiling weapons or planning to blow up a building. Or assassinate another leader. I truly wish I could have arrested Annie Phillips and her group long before Chicago. Some of the people I talked to who were into the streets that night blame Annie for everything that's happened since and I think that's why the authorities have kept her alive instead of killing her – so the old radicals could hate her more than the government.

After I talked to Annie, I understood why she turned violent, even if I didn't condone it. If her voice could have been heard in 1964, maybe all these voices could be heard now, though they might not have so much to say . . .

Oh, how melodramatic, "Davis". I can't help it. I was actually just like any of them in the year 1968 – I thought my country was in trouble and I was trying to do something about it. And –

And what the hell, we won the Viet Nam war. Hooray for America. The Viet Namese are all but extinct, but we brought the boys back home. We sent them right back out to the Middle East, and then down to Nicaragua, and to the Philippines, and to Europe, of course, where they don't protest our missile bases much any more. That big old stick. We've gone one better than talking softly and carrying a big stick. Now we don't talk at all . . .

In the weeks since I finally got out of the country, I've been having this recurring dream. I keep dreaming that things turned out differently, that there was even just one thing that didn't happen, or something else that did, and the country just . . . went on. And so I keep thinking about it. If Johnson hadn't run . . . if no one had been killed in Cicero four years earlier . . . if Reagan hadn't used so much force on campus. If someone hadn't thrown a rock at Allen Ginsburg. If that bomb hadn't gone off. If Kennedy hadn't been killed. If Dylan had showed up.

If Dylan had showed up . . . I wonder sometimes if that's it. God the world should be so simple. Instead of simple and brutal and crude.

Even after putting together this risky account, I'm not sure that I really know much more than I did in the beginning. I was hoping that I might figure it all out, how, instead of winning the battle and losing the war, we won the war and lost everything we had.

But it could have been different. I don't know why it's so important to me to believe that. Maybe because I don't want to believe that this was the way we were going no matter what. I don't want to believe that everything that was any value is stuck back there in the 1960s.

Papers found in a hastily vacated room in an Ecuadorian flop-house by occupying American forces during the third South American War, 13 October 1998

Catch That Zeppelin!

Fritz Leiber

This year on a trip to New York City to visit my son, who is a social historian at a leading municipal university there, I had a very unsettling experience. At black moments, of which at my age I have quite a few, it still makes me distrust profoundly those absolute boundaries in Space and Time which are our sole protection against Chaos, and fear that my mind – no, my entire individual existence – may at any moment at all and without any warning whatsoever be blown by a sudden gust of Cosmic Wind to an entirely different spot in a Universe of Infinite Possibilities. Or, rather, into another Universe altogether. And that my mind and individuality will be changed to fit.

But at other moments, which are still in the majority, I believe that my unsettling experience was only one of those remarkably vivid waking dreams to which old people become increasingly susceptible, generally waking dreams about the past, and especially waking dreams about a past in which at some crucial point one made an entirely different and braver choice than one actually did, or in which the whole world made such a decision, with a completely different future resulting. Golden glowing might-have-beens nag increasingly at the minds of some older people.

In line with this interpretation I must admit that my whole unsettling experience was structured very much like a dream. It began with startling flashes of a changed world. It continued into a longer period when I completely accepted the changed world and delighted in it and, despite fleeting quivers of uneasiness, wished I could bask in its glow forever. And it ended in horrors, or nightmares, which I hate to mention, let alone discuss, until I must.

Opposing this dream notion, there are times when I am completely convinced that what happened to me in Manhattan and in a certain famous building there was no dream at all, but absolutely real, and that I did indeed visit another Time Stream.

Finally, I must point out that what I am about to tell you I am necessarily describing in retrospect, highly aware of several transitions involved and, whether I want to or not, commenting on them and making deductions that never once occurred to me at the time.

No, at the time it happened to me – and now at this moment of writing I am convinced that it did happen and was absolutely real – one instant simply succeeded another in the most natural way possible. I questioned nothing.

As to why it all happened to me, and what particular mechanism was involved, well, I am convinced that every man and woman has rare brief moments of extreme sensitivity, or rather vulnerability, when his mind and entire being may be blown by the Change Winds to Somewhere Else. And then, by what I call the Law of the Conservation of Reality blown back again.

I was walking down Broadway somewhere near 34th Street. It was a chilly day, sunny despite the smog – a bracing day – and I suddenly began to stride along more briskly than is my cautious habit, throwing my feet ahead of me with a faint suggestion of the goose step. I also threw back my shoulders and took deep breaths, ignoring the fumes which tickled my nostrils. Beside me, traffic growled and snarled, rising at times to a machine-gun rata-tat-tat. While pedestrians were scuttling about with that desperate ratlike urgency characteristic of all big American cities, but which reaches its ultimate in New York. I cheerfully ignored that too. I even smiled at the sight of a ragged bum and a fur-coated grey-haired society lady both independently dodging across the street through the hurtling traffic with a cool practised skill one sees only in America's biggest metropolis.

Just then I noticed a dark, wide shadow athwart the street ahead of me. It could not be that of a cloud, for it did not move. I craned my neck sharply and looked straight up like the veriest yokel, a regular *Hans-Kopf-in-die-Luft* (Hans-Head-in-the-Air, a German figure of comedy).

My gaze had to climb up the giddy 102 storeys of the tallest building in the world, the Empire State. My gaze was strangely accompanied by the vision of a gigantic, long-fanged ape making the same ascent with a beautiful girl in one paw – oh, yes, I was recollecting the charming American fantasy film *King Kong*, or as they name it in Sweden, *Kong King*.

And then my gaze clambered higher still, up the 222-foot sturdy tower, to the top of which was moored the nose of the vast, breathtakingly beautiful, streamlined, silvery shape which was making the shadow.

Now here is a most important point. I was not at the time in the least startled by what I saw. I knew at once that it was simply the bow section of the German Zeppelin *Ostwald*, named for the great German pioneer of physical chemistry and electrochemistry, and queen of the mighty passenger and light-freight fleet of luxury airliners working out of Berlin, Baden-Baden, and Bremerhaven. That matchless Armada of Peace, each titanic airship named for a world-famous German scientist – the *Mach*, the *Nernst*, the *Humboldt*, the *Fritz Haber*, the French-named *Antoine Henri Becquerel*, the American-named *Edison*, the Polish-named *Sklodowska*, the American-Polish *T. Sklodowska Edison*, and even the Jewish-named *Einstein*! The great humanitarian navy in which I held a not unimportant position as international sales consultant and *Fachman* – I mean expert. My chest swelled with justified pride at this *edel* – noble achievement of *der Vaterland*.

I knew also without any mind-searching or surprise that the length of the *Ostwald* was more than one half the 1,472-foot height of the Empire State Building plus its mooring tower, thick enough to hold an elevator. And my heart swelled again with the thought that the Berlin *Zeppelinturm* (dirigible tower) was only a few metres less high. Germany, I told myself, need not strain for mere numerical records – her sweeping scientific and technical achievements speak for themselves to the entire planet.

All this literally took little more than a second, and I never broke my snappy stride. As my gaze descended, I cheerfully hummed under my breath *Deutschland, Deutschland über Alles*.

The Broadway I saw was utterly transformed, though at the time this seemed every bit as natural as the serene presence of the *Ostwald* high overhead, vast ellipsoid held aloft by helium. Silvery electric trucks and buses and private cars innumerable purred along far more evenly and quietly, and almost as swiftly, as had the noisy, stenchful, jerky gasoline-powered vehicles only moments before, though to me now the latter were completely forgotten. About two blocks ahead, an occasional gleaming electric car smoothly swung into the wide silver arch of a quick-battery-change station, while others emerged from under the arch to rejoin the almost dreamlike stream of traffic.

The air I gratefully inhaled was fresh and clean, without a trace of smog.

The somewhat fewer pedestrians around me still moved quite swiftly, but with a dignity and courtesy largely absent before, with the numerous blackamoors among them quite as well dressed and exuding the same quiet confidence as the Caucasians.

The only slightly jarring note was struck by a tall, pale, rather emaciated man in black dress and with unmistakably Hebraic features. His sombre clothing was somewhat shabby, though well kept, and his thin shoulders were hunched. I got the impression he had been looking closely at me, and then instantly glancing away as my eyes sought his. For some reason I recalled what my son had told me about the City College of New York – CCNY – being referred to surreptitiously and jokingly as Christian College Now Yiddish. I couldn't help chuckling a bit at that witticism, though I am glad to say it was a genial little guffaw rather than a malicious snicker. Germany in her well-known tolerance and noble-mindedness has completely outgrown her old, disfiguring anti-Semitism – after all, we must admit in all fairness that perhaps a third of our great men are Jews or carry Jewish genes, Haber and Einstein among them – despite what dark and, yes, wicked memories may lurk in the subconscious minds of oldsters like myself and occasionally briefly surface into awareness like submarines bent on ship murder.

My happily self-satisfied mood immediately reasserted itself, and with a smart, almost military gesture I brushed to either side with a thumbnail the short, horizontal black moustache which decorates my upper lip, and I automatically swept back into place the thick comma of black hair (I confess I dye it) whch tends to fall down across my forehead.

I stole another glance up at the *Ostwald*, which made me think of the matchless amenities of that wondrous deluxe airliner: the softly purring motors that powered its propellers – electric motors, naturally, energized by banks of lightweight TSE batteries and as safe as its helium; the Grand Corridor running the length of the passenger deck from the Bow Observatory to the stern's like-windowed Games Room, which becomes the Grand Ballroom at night; the other peerless room letting off that corridor – the *Gesellschaftsraum der Kapitan* (Captain's Lounge) with its dark woodwork, manly cigar smoke and *Damentische* (Tables for Ladies), the Premier Dining Room with its linen napery and silver-plated aluminium dining service, the Ladies' Retiring Room always set out profusely with fresh flowers, the Schwartzwald bar, the gaming casino with its roulette, baccarat, chemmy, blackjack (*vingt-et-un*), its tables for skat and bridge and dominoes and sixty-six, its chess tables presided over by the delightfully eccentric world's champion Nimzowitch, who would defeat you blindfold, but always brilliantly, simultaneously or one at a time, in charmingly baroque brief games for only two gold pieces per person per game (one gold piece to nutsy Nimzy, one to the DLG), and the supremely luxurious staterooms with costly veneers of mahogany over balsa; the hosts of attentive stewards, either as short and skinny as jockeys or else actual dwarfs, both types chosen to save weight; and the titanium elevator rising through the countless bags of helium to the two-decked Zenith Observatory, the sun deck wind-screened but roofless to let in the ever-changing clouds, the mysterious fog, the rays of the stars and good old Sol, and all the heavens. Ah, where else on land or sea could you buy such high living?

I called to mind in detail the single cabin which was always mine when I sailed on the *Ostwald – meine Stammkabine.* I visualized the Grand Corridor thronged with wealthy passengers in evening dress, the handsome officers, the unobtrusive ever-attentive stewards, the gleam of white shirt fronts, the glow of bare shoulders, the muted dazzle of jewels, the music of conversation like string quartets, the lilting low laughter that travelled along.

Exactly on time I did a neat *'Links, marschieren!'* ('To the left, march!') and passed through the impressive portals of the Empire State and across its towering lobby to the mutedly silver-glowing date: 6 May 1937 and the time of day: 1.07 p.m. Good! – since the *Ostwald* did not cast off until the tick of 3 p.m., I would be left plenty of time for a leisurely lunch and good talk with my son, if he had remembered to meet me – and there was actually no doubt about that, since he is the most considerate and orderly minded of sons, a real German mentality, though I say it myself.

I headed for the express bank, enjoying my passage through the clusters of high-class people who thronged the lobby without any unseemly crowding, and placed myself before the doors designated "Dirigible Departure Lounge" and in briefer German *"Zum Zeppelin"*.

The elevator hostess was an attractive Japanese girl in skirt of dull silver with the DLG, Double Eagle and Dirigible insignia of the German Airship Union emblazoned in small on the left breast of her mutedly silver jacket. I noted with unvoiced approval that she appeared to have an excellent command of both German and English and was uniformly courteous to the passengers in her smiling but unemotional Nipponese fashion, which is so like our German scientific precision of speech, though without the latter's warm underlying passion. How good that our two federations, at opposite sides of the globe, have strong commercial and behavioural ties!

My fellow passengers in the lift, chiefly Americans and Germans, were of the finest type, very well dressed – except that just as the doors were about to close, there pressed in my doleful Jew in black. He seemed ill at ease, perhaps because of his shabby clothing. I was surprised, but made a point of being particularly polite towards him, giving him a slight bow and brief but friendly smile, while flashing my eyes. Jews have as much right to the acme of luxury travel as any other people on the planet, if they have the money – and most of them do.

During our uninterrupted and infinitely smooth passage upward, I touched my outside left breast pocket to reassure myself that my ticket – first class on the *Ostwald*! – and my papers were there. But actually I got far more reassurance and even secret joy from the feel and thought of the documents in my tightly zippered inside left breast pocket: the signed preliminary agreements that would launch America herself into the manufacture of passenger Zeppelins. Modern Germany is always generous in sharing her great technical achievements with responsible sister nations, supremely confident that the genius of her scientists and engineers will continue to keep her well ahead of all other lands; and after all, the genius of two Americans, father and son, had made vital though indirect contributions to the development of safe airship travel (and not forgetting the part played by the Polish-born wife of the one and the mother of the other).

The obtaining of those documents had been the chief and official reason for my trip to New York City, though I had been able to combine it most pleasurably with a long overdue visit with my son, the social historian, and with his charming wife.

These happy reflections were cut short by the jarless arrival of our elevator at its lofty terminus on the 100th floor. The journey old love-smitten King Kong had made only after exhausting exertion we had accomplished effortlessly. The silvery doors spread wide. My fellow passengers hung back for a moment in awe and perhaps a little trepidation at the thought of the awesome journey ahead of them, and I – seasoned airship traveller that I am – was the first to step out, favouring with a smile and nod of approval my pert yet cool Japanese fellow employee of the lower echelons.

Hardly sparing a glance towards the great, fleckless window confronting the doors and showing a matchless view of Manhattan from an elevation of 1,250 feet minus two storeys, I briskly turned, not right to the portals of the Departure Lounge and tower elevator, but left to those of the superb German restaurant *Krahenest* (Crow's Nest).

I passed between the flanking three-foot-high bronze statuettes of Thomas Edison and Maria Sklodowska Edison niched in one wall and those of Count von Zeppelin and Thomas Sklodowska Edison facing them from the other, and entered the select precincts of the finest German dining place outside the Fatherland. I paused while my eyes travelled searchingly around the room with its restful, dark wood panelling deeply carved with beautiful representations of the Black Forest and its grotesque supernatural denizens – kobolds, elves, gnomes, dryads (tastefully sexy) and the like. They interest me since I am what Americans call a Sunday painter, though almost my sole subject matter is zeppelins seen against blue sky and airy, soaring clouds.

The *Oberkellner* came hurrying towards me with menu tucked under his left elbow and saying, "*Mein Herr!* Charmed to see you once more! I have a perfect table-for-one with porthole looking out across the Hudson."

But just then a youthful figure rose springily from behind a table set against the far wall, and a dear and familiar voice rang out to me with "*Hier, Papa!*"

"*Nein, Herr Ober,*" I smilingly told the head waiter as I walked past him, "*heute hab ich ein Gesellschafter. Mein Sohn.*"

I confidently made my way between tables occupied by well-dressed folk, both white and black.

My son wrung my hand with fierce family affection, though we had last parted only that morning. He insisted that I take the wide, dark, leather-upholstered seat against the wall, which gave me a fine view of the entire restaurant, while he took the facing chair.

"Because during this meal I wish to look only on you, Papa," he assured me with manly tenderness. "And we have at least an hour and a half together, Papa – I have checked your luggage through, and it is likely already aboard the *Ostwald*." Thoughtful, dependable boy!

"And now, Papa, what shall it be?" he continued after we had settled ourselves. "I see that today's special is *Sauerbraten mit Spatzel* and sweet-sour red cabbage. But there is also *Praprikahuhn* and—"

"Leave the chicken to flaunt her paprika in lonely red splendour today," I interrupted him. "*Sauerbraten* sounds fine."

Ordered by my Herr Ober, the aged wine waiter had already approached our table. I was about to give him directions when my son took upon himself that task with an authority and a hostfulness that warmed my heart. He scanned the wine menu rapidly but thoroughly.

"The Zinfandel 1933," he ordered with decision, though glancing my way to see if I concurred with his judgment. I smiled and nodded.

"And perhaps *ein Tropfchen Schnapps* to begin with?" he suggested.

"A brandy? – yes!" I replied. "And not just a drop, either. Make it a double. It is not every day I lunch with that distinguished scholar, my son."

"Oh, Papa," he protested, dropping his eyes and almost blushing. Then firmly to the bent-backed, white-haired wine waiter, "*Schnapps also. Doppel.*" The old waiter nodded his approval and hurried off.

We gazed at each other fondly for a few blissful seconds. Then I said, "Now tell me more fully about your achievements as a social historian on an exchange professorship in the New World. I know we have spoken about this several times, but only rather briefly and generally when various of your friends were present, or at least your lovely wife. Now I would like a more leisurely man-to-man account of your great work. Incidentally, do you find the scholarly apparatus – books, *und so weiter* (et cetera) – of the Municipal Universities of New York City adequate to your needs after having enjoyed those of Baden-

Baden University and the institutions of higher learning in the German Federation?"

"In some respects they are lacking," he admitted. "However, for my purposes they have proved completely adequate." Then once more he dropped his eyes and almost blushed. "But, Papa, you praise my small efforts far too highly." He lowered his voice. "They do not compare with the victory for international industrial relations you yourself have won in a fortnight."

"All in a day's work for the DLG," I said self-deprecatingly, though once again lightly touching my left chest to establish contact with those most important documents safely stowed in my inside left breast pocket. "But now, no more polite fencing!" I went on briskly. "Tell me about those 'small efforts', as you modestly refer to them."

His eyes met mine. "Well, Papa," he began in suddenly matter-of-fact fashion, "all my work these last two years has been increasingly dominated by a firm awareness of the fragility of the underpinnings of the good world-society we enjoy today. If certain historically minute key-events, or cusps, in only the past one hundred years had been decided differently – if another course had been chosen than the one that was – then the whole world might now be plunged in wars and worse horrors than we ever dream of. It is a chilling insight, but it bulks continually larger in my entire work, my every paper."

I felt the thrilling touch of inspiration. At that moment the wine waiter arrived with our double brandies in small goblets of cut glass. I wove the interruption into the fabric of my inspiration. "Let us drink then to what you name your chilling insight," I said. "*Prosit!*"

The bite and spreading warmth of the excellent *schnapps* quickened my inspiration further. "I believe I understand exactly what you're getting at . . ." I told my son. I set down my half-emptied goblet and pointed at something over my son's shoulder.

He turned his head around, and after one glance back at my pointing finger, which intentionally waggled a tiny bit from side to side, he realized that I was not indicating the entry of the *Krahenest*, but the four sizeable bronze statuettes flanking it.

"For instance," I said, "if Thomas Edison and Maria

Sklodowska had not married, and especially if they had not had their super-genius son, then Edison's knowledge of electricity and hers of radium and other radioactives might never have been joined. There might never have been developed the fabulous T. S. Edison battery, which is the prime mover of all today's surface and air traffic. Those pioneering electric trucks introduced by the *Saturday Evening Post* in Philadelphia might have remained an expensive freak. And the gas helium might never have been produced industrially to supplement earth's meagre subterranean supply."

My son's eyes brightened with the flame of pure scholarship. "Papa," he said eagerly, "you are a genius yourself! You have precisely hit on what is perhaps the most important of those cusp-events I referred to. I am at this moment finishing the necessary research for a long paper on it. Do you know, Papa, that I have firmly established by researching Paris records that there was in 1894 a close personal relationship between Maria Sklodowska and her fellow radium researcher Pierre Curie, and that she might well have become Madame Curie – or perhaps Madame Becquerel, for he too was in that work – if the dashing and brilliant Edison had not most opportunely arrived in Paris in December 1894 to sweep her off her feet and carry her off to the New World to even greater achievements?

"And just think, Papa," he went on, his eyes aflame, "what might have happened if their son's battery had not been invented – the most difficult technical achievement, hedged by all sorts of scheming scientific impossibilities, in the entire millennium-long history of industry. Why, Henry Ford might have manufactured automobiles powered by steam or by exploding natural gas or conceivably even vaporized liquid gasoline, rather than the mass-produced electric cars which have been such a boon to mankind everywhere – not our smoke-less cars, but cars spouting all sorts of noxious fumes to pollute the environment."

Cars powered by the danger-fraught combustion of vaporized liquid gasoline! – it almost made me shudder and certainly it was a fantastic thought, yet not altogether beyond the bounds of possibility, I had to admit.

Just then I noticed my gloomy, black-clad Jew sitting only two tables away from us, though how he got himself into the exclusive *Krahenest* was a wonder. Strange that I had missed his entry – probably immediately after my own, while I had eyes only for my son. His presence somehow threw a dark though only momentary shadow over my bright mood. Let him get some good German food inside him and some fine German wine, I thought generously – it will fill that empty belly of his and even put a bit of a good German smile into those sunken Yiddish cheeks! I combed my little moustache with my thumbnail and swept the errant lock of hair off my forehead.

Meanwhile my son was saying, "Also, Father, if electric transport had not been developed, and if during the last decade relations between Germany and the United States had not been so good, then we might never have got from the wells in Texas the supply of natural helium our Zeppelins desperately needed during the brief but vital period before we had put the artificial creation of helium on to an industrial footing. My researchers at Washington have revealed that there was a strong movement in the US military to ban the sale of helium to any other nation, Germany in particular. Only the powerful influence of Edison, Ford, and a few other key Americans, instantly brought to bear, prevented that stupid injunction. Yet if it had gone through, Germany might have been forced to use hydrogen instead of helium to float her passenger dirigibles. That was another crucial cusp."

"A hydrogen-supported Zeppelin – ridiculous! Such an airship would be a floating bomb, ready to be touched off by the slightest spark," I protested.

"Not ridiculous, Father," my son calmly contradicted me, shaking his head. "Pardon me for trespassing in your field, but there is an inescapable imperative about certain industrial developments. If there is not a safe road of advance, then a dangerous one will invariably be taken. You must admit, Father, that the development of commercial airships was in its early stages a most perilous adventure. During the 1920s there were the dreadful wrecks of the American dirigibles *Roma*, *Shenandoah*, which broke in two, *Akron*, and *Macon*, the British

R-38, which also broke apart in the air, and *R-101*, the French *Dixmude*, which disappeared in the Mediterranean, Mussolini's *Italia*, which crashed trying to reach the North Pole, and the Russian *Maxim Gorky*, struck down by a plane, with a total loss of no fewer than 350 crew members for the nine accidents. If that had been followed by the explosions of two or three hydrogen Zeppelins, world industry might well have abandoned for ever the attempt to create passenger airships and turned instead to the development of large propeller-driven heavier-than-air craft."

Monster aeroplanes, in danger every moment of crash from engine failure, competing with good old unsinkable Zeppelins? – impossible, at least at first thought. I shook my head, but not with as much conviction as I might have wished. My son's suggestion was really a valid one.

Besides, he had all his facts at his fingertips and was complete master of his subject, as I also had to allow. Those nine fearful airship disasters he mentioned had indeed occurred, as I knew well, and might have tipped the scale in favour of long-distance passenger and troop-carrying aeroplanes, had it not been for helium, the T. S. Edison battery, and German genius.

Fortunately I was able to dump from my mind these uncomfortable speculations and immerse myself in admiration of my son's multisided scholarship. That boy was a wonder! – a real chip off the old block, and, yes, a bit more.

"And now, Dolfy," he went on, using my nickname (I did not mind), "may I turn to an entirely different topic? Or rather to a very different example of my hypothesis of historical cusps?"

I nodded mutely. My mouth was busily full with fine *Sauerbraten* and those lovely, tiny German dumplings, while my nostrils enjoyed the unique aroma of sweet-sour red cabbage. I had been so engrossed in my son's revelations that I had not consciously noted our luncheon being served. I swallowed, took a slug of the good, red Zinfandel, and said, "Please go on."

"It's about the consequences of the American Civil War, Father," he said surprisingly. "Did you know that in the decade after that bloody conflict, there was a very real danger that the whole cause of Negro freedom and rights – for which the war

was fought, whatever they say – might well have been
completely smashed? The fine work of Abraham Lincoln,
Thaddeus Stevens, Charles Sumner, the Freedmen's Bureau,
and the Union League Clubs put to naught? and even the Ku
Klux Klan underground allowed free reign rather than being
sternly repressed? Yes, Father, my thoroughgoing researchings
have convinced me such things might easily have happened,
resulting in some sort of re-enslavement of the Blacks, with the
whole war to be refought at an indefinite future date, or at any
rate Reconstruction brought to a dead halt for many decades –
with what disastrous effects on the American character, turning
its deep simple faith in freedom to hypocrisy, it is impossible to
exaggerate. I have published a sizeable paper on this subject in
the *Journal of Civil War Studies.*"

I nodded sombrely. Quite a bit of this new subject matter of
his was *terra incognita* to me; yet I knew enough of American
history to realize he had made a cogent point. More than ever
before, I was impressed by his multifaceted learning – he was
indubitably a figure in the great tradition of German scholarship, a profound thinker, broad and deep. How fortunate to be
his father. Not for the first time, but perhaps with the greatest
sincerity yet, I thanked God and the Laws of Nature that I had
early moved my family from Braunau, Austria, where I had
been born in 1899, to Baden-Baden where he had grown up in
the ambience of the great new university on the edge of the
Black Forest and only 150 kilometres from Count Zeppelin's
dirigible factory in Wurttemberg, at Friedrichshafen on Lake
Constance.

I raised my glass of *Kirschwasser* to him in a solemn, silent
toast – we had somehow got to that stage in our meal – and
downed a sip of the potent, fiery, white cherry brandy.

He leaned towards me and said, "I might as well tell you,
Dolf, that my big book, at once popular and scholarly, my
Meisterwerk, to be titled *If Things Had Gone Wrong*, or perhaps *If
Things Had Turned for the Worse*, will deal solely – though illuminated by dozens of diverse examples – with my theory of
historical cusps, a highly speculative concept but firmly footed
in fact." He glanced at his wristwatch, muttered, "Yes, there's

still time for it. So now – " his face grew grave, his voice clear though small – "I will venture to tell you about one more cusp, the most disputable and yet most crucial of them all." He paused. "I warn you, dear Dolf, that this cusp may cause you pain."

"I doubt that," I told him indulgently. "Anyhow, go ahead."

"Very well. In November of 1918, when the British had broken the Hindenburg Line and the weary German Army was defiantly dug in along the Rhine, and just before the Allies, under Marshal Foch, launched the final crushing drive which would cut a bloody swath across the heartland to Berlin—"

I understood his warning at once. Memories flamed in my mind like the sudden blinding flares of the battlefield with their deafening thunder. The company I had commanded had been among the most desperately defiant of those he mentioned, heroically nerved for a last-ditch resistance. And then Foch had delivered that last vast blow, and we had fallen back and back before the overwhelming numbers of our enemies with their field guns and tanks and armoured cars innumerable and above all their huge aerial armadas of De Haviland and Handley-Page and other big bombers escorted by insect-buzzing fleets of Spads and other fighters shooting to bits our last Fokkers and Pfalzes and visiting on Germany a destruction greater by far than our Zeps had worked on England. Back, back, back, endlessly reeling and regrouping, across the devastated German countryside, a dozen times decimated yet still defiant until the end came at last amid the ruins of Berlin, and the most bold among us had to admit we were beaten and we surrendered unconditionally –

These vivid, fiery recollections came to me almost instantaneously.

I heard my son continuing, "At that cusp moment in November 1918, Dolf, there existed a very strong possibility – I have established this beyond question – that an immediate armistice would be offered and signed, and the war ended inconclusively. President Wilson was wavering, the French were very tired, and so on.

"And if that had happened in actuality – harken closely to me now, Dolf – then the German temper entering the decade of the 1920s would have been entirely different. She would have felt she had not been really licked, and there would inevitably have been a secret recrudescence of pan-German militarism. German scientific humanism would not have won its total victory over the Germany of the – yes! – Huns.

"As for the Allies, self-tricked out of the complete victory which lay within their grasp, they would in the long run have treated Germany far less generously than they did after their lust for revenge had been sated by that last drive to Berlin. The League of Nations would not have become the strong instrument for world peace that it is today; it might well have been repudiated by America and certainly secretly detested by Germans. Old wounds would not have healed because, paradoxically, they would not have been deep enough.

"There, I've had my say. I hope it hasn't bothered you too badly, Dolf."

I let out a gusty sigh. Then my wincing frown was replaced by a brow serene. I said very deliberately, "Not one bit, my son, though you have certainly touched my old wounds to the quick. Yet I feel in my bones that your interpretation is completely valid. Rumours of an armistice were indeed running like wild-fire through our troops in that black autumn of 1918. And I know only too well that if there had been an armistice at that time, then officers like myself would have believed that the German soldier had never really been defeated, only betrayed by his leaders and by red incendiaries, and we would have begun to conspire endlessly for a resumption of the war under happier circumstances. My son, let us drink to your amazing cusps."

Our tiny glasses touched with a delicate ting, and the last drops went down of biting, faintly bitter *Kirschwasser*. I buttered a thin slice of pumpernickel and nibbled it – always good to finish off a meal with bread. I was suddenly filled with an immeasurable content. It was a golden moment, which I would have been happy to have go on for ever, while I listened to my son's wise words and fed my satisfaction in him. Yes, indeed, it was a golden nugget of pause in the terrible rush of time – the enriching conversation, the peerless food and drink, the darkly pleasant surroundings –

At that moment I chanced to look at my discordant Jew two tables away. For some weird reason he was glaring at me with naked hate, though he instantly dropped his gaze –

But even that strange and disquieting event did not disrupt my mood of golden tranquillity, which I sought to prolong by saying in summation, "My dear son, this has been the most exciting though eerie lunch I have ever enjoyed. Your remarkable cusps have opened to me a fabulous world in which I can nevertheless utterly believe. A horridly fascinating world of sizzling hydrogen Zeppelins, of countless evil-smelling gasoline cars built by Ford instead of his electrics, of re-enslaved American blackamoors, of Madame Becquerels or Curies, a world without the T. S. Edison battery and even T. S. himself, a world in which German scientists are sinister pariahs instead of tolerant, humanitarian, great-souled leaders of world thought, a world in which a mateless old Edison tinkers forever at a powerful storage battery he cannot perfect, a world in which Woodrow Wilson doesn't insist on Germany being admitted at once to the League of Nations, a world of festering hatreds reeling towards a second and worse world war. Oh, altogether an incredible world, yet one in which you have momentarily made me believe, to the extent that I do actually have the fear that time will suddenly shift gears and we will be plunged into that bad dream world; and our real world will become a dream—"

I suddenly chanced to see the face of my watch –

At the same time my son looked at his own left wrist –

"Dolf," he said, springing up in agitation, "I do hope that with my stupid chatter I haven't made you miss—"

I had sprung up too –

"No, no, my son," I heard myself say in a fluttering voice, "but it's true I have little time in which to catch the *Ostwald. Auf Wiedersehn, mein Sohn, auf Weidersehn!*"

And with that I was hastening, indeed almost running, or else sweeping through the air like a ghost – leaving him behind to settle our reckoning – across a room that seemed to waver with my feverish agitation, alternately darkening and brightening like an electric bulb with its fine tungsten filament about to fly to powder and wink out forever –

Inside my head a voice was saying in calm yet death-knell tones, "The lights of Europe are going out. I do not think they will be rekindled in my generation—"

Suddenly the only important thing in the world for me was to catch the *Ostwald*, get aboard her before she unmoored. That and only that would reassure me that I was in my rightful world. I would touch and feel the *Ostwald*, not just talk about her –

As I dashed between the four bronze figures, they seemed to hunch down and become deformed, while their faces became those of grotesque, aged witches – four evil kobolds leering up at me with a horrid knowledge bright in their eyes –

While behind me I glimpsed in pursuit a tall, black, white-faced figure, skeletally lean –

The strangely short corridor ahead of me had a blank end – the Departure Lounge wasn't there –

I instantly jerked open the narrow door to the stairs and darted nimbly up them as if I were a young man again and not forty-eight years old –

On the third sharp turn I risked a glance behind and down –

Hardly a flight behind me, taking great pursuing leaps, was my dreadful Jew –

I tore open the door to the 102nd floor. There at last, only a few feet away, was the silver door I sought of the final elevator and softly glowing above it the words, *"Zum Zeppelin"* . At last I would be shot aloft to the *Ostwald* and reality.

But the sign began to blink as the *Krahenest* had, while across the door was pasted askew a white cardboard sign which read "Out of Order".

I threw myself at the door and scrabbled at it, squeezing my eyes several times to make my vision come clear. When I finally fully opened them the cardboard sign was gone.

But the silver door was gone too, and the words above it forever. I was scrabbling at seamless pale plaster.

There was a touch on my elbow. I spun around.

"Excuse me, sir, but you seem troubled," my Jew said solicitously. "Is there anything I can do?"

I shook my head, but whether in negation or rejection or to clear it, I don't know. "I'm looking for the *Ostwald*," I gasped only now realizing I'd winded myself on the stairs. "For the Zeppelin," I explained when he looked puzzled.

I may be wrong, but it seemed to me that a look of secret glee flashed deep in his eyes, though his general sympathetic expression remained unchanged.

"Oh, the Zeppelin," he said in a voice that seemed to me to have become sugary in its solicitude. "You must mean the *Hindenburg*."

Hindenburg? – I asked myself. There was no Zeppelin named *Hindenburg*. Or was there? Could it be that I was mistaken about such a simple and, one would think, immutable matter? My mind had been getting very foggy the last minute or two. Desperately I tried to assure myself that I was indeed myself and in my right world. My lips worked and muttered to myself, *Bin Adolf Hitler, Zeppelin Fachman* . . .

"But the *Hindenburg* doesn't land here, in any case," my Jew was telling me, "though I think some vague intention once was voiced about topping the Empire State with a mooring mast for dirigibles. Perhaps you saw some news story and assumed—"

His face fell, or he made it seem to fall. The sugary solitude in his voice became unendurable as he told me, "But apparently you can't have heard today's tragic news. Oh, I do hope you weren't seeking the *Hindenburg* so as to meet some beloved family member or close friend. Brace yourself, sir. Only hours ago, coming in for her landing at Lakehurst, New Jersey, the *Hindenburg* caught fire and burned up entire in a matter of seconds. Thirty or forty at least of her passengers and crew were burned alive. Oh, steady yourself, sir."

"But the *Hindenburg* – I mean the *Ostwald*! – couldn't burn like that," I protested. "She's a helium Zeppelin."

He shook his head. "Oh, no. I'm no scientist, but I know the *Hindenburg* was filled with hydrogen – a wholly typical bit of reckless German risk-running. At least we've never sold helium to the Nazis, thank God."

I stared at him, wavering my face from side to side in feeble denial.

While he stared back at me with obviously a new thought in mind.

"Excuse me once again," he said, "but I believe I heard you start to say something about Adolf Hitler. I suppose you know that you bear a certain resemblance to that execrable dictator. If I were you, sir, I'd shave my moustache."

I felt a wave of fury at this inexplicable remark with all its baffling references, yet withal a remark delivered in the unmistakeable tones of an insult. And then all my surrounding momentarily reddened and flickered, and I felt a tremendous wrench in the inmost core of my being, the sort of wrench one might experience in transiting timelessly from one universe into another parallel to it. Briefly I became a man still named Adolf Hitler, same as the Nazi dictator and almost the same age, a German-American born in Chicago, who had never visited Germany or spoke German, whose friends teased him about his chance resemblance to the other Hitler, and who used stubbornly to say, "No, I won't change my name! Let that *Fuehrer* bastard across the Atlantic change his! Ever hear about the British Winston Churchill writing the American Winston Churchill, who wrote *The Crisis* and other novels, and suggesting he change his name to avoid confusion, since the Englishman had done some writing too? The American wrote back it was a good idea, but since he was three years older, he was senior and so the Britisher should change *his* name. That's exactly how I feel about that son of a bitch Hitler."

The Jew still stared at me sneeringly. I started to tell him off, but then I was lost in a second weird, wrenching transition. The first had been directly from one parallel universe to another. The second was also in time – I aged fourteen or fifteen years in a single infinite instant while transiting from 1937 (where I had been born in 1889 and was forty-eight) to 1973 (where I had been born in 1910 and was sixty-three). My name changed back to my truly own (but what is that?), and I no longer looked one bit like Adolf Hitler the Nazi dictator (or dirigible expert?), and

I had a married son who was a sort of social historian in a New York City municipal university, and he had many brilliant theories, but none of historical cusps.

And the Jew – I mean the tall, thin man in black with possibly Semitic features – was gone. I looked around and around but there was no one there.

I touched my outside left breast pocket, then my hand darted trembling underneath. There was no zipper on the pocket inside and no precious documents; only a couple of grimy envelopes with notes I'd scribbled on them in pencil.

I don't know how I got out of the Empire State Building. Presumably by elevator. Though all my memory holds for that period is a persistent image of King Kong tumbling down from its top like a ridiculous yet poignantly pitiable giant teddy bear.

I do recollect walking in a sort of trance for what seemed hours through a Manhattan stinking with monoxide and carcinogens innumerable, half waking from time to time (usually while crossing streets that snarled, not purred) and then relapsing into trance. There were big dogs.

When I at last fully came to myself, I was walking down a twilit Hudson Street at the north end of Greenwich Village. My gaze was fixed on a distant and unremarkable pale-grey square of building top. I guessed it must be that of the World Trade Center, 1,350 feet tall.

And then it was blotted out by the grinning face of my son, the professor.

"Justin!" I said.

"Fritz!" he said. "We'd begun to worry a bit. Where did you get off to, anyhow? Not that it's a damn bit of my business. If you had an assignation with a go-go girl, you needn't tell me."

"Thanks," I said. "I do feel tired, I must admit, and somewhat cold. But no, I was just looking at some of my old stamping grounds," I told him, "and taking longer than I realized. Manhattan's changed during my years on the West Coast, but not all that much."

"It's getting chilly," he said. "Let's stop in that place ahead with the black front. It's the White Horse. Dylan Thomas used to drink there. He's supposed to have scribbled a poem on the wall of the can, only they painted it over. But it has the authentic sawdust."

"Good," I said, "only we'll make mine coffee, not ale. Or if I can't get coffee, then cola."

I am not really a *Prosit!*-type person.

A Very British History

Paul McAuley

It's about time someone produced a proper history of the space race.

After all, here we are in this year 2001, with two permanent colonies on the Moon, and outposts on Mars, Mercury, and the moons of Jupiter and Saturn. Not to mention close to a hundred low Earth orbit factories, hotels, laboratories and solar power farms, and the even dozen habitats orbiting the L5 point between Earth and the Moon. Why, at the Aldermaston Jet Propulsion Laboratories they're building the first robotic inter-stellar probes, and blueprints for multi-generation arks capable of transporting colonists to new Earths around other suns are already on the drawing boards. We've had plenty of readable, thoughtful but rapidly dated pieces of space boosterism by enthusiasts like Clarke and Asimov and Sagan. We've had far too many dry-as-dust official histories written by committees, and a plethora of self-serving, ghostwritten autobiographies by minor rocket scientists and second-string astronauts. We've had more than enough heavyweight commentaries by the likes of C. P. Snow, Norman Mailer, and Gore Vidal which, although ostensibly about the first men on the Moon or the second American revolution or the race for the outer system, are really about the authors' egos and hang-ups. And we've certainly had enough quickie pieces of crap knocked up from press releases by sci-fi hacks and penny ante journos, and more than enough half-baked manifestos cranked out by greedy shills masquerading as space-age messiahs (I can dig George Adamski's for-real craziness, and chortled my way through Baudrillard's *The Space Race Did Not Happen*, but *L. Ron Hubbard*?).

Yes, it's about time that we had a proper history of space colonization by a real historian: rigorous, heavily researched, determinedly fair-minded, leavened with some cerebral wackiness, and big enough to do some serious damage if you dropped it on your foot, even here on the Moon. A capstone to the first instalment of space exploration. Of course, it could only have been written by a Brit.

So here it is, Professor Sir William Coxton's *A Brief History of the Colonization of Space* (University of Oxford Press, 858 pp, with another cccxxvi pages of appendices, references and an exhaustive index, £75.00). And I'm very pleased to tell you that, despite the dry semi-detached style, for someone like me, who lived through part of this, it's the Real Deal. It makes you kind of proud to be in it, even if not much more than a footnote (page 634 if you're interested).

But I should warn you that despite appearing to bend over backward to be fair-minded, Sir Bill is never shy of elevating the contributions of his own country above those of the States and the former Soviet Union whenever the opportunity arises, as might be expected from someone who has, after all, benefited from the touch of the Queen's sword on his shoulder. Sir Bill isn't an actual aristo, having been born into a coal-mining family in a Yorkshire village that is, as far as I can make out, more like one of the hard-scrabble towns in Kentucky than the landscaped acres of some ancestral pile. But like a lot of heavyweight Brit academics, he's far more pro-establishment than most of the actual establishment, and despite the many hours he spent in the archives, and the many more hours he spent interviewing the surviving principals of the keynote dramas (he even wasted a couple of hours talking to yours truly), he's prone to a certain partiality.

As shown by the fact that he doesn't begin his story in the usual places – Tsiolkovski's schoolroom, Goddard's machined fireworks – but with the race for Peenemünde at the end of the Second World War. Sir Bill is famous for his theories on hinge points in history, and has edited a fat book of counterfactual essays in which historians imagined what might have happened if, for instance, that ur-student radical Gavrilo Princip's revolver shots had missed Archduke Ferdinand and his wife in Sarajevo in 1914. And here he spends a lot of time arguing that, as far as the space race is concerned, the capture of the Nazi rocket scientists is the crucial hinge point in the history of space exploration. In fact, he's so consumed by this notion that he wastes a whole chapter speculating about what would have happened if the Brits didn't get there first. But I'm not going to depress us all by arguing the details of Sir Bill's imaginary account of the failures of nerve, the overriding requirements of the military-industrial complexes of the USA and the former Soviet Union, and the political, budgetary and managerial blunders that might have aborted NASA's exploration of the Moon and prematurely curtailed the slower but in many ways more ambitious Russian space program. After all, none of that actually happened, and even if the US army had managed to get to Peenemünde before the Brits, it still might not have happened. In the end, I'm pretty sure that Sir Bill's counter-factual is just one more of his ploys to convince us all that only the Brits were fit to be the first true space pioneers.

So we can skip all that theoretical gloom with a clear conscience, and get our teeth into the meat of the book. The story of the British army's capture of Peenemünde has been told many times before, but Sir Bill spices his account with an extensive reimagining from the point of view of a certain Sergeant Stapledon, who claims to have led the mission and who remained to his death (Sir Bill interviewed him ten years ago) sorely pissed off that he was written out of history by his superiors. It's exciting, full of hectic detail, and permeated with the intricacies of the British class system (Sergeant Stapledon was, like Sir Bill, a committed socialist, and ignored the order of the day because he despised his officers as effete fops).

It was because of Stapledon's initiative, Sir Bill claims, that the space age began in the ruins of Europe at the end of the

Second World War, when the Brits won the race to capture the secrets of the V-2 bunkers. Winston Churchill cannily arranged a swap of a few of the debriefed German personnel and a number of V-2s for American atomic technology, while spiriting much equipment, several half-completed V-3s, and a large contingent of technicians led by the formidable Wernher Von Braun, to the new rocket ranges at Woomera in the Australian outback. One of Churchill's last acts before the postwar election was to secure the future of the Woomera facility by encouraging engineering luminaries such as Barnes-Wallis, Christopher Cockerel and Frank Whittle to work with the Germans and, in Churchill's words, "extend the British ideal of freedom and fair play towards the stars". What he was about, of course, was building a new British Empire.

The next half-dozen chapters dig deep into the crazy stiff-upper-lipped heroics of early Brit space pioneers, who defied death atop barely tested rockets for the glory of King and country. Sir Bill is no sentimentalist, but it's easy to detect a sneaking admiration for those rocket boys in his account, which in taut, laconic prose captures the reckless mood of volunteers who, like Battle of Britain Spitfire pilots, made almost inevitable death seem like no more than an awfully big adventure: boys who could never grow up. The most famous of them all, Maurice Gray, now retired and tending his beehives and rose garden in Devon, still sounds like a fey mix of Peter Pan and Christopher Robin, a boy laughing lightly at inconceivable death, the British version of a zen master.

These were necessary heroics. While the Russians were racing to launch the first satellite, using big chemical multistage rockets designed by their own native genius, the legendary Chief Engineer, Sergei Koryolev, and the Americans were developing a military space program centred on the X-series rocketships, the British were concentrating on true manned space flight. The first man to ascend beyond the tropopause, to a height of more than twenty miles, was sixteen-year-old Maurice Gray, in a helium balloon in 1955; he also broke the current airspeed record by breaking the sound barrier when he plummeted nineteen miles back to Earth in free fall before opening his parachute. This was quickly followed by several suborbital lobs of RAF volunteers atop modified V-3s in 1956 and 1957, but after several fatal crashes of the two-stage A.20, British scientists became dissatisfied with mere chemical rockets and decided to develop a more powerful atomic technology, despite a couple of hair-raising (and hitherto suppressed) accidents which could have rendered most of Australia uninhabitable for 1,000 years.

Meanwhile, the Russians were the first to orbit a satellite in 1957, swiftly following that with a capsule containing a dog, and then a capsule containing a man, and with the X-20 the American Air Force developed a reusable chemically powered space plane which achieved orbit in 1960. But even as the two superpowers vied for military and political supremacy in Earth orbit, Britain's space program looked further, developing a reusable space ship using the highly advanced White Streak atomic motor, whose power both the Russians and the Americans grievously underestimated. In July 1962, two Brit scientists, Savage and Kingston, landed on the Moon, where they spent an entire Lunar day, two weeks, exploring and collecting rocks before returning to a hero's welcome.

The American government's space program remained strictly military. But the brilliant and ruthless entrepreneur Delos Harriman, spurred on by the British example, started a commercially funded space program in the States, and in 1970 finally reached the Moon using conventional multistage chemical boosters. Sir Bill's account of Harriman's achievement is curiously muted; it's clear he doesn't think much of the Yankee mix of rabid capitalism and pioneer individualism. And of course the British, using their atomic technology, had already reached Mars in 1968 – here, drawing upon extensive interviews with the protagonists, Sir Bill deftly improves upon Patrick Moore's classic account, in *Mission to Mars*, of how the first expedition was stranded because the motor of their craft was damaged on landing, and of how they survived for a year before a second expedition rescued them.

With the Moon and Mars secured by the British government and American free enterprise, the Russians turned their attention to the inner solar system. Only recently, after the fall of the Communist state, has the tragic fate of the first manned expedition to Venus been revealed. No one who has heard the recordings will forget the screams of the two unlucky cosmonauts as their descent capsule was cooked and crushed in Venus's infernal atmosphere. There's no derring-do here: only horror. What had been intended as a *coup de théâtre* to trump the British expedition to Mars became a tragedy that was hastily covered over, and Sir Bill has cannily exploited the recent openness of the new Russian government to secure at first hand accounts of the Venus disaster. The first Russian landing on Mercury, four years later, in 1972, was of course more successful, establishing solar-powered robot mining facilities and a rail gun which within a year began to launch back to Earth packages of refined precious metals, immensely enriching the Russian economy, and starting in earnest the race to commercially exploit the solar system.

By this time the British had established a permanent colony on the Moon, and a dozen expeditions were exploring her surface in powerful tractors. Early space suits, which had borrowed their design from deep sea diving outfits, heavily armoured and with pincers instead of gloves, had given way to more comfortable suits based on the indestructible cloth invented by Sidney Stratton, with integral life support backpacks instead of heavy metal air cylinders. There was also a semi-permanent scientific station on Mars. After the disappointment that the fabulous canals of Lowell had been no more than optical illusions and wishful thinking, the British Geological Society was busily exploring vast canyons, craters and volcanoes, and drilling deep for signs of life in the Martian crust. In 1977, to celebrate the Queen's Jubilee, a British climbing expedition planted the Union Jack on top of Mount Elizabeth, the largest volcano in the solar system.

All of this was no longer under the control of the military, but was funded by a mixture of public subscription, commercial money (especially from the BBC's Relay Chain satellite network), and money earned by transporting material for American and Russian projects – just as in the old British

Empire, the new colonies were largely self-funding. Meanwhile, British atomic-powered space ships were carrying out the first surveys of the moons of Jupiter and Saturn. Life was discovered in Europa's salty sub-ice ocean in 1982; the first expedition landed, if that's the right word for a descent to a surface covered in liquid ethane, on Titan in 1988.

While British expeditions are bringing back treasures to the Science Museum, and the British government has built an extensive spaceport in Ceylon to service almost daily flights to Earth orbit and the Moon, the official US space program is still recovering from the political and economic fallout of the Second American Revolution. The Lunar colony founded by Harriman's company had been taken over by the feds in 1977, and used as a dumping ground for dissidents after Nixon was elected to his third term as president. In 1979, a revolt by the imprisoned dissidents led to the foundation of the Lunar Republic and the fall of the Nixon government after a brief bombardment of the American mainland by rocks launched by the Lunar rail gun. Sir Bill's account of the revolt, the former Lunar prison's declaration of independence and the brief war quite rightly highlights the way mainstream history (heavily influenced by Heinlein's colourful but disapproving popular account in *The Moon is a Harsh Mistress*, whose claims that libertarian heroes were suppressed by evil socialist radicals and drug-crazed hippies would be pitiful if they weren't, thanks to the movie version, still so widely held) has unfairly dismissed the discreet but vital help given by the British Lunar colonists to the former prisoners. For as this writer can affirm from personal experience, the phlegmatic Brit scientists were surprisingly sympathetic to us hepcat hippie rebels.

After the revolution, some of the rebels, including William Burroughs and Jack Kerouac, chose to return to Earth, but this wasn't, as Sir Bill claims, a split in our ranks, merely a natural shakedown amongst a bunch of highly creative and mostly anarchic individuals. Many others, including Ken Kesey, Allen Ginsberg, Neil Cassady, Tom Hayden and Noam Chomsky, stayed on to found a new republic that attempted to marry the artistic impulses of many of its members with the technology required for survival. Very soon, we in the New Lunar Utope became expert at building habitats from scratch, and furnishing them with self-sufficient closed ecosystems; something we developed by ourselves by the way, despite Sir Bill's crude hints that we were dependent on British expertise. It just wasn't so, Bill: we *had* to learn to develop efficient closed-loop systems quickly or perish, and as this veteran of Ken Kesey's magic bus tour of the Martian highlands can affirm from personal experience, it was all down to good old Yankee ingenuity.

After the fall of Nixon and the election of Ronald Reagan, détente with the Russians swiftly followed, and the end of the cold war has led to a welcome diversion of funding from the US military space program to the construction of habitats and factories and solar power farms in Earth orbit and at the L5 point between Earth and the Moon. It's a healthy sign, surely, that the habitats are not the transplanted whitebread suburbias of NASA's drawing boards, but are designed by the New Lunar Utope as diverse multicultural centres for any artistic and scientific community that can afford the one-way ticket out of Earth's gravity well.

Meanwhile, the Russians have consolidated their exploitation of the vast resources of Mercury and have begun to mine many near-Earth asteroids. After the fall of Communism, Mercury declared itself an independent republic, and dozens of mining communities scattered through the asteroid belt have declared their autonomy too. Sir Bill's explication of the political links between the former Soviet mining stations and the Free Lunar Utope is enjoyably disapproving. He's forced to admit that the British hegemony is now strongly compromised by plans to extend the alliance to the outer reaches of the solar system by slingshotting seed colonies past Venus towards the newly discovered planetoids of the Kuiper Belt, and his speculation that the Free Lunar Utope and the Autonomous Space Republics have transformed the comet fragment Neo-8 into a multi-generation starship aimed at Tau Ceti reeks of panicky paranoia.

It's understandable that the Brits are nervous. It turns out that the bustling solar system hasn't become the new British

Empire after all, and it's natural that they don't want their tremendous investment in the first robot interstellar probes – due to be launched within the next two years towards the eight extra-solar systems with Earth-like planets discovered by the Newton space telescope on the far side of the Moon – to be upstaged. But hey, whatever happens, and here I'm in complete agreement with Sir Bill: we can only look back fondly and admiringly on the writings of the first prophets of the space age, and marvel at how timid their once outrageously optimistic predictions now seem. Let a thousand flowers bloom!

The Imitation Game

Rudy Rucker

It was a rainy Sunday night, 6 June, 1954. Alan Turing was walking down the liquidly lamp-lit street to the Manchester train station, wearing a long raincoat with a furled umbrella concealed beneath. His Greek paramour Zeno was due on the 9 p.m. train, having taken a ferry from Calais. And, no, the name had no philosophical import, it was simply the boy's name. If all went well, Zeno and Alan would be spending the night together in the sepulchral Manchester Midland travellers' hotel – Alan's own home nearby was watched. He'd booked the hotel room under a pseudonym.

Barring any intrusions from the morals squad, Alan and Zeno would set off bright and early tomorrow for a lovely week of tramping across the hills of the Lake District, free as rabbits, sleeping in serendipitous inns. Alan sent up a fervent prayer, if not to God, then to the deterministic universe's initial boundary condition.

"Let it be so."

Surely the cosmos bore no distinct animus towards homosexuals, and the world might yet grant some peace to the tormented, fretful gnat labelled Alan Turing. But it was by no means a given that the assignation with Zeno would click. Last spring, the suspicious authorities had deported Alan's Norwegian flame Kjell straight back to Bergen before Alan even saw him.

It was as if Alan's persecutors supposed him likely to be teaching his men top-secret code-breaking algorithms, rather than sensually savouring his rare hours of private joy. Although, yes, Alan did relish playing the tutor, and it was in fact conceivable that he might feel the urge to discuss those topics upon which he'd worked during the war years. After all, it was no one but he, Alan Turing, who'd been the brains of the British cryptography team at Bletchley Park, cracking the Nazi Enigma code and shortening the war by several years – little thanks that he'd ever got for that.

The churning of a human mind is unpredictable, as is the anatomy of the human heart. Alan's work on universal machines and computational morphogenesis had convinced him that the world is both deterministic *and* overflowing with endless surprise. His proof of the unsolvability of the Halting Problem had established, at least to Alan's satisfaction, that there could never be any shortcuts for predicting the figures of Nature's stately dance.

Few but Alan had as yet grasped the new order. The prating philosophers still supposed, for instance, that there must be some element of randomness at play in order that each human face be slightly different. Far from it. The differences were simply the computation-amplified results of disparities among the embryos and their wombs – with these disparities stemming in turn from the cosmic computation's orderly unpacking of the universe's initial conditions.

Of late Alan had been testing his ideas with experiments involving the massed cellular computations by which a living organism transforms egg to embryo to adult. Input acorn; output oak. He'd already published his results involving the dappling of a brindle cow, but his latest experiments were so close to magic that he was holding them secret, wanting to refine the work in the alchemical privacy of his starkly under-furnished home. Should all go well, a Nobel prize might grace the burgeoning field of computational morphogenesis. This time Alan didn't want a droning gasbag like Alonzo Church to steal his thunder – as had happened with the Hilbert *Entscheidungsproblem*.

Alan glanced at his watch. Only three minutes till the train arrived. His heart was pounding. Soon he'd be committing lewd and lascivious acts (luscious phrase) with a man in England. To avoid a stint in jail, he'd sworn to abjure this practice – but he'd found wiggle room for his conscience. Given that Zeno was a visiting Greek national, he wasn't, strictly speaking, a "man in England", assuming that "in" was construed to mean "who is a member citizen of". Chop the logic and let the tree of the Knowledge of Good and Evil fall, soundless in the mouldering woods.

It had been nearly a year since Alan had enjoyed manly love – last summer on the island of Corfu with none other than Zeno, who'd taken Alan for a memorable row in his dory. Alan had just been coming off his court-ordered oestrogen treatments, and thanks to the lingering effects of the libido-reducing hormones, the sex had been less intense than one might wish. This coming week would be different. Alan felt randy as a hat rack; his whole being was on the surface of his skin.

Approaching the train station, he glanced back over his shoulder – reluctantly playing the socially assigned role of furtive perv – and sure enough, a weedy whey-faced fellow was mooching along half a block behind, a man with a little round mouth like a lamprey eel's. Officer Harold Jenkins. Devil take the beastly prig!

Alan twitched his eyes forward again, pretending not to have seen the detective. What with the growing trans-Atlantic hysteria over homosexuals and atomic secrets, the security minders grew ever more officious. In these darkening times, Alan sometimes mused that the United States had been colonized by the lowest dregs of British society: sexually obsessed zealots, degenerate criminals, and murderous slave masters.

On the elevated tracks, Zeno's train was pulling in. What to do? Surely Detective Jenkins didn't realize that Alan was meeting this particular train. Alan's incoming mail was vetted by the censors – he estimated that by now Her Majesty was employing the equivalent of two point seven workers full time to torment that disgraced boffin, Professor A. M. Turing. But –

score one for Prof. Turing – his written communications with Zeno had been encrypted via a sheaf of one-time pads he'd left in Corfu with his golden-eyed Greek god, bringing a matching sheaf home. Alan had made the pads from clipped-out sections of identical newspapers; he'd also built Zeno a cardboard cipher wheel to simplify the look-ups.

No, no, in all likelihood, Jenkins was in this louche district on a routine patrol, although now, having spotted Turing, he would of course dog his steps. The arches beneath the elevated tracks were the precise spot where, two years ago, Alan had connected with a sweet-faced boy whose dishonesty had led to Alan's conviction for acts of gross indecency. Alan's arrest had been to some extent his own doing; he'd been foolish enough to call the police when one of the boy's friends burgled his house. "Silly ass", Alan's big brother had said. Remembering the phrase made Alan wince and snicker. A silly ass in a dunce's cap, with donkey ears. A suffering human being nonetheless.

The train screeched to stop, puffing out steam. The doors of the carriages slammed open. Alan would have loved to sashay up there like Snow White on the palace steps. But how to shed Jenkins?

Not to worry; he'd prepared a plan. He darted into the men's public lavatory, inwardly chuckling at the vile, voyeuristic thrill that disc-mouthed Jenkins must feel to see his quarry going to earth. The echoing stony chamber was redolent with the rich scent of putrefying urine, the airborne biochemical signature of an immortal colony of micro-organisms indigenous to the standing waters of the train station *pissoir*. It put Alan in mind of his latest Petri-dish experiments at home. He'd learned to grow stripes, spots and spirals in the flat mediums, and then he'd moved into the third dimension. He'd grown tentacles, hairs, and, just yesterday, a congelation of tissue very like a human ear.

Like a thieves' treasure cave, the wonderful lavatory ran straight through to the other side of the elevated track – with an exit on the far side. Striding through the room's length, Alan drew out his umbrella, folded his mackintosh into a small bundle tucked beneath one arm, and hiked up the over-long

pants of his dark suit to display the prominent red tartan spats
that he'd worn, the spats a joking gift from a Cambridge friend.
Exiting the jakes on the other side of the tracks, Alan opened his
high-domed umbrella and pulled it low over his head. With the
spats and dark suit replacing the beige mac and ground-
dragging cuffs, he looked quite the different man from before.

Not risking a backward glance, he clattered up the stairs to
the platform. And there was Zeno, his handsome, bearded face
alight. Zeno was tall for a Greek, with much the same build as
Alan's. As planned, Alan paused briefly by Zeno as if asking a
question, privily passing him a little map and a key to their room
at the Midland Hotel. And then Alan was off down the street,
singing in the rain, leading the way.

Alan didn't notice Detective Jenkins following him in an
unmarked car. Once Jenkins had determined where Alan and
Zeno were bound, he put in a call to the security office at MI5.
The matter was out of his hands now.

The sex was even more enjoyable than Alan had hoped. He
and Zeno slept till mid-morning, Zeno's leg heavy across his,
the two of them spooned together in one of the room's twin
beds. Alan awoke to a knocking on the door, followed by a
rattling of keys.

He sprang across the carpet and leaned against the door.
"We're still asleep," he said, striving for an authoritative tone.

"The dining room's about to close," whined a woman's
voice. "Might I bring the gentlemen their breakfast in the
room?"

"Indeed," said Alan through the door. "A British breakfast
for two. We have a train to catch rather soon." Earlier this week,
he'd had his housekeeper send his bag ahead to Cumbria in the
Lake District.

"Very good, sir. Full breakfast for two."

"Wash," said Zeno, sticking his head out of the bathroom. At
the sound of the maid, he'd darted right in there and started the
tub. He looked happy. "Hot water."

Alan joined Zeno in the bath for a minute, and the dear boy
brought him right off. But then Alan grew anxious about the
return of the maid. He donned his clothes and rucked up the

second bed so it would look slept in. Now Zeno emerged from his bath, utterly lovely in his nudity. Anxious Alan shooed him into his clothes. Finally the maid appeared with the platters of food, really quite a nice-looking breakfast, with kippers, sausages, fried eggs, toast, honey, marmalade, cream and a lovely great pot of tea, steaming hot.

Seeing the maid face to face, Alan realized they knew each other; she was the cousin of his housekeeper. Although the bent little woman feigned not to recognize him, he could see in her eyes that she knew exactly what he and Zeno were doing here. And there was a sense that she knew something more. She gave him a particularly odd look when she poured out the two mugs of tea. Wanting to be shut of her, Alan handed her a coin and she withdrew.

"Milk tea," said Zeno, tipping half his mug back into the pot and topping it up with cream. He raised the mug as if in a toast, then slurped most of it down. Alan's tea was still too hot for his lips, so he simply waved his mug and smiled.

It seemed that even with the cream, Zeno's tea was very hot indeed. Setting his mug down with a clatter, he began fanning his hands at his mouth, theatrically gasping for breath. Alan took it for a joke, and let out one of his grating laughs. But this was no farce.

Zeno squeaked and clutched at his throat; beads of sweat covered his face; foam coated his lips. He dropped to the floor in a heap, spasmed his limbs like a starfish, and beat a tattoo on the floor.

Hardly knowing what to think, Alan knelt over his inert friend, massaging his chest. The man had stopped breathing; he had no pulse. Alan made as if to press his mouth to Zeno's, hoping to resuscitate him. But then he smelled bitter almonds – the classic sign of cyanide poisoning.

Recoiling as abruptly as a piece of spring-loaded machinery, Alan ran into the bathroom and rinsed out his mouth. Her Majesty's spy-masters had gone mad; they'd meant to murder them both. In the Queen's eyes, Alan was an even greater risk than a rogue atomic scientist. Alan's cryptographic work on breaking the Enigma code was a secret secret – the very existence of his work was unknown to the public at large.

His only hope was to slip out of the country and take on a new life. But how? He thought distractedly of the ear-shaped form he'd grown in the Petri dish at home. Why not a new face?

Alan leaned over Zeno, rubbing his poor, dear chest. The man was very dead. Alan went and listened by the room's door. Were MI5 agents lurking without, showing their teeth like hideous omnivorous ghouls? But he heard not a sound. The likeliest possibility was that some low-ranking operative had paid the maid to let him dose the tea – and had then got well out of the way. Perhaps Alan had a little time.

He imagined setting his internal computational system to double speed. Stepping lively, he exchanged clothes with Zeno – a bit tricky as the other man's body was so limp. Better than rigor mortis, at any rate.

Finding a pair of scissors in Zeno's travel kit, Alan trimmed off the pathetic, noble beard, sticking the whiskers to his own chin with smears of honey. A crude initial imitation, a first-order effect.

Alan packed Zeno's bag and made an effort to lift the corpse to his feet. Good lord but this was hard. Alan thought to tie a necktie to the suitcase, run the tie over his shoulder and knot it around Zeno's right arm. If Alan held the suitcase in his left hand, it made a useful counterweight.

It was a good thing that, having survived the oestrogen treatments, Alan had begun training again. He was very nearly as fit as in his early thirties. Suitcase in place, right arm tightly wrapped around Zeno's midriff and grasping the man's belt, Alan waltzed his friend down the hotel's back stairs, emerging into a car park where, thank you Great Algorithmist, a cabbie was having a smoke.

"My friend Turing is sick," said Alan, mustering an imitation of a Greek accent. "I want take him home."

"Blind pissed of a Monday morn," cackled the cabbie, jumping to his own conclusions. "That's the high life for the fair. And red spats! What's our toff's address?"

With a supreme effort, Alan swung Zeno into the cab's rear seat and sat next to him. Alan reached into the body's coat and pretended to read off his home address. Nobody seemed to be tailing the cab. The spooks were lying low, lest blame for the murder fall upon them.

As soon as the cab drew up to Alan's house, he overpaid the driver and dragged Zeno to his feet, waving off all offers of assistance. He didn't want the cabbie to get a close look at the crude honey-sticky beard on his chin. And then he was in his house, which was blessedly empty, Monday being the house-keeper's day off. Moving from window to window, Alan drew the curtains.

He dressed Zeno in Turing pajamas, laid him out in the professorial bed, and vigorously washed the corpse's face, not forgetting to wash his own hands afterwards. Seeking out an apple from the kitchen, he took two bites, then dipped the rest of the apple into a solution of potassium cyanide that he happened to have about the place in a jam jar. He'd always loved the scene in *Snow White and the Seven Dwarfs* when the Wicked Witch lowers an apple into a cauldron of poison. Dip the apple in the brew, let the sleeping death seep through!

Alan set the poison apple down beside Zeno. A Snow White suicide. Now to perfect the imitation game.

He laboured all afternoon. He found a pair of baking sheets in the kitchen – the housekeeper often did baking for him. He poured a quarter-inch of his specially treated gelatin solution onto each sheet – as it happened, the gelatin was from the bones of a pig. Man's best friend. He set the oven on its lowest heat, and slid in the baking sheets, leaving the oven door wide open so he could watch. Slowly the medium jelled. Alan's customized jelly contained a sagacious mixture of activator and inhibitor compounds; it was tailored to promote just the right kind of embryological reaction-diffusion computation.

Carefully wielding a scalpel, Alan cut a tiny fleck of skin from the tip of Zeno's cold nose. He set the fleck into the middle of the upper cookie sheet, and then looked in the mirror, preparing to repeat the process on himself. Oh blast, he still had honey and hair on his chin. Silly ass. Carefully he swabbed off the mess with toilet paper, flushing the evidence down the commode. And then he took the scalpel to his own nose.

After he set his fleck of tissue into place on the lower pan, his tiny cut *would* keep on bleeding, and he had to spend nearly half an hour staunching the spot, greatly worried that he might scatter drops of blood around. Mentally he was running double-strength error-checking routines to keep himself from mucking things up. It was so very hard to be tidy.

When his housekeeper arrived tomorrow morning, Alan's digs should look chaste, sarcophagal, Egyptian. The imitation Turing corpse would be a mournful memento mori of a solitary life gone wrong, and the puzzled poisoners would hesitate to intervene. The man who knew too much would be dead; that was primary desideratum. After a perfunctory inquest, the Turing replica would be cremated, bringing the persecution to a halt. And Alan's mother might forever believe that her son's death was an accident. For years she'd been chiding him over his messy fecklessness with the chemicals in his home lab.

Outside a car drove past very slowly. The brutes were wondering what was going on. Yet they hesitated to burst in, lest the neighbours learn of their perfidy. With shaking hands, Alan poured himself a glass of sherry. Steady, old man. See this through.

He pulled up a kitchen chair and sat down to stare through the open oven door. Like puffing pastry, the flecks of skin were rising up from the cookie sheets, with discs of cellular growth radiating out as the tissues grew. Slowly the noses hove into view, and then the lips, the eye holes, the forehead, the chins. As the afternoon light waned, Alan saw the faces age, Zeno on the top, Alan on the bottom. They began as innocent babes, became pert boys, spotty youths, and finally grown men.

Ah, the pathos of biology's irreversible computations, thought Alan, forcing a wry smile. But the orotund verbiage of academe did little to block the pain. Dear Zeno was dead. Alan's life as he'd known it was at an end. He wept.

It was dark outside now. Alan drew the pans from the oven, shuddering at the enormity of what he'd wrought. The uncanny empty-eyed faces had an expectant air; they were like holiday piecrusts, waiting for steak and kidney, for mincemeat and plums.

Bristles had pushed out of the two flaccid chins, forming little beards. Time to slow down the computation. One didn't want the wrinkles of extreme old age. Alan doused the living faces with inhibitor solution, damping their cellular computations to a normal rate.

He carried the bearded Turing face into his bedroom and pressed it onto the corpse. The tissues took hold, sinking in a bit, which was good. Using his fingers, Alan smoothed the joins at the edges of the eyes and lips. As the living face absorbed cyanide from the dead man's tissues, its colour began to fade. A few minutes later, the face was waxen and dead. The illusion was nearly complete.

Alan momentarily lost his composure and gagged; he ran to the toilet and vomited, though little came up. He'd neglected to eat anything today other than those two bites of apple. Finally his stomach-spasms stopped. In full error-correction mode, he remembered to wash his hands several times before wiping his face. And then he drank two pints of water from the tap.

He took his razor and shaved the still-bearded dead Turing face in his bed. The barbering went faster than when he'd shaved Zeno in the hotel. It was better to stand so that he saw the face upside down. Was barbering a good career? Surely he'd never work as a scientist again. Given any fresh input, the halted Turing persecution would resume.

Alan cleaned up once more and drifted back into the kitchen. Time to skulk out through the dark garden with Zeno's passport, bicycle through the familiar woods to a station down the line, and catch a train. Probably the secret police wouldn't be much interested in pursuing Zeno. They'd be glad Zeno had posed their murder as a suicide, and the less questions asked the better.

But to be safe, Turing would flee along an unexpected route. He'd take the train to Plymouth, the ferry from there to Santander on the north coast of Spain, a train south through Spain to the Mediterranean port of Tarifa, and another ferry from Tarifa to Tangiers.

Tangiers was an open city, an international zone. He could buy a fresh passport there. He'd be free to live as he liked – in a small way. Perhaps he'd master the violin. And read the *Iliad* in Greek. Alan glanced down at the flaccid Zeno face, imagining himself as a Greek musician.

If you were me, from A to Z, if I were you, from Z to A . . .

Alan caught himself. His mind was spinning in loops, avoiding what had to be done next. It was time.

He scrubbed his features raw and donned his new face.

Weinachtsabend

Keith Roberts

1

The big car moved slowly, nosing its way along narrowing lanes. Here, beyond the little market town of Wilton, the snow lay thicker. Trees and bushes loomed in the headlights, coated with driven white. The tail of the Mercedes wagged slightly, steadied. Mainwaring heard the chauffeur swear under his breath. The link had been left live.

Dials let into the seat back recorded the vehicle's mechanical well-being; oil pressure, temperature, revs, kph. Lights from the repeater glowed softly on his companion's face. She moved, restlessly; he saw the swing of yellow hair. He turned slightly. She was wearing a neat, brief kilt, heavy boots. Her legs were excellent.

He clicked the dial lights off. He said, "Not much farther."

He wondered if she was aware of the open link. He said, "First time down?"

She nodded in the dark. She said, "I was a bit overwhelmed."

Wilton Great House sprawled across a hilltop five miles or more beyond the town. The car drove for some distance beside the wall that fringed the estate. The perimeter defences had been strengthened since Mainwaring's last visit. Watchtowers reared at intervals; the wall itself had been topped by multiple strands of wire.

The lodge gates were commanded by two new stone

pillboxes. The Merc edged between them, stopped. On the road from London, the snow had eased; now big flakes drifted again, lit by the headlights. Somewhere, orders were barked.

A man stepped forward, tapped at the window. Mainwaring buttoned it open. He saw a GFP armband, a hip holster with the flap tucked back. He said, "Good evening, Captain."

"*Guten Abend, mein Herr. Ihre Ausweis Karte?*"

Cold air gusted against Mainwaring's cheek. He passed across his identity card and security clearance. He said, "*Richard Mainwaring. Die rechte Hand zu dem Gesanten. Fraülein Hunter, von meiner Abteilung.*"

A torch flashed over the papers, dazzled into his eyes, moved to examine the girl. She sat stiffly, staring ahead. Beyond the Security officer Mainwaring made out two steel-helmeted troopers, automatics slung. In front of him, the wipers clicked steadily.

The GFP man stepped back. He said, "*In einer Woche, Ihre Ausweis Karte ist ausgelaufen. Erneuen Sie Ihre Karte.*"

Mainwaring said, "*Vielen Dank, Herr Hauptmann. Frohe Weihnacht.*"

The man saluted stiffly, unclipped a walkie-talkie from his belt. A pause, and the gates swung back. The Merc creamed through. Mainwaring said, "*Bastard . . .*"

She said, "Is it always like this?"

He said, "They're tightening up all round."

She pulled her coat round her shoulders. She said, "Frankly, I find it a bit scary."

He said, "Just the Minister taking care of his guests."

Wilton stood in open downland set with great trees. Hans negotiated a bend, carefully, drove beneath half-seen branches. The wind moaned, zipping round a quarterlight. It was as if the car butted into a black tunnel, full of swirling pale flakes. He thought he saw her shiver. He said, "Soon be there."

The headlamps lit a rolling expanse of snow. Posts, buried nearly to their tops, marked the drive. Another bend, and the house showed ahead. The car lights swept across a facade of mullioned windows, crenellated towers. Hard for the uniniti-ated to guess, staring at the skilfully weathered stone, that the shell of the place was of reinforced concrete. The car swung right with a crunching of unseen gravel, and stopped. The ignition repeater glowed on the seat back.

Mainwaring said, "Thank you, Hans. Nice drive."

Hans said. "My pleasure, sir."

She flicked her hair free, picked up her handbag. He held the door for her. He said, "OK, Diane?"

She shrugged. She said, "Yes. I'm a bit silly sometimes." She squeezed his hand, briefly. She said, "I'm glad you'll be here. Somebody to rely on."

Mainwaring lay back on the bed and stared at the ceiling. Inside as well as out, Wilton was a triumph of art over nature. Here, in the Tudor wing where most of the guests were housed, walls and ceilings were of wavy plaster framed by heavy oak beams. He turned his head. The room was dominated by a fireplace of yellow Ham stone; on the overmantel, carved in bold relief, the *hakenkreuz* was flanked by the lion and eagle emblems of the Two Empires. A fire burned in the wrought-iron basket; the logs glowed cheerfully, casting wavering warm reflections across the ceiling. Beside the bed a bookshelf offered required reading; the Fuehrer's official biography, Shirer's *Rise of the Third Reich*, Cummings' monumental *Churchill: the Trial of Decadence*. There were a nicely bound set of Buchan novels, some Kiplings, a Shakespeare, a complete Wilde. A side table carried a stack of current magazines; *Connoisseur, The Field, Der Spiegel, Paris Match.* There was a washstand, its rail hung with dark blue towels; in the corner of the room were the doors to the bathroom and wardrobe, in which a servant had already neatly disposed his clothes.

He stubbed his cigarette, lit another. He swung his legs off the bed, poured himself a whisky. From the grounds, faintly, came voices, snatches of laughter. He heard the crash of a pistol, the rattle of an automatic. He walked to the window, pushed the curtain aside. Snow was still falling, drifting silently from the black sky; but the firing pits beside the big house were brightly lit. He watched the figures move and bunch for a while, let the curtain fall. He sat by the fire, shoulders hunched, staring into the flames. He was remembering the trip through London; the flags hanging limp over Whitehall, slow, jerking movement of traffic, the light tanks drawn up outside St James. The Kensington Road had been crowded, traffic edging and hooting; the vast frontage of Harrods looked grim and oriental against the louring sky. He frowned, remembering the call he had had before leaving the Ministry.

Kosowicz had been the name. From *Time International*; or so he had claimed. He'd refused twice to speak to him; but Kosowicz had been insistent. In the end, he'd asked his secretary to put him through.

Kosowicz had sounded very American. He said, "Mr Mainwaring, I'd like to arrange a personal interview with your Minister."

"I'm afraid that's out of the question. I must also point out that this communication is extremely irregular."

Kosowicz said, "What do I take that as, sir? A warning, or a threat?"

Mainwaring said carefully, "It was neither. I merely observed that proper channels of approach do exist."

Kosowicz said, "Uh-huh. Mr Mainwaring, what's the truth behind this rumour that Action Groups are being moved into Moscow?"

Mainwaring said, "Deputy-Fuehrer Hess has already issued a statement on the situation. I can see that you're supplied with a copy."

The phone said, "I have it before me. Mr Mainwaring, what are you people trying to set up? Another Warsaw?"

Mainwaring said, "I'm afraid I can't comment further, Mr Kosowicz. The Deputy-Fuehrer deplored the necessity of force. The *Einsatzgruppen* have been alerted; at this time, that is all. They will be used if necessary to disperse militants. As of this moment, the need has not arisen."

Kosowicz shifted his ground. "You mentioned the Deputy-Fuehrer, sir. I hear there was another bomb attempt two nights ago, can you comment on this?"

Mainwaring tightened his knuckles on the handset. He said,

"I'm afraid you've been misinformed. We know nothing of any such incident."

The phone was silent for a moment. Then it said, "Can I take your denial as official?"

Mainwaring said, "This is not an official conversation. I'm not empowered to issue statements in any respect."

The phone said, "Yeah, channels do exist. Mr Mainwaring, thanks for your time."

Mainwaring said, "Goodbye." He put the handset down, sat staring at it. After a while he lit a cigarette.

Outside the windows of the Ministry the snow still fell, a dark whirl and dance against the sky. His tea, when he came to drink it, was half cold.

The fire crackled and shifted. He poured himself another whisky, sat back. Before leaving for Wilton, he'd lunched with Winsby-Walker from Productivity. Winsby-Walker made it his business to know everything; but he had known nothing of a correspondent called Kosowicz. He thought, "I should have checked with Security." But then, Security would have checked with him.

He sat up, looked at his watch. The noise from the ranges had diminished. He turned his mind with a deliberate effort into another channel. The new thoughts brought no more comfort. Last Christmas he had spent with his mother; now, that couldn't happen again. He remembered other Christmases, back across the years. Once, to the child unknowing, they had been gay affairs of crackers and toys. He remembered the scent and texture of pine branches, closeness of candlelight; and books read by torchlight under the sheets, the hard angles of the filled pillowslip, heavy at the foot of the bed. Then, he had been complete; only later, slowly, had come the knowledge of failure. And with it, loneliness. He thought, "She wanted to see me settled. It didn't seem much to ask."

The Scotch was making him maudlin. He drained the glass, walked through to the bathroom. He stripped, and showered. Towelling himself, he thought, "Richard Mainwaring, Personal Assistant to the British Minister of Liaison." Aloud he said, "One must remember the compensations."

He dressed, lathered his face and began to shave. He thought, 'Thirty-five is the exact middle of one's life.' He was remembering another time with the girl Diane when just for a little while some magic had interposed. Now, the affair was never mentioned between them. Because of James. Always, of course, there is a James.

He towelled his face, applied aftershave. Despite himself, his mind had drifted back to the phone call. One fact was certain; there had been a major security spillage. Somebody somewhere had supplied Kosowicz with closely guarded information. That same someone, presumably, had supplied a list of ex-directory lines. He frowned, grappling with the problem. One country, and one only, opposed the Two Empires with gigantic, latent strength. To that country had shifted the focus of Semitic nationalism. And Kosowicz had been an American.

He thought, 'Freedom, schmeedom. Democracy is Jew-shaped.' He frowned again, fingering his face. It didn't alter the salient fact. The tip-off had come from the Freedom Front; and he had been contacted, however obliquely. Now, he had become an accessory; the thought had been nagging at the back of his brain all day.

He wondered what they could want of him. There was a rumour – a nasty rumour – that you never found out. Not till the end, till you'd done whatever was required from you. They were untiring, deadly and subtle. He hadn't run squalling to Security at the first hint of danger; but that would have been allowed for. Every turn and twist would have been allowed for.

Every squirm, on the hook.

He grunted, angry with himself. Fear was half their strength. He buttoned his shirt remembering the guards at the gates, the wire and pillboxes. Here, of all places, nothing could reach him. For a few days, he could forget the whole affair. He said aloud, "Anyway, I don't even matter. I'm not important." The thought cheered him, nearly.

He clicked the light off, walked through to his room, closed the door behind him. He crossed to the bed and stood quite still, staring at the bookshelf. Between Shirer and the Churchill tome there rested a third slim volume. He reached to touch the spine, delicately; read the author's name, Geissler, and the title. *Toward Humanity.* Below the title, like a topless Cross of Lorraine, were the twin linked Fs of the Freedom Front.

Ten minutes ago, the book hadn't been there.

He walked to the door. The corridor beyond was deserted. From somewhere in the house, faintly, came music; *Till Eulenspiegel.* There were no nearer sounds. He closed the door again, locked it. Turned back and saw the wardrobe stood slightly ajar.

His case still lay on the sidetable. He crossed to it, took out the Luger. The feel of the heavy pistol was comforting. He pushed the clip home, thumbed the safety forward, chambered a round. The breach closed with a hard snap. He walked to the wardrobe, shoved the door wide with his foot.

Nothing there.

He let his held breath escape with a little hiss. He pressed the clip release, ejected the cartridge, laid the gun on the bed. He stood again looking at the shelf. He thought, 'I must have been mistaken.'

He took the book down, carefully. Geissler had been banned since publication in every Province of the Two Empires; Mainwaring himself had never even seen a copy. He squatted on the edge of the bed, opened the thing at random.

"The doctrine of Aryan co-ancestry, seized on so eagerly by the English middle classes, had the superficial reason-ableness of most theories ultimately traceable to Rosenberg. Churchill's answer, in one sense, had already been made; but Chamberlain, and the country, turned to Hess . . ."

"The Cologne settlement, though seeming to offer hope of security to Jews already domiciled in Britain, in fact paved the way for campaigns of intimidation and extortion similar to those already undertaken in history, notably by King John. The comparison is not unapt; for the English *bourgeoisie,* anxious to construct a rationale, discovered many unassailable precedents. A true Sign of the Times, almost certainly, was the resurgence of interest in the novels of Sir Walter Scott. By 1942 the lesson had been learned on both sides; and the Star of David was a common sight on the streets of most British cities."

The wind rose momentarily in a long wail, shaking the window casement. Mainwaring glanced up, turned his attention back to the hook. He leafed through several pages.

"In 1940, her Expeditionary Force shattered, her allies quiescent or defeated, the island truly stood alone. Her proletariat, bedevilled by bad leadership, weakened by a gigantic depression, was effectively without a voice. Her aristocracy, like their *Junker* counterparts, embraced coldly what could no longer be ignored; while after the Whitehall *Putsch* the Cabinet was reduced to the status of an Executive Council . . ."

The knock at the door made him start, guiltily. He pushed the book away. He said, "Who's that?"

She said, "Me. Richard, aren't you ready?"

He said, "Just a minute." He stared at the book, then placed it back on the shelf. He thought, 'That at least wouldn't be expected.' He slipped the Luger into his case and closed it. Then he went to the door.

She was wearing a lacy black dress. Her shoulders were bare; her hair, worn loose, had been brushed till it gleamed. He stared at her a moment, stupidly. Then he said, "Please come in."

She said, "I was starting to wonder . . . Are you all right?"

"Yes. Yes, of course."

She said, "You look as if you'd seen a ghost."

He smiled. He said, "I expect I was taken aback. Those Aryan good looks."

She grinned at him. She said, "I'm half Irish, half English, half Scandinavian. If you have to know."

"That doesn't add up."

She said, "Neither do I, most of the time."

"Drink?"

"Just a little one. We shall be late."

He said, "It's not very formal tonight." He turned away, fiddling with his tie.

She sipped her drink, pointed her foot, scuffed her toe on the carpet. She said, "I expect you've been to a lot of houseparties."

He said, "One or two."

She said, "Richard, are they . . ."

"Are they what?"

She said, "I don't know. You can't help hearing things."

He said, "You'll be all right. One's very much like the next."

She said, "Are you honestly OK?"

"Sure."

She said, "You're all thumbs. Here, let me." She reached up, knotted deftly. Her eyes searched his face for a moment, moving in little shifts and changes of direction. She said, "There. I think you just need looking after."

He said carefully, "How's James?"

She stared a moment longer. She said, "I don't know. He's in Nairobi. I haven't seen him for months."

He said, "I am a bit nervous, actually."

"Why?"

He said, "Escorting a rather lovely blonde."

She tossed her head, and laughed. She said, "You need a drink as well then."

He poured whisky, said, "Cheers." The book, now, seemed to be burning into his shoulderblades.

She said, "As a matter of fact you're looking rather fetching yourself."

He thought, 'This is the night, when all things come together. There should be a word for it.' Then he remembered about *Till Eulenspiegel*.

She said, "We'd honestly better go down."'

Lights gleamed in the Great Hall, reflecting from polished boards, dark linenfold panelling. At the nearer end of the chamber a huge fire burned. Beneath the minstrels' gallery long tables had been set. Informal or not, they shone with glass and silverware. Candles glowed amid wreaths of dark evergreen; beside each place was a rolled crimson napkin.

In the middle of the Hall, its tip brushing the coffered ceiling, stood a Christmas tree. Its branches were hung with apples, baskets of sweets, red paper roses; at its base were piled gifts in gay-striped wrappers. Round the tree folk stood in groups, chatting and laughing. Richard saw Müller the Defence Minister, with a striking-looking blonde he took to be his wife; beside them was a tall, monocled man who was something or other in Security. There was a group of GSP officers in their dark, neat uniforms, beyond them half a dozen Liaison people. He saw Hans the chauffeur standing head bent, nodding intently, smiling at some remark, and thought as he had thought before how he looked like a big, handsome ox.

Diane had paused in the doorway, and linked her arm through his. But the Minister had already seen them. He came weaving through the crowd, a glass in his hand. He was wearing tight black trews, a dark blue roll-neck shirt. He looked happy and relaxed. He said, "Richard. And my dear Miss Hunter. We'd nearly given you up for lost. After all, Hans Trapp is about. Now, some drinks. And come, do come; please join my friends. Over here, where it is warm."

She said, "Who's Hans Trapp?"

Mainwaring said, "You'll find out in a bit."

A little later the Minister said, "Ladies and gentlemen, I think we may be seated."

The meal was superb, the wine abundant. By the time the brandy was served Richard found himself talking more easily, and the Geissler copy pushed nearly to the back of his mind. The traditional toasts – King and Fuehrer, the Provinces, the Two Empires – were drunk; then the Minister clapped his hands for quiet. "My friends," he said, "tonight, this special night when we can all mix so freely, is *Weihnachtsabend.* It means, I suppose, many things to the many of us here. But let us remember, first and foremost, that this is the night of the children. Your children, who have come with you to share part at least of this very special Christmas."

He paused. "Already," he said, "they have been called from their crèche; soon, they will be with us. Let me show them to you." He nodded; at the gesture servants wheeled forward a heavy, ornate box. A drape was twitched aside, revealing the grey surface of a big TV screen. Simultaneously, the lamps that lit the Hall began to dim. Diane turned to Mainwaring, frowning; he touched her hand, gently, and shook his head.

Save for the firelight, the Hall was now nearly dark. The candles guttered in their wreaths, flames stirring in some draught; in the hush, the droning of the wind round the great facade of the place was once more audible. The lights would be out, now, all over the house.

"For some of you," said the Minister, "this is your first visit here. For you, I will explain.

"On *Weinachtsabend*, all ghosts and goblins walk. The demon Hans Trapp is abroad; his face is black and terrible, his clothing the skins of bears. Against him comes the Lightbringer, the Spirit of Christmas. Some call her Lucia Queen, some *Das Christkind*. See her now."

The screen lit up.

She moved slowly, like a sleepwalker. She was slender, and robed in white. Her ashen hair tumbled round her shoulders; above her head glowed a diadem of burning tapers. Behind her trod the Star Boys with their wands and tinsel robes; behind again came a little group of children. They ranged in age from eight- and nine-year-olds to toddlers. They gripped each other's hands, apprehensively, setting feet in line like cats, darting terrified glances at the shadows to either side.

"They lie in darkness, waiting," said the Minister softly. "Their nurses have left them. If they cry out, there is none to hear. So they do not cry out. And one by one, she has called them. They see her light pass beneath the door; and they must rise and follow. Here, where we sit, is warmth. Here is safety. Their gifts are waiting; to reach them, they must run the gauntlet of the dark."

The camera angle changed. Now they were watching the procession from above. The Lucia Queen stepped steadily; the shadows she cast leaped and flickered on panelled walls.

"They are in the Long Gallery now," said the Minister. "Almost directly above us. They must not falter, they must not look back. Somewhere, Hans Trapp is hiding. From Hans, only

Das Christkind can protect them. See how close they bunch behind her light!"

A howling began, like the crying of a wolf. In part it seemed to come from the screen, in part to echo through the Hall itself. The *Christkind* turned, raising her arms; the howling split into a many-voiced cadence, died to a mutter. In its place came a distant huge thudding, like the beating of a drum.

Diane said abruptly, "I don't find this particularly funny."

Mainwaring said, "It isn't supposed to be. Shh."

The Minister said evenly, "The Aryan child must know, from earliest years, the darkness that surrounds him. He must learn to fear, and to overcome that fear. He must learn to be strong. The Two Empires were not built by weakness; weakness will not sustain them. There is no place for it. This in part your children already know. The house is big, and dark; but they will win through to the light. They fight as the Empires once fought. For their birthright."

The shot changed again, showed a wide, sweeping staircase. The head of the little procession appeared, began to descend. "Now, where is our friend Hans?" said the Minister. "*Ah . . .*"

Her grip tightened convulsively on Mainwaring's arm. A black-smeared face loomed at the screen. The bogey snarled, clawing at the camera; then turned, loped swiftly towards the staircase. The children shrieked, and bunched; instantly the air was wild with din. Grotesque figures capered and leaped; hands grabbed, clutching. The column was buffeted and swirled; Mainwaring saw a child bowled completely over. The screaming reached a high pitch of terror; and the *Christkind* turned, arms once more raised. The goblins and werethings backed away, growling, into shadow; the slow march was resumed.

The Minister said, "They are nearly here. And they are good children, worthy of their race. Prepare the tree."

Servants ran forward with tapers to light the many candles. The tree sprang from gloom, glinting, black-green; and Mainwaring thought for the first time what a dark thing it was, although it blazed with light.

The big doors at the end of the Hall were flung back; and the children came tumbling through. Tearstained and sobbing they were, some bruised; but all, before they ran to the tree, stopped, made obeisance to the strange creature who had brought them through the dark. Then the crown was lifted, the tapers extinguished; and Lucia Queen became a child like the rest, a slim, barefooted girl in a gauzy white dress.

The Minister rose, laughing. "Now," he said, "music, and some more wine. Hans Trapp is dead. My friends, one and all, and children; *Frohe weihnacht!*"

Diane said, "Excuse me a moment."

Mainwaring turned. He said, "Are you all right?"

She said, "I'm just going to get rid of a certain taste."

He watched her go, concernedly; and the Minister had his arm, was talking. "Excellent, Richard," he said. "It has gone excellently so far, don't you think?"

Richard said, "Excellently, sir."

"Good, good. Eh, Heidi, Erna . . . and Frederick, is it Frederick? What have you got there? Oh, very fine . . ." He steered Mainwaring away, still with his fingers tucked beneath his elbow. Squeals of joy sounded; somebody had discovered a sled, tucked away behind the tree. The Minister said, "Look at them; how happy they are now. I would like children, Richard. Children of my own. Sometimes I think I have given too much . . . Still, the opportunity remains. I am younger than you, do you realize that? This is the Age of Youth."

Mainwaring said, "I wish the Minister every happiness."

"Richard, Richard, you must learn not to be so very correct at all times. Unbend a little, you are too aware of dignity. You are my friend. I trust you; above all others, I trust you. Do you realize this?"

Richard said, "Thank you, sir. I do."

The Minister seemed bubbling over with some inner pleasure. He said, "Richard, come with me. Just for a moment. I have prepared a special gift for you. I won't keep you from the party very long."

Mainwaring followed, drawn as ever by the curious dynamism of the man. The Minister ducked through an arched doorway, turned right and left, descended a narrow flight of stairs. At the bottom the way was barred by a door of plain grey steel. The Minister pressed his palm flat to a sensor plate; a click, the whine of some mechanism, and the door swung inward. Beyond was a further flight of concrete steps, lit by a single lamp in a heavy well-glass. Chilly air blew upward. Mainwaring realized, with something approaching a shock, that they had entered part of the bunker system that honeycombed the ground beneath Wilton.

The Minister hurried ahead of him, palmed a further door. He said, "Toys, Richard. All toys. But they amuse me." Then, catching sight of Mainwaring's face, "Come, man, come! You are more nervous than the children, frightened of poor old Hans!"

The door gave onto a darkened space. There was a heavy, sweetish smell that Mainwaring, for a whirling moment, couldn't place. His companion propelled him forward gently. He resisted, pressing back; and the Minister's arm shot by him. A click, and the place was flooded with light. He saw a wide, low area, also concrete-built. To one side, already polished and gleaming, stood the Mercedes, next it the Minister's private Porsche. There were a couple of Volkswagens, a Ford Executive; and in the farthest corner, a vision in glinting white. A Lamborghini. They had emerged in the garage underneath the house.

The Minister said, "My private short cut." He walked forward to the Lamborghini, stood running his fingers across the low, broad bonnet. He said, "Look at her, Richard. Here, sit in. Isn't she a beauty? Isn't she fine?"

Mainwaring said, "She certainly is."

"You like her?"

Mainwaring smiled. He said, "Very much sir. Who wouldn't?"

The Minister said, "Good, I'm so pleased. Richard, I'm upgrading you. She's yours. Enjoy her."

Mainwaring stared.

The Minister said, "Here, man. Don't look like that, like a fish. Here, see. Logbook, your keys. All entered up, finished." He gripped Mainwaring's shoulders, swung him round laughing. He said, "You've worked well for me. The Two Empires don't forget. Their good friends, their servants."

Mainwaring said, "I'm deeply honoured, sir."

"Don't be honoured. You're still being formal, Richard . . ."

"Sir?"

The Minister said, "Stay by me. Stay by me. Up there they don't understand. But we understand . . . eh? These are difficult times. We must be together, always together. Kingdom, and Reich. Apart . . . we could be destroyed." He turned away, placed clenched hands on the roof of the car. He said, "Here, all this. Jewry, the Americans . . . Capitalism. They must stay afraid. Nobody fears an Empire divided. It would fall!"

Mainwaring said, "I'll do my best, sir. We all will."

The Minister said, "I know, I know. But Richard, this afternoon. I was playing with swords. Silly little swords."

Mainwaring thought, 'I know how he keeps me. I can see the mechanism. But I mustn't imagine I know the entire truth.'

The Minister turned back, as if in pain. He said, "Strength is Right. It has to be. But Hess . . ."

Mainwaring said slowly, "We've tried before, sir . . ."

The Minister slammed his fist onto the metal. He said, "Richard, don't you see? It wasn't us. Not this time. It was his own people. Baumann, von Thaden . . . I can't tell. He's an old man, he doesn't matter any more. It's an idea they want to kill, Hess is an idea. Do you understand? It's *Lebensraum*. Again . . . Half the world isn't enough."

He straightened. He said, "The worm, in the apple. It gnaws, gnaws . . . But we are Liaison. We matter, so much. Richard, be my eyes. Be my ears."

Mainwaring stayed silent, thinking about the book in his room; and the Minister once more took his arm. He said, "The shadows, Richard. They were never closer. Well might we teach our children to fear the dark. But . . . not in our time. Eh? Not for us. There is life, and hope. So much we can do . . ."

Mainwaring thought, 'Maybe it's the wine I drank. I'm being pressed too hard.' A dull, queer mood, almost of indifference, had fallen on him. He followed his Minister without complaint, back through the bunker complex, up to where the great fire burned low and the tapers on the tree. He heard the singing mixed with the wind-voice, watched the children rock heavy-eyed, carolling sleep. The house seemed winding down, to rest; and she had gone of course. He sat in a corner and drank wine and brooded, watched the Minister move from group to group until he too was gone, the Hall nearly empty and the servants clearing away.

He found his own self, his inner self, dozing at last as it dozed at each day's end. Tiredness, as ever, had come like a benison. He rose carefully, walked to the door. He thought, "I shan't be missed here." Shutters closed, in his head.

He found his key, unlocked his room. He thought, 'Now, she will be waiting. Like all the letters that never came, the phones that never rang.' He opened the door.

She said, "What kept you?"

He closed the door behind him, quietly. The fire crackled in the little room, the curtains were drawn against the night. She sat by the hearth, barefooted, still in her party dress. Beside her on the carpet were glasses, an ashtray with half-smoked stubs. One lamp was burning; in the warm light her eyes were huge and dark.

He looked across to the bookshelf. The Geissler stood where he had left it. He said, "How did you get in?"

She chuckled. She said, "There was a spare key on the back of the door. Didn't you see me steal it?"

He walked towards her, stood looking down. He thought, 'Adding another fragment to the puzzle. Too much, too complicated.'

She said, "Are you angry?"

He said, "No."

She patted the floor. She said gently, "Please, Richard. Don't be cross."

He sat, slowly, watching her.

She said, "Drink?" He didn't answer. She poured one anyway. She said, "What were you doing all this time? I thought you'd be up hours ago."

He said, "I was talking to the Minister."

She traced a pattern on the rug with her forefinger. Her hair fell forward, golden and heavy, baring the nape of her neck. She said, "I'm sorry about earlier on. I was stupid. I think I was a bit scared too."

He drank slowly. He felt like a run-down machine. Hell to have to start thinking again at this time of night. He said, "What were you doing?"

She watched up at him. Her eyes were candid. She said, "Sitting here. Listening to the wind."

He said, "That couldn't have been much fun."

She shook her head, slowly, eyes fixed on his face. She said softly, "You don't know me at all."

He was quiet again. She said, "You don't believe in me, do you?"

He thought, 'You need understanding. You're different from the rest; and I'm selling myself short.' Aloud he said, "No."

She put the glass down, smiled, took his glass away. She hotched towards him across the rug, slid her arm round his neck. She said, "I was thinking about you. Making my mind up." She kissed him. He felt her tongue pushing, opened his lips. She said, "*Mmm . . .*" She sat back a little, smiling. She said, "Do you mind?"

"No."

She pressed a strand of hair across her mouth, parted her teeth, kissed again. He felt himself react, involuntarily; and felt her touch and squeeze.

She said, "This is a silly dress. It gets in the way." She reached behind her. The fabric parted; she pushed down, to the waist. She said, "Now it's like last time."

He said slowly, "Nothing's ever like last time."

She rolled across his lap, lay watching up. She whispered, "I've put the clock back."

Later in the dream she said, "I was so silly."

"What do you mean?"

She said, "I was shy. That was all. You weren't really supposed to go away."

He said, "What about James?"

"He's got somebody else. I didn't know what I was missing."

He let his hand stray over her; and present and immediate

past became confused so that as he held her he still saw her kneeling, firelight dancing on her body. He reached for her and she was ready again; she fought, chuckling, taking it bareback, staying all the way.

Much later he said, "The Minister gave me a Lamborghini."

She rolled onto her belly, lay chin in hands watching under a tangle of hair. She said, "And now you've got yourself a blonde. What are you going to do with us?"

He said, "None of it's real."

She said, "*Oh* . . ." She punched him. She said, "Richard, you make me cross. It's happened, you idiot. That's all. It happens to everybody." She scratched again with a finger on the carpet. She said, "I hope you've made me pregnant. Then you'd have to marry me."

He narrowed his eyes; and the wine began again, singing in his head.

She nuzzled him. She said, "You asked me once. Say it again."

"I don't remember."

She said, "Richard, please . . ." So he said, "Diane, will you marry me?" And she said, "Yes, yes, yes," then afterwards awareness came and though it wasn't possible he took her again and that time was finest of all, tight and sweet as honey. He'd fetched pillows from the bed and the counterpane, they curled close and he found himself talking, talking, how it wasn't the sex, it was shopping in Marlborough and having tea and seeing the sun set from White Horse Hill and being together, together; then she pressed fingers to his mouth and he fell with her in sleep past cold and loneliness and fear, past deserts and unlit places, down maybe to where spires reared gold and tree leaves moved and dazzled and white cars sang on roads and suns burned inwardly, lighting new worlds.

He woke, and the fire was low. He sat up, dazed. She was watching him. He stroked her hair awhile, smiling; then she pushed away. She said, "Richard, I have to go now."

"Not yet."

"It's the middle of the night."

He said, "It doesn't matter."

She said, "It does. He mustn't know."

"Who?"

She said, "You know who. You know why I was asked here."

He said, "He's not like that. Honestly."

She shivered. She said, "Richard, please. Don't get me in trouble." She smiled. She said, "It's only till tomorrow. Only a little while."

He stood, awkwardly, and held her, pressing her warmth close. Shoeless, she was tiny; her shoulder fitted beneath his armpit.

Halfway through dressing she stopped and laughed, leaned a hand against the wall. She said, "I'm all woozy."

Later he said, "I'll see you to your room."

She said, "No, please. I'm all right." She was holding her handbag, and her hair was combed. She looked, again, as if she had been to a party.

At the door she turned. She said, "I love you, Richard. Truly." She kissed again, quickly; and was gone.

He closed the door, dropped the latch. He stood a while looking round the room. In the fire a burned-through log broke with a snap, sending up a little whirl of sparks. He walked to the washstand, bathed his face and hands. He shook the counterpane out on the bed, rearranged the pillows. Her scent still clung to him; he remembered how she had felt, and what she had said.

He crossed to the window, pushed it ajar. Outside, the snow lay in deep swaths and drifts. Starlight gleamed from it, ghost-white; and the whole great house was mute. He stood feeling the chill move against his skin; and in all the silence, a voice drifted far-off and clear. It came maybe from the guardhouses, full of distance and peace.

"*Stille Nacht, heilige Nacht,*
alle's schläfte, einsam wacht . . ."

He walked to the bed, pulled back the covers. The sheets were crisp and spotless, fresh-smelling. He smiled, and turned off the lamp.

"*Nur das traute, hoc heilige Paar.*
Holder Knabe im lochigen Haar . . ."

In the wall of the room, an inch behind the plasterwork, a complex little machine hummed. A spool of delicate golden wire shook slightly; but the creak of the opening window had been the last thing to interest the recorder, the singing alone couldn't activate its relays. A micro-switch tripped, inaudibly; valve filaments faded, and died. Mainwaring lay back in the last of the firelight, and closed his eyes.

"*Schlaf' in himmlischer Ruh,*
Schlaf' in himmlischer Ruh . . ."

2

Beyond drawn curtains, brightness flicks on.

The sky is a hard, clear blue; icy, full of sunlight. The light dazzles back from the brilliant land. Far things – copses, hills, solitary trees – stand sharp-etched. Roofs and eaves carry hummocks of whiteness, twigs a three-inch crest. In the stillness, here and there, the snow cracks and falls, powdering.

The shadows of the riders jerk and undulate. The quiet is interrupted. Hooves ring on swept courtyards or stamp muffled, churning the snow. It seems the air itself has been rendered crystalline by cold; through it the voices break and shatter, brittle as glass.

"*Guten morgen, Hans . . .*"

"*Verflucht Kalt!*"

"*Der Hundenmeister sagt, sehr Gefährlich!*"

"*Macht nichts! Wir erwischen es bevor dem Wald!*"

A rider plunges beneath an arch. The horse snorts and curvets.

"*Ich wette dier fünfzig amerikanische Dollar!*"

"*Einverstanden! Heute, habe ich Glück!*"

The noise, the jangling and stamping, rings back on itself. Cheeks flush, perception is heightened; for more than one of the riders, the early courtyard reels. Beside the house door trestles have been set up. A great bowl is carried, steaming. The cups are raised, the toasts given; the responses ring again, crashing.

"The Two Empires . . !"
"The Hunt . . !"

Now, time is like a tight-wound spring. The dogs plunge forward, six to a handler, leashes straining, choke links creaking and snapping. Behind them jostle the riders. The bobbing scarlet coats splash across the snow. In the house drive, an officer salutes; another strikes gloved palms together, nods. The gates whine open.

And across the country for miles around doors slam, bolts are shot, shutters closed, children scurried indoors. Village streets, muffled with snow, wait dumbly. Somewhere a dog barks, is silenced. The houses squat sullen, blind-eyed. The word has gone out, faster than horses could gallop. Today the Hunt will run; on snow.

The riders fan out, across a speckled waste of fields. A check, a questing; and the horns begin to yelp. Ahead the dogs bound and leap, black spots against whiteness. The horns cry again; but these hounds run mute. The riders sweep forward, onto the line.

Now, for the hunters, time and vision are fragmented. Twigs and snow merge in a racing blur; and tree-boles, ditches, gates. The tide reaches a crest of land, pours down the opposing slope. Hedges rear, mantled with white; and muffled thunder is interrupted by sailing silence, the smash and crackle of landing. The View sounds, harsh and high; and frenzy, and the racing blood, discharge intelligence. A horse goes down, in a gigantic flailing; another rolls, crushing its rider into the snow. A mount runs riderless. The Hunt, destroying, destroys itself unaware.

There are cottages, a paling fence. The fence goes over, unnoticed. A chicken house erupts in a cloud of flung crystals; birds run squawking, under the hooves. Caps are lost, flung away; hair flows wild. Whips flail, spurs rake streaming flanks; and the woods are close. Twigs lash, and branches; snow falls, thudding. The crackling, now, is all around.

At the end, it is always the same. The handlers close in, yodelling, waist-high in trampled brush; the riders force close and closer, mounts sidling and shaking; and silence falls. Only the quarry, reddened, flops and twists; the thin high noise it makes is the noise of anything in pain.

Now, if he chooses, the *Jagdmeister* may end the suffering. The crash of the pistol rings hollow; and birds erupt, high from frozen twigs, wheel with the echoes and cry. The pistol fires again; and the quarry lies still. In time, the shaking stops; and a dog creeps forward, begins to lick.

Now a slow movement begins; a spreading out, away from the place. There are mutterings, a laugh that chokes to silence. The fever passes. Somebody begins to shiver; and a girl, blood glittering on cheek and neck, puts a glove to her forehead and moans. The Need has come and gone; for a little while, the Two Empires have purged themselves.

The riders straggle back on tired mounts, shamble in through the gates. As the last enters a closed black van starts up, drives away. In an hour, quietly, it returns; and the gates swing shut behind it.

Surfacing from deepest sleep was like rising, slowly, through a warm sea. For a time, as Mainwaring lay eyes closed, memory and awareness were confused so that she was with him and the room a recollected, childhood place. He rubbed his face, yawned, shook his head; and the knocking that had roused him came again. He said, "Yes?"

The voice said, "Last breakfasts in fifteen minutes, sir."

He called, "Thank you," heard the footsteps pad away.

He pushed himself up, groped on the sidetable for his watch, held it close to his eyes. It read ten forty-five.

He swung the bedclothes back, felt air tingle on his skin. She had been with him, certainly, in the dawn; his body remembered the succubus, with nearly painful strength. He looked down smiling, walked to the bathroom. He showered, towelled himself, shaved and dressed. He closed his door and locked it, walked to the breakfast room. A few couples still sat over their coffee; he smiled a good morning, took a window seat. Beyond the double panes the snow piled thickly; its reflection lit the room with a white, inverted brilliance. He ate slowly, hearing distant shouts. On the long slope behind the house, groups of children pelted each other vigorously. Once a toboggan came into sight, vanished behind a rising swell of ground.

He had hoped he might see her, but she didn't come. He drank coffee, smoked a cigarette. He walked to the television lounge. The big colour screen showed a children's party taking place in a Berlin hospital. He watched for a while. The door behind him clicked a couple of times, but it wasn't Diane.

There was a second guests' lounge, not usually much frequented at this time of the year; and a reading room and library. He wandered through them, but there was no sign of her. It occurred to him she might not yet be up; at Wilton, there were few hard-and-fast rules for Christmas Day. He thought, 'I should have checked her room number.' He wasn't even sure in which of the guest wings she had been placed.

The house was quiet; it seemed most of the visitors had taken to their rooms. He wondered if she could have ridden with the Hunt; he'd heard it vaguely, leaving and returning. He doubted if the affair would have held much appeal.

He strolled back to the TV lounge, watched for an hour or more. By lunchtime he was feeling vaguely piqued; and sensing too the rising of a curious unease. He went back to his room, wondering if by any chance she had gone there; but the miracle was not repeated. The room was empty.

The fire was burning, and the bed had been remade. He had forgotten the servants' pass keys. The Geissler copy still stood on the shelf. He took it down, stood weighing it in his hand and frowning. It was, in a sense, madness to leave it there.

He shrugged, put the thing back. He thought, 'So who reads bookshelves anyway?' The plot, if plot there had been, seemed absurd now in the clearer light of day. He stepped into the corridor, closed the door and locked it behind him. He tried as far as possible to put the book from his mind. It represented a problem; and problems, as yet, he wasn't prepared to cope with. Too much else was going on in his brain.

He lunched alone, now with a very definite pang; the process was disquietingly like that of other years. Once he thought he caught sight of her in the corridor. His heart thumped; but it was the other blonde, Müller's wife. The gestures, the fall of the hair, were similar; but this woman was taller.

He let himself drift into a reverie. Images of her, it seemed, were engraved on his mind; each to be selected now, studied, placed lovingly aside. He saw the firelit texture of her hair and skin, her lashes brushing her cheek as she lay in his arms and slept. Other memories, sharper, more immediate still, throbbed like little shocks in the mind. She tossed her head, smiling; her hair swung, touched the point of a breast.

He pushed his cup away, rose. At fifteen hundred, patriotism required her presence in the TV lounge. As it required the presence of every other guest. Then, if not before, he would see her. He reflected, wryly, that he had waited half a lifetime for her; a little longer now would do no harm.

He took to prowling the house again; the Great Hall, the Long Gallery where the *Christkind* had walked. Below the windows that lined it was a snow-covered roof. The tart, reflected light struck upward, robbing the place of mystery. In the Great Hall, they had already removed the tree. He watched household staff hanging draperies, carrying in stacks of gilded cane chairs. On the Minstrels' Gallery a pile of odd-shaped boxes proclaimed that the orchestra had arrived.

At fourteen hundred hours he walked back to the TV lounge. A quick glance assured him she wasn't there. The bar was open; Hans, looking as big and suave as ever, had been pressed into service to minister to the guests. He smiled at Mainwaring and said, "Good afternoon, sir." Mainwaring asked for a lager beer, took the glass to a corner seat. From here he could watch both the TV screen and the door.

The screen was showing the world-wide link-up that had become hallowed Christmas afternoon fare within the Two Empires. He saw, without particular interest, greetings flashed from the Leningrad and Moscow garrisons, a lightship, an Arctic weather station, a Mission in German East Africa. At fifteen hundred, the Fuehrer was due to speak; this year, for the first time, Ziegler was preceding Edward VIII.

The room filled, slowly. She didn't come. Mainwaring finished the lager, walked to the bar, asked for another and a pack of cigarettes. The unease was sharpening now into something very like alarm. He thought for the first time that she might have been taken ill.

The time signal flashed, followed by the drumroll of the German anthem. He rose with the rest, stood stiffly till it had finished. The screen cleared, showed the familiar room in the Chancellery; the dark, high panels, the crimson drapes, the big *hakenkreuz* emblem over the desk. The Fuehrer, as ever, spoke impeccably; but Mainwaring thought with a fragment of his mind how old he had begun to look.

The speech ended. He realized he hadn't heard a word that was said.

The drums crashed again. The King said, "Once more, at Christmas, it is my . . . duty and pleasure . . . to speak to you."

Something seemed to burst inside Mainwaring's head. He rose, walked quickly to the bar. He said, "Hans, have you seen Miss Hunter?"

The other jerked round. He said, "Sir, *shh* . . . please . . ."

"*Have you seen her?*"

Hans stared at the screen, and back to Mainwaring. The King was saying, "There have been . . . troubles, and difficulties. More perhaps lie ahead. But with . . . God's help, they will be overcome."

The chauffeur licked his mouth. He said, "I'm sorry, sir. I don't know what you mean."

"Which was her room?"

The big man looked like something trapped. He said, "Please, Mr Mainwaring. You'll get me into trouble . . ."

"*Which was her room?*"

Somebody turned and hissed, angrily. Hans said, "I don't understand."

"For God's sake man, you carried her things upstairs. I saw you!"

Hans said, "No, sir . . ."

Momentarily, the lounge seemed to spin.

There was a door behind the bar. The chauffeur stepped back. He said, "Sir. Please . . ."

The place was a storeroom. There were wine bottles racked,

a shelf with jars of olives, walnuts, eggs. Mainwaring closed the
door behind him, tried to control the shaking. Hans said, "Sir,
you must not ask me these things I don't know a Miss Hunter.
I don't know what you mean."

Mainwaring said, "Which was her room? I demand that you
answer."

"I can't!"

"You drove me from London yesterday. Do you deny that?"

"No, sir."

"You drove me with Miss Hunter."

"No, sir!"

"*Damn your eyes, where is she?*"

The chauffeur was sweating. A long wait; then he said, "Mr
Mainwaring, please. You must understand. I can't help you."
He swallowed, and drew himself up. He said, "I drove you from
London. I'm sorry. I drove you . . . *on your own.*"

The lounge door swung shut behind Mainwaring. He half-
walked, half-ran to his room. He slammed the door behind him,
leaned against it panting. In time the giddiness passed. He
opened his eyes, slowly. The fire glowed; the Geissler stood on
the bookshelf. Nothing was changed.

He set to work, methodically. He shifted furniture, peered
behind it. He rolled the carpet back, tapped every foot of floor.
He fetched a flashlight from his case and examined, minutely,
the interior of the wardrobe. He ran his fingers lightly across the
walls, section by section, tapping again. Finally he got a chair,
dismantled the ceiling lighting fitting.

Nothing.

He began again. Halfway through the second search he froze,
staring at the floorboards. He walked to his case, took the
screwdriver from the pistol holster. A moment's work with the
blade and he sat back, staring into his palm. He rubbed his face,
placed his find carefully on the side table. A tiny earring, one of
the pair she had worn. He sat awhile breathing heavily, his head
in his hands.

The brief daylight had faded as he worked. He lit the standard
lamp, wrenched the shade free, stood the naked bulb in the
middle of the room. He worked round the walls again peering,

tapping, pressing. By the fireplace, finally, a foot-square section of plaster rang hollow.

He held the bulb close, examined the hairline crack. He inserted the screwdriver blade delicately, twisted. Then again. A click; and the section hinged open.

He reached inside the little space, shaking, lifted out the recorder. He stood silent a time, holding it; then raised his arms, brought the machine smashing down on the hearth. He stamped and kicked, panting, till the thing was reduced to fragments.

The droning rose to a roar, swept low over the house. The helicopter settled slowly, belly lamps glaring, down-draught raising a storm of snow. He walked to the window, stood staring. The children embarked, clutching scarves and gloves, suitcases, boxes with new toys. The steps were withdrawn, the hatch dogged shut. Snow swirled again; the machine lifted heavily, swung away in the direction of Wilton.

The party was about to start.

Lights blaze, through the length and breadth of the house. Orange-lit windows throw long bars of brightness across the snow. Everywhere is an anxious coming and going, the pattering of feet, clink of silver and glassware, hurried commands. Waiters scuttle between the kitchens and the Green Room where dinner is laid. Dish after dish is borne in, paraded. Peacocks, roast and gilded, vaunt their plumes in shadow and candleglow, spirit-soaked wicks blazing in their beaks. The Minister rises, laughing; toast after toast is drunk. To five thousand tanks, ten thousand fighting aeroplanes, a hundred thousand guns. The Two Empires feast their guests, royally.

The climax approaches. The boar's head, garnished and smoking, is borne shoulder-high. His tusks gleam; clamped in his jaws is the golden sun-symbol, the orange. After him march the waits and mummers, with their lanterns and begging-cups. The carol they chant is older by far than the Two Empires; older than the Reich, older than Great Britain.

"*Alive he spoiled, where poor men toiled, which made kind Ceres sad . . .*"

The din of voices rises. Coins are flung, glittering; wine is poured. And more wine, and more and more. Bowls of fruit are passed, and trays of sweets; spiced cakes, gingerbread, marzipans. Till at a signal the brandy is brought and boxes of cigars.

The ladies rise to leave. They move flushed and chattering through the corridors of the house, uniformed link-boys grandly lighting their way. In the Great Hall, their escorts are waiting. Each young man is tall, each blond, each impeccably uniformed. On the Minstrels' Gallery a baton is poised; across the lawns, distantly, floats the whirling excitement of a waltz.

In the Green Room, hazed now with smoke, the doors are once more flung wide. Servants scurry again, carrying in boxes, great gay-wrapped parcels topped with scarlet satin bows. The Minister rises, hammering on the table for quiet.

"My friends, good friends, friends of the Two Empires. For you, no expense is spared. For you, the choicest gifts. Tonight, nothing but the best is good enough; and nothing but the best is here. Friends, enjoy yourselves. Enjoy my house. *Frohe Weinacht . . .*"

He walks quickly into shadow, and is gone. Behind him, silence falls. A waiting; and slowly, mysteriously, the great heap of gifts begins to stir. Paper splits, crackling. Here a hand emerges, here a foot. A breathless pause; and the first of the girls rises slowly, bare in flamelight, shakes her glinting hair.

The table roars again.

The sound reached Mainwaring dimly. He hesitated at the foot of the main staircase, moved on. He turned right and left, hurried down a flight of steps. He passed kitchens, and the servants' hall. From the hall came the blare of a record player. He walked to the end of the corridor, unlatched a door. Night air blew keen against his face.

He crossed the courtyard, opened a further door. The space beyond was bright-lit; there was the faint, musty stink of animals. He paused, wiped his face. He was shirt-sleeved; but despite the cold he was sweating.

He walked forward again, steadily. To either side of the corridor were the fronts of cages. The dogs hurled themselves at the bars, thunderously. He ignored them.

The corridor opened into a square concrete chamber. To one side of the place was a ramp. At its foot was parked a window-less black van.

In the far wall, a door showed a crack of light. He rapped sharply, and again.

"*Hundenmeister . . .*"

The door opened. The man who peered up at him was as wrinkled and pot-bellied as a Nast Santa Claus. At sight of his visitor's face he tried to duck back; but Mainwaring had him by the arm. He said, "*Herr Hundenmeister*, I must talk to you."

"Who are you? I don't know you. What do you want . . ."

Mainwaring showed his teeth. He said, "The van. You drove the van this morning. What was in it?"

"I don't know what you mean . . ."

The heave sent him stumbling across the floor. He tried to bolt; but Mainwaring grabbed him again.

"*What was in it . . .*"

"I won't talk to you! Go away!"

The blow exploded across his cheek. Mainwaring hit him again, backhanded, slammed him against the van.

"*Open it . . .!*"

The voice rang sharply in the confined space.

"*Wer ist da? Was ist passiert?*"

The little man whimpered, rubbing at his mouth.

Mainwaring straightened, breathing heavily. The GFP captain walked forward, staring, thumbs hooked in his belt.

"*Wer sind Sie?*"

Mainwaring said, "You know damn well. And speak English, you bastard. You're as English as I am."

The other glared. He said, "You have no right to be here. I should arrest you. You have no right to accost *Herr Hundenmeister*."

"What is in that van?"

"Have you gone mad? The van is not your concern. Leave now. At once."

"*Open it!*"

The other hesitated, and shrugged. He stepped back. He said, "Show him, *mein Herr*."

The *Hundenmeister* fumbled with a bunch of keys. The van doors grated. Mainwaring walked forward, slowly.

The vehicle was empty.

The captain said, "You have seen what you wished see. You are satisfied. Now go."

Mainwaring stared round. There was a further door, recessed deeply into the wall. Beside it controls like the controls of a bank vault.

"What is in that room?"

The GFP man said, "You have gone too far. I order you to leave."

"You have no authority over me!"

"Return to your quarters!"

Mainwaring said, "I refuse."

The other slapped the holster at his hip. He gut-held the Walther, wrists locked, feet apart. He said, "*Then you will be shot.*"

Mainwaring walked past him, contemptuously. The baying of the dogs faded as he slammed the outer door.

"It was among the middle classes that the seeds had first been sown; and it was among the middle classes that they flourished. Britain had been called often enough a nation of shopkeepers; now for a little while the tills were closed, the blinds left drawn. Overnight it seemed, an effete symbol of social and national disunity became the *Einsatzegruppefuehrer*; and the wire for the first detention camps was strung . . ."

Mainwaring finished the page, tore it from the spine, crumpled it and dropped it on the fire. He went on reading. Beside him on the hearth stood a part-full bottle of whisky and a glass. He picked the glass up mechanically, drank. He lit a cigarette. A few minutes later a new page followed the last.

The clock ticked steadily. The burning paper made a little rustling. Reflections danced across the ceiling of the room.

Once Mainwaring raised his head, listened; once put the ruined book down, rubbed his eyes. The room, and the corridor outside, stayed quiet.

"Against immeasurable force, we must pit cunning; against immeasurable evil, faith and a high resolve. In the war we wage, the stakes are high; the dignity of man, the freedom of the spirit, the survival of humanity. Already in that war, many of us have died; many more, undoubtedly, will lay down their lives. But always, beyond them, there will be others; and still more. We shall go on, as we must go on, till this thing is wiped from the earth.

"Meanwhile, we must take fresh heart. Every blow, now, is a blow for freedom. In France, Belgium, Finland, Poland, Russia, the forces of the Two Empires confront each other uneasily. Greed, jealousy, mutual distrust; these are the enemies, and they work from within. This, the Empires know full well. And, knowing, for the first time in their existence, fear . . ."

The last page crumpled, fell to ash. Mainwaring sat back, staring at nothing. Finally he stirred, looked up. It was zero three hundred; and they hadn't come for him yet.

The bottle was finished. He set it to one side, opened another. He swilled the liquid in the glass, hearing the magnified ticking of the clock.

He crossed the room, took the Luger from the case. He found a cleaning rod, patches and oil. He sat awhile dully, looking at the pistol. Then he slipped the magazine free, pulled back on the breech toggle, thumbed the latch, slid the barrel from the guides.

His mind, wearied, had begun to play aggravating tricks. It ranged and wandered, remembering scenes, episodes, details sometimes from years back; trivial, unconnected. Through and between the wanderings, time after time, ran the ancient, lugubrious words of the carol. He tried to shut them out, but it was impossible.

"Living he spoiled where poor men toiled, which made kind Ceres sad . . ."

He pushed the link pin clear, withdrew the breech block, stripped the firing pin. He laid the parts out, washed them with oil and water, dried and re-oiled. He reassembled the pistol, working carefully; inverted the barrel, shook the link down in front of the hooks, closed the latch, checked the recoil spring engagement. He loaded a full clip, pushed it home, chambered a round, thumbed the safety to GESICKERT. He released the clip, reloaded.

He fetched his briefcase, laid the pistol inside carefully, grip uppermost. He filled a spare clip, added the extension butt and a fifty box of Parabellum. He closed the flap and locked it, set the case beside the bed. After that there was nothing more to do. He sat back in the chair, refilled his glass.

"*Toiling he boiled, where poor men spoiled . . .*"

The firelight faded, finally.

He woke, and the room was dark. He got up, felt the floor sway a little. He understood that he had a hangover. He groped for the light switch. The clock hands stood at zero eight hundred.

He felt vaguely guilty at having slept so long.

He walked to the bathroom. He stripped and showered, running the water as hot as he could bear. The process brought him round a little. He dried himself, staring down. He thought for the first time what curious things these bodies were; some with their yellow cylinders, some their indentations.

He dressed and shaved. He had remembered what he was going to do; fastening his tie, he tried to remember why. He couldn't. His brain, it seemed, had gone dead.

There was an inch of whisky in the bottle. He poured it, grimaced and drank. Inside him was a fast, cold shaking. He thought, 'Like the first morning at a new school.'

He lit a cigarette. Instantly his throat filled. He walked to the bathroom and vomited. Then again. Finally there was nothing left to come.

His chest ached. He rinsed his mouth, washed his face again. He sat in the bedroom for a while, head back and eyes closed. In time the shaking went away. He lay unthinking, hearing the clock tick. Once his lips moved. He said, "They're no better than us."

At nine hundred hours he walked to the breakfast room. His stomach, he felt, would retain very little. He ate a slice of toast, carefully, drank some coffee. He asked for a pack of cigarettes, went back to his room. At ten hundred hours he was due to meet the Minister.

He checked the briefcase again. A thought made him add a pair of stringback motoring gloves. He sat again, stared at the ashes where he had burned the Geissler. A part of him was willing the clock hands not to move. At five to ten he picked the briefcase up, stepped into the corridor. He stood a moment staring round him. He thought, 'It hasn't happened yet. I'm still alive.' There was still the flat in town to go back to, still his office; the tall windows, the telephones, the khaki utility desk.

He walked through sunlit corridors to the Minister's suite.

The room to which he was admitted was wide and long. A fire crackled in the hearth; beside it on a low table stood glasses and a decanter. Over the mantel, conventionally, hung the Fuehrer's portrait. Edward VIII faced him across the room. Tall windows framed a prospect of rolling parkland. In the distance, blue on the horizon, were the woods.

The Minister said, "Good morning, Richard. Please sit down. I don't think I shall keep you long."

He sat, placing the briefcase by his knee.

This morning everything seemed strange. He studied the Minister curiously, as if seeing him for the first time. He had that type of face once thought of as peculiarly English; short-nosed and slender, with high, finely shaped cheekbones. The hair, blond and cropped close to the scalp, made him look nearly boyish. The eyes were candid, flat, dark-fringed. He looked, Mainwaring decided, not so much Aryan as like some fierce nursery toy; a feral Teddy Bear.

The Minister riffled papers. He said, "Several things have cropped up; among them I'm afraid, more trouble in Glasgow. The fifty-first Panzer division is standing by; as yet, the news hasn't been released."

Mainwaring wished his head felt less hollow. It made his own voice boom so unnecessarily. He said, "Where is Miss Hunter?"

The Minister paused. The pale eyes stared; then he went on speaking.

"I'm afraid I may have to ask you to cut short your stay here. I shall be flying back to London for a meeting; possibly tomorrow, possibly the day after. I shall want you with me of course."

"*Where is Miss Hunter?*"

The Minister placed his hands flat on the desk top, studied the nails. He said, "Richard, there are aspects of Two Empires culture that are neither mentioned nor discussed. You of all people should know this. I'm being patient with you; but there are limits to what I can overlook."

"*Seldom he toiled, while Ceres roiled, which made poor kind men glad . . .*"

Mainwaring opened the flap of the case and stood up. He thumbed the safety forward and levelled the pistol.

There was silence for a time. The fire spat softly. Then the Minister smiled. He said, "That's an interesting gun, Richard. Where did you get it?"

Mainwaring didn't answer.

The Minister moved his hands carefully to the arms of his chair, leaned back. He said, "It's the Marine model of course. It's also quite old. Does it by any chance carry the Erfurt stamp? Its value would be considerably increased."

He smiled again. He said, "If the barrel is good, I'll buy it. For my private collection."

Mainwaring's arm began to shake. He steadied his wrist, gripping with his left hand.

The Minister sighed. He said, "Richard, you can be so stubborn. It's a good quality; but you do carry it to excess." He shook his head. He said, "Did you imagine for one moment I didn't know you were coming here to kill me? My dear chap, you've been through a great deal. You're overwrought. Believe me, I know just how you feel."

Mainwaring said, "You murdered her."

The Minister spread his hands. He said, "What with? A gun? A knife? Do I honestly look such a shady character?"

The words made a cold pain, and a tightness in the chest. But they had to be said.

The Minister's brows rose. Then he started to laugh. Finally he said, "At last I see. I understood, but I couldn't believe. So you bullied our poor little *Hundenmeister*, which wasn't very worthy; and seriously annoyed the *Herr Hauptmann*, which wasn't very wise. Because of this fantasy, stuck in your head. Do you really believe it, Richard? Perhaps you believe in *Struwwelpeter* too." He sat forward. He said, "The Hunt ran. And killed . . . a deer. She gave us an excellent chase. As for your little Huntress . . . Richard, she's gone. She never existed. She was a figment of your imagination. Best forgotten."

Mainwaring said, "We were in love."

The Minister said, "Richard, you really are becoming tiresome." He shook his head again. He said, "We're both adult. We both know what that word is worth. It's a straw, in the wind. A candle, on a night of gales. A phrase that is meaningless. *Lächerlich.*" He put his hands together, rubbed a palm. He said, "When this is over, I want you to go away. For a month, six weeks maybe. With your new car. When you come back . . . well, we'll see. Buy yourself a girlfriend, if you need a woman that much. *Einen Schatz.* I never dreamed; you're so remote, you should speak more of yourself. Richard, I understand; it isn't such a very terrible thing."

Mainwaring stared.

The Minister said, "We shall make an arrangement. You will have the use of an apartment, rather a nice apartment. So your lady will be close. When you tire of her . . . buy another. They're unsatisfactory for the most part, but reasonable. Now sit down like a good chap, and put your gun away. You look so silly, standing there scowling like that."

It seemed he felt all life, all experience, as a grey weight pulling. He lowered the pistol, slowly. He thought, 'At the end, they were wrong. They picked the wrong man.' He said, "I suppose now I use it on myself."

The Minister said, "No, no, no. You still don't understand." He linked his knuckles, grinning. He said, "Richard, the *Herr Hauptmann* would have arrested you last night. I wouldn't let him. This is between ourselves. Nobody else. I give you my word."

Mainwaring felt his shoulders sag. The strength seemed drained from him; the pistol, now, weighed too heavy for his arm.

The Minister said, "Richard, why so glum? It's a great occasion, man. You've found your courage. I'm delighted."

He lowered his voice. He said, "Don't you want to know why I let you come here with your machine? Aren't you even interested?"

Mainwaring stayed silent.

The Minister said, "Look around you, Richard. See the world. I want men near me, serving me. Now more than ever. Real men, not afraid to die. Give me a dozen . . . but you know the rest. I could rule the world. But first . . . I must rule them. My men. Do you see now? Do you understand?"

Mainwaring thought, 'He's in control again. But he was always in control. He owns me.'

The study spun a little.

The voice went on, smoothly. "As for this amusing little plot by the so-called Freedom Front; again, you did well. It was difficult for you. I was watching; believe me, with much sympathy. Now, you've burned your book. Of your own free will. That delighted me."

Mainwaring looked up, sharply.

The Minister shook his head. He said, "The real recorder is rather better hidden, you were too easily satisfied there. There's also a TV monitor. I'm sorry about it all, I apologise. It was necessary."

A singing started, inside Mainwaring's head.

The Minister sighed again. He said, "Still unconvinced, Richard? Then I have some things I think you ought to see. Am I permitted to open my desk drawer?"

Mainwaring didn't speak. The other slid the drawer back slowly, reached in. He laid a telegram flimsy on the desk top. He said, "The addressee is Miss D. J. Hunter. The message consists of one word. 'ACTIVATE.'"

The singing rose in pitch.

"This as well," said the Minister. He held up a medallion on a thin gold chain. The little disc bore the linked motif of the Freedom Front. He said, "Mere exhibitionism; or a death wish. Either way, a most undesirable trait."

He tossed the thing down. He said, "She was here under surveillance of course, we'd known about her for years. To them, you were a sleeper. Do you see the absurdity? They really thought you would be jealous enough to assassinate your Minister. This they mean in their silly little book, when they talk of subtlety. Richard, I could have fifty blonde women if I chose. A hundred. Why should I want yours?" He shut the drawer with a click, and rose. He said, "Give me the gun now. You don't need it any more." He extended his arm; then he was flung heavily backward. Glasses smashed on the sidetable. The decanter split; its contents poured dark across the wood.

Over the desk hung a faint haze of blue. Mainwaring walked forward, stood looking down. There were blood-flecks, and a little flesh. The eyes of the Teddy Bear still showed glints of white. Hydraulic shock had shattered the chest; the breath drew ragged, three times, and stopped. He thought, 'I didn't hear the report.'

The communicating door opened. Mainwaring turned. A secretary stared in, bolted at the sight of him. The door slammed.

He pushed the briefcase under his arm, ran through the outer office. Feet clattered in the corridor. He opened the door, carefully. Shouts sounded, somewhere below in the house.

Across the corridor hung a loop of crimson cord. He stepped over it, hurried up a flight of stairs. Then another. Beyond the private apartments the way was closed by a heavy metal grille. He ran to it, rattled. A rumbling sounded from below. He glared round. Somebody had operated the emergency shutters; the house was sealed.

Beside the door an iron ladder was spiked to the wall. He climbed it, panting. The trap in the ceiling was padlocked. He clung one-handed, awkward with the briefcase, held the pistol above his head.

Daylight showed through splintered wood. He put his shoulder to the trap, heaved. It creaked back. He pushed head and shoulders through, scrambled. Wind stung at him, and flakes of snow.

His shirt was wet under the arms. He lay face down, shaking. He thought, 'It wasn't an accident. None of it was an accident.' He had underrated them. They understood despair.

He pushed himself up, stared round. He was on the roof of Wilton. Beside him rose gigantic chimney stacks. There was a lattice radio mast. The wind hummed in its guy wires. To his right ran the balustrade that crowned the facade of the house. Behind it was a snow-choked gutter.

He wriggled across a sloping scree of roof, ran crouching. Shouts sounded from below. He dropped flat, rolled. An automatic clattered. He edged forward again, dragging the briefcase. Ahead, one of the corner towers rose dark against the sky. He crawled to it, crouched sheltered from the wind. He opened the case; pulled the gloves on. He clipped the stock to the pistol, laid the spare magazine beside him and the box of rounds.

The shouts came again. He peered forward, through the balustrade. Running figures scattered across the lawn. He sighted on the nearest, squeezed. Commotion below. The automatic zipped; stone chips flew, whining. A voice called, "Don't expose yourselves unnecessarily." Another answered.

"*Die kommen mit dem Hubschrauber . . .*"

He stared round him, at the yellow-grey horizon. He had forgotten the helicopter.

A snow flurry drove against his face. He huddled, flinching. He thought he heard, carried on the wind, a faint droning.

From where he crouched he could see the nearer trees of the park, beyond them the wall and gatehouses. Beyond again, the land rose to the circling woods.

The droning was back, louder than before. He screwed his eyes, made out the dark spot skimming above the trees. He shook his head. He said, "We made a mistake. We all made a mistake."

He settled the stock of the Luger to his shoulder, and waited.

The Lucky Strike

Kim Stanley Robinson

War breeds strange pastimes. In July of 1945 on Tinian Island in the North Pacific, Captain Frank January had taken to piling pebble cairns on the crown of Mount Lasso – one pebble for each B-29 take-off, one cairn for each mission. It was a mindless pastime, but so was poker. The men of the 509th had played a million hands of poker, sitting in the shade of a palm around an upturned crate, sweating in their skivvies, swearing and betting all their pay and cigarettes, playing hand after hand, until the cards got so soft and dog-eared you could have used them for toilet paper. Captain January had got sick of it, and after he lit out for the hilltop a few times some of his crewmates started trailing him. When their pilot, Jim Fitch, joined them it became an official pastime, like throwing flares into the compound or going hunting for stray Japs. What Captain January thought of the development he didn't say. The others grouped near Captain Fitch, who passed around his battered flask. "Hey, January," Fitch called. "Come and have a shot."

January wandered over and took the flask. Fitch laughed at his pebble. "Practising your bombing up here, eh, Professor?"

"Yeah," January said sullenly. Anyone who read more than the funnies was Professor to Fitch. Thirstily January knocked back some rum. He passed the flask on to Lieutenant Matthews, their navigator.

"That's why he's the best," Matthews joked. "Always practising."

Fitch laughed. "He's best because I make him the best, right, Professor?"

January frowned. Fitch was a bulky youth, thick-featured, pig-eyed – a thug, in January's opinion. The rest of the crew were all in their mid-twenties, like Fitch, and they liked the captain's bossy roughhouse style. January, who was thirty-seven, didn't go for it. He wandered away, back to the cairn he had been building. From Mount Lasso they had an overview of the whole island, from the harbour at Wall Street to the north field in Harlem. January had observed hundreds of B-29s roar off the four parallel runways of the north field and head for Japan. The last quartet of this particular mission buzzed across the width of the island, and January dropped four more pebbles, aiming for crevices in the pile. One of them stuck nicely.

"There they are!" said Matthews. "They're on the taxiing strip."

January located thc 509th's first plane. Today, the first of August, there was something more interesting to watch than the usual Superfortress parade. Word was out that General LeMay wanted to take the 500th's mission away from it. Their commander, Colonel Tibbets, had gone and hitched to LeMay in person, and the general had agreed the mission was theirs, but on one condition – one of the general's men was to make a test flight with the 509th to make sure they were fit for combat over Japan. The general's man had arrived, and now he was down there in the strike plane with Tibbets and the whole first team. January sidled back to his mates to view the take-off with them.

"Why don't the strike plane have a name, though?" Haddock was saying.

Fitch said, "Lewis won't give it a name because it's not his plane, and he knows it." The others laughed. Lewis and his crew were naturally unpopular, being Tibbets's favourites.

"What do you think he'll do to the general's man?" Matthews asked.

The others laughed at the very idea. "He'll kill an engine at take-off, I bet you anything," Fitch said. He pointed at the wrecked B-29s that marked the end of every runway. "He'll want to show that he wouldn't go down if it happened to him."

"Course he wouldn't!" Matthews said.

"You hope," January said under his breath.

"They let those Wrights out too soon," Haddock said seriously. "They keep busting under the take-off load."

"Won't matter to the old bull," Matthews said. Then they all started in about Tibbets's flying ability, even Fitch. They all thought Tibbets was the greatest. January, on the other hand, liked Tibbets even less than he liked Fitch. That had started right after he was assigned to the 509th. He had been told he was part of the most important group in the war and then given a leave. In Vicksburg a couple of fliers just back from England had bought him a lot of whiskeys, and since January had spent several months stationed near London they had talked for a good long time and got pretty drunk. The two were really curious about what January was up to now, but he had stayed vague on it and kept returning the talk to the blitz. He had seen an English nurse, for instance, whose flat had been bombed, family killed . . . But they had really wanted to know. So he had told them he was onto something special, and they had flipped out their badges and told him they were Army Intelligence, and that if he ever broke security like that again he'd be transferred to Alaska. It was a dirty trick. January had gone back to Wendover and told Tibbets so to his face, and Tibbets had turned red and threatened him some more. January despised him for that. During their year's training he had bombed better than ever, as a way of showing the old bull he was wrong. Every time their eyes had met it was clear what was going on. But Tibbets never backed off no matter how precise January's bombing got. Just thinking about it was enough to cause January to line up a pebble over an ant and drop it.

"Will you cut that out?" Fitch complained.

January pointed. "They're going."

Tibbets's plane had taxied to runway Baker. Fitch passed the flask around again. The tropical sun beat on them, and the ocean surrounding the island blazed white. January put up a sweaty hand to aid the bill of his baseball cap.

The four props cut in hard, and the sleek Superfortress quickly trundled up to speed and roared down Baker. Three-quarters of the way down the strip the outside right prop feathered.

"Yow!" Fitch crowed. "I told you he'd do it!"

The plane nosed off the ground and slewed right, then pulled back on course to cheers from the four young men around January. January pointed again. "He's cut number three, too."

The inside right prop feathered, and now the plane was pulled up by the left wing only, while the two right props wind-milled uselessly. "Holy smoke!" Haddock cried. "Ain't the old bull something?"

They whooped to see the plane's power and Tibbets's nervy arrogance.

"By God, LeMay's man will remember this flight," Fitch hooted. "Why, look at that! He's banking!"

Apparently taking off on two engines wasn't enough for Tibbets; he banked the plane right until it was standing on its dead wing, and it curved back towards Tinian.

Then the inside left engine feathered.

War tears at the imagination. For three years Frank January had kept his imagination trapped, refusing to give it any play whatsoever. The dangers threatening him, the effects of the bombs, the fate of the other participants in the war – he had refused to think about any of it. But the war tore at his control. That English nurse's flat. The missions over the Ruhr. The bomber just below him blown apart by flak. And then there had been a year in Utah, and the vicelike grip that he had once kept on his imagination had slipped away.

So when he saw the number two prop feather, his heart gave a little jump against his sternum, and helplessly he was up there with Ferebee, the first-team bombardier. He would be looking over the pilots' shoulders . . .

"Only one engine?" Fitch said.

"That one's for real," January said harshly. Despite himself he *saw* the panic in the cockpit, the frantic rush to power the two right engines. The plane was dropping fast and Tibbets levelled it off, leaving them on a course back towards the island. The two right props spun, blurred to a shimmer. January held his breath. They needed more lift; Tibbets was trying to pull it over the island. Maybe he was trying for the short runway on the south half of the island.

But Tinian was too tall, the plane too heavy. It roared right into the jungle above the beach, where Forty-second Street met their East River. It exploded in a bloom of fire. By the time the sound of it struck them they knew no one in the plane had survived.

Black smoke towered into white sky. In the shocked silence on Mount Lasso, insects buzzed and creaked. The air left January's lungs with a gulp. He had been with Ferebee, he had heard the desperate shouts, seen the last green rush, been stunned by the dentist-drill-all-over pain of the impact.

"Oh my God," Fitch was saying. "Oh my God." Matthews was sitting. January picked up the flask, tossed it at Fitch.

"C-come on," he stuttered. He hadn't stuttered since he was sixteen. He led the others in a rush down the hill. When they got to Broadway a jeep careered towards them and skidded to a halt. It was Colonel Scholes, the old bull's exec. "What happened?"

Fitch told him.

"Those damned Wrights," Scholes said as the men piled in. This time one had failed at just the wrong moment; some welder in the States had kept flame to metal a second less than usual – or something equally minor, equally trivial – and that had made all the difference.

They left the jeep at Forty-second and Broadway and hiked east over a narrow track to the shore. A fairly large circle of trees was burning. The fire trucks were already there.

Scholes stood beside January, his expression bleak. "That was the whole first team," he said.

"I know," said January. He was still in shock, his imagination crushed, incinerated, destroyed. Once as a kid he had tied sheets to his arms and waist, jumped off the roof, and landed right on his chest; this felt like that had. He had no way of knowing what would come of this crash, but he had a suspicion that he had indeed smacked into something hard.

Scholes shook his head. A half-hour had passed, the fire was nearly out. January's four mates were over chattering with the Seabees. "He was going to name the plane after his mother," Scholes said to the ground. "He told me that just this morning. He was going to call it *Enola Gay*."

At night the jungle breathed, and its hot wet breath washed over the 509th's compound. January stood in the doorway of his Quonset barracks hoping for a real breeze. No poker tonight. Noises were hushed, faces solemn. Some of the men had helped box up the dead crew's gear. Now most lay on their bunks. January gave up on the breeze, climbed onto his top bunk to stare at the ceiling.

He observed the corrugated arch over him. Cricket song sawed through his thoughts. Below him a rapid conversation was being carried on in guilty undertones, Fitch at its centre. "January is the best bombardier left," he said. "And I'm as good as Lewis was."

"But so is Sweeney," Matthews said. "And he's in with Scholes."

They were figuring out who would take over the strike. January scowled. Tibbets and the rest were less than twelve hours dead, and they were squabbling over who would replace them.

January grabbed a shirt, rolled off his bunk, put the shirt on.

"Hey, Professor," Fitch said, "where you going?"

"Out."

Though midnight was near, it was still sweltering. Crickets shut up as he walked by, started again behind him. He lit a cigarette. In the dark the MPs patrolling their compound were like pairs of walking armbands. Forcefully January expelled smoke, as if he could expel his disgust with it. They were only kids, he told himself. Their minds had been shaped in the war, by the war, and for the war. They knew you couldn't mourn the dead for long; carry around a load like that and your own engines might fail. That was all right with January. It was an attitude that Tibbets had helped to form, so it was what he deserved. Tibbets would *want* to be forgotten in favour of the mission; all he had lived for was to drop the gimmick on the Japs, and he was oblivious to anything else – men, wife, family, anything.

So it wasn't the lack of feeling in his mates that bothered January. And it was natural of them to want to fly the strike they had been training a year for. Natural, that is, if you were a kid with a mind shaped by fanatics like Tibbets, shaped to take orders and never imagine consequences. But January was not a kid, and he wasn't going to let men like Tibbets do a thing to his mind. And the gimmick . . . the gimmick was not natural. A chemical bomb of some sort, he guessed. Against the Geneva Convention. He stubbed his cigarette against the sole of his sneaker, tossed the butt over the fence. The tropical night breathed over him. He had a headache.

For months now he had been sure he would never fly a strike. The dislike Tibbets and he had exchanged in their looks (January was acutely aware of looks) had been real and strong. Tibbets had understood that January's record of pinpoint accuracy in the runs over the Salton Sea had been a way of showing contempt. The record had forced him to keep January on one of the four second-string teams, but with the fuss they were making over the gimmick January had figured that would be far enough down the ladder to keep him out of things.

Now he wasn't so sure. Tibbets was dead. He lit another cigarette, found his hand shaking. The Camel tasted bitter. He threw it over the fence at a receding armband and regretted it instantly. A waste. He went back inside.

Before climbing on to his bunk he got a paperback out of his foot-locker. "Hey, Professor, what you reading now?" Fitch said, grinning.

January showed him the blue cover. *Winter's Tales*, by an Isak Dinesen. Fitch examined the little wartime edition. "Pretty racy, eh?"

"You bet," January said heavily. "This guy puts sex on every page." He climbed onto his bunk, opened the book. The stories were strange, hard to follow. The voices below bothered him. He concentrated harder.

As a boy on the farm in Arkansas, January had read everything he could lay his hands on. On Saturday afternoons he

would race his father down the muddy lane to the mailbox (his
father was a reader too), grab the *Saturday Evening Post*, and
run off to devour every word of it. That meant he had another
week with nothing new to read, but he couldn't help it. It was a
way off the farm, a way into the world. He had become a man
who could slip between the covers of a book whenever he chose.

But not on this night.

The next day the chaplain gave a memorial service, and on
the morning after that Colonel Scholes looked in the door of
their hut right after mess. "Briefing at eleven," he announced.
His face was haggard. "Be there early." He looked at Fitch with
bloodshot eyes, crooked a finger. "Fitch, January, Matthews –
come with me."

January put on his shoes. The rest of the men sat on their
bunks and watched them wordlessly. January followed Fitch
and Matthews out of the hut.

"I've spent most of the night on the radio with General
LeMay," Scholes said. He looked them each in the eye. "We've
decided you're to be the first crew to make a strike."

Fitch was nodding, as if he had expected it.

"Think you can do it?" Scholes said.

"Of course," Fitch replied. Watching him, January understood why they had chosen him to replace Tibbets. Fitch was
like the old bull, he had that same ruthlessness. The young bull.

"Yes sir," Matthews said.

Scholes was looking at him. "Sure," January said, not
wanting to think about it. "Sure." His heart was pounding
directly on his sternum. But Fitch and Matthews looked serious
as owls, so he wasn't going to stick out by looking odd. It was
big news, after all; anyone would be taken aback by it.
Nevertheless, January made an effort to nod.

"Okay," Scholes said. "McDonald will be flying with you as
co-pilot." Fitch frowned. "I've got to go tell those British officers that LeMay doesn't want them on the strike with you. See
you at the briefing."

"Yes sir."

As soon as Scholes was around the corner Fitch swung a fist
at the sky. "Yow!" Matthews cried. He and Fitch shook hands.

"We did it!" Matthews took January's hand and wrung it, his face plastered with a goofy grin. "We did it!"

"Somebody did it, anyway," January said.

"Ah, Frank," Matthews said. "Show some spunk. You're always so cool."

"Old Professor Stoneface," Fitch said, glancing at January with a trace of amused contempt. "Come on, let's get to the briefing."

The briefing hut, one of the longer Quonsets, was completely surrounded by MPs holding carbines. "Gosh," Matthews said, subdued by the sight. Inside, it was already smoky. The walls were covered by the usual maps of Japan. Two blackboards at the front were draped with sheets. Captain Shepard, the naval officer who worked with the scientists on the gimmick, was in back with his assistant Lieutenant Stone, winding a reel of film onto a projector. Dr Nelson, the group psychiatrist, was already seated on a front bench near the wall. Tibbets had recently sicced the psychiatrist on the group – another one of his great ideas, like the spies in the bar. The man's questions had struck January as stupid. He hadn't even been able to figure out that Easterly was a flake, something that was clear to anybody who flew with him or even played him in a single round of poker. January slid onto a bench beside his mates.

The two Brits entered, looking furious in their stiff-upper-lip way. They sat on the bench behind January. Sweeney's and Easterly's crews filed in, followed by the other men, and soon the room was full. Fitch and the rest pulled out Lucky Strikes and lit up; since they had named the plane only January had stuck with Camels.

Scholes came in with several men January didn't recognize and went to the front. The chatter died, and all the smoke plumes ribboned steadily into the air.

Scholes nodded, and two intelligence officers took the sheets off the blackboards, revealing aerial reconnaissance photos.

"Men," Scholes said, "these are the target cities."

Someone cleared his throat.

"In order of priority they are Hiroshima, Kokura, and Nagasaki. There will be three weather scouts – *Straight Flush* to

Hiroshima, *Strange Cargo* to Kokura, and *Full House* to Nagasaki. *The Great Artiste* and *Number 91* will be accompanying the mission to take photos. And *Lucky Strike* will fly the bomb."

There were rustles, coughs. Men turned to look at January and his mates, and they all sat up straight. Sweeney stretched back to shake Fitch's hand, and there were some quick laughs. Fitch grinned.

"Now listen up," Scholes went on. "The weapon we are going to deliver was successfully tested stateside a couple weeks ago. And now we've got orders to drop it on the enemy." He paused to let that sink in. "I'll let Captain Shepard tell you more—"

Shepard walked to the blackboard slowly, savouring his entrance. His forehead was slimy with sweat, and January realized he was excited or nervous. He wondered what the psychiatrist would make of that.

"I'm going to come right to the point," Shepard said. "The bomb you are going to drop is something new in history. We think it will knock out everything within four miles."

Now the room was completely still. January noticed that he could see a great deal of his nose, eyebrows, and cheeks; it was as if he were receding back into his body, like a fox into its hole. He kept his gaze rigidly on Shepard, steadfastly ignoring the feeling. Shepard pulled a sheet back over a blackboard while someone else turned down the lights.

"This is a film of the only test we have made," Shepard said. The film started, caught, started again. A wavery cone of bright cigarette smoke speared the length of the room, and on the sheet sprang a dead grey landscape – a lot of sky, a smooth desert floor, hills in the distance. The projector went *click-click-click-click, click-click-click-click.* "The bomb is on top of the tower," Shepard said, and January focused on the pinlike object sticking out of the desert floor, off against the hills. It was between eight and ten miles from the camera, he judged; he had got good at calculating distances. He was still distracted by his face.

Click-click-click-click, click – then the screen went white for a second, filling even their room with light. When the picture returned the desert floor was filled with a white bloom of fire. The fireball coalesced, and then quite suddenly it leaped off the earth all the way into the *stratosphere*, by God, like a tracer bullet leaving a machine gun, trailing a whitish pillar of smoke behind it. The pillar gushed up, and a growing ball of smoke billowed outward, capping the pillar. January calculated the size of the cloud but was sure he got it wrong. There it stood. The picture flickered, and then the screen went white again, as if the camera had melted or that part of the world had come apart. But the flapping from the projector told them it was the end of the film.

January felt the air suck in and out of his open mouth. The lights came on in the smoky room, and for a second he panicked. He struggled to shove his features into an accepted pattern – the psychiatrist would be looking around at them all and then he glanced around and realized he needn't have worried, that he wasn't alone. Faces were bloodless, eyes were blinky or bugged out with shock, mouths hung open or were clamped whitely shut. For a few moments they all had to acknowledge what they were doing. January, scaring himself, felt an urge to say, "Play it again, will you?" Fitch was pulling his curled black hair off his thug's forehead uneasily. Beyond him January saw that one of the Limeys had already reconsidered how mad he was about missing the flight. Now he looked sick. Someone let out a long *whew*, another whistled. January looked to the front again, where Dr Nelson watched them, undisturbed.

Shepard said, "It's big, all right. And no one knows what will happen when it's dropped from the air. But the mushroom cloud you saw will go to at least thirty thousand feet, probably sixty. And the flash you saw at the beginning was hotter than the sun."

Hotter than the sun. More licked lips, hard swallows, readjusted baseball caps. One of the intelligence officers passed out tinted goggles like welders glasses. January took his and twiddled the opacity dial.

Scholes said, "You're the hottest thing in the armed forces, now. So no talking even among yourselves." He took a deep breath. "Let's do it the way Tibbets would have wanted us to. He picked every one of you because you were the best, and now's the time to show he was right. So – let's make the old man proud."

The briefing was over. Men filed out into the sudden sunlight. Into the heat and glare. Captain Shepard approached Fitch. "Stone and I will be flying with you to take care of the bomb," he said.

Fitch nodded. "Do you know how many strikes we'll fly?"

"As many as it takes to make them quit." Shepard stared hard at all of them. "But it will only take one."

War breeds strange dreams. That night, January writhed over his sheets in the hot, wet, vegetable night, in that frightening half-sleep when you sometimes know you are dreaming but can do nothing about it, and he dreamed he was walking . . .

. . . walking through the streets when suddenly the sun swoops down, the sun touches down and everything is instantly darkness and smoke and silence, a deaf roaring. Walls of fire. His head hurts and in the middle of his vision is a blue-white blur as if God's camera went off in his face. Ah – the sun fell, he thinks. His arm is burned. Blinking is painful. People stumbling by, mouths open, horribly burned –

He is a priest, he can feel the clerical collar, and the wounded ask him for help. He points to his ears, tries to touch them but can't. Pall of black smoke over everything, the city has fallen into the streets. Ah, it's the end of the world. In a park he finds shade and cleared ground. People crouch under bushes like animals. Where the park meets the river, red and black figures crowd into steaming water. A figure gestures from a copse of bamboo. He enters it, finds five or six faceless soldiers huddling. Their eyes have melted, their mouths are holes. Deafness spares him their words. The sighted soldier mimes drinking. The soldiers are thirsty. He nods and goes to the river in search of a container. Bodies float downstream.

Hours pass as he hunts fruitlessly for a bucket. He pulls people from the rubble. He hears a bird screeching, and he realizes that his deafness is the roar of the city burning, a roar like the blood in his ears, but he is not deaf, he only thought he was because there are no human cries. The people are suffering in silence. Through the dusky night he stumbles back to the river, pain crashing through his head. In a field, men are pulling potatoes out of the ground that have been baked well enough to eat. He shares one with them. At the river everyone is dead –

– and he struggled out of the nightmare drenched in rank sweat, the taste of dirt in his mouth, his stomach knotted with horror. He sat up, and the wet, rough sheet clung to his skin. His heart felt crushed between lungs desperate for air. The flowery rotting-jungle smell filled him, and images from the dream flashed before him so vividly that in the dim hut he saw nothing else. He grabbed his cigarettes and jumped off the bunk, hurried out into the compound. Trembling, he lit up, started pacing around. For a moment he worried that the idiot psychiatrist might see him, but then he dismissed the idea. Nelson would be asleep. They were all asleep. He shook his head, looked down at his right arm, and almost dropped his cigarette – but it was just his stove scar, an old scar. He'd had it most of his life, since the day he'd pulled the frypan off the stove and onto his arm, burning it with oil. He could still remember the round O of fear that his mother's mouth had made as she rushed in to see what was wrong. Just an old burn scar, he thought, let's not go overboard here. He pulled his sleeve down.

For the rest of the night he tried to walk it off, cigarette after cigarette. The dome of the sky lightened until all the compound and the jungle beyond it was visible. He was forced by the light of day to walk back into his hut and lie down as if nothing had happened.

Two days later Scholes ordered them to take one of LeMay's men over Rota for a test run. This new lieutenant colonel ordered Fitch not to play with the engines on take-off. They flew a perfect run, January put the dummy gimmick right on the aiming point, and Fitch powered the plane down into the violent bank that started their 150-degree turn and flight for safety. Back on Tinian the lieutenant colonel congratulated them and shook each of their hands. January smiled with the rest, palms cool, heart steady. It was as if his body were a shell, something he could manipulate from without, like a bombsight. He ate well, he chatted as much as he ever had, and when the psychiatrist ran him to earth for some questions, he was friendly and seemed open.

"Hello, Doc."

"How do you feel about all this, Frank?"

"Just like I always have, sir. Fine."

"Eating well?"

"Better than ever."

"Sleeping well?"

"As well as I can in this humidity. I got used to Utah, I'm afraid." Dr Nelson laughed. Actually January had hardly slept since his dream. He was afraid of sleep. Couldn't the man see that?

"And how do you feel about being part of the crew chosen to make the first strike?"

"Well, it was the right choice, I reckon. We're the b— the best crew left."

"Do you feel sorry about Tibbets's crew's accident?"

"Yes sir, I do." You better believe it.

After the jokes that ended the interview, January walked out into the blaze of the tropical noon and lit a cigarette. He allowed himself to feel how much he despised the psychiatrist and his blind profession at the same time he was waving good-bye to the man. Ounce brain. Why couldn't he have seen? Whatever happened it would be his fault . . . With a rush of smoke out of him January realized how painfully easy it was to fool someone if you wanted to. All action was no more than a mask that could be perfectly manipulated from somewhere else. And all the while in that somewhere else, January lived in a *click-click-click* of film, in the silent roaring of a dream, struggling against images he couldn't dispel. The heat of the tropical sun – ninety-three million miles away, wasn't it? – pulsed painfully on the back of his neck.

As he watched the psychiatrist collar their tail gunner, Kochenski, he thought of walking up to the man and saying *I quit. I don't want to do this.* In imagination he saw the look that would form in the man's eye, in Fitch's eye, in Tibbets's eye, and his mind recoiled from the idea. He felt too much contempt for them. He wouldn't for anything give them a means to despise him, a reason to call him coward. Stubbornly he banished the whole complex of thought. Easier to go along with it.

And so a couple of disjointed days later, just after midnight of 9 August, he found himself preparing for the strike. Around him Fitch and Matthews and Haddock were doing the same. How odd were the everyday motions of getting dressed when you were off to demolish a city! January found himself examining his hands, his boots, the cracks in the linoleum. He put on his survival vest, checked the pockets abstractedly for fishhooks, water kit, first-aid package, emergency rations. Then the parachute harness, and his coveralls over it all. Tying his bootlaces took minutes; he couldn't do it when watching his fingers so closely.

"Come on, Professor!" Fitch's voice was tight. "The big day is here."

He followed the others into the night. A cool wind was blowing. The chaplain said a prayer for them. They took jeeps down Broadway to runway Able. *Lucky Strike* stood in a circle of spotlights and men, half of them with cameras, the rest with reporters' pads. They surrounded the crew; it reminded January of a Hollywood première. Eventually he escaped up the hatch and into the plane. Others followed. Half an hour passed before Fitch joined them, grinning like a movie star. They started the engines, and January was thankful for their vibrating, thought-smothering roar. They taxied away from the Hollywood scene, and January felt relief for a moment, until he remembered where they were going. On runway Able the engines pitched up to their twenty-three-hundred-RPM whine, and looking out the clear windscreen, he saw the runway paint marks move by ever faster. Fitch kept them on the runway till Tinian had run out from under them, then quickly pulled up. They were on their way.

When they got to altitude, January climbed past Fitch and McDonald to the bombardier's seat and placed his parachute on it. He leaned back. The roar of the four engines packed around him like cotton batting. He was on the flight, nothing to be done about it now. The heavy vibration was a comfort, he liked the feel of it there in the nose of the plane. A drowsy, sad acceptance hummed through him.

Against his closed eyelids flashed a black eyeless face, and he jerked awake, heart racing. He was on the flight, no way out. Now he realized how easy it would have been to get out of it. He could have just said he didn't want to. The simplicity of it appalled him. Who gave a damn what the shrink or Tibbets or anyone else thought, compared to this? Now there was no way out. It was a comfort, in a way. Now he could stop worrying, stop thinking he had any choice.

Sitting there with his knees bracketing the bombsight, January dozed, and as he dozed he daydreamed his way out. He could climb the step to Fitch and McDonald and declare he had been secretly promoted to major and ordered to redirect the mission. They were to go to Tokyo and drop the bomb in the bay. The Jap War Cabinet had been told to watch this demonstration of the new weapon, and when they saw that fireball boil the bay and bounce into heaven they'd run and sign surrender papers as fast as they could write, kamikazes or not. They weren't crazy, after all. No need to murder a whole city. It was such a good plan that the generals were no doubt changing the mission at this very minute, desperately radioing their instructions to Tinian, only to find out it was too late . . . so that when they returned to Tinian, January would become a hero for guessing what the generals really wanted and for risking all to do it. It would be like one of the Hornblower stories he had read in the *Saturday Evening Post*.

Once again January jerked awake. The drowsy pleasure of the fantasy was replaced with desperate scorn. There wasn't a chance in hell that he could convince Fitch and the rest that he had secret orders superseding theirs. And he couldn't go up there and wave his pistol around and *order* them to drop the bomb in Tokyo Bay, because he was the one who had to actually drop it, and he couldn't be down in front dropping the bomb and up ordering the others around at the same time. Pipe dreams.

Time swept on, slow as a second hand. January's thoughts,

however, matched the spin of the props; desperately they cast about, now this way now that, like an animal caught by the leg in a trap. The crew was silent. The clouds below were a white scree on the black ocean. January's knee vibrated against the bombsight. He was the one who had to drop the bomb. No matter where his thoughts lunged, they were brought up short by that. He was the one, not Fitch or the crew, not LeMay, not the generals and scientists back home, not Truman and his advisers. Truman – suddenly January hated him. Roosevelt would have done it differently. If only Roosevelt had lived! The grief that had filled January when he learned of Roosevelt's death reverberated through him more strongly than ever. It was unfair to have worked so hard and then not see the war's end. And FDR would have ended it differently. Back at the start of it all he had declared that civilian centres were never to be bombed, and if he had lived, if, if, if. But he hadn't. And now it was smiling bastard Harry Truman, ordering *him*, Frank January, to drop the sun on two hundred thousand women and children. Once his father had taken him to see the Browns play before twenty thousand, a giant crowd – "I never voted for you," January whispered viciously and jerked to realize he had spoken aloud. Luckily his microphone was off. And Roosevelt would have done it differently, he *would have*.

The bombsight rose before him, spearing the black sky and blocking some of the hundreds of little cruciform stars. *Lucky Strike* ground on towards Iwo Jima, minute by minute flying four miles closer to their target. January leaned forward and put his face in the cool headrest of the bombsight, hoping that its grasp might hold his thoughts as well as his forehead. It worked surprisingly well.

His earphones crackled and he sat up. "Captain January." It was Shepard. "We're going to arm the bomb now, want to watch?"

"Sure thing." He shook his head, surprised at his own duplicity. Stepping up between the pilots, he moved stiffly to the roomy cabin behind the cockpit. Matthews was at his desk taking a navigational fix on the radio signals from Iwo Jima and Okinawa, and Haddock stood beside him. At the back of the compartment was a small circular hatch, below the larger tunnel leading to the rear of the plane. January opened it, sat down, and swung himself feet-first through the hole.

The bomb bay was unheated, and the cold air felt good. He stood facing the bomb. Stone was sitting on the floor of the bay; Shepard was laid out under the bomb, reaching into it. On a rubber pad next to Stone were tools, plates, several cylindrical blocks. Shepard pulled back, sat up, sucked a scraped knuckle. He shook his head ruefully. "I don't dare wear gloves with this one."

"I'd be just as happy myself if you didn't let something slip," January joked nervously. The two men laughed.

"Nothing can blow till I change those wires," Stone said.

"Give me the wrench," Shepard said. Stone handed it to him, and he stretched under the bomb again. After some awkward wrenching inside it he lifted out a cylindrical plug. "Breech plug," he said, and set it on the mat.

January found his skin goose-pimpling in the cold air. Stone handed Shepard one of the blocks. Shepard extended under the bomb again. Watching them, January was reminded of auto mechanics on the oily floor of a garage, working under a car. He had spent a few years doing that himself, after his family moved to Vicksburg. Hiroshima was a river town. One time a flatbed truck carrying bags of cement powder down Fourth Street hill had lost its brakes and careered into the intersection with River Road, where, despite the driver's efforts to turn, it smashed into a passing car. Frank had been out in the yard playing and heard the crash and saw the cement dust rising. He had been one of the first there. The woman and child in the passenger seat of the Model T had been killed. The woman driving was okay. They were from Chicago. A group of folks subdued the driver of the truck, who kept trying to help at the Model T, though he had a bad cut on his head and was covered with white dust.

"Okay, let's tighten the breech plug." Stone gave Shepard the wrench. "Sixteen turns exactly," Shepard said. He was sweating even in the bay's chill, and he paused to wipe his forehead. "Let's hope we don't get hit by lightning." He put the wrench down, shifted onto his knees, and picked up a circular plate.

Hubcap, January thought. Stone connected wires, then helped Shepard install two more plates. Good old American know-how, January thought, goose pimples rippling across his skin like cat's paws over water. There was Shepard, a scientist, putting together a bomb like he was an auto mechanic changing oil. January felt a tight rush of rage at the scientists who had designed the bomb. They had worked on it for over a year. Had none of them in all that time ever stopped to think what they were doing?

But none of them had to drop it. January turned to hide his face from Shepard, stepped down the bay. The bomb looked like a big long trash can, with fins at one end and little antennae at the other. Just a bomb, he thought, damn it, it's just another bomb.

Shepard stood and patted the bomb gently. "We've got a live one now." Never a thought about what it would do. January hurried by the man, afraid that hatred would crack his shell and give him away. The pistol strapped to his belt caught on the hatchway, and he imagined shooting Shepard – shooting Fitch and McDonald and plunging the controls forward so that *Lucky Strike* tilted and spun down into the sea like a spent tracer bullet, like a plane broken by flak, following the arc of all human ambition. Nobody would ever know what had happened to them, and their trash can would be dumped to the bottom of the Pacific. He could even shoot everyone, parachute out, and perhaps be rescued by one of the Superdumbos following them . . .

The thought passed, and remembering it January squinted with disgust. But another part of him agreed that it was a possibility. It could be done. It would solve his problem.

"Want some coffee?" Matthews asked.

"Sure," January said, and took a cup. He sipped – hot. He watched Matthews and Benton tune the loran equipment. As the beeps came in Matthews took a straightedge and drew lines from Okinawa and Iwo Jima. He tapped a finger on the inter-section. "They've taken the art out of navigation," he said to January. "They might as well stop making the navigator's dome," thumbing up at the little Plexiglas bubble over them.

"Good old American know-how," January said.

Matthews nodded. With two fingers he measured the distance between their position and Iwo Jima. Benton measured with a ruler.

"Rendezvous at five thirty-five, eh?" Matthews said. They were to rendezvous with the two trailing planes over Iwo.

Benton disagreed. "I'd say five-fifty."

"What? Check again, guy, we're not in no tugboat here."

"The wind—"

"Yeah, the wind. Frank, you want to add a bet to the pool?"

"Five thirty-six," January said promptly.

They laughed. "See, he's got more confidence in me," Matthews said with a dopey grin.

January recalled his plan to shoot the crew and tip the plane into the sea, and he pursed his lips, repelled. Not for anything would he be able to shoot these men, who, if not friends, were at least companions. They passed for friends. They meant no harm.

Shepard and Stone climbed into the cabin. Matthews offered them coffee. "The gimmick's ready to kick their ass, eh?" Shepard nodded and drank.

January moved forward, past Haddock's console. Another plan that wouldn't work. What to do? All the flight engineer's dials and gauges showed conditions were normal. Maybe he could sabotage something? Cut a line somewhere?

Fitch looked back at him and said, "When are we due over Iwo?"

"Five-forty, Matthews says."

"He better be right."

A thug. In peacetime Fitch would be hanging around a pool table giving the cops trouble. He was perfect for war. Tibbets had chosen his men well – most of them, anyway. Moving back past Haddock, January stopped to stare at the group of men in the navigation cabin. They joked, drank coffee. They were all a bit like Fitch – young toughs, capable and thoughtless. They were having a good time, an adventure. That was January's dominant impression of his companions in the 509th; despite all the bitching and the occasional moments of overmastering fear, they were having a good time. His mind spun forward, and he saw what these young men would grow up to be like as clearly as if they stood before him in businessmen's suits, prosperous and balding. They would be tough and capable and thoughtless, and as the years passed and the great war receded in time they would look back on it with ever-increasing nostalgia, for they would be the survivors and not the dead. Every year of this war would feel like ten in their memories, so that the war would always remain the central experience of their lives – a time when history lay palpable in their hands, when each of their acts affected it, when moral issues were simple, and others told them what to do – so that as more years passed and the survivors aged, bodies falling apart, lives in one rut or another, they would unconsciously push harder and harder to thrust the world into war again, thinking somewhere inside themselves that if they could only return to world war then they would magically be again as they were in the last one – young and free and happy. And by that time they would hold the positions of power, they would be capable of doing it.

So there would be more wars, January saw. He heard it in Matthews's laughter, saw it in their excited eyes. "There's Iwo, and it's five thirty-one. Pay up! I win!" And in future wars they'd have more bombs like the gimmick, hundreds of them no doubt. He saw more planes, more young crews like this one, flying to Moscow, no doubt, or to wherever, fireballs in every capital. Why not? And to what end? To what end? So that the old men could hope to become magically young again. Nothing more sane than that. It made January sick.

They were over Iwo Jima. Three more hours to Japan. Voices from *The Great Artiste* and *Number 91* crackled on the radio. Rendezvous accomplished, the three planes flew northwest, towards Shikoku, the first Japanese island in their path. January manoeuvred down into the nose. "Good shooting," Matthews called after him.

Forward it seemed quieter. January got settled, put his headphones on, and leaned forward to look out the ribbed Plexiglas.

Dawn had turned the whole vault of the sky pink. Slowly the radiation shade shifted through lavender to blue, pulse by pulse a different colour. The ocean below was a glittering blue plane, marbled by a pattern of puffy pink cloud. The sky above was a vast dome, darker above than on the horizon. January had always thought that dawn was the time when you could see most clearly how big the earth was and how high above it they flew. It seemed they flew at the very upper edge of the atmosphere, and January saw how thin it was, how it was just a skin of air really, so that even if you flew up to its top the earth still extended away infinitely in every direction. The coffee had warmed January, he was sweating. Sunlight blinked off the Plexiglas. His watch said six. Plane and hemisphere of blue were split down the middle by the bombsight. His earphones crackled and he listened in to the reports from the lead planes flying over the target cities. Kokura, Nagasaki, Hiroshima, all of them had six-tenths cloud cover. Maybe they would have to cancel the whole mission because of weather. "We'll look at Hiroshima first," Fitch said. January peered down at the fields of miniature clouds with renewed interest. His parachute slipped under him. Readjusting it, he imagined putting it on, sneaking back to the central escape hatch under the navigator's cabin, opening the hatch . . . He could be out of the plane and gone before anyone noticed. They could bomb or not but it wouldn't be January's doing. He could float down onto the world like a puff of dandelion, feel cool air rush around him, watch the silk canopy dome hang over him like a miniature sky, a private world.

An eyeless black face. January shuddered; it was as though the nightmare could return any time. If he jumped nothing would change, the bomb would still fall – would he feel any better, floating on his Inland Sea? Sure, one part of him shouted; maybe, another conceded; the rest of him saw that face . . .

Earphones crackled. Shepard said, "Lieutenant Stone has now armed the bomb, and I can now tell you all what we are carrying. Aboard with us is the world's first atomic bomb."

Not exactly, January thought. Whistles squeaked in his earphones. The first one went off in New Mexico. Splitting atoms. January had heard the term before. Tremendous energy in every atom, Einstein had said. Break one and – he had seen the result on film. Shepard was talking about radiation; which brought back more to January. Energy released in the form of X-rays. Killed by X-rays! It would be against the Geneva Convention if they had thought of it.

Fitch cut in. "When the bomb is dropped Lieutenant Benton will record our reaction to what we see. This recording is being made for history, so watch your language." Watch your language! January choked back a laugh. Don't curse or blaspheme God at the sight of the first atomic bomb incinerating a city with X-rays!

Six-twenty. January found his hands clenched together on the headrest of the bombsight. He felt as if he had a fever. In the harsh wash of morning light the skin on the backs of his hands appeared slightly translucent. The whorls in the skin looked like the delicate patterning of waves on the sea's surface. His hands were made of atoms. Atoms were the smallest building blocks of matter. It took billions of them to make those tense, trembling hands. Split one atom and you had the fireball. That meant that the energy contained in even one hand . . . He turned up a palm to look at the lines and the mottled flesh under the transparent skin. A person was a bomb that could blow up the world. January felt that latent power stir in him, pulsing with every hard heart knock. What beings they were, and in what a blue expanse of a world! And here they spun on to drop a bomb and kill a hundred thousand of these astonishing beings.

When a fox or raccoon is caught by the leg in a trap, it lunges until the leg is frayed, twisted, perhaps broken, and only then does the animal's pain and exhaustion force it to quit. Now in the same way January wanted to quit. His mind hurt. His plans to escape were so much crap – stupid, useless. Better to quit. He tried to stop thinking, but it was hopeless. How could he stop? As long as he was conscious he would be thinking. The mind struggles longer than any fox.

Lucky Strike tilted up and began the long climb to bombing altitude. On the horizon the clouds lay over a green island. Japan. Surely it had got hotter. The heater must be broken, he thought. Don't think. Every few minutes Matthews gave Fitch

small course adjustments. "Two seventy-five, now. That's it."
To escape the moment, January recalled his childhood.
Following a mule and plough. Moving to Vicksburg (rivers).
For a while there in Vicksburg, since his stutter made it hard to
gain friends, he had played a game with himself. He had passed
the time by imagining that everything he did was vitally important and determined the fate of the world. If he crossed a road
in front of a certain car, for instance, then the car wouldn't
make it through the next intersection before a truck hit it, and
so the man driving would be killed and wouldn't be able to
invent the flying boat that would save President Wilson from
kidnappers, so he had to wait for that car, oh damn it, he
thought, damn it, think of something *different*. The last
Hornblower story he had read – how would *he* get out of this?
The round O of his mother's face as she ran in and saw his arm
– The Mississippi, mud-brown behind its levees – Abruptly he
shook his head, face twisted in frustration and despair, aware at
last that no possible avenue of memory would serve as an escape
for him now; for now there was no part of his life that did not
apply to the situation he was in, and no matter where he cast his
mind it was going to shore up against the hour facing him.

Less than an hour. They were at thirty thousand feet,
bombing altitude. Fitch gave him altimeter readings to dial into
the bombsight. Matthews gave him wind speeds. Sweat got in
his eye and he blinked furiously. The sun rose behind them like
an atomic bomb, glinting off every corner and edge of the
Plexiglas, illuminating his bubble compartment with a fierce
glare. Broken plans jumbled together in his mind, his breath
was short, his throat dry. Uselessly and repeatedly he damned
the scientists, damned Truman. Damned the Japanese for
causing the whole mess in the first place, damned yellow killers,
they had brought this on themselves. Remember Pearl.
American men had died under bombs when no war had been
declared; they had started it and now it was coming back to
them with a vengeance. And they deserved it. And an invasion
of Japan would take years, cost millions of lives. End it now, end
it, they deserved it, they deserved it, steaming river full of charcoal people silently dying, damned stubborn race of maniacs!

"There's Honshu," Fitch said, and January returned to the world of the plane. They were over the Inland Sea. Soon they would pass the secondary target, Kokura, a bit to the south. Seven-thirty. The island was draped more heavily than the sea by clouds, and again January's heart leaped with the idea that weather would cancel the mission. But they did deserve it. It was a mission like any other mission. He had dropped bombs on Africa, Sicily, Italy, all Germany . . . He leaned forward to take a look through the sight. Under the X of the cross hairs was the sea, but at the lead edge of the sight was land. Honshu. At two hundred and thirty miles an hour that gave them about a half hour to Hiroshima. Maybe less. He wondered if his heart could beat so hard for that long.

Fitch said, "Matthews, I'm giving over guidance to you. Just tell us what to do."

"Bear south two degrees," was all Matthews said. At last their voices had taken on a touch of awareness.

"January, are you ready?" Fitch asked.

"I'm just waiting," January said. He sat up so Fitch could see the back of his head. The bombsight stood between his legs. A switch on its side would start the bombing sequence – the bomb would not leave the plane immediately upon the flick of the switch but would drop after a fifteen-second radio tone warned the following planes. The sight was adjusted accordingly.

"Adjust to a heading of two sixty-five," Matthews said. "We're coming in directly upwind." This was to make any side-drift adjustments for the bomb unnecessary. "January, dial it down to two hundred and thirty-one miles per hour."

"Two thirty-one."

Fitch said, "Everyone but January and Matthews, get your goggles on."

January took the darkened goggles from the floor. One needed to protect one's eyes or they might melt. He put them on, put his forehead on the headrest. They were in the way. He took them off. When he looked through the sight again there was land under the cross hairs. He checked his watch. Eight o'clock. Up and reading the papers, drinking tea.

"Ten minutes to AP," Matthews said. The aiming point was

Aioi Bridge, a T-shaped bridge in the middle of the delta-straddling city. Easy to recognize.

"There's a lot of cloud down there," Fitch noted. "Are you going to be able to see?"

"I won't be sure until we try it," January said.

"We can make another pass and use radar if we need to," Matthews said.

Fitch said, "Don't drop it unless you're sure, January."

"Yes sir."

Through the sight a grouping of rooftops and grey roads was just visible between broken clouds. Around it green forest. "All right," Matthews exclaimed, "here we go! Keep it right on this heading, Captain! January, we'll stay at two thirty-one."

"And same heading," Fitch said. "January, she's all yours. Everyone be ready for the turn."

January's world contracted to the view through the bombsight. A stippled field of cloud and forest. Over a small range of hills and into Hiroshima's watershed. The broad river was mud brown, the land pale hazy green, the growing network of roads flat grey. Now the tiny rectangular shapes of buildings covered almost all the land, and swimming into the sight came the city proper, narrow islands thrusting into a dark blue bay. Under the cross hairs the city moved island by island, cloud by cloud. January had stopped breathing. His fingers were rigid as stone on the switch. And there was Aioi Bridge. It slid right under the cross hairs, a tiny T right in a gap in the clouds. January's fingers crushed the switch. Deliberately he took a breath, held it. Clouds swam under the cross hairs, then the next island. "Almost there," he said calmly into his microphone. "Steady." Now that he was committed his heart was humming like the Wrights. He counted to ten. Now flowing under the cross hairs were clouds alternating with green forest, leaden roads. "I've turned the switch, but I'm not getting a tone!" he croaked into the mike. His right hand held the switch firmly in place. Behind him Fitch was shouting something; Matthews's voice cracked across it. "Flipping it b-back and forth," January shouted, shielding the bombsight with his body from the eyes of the pilots. "But *still* – wait a second—"

He pushed the switch down. A low hum filled his ears. "That's it! It started!"

"But where will it land?" Matthews cried.

"Hold steady!" January shouted.

Lucky Strike shuddered and lofted up ten or twenty feet. January twisted to look down, and there was the bomb, flying just below the plane. Then with a wobble it fell away.

The plane banked right and dived so hard that the centrifugal force threw January against the Plexiglas. Several thousand feet lower, Fitch levelled it out and they hurtled north.

"Do you see anything?" Fitch cried.

From the tail gun Kochenski gasped, "Nothing." January struggled upright. He reached for the welder's goggles, but they were no longer on his head. He couldn't find them. "How long has it been?" he said.

"Thirty seconds," Matthews replied.

January shut his eyes.

The blood in his eyelids lit up red, then white.

On the earphones a clutter of voices – "Oh my God. Oh my God." The plane bounced and tumbled, metallic shrieking. January pressed himself off the Plexiglas. "'Nother shock wave!" Kochenski yelled. The plane rocked again. This is it, January thought, end of the world, I guess that solves my problem.

He opened his eyes and found he could still see. The engines still roared, the props spun. "Those were the shock waves from the bomb," Fitch called. "We're okay now. Look at that! Will you look at that son of a bitch go!"

January looked. The cloud layer below had burst apart, and a black column of smoke billowed up from a core of red fire. Already the top of the column was at their height. Exclamations of shock hurt January's ears. He stared at the fiery base of the cloud, at the scores of fires feeding into it. Suddenly he could see past the cloud, and his fingernails cut into his palms. Through a gap in the clouds he saw it clearly, the delta, the six rivers, there off to the left of the tower of smoke – the city of Hiroshima, untouched.

"We missed!" Kochenski yelled. "We missed it!"

January turned to hide his face from the pilots; on it was a grin like a rictus. He sat back in his seat and let the relief fill him.

Then it was back to it. "Goddamn it!" Fitch shouted down at him. McDonald was trying to restrain him. "January, get up here!"

"Yes sir." Now there was a new set of problems.

January stood and turned, legs weak. His right fingertips throbbed painfully. The men were crowded forward to look out the Plexiglas. January looked with them.

The mushroom cloud was forming. It rolled out as if it might continue to extend forever, fed by the inferno and the black stalk below it. It looked about two miles wide and half a mile tall, and it extended well above the height they flew at, dwarfing their plane entirely "Do you think we'll all be sterile?" Matthews said.

"I can taste the radiation," McDonald declared. "Can you? It tastes like lead."

Bursts of flame shot up into the cloud from below, giving a purplish tint to the stalk. There it stood – lifelike, malignant, sixty thousand feet tall. One bomb. January shoved past the pilots into the navigation cabin, overwhelmed.

"Should I start recording everyone's reactions, Captain?" asked Benton.

"To hell with that," Fitch said, following January back. But Shepard got there first, descending quickly from the navigation dome. He rushed across the cabin, caught January on the shoulder. "You bastard!" he screamed as January stumbled back. "You lost your nerve, coward!"

January went for Shepard, happy to have a target at last, but Fitch cut in and grabbed him by the collar, pulled him around until they were face to face.

"Is that right?" Fitch cried, as angry as Shepard. "Did you screw up on purpose?"

"No," January grunted, and knocked Fitch's hands away from his neck. He swung and smacked Fitch on the mouth, caught him solid. Fitch staggered back, recovered, and no doubt would have beaten January up, but Matthews and Benton and Stone leaped in and held him back, shouting for order. "Shut up! Shut up!" McDonald screamed from the cockpit and for a moment it was bedlam. But Fitch let himself be restrained, and soon only McDonald's shouts for quiet were heard. January retreated to between the pilot seats, right hand on his pistol holster.

"The city was in the cross hairs when I flipped the switch," he said. "But the first couple of times I flipped it nothing happened—"

"That's a lie!" Shepard shouted. "There was nothing wrong with the switch, I checked it myself. Besides the bomb exploded *miles* beyond Hiroshima, look for yourself! That's *minutes*." He wiped spit from his chin and pointed at January. "You did it."

"You don't know that," January said. But he could see the men had been convinced by Shepard, and he took a step back. "You just get me to a board of inquiry, quick. And leave me alone till then. If you touch me again," glaring venomously at Fitch and then Shepard, "I'll shoot you." He turned and hopped down to his seat, feeling exposed and vulnerable, like a treed raccoon.

"They'll shoot *you* for this," Shepard screamed after him. "Disobeying orders – treason—" Matthews and Stone were shutting him up.

"Let's get out of here," he heard McDonald say. "I can taste the lead, can't you?"

January looked out the Plexiglas. The giant cloud still burned and roiled. One atom . . . Well, they had really done it to that forest. He almost laughed but stopped himself, afraid of hysteria. Through a break in the clouds he got a clear view of Hiroshima for the first time. It lay spread over its islands like a map, unharmed. Well, that was that. The inferno at the base of the mushroom cloud was eight or ten miles around the shore of the bay and a mile or two inland. A certain patch of forest would be gone, destroyed – utterly blasted from the face of the earth. The Japs would be able to go out and investigate the damage. And if they were told it was a demonstration, a warning – and if they acted fast – well, they had their chance. Maybe it would work.

The release of tension made January feel sick. Then he recalled Shepard's words, and he knew that whether his plan worked or not he was still in trouble. In trouble! It was worse than that. Bitterly he cursed the Japanese. He even wished for a moment that he *had* dropped it on them. Wearily he let his despair empty him.

A long while later he sat up straight. Once again he was a trapped animal. He began lunging for escape, casting about for plans. One alternative after another. All during the long, grim flight home he considered it, mind spinning at the speed of the props and beyond. And when they came down on Tinian he had a plan. It was a long shot, he reckoned, but it was the best he could do.

The briefing hut was surrounded by MPs again. January stumbled from the truck with the rest and walked inside. He was more than ever aware of the looks given him, and they were hard, accusatory. He was too tired to care. He hadn't slept in more than thirty-six hours and had slept very little since the last time he had been in the hut, a week before. Now the room quivered with the lack of engine vibration to stabilize it, and the silence roared. It was all he could do to hold on to his plan. The glares of Fitch and Shepard, the hurt incomprehension of Matthews, they had to be thrust out of his focus. Thankfully he lit a cigarette.

In a clamour of question and argument the others described the strike. Then the haggard Scholes and an intelligence officer led them through the bombing run. January's plan made it necessary to hold to his story. ". . . and when the AP was under the cross hairs I pushed down the switch, but got no signal. I flipped it up and down repeatedly until the tone kicked in. At that point there was still fifteen seconds to the release."

"Was there anything that may have caused the tone to start when it did?"

"Not that I noticed immediately, but—"

"It's impossible," Shepard interrupted, face red. "I checked the switch before we flew and there was nothing wrong with it. Besides, the drop occurred over a minute—"

"Captain Shepard," Scholes said. "We'll hear from you presently."

"But he's obviously lying—"

"Captain Shepard! It's not at all obvious. Don't speak unless questioned."

"Anyway," January said, hoping to shift the questions away from the issue of the long delay, "I noticed something about the bomb when it was falling that could explain why it stuck. I need to discuss it with one of the scientists familiar with the bomb's design."

"What was that?" Scholes asked suspiciously.

January hesitated. "There's going to be an inquiry, right?"

Scholes frowned "This is the inquiry, Captain January. Tell us what you saw."

"But there will be some proceeding beyond this one?"

"It looks like there's going to be a court-martial, yes, Captain."

"That's what I thought. I don't want to talk to anyone but my counsel, and some scientist familiar with the bomb."

"*I'm* a scientist familiar with the bomb," Shepard burst out. "You could tell me if you really had anything, you—"

"I said I need a scientist!" January exclaimed, rising to face the scarlet Shepard across the table. "Not a g-goddamned mechanic." Shepard started to shout, others joined in, and the room rang with argument. While Scholes restored order January sat down, and he refused to be drawn out again.

"I'll see you're assigned counsel and initiate the court-martial," Scholes said, clearly at a loss. "Meanwhile you are under arrest, on suspicion of disobeying orders in combat." January nodded, and Scholes gave him over to MPs.

"One last thing," January said, fighting exhaustion. "Tell General LeMay that if the Japs are told this drop was a warning, it might have the same effect as—"

"I told you!" Shepard shouted, "I told you he did it on purpose!"

Men around Shepard restrained him. But he had convinced most of them, and even Matthews stared at him with surprised anger.

January shook his head wearily. He had the dull feeling that his plan, while it had succeeded so far, was ultimately not a good one. "Just trying to make the best of it." It took all of his remaining will to force his legs to carry him in a dignified manner out of the hut.

His cell was an empty NCO's office. MPs brought his meals. For the first couple of days he did little but sleep. On the third day he glanced out the office's barred window and saw a tractor pulling a tarpaulin-draped trolley out of the compound, followed by jeeps filled with MPs. It looked like a military funeral. January rushed to the door and banged on it until one of the young MPs came.

"What's that they're doing out there?" January demanded.

Eyes cold and mouth twisted, the MP said, "They're making another strike. They're going to do it right this time."

"No!" January cried. "No!" He rushed the MP, who knocked him back and locked the door. "*No!*" He beat the door until his hands hurt, cursing wildly. "You don't *need* to do it, it isn't *necessary.*" Shell shattered at last, he collapsed on the bed and wept. Now everything he had done would be rendered meaningless. He had sacrificed himself for nothing.

A day or two after that the MPs led in a colonel, an iron-haired man who stood stiffly and crushed January's hand when he shook it. His eyes were a pale icy blue.

"I am Colonel Dray," he said. "I have been ordered to defend you in court-martial." January could feel the dislike pouring from the man. "To do that I'm going to need every fact you have, so let's get started."

"I'm not talking to anybody until I've seen an atomic scientist."

"I am your *defence* counsel—"

"I don't care who you are," January said. "Your defence of me depends on you getting one of the scientists *here*. The higher up he is, the better. And I want to speak to him alone."

"I will have to be present."

So he would do it. But now January's counsel, too, was an enemy.

"Naturally," January said. "You're my counsel. But no one else. Our atomic secrecy may depend on it."

"You saw evidence of sabotage?"

"Not one word more until that scientist is here."

Angrily the colonel nodded and left.

Late the next day the colonel returned with another man. "This is Dr Forest."

"I helped develop the bomb," Forest said. He had a crew cut and was dressed in fatigues, and to January he looked more Army than the colonel. Suspiciously he stared back and forth at the two men.

"You'll vouch for this man's identity on your word as an officer?" he asked Dray.

"Of course," the colonel said stiffly, offended.

"So," Dr Forest said. "You had some trouble getting it off when you wanted to. Tell me what you saw."

"I saw nothing," January said harshly. He took a deep breath; it was time to commit himself. "I want you to take a message back to the scientists. You folks have been working on this thing for years, and you must have had time to consider how the bomb should have been used. You know we could have convinced the Japs to surrender by showing them a demonstration—"

"Wait a minute," Forest said. "You're saying you didn't see anything? There wasn't a malfunction?"

"That's right," January said, and cleared his throat. "It wasn't *necessary*, do you understand?"

Forest was looking at Colonel Dray. Dray gave him a disgusted shrug. "He told me he saw evidence of sabotage."

"I want you to go back and ask the scientists to intercede for me," January said, raising his voice to get the man's attention. "I haven't got a chance in that court-martial. But if the scientists defend me then maybe they'll let me live, see? I don't want to get shot for doing something every one of you scientists would have done."

Dr Forest backed away. Colour rising, he said, "What makes you think that's what we would have done? Don't you think we considered it? Don't you think men better qualified than you made the decision?" He waved a hand. "Goddamn it – what made you think you were competent to decide something as important as that!"

January was appalled at the man's reaction; in his plan it had gone differently. Angrily he jabbed a finger at Forest. "Because *I* was the man doing it, *Doctor* Forest. You take even one step back from that and suddenly you can pretend it's not your doing. Fine for you, but *I was there*."

At every word the man's colour was rising. It looked like he might pop a vein in his neck. January tried once more. "Have you ever tried to imagine what one of your bombs would do to a city full of people?"

"I've had enough!" the man exploded. He turned to Dray. "I'm under no obligation to keep what I've heard here confidential. You can be sure it will be used as evidence in Captain January's court-martial." He turned and gave January a look of such blazing hatred that January understood it. For these men to admit he was right would mean admitting that they were wrong – that every one of them was responsible for his part in the construction of the weapon January had refused to use. Understanding that, January knew he was doomed.

The bang of Dr Forest's departure still shook the little office. January sat on his cot, got out a smoke. Under Colonel Dray's cold gaze he lit one shakily, took a drag. He looked up at the colonel and shrugged. "It was my best chance," he explained. That did something – for the first and only time the cold disdain in the colonel's eyes shifted, to a little, hard, lawyerly gleam of respect.

The court-martial lasted two days. The verdict was guilty of disobeying orders in combat and of giving aid and comfort to the enemy. The sentence was death by firing squad.

For most of his remaining days January rarely spoke, drawing ever further behind the mask that had hidden him for so long. A clergyman came to see him, but it was the 509th's chaplain, the one who had said the prayer blessing the *Lucky Strike*'s mission before they took off. Angrily January sent him packing.

Later, however, a young Catholic priest dropped by. His name was Patrick Getty. He was a little pudgy man, bespectacled and, it seemed, somewhat afraid of January. January let the man talk to him. When he returned the next day January talked back a bit, and on the day after that he talked some more. It became a habit.

Usually January talked about his childhood. He talked of ploughing mucky black bottomland behind a mule. Of running down the lane to the mailbox. Of reading books by the light of the moon after he had been ordered to sleep. And of being beaten by his mother for it with a high-heeled shoe. He told the priest the story of the time his arm had been burned, and about the car crash at the bottom of Fourth Street. "It's the truck driver's face I remember, do you see, Father?"

"Yes," the young priest said. "Yes."

And he told him about the game he had played in which every action he took tipped the balance of world affairs. "When I remembered that game I thought it was dumb. Step on a side-walk crack and cause an earthquake – you know, it's stupid. Kids are like that." The priest nodded. "But now I've been thinking that if everybody were to live their whole lives like that, thinking that every move they made really was important, then . . . it might make a difference." He waved a hand vaguely, expelled cigarette smoke. "You're accountable for what you do."

"Yes," the priest said. "Yes, you are."

"And if you're given orders to do something wrong, you're still accountable, right. The orders don't change it."

"That's right."

"Hmph." January smoked a while. "So they say, anyway. But look what happens." He waved at the office. "I'm like the guy in a story I read – he thought everything in books was true, and after reading a bunch of westerns he tried to rob a train. They tossed him in jail." He laughed shortly. "Books are full of crap."

"Not all of them," the priest said. "Besides, you weren't trying to rob a train."

They laughed at the notion. "Did you read that story?"

"No."

"It was the strangest book – there were two stories in it, and they alternated chapter by chapter, but they didn't have a thing to do with each other! I didn't get it."

"Maybe the writer was trying to say that everything connects to everything else."

"Maybe. But it's a funny way to say it."

"I like it."

And so they passed the time, talking.

So it was the priest who was the one to come by and tell January that his request for a presidential pardon had been refused. Getty said awkwardly, "It seems the President approves the sentence."

"That bastard," January said weakly. He sat on his cot.

Time passed. It was another hot, humid day.

"Well," the priest said. "Let me give you some better news. Given your situation I don't think telling you matters, though I've been told not to. The second mission – you know there was a second strike?"

"Yes."

"Well, they missed too."

"What?" January cried, and bounced to his feet. "You're kidding!"

"No. They flew to Kokura but found it covered by clouds. It was the same over Nagasaki and Hiroshima, so they flew back to Kokura and tried to drop the bomb using radar to guide it, but apparently there was a genuine equipment failure this time, and the bomb fell on an island."

January was hopping up and down, mouth hanging open, "So we n-never—"

"We never dropped an atom bomb on a Japanese city. That's right." Getty grinned. "And get this – I heard this from my superior – they sent a message to the Japanese Government telling them that the two explosions were warnings, and that if they didn't surrender by September we would drop bombs on Kyoto and Tokyo, and then wherever else we had to. Word is that the Emperor went to Hiroshima to survey the damage, and when he saw it he ordered the Cabinet to surrender. So . . ."

"So it worked," January said. He hopped around. "It worked, it worked!"

"Yes."

"Just like I said it would!" he cried, and hopping in front of the priest he laughed.

Getty was jumping around a little too, and the sight of the priest bouncing was too much for January. He sat on his cot and laughed till the tears ran down his cheeks.

"So—" He sobered quickly. "So Truman's going to shoot me anyway, eh?"

"Yes," the priest said unhappily. "I guess that's right."

This time January's laugh was bitter. "He's a bastard, all right. And proud of being a bastard, which makes it worse." He shook his head. "If Roosevelt had lived . . ."

"It would have been different," Getty finished. "Yes. Maybe so. But he didn't." He sat beside January. "Cigarette?" He held out a pack, and January noticed the green wrapper, the round bull's-eye. He frowned.

"You haven't got a Camel?"

"Oh. Sorry."

"Oh well. That's all right." January took one of the Lucky Strikes, lit up. "That's awfully good news." He breathed out. "I never believed Truman would pardon me anyway, so mostly you've brought good news. Ha. They *missed*. You have no idea how much better that makes me feel."

"I think I do."

January smoked the cigarette.

"So I'm a good American after all. I *am* a good American," he insisted, "no matter what Truman says."

"Yes," Getty replied, and coughed. "You're better than Truman any day."

"Better watch what you say, Father." He looked into the eyes behind the glasses, and the expression he saw there gave him pause. Since the drop every look directed at him had been filled with contempt. He'd seen it so often during the court-martial that he'd learned to stop looking; and now he had to teach himself to see again. The priest looked at him as if he were . . . as if he were some kind of hero. That wasn't exactly right. But seeing it . . .

January would not live to see the years that followed, so he would never know what came of his action. He had given up casting his mind forward and imagining possibilities, because there was no point to it. His planning was ended. In any case he would not have been able to imagine the course of the postwar years. That the world would quickly become an armed camp pitched on the edge of atomic war, he might have predicted. But he never would have guessed that so many people would join a January Society. He would never know of the effect the Society had on Dewey during the Korean crisis, never know of the Society's successful campaign for the test-ban treaty, and never learn that, thanks in part to the Society and its allies, a treaty would be signed by the great powers that would reduce the number of atomic bombs year by year, until there were none left.

Frank January would never know any of that. But in that moment on his cot looking into the eyes of young Patrick Getty, he guessed an inkling of it – he felt, just for an instant, the impact on history.

And with that he relaxed. In his last week everyone who met him carried away the same impression – that of a calm, quiet man, angry at Truman and others, but in a withdrawn, matter-of-fact way. Patrick Getty, a strong force in the January Society ever after, said January was talkative for some time after he learned of the missed attack on Kokura. Then he got quieter, as the day approached. On the morning that they woke him at dawn to march him out to a hastily constructed execution shed, his MPs shook his hand. The priest was with him as he smoked a final cigarette, and they prepared to put the hood over his head. January looked at him calmly. "They load one of the guns with a blank cartridge, right?"

"Yes," Gerry said.

"So each man in the squad can imagine he may not have shot me?"

"Yes. That's right."

A tight, unhumorous smile was January's last expression. He threw down the cigarette, ground it out, poked the priest in the arm. "But I *know*." Then the mask slipped back into place for good, making the hood redundant, and with a firm step January went to the wall. One might have said he was at peace.

His Powder'd Wig,
His Crown of Thornes

Marc Laidlaw

Grant Innes first saw the icon in the Indian ghettos of London, but thought nothing of it. There were so many gewgaws of native "art" being thrust in his face by faddishly war-painted Cherokees that this was just another nuisance to avoid, like the huge radios blaring obnoxious "Choctawk" percussions and the high-pitched warbling of Tommy Hawkes and the effeminate Turquoise Boys; like the young Mohawk ruddies practising skateboard stunts for sluttish cockney girls whose kohled black eyes and slack blue lips betrayed more interest in the dregs of the bottles those boys carried than in the boys themselves. Of course, it was not pleasure or curiosity that brought him into the squalid district, among the baggy green canvas street-teepees and graffitoed storefronts. Business alone could bring him here. He had paid a fair sum for the name and number of a Mr Cloud, dealer in Navaho jewellery, whose samples had proved of excellent quality and would fetch the highest prices, not only in Europe but in the Colonies as well. Astute dealers knew that the rage for turquoise had nearly run its course, thank God; following the popularity of the lurid blue stone, the simplicity of black-patterned silver would be a welcome relief indeed. Grant had hardly been able to tolerate the sight of so much garish rock as he'd been forced to stock in order to suit his customers; he was looking forward to this next trend. He'd already laid the ground for several showcase presentations in Paris; five major glossies were bidding for rights to photograph his collector's pieces, antique sand-cast *najas* and squash-blossom necklaces, for a special fashion portfolio.

Here in the slums, dodging extruded plastic kachina dolls and machine-woven blankets, his fine-tuned eye was offended by virtually everything he saw. It was trash for tourists. Oh, it had its spurts of cheap popularity, like the war bonnets which all the cyclists had worn last summer, but such moments were as fleeting as pop hits, thank God. Only true quality could ever transcend the dizzying gyres of public favour. Fine art, precious stones, pure metal: these were investments that would never lose their value.

So much garbage ultimately had the effect of blinding him to his environment; avoidance became a mental as well as a physical trick. He was dreaming of silver crescents gleaming against ivory skin when he realized that he must have passed the street he sought. He stopped in his tracks, suddenly aware of the hawkers' cries, the pulse of hide-drums and synthesizers. He spun about searching for a number on any of the shops.

"Lost, guv?" said a tall young brave with gold teeth, his bare chest ritually scarified. He carried a tall pole strung with a dozen gruesome rubber scalps, along with several barristers' wigs. They gave the brave the appearance of a costume merchant, except for one morbid detail: each of the white wigs was spattered with blood . . . red dye, rather, liberally dripped among the coarse white strands.

"You *look* lost."

"Looking for a shop," he muttered, fumbling Mr Cloud's card from his pocket.

"No, I mean really lost. Out of balance. *Koyaanisqatsi*, guv. Like the whole world."

"I'm looking for a shop," Grant repeated firmly.

"That all, then? A shop? What about the things you really lost? Things we've all lost, I'm talking about. Here."

He patted his bony hip, which was wrapped in a black leather loincloth. Something dangled from his belt, a doll-like object on a string, a charm of some sort. Grant looked over the brave's head and saw the number he sought, just above a doorway. The damn ruddy was in his way. As he tried to slip past, avoiding contact with the rubbery scalps and bloodied wigs, the brave unclipped the charm from his belt and thrust it into his face.

Grant recoiled, nearly stumbling backward in the street. It was an awful little mannequin, face pinched and soft, its agonized expression carved from a withered apple.

'Here – here's where we lost it," the brave said, thrusting the doll up to his cheek, as if he would have it kiss or nip him with its rice-grain teeth. Its limbs were made of jerked beef, spread-eagled on wooden crossbars, hands and feet fixed in place with four tiny nails. It was a savage Christ – an obscenity.

"He gave His life for you," the brave said. "Not just for one people, but for everyone. Eternal freedom, that was His promise."

"I'm late for my appointment," Grant said, unable to hide his disgust.

"Late and lost," the brave said. "But you'll never catch up – the time slipped past. And you'll never find your way unless you follow Him."

"Just get out of my way!"

He shoved the brave aside, knocking the hideous little idol out of the Indian's grasp. Fearing reprisal, he forced an apologetic expression as he turned back from the hard-won doorway. But the brave wasn't watching him. He crouched over the filthy street, retrieving his little martyr. Lifting it to his lips, he kissed it gently.

"I'm sorry," Grant said.

The brave glanced up at Grant and grinned fiercely, baring his gold teeth; then he bit deep into the dried brown torso of the Christ and tore away a ragged strip of jerky.

Nauseous, Grant hammered on the door behind him. It opened abruptly and he almost fell into the arms of Mr Cloud.

He next saw the image the following summer, in the District of Cornwallis. Despite the fact that Grant specialized in provincial art, most of his visits to the colonies had been for business purposes, and had exposed him to no more glorious surroundings than the interiors of banks and mercantile offices, with an occasional jaunt into the Six Nations to meet with the creators of the fine pieces that were his trade. Sales were brisk, his artisans had been convinced to ply their craft with gold as well as silver, supplanting turquoise and onyx with diamonds and other precious stones; the trend towards high-fashion American jewellery had already surpassed his highest expectations. Before the inevitable decline and a panicked search for the next sure thing, he decided to accept the offer of an old colonial acquaintance who had long extended an open invitation to a tour of great American monuments in the capital city.

Arnoldsburg, D.C., was sweltering in a humid haze, worsened by exhaust fumes from the taxis that seemed the city's main occupants. Eyes burning, lungs fighting against collapse, he and his guide crawled from taxi after taxi and plunged into cool marble corridors reeking of urine and crowded with black youths selling or buying opiates. It was hard not to mock the great figures of American history, thus surrounded and entrapped by the ironic fruits of their victories. The huge seated figure of Burgoyne looked mildly bemused by the addicts sleeping between his feet; the bronze brothers Richard and William Howe stood back to back embattled in a waist-high mob, as though taking their last stand against colonial Lilliputians.

His host, David Mickelson, was a transplanted Irishman. He had first visited America as a physician with the Irish Royal Army, and after his term expired had signed on for a stint in the Royal American Army. He had since opened a successful dermatological practice in Arnoldsburg. He was a collector of native American art, which practice had led him to deal with Grant Innes. Mickelson had excellent taste in metalwork, but Grant chided him for his love of "these marble monstrosities".

"But these are heroes, Grant. Imagine where England would be without these men. An island with few resources and limited room for expansion? How could we have kept up the sort of healthy growth we've had since the Industrial Revolution? It's impossible. And without these men to secure this realm for us, how could we have held onto it? America is so vast – really, you have no concept of it. These warriors laid the way for peace and proper management, steering a narrow course between Spain and France. Without such fine ambassadors to put down the early rebellion and ease the co-settling of the Six Nations, America might still be at war. Instead its resources belong to the crown. This is our treasure house, Grant, and these are the keepers of that treasure."

"Treasure," Grant repeated, with an idle nudge at the body of an old squaw who lay unconscious on the steps of the Howe Monument.

"Come with me, then," Mickelson said. "One more sight, and then we'll go wherever you like."

They boarded another taxi which progressed by stops and starts through the iron river of traffic. A broad, enormous dome appeared above the cars.

"Ah," said Grant. "I know what that is."

They disembarked at the edge of a huge circular plaza. The dome that capped the plaza was supported by a hundred white columns. They went into the lidded shadow, into darkness, and for a moment Grant was blinded.

"Watch out, old boy," Mickelson said. "Here's the rail. Grab on. Wouldn't want to stumble in here."

His hands closed on polished metal. When he felt steady again, he opened his eyes and found himself staring into a deep pit. The walls of the shaft were perfectly smooth, round as a bullet hole drilled deep into the earth. He felt a cold wind coming out of it, and then the grip of vertigo.

"The depths of valour, the inexhaustible well of the human spirit," Mickelson was saying. "Makes you dizzy with pride, doesn't it?"

"I'm . . . feeling . . . sick . . ." Grant turned and hurried towards daylight.

Out in the sunshine again, his sweat gone cold, he leaned against a marble podium and gradually caught his breath. When his mind had cleared somewhat, he looked up and saw that the podium was engraved with the name of the hero whose accomplishments the shaft commemorated. His noble bust surmounted the slab.

BENEDICT ARNOLD

First American President-General, appointed such by King George III as reward for his valiant role in suppressing the provincial revolt of 1776–79.

David Mickelson caught up with him.

"Feeling all right, Grant?"

"Better. I – I think I'd like to get back to my rooms. It's this heat."

"Surely. I'll hail a cab, you just hold on here for a minute."

As Grant watched Mickelson hurry away, his eyes strayed over the circular plaza where the usual hawkers had laid out the usual souvenirs. Habit, more than curiousity, drove him out among the ragged blankets, his eyes swiftly picking through the merchandise and discarding it all as garbage.

Well, most of it. This might turn out to be another fortunate venture after all. His eyes had been caught by a display of absolutely brilliant designs done in copper and brass. He had never seen anything quite like them. Serpents, eagles, patterns of stars. The metal was all wrong, but the artist had undoubtedly chosen them by virtue of their cheapness and could be easily convinced to work in gold. He looked up at the proprietor of these wares and saw a young Indian woman, bent on her knees, threading coloured beads on a string.

"Who made these?" he said, softening the excitement he felt into a semblance of mild curiosity.

She gazed up at him. "My husband."

"Really? I like them very much. Does he have a distributor?"

She didn't seem to know what he meant.

"That is . . . does anyone else sell these pieces?"

She shook her head. "This is all he makes, right here. When he makes more, I sell those."

In the distance, he heard Mickelson shouting his name. The dermatologist came running over the marble plaza. "Grant, I've got a cab!"

Grant gestured as if to brush him away. "I'll meet you later, David, all right? Something's come up."

"What have you found?" Mickelson tried to look past him at the blanket, but Grant spun him around in the direction of the taxis – perhaps a bit too roughly. Mickelson stopped for a moment, readjusted his clothes, then stalked away peevishly towards the cars. So be it.

Smiling, Grant turned back to the woman. His words died on his tongue when he saw what she was doing with beads she'd been stringing.

She had formed them into a noose, a bright rainbow noose, and slipped this over the head of a tiny brown doll.

He knew that doll, knew its tough leathered flesh and pierced limbs, the apple cheeks and teeth of rice. The cross from which she'd taken it lay discarded on the blanket, next to the jewellery that suddenly seemed of secondary importance.

While he stood there unspeaking, unmoving, she lifted the dangling doll to her lips and daintily, baring crooked teeth, tore off a piece of the leg.

"What . . . what . . ."

He found himself unable to ask what he wished to ask. Instead, fixed by her gaze, he stammered, "What do you want for all of these?"

She finished chewing before answering. "All?"

"Yes, I . . . I'd like to buy all of them. In fact, I'd like to buy more than this. I'd like to commission a piece, if I might."

The squaw swallowed.

"My husband creates what is within the soul. He makes dreams into metal. He would have to see your dreams."

"My dreams? Well, yes, I'll tell him exactly what I want. Could I meet him to discuss this?"

The squaw shrugged. She patiently unlooped the noose from the shrivelled image, spread it back onto its cross and pinned the three remaining limbs into place, then tucked it away in a bag at her belt. Finally, rising, she rolled up the blanket with all the bangles and bracelets inside it, and tucked the parcel under her arm.

"Come with me," she said.

He followed her without another word, feeling as though he were moving down an incline, losing his balance with every step, barely managing to throw himself in her direction. She was his guide through the steaming city, through the crowds of ragged cloth, skins ruddy and dark. He pulled off his customary jacket, loosened his tie, and struggled after her. She seemed to dwindle in the distance; he was losing her, losing himself, stretching into a thin strand of beads, beads of sweat, sweat that dripped through the gutters of Arnoldsburg and offered only brine to the thirsty . . .

But when she once looked back and saw him faltering, she put out her hand and he was standing right beside her, near a metal door. She put her hand upon it and opened the way.

It was cool inside, and dark except for the tremulous light of candles that lined a descending stairway. He followed, thinking of catacombs, the massed and desiccated ranks of the dead he had seen beneath old missions in Spanish Florida. There was a dusty smell, and far off the sound of hammering. She opened another door and the sound was suddenly close at hand.

They had entered a workshop. A man sat at a metal table cluttered with coils of wire, metal snips, hand torches. The woman stepped out and closed the door on them.

"Good afternoon," Grant said. "I . . . I'm a great admirer of your work."

The man turned slowly, the metal stool creaking under his weight, although he was not a big man. His skin was very dark, like his close-cropped hair. His face was soft, as though made of chamois pouches; but his eyes were hard. He beckoned.

"Come here," he said. "You like my stuff? What is it that you like?"

Grant approached the workbench with a feeling of awe. Samples of the man's work lay scattered about, but these were not done in copper or brass. They were silver, most of them, and gleamed like moonlight.

"The style," he said. "The . . . substance."

"How about this?" The Indian fingered a large eagle with spreading wings.

"It's beautiful – almost alive."

"It's a sign of freedom." He laid it down. "What about this one?"

He handed Grant a small rectangular plaque inscribed with an unusual but somehow familiar design. A number of horizontal stripes, with a square inset in the lower right corner, and in that square a wreath of thirteen stars.

"Beautiful," Grant said. "You do superior work."

"That's not what I mean. Do you know the symbol?"

"I . . . I think I've seen it somewhere before. An old Indian design, isn't it?"

The Indian grinned. Gold teeth again, bridging the distance between London and Arnoldsburg, reminding him of the jerked beef martyr, the savage Christ.

"Not an Indian sign," he said. "A sign for all people."

"Really? Well, I'd like to *bring* it to all people. I'm a dealer in fine jewellery. I could get a very large audience for these pieces. I could make you a very rich man."

"Rich?" The Indian set the plaque aside. "Plenty of Indians are rich. The tribes have all the land and factories they want – as much as you have. But we lack what you also lack: freedom. What is wealth when we have no freedom?"

"Freedom?"

"It's a dim concept to you, isn't it? But not to me." He put his hand over his heart. "I hold it here, safe with the memory of how we lost it. A precious thing, a cup of holy water that must never be spilled until it can be swallowed in a single draft. I carry the cup carefully, but there's enough for all. If you wish to drink, it can be arranged."

"I don't think you understand," Grant said, recovering some part of himself that had begun to drift off through the mystical fog in which the Indians always veiled themselves. He must do something concrete to counteract so much vagueness. "I'm speaking of a business venture. A partnership."

"I hear your words. But I see something deeper in you. Something that sleeps in all men. They come here seeking what is lost, looking for freedom and a cause. But all they find are the things that went wrong. Why are you so out of balance, eh? You stumble and crawl, but you always end up here with that same empty look in your eyes. I've seen you before. A dozen just like you."

"I'm an art dealer," Grant said. "Not a – a pilgrim. If you can show me more work like this, I'd be grateful. Otherwise, I'm sorry for wasting your time, and I'll be on my way."

Suddenly he was anxious to get away, and this seemed a reasonable excuse. But the jeweller now seemed ready to accommodate him.

"Art, then," he said. "All right. I will show you the thing that speaks to you, and perhaps then you will understand. Art is also a way to the soul."

He slipped down from the stool and moved towards the door, obviously intending Grant to follow.

"I'll show you more than this," the Indian said. "I'll show you inspiration."

After another dizzying walk, they entered a derelict museum in a district that stank of danger. Grant felt safe only because of his companion; he was obviously a stranger here, in these oppressive alleys. Even inside the place, which seemed less a museum than a warehouse, he sensed that he was being watched. It was crowded by silent mobs, many of them children, almost all of them Negro or Indian. Some sat in circles on the cement floors, talking quietly among themselves, as though taking instruction. Pawnee, Chickasaw, Blackfoot, Cheyenne, Comanche . . . Arnoldsburg was a popular site for tourists, but these didn't have the look of the ruddy middle-class traveller; these were lower-class ruddies, as tattered as the people in the street. Some had apparently crossed the continent on foot to come here. He felt as if he had entered a church.

"Now you shall see," said the jeweller. "This is the art of the patriots. The forefathers. The hidden ones."

He stopped near a huge canvas that leaned against a steel beam; the painting was caked with grease, darkened by time, but even through the grime he could see that it was the work of genius. An imitation of da Vinci's *Last Supper*, but strangely altered . . .

The guests at Christ's table wore not biblical attire, but that of the eighteenth century. It was no windowed building that sheltered them, but a tent whose walls gave the impression of a strong wind beating against them from without. The thirteen were at table, men in military outfits, and in their midst a figure of mild yet radiant demeanour, humble in a powdered wig, a mere crust of bread on his plate. Grant did not recognize him, this figure in Christ's place, but the man in Judas's place was recognizable enough from the numerous busts and portraits in Arnoldsburg. That was Benedict Arnold.

The Indian pointed at several of the figures, giving them names: "Henry Knox, Nathaniel Greene, Light-Horse Harry Lee, Lafayette, General Rochambeau—"

"Who painted this?"

"It was the work of Benjamin Franklin," said his guide. "Painted not long after the betrayal at West Point, but secretly, in sadness, when the full extent of our tragedy became all too apparent. After West Point, the patriots continued to fight. But this man, this one man, was the glue that held the soldiers together. After His death, the army had many commanders, but none could win the trust of all men. The revolution collapsed and our chance for freedom slipped away. Franklin died without finishing it, his heart broken."

"But that man in the middle?"

The Indian led him to another painting. This was much more recent, judging from the lack of accumulated soot and grease. Several children stood gazing at it, accompanied by a darkie woman who was trying to get them to analyse the meaning of what was essentially a simple image.

"What is this?" she asked.

Several hands went up. "The cherry tree!" chimed a few voices.

"That's right, the cherry tree. Who can tell us the story of the cherry tree?"

One little girl pushed forward. "He chopped it down and when He saw what He had done, He said, 'I cannot let it die.' So He planted the piece He cut off and it grew into a new tree, and the trunk of the old tree grew too, because it was magic."

"Very good. Now that's a fable, of course. Do you know what it really means? What the cherry tree represents?"

Grant felt like one of her charges, waiting for some explanation, innocent.

"It's an English cherry," the teacher hinted.

Hands went up. "The tree!" "I know!" "It's England."

"That's right. And the piece He transplanted?"

"America!"

"Very good. And do you remember what happened next? It isn't shown in this painting, but it was very sad. Tinsha?"

"When His father saw what He had done, he was very scared. He was afraid his son was a devil or something, so he tore up the little tree by the roots. He tore up America."

"And you know who the father really was, don't you?"

"The . . . king?" said Tinsha.

Grant and his guide went on to another painting, this one showing a man in a powdered wig and a ragged uniform walking across a river in midwinter – not stepping on the floes, but moving carefully between them, on the breast of the frigid water. With him came a band of barefoot men, lightly touching hands, the first of them resting his fingers on the cape of their leader. The men stared at the water as if they could not believe their eyes, but there was only confidence in the face of their commander – that and a serene humility.

"This is the work of Sully, a great underground artist," said the jeweller.

"These . . . these are priceless."

The Indian shrugged. "If they were lost tomorrow, we would still carry them with us. It is the feelings they draw from our hearts that are truly beyond price. He came for all men, you see. If you accept Him, if you open your heart to Him, then His death will not have been in vain."

"Washington," Grant said, the name finally coming to him. An insignificant figure of the American Wars, an arch-traitor whose name was a mere footnote in the histories he'd read. Arnold had defeated him, hadn't he? Was that what had happened at West Point? The memories were vague and unreal, textbook memories.

The jeweller nodded. "George Washington," he repeated. "He was leading us to freedom, but He was betrayed and held out as an example. In Philadelphia He was publicly tortured to dispirit the rebels, then hung by His neck after his death, and His corpse toured through the colonies. And that is our sin, the penance which we must pay until every soul has been brought back into balance."

"Your sin?"

The Indian nodded, drawing from the pouch at his waist another of the shrivelled icons, Christ – no, Washington – on the cross.

"We aided the British in that war. Cherokee and Iroquois, others of the Six Nations. We thought the British would save us from the colonists; we didn't know that they had different ways of enslavement. My ancestors were master torturers. When Washington was captured it fell to them – to us – to do the bloodiest work."

His hands tightened on the figure of flesh; the splintered wood dug into his palm.

"We nailed Him to the bars of a cross, borrowing an idea that pleased us greatly from your own religion."

The brown hand shook. The image rose to the golden mouth.

"First, we scalped Him. The powdered hair was slung from a warrior's belt. His flesh was pierced with thorns and knives. And then we flayed Him alive."

"Flayed . . ."

Grant winced as golden teeth nipped a shred of jerky and tore it away.

"Alive . . . ?"

"He died bravely. He was more than a man. He was our deliverer, saviour of all men, white, red, and black. And we murdered Him. We pushed the world off balance."

"What is this place?" Grant asked. "It's more than a museum, isn't it? It's also a school."

"It is a holy place. His spirit lives here, in the heart of the city named for the man who betrayed Him. He died to the world two hundred years ago, but He still lives in us. He is champion of the downtrodden, liberator of the enslaved." The jeweller's voice was cool despite the fervour of his theme. "You see . . . I have looked beyond the walls of fire that surround this world. I have looked into the world that should have been, that would have been if He had lived. I saw a land of the free, a land of life, liberty, and happiness, where the red men lived in harmony with the white. Our plains bore fruit instead of factories. And the holy cause, that of the republic, spread from the hands of the Great Man. The king was dethroned and England too made free. The bell of liberty woke the world; the four winds carried the cause." The jeweller bowed his head. "That is how it would have been. This I have seen in dreams."

Grant looked around him at the paintings, covered with grime but carefully attended; the people, also grimy but with an air of reverence. It was a shame to waste them here, on these people. He imagined the paintings hanging in a well-lit gallery, the patina of ages carefully washed away; saw crowds of people in fine clothes, decked in his gold jewellery, each willing to pay a small fortune for admission. With the proper sponsorship, a world tour could be brought off. He would be a wealthy man, not merely a survivor, at the end of such a tour.

The Indian watched him, nodding. "I know what you're thinking. You think it would be good to tell the world of these things, to spread the cause. You think you can carry the message to all humanity, instead of letting it die here in the dark. But I tell you . . . it thrives here. Those who are oppressed, those who are broken and weary of spirit, they are the caretakers of liberty."

Grant smiled inwardly; there was a bitter taste in his mouth.

"I think you underestimate the worth of all this," he said. "You do it a disservice to hide it from the eyes of the world. I think everyone can gain something from it."

"Yes?" The Indian looked thoughtful. He led Grant towards a table where several old books lay open, their pages swollen with humidity, spines cracking, paper flaking away.

"Perhaps you are right," he said, turning the pages of one book entitled *The Undying Patriot*, edited by a Parson Weems. "It may be as Doctor Franklin says . . ."

Grant bent over the page, and read:

Let no man forget His death. Let not the memory of our great Chief and Commander fade from the thoughts of the common people, who stand to gain the most from its faithful preservation. For once these dreams have fad'd, there is no promise that they may again return. In this age and the next, strive to hold true to the honor'd principals for which He fought, for which he was nail'd to the rude crucifix and his flesh stript away. Forget not His sacrifice, His powder'd wig and crown of thornes. Forget not that a promise Ï can never be repair'd.

"I think you are right," said the jeweller. "How can we take it upon ourselves to hide this glory away? It belongs to the world, and the world shall have it."

He turned to Grant and clasped his hands. His eyes were afire with a patriotic light. "He brought you to me, I see that now. This is a great moment. I thank you, brother, for what you will do."

"It's only my duty," Grant said.

Yes. Duty.

And now he stood in the sweltering shadows outside the warehouse, the secret museum, watching the loading of several large vans. The paintings were wrapped in canvas so that none could see them. He stifled an urge to rush up to the loading men and tear away the cloth, to look once more on that noble face. But the police were thick around the entrance.

"Careful," said David Mickelson at his elbow.

News of the find had spread through the city and a crowd had gathered, in which Grant was just one more curious observer. He supposed it was best this way, though he would rather it was his own people moving the paintings. The police were unwontedly rough with the works, but there was nothing he could do about that.

Things had got a little out of hand.

"Hard to believe it's been sitting under our noses all this time," said Mickelson. "You say you actually got a good look at it?"

Grant nodded abstractedly. "Fairly good. Of course, it was dark in there."

"Even so . . . what a catch, eh? There have been rumours of this stuff for years, and you stumble right into it. Amazing idea you had, though, organizing a tour. As if anyone would pay to see that stuff aside from ruddies and radicals. Even if it weren't completely restricted."

"What . . . what do you think they'll do with it?" Grant asked.

"Same as they do with other contraband, I'd imagine. Burn it."

"Burn it," Grant repeated numbly.

Grant felt a restriction of the easy flow of traffic; suddenly the crowd, mainly black and Indian, threatened to change into something considerably more passionate than a group of disinterested onlookers. The police loosened their riot gear as the mob began to shout insults.

"Fall back, Grant," Mickelson said.

Grant started to move away through the crowd, but a familiar face caught his attention. It was the Indian, the jeweller; he hung near a corner of the museum, his pouchy face unreadable. Somehow, through all the confusion, among the hundred or so faces now mounting in number, his eyes locked onto Grant's.

Grant stiffened. The last of the vans shut its doors and rushed away. The police did not loiter in the area. He had good reason to feel vulnerable.

The jeweller stared at him. Stared without moving. Then he brought up a withered brown object and set it to his lips. Grant could see him bite, tear, and chew.

"What is it, Grant? We should be going now, don't you think? There's still time to take in a real museum, or perhaps the American Palace."

Grant didn't move. Watching the Indian, he put his thumb to his mouth and caught a bit of cuticle between his teeth. He felt as if he were dreaming. Slowly, he tore off a thin strip of skin, ripping it back almost down to the knuckle. The pain was excruciating, but it didn't seem to wake him. He chewed it, swallowed.

"Grant? Is anything wrong?"

He tore off another.

Roncesvalles

Judith Tarr

Spain, AD 778/161 AH

1

Charles, king of the Franks and the Lombards, sometime ally of Baghdad and Byzantium, sat at table in the midst of his army, and considered necessity. He had had the table set in full view of it: namely, the walls of Saragossa, and the gate which opened only to expel curses and the odd barrel of refuse. The city was won for Baghdad against the rebels in Córdoba, but precious few thanks Charles had for his part in it. He was an infidel, and a pagan at that. Saragossa did not want him defiling its Allah-sanctified streets with his presence. Even if it had been he who freed them.

He thrust his emptied plate aside and rose. He was a big man even for a Frank, and a month of playing beggar at Saragossa's door, with little else to do but wait and eat and glare at the walls, had done nothing to lessen his girth. He knew how he towered, king enough even in his plain unkingly clothes; he let the men about him grow still before he spoke. He never shouted: he did not have the voice for it. He always spoke softly, and made men listen, until they forgot the disparity between the clear light voice and the great bear's body. "Tomorrow," he said, "we leave this place. Spain has chosen to settle itself. Let it. We have realms to rule in Gaul, and enemies to fight. We gain no advantage in lingering here."

Having cast the fox among the geese, Charles stood back to watch the spectacle. The Franks were torn between homesickness and warrior honour; between leaving this alien and unfriendly country, and retreating from a battle barely begun. The Arabs howled in anguish. How could he, their ally, abandon them now? The Byzantines stood delicately aside and refrained from smiles.

One voice rose high above the others. Not as high as Charles', but close enough for kin, though the man it came from had a body more fitted to it: a slender dark young firebrand who was, everyone agreed, the very image of the old king. "Leave? *Leave,* my lord? My lord, how can we leave? We've won nothing yet. We've lost men, days, provisions. And for what? To slink back to Gaul with our tails between our legs? By Julian and holy Merovech, I will not!"

The reply came with the graceful inevitability of a Christian antiphon. "You will not? And who are you, young puppy? Are you wisdom itself, that you should command our lord, the king?"

Our lord the king pulled at his luxuriant moustaches and scowled. He loved his sister Gisela dearly, but she had a penchant for contentious males. Her son, who was her image as well as her father the old king's, took after his father when it came to temper. Her husband that was now, barely older than the son who faced him with such exuberant hostility, looked enough like the boy to prompt strangers to ask if they were brothers; but Roland's forthright insolence clashed head-on with Ganelon's vicious urbanity. There was a certain Byzantine slither in the man, but his temper was all Frank, and his detestation of his stepson as overt as ever a savage could wish. He was a Meroving, was Ganelon; they hated best where the blood-tie was closest. What Gisela saw in him, Roland would never comprehend; but Charles could see it well enough. Clever wits, a comely face, and swift mastery of aught he set his hand to. He was not, all things considered, an ill match for the daughter of a king. But Charles could wish, on occasion, that Gisela had not come to her senses after the brief madness of her youth, and abandoned the

Christians' nunnery for a pair of bold black eyes.

Her son and her husband stood face to face across the laden table: two small, dark, furious men, bristling and spitting like warring cats. "Puppy, you call me?" cried Roland. "Snake's get, you, crawling and hissing in corners, tempting my lord to counsels of cowardice."

"Counsels of wisdom," said Ganelon, all sweet reason. "Counsels of prudence. Words you barely know, still less understand."

"Cowardice!" Roland cried, louder. Charles was reminded forcibly of his own determination never to shout. Yes; it was almost as high as a woman's, or like a boy's just broken. In Roland, it seemed only a little ridiculous. "A word *you* can never understand, simply be. Where were you when I led the charge on Saragossa? Did you even draw your sword? Or were you too preoccupied with piddling in your breeches?"

Men round about leaped before either of the kinsmen could move, and wrestled them down. Roland was laughing as he did when he fought, high and light and wild. Ganelon was silent. Until there was a pause in the laughter Then he said calmly, "Better a coward than an empty braggart."

"That," said Charles, "will be enough."

He was heard. He met the eyes of the yellow-haired giant who sat with some effort on Roland. The big man settled his weight more firmly, and mustered a smile that was half a grimace. Charles shifted his stare to Ganelon. His counsellor had freed himself, and stood shaking his clothing into place, smiling a faint, mirthless smile. After a judicious pause he bowed to the king and said, "My lord knows the path of wisdom. I regret that he must hear the counsel of fools."

Charles had not known how taut his back was, until he eased it, leaning forward over the table, running his eyes over all their faces. "I give ear to every man who speaks. But in the end, the choice is mine. I have chosen. Tomorrow we return to Gaul." He stood straight. "Sirs. My lords. You know your duties. You have my leave to see to them."

★   ★   ★

Once Roland was out of Ganelon's sight, he regained most of his sanity. Never all of it, where his stepfather was concerned, but enough to do as his king had bidden. Even before he was Ganelon's enemy, he was the king's man, Count of the Breton Marches, with duties both many and various. Oliver, having seen him safely engaged in them, withdrew for a little himself, to look to his own duties and, if truth be told, to look for the girl who sold sweets and other delights to the soldiers. She was nowhere in sight; he paused by his tent, nursing a new bruise. It never ceased to amaze him how so little a man as Roland could be so deadly a fighter. The best in Frankland, Oliver was certain. One of the three or four best, Roland himself would say. Roland was no victim of modesty. He called it a Christian vice. A good pagan knew himself; and hence, his virtues as well as his vices.

Oliver, whose mother had been Christian but whose father had never allowed her to raise her son in that faith, had no such simplicity of conviction. He was not a good pagan. He could not be a Christian; Christians tried to keep a man from enjoying women. Maybe he would make a passable Muslim. War was holy, in Islam. And a man who did not enjoy the pleasures of the flesh, was no man at all.

"Sir? Oliver?"

He had heard the man's approach. He turned now, and raised a brow. His servant bowed, which was for anyone who might be watching, and met his eyes steadily, which was for the two of them. "Sir," said Walthar, "there's something you ought to see."

His glance forbade questions; his tone forestalled objection. Oliver set his lips tight together, and followed where Walthar led.

Walthar led him by a twisting way, more round the camp than through it, keeping to the backs of tents, pausing when it seemed that anyone might stop to put names to two men moving swiftly in shadows. Oliver crouched as low as he could, for what good it did: he was still an extraordinarily large shadow.

He had kept count of where they went, and whose portions of the encampment they passed. From one end to the other, from Roland's to – yes, this was Ganelon's circle of tents, and Ganelon's in the middle. Turbulent as the camp was, stung into action by the king's command, here was almost quiet. There were guards at the tent's flap, but no one in the dusk behind, where Walthar led Oliver with hunter's stealth and beckoned him to kneel and listen.

At first he heard nothing. He was on the verge of rising and dragging his meddlesome servant away to chastisement, when a voice spoke. It was not Ganelon's. It spoke Greek, of which Oliver knew a little. Enough to piece together what it said. "No. No, my friend. I do not see the wisdom in it."

The man who replied, surely, was Ganelon. Ganelon, who pretended to no more Greek than the king had, which was just enough to understand an ambassador's speech, never sufficient for speech of his own, Ganelon, speaking Greek with ease and, as far as Oliver's untutored ears could tell, hardly a trace of Frankish accent. "Then, my friend" – irony there, but without overt malice – "you do not know the king, Yes, he withdraws from Saragossa. Yes, he seems by that to favour our cause. But the king is never a simple man. Nor should you take him for such, because his complexity is never Byzantine complexity."

The Greek was silken, which meant that he was angry. "I have yet to make the mistake of underestimating your king. Yet still I see no utility in what you propose. Saragossa has done nothing to advance the cause of its caliph, by casting out the ally who won it from the rebels. His departure is prudence, and anger. Best to foster that, yes. But to embellish it – that is not necessary, and if it fails, it is folly; it may lose us all that we have gained. There are times when even a Byzantine can see the value in simplicity."

"Simple, yes. As that nephew of his is simple. There is a man who will never rest until he has a war to fight. He sees this withdrawal not as strategy but as cowardice. Let him work on the king, let him bring in his toadies and their warmongering, and the king well may change his mind. More: he may turn from our cause altogether, and embrace Islam. You may not see it, but I am all too well aware of it. He is attracted to the faith of Muhammad. It speaks to the heart of him. The sacredness of war. The allurements of the flesh both in this life and in the next. The dreams of empire. And what have we to offer in return?"

"The reality of empire," said the Greek.

Ganelon snorted indelicately. "Oh, come! We're both conspirators here. You know as well as I, that our sacred empress will never consent to bed with a heathen Frank. However passionately he may profess his conversion to the true faith."

"No," said the Greek, too gently. "I do not know it. Irene is empress. She understands practicalities. She knows what the empire needs. If her lord had lived a year or two longer . . ." He sighed "'If' wins no battles. The Basileus is dead, and the Basilissa requires a strong consort. Your king has that strength, and the lands to accompany it."

"But will he suffer Byzantium to call them its own? He has no reason to love the empire; he resists its faith, as his fathers resisted it before him. To him Our Lord is a felon who died on a tree, less noble and less worthy to be worshipped than the Saxons' Wotan, our Church has no power where he can perceive it, only a gaggle of half-mad priests on the edges of the world, and an impotent nobody in Rome who calls himself the successor of Peter, and quarrels incessantly with the Patriarch in Constantinople. Simpler and more expedient for him to subscribe to the creed of the Divine Julian, which allows him to rule his own lands in his own fashion, and leaves him free to live as he pleases."

"Divine," said the Greek in distaste. "Apostate, and damned, not least for the world he left us. Our empire divided, the West fallen to barbarian hordes, the light of Christ extinguished there wherever it has kindled; and now the terror out of east and south and west, the armies of Islam circling for the kill. Charles must choose between us, or be overwhelmed. He is the key to Europe. Without him, we can perhaps hold our ground in the East, but the West is lost to us. With him, we gain the greater part of our old empire, and stand to gain the rest."

Ganelon spoke swiftly, with passion enough to rock Oliver where he crouched. "And if he turns to Islam, not only is Europe lost; Byzantium itself may fall. Charles the pagan fancies himself an enlightened man, a man of reason, dreaming of Rome restored. Charles the Muslim would see naught but sheer, red war."

"Therefore," asked the Greek, "you would force a choice?"

Ganelon had calmed himself, but his voice was tight, and grimly quiet. "You are wise, and you are skilled in the ways of war and diplomacy. But I know my king. We are not wise to leave matters to fate, or to God if you will. It is not enough to trust that our memory of Rome will speak more clearly to his heart than the raw new faith of Islam. He is, after all, a follower of Julian the Apostate. As is his hotspur of a nephew – who has been heard to swear that he will never bow his head to any God Who makes a virtue of virginity." Ganelon paused as if to gather the rags of his temper, and the threads of his argument. "Count Roland is a danger to us and to our purpose. While he lives, the king will not turn Christian. Of that, I am certain. He were best disposed of, and quickly. How better than by such a means, which should serve also to turn the king to our cause?"

"And if it fails? What then, my friend?"

"It will not fail. You have my oath on it."

That was all they said that mattered to Oliver. He lingered for a dangerous while, until it was clear that they were done with their conspiring. There was a stir near the front of the tent: guards changing; a mutter of Greek. Oliver beat a rapid retreat.

It was an age before he could catch Roland alone. The count, having recovered his temper, had thrown himself into his duties. Oliver's return he greeted with a flurry of commands, all of them urgent and most of them onerous. Oliver set his teeth and obeyed them. But he kept his eye on Roland, as much as he might in the uproar.

A little before dawn, when the camp had quieted at last, to rest for an hour or two and restore its strength for the march, Oliver followed the count into his tent. It was not the first time he had done that; Roland looked at him without surprise. "I think you should sleep tonight," he said with careful gentleness.

Oliver blushed. That was not what he had been thinking of at all. He said so, bluntly.

Roland's brows went up. Perhaps he believed it. Perhaps he did not. After a moment he shrugged, one-sided, and went about stripping for sleep.

"Roland," said Oliver.

Something in his tone brought Roland about. He had his drawers in his hand. Oliver could count all the scars on the fine brown skin, the bruises of his struggle tonight and his hunt this morning, and one on his neck that men in the camp called the sweetseller's brand.

"Roland," Oliver said again. "There's something you should know."

And Oliver told him, all of it, word for word as he remembered it. Roland listened in silence that deepened the longer it lasted.

"I may have misunderstood everything," Oliver said at the end. "You know how bad my Greek is."

"Yes," said Roland, soft and still. "I know." His eyes were wide; in rushlight they seemed blurred, as if with sleep.

He shook himself suddenly, blinked, was Roland again. But not, quite, Roland. Roland was a wild man, everyone knew it. Such news as this should have driven him raving mad.

But Oliver was not everyone, and he had known Roland since they shared the nurse's breast. He laid a hand on the slender shoulder, "Brother. Don't think it."

"Why?" asked Roland. "What am I thinking?"

"You know what will happen if you kill your father. Even a stepfather. You can't do it. The king needs you too badly."

"Kill? Did I say kill?"

"Roland – "

"Oliver." Roland closed his hand over Oliver's. "Brother, I won't kill him. Even I am hardly that vast a fool."

"Then what will you do?"

"Nothing." Roland said it with appalling lightness. "Except thank you for the knowledge. And – yes, brother nurse, keep watch against treachery."

"You're too calm," said Oliver.

He was. He was not trembling, that Oliver could see or feel or sense. He looked as if he had learned nothing more terrible than that his third-best charger had - a girth-gall. "I'm . . . almost . . . Yes, I'm glad," he said. "I've always known what a snake that man is. Now he lays the proof in my hands. Let him strike at me. Then the king can deal with him."

"And if you die of the stroke?"

"I won't die. I gave you my oath, don't you remember? I'll never die before you. We'll go together, or not at all. And," said Roland, "it's not you he wants, or will touch."

Oliver was by no means comforted. But Roland had heard all he wanted to hear. He flung his arms about his milkbrother and hugged him till his ribs creaked, and thrust him away. "Go to bed, brother nurse. Here, if you will, but I tell you truly, I intend to do no more than sleep."

"Here, then," said Oliver, not even trying to match his lightness. And he kept his word. Two cloaks and a blanket were ample for them both; and Roland humoured a friend. He let Oliver take the outside.

2

Oliver did not know whether to be glad or to be more wary than ever. Days, they had marched. They had broken down the walls of Pamplona, almost for sport, to soothe the Arabs' fears, and left them there with the pick of the spoil. The ambassador from Baghdad lingered, and would linger, it was clear, until the king saw fit to dismiss him or his own caliph called him back. Likewise the envoys from Byzantium. The king was a battleground, and well he knew it; he seemed to find it amusing, when he troubled to think of it at all.

No one had moved to strike Roland. No dagger out of the dark. No poison in his cup. Not even a whisper in the king's ear, to shake Charles's confidence in his nephew's loyalty. All that Oliver had heard might have been a dream. Or the Greek had prevailed, and Ganelon had turned his mind elsewhere, to other and easier prey.

Roland acted no differently towards him. For Oliver it was harder. Oliver was a very bad liar. He kept out of the traitor's path, not gladly, but with every ounce of prudence in him. Ganelon murdered by Oliver was hardly less shocking a prospect than Ganelon murdered by Roland, and equally likely to ruin the Breton count. Which dilemma, too, the subtle snake might well have wished upon them.

Therefore they did nothing, not even to tell the king; for after all they had no proof. The days went on in marching and in encampments, and once the diversion of Pamplona. Beyond the broken walls, where the Pyrenees rose like walls shattered by gods, the army moved a little lighter. There were the ramparts; beyond them lay the fields and forests of Gaul.

It was the custom, and Roland's own preference, that the Bretons with their heavy cavalry kept either the van or the rear. Through most of Spain, Roland himself had ridden first of all except the scouts; but as the hills rose into mountains, the king called him to the centre. Oliver followed, unquestioned; the count's milkbrother and swordbrother, as inseparable as his shadow. Already the way grew steep; they had left their horses ahead with their armour bearers, and taken to surefooted mules. Not a few along the line chaffed them for that; Roland laughed and chaffed back, but Oliver set his teeth and endured.

The king, who was above all a practical man, had mounted his lordly bulk on a brother of their own beasts. No one, Oliver noticed, even looked askance at him. As always when he was at war, he wore nothing to mark him out from any common soldier, except the circlet of gold on his helmet. He greeted them both with his usual gladness.

Neither was quick to match him. He was attended, as always. The Byzantines were there, and the men from Baghdad. And Ganelon, close at his side, riding a horse with an Arab look about the head. The man was all limpid innocence, the loyal counsellor attending his king.

Charles beckoned Roland in. Ganelon drew back with every appearance of good will, no dagger flashing in his hand, no hatred in his glance. Roland would not meet it at all. There was a pause while the mules settled precedence; then the king said,

"Roland, sister-son, now that the land is changing, I've a mind to change the army to fit it. The way ahead should be clear enough for lesser forces. It's the rear I'm wary of; the brigands' portion. And the baggage can't move any faster than it's moving. I need you and your Bretons there. Will you take it?"

Oliver's hackles quivered and rose. It was a perfectly reasonable order, presented in the king's usual fashion: as a request, to be accepted or refused. The Bretons with their armour and their great lumbering horses would deter anything that a brigand might think of. And a brigand would think of, and covet, the baggage and the booty.

It was not the prospect of robbery that chilled Oliver's nape. It was Ganelon's expression. Calm; innocent. Barely listening, as if the hawk on the wing mattered more than the count in the rearguard.

It was too well done. He should be sneering, making it clear whose counsel it was that Roland breathe the army's dust and shepherd its baggage.

As if he had realized the oversight, he lowered his eyes from the sky and smiled at his stepson. Oliver did not need to be a seer to foretell what Roland would do. Roland bristled; his mule jibbed and lashed out. Ganelon's mare eluded it with contemptuous ease. "You," said Roland. "What are you plotting? Why this change, now, when we're so close to Gaul?"

"My lord king," Ganelon said with sweet precision, "has been apprised by his scouts that the way ahead of us is steep, the passage narrow. He has need of both valour and vigilance, and in the rear most of all, where robbers most often strike. Who better to mount guard there, than the knights of Brittany?"

Smooth words, irreproachable even in tone. Oliver would happily have throttled the man who uttered them. Roland raised his head, his black eyes narrow, searching his stepfather's face. It gave him nothing back. "You want me there," he said. "What if I refuse?"

"Then another will be sent," said the king before Ganelon could speak. He sensed something, Oliver could tell, but he was too preoccupied or too accustomed to his kinsmen's enmity to take notice. "I have reason to think that there may be one last stroke before we ride out of Spain: revenge for Pamplona, or a final blow from the rebels of Córdoba. Will you guard my back?"

Roland sat erect in the saddle, neatly and inextricably trapped. Ganelon himself could have done no better. Roland's voice rang out over the song of wind, echoing in the passes. "Always, my king."

Charles smiled and, leaning out of the saddle, pulled him into an embrace. "Watch well, sister-son. Half the treasure on my wagon is yours to share with your men."

Roland laughed. "All the more reason to guard it! Come, Oliver. We've a king to serve."

"This is it," said Oliver as they worked their way back up through the army. "This is what he was waiting for."

Roland's eyes were bright, his nostrils flared to catch the scent of danger. But he said, "You can't know that. Probably he wants to poison the beer I'll drink with supper, and needs me out of the way to do it. I'll drink wine tonight, or water. Will that content you?"

Oliver shook his head. He could see their banner now, their men waiting beside the steep stony track, held there by the king's messenger. They seemed glad enough of the chance to pause, rest, inspect girths and hoofs and harness buckles. The army toiled up past them. No chaffing now: it took too much breath simply to move.

Slowly, by excruciating inches, the rear came in sight. The men who had been guarding it were pleased to move up, away from the lumbering wagons, the oxen groaning and labouring, the drivers cursing in an endless half-chant. Roland's Bretons fell in behind. They had all, uncommanded, shifted to remounts.

"You scent trouble, too, then?"

Oliver started, stared. Not all of the former rearguard had gone ahead. The Count of the Palace was there, watching over his charge, which was all here but the king himself; and Ekkehard, the king's seneschal, riding on the wain with the royal plate. And, on a horse that had been bred in Roland's own pastures, Turpin the high priest of Mithras in Rheims. As befit the priest of a warrior creed, he rode armed and armoured and his acolytes were also his armour-bearers. He grinned at Oliver, old warhound that he was, and breathed deep of the thin air. "There'll be an ambush ahead. Do you remember this way, when we came out of Gaul? It narrows and steepens, and where it's narrowest and steepest, the gorge they call Roncesvalles – they'll strike there, if they strike at all."

"'They'?" asked Oliver.

"Basques, most likely: savages of these mountains. Pamplona is theirs, you know; it's not Saracen, though sometimes it suits them to dance to Córdoba's tune. I expect they'll want to claim back what we took from them."

He seemed remarkably undismayed at the prospect. Oliver eyed his greying beard and his eager face, and castigated himself for a fool. If there was a battle, it would be one that they could easily win. If it aimed chiefly at Roland, then his men would make themselves a wall about him. There was nothing to fret over but a few words spoken in a tongue he barely knew, and which he might well have misunderstood.

The steeper the way grew, the closer the walls drew in, the slower the baggage train travelled. The clamour of the army, echoing in the gorges, began little by little to fade. They had drawn ahead. Too far, Oliver began to suspect. There were only their small company, and the drivers, and such of the women and servants as had not gone ahead with their masters; and the wains lurching and struggling up the mountainside. Behind, there was nothing to see but stone and scree and steep descent. Ahead, Oliver remembered dimly, was a bit of almost level, then another bitter ascent, little more than a roofless corridor, to the summit of the pass. Already it was growing dim below, though the sky was bright still. If night found them on the mountain . . .

Roland had sent scouts ahead and, while the cliffs were still scalable, to the side. None of them had come back.

A signal went down the line. *Dismount and lead your horses.* Oliver obeyed it, but struggled forward, to draw level with

Roland. For a long while he could do nothing but breathe. Roland climbed in silence, not even cursing when his horse stumbled.

"You might," said Oliver between hard breaths, "sound your horn. Just for prudence. So that the king knows how far back we are."

Roland's hand found the horn where it hung at his side: a beauty of a thing, an olifant bound with gold and hung on a gold-worked baldric; the only adornment he would wear, whose sword and armour were as plain as a trooper's. But he did not move to raise the horn.

Roland," said Oliver, "brother, sound the horn. If we're caught here we're too few, the pass is too steep; we'll barely hold till the king can come back."

"No," said Roland.

Oliver drew breath once again, and flung all his passion into it. "Roland, brother, sound the horn! It's I who beg you. I'll bear the shame if shame there is, and no army waits for us above."

"No one will bear the shame for me," Roland said. "How large an army can a pack of savages muster? We'll fight them off. Or don't you think I'm strong enough for that?"

"I think your stepfather has something hidden here, and that is your death."

"Are you calling my mother's husband a traitor?"

Mad, thought Oliver in despair. God-mad, as they said men were when they were chosen to be sacrificed: going to their deaths willingly and even with joy. And gods help the man who spoke ill of the man he hated.

Oliver shut his mouth and set himself to climb and watch, both at once, as much as his struggling body would allow. He kept close to Roland's side, his battle-station, though his wonted place on the march was well apart from the count.

At the level they paused, a moment only, to replenish their strength. The cliff-walls closed in above. There was still no sign of the scouts. Roland did not mention them; Oliver did not want to. When they moved on again, Turpin was beside them, leading his fine warhorse, whistling tunelessly between his teeth.

The creaking of wains echoed and re-echoed from the walls. The lead ox threw up its head and snorted, balking in the gate of the defile. Its driver cursed and thrust in the goad. The ox lowed in pain, but stood fast.

Through the echoes of its cry, Oliver heard thunder.

Not thunder. Stones. Great boulders, roaring and tumbling down the cliffsides, and men howling behind them. Howling in Arabic. *Allah-il-allah!*

Saracens. They fell like hail out of the sky, bearded, turbaned, shrilling sons of Allah; they filled the pass behind, thick as locusts in the plains of Granada. The trap was sprung. The bait could not even cower in it. There was no room.

Oliver almost laughed. So, then. That was what they had meant, the conspirators, when they spoke of turning the king against the enemies of Byzantium. It would not have been hard to win Córdoba to their cause, if it cost Baghdad its ally. Then the traitor need but see to it that Roland was given the rearguard and led to expect nothing worse than a pack of brigands; and leave the rest to the armies of Córdoba.

They were, at most, fifty men. If there were less than a thousand about them, then Oliver had lost his ability to reckon armies. And the wagons to defend, and the way closed on all sides, and no escape but through the armies of Islam.

Roland saw them and laughed. By some freak of fate and the army and the echoes about them, his laughter sounded light and clear in almost silence, the laughter of a man who loves a battle. It danced with mockery. It dared death to take him. He leaped up on a wain though darts rained down, and called out: "Here, men! Here's a fight for us. Who'll take first blood? Who'll die for our king?"

"I!" they shouted back. And in a rising roar, till even the echoes fled in terror: "Montjoie! Montjoie! *Montjoie!*"

The enemy faltered. But they could count as well as Oliver, and they had seen how ill the train was disposed, sprawled all down the narrow pass, no room to draw together and make a stand. The small company that clustered in the rear, their horses useless on that steep and broken ground, the enemy all but ignored; they fell on the train itself, their howls drowning out even the shrieks of women and the death-cries of horses and cattle.

The Bretons frayed at the edges. Hands reached for pommels, men braced to spring astride their horses. Roland's voice lashed them back, away from the stumbling, hindering, helpless beasts, into a formation they all knew. Then, fiercely, forward.

They drove like a lance into the column. And for a little while, no one resisted them. Oliver grinned in his helmet. There was a use after all for the Roman foot-drill that the king had inflicted on them – a game, he said; an idea he had, that Roland, always apt for mischief, was willing to try. Now it served them in this most impossible of places, drove them into the enemy, mowed the attackers down and swept them aside under the hoofs of panicked beasts.

But there were too many of them; and the cavalry shield was little use in building the Roman shieldwall. Frayed already by startlement and rage and the Franks' inborn resistance to marching in step, they tore apart as the enemy rallied. Men were down. Oliver could not count, could not reckon. He had his own life to look after, and his brother's.

Roland was always calm enough when a battle began, well able to array his troops and judge their moment. But let his sword taste blood and he was lost.

Someone was on Roland's other side, sword-side to Oliver's shield-side. Turpin, again. He had the bull of Mithras on his shield. It seemed to dance among the fallen, its white hide speckled with blood.

Oliver's foot slipped. He spared a glance for it: blood, entrails, a hand that cracked like bunched twigs under his boot. His eye caught a flash; his spear swung round, swift, swift, but almost too late. Fool's recompense, for casting eye on aught but the enemy. The good ash shaft jarred on steel and shattered. He thrust it in a howling face, let it fall, snatched out his sword. Roland's was out already, his named-blade Durandal, running with blood.

Most often a battle runs like the sea: in ebbs and flows, in eddies and swirls and moments of stillness. But that is where armies are matched, and one side cannot count twenty men for every man of the other. Here, there were no respites. Only battle, and battle, and more battle. Death on every side, no time even for despair. They three had fought their way clear to the front of the battle and backed against the wall of the pass, as high up as the fallen stones would allow. Through the press of the fight they could see the downward way: a roil of ants in the nest, no head raised that did not wear a turban, and everywhere the sight and stench of slaughter.

Oliver, turning a bitter blow, was numb to the marrow. So soon? he wondered. So soon, they are all fallen?

So soon, in their heavy armour that was never made for fighting on foot, dragged down and slaughtered by the sheer mass of their enemies. His arm was leaden. He flailed at a stroke he barely saw, and never saw the one that glanced off his helmet. He staggered, head ringing, and fell to one knee. Lightning smote the man who stooped to the kill.

Durandal, and Roland's face behind it, white in the helmet, burning-eyed. He had dropped his shield, or lost it. His olifant was in his hand.

Oliver cursed him, though he had no breath to spare for it. "What use now? It will never bring the king. He's too far ahead."

Roland gave a yelling savage a second, blood-fountained mouth, and sent him reeling back among his fellows. For an impossible moment, none came forward in his place. There were easier pickings elsewhere; a whole baggage train to plunder. Roland set the horn to his lips.

Oliver, who knew what he would hear, clapped hands to his ears. Even that was barely enough to blunt the edge of it. The great horn roared like the aurochs from which it was won; shrieked up to heaven; sang a long plaint of wrath and valour and treachery. Roland's face was scarlet. A thin trail of blood trickled down from his ear.

The horn dropped, swung on its baldric. Roland half-fell against Oliver. Turpin caught him; they clung to one another. The enemy had frozen in their places. Many had fallen, smitten down by the power of the horn.

They rose like grass when the wind has faded. They turned

their faces towards the three of all their prey who yet lived. They reckoned anew their numbers, and the number that opposed them. They laughed, and fell upon them.

Oliver could not reckon the moment when he knew that one of his wounds was mortal. It was not when he took the wound, he was reasonably sure of that. He had others in plenty, and they were in his way, shedding blood to weaken his arm and foul his footing. But this one was weakening him too quickly. He found himself on the ground, propped against the rock, trying to lift his sword. A foot held him down. It was Roland's; that came to him when he tried to hack at it and the voice over his head cursed him in his brother's voice. "Sorry," he tried to say. "Can't see. Can't—"

"Be quiet," said Roland fiercely. Oliver was too tired to object. Except that he wanted to say something. He could not remember what. Something about horns. And kings. And turbans, with faces under them. Faces that should be – should be –

"Oliver."

Somebody was crying. It sounded like Roland. Roland did not often cry. Oliver wondered why he was doing it now. Had something happened? Was the king hurt? Dead? No, Oliver could not conceive of that. The king would never die. The king would live forever.

Oliver blinked. There was Roland's face, hanging over him. Another by it: Turpin's. They looked like corpses. "Am I dead?" Oliver asked, or tried to. "Is this Hades? Or the Muslims' Paradise? Or—"

"You talk too much," Roland growled.

They were alive. But it was very quiet. Too quiet. No shrilling of enemy voices. Unless that were they, faint and far away and fading slowly, like wind in empty places.

"They're gone," the priest said, as if he could understand what Oliver was thinking. Maybe he could. Priests were unchancy folk. But good: very good, in a fight. "They took what they came for."

"Did they?"

They both heard that. Roland glared. "Wasn't the king's whole baggage train enough?"

You," Oliver said. "You live. Still."

Roland burst into tears again. But he looked worse than furious. He looked deadly dangerous.

The dark was closing in. "Brother," Oliver said through it, shouting in full voice against the failing of his body. "Brother, look. The enemy. Turbans – turbans wrong. Not Saracen. Can you understand? *Not Saracen.*"

Maybe Oliver dreamed it. Maybe he only needed to hear it. But it was there, on the other side of the night. "I understand."

"I understand," Roland said. The weight in his arms was no greater and no less. But suddenly it was the weight of a world.

He knew the heft of death in his arms. Not Oliver, not now: not those wide blue eyes, emptying of life as they had, moments since, emptied of light.

He flung his head back and keened.

"My lord." Dry voice, with calm behind it. Turpin was weary: he had lain down beside Oliver, maybe with some vanishing hope of keeping him warm.

Or himself. Not all the blood on him was the enemy's. Some of it was bright with newness, glistening as it welled from a deep spring.

Dying, all of them. Roland, too. The enemy had seen to that before they left. He had not intended to tell either of his companions about the blade that stabbed from below, or the reason why he held himself so carefully when he rose. When he had finished doing what he must do, he would let go. It would not be a slow death, or an easy one, but it was certain. A good death for a fool, when all was considered.

He spoke lightly; he was proud of that lightness. "I'm going to see if I can find our fellows," he said to the one who could hear him and the one who was past it: "give them a word of passage; cast earth on the ones who'll need it."

Turpin nodded. He did not offer to rise. But there was, Roland judged, a little life in him yet. Enough to mount guard over Oliver, and keep the crows from his eyes. They were feasting already and long since, and the vultures with them: racing against the fall of the dark.

He walked the field in the gathering twilight, dim-lit by the glow of the sky above him. The birds of battle were as thick as flies; but where they were thickest, there he knew he would find his men. Two here, three there, five fallen together in the remnant of a shieldring. The king's seneschal, the count of his palace, the *palatium* that was not a thing of walls and stone but of the household that went with the king wherever he journeyed. Lost, here, gone down the long road with men in knotted turbans.

But not all of those who had come to seize it had left the field. Many of their dead, they had taken, but they had left many, pressed by the fall of the dark and the need to escape with their booty before the King of the Franks swept down in the full force of his wrath. There at Roland's feet, locked in embrace like lovers, lay a camp follower who had lost her man at Pamplona, and a brigand; but there was a knife in his heart and a look of great surprise on his face. Roland could not tell if she smiled. There was too little left of her

The man, sheltered by her body, was barely touched by the crows. Roland grasped him by the foot and dragged him into what light there was. The turban fell from a matted and filthy head. Roland bent to peer. The face – anonymous dead face. But odd. Ruthlessly he rent the tunic away from neck and breast and belly. The trousers, he need hardly tear at. He saw beneath them all that he needed to see.

His breath left him in a long sigh. With care, holding his middle lest his entrails spill upon the ground, he made his way among the enemy's dead. All; all alike.

Not far from the place where Oliver had died, he found the last thing, the thing that drained the strength from his legs, the life from his body. But he smiled. He took what he needed, and the body with it, crawling now. The night, which seemed to have waited for him, fell at last.

Turpin was stiff and still. Oliver lay untouched beside him, familiar bulk gone unfamiliar in death. Roland kissed him, and with every last vestige of his strength, staggered upright. The stars stared down. "Allah!" he called out. His voice rang in the gorge. "Allah! Will you take us all, if I speak for us? Will you, then? He'd like your Paradise, my brother. All the lovely maidens. Will you take him if I ask?"

The stars were silent. Roland laughed and flung up Durandal. He had, somehow, remembered to scour the blade of blood: prudence worn to habit. A pity for a good sword to die, though its master must. Take my sword, Allah. Take my soul and my oath; if only you take my brother with it. You'll find him waiting hereabout. Come, do you hear him whispering? He'd say it with me if he could. Listen! *There is no god but God, and Muhammad is the Prophet of God.*"

The echoes throbbed into silence. Roland sank down in them. His heart was light. In a little while he was going to convulse in agony, but for this moment, he knew no pain. Only a white, mad joy. To have chosen, and chosen so. To have taken the purest revenge of all, on Ganelon who had betrayed him.

Oliver was waiting. Roland laid Durandal on the broad breast, and his head beside it, and sighed. Then at last, with all the courage that was left in him, he let go.

3

Charles the king stood once more on the sweet soil of Gaul, the horrors of the pass behind him, the army finding new vigour in the sight of their own country spread below. But he was not easy in his mind. Word from the rear was unvarying. No sign of the baggage. A scout or two, sent out, did not return.

As the sun sank low, he called a halt. Without the baggage they could not raise a proper camp, but every man had his store of food and drink, and many had women who marched with them and carried the necessities of living. They settled willingly enough.

The king left his servants to make what shift they could with what they had, and rode back a little, up towards the pass. One or two men rode with him. The empress' ambassador; the caliph's man, not to be outflanked; Ganelon. Beyond the fringe of the army, the king paused.

"Do you hear a horn?" he asked.

They glanced at one another. "A horn?" Ganelon inquired. "No, sire. I hear nothing but the wind."

"Yes," said Charles. "The wind. That's what it must be. But I could have sworn . . ."

"My lord's ears are excellent," the Arab said. No; Charles should be precise, even in his mind. The man was a Persian. The Persian, then, and a smoothly smiling fellow he was, oily as a Greek, and yet, for all of that, a man worth liking. "Perhaps he hears the rearguard as it comes through the pass."

"Perhaps," said Ganelon. The Greek, for a marvel, said nothing at all.

They sat their tired horses, waiting, because the king waited. He could not bring himself to turn away. He had not liked the pass as he scaled it, and he had not liked the failure of his scouts to come back. Still less did he like his folly in letting the rearguard fall so far behind. He had been in haste to abandon the pass, to see his own lands again. He had let himself be persuaded to press on. The one man he sent back to find the rearguard, had not found him again.

In the falling dark, in silence barely troubled by the presence of an army, he saw what he had willed not to see. He saw it with brutal clarity; he knew it for what it was. There was no pain, yet. Later, there would be; a whole world of it. But now, only numbness that was not blessed. Oh, no. Not blessed at all. "They are dead," he said, "my Bretons. There was an ambush in the pass."

"My lord," said Ganelon, "you cannot know that. They will have been sensible: seen that night was falling, and stopped, and made camp. In time their messenger will come. Only wait, and rest. You can hardly ride back now. Night will catch you before you mount the pass."

"Yes," said Charles. "It will, won't it?"

His voice must have betrayed more than he knew. Ganelon stiffened; his mouth set. His eyes darted. Charles noticed where they fell first. The Byzantine refused them, gazing expressionless where Charles's mind and heart were.

With great care, the king unknotted his fists. He had no proof. He had nothing but the feeling in his bones, and the absence of his rearguard. His valiant, reluctant, pitifully inadequate rear-guard.

He was, first of all, king. He turned his back on the pass of Roncesvalles, and went to see his army.

The king did not sleep that night. When he drowsed, his mind deluded him: gave him the far cry of a horn, a great olifant, blown with the desperation of a dying man. Roland was dead. He knew it. Dead in battle; dead by treachery.

He rose before dawn. His army slept; he silenced the trum-peter who would have roused them. "Let them sleep," he said. "We go nowhere until the baggage comes."

When his horse came, others came with it. The Greek and the Persian, again and perpetually; Ganelon; a company of his guardsmen. He greeted them with a nod. They were all, like the king, armed as if to fight. It was odd to see the Byzantine in mail, carrying a sword. Charles had not known that he owned either.

Morning rose with them, surmounted the pass, sped above them while they went down. They picked their way with care, finding no trace of the baggage, and nothing ahead of them but fading darkness.

A wall of tumbled stones where none had been before, woke in the king no surprise, not even anger. Wordlessly he dismounted, handed his horse to the man nearest, and set himself to scale the barrier. It was not high, if much confused. At the top of it he paused.

He had expected nothing less than what he saw. He had seen sights like it ever since he could remember. But it was never an easy thing to see; even when the dead were all the enemy's.

Someone had seen to the dead of Gaul. Each was consecrated in his own fashion: a cross drawn in blood on the brow of the Christian, a scattering of earth for him who held to Julian's creed, a simple laying out in dignity for the follower of Mithras or of the old faith. But hope, having swelled, died swiftly. No living man walked that field.

Beyond them, as if they had made a last stand, lay three together. Turpin the priest of Mithras with his bones given to the birds of the air, and Roland and Oliver in one another's arms as they had been since they shared their milkmother's breast. They had died well, if never easily.

The king was aware, distantly but very clearly, of the men nearest him: Greek, Persian, Frankish counsellor. None ventured to touch the dead. He knelt beside them, and gently, as if the boy could feel it still, took Roland in his arms.

Roland clasped something to his breast, even in death. His olifant. Which Charles had heard; he was certain of it now. Heard, and never come. The king steadied it as it slipped. It was heavier than it should be, unwieldy. It eluded the king's hand and fell, spilling brightness on the grass.

Byzantine gold. And mingled with it, the rougher coin of Gaul, and Charles' face on every one.

He did not glance, even yet, at his companions. There was a message here; he was meant to read it. At the brothers' feet lay one of the enemy's dead, whom Charles had had no eyes to see. But there was no other close by, and this one looked to have been brought here.

Charles laid Roland again in Oliver's arms, and examined the body. He was perfectly, icily calm. Intent on his own dead, he had not seen more than that the enemy wore turbans over dark faces. This one's turban had fallen beside him; his tunic was rent and torn, baring white skin, skin too white for the face. And between them, a ragged line, the stain rubbed on in haste with no expectation of need for greater concealment. And, below, what Charles did not need the Persian to say for him.

"This man is not a Muslim. He is not circumcised."

"So," said Charles, "I notice."

Even dying, Roland had kept his wits about him. Gold of Byzantium, gold and silver of Gaul. An infidel in Muslim guise. Trap, and battle, and the deaths of great lords of the Franks.

Here was treachery writ large.

He read it, writ subtle, in Ganelon's face. He could never have thought to be so betrayed, and so simply. And by his brainless braggart of a stepson.

They had all drawn back from him. He seemed just now to realize it. He was white under his elegant beard, struggling to

maintain his expression of innocence. Ganelon, who had never
made a secret of his hatred for Roland; whose very openness
had been deceit. Who would have expected that he would turn
traitor? Open attack, surely, daggers drawn in hall, a challenge
to a duel; but this, no one had looked for. Least of all, and most
damnably of all, the king.

"It would have been better for you," Charles said, "if you had
killed him before my face. Clean murder bears a clean penalty.
For this, you will pay in your heart's blood."

"Pay, sire?" Ganelon struggled even yet to seem baffled.
"Surely, sire, you do not think—"

"I know," said Charles. His eyes burned. They were wide, he
knew, and pale, and terrible. When they fell on the Greek, the
man blanched.

"I am not," he said, "a part of this. I counselled against it. I
foresaw this very outcome."

"You sanctioned it with your empress' gold," said the king.

"For what an agent does with his wages, I bear no responsibility."

Charles laughed. His guards had drawn in, shoulder to
shoulder. If the traitor had any thought of escape, he quelled it.
He regarded his quondam ally with no surprise, if with nothing
approaching pleasure.

"You shall be tried," the king said to him, "where the law
commands, before my tribunal in Gaul. I expect that you will
receive the extremest penalty. I devoutly pray that you may
suffer every pang of guilt and grief and rage to which even a
creature of your ilk should be subject."

Ganelon stiffened infinitesimally, but not with dismay. Was
that the beginning of a smile? "You have no certain proof," he
said.

"God will provide," said Charles.

"God? Or Allah?"

Bold, that one, looking death in the face. If death it was that
he saw. It was a long way to Gaul, and his tongue was serpent-
supple. Had not Charles himself been taken in by it?

Charles met his eyes and made them fall. "Yes," he said,
answering the man's question. "There you have it. God, or

Allah? The Christians' God, or all the gods of my faith who in the end are one, or the God of the Prophet? Would you have me choose now? Julian is dead, his teachings forgotten everywhere but in my court. The Christ lives; the sons of the Prophet rule in Baghdad, and offer alliance. I know what I am in this world. Byzantium dares to hope in me, to hold back the armies of Islam. Islam knows that without me it can never rule in the north of the world. How does it twist in you, betrayer of kin, to know that I am the fulcrum on which the balance rests?"

"Islam," said Ganelon without a tremor, "offers you the place of a vassal king. Byzantium would make you its emperor."

"So it would. And such a marriage it would be, I ruling here in Gaul, and she on the Golden Horn. Or would I be expected to settle in Constantinople? Who then would rule my people? You, kinslayer? Is that the prize you played for?"

"Better I than a wild boy who could never see a battle without flinging himself into the heart of it."

The king's fist lashed out. Ganelon dropped. "Speak no ill of the dead," Charles said.

The others were silent. They did not press him; and yet it was there, the necessity, the making of choices. If he would take vengeance for this slaughter, he must move now.

He began to smile. It was not, he could well sense, pleasant to see. "Yes," he said. "Revenge. It's fortunate for my sister-son, is it not, that I'm pagan, and no Christian, to have perforce to forgive. You plotted well, kinslayer. You thought to turn me against Islam and cast me into the empress' arms. Would there be a dagger for me there? Or, more properly Greek, poison in my cup?"

Sire," said Ganelon, and that was desperation, now, at last. "Sire, do not judge the empire by the follies of a single servant."

"I would never do that," Charles said. "But proof of long conviction will do well enough. I will never set my people under the Byzantine heel. Even with the promise of a throne. Thrones can pass, like any other glory of this world; and swiftly, if those who offer them are so minded."

"Still, my lord, you cannot choose Islam. Would you betray

all that the Divine Julian fought for? Would you turn against Rome herself?"

If the Greek had said it, Charles would have responded altogether differently. But it was Ganelon who spoke, and Ganelon who felt the pain of it.

"I am," said Charles, "already, in the caliph's eyes, his emir over Spain. I am not able for the moment to press the claim. Gaul needs me, and Gaul is mine first. If Baghdad will want the justice in that, then," he said, "I choose Islam."

No thunder roared in the sky; no shaking rent the earth. There were only a handful of men in a narrow pass, and the dead, and the sun too low still to cast its light on them. Spain was behind them; the mountain before and beyond it, Gaul. What its king chose, it also would choose. He knew his power there.

He bent and took up Roland's horn. It rang softly, bearing still a weight of imperial gold. With it in his hands, he said the words which he must say. If his conviction was not yet as pure as it might be, then surely he would be forgiven. He was doing it for Gaul, and for the empire that would be. But before even that, for Roland who was his sister's son, who had died for Byzantine gold.

Charles was, when it came to it, a simple man. The choice had not been simple, until Ganelon made it so. A better traitor than he knew, that one. Traitor even to his own cause.

"*There is no god but God,*" said the king of the Franks and the Lombards, "*and Muhammad is the Prophet of God.*"

The English Mutiny

Ian R. MacLeod

I was there. I was fucking there.

I know that's what they say, all of us English anyway, and half the rest of the Empire besides. The fact that people think they can make that claim – tell anyone who'll listen to them how they survived the atrocities and sieges – is supposed to be evidence enough. But I was. I was *there*. Right at the beginning, and way, way earlier than that. I knew Private Sepoy Second Class Johnny Sponson of the Devonshires long before that name meant anything. *More* than knew the guy, the bastard, the sadhu, holy monster, the saint – whatever you want to call him. I loved him. I hated him. He saved my fucking life.

Me? I was just a soldier, a squaddie, another sepoy of the Mughal Empire. I really didn't count. Davey Whittings, sir, Sahib, and where do you want that latrine dug? Always was – just like my Dad and his Dad before him. All took the Resident's rupee and gave their blood. No real sense of what we were, other than targets for enemy cannon. Stand up and salute or drop down and die. Nobody much cared what the difference was, either, least of all us.

But Johnny Sponson was different. Johnny came out of nowhere with stories you wouldn't believe and a way of talking that sounded like he was forever taking the piss. In a way, he was. In a way, he was shitting us all with his tall good looks and his la di da. But he was also deadly earnest.

This was at the start of the Scottish campaign. One of them anyway – rebellious bastards that the Scots are, I know there's been a lot. Never really saw that much of Johnny at first as we marched north through England. But I knew there was this new guy with us who liked the look of his reflection and the sound of his voice. Could hear him sometimes as I lay trying to get some sleep. Holding forth.

But no – no . . . Already, I'm getting this wrong. The way I'm describing Johnny Sponson, someone like him would never have got as far as being torn apart by Scottish guns. He'd have copped it long before in a parade-ground misfire with some sepoy – oops, sorry Sarge, silly me – leaning the wrong way on his musket. Or maybe a garrotte in the night. Anything, really, just to shut the loudmouthed fucker up. But with Johnny, there was always something extra – a tale beyond the tale he was spinning or some new scam to make the half-blood NCOs look like even bigger cunts than they already were. Even then, even before the revolt, mutiny, freedom war, whatever you want to call it, Johnny simply didn't give the tiniest fuck about all the usual military bullshit. He was an original. He was a one-off.

Johnny might have been just a private, a sepoy, lowest of the low, but he'd grown up as Lord-in-waiting on one of the last English estates. Learned to read and fight and fence and dance and talk there, and do all the other things he could do so much better than the rest of us combined. Even I was listening to Johnny's stories by the time we crossed Hadrian's Wall. We all were. And the place he was describing that he'd come from didn't sound much like the England I knew. There were no factories or hovels or beggars. I pictured it as a world of magic – like so-called Mother India or heaven, but somehow different and better still. The landscapes were softer, the skies less huge. I saw green lawns and cosy rooms filled with golden warmth, and the whole thing felt real to me the way they only can when you're marching towards battle and your back aches and your feet hurt. It was a fine place, was Johnny's estate, and all of it was taken from him because some Indian vakil lawyer came up with a scrap of ancient paper which disproved the Sponson family title.

The way Johnny told his story, it span on like those northern roads we had to march. He used words we'd never heard. Words like *right* and *liberty* and *nation*. Words like *reversion*, which was how the Mughal Empire had swallowed up so much of England when the country was rightly ours. Bankrupted, disinherited, thrown out on the streets, Johnny had had no choice but to sign up for the Resident's rupee like the rest of us. And so here he was, marching north behind the elephants with the rest of us Devonshires to fight the savage bloody Scots.

Never seen such mountains before. Never felt such cold. The Scottish peasants, they live in slum hovels that would make a sorry dump like York or Bristol seem lovely as Hyderabad. They reek of burned dung. The women came to our camps at night, offering to let us fuck them for half a loaf of bread. They'd let you do it, as well, before they slipped a dagger into your ribs and scarpered off with the bread. Can't even remember how I got hit exactly. We were on this high, wind-bitten road. Elephants pulling the ordnance ahead. Then a whoosh. Then absolute silence, and I was staring at a pool of my own steaming guts. It seemed easy, just to lie there on the frozen road. I mean, what the hell difference did it make? Private Davey Whittings, second class. Snap your heels, stand up straight lad, salute the flag of Empire and pay good attention to the cleanliness of your gun. Death or glory, just like my Dad always used to say before beating me for something I hadn't done.

But the voice I heard was Private Johnny Sponson's, not my Dad's at all. My Dad's been dead these last fifteen years, and I hope the bastard didn't give the vultures too much bellyache. But I was raving about him – and how my dear Mum had then done the decent thing and walked into a furnace – as Johnny pushed my insides back where they belonged, then lifted me up and tied me to what was left of a wagon. Then, seeing as all the elephants were dead and the bullocks were all shot to mincemeat, he started to haul me himself back along that windy road for . . . I really don't know how many days, how many miles.

At the end of it, there was this military hospital. I already knew all about military fucking hospitals. If you wanted to live, you avoided such places like the plague. If you wanted to die, it was far better to die on a battlefield. Without Johnny Sponson there, I wouldn't have stood a chance. The whole place was freezing. Wet tents in a lake of mud. Got me through, though, Johnny did. Found me enough blankets to stop me freezing solid. Changed the dressings on my wound, nagged the nurses to give me some of the half-decent food they otherwise saved for themselves. Bastard saved my fucking life. So in a way I was the first of Johnny Sponson's famous miracles, least as far as I know. But Christ wasn't there, and neither was Mohammed or Shakti. Johnny wasn't some ghost or saint or angel like the way you'd hear some people talk. It was just him, and he was just being Johnny, and filling my head with his Johnny Sponson stories. Which was more than enough.

Told me how half the platoon had got killed or injured in that Scottish bombardment. Told me how he'd fluked his way around the cannonfire in the same way he'd fluked his way around most things. Then he'd seen me lying there with half of me insides out and decided I could do with some help. Suppose he could have saved someone else – someone with a far better chance of living than I ever had. Why me? All the time I knew him, I never thought to ask.

Johnny told me many things. How, for example, little England had once been a power to be reckoned with in the world. How this guy called William Hawkins had once sailed all the way around the Horn of Africa to India back in the days when the Mughal Empire didn't even cover all of India let alone Europe, and no one had even dreamed of the Egyptian Canal. How Hawkins arrived in pomp at the court of Jehangir. How, the way things had been back then, he'd been an emissary from equal kingdoms. No, *more* than that, because Hawkins had sailed from England to India, and not the other way around. After that, there'd been trade, of course. Spices and silks, mainly, from India – with English wool and the sort of cheap gewgaws we were already getting so good at manufacturing in return. The stuff became hugely fashionable, so Johnny assured me, which always helps.

So there we were, the English and the Mughals, equal part-ners, and safely half a world away from each other, and between us lay the Portuguese, who were travelling and trading as well. Then something changed. I was still half in and out of my fever, but I remember Johnny shaking his head. Like, for just this once, he didn't know the answer. *Something*, he kept saying, as if he couldn't figure what. Of course, these were difficult times, the sort the priests will still tell you about – when it snowed in England one sunless August and the starving ate the dead, and the Mughals down in India expanded across India looking for food and supplies – looking for allies, as well. They could have turned to England, I suppose. That was what Johnny said, anyway. But the Mughals turned to Portugal instead. A great armada was formed, and we English were defeated, and the Mughal Empire expanded all that way to the northerly fringes of Europe. I know, I know – I remember Johnny clapping his hands and laughing and shaking his head. Bloody ridiculous – England and India united by an Empire, which has since pushed south and west across France and Spain and Prussia, and east from India across all the lands of Araby. Half the world taken as if in some fit of forgetfulness, and who the hell knows why . . .

So I recovered in that hospital with a scar on my belly and a strange new way of looking at things. Sometimes, it sounded to me as if Johnny was just talking to himself. In a way, I think he was. Practising what he wanted to say in those famous speeches that came not long after. He certainly had a way of talking, did Johnny. So much of the truth's lost now, but Johnny really *was* an educated man. He'd say the words of writers written years ago in English, of all languages – instead of proper Persian or Hindi or Arabic – as if they were fresh as baked bread.

There was this Shakes-something, and I thought at first Johnny meant an Arab prince. I can even remember some. *If it is a sin to covert honour, then I am the most offending soul.* That was one of them. Learned from his tutors, who taught him about the old ways of England in that fine estate before the Mughals took it away from him like the greedy bloodsucking bastards they are. Not that Johnny would put it so bluntly, but I learned that from him as well – how it wasn't as simple as the Indians being in charge and us English being the servants, the sepoys, the ones who worked the mines and choked on our own blood to keep their palaces warm.

Death. Guns. Spit and blood and polish. How to use a bayonet in the daylight of battle and a garrotte in the dark. That was all I knew before Johnny Sponson came along. I was never that much of a drinker, or a chancer, or a gambler of any kind. Don't stand out – that was the only thing I'd ever learned from my dear-departed Dad, bastard that he was. I spent most of what little spare time I had, and even less spare thought, on wandering around whatever place I happened to be billeted. Liked to look up at the buildings and over the bridges and stand outside the temples, just studying the scene. Watch the sadhu beggars with their ash-smeared bodies, their thin ribs and twisted and amputated limbs. I was fascinated by the things they did, the way they adorned and painted what was left of themselves, affixed it with hooks and nails and bamboo pins. But what struck me most was the contrast – the beauty of their aspiration to be one with God, and the ugliness of what you actually saw. And the ways they smiled and rocked and moaned and screamed – was that pain, or was it ecstasy? I never really understood.

Those of us Devonshires considered alive enough to be worth saving were put on board this ship which was to take us to our next posting in London. The winter weather was kind to us on that journey south. The cold winds pushed us easily and the sea was smooth, and the sailors were good at turning a blind eye in the way that sailors generally are. We sepoys lay out there on the deck underneath the stars with the sconces burning, and we talked and we danced and we drank. And Johnny, being Johnny, talked and drank and danced most of all.

You remember what that time before the mutiny was like – you remember the rumours? The plans to extend the term of service for us sepoys from fifteen to twenty years? That, and the forced conversion to Islam? Not that we cared much about any kind of religion, but the business of circumcision – that got us as angry as you'd expect. It just needed *something* . . . I remember Johnny saying as I leaned with him looking out at the ship's white backwash and the wheeling gulls – how the Indians would be nothing without us English, how the whole of their Empire would collapse if someone finally pulled out just one tiniest bit like a house of cards . . .

There was a lot of other stuff as well. Hopes and plans. What we'd do come the day. And Johnny seemed at the centre of it, to me at least. But where all those rumours came from, whether they were his or someone else's or arose in several different places all at once, I really couldn't tell. But that whole idea that England was waiting for Johnny Sponson – like the people knew him already, or had invented him like something magical in their hour of need . . . I can't tell you that that was true. But there are many kinds of lies – that's one thing that being around Johnny Sponson taught me. And maybe the lie that there were whole regiments of sepoys just waiting for the appearance of something that had the size and shape and sheer fucking balls of Johnny Sponson . . . Well, maybe that's the closest lie there is to the truth.

So we ended up down in London, and were billeted in Whitehall barracks, and the air was already full of trouble even before that spring began. Everywhere now, there was talk. So much of it that even the officers – who mostly couldn't speak a word of English to save their lives, as many of them would soon come to regret – caught on. The restrictions, the rules, the regimental bullshit, got ever stupider – and that was saying a lot. The whole wretched city was under curfew, but Johnny and I still got out over the barracks walls. There used to be these bars in London then, down by Charing Cross – the sort where women and men could dance with each other, and you could buy proper drink. Illegal dives, of course. The sweat dripped down the walls, and there was worse on the floor. But that wasn't the point. The point was just to be there – your head filled up with pipesmoke and cheering and music loud enough to make your ears ring.

And afterwards when the booze and the dancing and maybe a few of the girls had finally worn everyone out, Johnny and I and the rest of us sepoys would stagger back through London's curfew darkness. I remember the last time we got out was the night before the Muharram parade when the mutiny began, and how Johnny danced the way even he had never danced before. Tabletops and bar-tops and crashed-over benches held no obstacle – there was already a wildness in his eyes. As if he already knew. And perhaps he did. After all, he was Johnny Sponson.

Johnny and I rolled arm in arm late that night along the ghats beside the Thames. And still he talked. He was saying how the Moslem Mughals were so nice and accommodating to the Hindus, and how the Hindus took everything they could in return. Something about an officer class and a merchant class, and the two getting on with each other nicely, the deal being that every other religion got treated like dogshit as a result. Like the Jews, for example. Or the Romanies. Even the Catholic Portuguese, who'd had centuries to regret helping conquer England for the Mughals. Or us Protestant Christians here in England – although anyone rich enough to afford it turns to Mecca or buys themselves into a caste. Why, Johnny, he could take me along this river, right within these city walls, and show me what was once supposed to have been a great new cathedral – a place called Saint Paul's. A half-built ruin, it was, even though it was started before the Mughals invaded more than two hundred years ago.

I remember how he disentangled himself from my arm and wavered over to a wall in that elegant way he still managed when he was drunk. The guy even *pissed* with a flourish! Never stopped talking, as well. About how this wall was part of something called the English Repository, where much of what used to belong to the lost English kings – the stuff, anyway, that hasn't been melted down and shipped back to India – had been left to rot. Thrones and robes. Great works of literature, too. Shakespeare, Chaucer – men no one in England has heard of now . . . Nobody came here, except a few mad scholars looking for a hint of English exoticism to spice up their dreary poems. That, and another kind of trade . . . Johnny was still pissing as he talked. "I believe the mollies frequent the darker aisles. Their customers call them Repository girls . . ." Finally, he hitched himself up, turned around and gave me the wink. "I believe they're quite reasonable. You should try them, Davey."

We wandered on. But, as any soldier will tell you, it's a whole lot easier to get out of barracks than it is to get back in, and Johnny and I were spotted by the sentries just as we were hanging our arses over the top of the wall. Which is how we ended up on punishment duty on next day's famous parade, and perhaps why everything else that happened came about.

It started out as a fine winter morning. People seem to forget that. Muharram, it was, and I remember thinking that this whole pestilential city seemed almost beautiful for once as we troops were mustered beside the Thames at dawn. Even the rancid river looked like velvet. And on it was passing all the traffic of Empire. Red-sailed tugs, and rowboats and barges. I remember how a naval aeropile came pluming by, the huge sphere of its engine turning, and how the sky flickered like spiderwebs with the lines of all the kites, and me thinking that, despite all Johnny said, perhaps this Empire which I'd spent my whole life defending wasn't such a bad thing after all.

Then the parade began. You know how the Indians love a bit of pomp, especially on holy days. And us Devonshires were there to celebrate the great victory we were supposed to have won against the savage Scots. Whatever, it was another fucking parade, and soon the clear skies darkened and it started sleeting, although I suppose it must still have looked some sight just like it always does. Elephants ploughing up Whitehall with those great howdahs swaying on their backs. Nautch girls casting flowers, and the dripping umbrella lines and prayer flags of the crowds who'd quit their sweatshops in Holborn, Clerkenwell and Chelsea for the day. The shining domes of balconies of the Resident's Palace along Downing Street. And camels and oxen and stallions and bagpipes and sitars.

Johnny and I had been given these long-handled shovels. It was our job to follow a cart behind the elephants and scrape up and toss their shit onto the back of it. Punishment duty, like I said, and we were lucky not to have got something a whole lot worse. But the crowd thought it was fucking hilarious – sheer bloody music hall, the way we slipped and slid, and I guess that Johnny's dignity was hurt, and he was tired and he was hung over as well, and maybe that was just one last hurt too many in a life full of hurts.

There was a guy in the crowd who thought me and Johnny scrabbling and falling in the sleet and shit in our best uniforms was even funnier than everyone else. He kept pushing on through the crowds so he could point and laugh some more. I hardly noticed, but Johnny gave this sudden roar and lunged towards him, waving his shit-caked shovel like it was a halberd. Not sure that he actually meant to hit anyone, but he *was* mad, and people started falling over and shouting just to get out of his way, and that spooked the elephants, and the next thing I knew a wave of chaos was spreading along the parade.

Soon, guns were firing. You could tell they were Indian repeaters rather than the slow old muskets which was all us sepoys were trusted with. It didn't feel like a parade any longer – more like some kind of battle, which is the one thing we sepoys know something about. The elephant's bellowing and rampaging added to the chaos. I remember how the whole side of this great gold crusted temple just crumbled when one lunged into it. I remember the way it fell apart, and how the bibis and the priests inside came screaming out, and the freezing English sleet just kept on pouring down. Fucking beautiful, it was.

London was in uproar, and I managed pretty well that day with just my bayonet and my shovel, even if I say so myself. Of course, there was bloodshed, but there was far less than anyone expected, or the tales would have you believe. The Indians – the so-called loyal troops, the camel regiments out of Hyderabad and all the cavalry – they just fired and fell back beyond the city walls. London didn't burn that day – although the temple monkeys got it, and of course the tigers in Hyde Park and anything else that didn't look English. Like I say, there had been rumours of an uprising, and most of the higher caste Indians and the rich merchants and the Resident and all of his staff had left London days or weeks before. The city just fell into our hands.

We were like kids, rampaging after years of being kept locked up. The shops and warehouses were gutted, of course, and so were all the bungalows of Chelsea and the temples of Whitefriars and the palaces of Whitechapel. It was like an army of ants at work in a kitchen, only people were carrying these huge sideboards and settees instead of grains of rice. Everything was spilling out of doors, and we were all dancing and laughing, and most of our gunshots were aimed in the air. Sepoy or Londoner, half-blood or English – on that first day of the uprising it really didn't matter. We were all on the same side.

Didn't see much of Johnny for a while – got myself lost in the cheering crowds. When I did find him it was already late in the afternoon. It was no surprise that the crowds were cheering most loudly around him – waving bits of curtain rod and bill-hooks and scythes, beating stolen temple drums. This was outside the great temple of Ganesh at Whitefriars, and I suppose most of its treasures must already have been looted, and its priests killed, and there was Johnny clambering high on the tower to speak to us all.

I won't bore you with most of what Johnny said. You either know it already or you don't care, and you can still get the pamphlets the censors haven't destroyed if you know who to tip the wink to. It was just . . . Well, for me, it was simply Johnny being Johnny. Going on the way he always did, only now he had a bigger audience. And some already knew he was the guy who had swung that first shovel which got the whole mutiny started, and the rest would have believed anything he said by then. That day, we all wanted to believe. The stuff he was saying as he clung to the lotus blossom carvings on that tower, to me it was all typical Johnny Sponson – and it was still sleeting, and the stones must have been slippery, and he'd have killed himself if he fell. Stuff about how, contrary to most outward appearances, London *was* a great city, and this whole country was great as well. Not some province of Empire, no, but England, England, in its own right! And he mentioned all the names I'd often heard – names which the other sepoys and the rest of London were soon chanting as well. Elizabeth! Arthur! King Henry the Something! No, no, he was telling us, this shouldn't be the temple of Ganesh. If it was anyone's temple, it should be the temple of Christ, for Christ was an Englishman, and so was God. And if the Indians thought we were rats, well, then we'd make it the temple of Karair Matr, the rat goddess, and we'd swarm all over them and eat out their eyes . . .! Once Johnny got going, there was nothing could make him stop, and we were all cheering and no one wanted him to. London was some place to be, on that first great day of the English Mutiny.

I found Johnny again some time later when it was fully dark. By then, people had lit many fires – after all, it was freezing and they needed to keep warm. The city glittered with broken things. It looked like a box of spilled jewels. And those who had gathered around him had already sorted themselves in the way that people who sense where power lies always do. Already, he was giving out orders, and all of London was taking them. I had a job to get to him as he sat by this huge bonfire on the padded bench of a broken palanquin surrounded by bodyguards. Nearly got knifed in the process, until Johnny saw who it was and shouted for them to let me through.

"Well, Davey," he said. "Something *has* happened. Birnam Wood has moved, perhaps. Or Hampstead Heath, perhaps . . ." It was still his old way of talking, and I could tell from his eyes that he was long past being drunk.

"What happens now?"

He smiled at the fire. "That's up to us, isn't it? 'They that have the power to hurt, and will do none, they rightly do inherit heaven's graces.'"

Despite the flames, I felt myself going cold. Already, I was starting to hate such nonsense, and all the bloodshed and destruction that I already feared would follow. We've all suffered one way or another, I suppose, Indian and English, no matter what side we took in that mutiny or revolt. The odd thing to me is how little us sepoys, who know as much as anyone about battle, didn't see how it was bound to turn out. Thought we could just march out across England, that everything would fall to us as easily as London did on that first marvellous day.

It even seemed that it was going to happen that way – at least for a while. We got news from Chester about a revolt which had started there several days earlier, and how all the non-English in the city had been slaughtered, which helped explain why the Indian troops in London had been so edgy, and quick to pull out. News from Bath and Derby, as well. Not that I'm much at reading maps, but Johnny used to study them endlessly as his rebel regiments fanned out from London to mop up what then seemed like the flimsy Indian resistance. It really was like dominos or falling cards or some unstoppable tide – all of the fancy descriptions Johnny liked to use when he climbed high on that tower of that temple of Ganesh to speak to us all.

It's a lie to say we didn't have a plan. We were soldiers, we were disciplined – we knew how to fight, and we knew that this whole land was rightly ours. Of course, we needed supplies, and of course we took them, but that's no more than any army does. And as for the other things – well, armies do tend to do some of those, as well. It comes with the trade. But the rumours of bonfires being made of all the raped and mutilated bodies – that's just Indian talk. Bodies don't burn that easily in any case. And Johnny, he never wanted those things to happen, and he flew into towering rages when they did. And all the time the red of Empire was changing on his maps to English green, just as the English winter was warming to spring. We'd hear that yet another town had overthrown its oppressors, or another battalion or whole regiment which had gone over to the rightful English side. Seemed like just a matter of time before this whole country was ours. Seemed like it wouldn't be long before we heard news that the Resident himself had peacefully surrendered to the Zenana Guard who protected his women, and then we could put away our bayonets and guns and garrottes. And after that . . . After that, everything would be the same as it was before, only better.

But Johnny's dreams were bigger, and we needed those as well. We needed *him*. It's an odd thing, I suppose, that we were happy to kowtow to a high-caste omrah like Johnny Sponson when we were so busy despoiling the estates his likes had come from. But that was how it was, and it was something Johnny played up to. Set himself up in old Saint James Place, he did. Said the place could be defended, if push ever came to shove. Didn't exactly sit on a throne – he was always too busy pacing about and giving orders – but there was certainly a throne in the great hall in which he'd established his command, and its walls and floors were covered with beautiful rugs and many other fine things which had been looted from the Indian palaces across London. Every time he climbed that gold-encrusted tower of the Great Temple of Ganesh, he climbed a little bit higher, and the clothes he wore were that much grander. He spread his arms out to all the thousands who waited below him, and his red velvet robe set with jewels and gold encrustations spread out around him in the wind.

I might have been Johnny's oldest and best friend, but in most ways I was still nothing special. Had no appetite for giving out orders, for a start – got too much of that from my bastard Dad, and all the bullshit NCOs I've served under since. Anyway, there were plenty of others that did. In the new England we thought we were creating, that was one thing that hadn't changed one little bit – people were still telling other people what to do. Still, Johnny looked out for me, just as he always had. I passed messages. I listened. He asked me to be his eyes and ears.

I talked to people. Regiments which had arrived fresh at the capital, or ones which were returning bloodied and exhausted from some campaign. I didn't speak to those who were setting themselves up as captains and majors and generals – even wearing the sashes and badges of the men they'd tortured and killed, they were, by then – but to men like myself, ordinary sepoys, common soldiers, who still had to fight for their lives just like they'd always fought. And they spoke freely. They had no idea that I was any different to them.

That way, and using what I suppose you'd call my soldier's intuition, I started to get a picture of what was happening across England. Sometimes, it seemed to me that I understood things far better than Johnny's generals, or how they were drawn on his precious maps. The Indians and their loyal regiments had retreated, that was for certain, but they hadn't vanished. They'd mostly drawn back into the major cities we sepoys had laid siege to but still hadn't mustered the forces to attack. They were skulking in the huge new fortresses at Dover, for example, and hiding in the castles and ramparts surrounding Liverpool, Portsmouth and Bristol, which had all been recently enlarged. Basically, the way I saw it, the bastard Indians had made sure they kept control of the main ports apart from London, which they'd given up because they knew its walls were too old to properly defend. Kept, as well, the power of their navy, both merchant and marine, which – uncaring shits that sailors are – had remained loyal to them. For me, it seemed as if the Indians had anticipated our mutiny far better than we sepoys. I even heard about the ships and reinforcements coming from Portugal long before the story was believed.

At first Johnny listened to what I told him, but soon, being Johnny, he listened less and less, and talked more and more. Lord Johnny Sponson of all England just laughed and danced across his plundered carpets and around his gilded logpiles of half-ruined furniture in his great and echoing halls. Johnny did all the things he'd always been good at, and all his new friends and commanders – and mistresses – agreed and applauded and laughed and danced as well. The women, of course, were mad for him. For the ease of his limbs, and who he was, and what he could do for them. And if that look in his eyes, the way he smiled, wasn't quite the same as the Johnny I remembered, who the hell was there but me to care or notice?

Spring turned to summer, and the Indians with all their new supplies and fresh foreign troops pushed out from their fortresses. They defeated us at Bewdley and Oxford. They moved back across the Severn and the Thames. The weather turned hot, and food grew short because most of the farms in the area around London where we rebel sepoys were now pinned had been abandoned and no one had thought to harvest the crops. The Indian armies had the repeating rifles which they'd never allowed us sepoys to use. They had proper cannon instead of our antique ceremonial relics. They had fresh elephants, and armoured aeropiles to plough along the captured rivers, and barrels of terrible Greek Fire. Their victories weren't so much defeats for us as routs – organized destruction, and the revenge they took upon all the thousands of sepoys they captured was terrible. They tied our bodies to their new guns and blasted them to pieces because they thought that we Christian English feared for our souls if we weren't given a proper burial. They pierced us with hooks. They burned us on slow fires of charcoal. They fed us, half-roasted but still alive, to the crows.

It was late August by the time London was fully encircled, and the great sepoy army which Lord Johnny had drawn around him had gathered within its feeble walls. The place was hot and overcrowded. The sewers were shattered. The river stank. The wells had turned bad. Yet there was still hope. There was still dancing. The severed heads of freshly discovered collaborators and Indians were regularly borne along the streets whilst the Indians generals waited outside the city walls.

I remember I was wandering one morning in the strange place London had become. The temples were emptied, the buildings and bridges were torn. There were no sadhus now, no beggars – or we were all sadhus and beggars. It was hard to tell. A smog of burning hung over the city. It darkened the sky. It shaded out the sun. The streets seemed strangely paved in that odd twilight. I pushed through drifts of sheet music. My boots crunched on the shattered brass shells of pocketwatches looted from a store. Stooping to look at them more closely, I saw there were even a few broken scraps of gold. I remembered walking – it seemed, not so long ago – arm in arm with Johnny close to this same place as we headed back from that bar at Charing Cross. There was no beer now. There was scarcely any water. But ahead of me, although now daubed with fresh layers of slogans, was the wall of the English Repository against which Johnny had pissed.

A movement caught my eye. This city was no longer safe – my hand went straight to my bayonet – but what I saw was a female figure, smallish and seemingly youngish, dressed in a brocaded red sari. The figure beckoned. Although I had no idea what she wanted, I followed.

The entrance to the English Repository had once been grand. Filthy statues which I suppose had once been supposed to represent art, or love, leaned around its collapsing arch. It was dark outside that day, but inside the darkness was far greater. The sort of dark you get that piles up over ages from shadows and mildew and things long left to rot. A few muttonfat candles smoked, and I could see it was just as Johnny had said. Old stuff, once kingly and grand, but now so ruined as to have been ignored even by the rampaging mobs was piled everywhere. Rain-leaked ceremonial carriages. Beds like the bloated corpses you saw down by the river, their upholstery green and swollen. And books everywhere. Not just on shelves, but piled on the floors and spilling their leaves amid the puddles. It was a damp place, even in the middle of summer. Reeked of piss, as well. The English Repository would barely have smouldered when all the rest of London had burned.

The woman in the glittering, once-beautiful sari was still shuffling ahead of me. Beckoning me on, and talking all the while in this cracked voice – saying words which made no sense, but also sounded familiar. Something about the rags of time, and love knowing no season – nonsense really, but pretty, bookish nonsense of a kind I knew only too well. I understood what she was by now, and I saw as we entered some kind of courtyard filled with the dead remains of furniture and rusting suits of armour that there were many others of her kind. They looked like crows – roosting there, and cackling as well. Repository girls, Johnny had called them. What a strange and desolate place to live, I thought – but I let the woman pull me to her, even though she stank as sourly as the city itself.

She was fumbling beneath my trews with black crow fingers. And I could see the rotting spines of the books amid the mushroom shelves behind. Could even read the same names that Johnny had once said to me. Shakes-something. And Chancer – Chaucer? Donne – Dun, Donny, is that how you'd say it? Somebody called Marlow. All the old Johnny bullshit. At least, that was how it seemed to me. And beyond that, leaning against a mossy wall with dead bits of vine growing over it and half the paint peeled and blistered off, there was this huge old painting of some lost great English estate. You could tell that it no longer existed. You could tell that it came from an England which had been plundered and destroyed long ago. I pulled away from her and threw the scraps of gold I'd picked up outside that looted shop as I fled to stop the woman following – although, like everything else in this city, it was worthless. She was shouting after me about how she had a son, a nice boy, for sale as well.

London had stirred itself while I was in the English Repository's darkness. The streets were suddenly rivered with people. They were smashing what hadn't already been destroyed. They were chanting and wailing and pulling at their clothes. Guns were firing into the air – a waste of precious shot. I feared that the Indians had already breached our walls. But I know what a battle feels like, and I realized that this wasn't one, although there was so much noise and confusion that it took me some time to find out what had really happened. Even then, I still didn't believe. Johnny Sponson, Lord Protector of all of England, had been out walking this very morning, keeping up morale, touching the ill and the wounded who clamoured to be cured, showing his face to the adoring crowds. I'm sure he thought he was well protected, but the Indians must have positioned snipers close enough for one of them to pick him out. After all, he'd have made an obvious target, dressed as he now dressed. I grabbed arms and shouted into faces. Was he alive? Was he dead? No one seemed to know for sure.

I pushed on towards Saint James Palace. Try to go any other way, and I'd have been trampled for sure. You've never seen such sights – heard such sounds. And then, of all things, I heard my own name being shouted by the guards who were protecting the palace gates, and hands were all over me and I found myself being lifted up. Yes. Here's the one. Yes, this is Private Sepoy Davey Whittings. No, no, back, back you fucking idiots. This is *him*. I feared for my life, although death and I had long since reached an understanding. But there I was, being hauled over the crowds and shoved through the gates of Saint James Palace by Johnny Sponson's liveried guards, then led through ruined logfalls of gilded furniture which weren't so very different to those in the English Repository. Then a final door banged behind me, and I was standing alone in the great hall of Johnny's throne room.

The place seemed huge and oddly still, emptied of all the usual so-called generals, and fawning and laughing fools. But something big had been set in the middle of it – a tall thing of red curtains and lotus-carved pillars more than large enough to make a room of its own. When I peered inside it, I saw Johnny, and I realized that it was some kind of bed. He was half-lying, half-sitting, against these cushions, and he was smiling – almost chuckling – and he was wearing his usual cloak and a jewel-studded turban and many chains of office, and his right arm was hooked in a sling. It took me a moment to take in what I was seeing.

"So you're not dead?"

"Is that what they're saying?"

"No one knows for sure."

"And they're all crying, howling out my name?"

"What would you expect?"

He chuckled louder. "Glory," he muttered, "is like a circle of water, which never ceases to enlarge, till by broad spreading it disperses to nothing – haven't you found that to be the truth, Davey?"

"You know I don't understand that kind of fucking bollocks. I never did."

"Don't you?" He seemed surprised – almost pained. "Perhaps not."

"Why did you ask for me, Johnny? Why the fuck did you bring me here?"

Part of me wondered if he really had feared that he was dying, and had wanted to see his old pal Davey Whittings for one last time. But then, he didn't look so bad, and so many others were closer to him now – hangers-on, women who dressed like princesses and acted like whores, men who smelled like butchers because of the reek of death on their clothes. Old mates of mine, some of them, although you wouldn't have recognized them now. But I was still plain old Davey Whittings, sir, Sahib, Sepoy Second Class. With all of London wailing his name outside, I wondered if Johnny Sponson hadn't simply wanted to see me just to remind himself of how very far he'd come.

He didn't give a straight answer to my question, of course. He never could. He just gave another one of those Johnny chuckles. He just grinned a Johnny grin. And then he started talking about how England had needed someone. Not Johnny Sponson necessarily, but he'd been the one more than anyone else who had felt that need, and had known how to fill it. Said he was like the soil of England, this sceptred isle, this seat of majesty . . . all the usual bollocks. It really was like he was giving me his deathbed speech, even though he plainly wasn't dying. Or, more likely, he was doing the same thing that he'd done when he sat beside me in that filthy hospital, and was rehearsing what he was planned to say later to a much bigger audience when he climbed the Great Temple of Ganesh, or perhaps, seeing as he was wounded, got himself hoisted up there on a wooden cross.

I could imagine his words ringing out across the adoring crowds. And I knew that they'd love him all the more now that he'd cheated death itself. And he was right, as well – when he said he gave them the spirit they needed to fight. That they needed him as much as he needed them. Without him, they'd be a rabble of looters and cut-throats – soldiers without orders. And without them . . . he'd just be plain old Johnny Sponson. The man who'd saved my life. The man I'd once grown to love.

But this different Johnny Sponson seemed pleased, excited, by his brush with a sniper's bullet. He was full of new wildness and strange hope, and odd new theories to add to all of those he already had. How, for example, the reason that the Indians had spread this Empire so far was because of their simple need to survive those dreadful few summers and freezing winters of 200 and more years ago. How it all would have been different if something strange hadn't fallen out of the skies to darken our world. As ever, he was full of it. Nothing had changed. Part of him was just being more and more of what he already was.

Despite London being surrounded by a far larger and better-equipped army, Johnny was convinced that this wasn't the end of the English Mutiny. And, as he talked of how the Scots had seized the moment to attack beyond Hadrian's Wall and were marching south even now, and how the Lowland Hollanders would soon be breaking the Indian blockade and sailing up the Thames with fresh ships and supplies, he even began to convince me. I could feel it happening – I could see the colours returning to English green on his beloved maps, and I knew that others would believe him even more than I did. But the difference was, I hated the very thought of yet another battle, even if victory was the result. Nor could I understand why I was suddenly on the same side as the fucking Scots seeing as I'd nearly lost my life fighting them. All that would happen if we sepoys were able to break this siege and the Hollanders arrived and the Scots came to our aid was that there would be more destruction, and another year's harvest fallen to neglect as a result. Above all, there would be more deaths. Killing was the only thing that we sepoys were good for, when all was said and done. Try to get us to do anything else and we fucked up.

I looked around me at this great and empty throne room. Johnny was going on even more now about duty, and about flags, and the need for loyalty, the need to stand up straight before what mattered, and fight for your nation and obey orders and do the right thing, even if the right thing was death. Perhaps the wound in his arm was worse than I'd thought, or perhaps he'd already taken something to help with the pain, or maybe he was simply a little drunk, but he was ranting now – and all of it was stuff I'd heard before. On parade grounds and from the mouths of officers, and back when I was a kid in the hovel we used to call home.

I reached my hand into my pocket, and felt for the loop of wire I still carried there, just like the good soldier I still was. And I opened it out and held it there whilst Johnny was still talking. I think it took him a moment to realize what I was about to do. And even then he didn't exactly seem surprised. After all, part of him was still like me, still a sepoy. He knew death was always waiting around the next corner, especially at the moment when you thought you'd finally left it behind.

"Why . . . ?"

He struggled, but he was wounded – hampered by that sling and his ridiculous clothes – and my movements were quick, and by then I'd had more than enough of Johnny's bullshit talk. Still, it's not a swift death, or an easy one. You need strong hands, a strong will, to use a garrotte. His loosened hands batted against me. His legs spasmed. His faced reddened, then blued. His tongue went out. He leaked piss and blood. His eyes rolled. But I didn't let go. I was a soldier, a sepoy. Death was my job. But in truth, it wasn't the thought of all the fresh battles he'd urge us sepoys to fight which kept me pulling the wire. It wasn't even all the dead bodies and sobbing women and smoking skies and ruined towns that another season's fighting would bring. If the bastard had sounded like anyone towards the end in what he'd been saying, it was like my Dad when he was in his cups. So it wasn't for the glory or for the sake of saving anyone or rescuing London or preserving the Empire that I killed Johnny Sponson. I simply wanted to shut the fucker up.

Someone must have decided that I'd been alone with my supposed best mate in that throne room for a little too long. Perhaps, seeing as they knew what Johnny was like, it had gone a bit quiet, as well. Whatever it was, the guards burst in yelling, and they saw instantly what I had done. Word went out from there quicker than you could ever have imagined – beyond the palace gates and across London, right out over the city walls to the waiting Indian armies with their huge siege engines and repeating guns. Johnny Sponson, Lord of whatever he was lord of, our Prince and our King – private sepoy second-class, expert bullshitter, brilliant dancer and secret son of some English Repository whore – was dead. The grief and the chaos were incredible. London burned that night. It was wrecked even before the Indians moved in to occupy it the next morning. Or so I think I've been told.

I'd imagined Johnny's guards would simply kill me. I hadn't counted on the fact that they were sepoys just as I was, and understood that death wasn't something I'd care that much about – that it was like the face of someone you're given up trying to love. They knew, as well, that their own chances of survival and the success of this whole mutiny had vanished with Johnny Sponson's death. They'd probably even seen the bodies of their captured comrades – or, once the Indians had finished, what was left of them.

You can see what Johnny's sepoys did to me yourself. They had a whole night to work at it before the Indians breached the city walls. And work they did. Then they left me there, destroyed as I was, right there in Johnny's throne room, laid beside the body of the man I had killed as flames took hold of the rugs and tapestries and licked up the walls. Perhaps they wanted me to be a signal, a sign, although I doubt if they ever imagined I'd have survived for as long as I have.

As you will long ago have noticed, they left me my mouth and tongue after they'd cut away my legs and retwisted my arms. I miss my vanished sight the more, though, because I'd love to have seen what has been made of this newly rebuilt city on the cold northerly fringes of this great Empire. I'd like to believe it's as beautiful as sometimes, in the right fall of hope or light or darkness, I thought it might become. I can't hear you, either, kind sir, Sahib, Brahmin, Begum, Fakir, Lord, Lady, but I do not ask for words, or alms. Just touch here on my chest where the white ash is smeared. Tell me it's true that this city has been remade into something beautiful – that I'm propped on the marble steps of a fine new temple, filled with light and mosaic and the very breath of Christ, Mohammed, Brahma – that the skies above teem with kites and flags and spires and muezzin towers and the cries of mullahs and the clamour of bells. Touch me here, where the flesh isn't so burned. Then I'll know. Then I'll understand.

And don't worry about the ash, sir, Sahib, if your hands are clean or your clothes are smart. It'll wash off easily enough.

O One

Chris Roberson

Tsui stood in the golden morning light of the Ornamental Garden, looking over the still waters of the abacus fishponds and thinking about infinity. Beyond the walls, the Forbidden City already hummed with the activity of innumerable servants, eunuchs, and ministers bustling along in the Emperor's service, but in the garden itself there was only silence and serenity.

Apart from the Imperial House of Calculation, which Tsui had served as Chief Computator since the death of his predecessor and father years before, the Ornamental Garden was the only place he lingered. The constant susurration of beads shuttling and clacking over oiled rods was the only music he could abide, and as dear to him as the beating of his own heart, but there were times still when the rhythms of that symphony began to wear on him. On these rare occasions the silence of the fishponds and the sculpted grounds surrounding them was the only solace he had found.

His father, when he had been Chief Computator and Tsui not yet an apprentice, had explained that time and resources were the principal enemies of calculation. One man, with one abacus and an unlimited amount of time, could solve every mathematical operation imaginable, just as an unlimited number of men working with an infinite number of abacuses could solve every operation imaginable in an instant, but no man had an infinity in which to work, and no emperor could marshal to his service an infinite number of men. It was the task of the Chief Computator to strike the appropriate balance. The men of the Imperial House of Calculation worked in their hundreds delicately manipulating the beads of their abacuses to provide the answers the Emperor required. That every click of bead on bead was followed a moment of silence, however brief, served only to remind Tsui of the limits this balance demanded. In that brief instant the enemies of calculation were the victors.

As a child Tsui had dreamt of an endless plain, filled with men as far as the eye could see. Every man in his dream was hunched over a small wooden frame, his fingers dancing over cherrywood beads, and together they simultaneously solved every possible operation, a man for each calculation. In his dream, though, Tsui had not heard the same clatter and click he'd found so often at his father's side, with an endless number of permutations, every potential silence was filled with the noise of another bead striking bead somewhere else. The resulting sound was steady and even, a constant hum, no instant distinguishable from any other.

Only in pure silence had Tsui ever found another sensation quite like that, and the only silence he had found pure enough was that of the Ornamental Garden. Without speaking or moving, he could stand with eyes closed at the water's edge and imagine himself on that infinite plain, the answer to every problem close at hand.

The sound of feet scuffing on flagstone broke Tsui from his reverie, and he looked up to see Royal Inspector Bai walking leisurely through the garden's gate. Like Tsui, the Royal Inspector seemed to find comfort within the walls of silence, and the two men frequently exchanged a word of pleasantry on their chance encounters.

"A good morning, Chief Computator?" Bai asked. He approached the fishponds, a package of waxed paper in his hands. He stopped opposite Tsui at the water's edge of the southernmost of the two ponds and, unwrapping his package with deft maneuvers, revealed a slab of cold pork between two slices of bread. A concept imported from the cold and distant England on the far side of the world, it was a dish that had never appealed to Tsui, more traditional in his tastes than the adventurous Inspector.

"As good as I might deserve, Inspector," Tsui answered, inclining his head a fraction. As he was responsible for the work of hundreds, Tsui technically ranked above the Inspector in the hierarchy of palace life, but considering the extensive influence and latitude granted the latter by imperial decree, the Chief Computator always displayed respect shading into submissiveness as a matter of course.

Bai nodded in reply and, tearing pieces of bread from either slice, dropped them onto the water before him. The abacus fish in the southern pond, of a precise but slow strain, moved in a languid dance to nibble the crumbs floating on the water's surface. The brilliant gold hue of their scales, iridescent in the shifting light, prismed through the slowly shifting water's surface, sparkling from below like prized gems. The fish, the result of a failed experiment years before to remove man from the process of calculation, had been bred from ornamentals chosen for their instinct of swimming in schools of close formation. In tests of the system, though, with a single agent flashing a series of lights at the water's edge representing a string of digits and the appropriate operation, it was found that while accurate to a high degree, the slowness of their movements made them no more effective than any apprentice of the House of Calculation. The biological and chemical agents used in breeding them from true, however, had left the scales of the languid abacus fish and their descendants much more striking that those of the base stock, and so a place was found for the failed experiment in the gardens.

"Your pardon, O Chief Computator," Bai remarked, shaking the last dusty crumbs from the pork and moving to the northern pond. "But it seems to me, at such times, that the movements of these poor doomed creatures still suggest the motions of your beads over rods, for even in their feeding, the fish arrange themselves in columns and rows of varying number."

Tearing off strips of pork, the Inspector tossed them onto the water, which frothed and bubbled the instant the meat hit the surface. Silt, kicked up by the force of the sudden circulation, colored the water a dusty gray.

"I can only agree, of course," Tsui answered, drawing alongside the Inspector and looking down on the erratic dance beneath the surface of the pond. This strain of abacus fish was, in contrast to its languid neighbor, much swifter but likewise far less consistent. They had been mutated from a breed of carnivorous fish from the Western Hemisphere's southern continent, the instinct of hunger incarnate. The operations they performed, cued by motions in the air above and enticed by offerings of raw flesh, were done faster than any but the most accomplished human operator could match, but with an unacceptably high degree of error. Like their languid cousins before them these fierce creatures were highly prized for their appearance, their strangely iridescent scales offset by razor teeth and jagged fins, and so they were relocated from the Imperial Ministry of Experimentation into the garden when Tsui was only a child. "They mimic the process of calculation as a mynah bird does that of human speech. Ignorant, and without any comprehension. Man does not, as yet, have any replacement."

"Hmm," the Inspector hummed, tossing the last of the pork into the water. "But what does the abacus bead know of its use? Is it not the computator only who must understand the greater meaning?"

"Perhaps, O Inspector, this may be how the Emperor himself, the-equal-of-heaven and may-he-reign-ten-thousand-years, rules over the lives and destinies of men. Each of us need not know how we work in the grander scheme, so long as the Emperor's hand guides us." It was not a precise representation of Tsui's thoughts on the matter, but a more politic answer than that which immediately suggested itself, and one better fit for the ears of the Emperor's justice.

The Inspector hummed again, and wiped his fingers clean on the hems of his sleeves. Looking past Tsui's shoulder at the garden's entrance, Bai raised his eyebrows a fraction and nodded.

"You may be right, Chief Computator," the Inspector

answered, grinning slightly. "I believe either of two beads, you or I, will in short order be guided from here. Can you guess which?"

Tsui turned his chin over his shoulder, and saw the approach of the Imperial page.

"Neither can I," the Inspector said before Tsui could answer. When the page presented the parchment summons to the Chief Computator with an abbreviated bow, Bai smiled and nodded again, and turned his attention back to the abacus fish. The last of the pork was gone, but white foam still frothed over the silty gray waters.

★　★　★

Within the hall they waited, ministers and courtiers, eunuchs and servants, the Empress Dowager behind her screens, her ladies with faces made painted masks, and the Emperor himself upon the Golden Dragon Throne. All watching the still form of the infernal machine, squatting oily and threatening like a venomous toad on the lacquered wooden floor, its foreign devil master standing nervously to one side.

Tsui was met in the antechamber by the Lord Chamberlain. With a look of stern reproach for the Chief Computator's late arrival, the Chamberlain led Tsui into the hall, where they both knelt and kowtowed to the Emperor, touching foreheads to cold floor twice before waiting to be received.

"The Emperor does not like to be kept waiting," said the Emperor, lazily running his fingers along the surface of the scarlet and gold object in his hands. "Begin."

As the Emperor leaned forward, elbows resting on the carved arms of the ancient Manchurian throne, Tsui could see that the object in his hand was a representation in miniature of the proposed Imperial Space Craft. A much larger version, at fifty per cent scale, hung from the rafters of the hall overhead. It presented an imposing image of lacquered red cherrywood and finely wrought gold, with delicately sweeping fins and the imperial seal worked into the bulkheads above the forward viewing ports. That the Emperor did not like to be kept waiting was no secret. Since he'd first ascended to the Dragon Throne a decade before, he'd wanted nothing more than to travel to the heavens and had dedicated the resources of the world's most powerful nation to that end. His ancestors had conquered three-quarters of the world centuries before, his grandfather and then his father had gone on to bring the remaining rogue states under the red banner of China, and now the Emperor of the Earth would conquer the stars.

In the years of the Emperor's reign, four out of every five mathematical operations sent to the Imperial House of Calculation had been generated by the Ministry of Celestial Excursion, the bureau established to develop and perfect the art of flying into the heavens. Tsui had never given it a great deal of thought. When reviewing the produced solutions, approving the quality of each before affixing his chop and the ideogram that represented both "Completion" and "Satisfaction", he had never paused to wonder why the scientists, sages and alchemists might need these answers. The work of the Chief Computator was the calculation, and the use to which the results were put the concern of someone else.

Now, called for the first time to appear before his Emperor, it occurred to Tsui that he might, at last, be that someone else.

The Lord Chamberlain, at Tsui's side, motioned for the foreign devil to step forward. A tall, thin white man, he had a pile of pale brown hair on his head, and wispy mustaches that crept around the corners of his mouth towards his chin. A pair of round-framed glasses pinched the bridge of his nose, and his black wool suit was worn at the edges, the knees worn thin and shiny.

"Ten thousand pardons, your majesty," the Lord Chamberlain began, bowing from the waist, "but may I introduce to you the Proctor Napier, scientific attaché to the Imperial Capital from the subjugated land of Britain, conquered in centuries past by your glorious ancestors."

The Emperor inclined his head slightly, indicating that the foreign devil could continue.

"Many thanks for this indulgence, O Emperor," Proctor Napier began. "I come seeking your patronage."

The Emperor twitched the fingers of one hand, a precise motion.

"I was sent to these shores by your servant government in my home island," Napier continued, "to assist in Imperial research. My specialty is logic, and the ordering of information, and over the course of the past years I have become increasingly involved with the questions of computation. The grand designs of your majesty's long-range plans, whether to explore the moon and far planets, or to chart the course of the stars across the heavens, demand that complex calculations be performed at every step, and each of these calculations require both men, materials and time. It is my hope that each of these three prerequisites might be eliminated to a degree, so as to speed the progress towards your goals."

Tsui, not certain before this moment why he had been called before the Emperor, now harbored a suspicion, and stifled the desire to shout down the foreign devil. At the Chamberlain's side, he listened on, his hands curled into tense fists in his long sleeves.

"With your majesty's kind indulgence," Napier said, "I would take a moment to explain the fundamentals of my invention." With a timid hand, he gestured towards the oily contraption on the floor behind him. "The basic principle of its operation is a number system of only two values. I call this system 'binary'. Though an innovation of Europe, this system has its basis in the ancient wisdom of China, and as such it seems appropriate that your divine majesty is the one to whom it is presented.

"The trigrams of the I Ching are based on the structure of Yin and Yang, the complementary forces of nature. These trigrams, the building blocks of the I Ching, are composed either of broken or of unbroken lines. Starting from this pair of values, any number of combinations can be generated. Gottfried Liebniz, a German sage, adapted this basic structure some two hundred years ago into a full number system, capable of encoding any value using only two symbols. He chose the Arabic numerals '1' and '0', but the ideograms for Yin and Yang can be substituted and the system still functions the same.

The decoding is key. Using the Arabic notation, the number one is represented as '1', the number two as '10', the number three as '11', the number four as '100', and so on."

The Emperor sighed, pointedly, and glanced to the spacecraft model in his lap, signifying that he was growing weary of the presentation.

"Oh, dear," Napier whispered under his breath, and then hastened to add, "which which brings me to my invention." He turned, and stepped to the side of the construct of oily metal and wood on the floor. It was about the height of a man's knee, almost as wide, a roughly cubical shape of copper and iron plain and unadorned. The top face was surmounted by a brass frame, into which was set a series of wooden blocks, each face of which was carved with a number or symbol. On the cube face presented towards the Emperor was centered an array of articulated brass buttons, three rows of fifteen, the brassy sheen dulled by smudges of oil and grime.

"I call it the Analytical Engine. Powered by a simple motor, the engine comprises a series of switches, each of which can be set either to an 'on' or 'off' state by the manipulation of gears and cogs. By assigning a binary value to each of the two states, we are then able to represent with the engine any numerical value conceivable, so long as there are a sufficient number of switches available. With the inclusion of five operational variables, and the ability to display results immediately," he indicated the series of blocks crowning the device, "a fully functional Analytical Engine would theoretically be capable of solving quickly any equation put to it. Anyone with a rudimentary ability to read and input values can produce results more quickly and efficiently than a team of trained abacusists. This is only a prototype model, of course, capable of working only up to a limited number of digits, but with the proper funding I'm confident we could construct an engine free of this limitation."

Tsui's pulse raged in his ears, though he kept silent and calm in the view of the Emperor.

"If I may?" Napier said, glancing from the Emperor to his invention with an eyebrow raised.

The Emperor twitched, almost imperceptibly, and in response the Chamberlain stepped forward.

"You may exhibit your device," the Chamberlain announced, bowing his head fractionally but never letting his eyes leave Napier's.

Wiping his hands nervously on the thin fabric of his pants, Napier crouched down and gripped the wood-handled crank at the rear of the engine. Leaning in, the strain showing on his pale face, he cranked through a dozen revolutions that produced a grinding clatter that set Tsui's teeth on edge. Finally, when the Chief Computator was sure he could stand the torture no longer, the engine sputtered, coughed, and vibrated to clanking life. Little plumes of acrid smoke bellowed up from the corners of the metal cube, and a slow drip of oil from one side puddled in a growing pool on the lacquered floor.

Licking his lips, Napier worked his way around to the front of the device, and rested his fingers on the rows of brass buttons.

"I'll start with a simple operation," he announced. "Can anyone provide two numbers?"

No one ventured an answer, all too occupied with the clattering machine on the floor, afraid that it might do them some harm.

"You, sir?" Napier said, pointing at Tsui. "Can you provide me with two numbers for my experiment?"

All eyes on him, not least of which the Emperor's, Tsui could only nod, biting back the answer that crouched behind his teeth, hoping to pounce.

"One and two," Tsui answered simply, eyes on the floor.

With a last look around the assembled for any other response, Napier hit four buttons in sequence.

"I've just instructed the engine to compute the sum of the two provided values," he explained, pausing for a brief resigned sigh, "and when I press this final button the calculation will occur immediately and the result will be displayed above."

Demonstrating a flair for the dramatic, Napier reached back his hand, and stabbed a finger at the final button with a flourish. The engine smoked and wheezed even more than before, and with a final clatter the rightmost of the blocks crowning the device spun on its brass axis and displayed the symbol for "3" face up.

"There, you see?" Napier said. "The answer produced, without any human intervention beyond the initial input."

"I have seen horses," the Emperor replied in a quiet voice, "clopping their hoofs on cobblestones, do more complicated sums than this."

"Perhaps, your majesty," the Chamberlain said, stepping forward, "a more evaluative demonstration is in order. Chief Computator Tsui?" The Chamberlain motioned to him with a brief wave of his hand, and Tsui inched forward, his fingers laced fiercely together in front of him.

The Chamberlain then snapped his fingers, and a page glided out of the shadows into the center of the hall, a small stool in one hand, an abacus in the other. Setting the stool down a few paces from the foreign devil's instrument, the page presented the abacus to Tsui and, bowing low, glided back into the shadows.

"I would suggest, with your majesty's permission," the Chamberlain said, "that a series of calculations be performed, both by the Proctor Napier and his machine, and by our own Chief Computator and his abacus. Which of the two performs more reliably and efficiently will no doubt tell us more than any other demonstration could."

The Emperor twitched his eyebrows, slightly, suggesting a nod.

"Let us begin," said the Chamberlain.

Tsui seated himself on the stool. The abacus on his lap was cool and smooth at his touch, the beads when tested sliding frictionless over the frame of rods. Tilting the frame of the abacus up, he set the beads at their starting position, and then left his fingers hovering over the rightmost row, ready to begin.

★ ★ ★

The Chamberlain officiated, providing values and operations from a slip of paper he produced from his sleeve. That he'd anticipated this test of man and machine was obvious, though it was inappropriate for any involved to suggest the Chamberlain had orchestrated the events to his ends.

The first calculation was a simple addition, producing the sum of two six-digit numbers. Tsui had his answer while Napier's engine was still sputtering and wheezing, taking less than a third of the time needed for the machine to calculate and display the correct answer on blocks.

The second calculation was multiplication, and here again Tsui finished first. The lapse of time between Tsui calling out his answer and Napier calling out his, though, dwindled in this second round, the engine taking perhaps only twice as long.

The third calculation was division, a four-digit number divided into a six-digit one. Tsui, pulse racing, called out his answer only an instant before Napier. The ruling of the Chamberlain named the Chief Computator the victor, even after Napier protested that he had inadvertently set his engine to calculate to two decimal places, and that as a result his answer was in fact more accurate.

The fourth and final calculation was to find the cube root of a six-digit number. This time, with his previous failure in mind, Napier shouted out after the numbers had been read that the answer should be calculated to two decimal points. The Chamberlain, eyes on the two men, nodded gravely and agreed to this condition. Tsui, who was already fiercely at work on the solution, felt the icy grip of dread. Each additional decimal place in a cube root operation increased the time necessary for the computation exponentially, and even without them he wasn't sure if he would finish first.

Fingers racing over the beads, too tense even to breathe, Tsui labored. The answer was within reach, he knew, with only seconds until he would be named the victor. The abhorrent clattering machine of the foreign interloper would be exposed for a fraud, and the place of the Chief Computator, and of the Imperial House of Computation, would be secure.

"I have it!" Napier shouted, and stepped back from the Analytical Engine to let the assembled see the displayed solution. There was a manic gleam in his eyes, and he looked directly at the Emperor without reservation or shame, as though expecting something like applause.

Tsui was frozen, struck dumb. Reviewing his mental calculations, he realized he'd been nowhere near an answer, would have required minutes more even to come close. He looked up, saw the symbols displayed on the first blocks of the device, and knew that Napier's answer was the correct one.

"It is decided, then," the Chamberlain announced, striding to Tsui's side. "Of the four tests, the methods of our tradition won out more often than they did not, and only by changing the parameters of the examination after calculations had begun was the Proctor Napier able to prevail. Napier's device is a failure."

"But . . ." Napier began, on the edge of objection. Seeing the stern expression on the Chamberlain's face, and looking to the palace guards that ringed the room, the foreigner relented. He'd agreed that his machine should be judged by a majority of tests, and had to abide by the results. To object now would risk a loss of face, at best, and a loss of something much more dire at worst.

Tsui, too numb still to speak, rose shakily to his feet and handed the abacus back to the page who appeared again from the shadows. Bowing to the Emperor, he backed towards the exit, face burning with self-recrimination.

"The Emperor demands a brief moment," the Emperor announced, sitting forward with something resembling interest. "British, how much time and work would be needed for you to complete the improvements you mentioned earlier? How many of your countrymen are trained in the arts of this device, who could assist you in the process?"

Napier, already in the process of packing up his engine dejectedly, rose to his feet. Rubbing his lower lip with an oil-stained finger, he answered.

"A matter of months to eradicate the current limitations, your majesty," he said. "Perhaps a year. But I would need easily as much time to instruct a staff of men, as at present I am the only one who understands all the aspects of the engine's manufacture."

The Emperor, uncharacteristically demonstrative, nodded twice.

"Leave now," the Emperor commanded, and they did.

★   ★   ★

In the antechamber, while Napier led a collection of pages and eunuchs in dismantling and boxing up his device, the Chamberlain caught Tsui's elbow.

"A moment, Chief Computator," the Chamberlain said in a low voice, drawing him into an alcove well out of earshot.

"My thanks, O Lord Chamberlain," Tsui said, his tones hushed, "for allowing me to perform this small service for our master the Emperor."

"We all serve our part," the Chamberlain answered. "Remember, though, that the Emperor's remembrance of this good office will serve only to balance his displeasure that you kept him waiting."

"And for that, you have my apologies," Tsui answered. "But it is strange, I should think, that you would send for me at the House of Computation, in an hour during which it is well known to you that I am elsewhere at my leave. Would not one of my journeymen have been a suitable representative to hear the foreigner's presentation, and to offer any service you might require?"

"Perhaps," the Chamberlain replied, eyes narrowed. "Perhaps it slipped my memory that you would not be found in the House of Computation at this hour, and perhaps it did not occur to me that one of your able journeymen might be as suited for our purposes. But perhaps," the Chamberlain raised a long finger, "it was best that a member of the House of Computation in your position of leadership was present to see and hear what you have. I have always counted on you, O Chief Computator, to find solutions to problems others thought were without resolution. Even, I add, solutions to things others did not even see as problems."

Tsui nodded.

"Yes," he said, "but of the many hundreds who labor under

me in the art of calculation there are others very nearly as adept." He paused, and then added, "Many hundreds."

"Mmm," the Chamberlain hummed. "It is best, then, do you not think, that this device of the British does not meet the Emperor's standards, that so many hundreds of adepts are not removed from their productive positions?"

That the standards proposed had not been the Emperor's, but had instead been proposed by the Lord Chamberlain himself, was a point Tsui did not have to raise. The Emperor, in fact, as evidenced by his uncharacteristic inquiry into the production cycle of Napier's invention, seemed not entirely swayed by the Lord Chamberlain's stagecraft, the question of the utility of the Analytical Engine not nearly so closed as Tsui might have hoped.

"I could not agree more," Tsui answered, thin-lipped and grave. "I thank you for this consideration, and value our exchange."

The Chamberlain nodded, and drawing his robes around him, slid away into the antechamber and beyond, leaving Tsui alone.

★ ★ ★

The next morning found Tsui in the Ornamental Garden, eyes closed by the northernmost abacus fish pond.

The noise of shoes scuffing on gravel at his side startled him, and he opened his eyes to see Royal Inspector Bai standing at his side. He'd made no other sound in his approach.

"Good morning, Chief Computator," Bai said, a statement more than a question.

"Yes, Inspector," answered Tsui, looking down into the waters of the pond. They were silty and gray, the carnivorous fish almost hidden below the surface. "I would say that it is."

"Surprising, one might argue," Bai went on, "after the excitement of the evening." The Inspector pulled a wax-paper wrapped lump of meat and bread from within his sleeve and, unwrapping it, began to drop hunks of dried pork into the waters.

"Excitement?" Tsui asked, innocently.

"Hmm," the Inspector hummed, peering down into the water, quiet and still but for the ripples spreading out from the points where the meat had passed. "The fish seem not very hungry today," he said softly, distracted, before looking up and meeting Tsui's gaze. "Yes," he answered, "excitement. It seems that a visitor to the Forbidden City, a foreign inventor, went missing somewhere between the great hall and the main gate after enjoying an audience with the Emperor. The invention which he'd brought with him was found scattered in pieces in the Grand Courtyard, the box which held it appearing to have been dropped from a high-story balcony, though whether by accident or design we've been unable to determine. The Emperor has demanded the full attentions of my bureau be trained on this matter, as it seems that he had some service with which to charge this visitor. That the visitor is not in evidence, and this service might go unfilled, has done little to improve the temper of our master, equal-of-heaven and may-he-reign-ten-thousand-years."

Tsui nodded, displaying an appropriate mixture of curiosity and concern.

"As for the man himself," Bai said, shrugging, "as I've said, he seems just to have vanished." The Inspector paused again, and in a practiced casual tone added, "I believe you were present at the foreign inventor's audience yesterday, yes? You didn't happen to see him at any point following his departure from the hall, did you?"

Tsui shook his head, and in all sincerity answered, "No."

The Chief Computator had no fear. He'd done nothing wrong, after all, his involvement in the business beginning with a few choice words to his more perceptive journeymen and foremen on his hurried return to the Imperial House of Computation, and ending in the early morning hours when a slip of paper was delivered to him by one of his young apprentices. On the slip of paper, unsigned or marked by any man's chop, was a single ideogram, indicating "Completion" but suggesting "Satisfaction".

Tsui's business, since childhood, had been identifying problems and presenting solutions. To what uses those solutions might be put by other hands was simply not his concern.

"Hmm," the Inspector hummed again and, looking at the still waters of the pond, shook his head. "The abacus fish just don't seem interested today in my leavings. Perhaps they've already been fed, yes?"

"Perhaps," Tsui agreed.

The Inspector, with a resigned sigh, dropped the remainder of the meat into the northernmost pond, and then tossed the remaining bread into the southernmost, where the languid fish began their slow ballet to feed themselves.

"Well, the Emperor's service demands my attention," Inspector Bai said, brushing off his hands, "so I'll be on my way. I'll see you tomorrow, I trust?"

Tsui nodded.

"Yes," he answered, "I don't expect that I'll be going anywhere."

The Inspector gave a nod, which Tsui answered with a slight bow, and then left the Chief Computator alone in the garden.

Tsui looked down into the pond, and saw that the silt was beginning to settle on the murky bottom, revealing the abacus fish arranged in serried ranks, marking out the answer to some indefinable question. The Chief Computator closed his eyes, and in the silence imagined countless men working countless abacuses, tirelessly. His thoughts on infinity, Tsui smiled.

Islands in the Sea

Harry Turtledove

AH 152 (AD 769)

The Bulgar border guards had arrows nocked and ready as the Arab horsemen rode up from the south. Jalal ad-Din as-Stambuli, the leader of the Arab delegation, raised his right hand to show it was empty. "In the name of Allah, the Compassionate, the Merciful, I and my men come in peace," he called in Arabic. To be sure the guards understood, he repeated himself in Greek.

The precaution paid off. The guards lowered their bows. In Greek much worse than Jalal ad-Din's, one of them asked, "Why for you come in peace, whitebeard?"

Jalal ad-Din stroked his whiskers. Even without the Bulgar's mockery, he knew they were white. Not many men who had the right to style themselves *as-Stambuli*, the Constantinopolitan, still lived. More than fifty years had passed since the army of Suleiman and Maslama had taken Constantinople and put an end to the Roman Empire. Then Jalal ad-Din's beard had not been white. Then he could hardly raise a beard at all.

He spoke in Greek again: "My master the caliph Abd ar-Rahman asked last year if your khan Telerikh would care to learn more of Islam, of submission to the one God. This past spring Telerikh sent word that he would. We are the embassy sent to instruct him."

The Bulgar who had talked with him now used his own hissing language, Jalal ad-Din supposed, to translate for his comrades. They answered back, some of them anything but happily. Content in their paganism, Jalal ad-Din guessed – content to burn in hell forever. He did not wish that fate on anyone, even a Bulgar.

The guard who knew Greek confirmed his thought, saying, "Why for we want your god? Gods, spirits, ghosts good to us now."

Jalal ad-Din shrugged. "Your khan asked to hear more of Allah and Islam. That is why we are here." He could have said much more, but deliberately spoke in terms a soldier would understand.

"Telerikh want, Telerikh get," the guard agreed. He spoke again with his countrymen, at length pointed at two of them. "This Iskur. This Omurtag. They take you to Pliska, to where Telerikh is. Iskur, him know Greek a little, not so good like me."

"Know little your tongue too," Iskur said in halting Arabic, which surprised Jalal ad-Din and, evidently, the Bulgar who had been doing all the talking till now. The prospective guide glanced at the sun, which was a couple of hours from setting. "We ride," he declared, and started off with no more fanfare than that. The Bulgar called Omurtag followed.

So, more slowly, did Jalal ad-Din and his companions. By the time Iskur called a halt in deepening twilight, the mountains that made the northern horizon jagged were visibly closer.

"Those little ponies the Bulgars ride are ugly as mules, but they go and go and go," said Da'ud ibn Zubayr, who was a veteran of many skirmishes on the border between the caliph's land and Bulgaria. He stroked the mane of his elegant, Arab-bred mare.

"Sadly, my old bones do not." Jalal ad-Din groaned with relief as he slid off his own horse, a soft-gaited gelding. Once he had delighted in fiery stallions, but he knew that if he took a fall now he would shatter like glass.

The Bulgars stalked into the brush to hunt. Da'ud bent to the laborious business of getting a fire going. The other two Arabs,

Malik ibn Anas and Salman al-Tabari, stood guard, one with a bow, the other with a spear. Iskur and Omurtag emerged into firelight carrying partridges and rabbits. Jalal ad-Din took hard unleavened bread from a saddlebag: no feast tonight, he thought, but not the worst of fare either.

Iskur also had a skin of wine. He offered it to the Arabs, grinned when they declined. "More for me, Omurtag," he said. The two Bulgars drank the skin dry, and soon lay snoring by the fire.

Da'ud ibn Zubayr scowled at them. "The only use they have for wits is losing them," he sneered. "How can such folk ever come to acknowledge Allah and his Prophet?"

"We Arabs were wine-bibbers too, before Muhammad forbad it to us," Jalal ad-Din said. "My worry is that the Bulgars' passion for such drink will make khan Telerikh less inclined to accept our faith."

Da'ud dipped his head to the older man. "Truly it is just that you lead us, sir. Like a falcon, you keep your eye ever on our quarry."

"Like a falcon, I sleep in the evening," Jalal ad-Din said, yawning. "And like an old falcon, I need more sleep than I once did."

"Your years have brought you wisdom." Da'ud ibn Zubayr hesitated, as if wondering whether to go on. Finally he plunged: "Is it true, sir, that you once met a man who had known the Prophet?"

"It is true," Jalal ad-Din said proudly. "It was at Antioch, when Suleiman's army was marching to fight the Greeks at Constantinople. The grandfather of the innkeeper with whom I was quartered lived with him still: he was a Medinan, far older then than I am now, for he had soldiered with Khalid ibn al-Walid when the city fell to us. And before that, as a youth, he accompanied Muhammad when the Prophet returned in triumph from Medina to Mecca."

"*Allahu akbar*," Da'ud breathed: "God is great. I am further honored to be in your presence. Tell me, did – did the old man grant you any *hadith*, any tradition, of the Prophet that you might pass on to me for the sake of my enlightenment?"

"Yes," Jalal ad-Din said. "I recall it as if it were yesterday, just as the old man did when speaking of the journey to the Holy City. Abu Bakr, who was not yet caliph, of course, for Muhammad was still alive, started beating a man for letting a camel get loose. The Prophet began to smile, and said, 'See what this pilgrim is doing.' Abu Bakr was abashed, though the Prophet did not actually tell him to stop."

Da'ud bowed low. "I am in your debt." He repeated the story several times; Jalal ad-Din nodded to show him he had learned it perfectly. In the time-honored way, Da'ud went on, "I have this *hadith* from Jalal ad-Din as-Stambuli, who had it from – what was the old man's name, sir?"

"He was called Abd al-Qadir."

"—who had it from Abd al-Qadir, who had it from the Prophet. Think of it – only two men between Muhammad and me." Da'ud bowed again.

Jalal ad-Din returned the bow, then embarrassed himself by yawning once more. "Your pardon, I pray. Truly I must sleep."

"Sleep, then, and Allah keep you safe till the morning comes."

Jalal ad-Din rolled himself in his blanket. "And you, son of Zubayr."

"Those are no mean works," Da'ud said a week later, pointing ahead to the earthen rampart, tall as six men, that ringed Pliska, Telerikh's capital.

"That is a child's toy, next to the walls of Constantinople," Jalal ad-Din said. "A double wall, each one twice that height, all steep stone, well-ditched in front and between, with all the Greeks in the world, it seemed, battling from atop them." Across half a century, recalling the terror of the day of the assault, he wondered still how he had survived.

"I was born in Constantinople," Da'ud reminded him gently.

"Of course you were." Jalal ad-Din shook his head, angry at himself for letting past obscure present that way. It was something old men did, but who cares to remember he is old?

Da'ud glanced around to make sure Iskur was out of earshot, lowered his voice. "For pagan savages, those are no mean works. And see how much land they enclose – Pliska must be a city of greater size than I had supposed."

"No." Jalal ad-Din remembered a talk with a previous envoy to Telerikh. "The town itself is tiny. This earthwork serves chiefly to mark off the grazing lands of the khan's flocks."

"His flocks? Is that all?" Da'ud threw back his head and laughed. "I feel as I though I am transported to some strange new world, where nothing is as it seems."

"I have had that feeling ever since we came through the mountain passes," Jalal ad-Din said seriously. Da'ud gave him a curious look. He tried to explain: "You are from Constantinople. I was born not far from Damascus, where I dwell yet. A long journey from one to the other, much longer than from Constantinople to Pliska."

Da'ud nodded.

"And yet it is a journey through sameness," Jalal ad-Din went on. "Not much difference in weather, in crops, in people. Aye, more Greeks, more Christians in Constantinople still, for we have ruled there so much less time than in Damascus, but the difference is of degree, not of kind."

"That is all true," Da'ud said, nodding again. "Whereas here—"

"Aye, here," Jalal ad-Din said with heavy irony. "The olive will not grow here, the sun fights its way through mists that swaddle it as if it were a newborn babe, and even a Greek would be welcome, for the sake of having someone civilized to talk to. This is a different world from ours, and not one much to my liking."

"Still, we hope to wed it to ours through Islam," Da'ud said.

"So we do, so we do. Submission to the will of God makes all men one." Now Jalal ad-Din made sure Iskur was paying no attention. The nomad had ridden ahead. Jalal ad-Din went on, "Even Bulgars." Da'ud chuckled.

Iskur yelled something at the guards lounging in front of a wooden gate in Pliska's earthen outwall. The guards yelled back. Iskur shouted again, louder this time. With poor grace, the guards got up and opened the gate. They stared as they saw what sort of companions Iskur led.

Jalal ad-Din gave them a grave salute as he passed through the gate, as much to discomfit them as for any other reason. He pointed ahead to the stone wall of Pliska proper. "You see?"

"I see," Da'ud said. The rectangular wall was less than half a mile on a side. "In our lands, that would be a fortress, not a capital."

The gates of the stone wall were open. Jalal ad-Din coughed as he followed Iskur and Omurtag into the town: Pliska stank like – stank worse than – a big city. Jalal ad-Din shrugged. Sooner or later, he knew, he would stop noticing the stench.

Not far inside the gates stood a large building of intricately carven wood. "This is Telerikh's palace," Iskur announced.

Tethered in front of the palace were any number of steppe ponies like the ones Iskur and Omurtag rode and also, Jalal ad-Din saw with interest, several real horses and a mule whose trappings did not look like Arab gear. "To whom do those belong?" he asked, pointing.

"Not know," Iskur said. He cupped his hands and yelled towards the palace – yelling, Jalal ad-Din thought wryly, seemed the usual Bulgar approach towards any problem. After a little while, a door opened. The Arab had not even noticed it till then, so lost was its outline among carvings.

As soon as they saw someone come out of the palace, Iskur and Omurtag wheeled their horses and rode away without a backwards glance at the ambassadors they had guided to Pliska. The man who had emerged took a moment to study the new arrivals. He bowed. "How may I help you, my masters?" he asked in Arabic fluent enough to make Jalal ad-Din sit up and take notice.

"We are envoys of the caliph Abd ar-Rahman, come to your fine city" – Jalal ad-Din knew when to stretch a point – "at the bidding of your khan to explain to him the glories of Islam. I have the honor of addressing – ?" He let the words hang.

"I am Dragomir, steward to the mighty khan Telerikh. Dismount; be welcome here." Dragomir bowed again. He was, Jalal ad-Din guessed, in his late thirties, stocky and well made, with fair skin, a full brown beard framing rather a wide face, and gray eyes that revealed nothing whatever – a useful attribute in a steward.

Jalal ad-Din and his companions slid gratefully from their horses. As if by magic, boys appeared to hitch the Arabs' beasts to the rails in front of the palace and carry their saddlebags into it. Jalal ad-Din nodded at the other full-sized horses and the mule. "To whom do those belong, pray?" he asked Dragomir.

The steward's pale but hooded eyes swung towards the hitching rail, returned to Jalal ad-Din. "Those," he explained, "are the animals of the delegation of priests from the pope of Rome at the bidding of my khan to expound to him the glories of Christianity. They arrived earlier today."

Late that night, Da'ud slammed a fist against a wall of the chamber the four Arabs shared. "Better they should stay pagan than turn Christian!" he shouted. Not only was he angry that Telerikh had also invited Christians to Pliska as if intending to auction his land to the faith that bid highest, he was also short-tempered from hunger. The evening's banquet had featured pork. (It had *not* featured Telerikh; some heathen Bulgar law required the khan always to eat alone.)

"That is not so," Jalal ad-Din said mildly.

"And why not?" Da'ud glared at the older man.

"As Christians they would be *dhimmis* – people of the Book – and thus granted a hope of heaven. Should they cling to their pagan practices, their souls will surely belong to Satan till the end of time."

"Satan is welcome to their souls, whether pagan or Christian," Da'ud said. "But a Christian Bulgaria, allied to Rome, maybe even allied to the Franks, would block the true faith's progress northwards and could be the spearpoint of a thrust back towards Constantinople."

Jalal ad-Din sighed. "What you say is true. Still, the true faith is also true, and the truth surely will prevail against Christian falsehoods."

"May it be so," Da'ud said heavily. "But was this land not once a Christian country, back in the days before the Bulgars seized it from Constantinople? All the lands the Greeks held followed their usages. Some folk hereabouts must be Christian still, I'd wager, which might incline Telerikh towards their beliefs."

A knock on the door interrupted the argument. Da'ud kept one hand on his knife as he opened the door with the other. But no enemies stood outside, only four girls. Two were colored like Dragomir – to Jalal ad-Din's eyes, exotically fair. The other two were dark, darker than Arabs, in fact; one had eyes that seemed set at a slant. All four were pretty. They smiled and swayed their way in.

"Telerikh is no Christian," Jalal ad-Din said as he smiled back at one of the light-skinned girls. "Christians are not allowed concubines."

"The more fools they," Da'ud said. "Shall I blow out the lamps, or leave them burning?"

"Leave them," Jalal ad-Din answered. "I want to see what I am doing . . ."

Jalal ad-Din bowed low to khan Telerikh. A pace behind him, Da'ud did the same. Another pace back, Malik ibn Anas and Salman al-Tabari went to one knee, as suited their lower rank.

"Rise, all of you," Telerikh said in passable Arabic. The khan of the Bulgars was about fifty, swarthy, broad-faced, wide-nosed, with a thin beard going from black to gray. His eyes were narrow, hard, and shrewd. He looked like a man well able to rule a nation whose strength came entirely from the ferocity of its soldiers.

"Most magnificent khan, we bring the greetings of our master the caliph Abd ar-Rahman ibn Marwan, his prayers for your health and prosperity, and gifts to show that you stand high in his esteem," Jalal ad-Din said.

He waved Salman and Malik forward to present the gifts: silver plates from Persia, Damascus-work swords, fine enamel-ware from Constantinople, a robe of glistening Chinese silk, and, last but not least, a *Qu'ran* bound in leather and gold, its calligraphy the finest the scribes of Alexandria could provide.

Telerikh, though, seemed most interested in the robe. He rose from his wooden throne, undid the broad bronze belt he

wore, shrugged out of his knee-length fur caftan. Under it he
had on a linen tunic and trousers and low boots. Dragomir
came up to help him put on the robe. He smiled with pleasure
as he ran a hand over the watery-smooth fabric.

"Very pretty," he crooned. For a moment, Jalal ad-Din
hoped he was so taken by the presents as to be easily swayed.
But Telerikh, as the Arab had guessed from his appearance, was
not so simple. He went on, "The caliph gives lovely gifts. With
his riches, he can afford to. Now please take your places while
the envoys of the pope of Rome present themselves."

Dragomir waved the Arab delegation off to the right of the
throne, close by the turbaned boyars – the great nobles – who
made up Telerikh's court. Most were of the same stock as their
khan; a few looked more like Dragomir and the fair girl Jalal ad-
Din had so enjoyed the night before. Fair or dark, they smelled
of hard-run horses and ancient sweat.

As he had with the caliph's embassy, Dragomir announced
the papal legates in the throaty Bulgarian tongue. There were
three of them, as Jalal ad-Din had seen at the banquet. Two
were gorgeous in robes that reminded him of the ones the
Constantinopolitan grandees had worn so long ago as they
vainly tried to rally their troops against the Arabs. The third
wore a simple brown wool habit. Amid the Bulgar chatter,
meaningless to him, Jalal ad-Din picked out three names:
Niketas, Theodor and Paul.

The Christians scowled at the Arabs as they walked past them
to approach Telerikh. They bowed as Jalal ad-Din had.
"Stand," Telerikh said in Greek. Jalal ad-Din was not surprised
he knew that language; the Bulgars had dealt with
Constantinople before the Arabs took it, and many refugees had
fled to Pliska. Others had escaped to Italy, which no doubt
explained why two of the papal legates bore Greek names.

"Excellent khan," said one of the envoys (Theodore, Jalal ad-
Din thought it was), also in Greek, "we are saddened to see you
decked in raiment given you by our foes as you greet us. Does
this mean you hold us in contempt, and will give us no fair
hearing? Surely you did not invite us to travel so far merely for
that?"

Telerikh blinked, glanced down at the silk robe he had just put on. "No," he said. "It only means I like this present. What presents have you for me?"

Da'ud leaned forward, whispered into Jalal ad-Din's ear: "More avarice in that one than fear of hell." Jalal ad-Din nodded. That made his task harder, not easier. He would have to play politics along with expounding the truth of Islam. He sighed. Ever since he learned Telerikh had also bid the men from Rome hither, he'd expected no less.

The Christians were presenting their gifts, and making a great show of it to try to disguise their not being so fine as the ones their rivals had given – Jalal ad-Din's offerings still lay in a glittering heap beside Telerikh's throne. "Here," Theodore intoned, "is a copy of the Holy Scriptures, with a personal prayer for you inscribed therein by his holiness the pope Constantine."

Jalal ad-Din let out a quiet but scornful snort. "The words of Allah are the ones that count," he whispered to Da'ud ibn Zubayr, "not those of any man." It was Da'ud's turn to nod.

As he had with the Qu'ran, Telerikh idly paged through the Bible. Perhaps halfway through, he paused, glanced up at the Christians. "You have pictures in your book." It sounded almost like an accusation; had Jalal ad-Din said it, it would have been.

But the Christian in the plain brown robe, the one called Paul, answered calmly, "Yes, excellent khan, we do, the better to instruct the many who cannot read the words beside them." He was no longer young – he might have been close to Jalal ad-Din's age – but his voice was light and clear and strong, the voice of a man sure in the path he has chosen.

"Beware of that one," Da'ud murmured. "He has more holiness in him than the other two put together." Jalal ad-Din had already reached the same conclusion, and did not like it. Enemies, he thought, ought by rights to be rogues.

He got only a moment to mull on that, for Telerikh suddenly shifted to Arabic and called to him, "Why are there no pictures in your book, to show me what you believe?"

"Because Allah the one God is infinite, far too mighty for our tiny senses to comprehend, and so cannot be depicted," he said, "and man must not be depicted, for Allah created him in his image from a clot of blood. The Christians' own scriptures say as much, but they ignore any law which does not suit them."

"Liar! Misbeliever!" Theodore shouted. Torchlight gleamed off his tonsured pate as he whirled to confront Jalal ad-Din.

"No liar I," Jalal ad-Din said; not for nothing had he studied with men once Christian before they saw the truth of Muhammad's teaching. "The verse you deny is in the book called Exodus."

"Is this true?" Telerikh rumbled, scowling at the Christians.

Theodore started to reply; Paul cut him off. "Excellent khan, the verse is as the Arab states. My colleague did not wish to deny it." Theodore looked ready to argue. Paul did not let him, continuing, "But that law was given to Moses long ago. Since then, Christ the Son of God has appeared on Earth; belief in him assures one of heaven, regardless of the observance of the outdated rules of the Jews."

Telerikh grunted. "A new law may replace an old, if circumstances change. What say you to that, envoy of the caliph?"

"I will quote two verses from the Qu'ran, from the *sura* called The Cow," Jalal ad-Din said, smiling at the opening Paul had left him. "Allah says, 'The Jews say the Christians are astray, and the Christians say it is the Jews who are astray. Yet they both read the Scriptures.' Which is to say, magnificent khan, that they have both corrupted God's word. And again, 'They say: "Allah has begotten a son." Allah forbid!'"

When reciting from the Qu'ran, he had naturally fallen into Arabic. He was not surprised to see the Christians following his words without difficulty. They too would have prepared for any eventuality on this mission.

One of Telerikh's boyars called something to the khan in his own language. Malik ibn Anas, who was with Jalal ad-Din precisely because he knew a little of the Bulgar speech, translated for him: "He says that the sacred stones of their forefathers, even the pagan gods of the Slavs they rule, have served them well enough for years upon years, and calls on Telerikh not to change their usages now."

Looking around, Jalal ad-Din saw more than a few boyars nodding. "Great khan, may I speak?" he called. Telerikh nodded. Jalal ad-Din went on, "Great khan, you need but look about you to see proof of Allah's might. Is it not true that my lord the caliph Abd ar-Rahman, peace be unto him, rules from the Western Sea to India, from your borders to beyond the deserts of Egypt? Even the Christians, who know the one God imperfectly, still control many lands. Yet only you here in this small country follow your idols. Does this not show you their strength is a paltry thing?"

"There is more, excellent khan." Niketas, who had been quiet till then, unexpectedly spoke up. "Your false gods isolate Bulgaria. How, in dealing with Christians or even Muslims, can your folk swear an oath that will be trusted? How can you put the power of God behind a treaty, to ensure it will be enforced? In what way can one of you lawfully marry a Christian? Other questions like these will surely have occurred to you, else you would not have bid us come."

"He speaks the truth, khan Telerikh," Jalal ad-Din said. He had not thought a priest would have so good a grasp of matters largely secular, but Niketas did. Since his words could not be denied, supporting them seemed better than ignoring.

Telerikh gnawed on his mustaches. He looked from one delegation to the other, back again. "Tell me," he said slowly, "is it the same God both groups of you worship, or do you follow different ones?"

"That is an excellent question," Jalal ad-Din said; no, Telerikh was no fool. "It is the same God: there is no God but God. But the Christians worship him incorrectly, saying he is Three, not One."

"It is the same God," Paul agreed, once more apparently overriding Theodore. "Muhammad is not a true prophet and many of his preachings are lies, but it is the same God, who gave his only begotten Son to save mankind."

"Stop!" Telerikh held up a hand. "If it is the same God, what difference does it make how I and my people worship him. No matter what the prayers we send up to him, surely he will know what we mean."

Jalal ad-Din glanced towards Paul. The Christian was also
looking at him. Paul smiled. Jalal ad-Din found himself smiling
back. He too felt the irony of the situation: he and Paul had
more in common with each other than either of them did with
the naive Bulgar khan. Paul raised an eyebrow. Jalal ad-Din
dipped his head, granting the Christian permission to answer
Telerikh's question.

"Sadly, excellent khan, it is not so simple," Paul said. "Just as
there is only one true God, so there can be only one true way to
worship him, for while he is merciful, he is also just, and will not
tolerate errors in the reverence paid him. To use a homely
example, sir, would it please you if we called you 'khan of the
Avars'?"

"It would please me right well, were it true," Telerikh said
with a grim chuckle. "Worse luck for me, though, the Avars
have a khan of their own. Very well, priest, I see what you are
saying."

The Bulgar ruler rubbed his chin. "This needs more thought.
We will all gather here again in three days' time, to speak of it
further. Go now in peace, and remember" – he looked sternly
from Christians to Muslims – "you are all my guests here. No
fighting between you, or you will regret it."

Thus warned, the rival embassies bowed their way out.

Jalal ad-Din spent more time before his next encounter with the
priests exploring Pliska than he had hoped to. No matter how
delightful he found his fair-skinned pleasure girl, he was not a
young man: for him, between rounds meant between days.

After the barbarous richness of Telerikh's wooden palace, the
Arab found the rest of the town surprisingly familiar. He
wondered why until he realized that Pliska, like Damascus, like
Constantinople, like countless other settlements through which
he had passed at one time or another, had been a Roman town
once. Layout and architecture lingered long after overlords
changed.

Jalal ad-Din felt like shouting when he found a bath house not
only still standing but still used; from what his nose had told
him in the palace, he'd doubted the Bulgars even suspected

cleanliness existed. When he went in, he found most of the bathers were of the lighter-colored folk from whom Dragomir and his mistress had sprung. They were, he'd gathered, peasant Slavs over whom the Bulgars proper ruled.

He also found that, being mostly unacquainted with either Christianity or Islam, they let in women along with the men. It was scandalous; it was shocking; in Damascus it would have raised riots. Jalal ad-Din wished his eyes were as sharp as they'd been when he was forty, or even fifty.

He was happily soaking in a warm pool when the three Christian envoys came in. Theodore hissed in horror when he saw the naked women, spun on his heel, and stalked out. Niketas started to follow, but Paul took hold of his arm and stopped him. The older man shrugged out of his brown robe, sank with a sigh of pleasure into the same pool Jalal ad-Din was using. Niketas, by his expression still dubious, joined him a moment later.

"Flesh is flesh," Paul said calmly. "By pledging yourself to Christ, you have acknowledged that its pleasures are not for you. No point in fleeing, then."

Jalal ad-Din nodded to the Christians. "You have better sense, sir, than I would have looked for in a priest," he told Paul.

"I thank you." If Paul heard the undercurrent of irony in the Arab's voice, he did not let it affect his own tone, which briefly shamed Jalal ad-Din. Paul went on, "I am no priest in any case, only a humble monk, here to advise my superiors if they care to listen to me.

"'Only!'" Jalal ad-Din scoffed. But, he had to admit to himself, the monk sounded completely sincere. He sighed; hating his opponents would have been much easier were they evil. "They would be wise to listen to you," he said. "I think you are a holy man."

"You give me too much credit," Paul said.

"No, he does not," Niketas told his older colleague. "Not just by words do you instruct the barbarians hereabouts, but also through the life you live, which by its virtues illuminates your teachings."

Paul bowed. From a man squatting naked in waist-deep water, the gesture should have seemed ludicrous. Somehow it did not.

Niketas turned to Jalal ad-Din. "Did I hear correctly that you are styled as-Stambuli?"

"You did," the Arab answered proudly.

"How strange," Niketas murmured. "Perhaps here God grants me the chance to avenge the fall of the Queen of Cities."

He spoke as if the caliph's armies had taken Constantinople only yesterday, not long before he was born. Seeing Jalal ad-Din's confusion, Paul said, "Niketas' mother is Anna, the daughter of Leo."

"Yes?" Jalal ad-Din was polite, but that meant nothing to him. "And my mother was Zinawb, the daughter of Mu'in ibn Abd al-Wahhab. What of it?"

"Ah, but your grandfather, however illustrious he may have been (I do not slight him, I assure you) was never *Basileus ton Rhomaion* – Emperor of the Romans."

"*That* Leo!" Jalal ad-Din thumped his forehead with the heel of his hand. He nodded to Niketas. "Your grandfather, sir, was a very devil. He fought us with all he had, and sent too many brave lads to paradise before their time."

Niketas raised a dark eyebrow. His tonsured skull went oddly with those bushy brows and the thick beard that covered his cheeks almost to the eyes. "Too many, you say. I would say, not enough."

"So you would," Jalal ad-Din agreed. "Had Leo beaten us, you might be Roman Emperor yourself now. But Abd ar-Rahman the commander of the faithful rules Constantinople, and you are a priest in a foreign land. It is as Allah wills."

"So I must believe," Niketas said. "But just as Leo fought you with every weapon he had, I shall oppose you with all my means. The Bulgars must not fall victim to your false belief. It would be too great a blow for Christendom to suffer, removing from us all hope of greater growth."

Niketas' mind worked like an emperor's, Jalal ad-Din thought – unlike many of his Christian colleagues, he understood the long view. He'd shown that in debate, too, when he pointed out the problems attendant on the Bulgars' staying pagan. A dangerous foe – pope Constantine had sent to Pliska the best the Christians had.

Whether that would be enough . . . Jalal ad-Din shrugged. "It is as Allah wills," he repeated.

"And Telerikh," Paul said. When Jalal ad-Din looked at him in surprise, the monk went on, "Of course, Telerikh is in God's hands too. But God will not be influenced by what we do. Telerikh may."

"There is that," Jalal ad-Din admitted.

"No telling how long all this arguing will go on," Telerikh said when the Christian and Muslim embassies appeared before him once more. He spoke to Dragomir in his own language. The steward nodded, hurried away. A moment later, lesser servants brought in benches, which they set before Telerikh's throne. "Sit," the khan urged. "You may as well be comfortable."

"How would you have us argue?" Jalal ad-Din asked, wishing the bench had a back but too proud to ask for a chair to ease his old bones.

"Tell me of your one god," Telerikh said. "You say you and the Christians follow him. Tell me what you believe differently about him, so I may choose between your beliefs."

Jalal ad-Din carefully did not smile. He had asked his question to seize the chance to speak first. Let the Christians respond to him. He began where any Muslim would, with the *shahada*, the profession of faith: "*La illaha ill'Allah; Muhammadun rasulu'llah* – There is not God but Allah; Muhammad is the prophet of Allah. Believe that, magnificent khan, and you are a Muslim. There is more, of course, but that is of the essence."

"It is also a lie," Theodore broke in harshly. "Excellent khan, the books of the Old Testament, written hundreds of years before God's Son became flesh, foretold his coming. Neither Old nor New Testament speaks one word of the Arab charlatan who invented this false creed because he had failed as a camel-driver."

"There is no prophecy pertaining to Muhammad in the

Christians' holy books because it was deliberately suppressed," Jalal ad-Din shot back. "That is why God gave the Prophet his gifts, as the seal of prophecy."

"The seal of trickery is nearer the truth," Theodore said. "God's only begotten Son Jesus Christ said prophecy ended with John the Baptist, but that false prophets would continue to come. Muhammad lived centuries after John and Jesus, so he must be false, a trick of the devil to send men to hell."

"Jesus is no son of God. God is one, not three, as the Christians would have it," Jalal ad-Din said. "Hear God's own words in the Qu'ran: 'Say, God is one.' The Christians give the one God partners in the so-called Son and Holy Spirit. If he has two partners, why not three, or four, or more? Foolishness! And how could God fit into a woman's womb and be born like a man? More foolishness!"

Again it was Theodore who took up the challenge; he was a bad-tempered man, but capable all the same. "God is omnipotent. To deny the possibility of the Incarnation is to deny that omnipotence."

"That priest is twisty as a serpent," Da'ud ibn Zubayr whispered to Jalal ad-Din. The older man nodded, frowning. He was not quite sure how to respond to Theodore's latest sally. Who was he to say what Allah could or could not do?

Telerikh roused him from his unprofitable reverie by asking, "So you Arabs deny Jesus is the son of your one god, eh?"

"We do," Jalal ad-Din said firmly.

"What do you make of him, then?" the khan said.

"Allah commands us to worship none but himself, so how can he have a son? Jesus was a holy man and a prophet, but nothing more. Since the Christians corrupted his words, Allah inspired Muhammad to recite the truth once more."

"Could a prophet rise from the dead on the third day, as God's Son did?" Theodore snorted, clapping a dramatic hand to his forehead. "Christ's miracles are witnessed and attested in writing. What miracles did Muhammad work? None, the reason being that he could not."

"He flew to Jerusalem in the course of a night," Jalal ad-Din returned, "as the Qu'ran records – in writing," he added pointedly. "And the crucifixion and resurrection are fables. No man can rise from the dead, and another was set on the cross in place of Jesus."

"Satan waits for you in hell, blasphemer," Theodore hissed. "Christ healed the sick, raised the dead, stopped wind and rain in their tracks. Anyone who denies him loses all hope of heaven, and may garner for his sin only eternal torment."

"No, that is the fate reserved for those who make One into Three," Jalal ad-Din said. "You—"

"Wait, both of you." Telerikh held up a hand. The Bulgar khan, Jalal ad-Din thought, seemed more stunned than edified by the arguments he had heard. The Arab realized he had been quarreling with Theodore rather than instructing the khan. Telerikh went on, "I cannot find the truth in what you are saying, for each of you and each of your books makes the other a liar. That helps me not at all. Tell me instead what I and my people must do, if we follow one faith or the other."

"If you choose the Arabs' false creed, you will have to abandon both wine-drinking and eating pork," Theodore said before Jalal ad-Din could reply. "Let him deny it if he may." The priest shot the Arab a triumphant look.

"It is true," Jalal ad-Din said stoutly. "Allah has ordained it."

He tried to put a bold face on it, but knew Theodore had landed a telling blow. The mutter that went up from Telerikh's boyars confirmed it. A passion for wine inflamed most non-believers, Jalal ad-Din thought; sadly, despite the good counsel of the Qu'ran, it could capture Muslims as well. And as for pork – judging from the meals they served at Pliska, the Bulgars found it their favorite flesh.

"That is not good," Telerikh said, and the Arab's heart sank. A passion for wine . . . passion! "Magnificent khan, may I ask without offense how many wives you enjoy?"

Telerikh frowned. "I am not quite sure. How many is it now, Dragomir?"

"Forty-seven, mighty khan," the steward replied at once, competent as usual.

"And your boyars?" Jalal ad-Din went on. "Surely they also have more than one apiece."

"Well, what of it?" the khan said, sounding puzzled.

Now Jalal ad-Din grinned an unpleasant grin at Theodore. "If you become a Christian, magnificent khan, you will have to give up all your wives save one. You will not even be able to keep the others as concubines, for the Christians also forbid that practice."

"What?" If Telerikh had frowned before, the scowl he turned on the Christians now was thunderous. "Can this be true?"

"Of course it is true," Theodore said, scowling back. "Bigamy is a monstrous sin."

"Gently, my brother in Christ, gently," Paul said. "We do not wish to press too hard upon our Bulgar friends, who after all will be newly come to our observances."

"That one is truly a nuisance," Da'ud whispered.

"You are too right," Jalal ad-Din whispered back.

"Still, excellent khan," Paul went on, "you must not doubt that Theodore is correct. When you and your people accept Christianity, all those with more than one wife – or women with more than one husband, if any there be – will be required to repudiate all but their first marriages, and to undergo penance under the supervision of a priest."

His easy, matter-of-fact manner seemed to calm Telerikh. "I see you believe this to be necessary," the khan said. "It is so strange, though, that I do not see why. Explain further, if you will."

Jalal ad-Din made a fist. He had expected Christian ideas of marriage to appall Telerikh, not to intrigue him with their very alienness. Was a potential monk lurking under those fur robes, under that turban?

Paul said, "Celibacy, excellent khan, is the highest ideal. For those who cannot achieve it, marriage to a single partner is an acceptable alternative. Surely you must know, excellent khan, how lust can inflame men. And no sin is so intolerable to prophets and other holy men as depravity and sexual license, for the Holy Spirit will not touch the heart of a prophet while he is engaged in an erotic act. The life of the mind is nobler than that of the body; on this Holy Scripture and the wise ancient Aristotle agree."

"I never heard of this, ah, Aristotle. Was he a shaman?" Telerikh asked.

"You might say so," Paul replied, which impressed Jalal ad-Din. The Arab knew little of Aristotle, hardly more than that he had been a sage before even Roman times. He was certain, however, that Aristotle had been a civilized man, not a barbarous pagan priest. But that was surely the closest equivalent to sage within Telerikh's mental horizon, and Paul deserved credit for recognizing it.

The Bulgar khan turned to Jalal ad-Din. "What have you to say about this?"

"The Qu'ran permits a man four lawful wives, for those able to treat them equally well," Jalal ad-Din said. "For those who cannot, it enjoins only one. But it does not prohibit concubines."

"That is better," the khan said. "A man would get bored, bedding the same woman night after night. But this business of no pork and no wine is almost as gloomy." He gave his attention back to the priests. "You Christians allow these things."

"Yes, excellent khan, we do," Paul said.

"Hmm." Telerikh rubbed his chin. Jalal ad-Din did his best to hide his worry. The matter still stood balanced, and he had used his strongest weapon to incline the khan to Islam. If the Christians had any good arguments left, he – and the fate of the true faith in Bulgaria – were in trouble.

Paul said, "Excellent khan, these matters of practice may seem important to you, but in fact they are superficial. Here is the key difference between the Arabs' faith and ours: the religion Muhammad preached is one that loves violence, not peace. Such teaching can only come from Satan, I fear."

"That is a foul, stinking lie!" Da'ud ibn Zubayr cried. The other two Arabs behind Jalal ad-Din also shouted angrily.

"Silence!" Telerikh said, glaring at them. "Do not interrupt. I shall give you a chance to answer in due course."

"Yes, let the Christian go on," Jalal ad-Din agreed. "I am sure the khan will be fascinated by what he has to say."

Glancing back, he thought Da'ud about to burst with fury. The younger man finally forced out a strangled whisper: "Have you gone mad, to stand by while this infidel slanders the Prophet (may blessings be upon his head)?"

"I think not. Now be still, as Telerikh said. My ears are not what they once were; I cannot listen to you and Paul at once."

The monk was saying, "Muhammad's creed urges conversion by the sword, not by reason. Does not his holy book, if one may dignify it by that title, preach the holy war, the *jihad*" – he dropped the Arabic word into his polished Greek – "against all those who do not share his faith? And those who are slain in their murderous work, says the false prophet, attain heaven straight away." He turned to Jalal ad-Din. "Do you deny this?"

"I do not," Jalal ad-Din replied. "You paraphrase the third *sura* of the Qu'ran."

"There, you see?" Paul said to Telerikh. "Even the Arab himself admits the ferocity of his faith. Think also on the nature of the paradise Muhammad in his ignorance promises his followers—"

"Why do you not speak?" Da'ud ibn Zubayr demanded. "You let this man slander and distort everything in which we believe."

"Hush," Jalal ad-Din said again.

" – rivers of water and milk, honey and wine, and men reclining on silken couches and being served – served in all ways, including pandering to their fleshly lusts (as if souls could have such concerns!) – by females created especially for the purpose." Paul paused, needing a moment to draw in another indignant breath. "Such carnal indulgences – nay, excesses – have no place in heaven, excellent khan."

"No? What does, then?" Telerikh asked.

Awe transfigured the monk's thin, ascetic face as he looked within himself at the afterlife he envisioned. "Heaven, excellent khan, does not consist of banquets and wenches: those are for gluttons and sinners in this life, and lead to hell in the next. No: paradise is spiritual in nature, with the soul knowing the eternal joy of closeness and unity with God, peace of spirit and absence of all care. That is the true meaning of heaven."

"Amen," Theodore intoned piously. All three Christians made the sign of the cross over their breasts.

"That is the true meaning of heaven, you say?" Telerikh's blunt-featured face was impassive as his gaze swung towards Jalal ad-Din. "Now you may speak as you will, man of the caliph. Has this Christian told accurately of the world to come in his faith and in yours?"

"He has, magnificent khan." Jalal ad-Din spread his hands and smiled at the Bulgar lord. "I leave it to you, sir, to pick the paradise you would sooner inhabit."

Telerikh looked thoughtful. The Christian clerics' expressions went from confident to concerned to horrified as they gradually began to wonder, as Jalal ad-Din had already, just what sort of heaven a barbarian prince might enjoy.

Da'ud ibn Zubayr gently thumped Jalal ad-Din on the back. "I abase myself before you, sir," he said, flowery in apology as Arabs so often were. "You saw further than I." Jalal ad-Din bowed on his bench, warmed by the praise.

His voice urgent, the priest Niketas spoke up: "Excellent khan, you need to consider one thing more before you make your choice."

"Eh? And what might that be?" Telerikh sounded distracted. Jalal ad-Din hoped he was; the delights of the Muslim paradise were worth being distracted about. Paul's version, on the other hand, struck him as a boring way to spend eternity. But the khan, worse luck, was not altogether ready to abandon Christianity on account of that. Jalal ad-Din saw him focus his attention on Niketas. "Go on, priest."

"Thank you, excellent khan." Niketas bowed low. "Think on this, then: in Christendom the most holy pope is the leader of all things spiritual, true, but there are many secular rulers, each to his own state: the Lombard dukes, the king of the Franks, the Saxon and Angle kings in Britain, the various Irish princes, every one a free man. But Islam knows only one prince, the caliph, who reigns over all Muslims. If you decide to worship Muhammad, where is there room for you as ruler of your own Bulgaria?"

"No one worships Muhammad," Jalal ad-Din said tartly. "He is a prophet, not a god. Worship Allah, who alone deserves it."

His correction of the minor point did not distract Telerikh

from the major one. "Is what the Christian says true?" the khan
demanded. "Do you expect me to bend the knee to your khan
as well as your god? Why should I freely give Abd ar-Rahman
what he has never won in battle?"

Jalal ad-Din thought furiously, all the while damning Niketas.
Priest, celibate the man might be, but he still thought like a
Greek, like a Roman Emperor of Constantinople, sowing
distrust among his foes so they defeated themselves when his
own strength did not suffice to beat them.

"Well, Arab, what have you to say?" Telerikh asked again.

Jalal ad-Din felt sweat trickle into his beard. He knew he had
let silence stretch too long. At last, picking his words carefully,
he answered, "Magnificent khan, what Niketas says is not true.
Aye, the caliph Abd ar-Rahman, peace be unto him, rules all the
land of Islam. But he does so by right of conquest and right of
descent, just as you rule the Bulgars. Were you, were your
people, to become Muslim without warfare, he would have no
more claim on you than any brother in Islam has on another."

He hoped he was right, and that the jurists would not make a
liar of him once he got back to Damascus. All the ground here
was uncharted: no nation had ever accepted Islam without first
coming under the control of the caliphate. Well, he thought, if
Telerikh and the Bulgars did convert, that success in itself
would ratify anything he did to accomplish it.

If . . . Telerikh showed no signs of having made up his mind.
"I will meet with all of you in four days," the khan said. He rose,
signifying the end of the audience. The rival embassies rose too,
and bowed deeply as he stumped between them out of the hall
of audience.

"If only it were easy," Jalal ad-Din sighed.

The leather purse was small but heavy. It hardly clinked as Jalal
ad-Din pressed it into Dragomir's hand. The steward made it
disappear. "Tell me, if you would," Jalal ad-Din said, as casually as if the purse had never existed at all, "how your master is
inclined towards the two faiths about which he has been
learning."

"You are not the first person to ask me that question,"

Dragomir remarked. He sounded the tiniest bit smug: I've been bribed twice, Jalal ad-Din translated mentally.

"Was the other person who inquired by any chance Niketas?" the Arab asked.

Telerikh's steward dipped his head. "Why, yes, now that you mention it." His ice-blue eyes gave Jalal ad-Din a careful once-over: men who could see past their noses deserved watching.

Smiling, Jalal ad-Din said, "And did you give him the same answer you will give me?"

"Why, certainly, noble sir." Dragomir sounded as though the idea of doing anything else had never entered his mind. Perhaps it had not: "I told him, as I tell you now, that the mighty khan keeps his own counsel well, and has not revealed to me which faith – if either – he will choose."

"You are an honest man." Jalal ad-Din sighed. "Not as helpful as I would have hoped, but honest nonetheless."

Dragomir bowed. "And you, noble sir, are most generous. Be assured that if I knew more, I would pass it on to you." Jalal ad-Din nodded, thinking it would be a sorry spectacle indeed if one who served the caliph, the richest, mightiest lord in the world, could not afford a more lavish bribe than a miserable Christian priest.

However lavish the payment, though, it had not bought him what he wanted. He bowed his way out of Telerikh's palace, spent the morning wandering through Pliska in search of trinkets for his fair-skinned bedmate. Here too he was spending Abd ar-Rahman's money, so only the finest goldwork interested him.

He went from shop to shop, sometimes pausing to dicker, sometimes not. The rings and necklaces the Bulgar craftsmen displayed were less intricate, less ornate than those that would have fetched highest prices in Damascus, but had a rough vigor of their own. Jalal ad-Din finally chose a thick chain studded with fat garnets and pieces of polished jet.

He tucked the necklace into his robe, sat down to rest outside the jeweler's shop. The sun blazed down. It was not as high in the sky, not as hot, really, as it would have been in Damascus at the same season, but this was muggy heat, not dry, and seemed worse. Jalal ad-Din felt like a boiled fish. He started to doze.

"*Assalamu aleykum* – peace to you," someone said. Jalal ad-Din jerked awake, looked up. Niketas stood in front of him. Well, he'd long since gathered that the priest spoke Arabic, though they'd only used Greek between themselves till now.

"*Aleykum assalamu* – and to you, peace," he replied. He yawned and stretched and started to get to his feet. Niketas took him by the elbow, helped him rise. "Ah, thank you. You are generous to an old man, and one who is no friend of yours."

"Christ teaches us to love our enemies," Niketas shrugged. "I try to obey his teachings, as best I can."

Jalal ad-Din thought that a stupid teaching – the thing to do with an enemy was to get rid of him. The Christians did not really believe what they said, either; he remembered how they'd fought at Constantinople, even after the walls were breached. But the priest had just been kind – no point in churlishly arguing with him.

Instead, the Arab said, "Allah be praised, day after tomorrow the khan will make his choice known." He cocked an eyebrow at Niketas. "Dragomir tells me you tried to learn his answer in advance."

"Which can only mean you did the same." Niketas laughed dryly. "I suspect you learned no more than I did."

"Only that Dragomir is fond of gold," Jalal ad-Din admitted.

Niketas laughed again, then grew serious. "How strange, is it not, that the souls of a nation ride on the whim of a man both ignorant and barbarous. God grant that he choose wisely."

"From God come all things," Jalal ad-Din said. The Christian nodded; that much they believed in common. Jalal ad-Din went on, "That shows, I believe, why Telerikh will decide for Islam."

"No, you are wrong there," Niketas answered. "He must choose Christ. Surely God will not allow those who worship him correctly to be penned up in one far corner of the world, and bar them forever from access to whatever folk may lie north and east of Bulgaria."

Jalal ad-Din started to answer, then stopped and gave his rival a respectful look. As he had already noticed, Niketas' thought had formidable depth to it. However clever he was, though, the priest who might have been Emperor had to deal with his weakness in the real world. Jalal ad-Din drove that weakness home: "If God loves you so well, why has he permitted us Muslims dominion over so many of you, and why has he let us drive you back and back, even giving over Constantinople, your imperial city, into our hands?"

"Not for your own sake, I'm certain," Niketas snapped.

"No? Why then?" Jalal ad-Din refused to be nettled by the priest's tone.

"Because of the multitude of our own sins, I'm certain. Not only was – *is* – Christendom sadly riddled with heresies and false beliefs, even those who believe what is true all too often lead sinful lives. Thus your eruption from the desert, to serve as God's flail and as punishment for our errors."

"You have answers to everything – everything but God's true will. He will show that day after tomorrow, through Telerikh."

"That he will." With a stiff little bow, Niketas took his leave. Jalal ad-Din watched him go, wondering if hiring a knifeman would be worthwhile in spite of Telerikh's warnings. Reluctantly, he decided against it; not here in Pliska, he thought. In Damascus he could have arranged it and never been traced, but he lacked that sort of connections here. Too bad.

Only when he was almost back to the khan's palace to give the pleasure girl the trinket did he stop to wonder whether Niketas was thinking about sticking a knife in *him*. Christian priests were supposed to be above such things, but Niketas himself had pointed out what sinners Christians were these days.

Telerikh's servants summoned Jalal ad-Din and the other Arabs to the audience chamber just before the time for mid-afternoon prayers. Jalal ad-Din did not like having to put off the ritual; it struck him as a bad omen. He tried to stay serene. Voicing the inauspicious thought aloud would only give it power.

The Christians were already in the chamber when the Arabs entered. Jalal ad-Din did not like that either. Catching his eye, Niketas sent him a chilly nod. Theodore only scowled, as he did whenever he had anything to do with Muslims. The monk Paul, though, smiled at Jalal ad-Din as if at a dear friend. That only made him worry more.

Telerikh waited until both delegations stood before him. "I have decided," he said abruptly. Jalal ad-Din drew in a sudden, sharp breath. From the number of boyars who echoed him, he guessed that not even the khan's nobles knew his will. Dragomir had not lied, then.

The khan rose from his carven throne, stepped down between the rival embassies. The boyars muttered among themselves; this was not common procedure. Jalal ad-Din's nails bit into his palms. His heart pounded in his chest till he wondered how long it could endure.

Telerikh turned to face southeast. For a moment, Jalal ad-Din was too keyed up to notice or care. Then the khan sank to his knees, his face turned towards Mecca, towards the Holy City. Again Jalal ad-Din's heart threatened to burst, this time with joy.

"*La illaha ill'Allah; Muhammadun rasulu'llah*," Telerikh said in a loud, firm voice. "There is no God but Allah; Muhammad is the prophet of Allah." He repeated the *shahada* twice more, then rose to his feet and bowed to Jalal ad-Din.

"It is accomplished," the Arab said, fighting back tears. "You are a Muslim now, a fellow in submission to the will of God."

"Not I alone. We shall all worship the one God and his prophet." Telerikh turned to his boyars, shouted in the Bulgar tongue. A couple of nobles shouted back. Telerikh jerked his arm towards the doorway, a peremptory gesture of dismissal. The stubborn boyars glumly tramped out. The rest turned towards Mecca and knelt. Telerikh led them in the *shahada*, once, twice, three times. The khan faced Jalal ad-Din once more. "Now we are all Muslims here."

"God is most great," the Arab breathed. "Soon, magnificent khan, I vow, many teachers will come from Damascus to instruct you and your people fully in all details of the faith, though what you and your nobles have proclaimed will suffice for your souls until such time as the *ulama* – those learned in religion – may arrive."

"It is very well," Telerikh said. Then he seemed to remember that Theodore, Niketas, and Paul were still standing close by him, suddenly alone in a chamber full of the enemies of their faith. He turned to them. "Go back to your pope in peace, Christian priests. I could not choose your religion, not with heaven as you say it is – and not with the caliph's armies all along my southern border. Perhaps if Constantinople had not fallen so long ago, my folk would in the end have become Christian. Who can say? But in this world, as it is now, Muslims we must be, and Muslims we shall be."

"I will pray for you, excellent khan, and for God's forgiveness for the mistake you make this day," Paul said gently. Theodore, on the other hand, looked as if he was consigning Telerikh to the hottest pits of hell.

Niketas caught Jalal ad-Din's eye. The Arab nodded slightly to his defeated foe. More than anyone else in the chamber, the two of them understood how much bigger than Bulgaria was the issue decided here today. Islam would grow and grow, Christendom continue to shrink. Jalal ad-Din had heard that Ethiopia, far to the south of Egypt, had Christian rulers yet. What of it? Ethiopia was so far from the centre of affairs as hardly to matter. And the same fate would now befall the isolated Christian countries in the far northwest of the world.

Let them be islands in the Muslim sea, he thought, if that was what their stubbornness dictated. One day, *inshallah*, that sea would wash over every island, and they would read the Qu'ran in Rome itself.

He had done his share and more to make that dream real, as a youth helping to capture Constantinople and now in his old age by bringing Bulgaria the true faith. He could return once more to his peaceful retirement in Damascus.

He wondered if Telerikh would let him take along that fair-skinned pleasure girl. He turned to the khan. It couldn't hurt to ask.

Lenin in Odessa

George Zebrowski

"Lenin is a rotten little incessant intriguer . . . He just wants
power. He ought to be killed by some moral sanitary authority."
— H. G. Wells, in a letter dated July 1918,
sent to the *New York Weekly Review*

1

In 1918, Sidney Reilly, who had worked as a British agent
against the Germans and Japanese, returned to our newly
formed Soviet Russia. He was again working for England and
her allies, but this time he was also out for himself, intending to
assassinate Vladimir Ilyich Lenin and bring himself to power at
the head of the regime that he imagined his homeland deserved.

Jew though he was, Reilly saw himself as a Russian coming
home to make good. It angered him that another expatriate,
Lenin, had got there first – with German help, and with what
Reilly considered suspect motives. Reilly was convinced that his
own vision was the proper response to the problems of life in
Russia, which, as Sigmund Rosenblum, a bastard born in
Odessa, he had escaped in his youth. He believed that the right
man could, with sufficient thought and preparation, make of
history his own handiwork.

It was obvious to me that Reilly's thinking was a curious

patchwork of ideas, daring and naive at the same time, but lacking the systematic approach of a genuine scientific philosophy. His distaste for the bourgeois society that had oppressed him in his childhood was real, but he had developed a taste for its pleasures.

Of course, Reilly knew that he was sent in as a tool of the British and their allies, who opposed Bolshevism from the outset, and he let them continue to think that they could count on him, for at least as long as his aims would not conflict with theirs. Lenin himself had been eased back into Russia by the Germans, who hoped that he would take Russia out of the war in Europe. No German agent could have done that job better. Reilly was determined to remove or kill Lenin, as the prelude to a new Russia. What that Russia would be was not clear. The best that I could say about Reilly's intentions was that he was not a Czarist.

There was an undeniable effectiveness in Reilly, of which he was keenly aware. He was not a mere power seeker, even though he took pride in his physical prowess and craft as a secret agent; to see him as out for personal gain would be to underestimate the danger that he posed to those of us who understand power more fully than he did.

Reilly compared himself to Lenin. They had both been exiles from their homeland, dreaming of return, but Vladimir Ilyich Ulyanov had gone home on German hopes and seized power. Russia would be remade according to a heretical Marxism, in Reilly's view. Lenin's combination of revisionist ideology and good fortune was intolerable to Reilly; it wounded his craftsman's ego, which saw chance as a minor player in history. He ignored the evidence of Lenin's organizational skills, by which a spontaneous revolution had been shaped into one with purpose.

Reilly viewed himself and his hopes for Russia with romantic agony and a sense of personal responsibility that were at odds with his practical intellect and shrewdness, both of which should have told him that he could not succeed. But Reilly's cleverness delighted in craft and planning. His actions against the Germans and Japanese were all but inconceivable to the common man. Even military strategists doubted that one man could have carried out Reilly's decisive schemes. His greatest joy was in doing what others believed to be impossible.

Another clue to Reilly's personality lay in his love of technology, especially naval aviation. He was an accomplished flyer who looked to the future of transport. He was fascinated, for example, by the Michelson-Morley experiment to detect the aether wind, which was predicted on the idea of the Earth's motion through a stationary medium. When this detection failed, Reilly wrote a letter to a scientific journal (supplied to me by one of my intellectual operatives in London) insisting that the aether was too subtle a substance to register on current instruments. One day, he claimed, aether ships would move between the worlds.

Reilly's mind worried a problem until he found an imaginative solution; then his practical bent would find a way to accomplish the task. As a child he was able to remain invisible to his family simply by staying one step ahead of their house search for him. As a spy he once eluded his pursuers by joining them in the search for him. However rigorous and distasteful the means might be, Reilly would see what was possible and not flinch. With Lenin he understood that a single mind could change the world with thought and daring; but, unlike Vladimir Ilyich, Reilly's mind lacked the direction of historical truth. He was capable of bringing into being new things, but they were only short-lived sports, chimeras of an exceptional but misguided will. His self-imposed exile from his homeland had left divisions as incongruous as his Irish pseudonym.

Sidney Reilly sought escape from the triviality of his life, in which his skills had been used to prop up imperialism. He had been paid in money and women. By the time he returned to Russia, I already sensed that he would be useful to me. It seemed possible, on the basis of his revolutionary leanings, that I might win him to our cause.

2

"Comrade Stalin," Vladimir Ilyich said to me one gloomy summer morning, "tell me who is plotting against us this week?" He was sitting in the middle of a large red sofa, under a bare spot on the wall where a Czarist portrait had hung. He seemed very small as he sank into the dusty cushions.

"Only the ones I told you about last week. Not one of them is practical enough to succeed."

He stared at me for a moment, as if disbelieving, but I knew he was only tired. In a moment he closed his eyes and was dozing. I wondered if his bourgeois conscience would balk at the measures he would soon have to take to keep power. It seemed to me that he had put me on the Bolshevik Central Committee to do the things for which he had no stomach. Too many opportunists were ready to step into our shoes if we stumbled. Telling foe from ally was impossible; given the chance, anyone might turn on us.

Reilly was already in Moscow. I learned later that he had come by the usual northern route and had taken a cheap hotel room. On the following morning, he had abandoned that room, leaving behind an old suitcase with some work clothes in it. He had gone to a safe house, where he met a woman of middle years who knew how to use a handgun.

She was not an imposing figure – an impression she knew how to create; but there was no doubt in Reilly's mind that she would pull the trigger with no care for what happened to her afterward.

Lenin's death was crucial to Reilly's plot, even though he knew that it might make Vladimir Ilyich a Bolshevik martyr. Reilly was also depending on our other weaknesses to work for him. While Trotsky was feverishly organizing the Red Army, we were dependent on small forces – our original Red Guard, made up of factory workers and sailors, a few thousand Chinese railway workers, and the Latvian regiments, who acted as our Praetorian Guard. The Red Guard was loyal but militarily incompetent. The Chinese served in return for food. The Latvians hated the Germans for overrunning their country, but had to be paid. Reilly knew that he could bribe the Latvians and Chinese to turn against us, making it possible for the Czarist officers in hiding to unite and finish the job. With Lenin and myself either arrested or dead, he could then turn south and isolate Trotsky, who had taken Odessa back from the European allies and was busy shipping in supplies by sea. His position there would become impossible if the British brought in warships. If we failed in the north, we would be vulnerable from two sides.

Lenin's death would alter expectations in everyone. Reilly's cohorts would seize vital centers throughout Moscow. Our Czarist officers would go over to Reilly, taking their men with them. The opportunists among us would desert. Reilly's leaflets had already planted doubts in their minds. Lenin's death would be their weathervane. Even the martyrdom of Vladimir Ilyich, I realized, might not be enough to help us.

As I gazed at Lenin's sleeping face, I imagined him already dead and forgotten. His wife, Nadezhda Krupskaya, came into the room and covered him with a blanket. She did not look at where I sat behind the large library desk as she left.

3

"Comrade Lenin has been shot!" the messenger cried as he burst into the conference room.

I looked up from the table. "Is he dead?"

The young cadet was flushed from the cold. His teeth chattered as he shook his head in denial. "No – the doctors have him."

"Where?" I asked.

He shook his head. "You're to come with me, Comrade Stalin, for your own safety."

"What else do you know?" I demanded.

"Several of our units, including Cheka, are not responding to orders."

"They've gone over," I said, glancing down at the lists of names I had been studying.

The cadet was silent as I got up and went to the window. The grey courtyard below was deserted. There was no sign of the Latvian guards, and the dead horse I had seen earlier was gone. I turned my head slightly and saw the cadet in the window glass.

He was fumbling with his pistol holster. I reached under my long coat and grasped the revolver in my shoulder harness, then turned and pointed it at him under my coat. He had not drawn his pistol.

"No, Comrade Stalin!" he cried. "I was only unsnapping the case. It sticks."

I looked into his eyes. He was only a boy, and his fear was convincing.

"We must leave here immediately, Comrade Stalin," he added quickly. "We may be arrested at any moment."

I slipped my gun back into its sheath. "Lead the way."

"We'll go out the back," he said, his voice shaking with relief.

"Did it happen at the factory?" I asked.

"Just as he finished his speech, a woman shot him," he replied.

I tried to imagine what Reilly was doing at this very moment.

The cadet led me down the back stairs of the old office block. The iron railing was rusting, and the stairwell smelled of urine. On the first landing the cadet turned around and found his courage.

"You *are* under arrest, Comrade Stalin," he said with a nervous smile.

My boot caught him under the chin. I felt his neck break as he fired the pistol into the railing, scattering rust into my face. He fell backward onto the landing. I hurried down and wrenched the gun from his stiffening fingers, then went back up to the office.

There was a hiding place behind the toilet, but I would use it only if I had to. I came into the room and paused, listening, but there was only the sound of wind rattling the windows. Was it possible that they had sent only one person for me? Something had gone wrong, or the cadet had come for me on his own initiative, hoping to ingratiate himself with the other side. All of which meant I could expect another visit at any moment.

I hurried down the front stairs to the lobby, went out cautiously through the main doors, and spotted a motorcycle nearby – probably the cadet's. I rushed to it, got on, and started it on the first kick. I gripped the handlebars, gunned the engine into a roar, then turned the bike around with a screech and rolled into the street, expecting to see them coming for me.

But there was no one on the street. Something had gone wrong. The Latvians had been removed to leave me exposed, but the next step, my arrest and execution, had somehow been delayed. Only the cadet had shown up.

I tried to think. Where would they have taken Vladimir Ilyich? It had to be the old safe house outside of Moscow, just south of the city. That would be the only place now. I wondered if I had enough petrol to reach it.

4

Lenin was at the country house. He was not mortally wounded. His assassin was there also, having been taken prisoner by the Cheka guards who had gone with Lenin to the factory.

"Comrade Stalin!" Vladimir Ilyich exclaimed as I sat down by his cot in the book-lined study. "You are safe, but our situation is desperate."

"What has happened?" I asked, still unsteady from the long motorcycle ride.

"Moscow has fallen. Our Latvian regiments have deserted, along with our Chinese workers. Most of the Red Guard have been imprisoned. The Social Revolutionaries have joined the counter-revolution. My assassin is one of them. I suspect that killing me was to have been their token of good faith. There's no word from Trotsky's southern volunteers. There doesn't seem to be much we can do. We might even have to flee the country."

"Never," I replied.

He raised his hand to his massive forehead.

"Don't shout, I'm in terrible pain. The bullet struck my shoulder, but I have a headache that won't stop."

I looked around for Nadezhda, but she was not in the room. I saw several haggard, unfamiliar faces and realized that no one of great importance had escaped with Lenin from Moscow. By now they were in Reilly's hands, dead or about to be executed. He would not wait long. I had underestimated the Bastard of Odessa.

"What shall we do?" I asked.

Vladimir Ilyich sighed and closed his eyes. "I would like your suggestions."

"We must go where they won't find us easily," I replied. "I know several places in Georgia."

His eyes opened and fixed on me. "As long as you don't want to return to robbing banks."

His words irritated me, but I didn't show it.

"We needed the money," I said calmly, remembering that he had once described me as crude and vulgar. Living among émigré Russians in Europe had affected his practical sense.

"Of course, of course," he replied with a feeble wave of his hand. "You are a dedicated and useful man."

There was a muffled shot from outside. It seemed to relax Vladimir Ilyich. Dora Kaplan, his assassin, had been executed.

5

Just before leaving the safe house, we learned that Lenin's wife had been executed. Vladimir Ilyich began to rave as we led him out to the truck, insisting to me that Reilly could not have killed Nadezhda, and that the report had to be false. I said nothing; to me her death had been inevitable. As Lenin's lifelong partner, and a theoretician herself, she would have posed a threat in his absence. Reilly's swiftness in removing her impressed me. Lenin's reaction to her death was unworthy of a Bolshevik; suddenly his wife was only an unimportant woman. Nadezhda Krupskaya had not been an innocent.

We fled south, heading for a railway station that was still in our hands, just south of Moscow, where a special train was waiting to take us to Odessa. If the situation in that city turned out to be intractable, we would attempt to reach a hiding place in my native Georgia.

Three Chekas came with us in the truck – a young lieutenant and two privates, both of whom had abandoned the Czar's forces for the revolution. I watched the boyish faces of the two privates from time to time, looking for signs of doubt. The lieutenant, who was also a mechanic, drove the old Ford, nursing the truck through the muddy ten kilometers to the station.

"He could have held her hostage," Vladimir Ilyich insisted as the truck sputtered and coughed along. "Don't you think so? Maybe he thought we were dead, and she would be of no use to him as a hostage?"

For the next hour he asked his own questions and gave his own impossible answers. It depressed me to hear how much of the bourgeois there was still in him. I felt the confusion in the minds of the two Chekas.

It began to rain as the sun went down. We couldn't see the road ahead. The lieutenant pulled over and waited. Water seeped in on us through the musty canvas. Vladimir Ilyich began to weep.

"She was a soldier in our cause," I said loudly, hating his sentimentality.

He stared out into the rainy twilight. Lightning flashed as he turned to look at me, and for a moment it seemed that his face had turned to marble. "You're right," he said, eyes wild with conviction, "I must remember that."

Of course, I had always disliked Nadezhda's hovering, familiar-like ways. She had been a bony raven at his shoulder, forever whispering asides, but I had always taken great care to be polite to her. Now more than ever I realized what a buttress she had been to Vladimir Ilyich.

The rain lessened. The lieutenant tried to start the Ford, but it was dead.

"There's not much time," I said. "How much farther?"

"Less than half a kilometer."

"We'll go on foot," I said. "There's no telling who may be behind us."

I helped Vladimir Ilyich down from the truck. He managed to stand alone and refused my arm as we began our march on the muddy road. He moved steadily at my side, but his breathing was labored.

We were within sight of the station when he collapsed.

"Help!" I called out.

The lieutenant and one of the privates came back, lifted Vladimir Ilyich onto their shoulders, and hurried ahead with him. It was like a scene from the street rallies, but without the crowds.

"Is he very ill?" the other private asked me as I caught up.

I did not answer. Ahead, the train waited in a conflagration of storm lamps and steam.

6

Our train consisted of a dining car, a kitchen, one supply car, and the engine. A military evacuation train was being readied on the track next to ours, to carry away those who would be fleeing out of Moscow in the next day or two. I was surprised at this bit of organization. When I asked how it had been accomplished, a sergeant said one word to me: "Trotsky."

We sped off into the warm, misty night. Vladimir Ilyich recovered enough to have dinner with me and our three soldiers. The plush luxury of the Czarist interior seemed to brighten his mood.

"I only hope that Trotsky is in Odessa when we arrive," he said, sipping his brandy, "and that he can raise a force we can work with. Our foreign venders have been paid, fortunately, but we will have to keep our southern port open to be supplied."

He was looking into the large mirror at our right as he spoke. I nodded to his reflection.

"The troops behind us," the youthful lieutenant added, "will help ensure that."

Vladimir Ilyich put down his glass and looked at me directly. "Do you think, Comrade Stalin, that we hoped for too much?" He sounded lost.

"No," I answered. "We have popular support. The people are waiting to hear from you. Reilly's pamphlets have struck a nerve of longing with promises of foreign help and bourgeois progress, but he is actually depending only on the uncertainty of our followers. His mercenaries won't count for much when the news that you are alive gets out. Most of his support can be taken from him with that alone, but we will have to follow our victory with a period of terror, to compel loyalty among the doubters."

He nodded to me, then looked into the darkness of the window. In that mirror we rode not only in a well-appointed, brightly lit dining room, but in the cave of all Russia.

"You must get some sleep," I said.

We found blankets and made ourselves comfortable on the leather couches. The lieutenant turned down the lights.

I tried to sleep, but my thoughts seemed to organize themselves to the clatter of the train wheels. Contempt for my own kind crept into me, especially for the idealists in our party. Too many utopian fools were setting themselves up against their own nature and what was possible. They did not grasp that progress was like the exponent in one of Einstein's fashionable equations – a small modifying quantity that has an effect only when the big term grew very large. They failed to see that only when the biggest letter of human history, material wealth, became sufficiently large would there be a chance for social progress. Only then would we be able to afford to become humane. My role in this revolution was to remember this fact, and to act when it was neglected . . .

7

Our mood was apprehensive as our train pulled into Odessa. We stepped out into bright sunlight, and a deserted station.

"We don't know what may have happened here," I said.

"There hasn't been time," Vladimir Ilyich replied. His voice was gruff after three days on the train, and he seemed ready to bark at me in his usual way. I felt reassured. This was the Lenin who had taken a spontaneous uprising and interpreted the yearning of the masses so they would know what to do; the Lenin who would make ours a Communist revolution despite Marx. Like Reilly, Lenin was irreplaceable. Without him there would only be a struggle for power, with no vision justifying action.

Suddenly, a Ford Model T sedan pulled into the station and rattled towards us down the platform. I took Lenin's arm, ready to shove him out of harm's way, but the car slowed and stopped.

"Welcome!" the driver shouted as he threw open the door and got out. When he opened the back door for us, I saw that he was Trotsky's youngest son, Sergei. I greeted him and smiled, but his eyes worshiped only Lenin, as if I didn't exist, as we got into the back seat.

Sergei drove quickly, but the ride was comfortable. With the windows closed, Odessa seemed distant. We climbed a hill and saw the sun glistening on the Black Sea. I remembered the smell of leather in my father's shoe shop. Warm days gave the shop a keener odour. I pictured myself in the small church library, which was open to sons who might one day be priests. The books had been dusty, the air full of waxy smells from the lamps and candles. I remembered the young girl I had seduced on a sunny afternoon, and for an instant the world's failings seemed far away. I began to wonder if we were driving into a betrayal.

A crowd surrounded us as we pulled into the center of the city. They peered inside, saw Lenin, and cheered.

Trotsky was waiting for us with a company of soldiers on the courthouse steps. We climbed out into a bright paradise of good feeling. Trotsky saluted us, then came down and embraced Vladimir Ilyich, who looked shabby in his brown waistcoat under that silky blue sky.

The crowd cheered them. As Lenin turned to address the throng, I felt Reilly plotting against us in Moscow, and I knew in that moment what it would take to stop him.

"Comrades!" Lenin cried, regaining his old self with one word. "A dangerous counter-revolution has seized Moscow! It is supported by the foreign allies, who are not content with defeating Germany. They also want our lands. But we will regroup here, and strike north. With Comrade Trotsky's Red Army, and your bravery, we shall prevail . . . "

As he spoke, I wondered if anyone in Moscow would believe that he was still alive, short of seeing him there. Open military actions would not defeat Reilly in any reasonable time. It would take years, while the revolution withered, especially if Reilly avoided decisive battles. Reilly had to be killed as quickly and as publicly as possible. Like Lenin he was a leader who needed his followers as much as they needed him. There was no arguing with this fact of human attachment. Without Reilly, the counter-revolution would collapse in a matter of days. His foreign supporters would not easily shift their faith to another figure.

He had to die in a week, two at the latest, and I knew how it would have to be done. There was no other way.

"Long live Comrade Lenin!" the crowd chanted – loudly enough, it seemed to me, for Reilly to hear it in his bed in Moscow.

8

From the reports I had read about Reilly's life and activities, I suspected that he was a man who liked to brood. It was a way of searching, of pointing himself towards his hopes. He prayed to himself, beseeching a hidden center, where the future sang of sweet possibilities.

As head of his government, he would have to act against both Czarists and Bolsheviks. He could count on Czarists joining his regime, but he would never trust a Bolshevik. Czarists would be fairly predictable in their military actions, but Bolsheviks, he knew, would spare no outrage to bring him down.

He was probably in what remained of the British Embassy in Moscow, sipping brandy in the master bedroom, perhaps playing with the idea that he might have joined us. I knew there had been efforts to recruit him for our intelligence service. He would have disappeared and re-emerged as another man, as he did when he left Odessa for South America in his youth, to escape his adulterous family's bourgeois pesthole. It would have been simple justice for him to return in the same way, even as a Bolshevik.

But for the moment, Russia was his to mold. I could almost hear the Jew congratulating himself in that great bed of English oak.

Within the week there would be a knock on his bedroom door, and a messenger would bring him word that Lenin was in Odessa. Reilly would sit up and lean uncomfortably against the large wooden headboard, where once there had been luxurious pillows (a pity that the mobs had torn them to pieces). He would read the message with a rush of excitement and realize that a British seaplane could get him to Odessa within a day. The entire mission would flash through his mind, as if he were remembering the past.

He would fly to the Black Sea, then swing north to Odessa, using the night for cover. What feelings would pass through him as he landed on the moonlit water? Here he was, returning to the city of his childhood in order to test himself against his greatest enemies. The years would run back in his mind as he sat in the open doorway of the amphibious aircraft, breathing in the night air and remembering the youth who had startled himself with his superiority to the people around him. He had blackmailed his mother's lover for the money to escape Odessa. The man had nearly choked when Reilly had called him Father.

He would know that he was risking his counter-revolution by coming here alone. The Bolsheviks would be able to pull down any of his possible successors. But it was the very implausibility of his coming here alone that would protect him, he would tell himself. Tarnishing Lenin's name by revealing Germany's hand in his return was not enough. Lenin had to die before his followers could regroup, before reports of his death were proven false. Only then would the counter-revolution be able to rally the support of disenchanted Czarists, moderate democrats, churchmen, and Mensheviks – all those who still hoped for a regime that would replace monarchy but avoid bolshevism.

Reilly was a hopeless bourgeois, but more intelligent than most, hence more dangerous, despite his romantic imagination. He sincerely believed that bolshevism would only gain Russia the world's animosity and ensure our country's cultural and economic poverty.

He would come into Odessa one morning, in a small boat, perhaps dressed as a fisherman. Wearing old clothes, following the pattern of all his solo missions, he would savor the irony of his return to the city of his youth. It was a form of rebirth. He trusted it, and so would I.

9

The warmer climate of Odessa speeded Lenin's physical recovery. He would get up with the sun and walk along the street that led to the Great Steps (the site of the 1905 massacre of the townspeople by Czarist Cossacks, which the expatriate homosexual director, Sergei Eisenstein, later filmed in Hollywood). I let the Cheka guards sleep late and kept an eye on Vladimir Ilyich myself.

One morning, as I watched him through field glasses from the terrace of our hotel, he stopped and gazed out over city and sea, then sat down on the first step, something he had not done before. His shoulders slumped in defeat. He was probably reminiscing about his bourgeois European life with Krupskaya and regretting their return to Russia. His euphoric recovery during the first week after our arrival had eroded, and he had slowly slipped back into a brooding silence.

As I watched, a man's head floated up from the steps below the seated Lenin. The figure of a fisherman came into view, stopped next to Vladimir Ilyich, and tipped his hat to him. I turned my glasses to the sea and searched. Yes! There was something on the horizon – a small boat, or the wings of a seaplane. The reports I had received of engine sounds in the early morning had been correct.

I whipped back to the two figures. They were conversing amiably. Vladimir Ilyich seemed pleased by the encounter, but then he had always shown a naive faith in simple folk, and sometimes spoke to them as if he were confessing. Krupskaya's death had made him unobservant, and Reilly was a superb actor.

Reilly was taking his time out of sheer vanity, it seemed to me. He would not kill his great rival without first talking to him.

I put down the field glasses, checked my revolver, then slipped it into my shoulder holster and hurried downstairs, wearing only my white shirt and trousers. I ran through the deserted streets, sweating in the warm morning air, expecting at any moment to hear a shot. I reached the row of houses just above the Great Steps, slipped into a doorway, then crept out.

The blood was pounding in my ears as I peered around the corner. Lenin and the fisherman were sitting on the top step with their back to me. Vladimir Ilyich was gesturing with his right hand. I could almost hear him. The words sounded familiar.

I waited, thinking that the man was a fisherman, and that I had expected too much of Reilly.

Then the stranger put his arm around Vladimir Ilyich's shoulders. What had they been saying to each other? Had they reached some kind of rapprochement? Perhaps Lenin was in fact a German agent, and these two had been working together all along. Could I have been so wrong? The sight of them sitting side by side like old friends unnerved me.

The fisherman gripped Lenin's head with both hands and twisted it. The neck snapped, and in that long moment it seemed to me that he would tear the head from the body. I drew my revolver and rushed forward.

"Did you think it would be that easy, Rosenblum?" I said as I came up behind him.

The fisherman turned and looked up at me, not with surprise, but with irritation, and let go of Lenin.

"Don't move," I said as the corpse slumped face down across the stairs.

The fisherman seemed to relax, but he was watching me carefully. "So you used him as bait," he said, gesturing at the body. "Why didn't you just kill him yourself?"

His question was meant to annoy me.

He looked out to sea. "Yes, an economical solution to counter-revolution. You liquidate us both while preserving the appearance of innocence. You're certain that Moscow will fall without me."

I did not reply.

He squinted up at me. "Are you sure it's me you've captured? I may have sent someone else." He laughed.

I gestured with my revolver. "The seaplane – only Sidney

Reilly would have come here in one. You had to come quickly."

He nodded to himself, as if admitting his sins.

"What did Vladimir Ilyich say to you?" I asked.

His mood changed, as if I had suddenly given him what he needed.

"Well?" I demanded.

"You're very curious about that," he said without looking at me. "I may not tell you."

"Suit yourself."

He considered for a moment. "I will tell you. He feared for Russia's future, and that moved me, Comrade Stalin. He was afraid because there are too many of the likes of you. I was surprised to hear it from him."

"The likes of me?"

"Yes, the cynics and doubters who won't be content until they've made the world as barren for everyone else as they've made it for themselves. His wife's death brought it all home to him, as nothing else could have. His words touched me."

"Did you tell him that you killed her?"

"I was too late to save her."

"And he believed you?"

"Yes. I told him who I was. His dreams were dead. He wanted to die."

My hand was sweaty on the revolver. "Bourgeois sentiments destroyed him. I hope you two enjoyed exchanging idealist bouquets. Did you tell him what you would have done if you had caught us in Moscow?"

He looked up and smiled at me. "I would have paraded all of you through the street without your pants and underwear, shirt-tails flapping in the breeze!"

"And then killed us."

"No, I wouldn't have made martyrs. Prison would have served well enough after such ridicule."

"But you came here to kill him."

"Perhaps not," he said with a sigh. "I might have taken him back as my prisoner, but he wanted to die. I killed him as I would have an injured dog. In any case, Moscow believes that he died weeks ago."

"Well, you've botched it all now, haven't you?"

"At least I know that Lenin died a true Bolshevik."

"So now you claim to understand bolshevism?"

"I always have. True bolshevism contains enough constructive ideas to make possible a high social justice. It shares that with Christianity and the French Revolution, but it's the likes of you, Comrade Stalin, who will prevent a proper wedding of ideals and practical government." He smiled. "Well, perhaps the marriage will take place despite you. The little Soviets may hold fast to their democratic structures and bring you down in time. Who knows, they may one day lead the world to the highest ideal of statesmanship – internationalism."

"Fine words," I said, tightening my grip on the revolver, "but the reality is that you've done our Soviet cause a great service – by being a foreign agent, a counter-revolutionary, a Jewish bastard, and Lenin's assassin, all in one."

"I've only done *you* a service," he said bitterly, and I felt his hatred and frustration.

"You simply don't understand the realities of power, Rosenblum!"

"Do tell," he said with derision.

"Only limited things are possible with humanity," I replied. "The mad dog within the great mass of people must be kept muzzled. Civil order is the best any society can hope to achieve."

The morning sun was hot on my face. As I reached up to wipe my forehead with my sleeve, Reilly leaped over Lenin's body and fled down the long stairs.

I aimed and fired, but my fingers had stiffened during our little dialogue. My bullet got off late and missed. I fired again as he jumped a dozen steps, but the bullet hit well behind him.

"Stop him!" I shouted to a group of people below him. They had just come out of the church at the foot of the stairs. "He's killed Comrade Lenin!"

Reilly saw that he couldn't get by them. He turned and started back towards me, drawing a knife as he went. He stopped and threw it, but it struck the steps to my right. I laughed, and he came for me with his bare hands. I aimed, knowing that he might reach me if I missed. It impressed me that he would gamble on my aim rather than risk the drop over the great railings.

I pulled the trigger. The hammer struck a defective cartridge. Reilly grunted as he sensed victory, and kept coming.

I fired again.

The bullet pierced his throat. He staggered up and fell bleeding at my feet, one hand clawing at my heavy boots. His desperation was both strange and unexpected. Nothing had ever failed for him in quite this way. Its simplicity affronted his intelligence.

"I also feel for dogs," I said, squeezing a round into the back of his head. He lay still, free of life's metaphysics.

I holstered my revolver and nudged his body forward. It sprawled next to Lenin, then rolled down to the next landing. The people from the church came up, paused around Vladimir Ilyich, then looked up to me.

"Vladimir Ilyich's assassin is dead!" I shouted. "The counter-revolution has failed." A breeze blew in from the sea and cooled my face. I breathed deeply and looked saddened.

Reilly was hung by his neck in his hometown, but I was the only one who knew enough to appreciate the irony. Fishermen sailed out and towed his seaplane to shore.

Lenin's body was placed in a tent set up in the harbor area, where all Odessans could come to pay their last respects. Trotsky and I stood in line with everyone else. One of our warships fired its guns in a final salute.

10

We sent the news to Moscow in two carefully timed salvos.

First, that Reilly, a British agent, had been killed during an attempt on Lenin's life; then, that our beloved Vladimir Ilyich had succumbed to wounds received, after a valiant struggle.

We went north with our troops, carrying Lenin's coffin, recruiting all the way. Everywhere people met our train with shouts of allegiance. Trotsky appointed officers, gathered arms, and kept records. He also scribbled in his diary like a schoolgirl.

I knew now that I was Lenin's true heir, truer than he had been to himself in his last weeks. I would hold fast to that and to Russia, especially when Trotsky began to lecture me again about the urgent need for world revolution.

In the years that followed, I searched for men like Reilly to direct our espionage and intelligence services. If he had been turned, our KGB would have been built on a firmer foundation of skills and techniques. He would have recruited English agents for us with ease, especially from their universities, where the British played at revolution and ideology, and sentimental-ized justice. I could not rid myself of the feeling that in time Rosenblum would have turned back to his mother country; he had never been, after all, a Czarist. I regretted having had to kill him on that sunny morning in Odessa, because in later years I found myself measuring so many men against him. I wondered if a defective cartridge or a jammed revolver could have changed the outcome. Probably not. I would have been forced to club him to death. Still, he might have disarmed me . . .

But on that train in 1918, on the snowy track to Moscow, I could only wonder at Reilly's naive belief that he could have altered the course of Soviet inevitability, which now so clearly belonged to me.

The Einstein Gun

Pierre Gévart

Right now, pen in hand, I'm well aware that what I'm about to do is probably of no use whatsoever. Yet it seems to me that I ought to write this memoir, even if nobody ever reads it; even if I myself, at some point, *lose the ability* to remember the events I'm describing! Even if all of this has never actually been.

My name is Otto-Abram Siesienthal. I was born in Gloggnitz about 100 kilometers south of Vienna, where my father was a watchmaker. However, this noble profession didn't appeal to me. I preferred to study history at university in the capital. Thanks to the old Emperor Franz-Joseph, I won a scholarship and obtained my diploma in 1913. A year later, I had the great good fortune to follow my supervisor Albrecht Finnmayer as head of Modern History in Linz, before returning to the University of Vienna three years later.

What changed my life radically – and the lives of millions of others – was the ill-omened 6 February 1934.

As the century wore on, increasingly dominated by uncertainty caused by the financial crisis which began seven years earlier, that very same 6 February saw the French aviator Georges Guynemer become the first person to complete a transatlantic crossing by airship. Everybody had thought that Von Richtoffen would win the race. In Berlin they were getting ready to celebrate; they'd hung up paper lanterns and decked the streets with bunting. A fervent supporter of the Germans, poor Albert was almost sick at the news of the Frenchman's victory. An exceptional fellow, Albert, very wide-ranging in his interests!

Of course nowadays there's only one reason to remember that date. The election to the Diet had taken place three weeks earlier. That very day, the Emperor named a new Chancellor, who was supposed to figure out – at last! – a way out of the political crisis. Franz-Ferdinand was definitely less gifted and diligent than his predecessor Franz-Joseph. He also had some scary notions. His support for the Czechs during the second decade had slid bit by bit into wholesale antipathy towards the Slavs, which quickly shook hands with the new Chancellor's gut-instinct anti-Semitism. For long enough the Emperor had been lending an all too willing ear to all those extremists who unhesitatingly blamed the Slavs or the Jews for being at the root of the crisis. As though the crisis wasn't incurably global, tied up with the excesses of free trade politics; or at least in my opinion.

This Adolph Hitler didn't tick the box for me at all. For years he'd hung around the disreputable world of would-be artists in our capital before he found his vocation as an orator. He created an opposition group and, during his time in jail after a failed attempted murder, he even wrote a book called *My Protest*. You'd think a book with a title like that would go nowhere, but you'd be wrong. Hitler's star was forever on the rise thanks to his masterly use of the timeworn cliché of the scapegoat. Well, a double-headed goat in this case: Slavic and Jewish. So long as Hitler only had a few deputies in the Diet, that didn't matter too much. But after the Great Crash in '26, "Black Friday" on the Budapest Stock Exchange, and the explosion of unemployment that followed, his constituency swelled with every election.

The date, 6 February 1934 remains a sad day in all our memories: after Hitler had allied with the Liberals and the Conservatives, who were under pressure from the Emperor, he was appointed Chancellor.

Surprisingly, Albert didn't seem to pay much heed to this. You'd think his attention was all taken up by his own research – and by Guynemer. That was *so* Albert: one day passionately defending a righteous cause and the next day getting all wrapped up in the products of his mighty brain.

That was also the very day when Albert decided to reveal the results of an experiment to a close circle of Viennese intellectuals from various backgrounds. I was among the guests as much due to my friendship with Albert as my status in the Faculty of History.

As soon as the maid shut the door behind me, Albert welcomed me with words which I recall precisely: "Otto, I do believe we're well on our way to a *third of those things*!" I didn't need to ask what he meant. I *knew* he was implying a third Nobel Prize!

"Watch this clock", he carried on without troubling to introduce me to the other guests already present, most of whom I knew in any case, such as Freud, the doctor who strove to analyse the human mind; and from abroad there was an Italian scientist I'd met the previous year at a conference in Trieste – he'd constructed in the science labs of the university some kind of atomic pile, as he called it. Fermo? *Fermi?* Many other eminences were present, as well as various artists and journalists. However, Albert seemed to have forgotten their very existence, and insisted I focus my attention on a pendulum clock standing on a lab bench next to something covered by a piece of old cloth. The clock seemed nothing out of the ordinary – unless somehow it worked by atomic energy, which might explain the presence of the Italian, he of the atomic pile! By now there was a similar experimental pile in Vienna, on which the Italian may have been advising. If I recall aright, Fermi's pile – that was his name for sure – required something the size of a swimming pool and all we had here was a little clock. But I bided my time. I knew that Albert liked a joke, yet this didn't seem on the cards at such a moment.

"Yesterday this clock and its exact duplicate were set in exactly the same way in the presence of Herr Zacharius, Watchmaker to His Majesty the Emperor, and of Dr Dummliebe, who kindly agreed to seal the two clocks." While Albert was explaining to us what was presumably the prelude to some scientific experiment, the two men in question rose to take a bow. Zacharius acknowledged me with a friendly smile, since he'd been my father's apprentice. Somehow I felt unsettled. This seemed like a magic act in some variety show. Albert placed his hand on the cloth. "And here is the second clock!" he declared in a tone which I thought frivolous, and whisked away the cloth to reveal that second sealed clock, which looked identical . . . except that the time it showed was three minutes faster.

Albert made us take special note of this fact. Whereupon Freud responded that, so far as he was concerned, he had better things to waste his time on. Still, he pulled out a notebook and scribbled a few lines. An officer whom I didn't know declared his amazement that clocks made by Herr Zacharius could fall out of line in such a brief period. The Imperial Watchmaker angrily retorted that his clocks never ever . . . The officer retorted that nevertheless . . . Somebody got up and departed without a word of goodbye. Albert rapped the side of the bench with a piece of metal to call for silence.

"Herr Zacharius' clocks are in perfect synchrony. *The second one simply benefitted by spending three minutes in the future.* What you have here in front of you is proof that it's possible to travel in time, provided that the necessary energy is available."

This was greeted at first by a leaden silence. Then came an outburst of protest. I myself rebuked Albert with having confused 6 February with 1 April and departed, slamming the door; and I don't believe I was the only one. It has to be said we were all of us preoccupied by Hitler's rise to power, and with all that that might imply.

Time flew faster than we cared for. Franz-Ferdinand rushed into force the Laws of July, and Albert left for Paris. He was heeding President Pergaud's call (only the French could elect a writer to be their Head of State) and was appointed to the chair of the recently deceased Madame Curie. I had no chance to see him again before his departure.

As for me, I tried my best to hold on despite the July Laws. Since I was Jewish, I must needs yield my chair of modern history to a Hungarian. From now on, only non-Jewish Austrians, Magyars and Czechs had the right to teach at the university. Nevertheless I tried to get as much joy as I could from my new job as history teacher in high school.

After the Laws of July, came the decrees of May 1936. While the socialist revolution triumphed in France, with the French granting equality to the inhabitants of their far-flung colonies, and making Dakar the second capital of their nation, the Austro-Hungarian Empire was making its subjects increasingly unequal. Like many others, I had to bow to a total ban on Jews teaching anywhere, and be satisfied with a post as a clerk in the city archives. Many of my old colleagues preferred exile, but I was too fond of Emma and her parents to go to such an extreme. In 1939, we even lost the right to be public officials and I needed to live from hand to mouth while putting up with harassment from groups of self-styled "Young Aryans".

It was at this point that the Network contacted me.

I'd been aware of the existence of a mutual aid association for the victims of persecution, but I'd preferred to keep my distance. For one thing, such an association might be used as an excuse to validate some of the accusations that the powers-that-be made against us. Nevertheless, I agreed to join, if only in the hope that they might be able to help me leave the country if things turned really nasty.

About then, I received a letter from Albert, asking me to join him in Paris. The departure of many professors for the new universities set up in Africa or Indochina had resulted in vacancies, which meant interesting teaching opportunities for me in France. Albert also asked me to fetch him some papers he'd left at the university, which would be languishing in a cupboard.

This brought home to me how much things had changed for us Jewish people. I'd never really thought of myself as Jewish until I lost my right to teach. What's more, I was encumbered with an internal passport bearing a huge, reddish stamp which I had to show at almost every street corner; not to mention being obliged to wear a yellow star since 1938. In fact I couldn't even enter certain premises, as I found when I went to the university for Albert's papers. I think it was only that day when I became fully conscious, after a long time in the doldrums, of the extent of my humiliation and decided that I *had* to do something to stop this government from destroying us all. How well I recall the gate I'd gone through so many times in the past, and the policeman, belonging to the Party, disdainfully handing my passport back, barring my way, and advising me to make myself scarce before a gang of Young Aryans spotted me. It was true enough that former Jewish professors and civil servants were often beaten up or jeered at in the streets before the indifferent gaze of passers-by. And of course when the imperial police turned up, they merely dispersed the aggressors but never arrested any of them.

That very evening I decided to visit Rolf and Gertrud Oppenheim. They'd been good colleagues, almost friends, though I hadn't seen them since my expulsion. They admired Albert and certainly wouldn't refuse to help him.

They were still at the same place, a smart apartment in Franz-Josef Strasse. Outside their door my worn-out clothes, so often mended, and my old shoes made me ashamed. Of a sudden I imagined myself to be giving off the same tramp-like odour of misery and filth as had disgusted me in the past.

I rang the bell. A servant girl whom I didn't know opened the door. From within came the chatter of voices and then familiar music: one of those wonderful Schubert lieder. Evidently they were holding a reception, so I'd arrived at a bad moment. The servant girl took my card disgustedly, wrinkling her nose. "I'd be surprised if my master . . ."

But her master did come. Rolf had changed. He seemed older and fatter than since I quit the university. I too had altered for sure in the twenty years since that wonderful 1916 when both of us had journeyed across half of Europe from one railway to another!

Rolf seemed distinctly unthrilled to see me. He forced a meagre smile and darted an anxious glance along the hallway before letting me in. He didn't take me to the music room but to a closet where he would deal with tradesmen. Briefly I explained the help I needed; his features creased even as I spoke. Peals of laughter resounded; I thought I heard Gertrud's voice.

Rolf sighed. "No, Otto, I can't. Truly I can't." Just at that moment I noticed his Party badge, half-hidden by the handkerchief in his breast pocket.

"I understand," I said disappointedly. "How's Gertrud?"

"She's fine, thanks, and very busy with our guests."

Without asking after my own family or offering any other courtesy, he gripped me by the elbow and steered me to the door, which he shut smartly behind me.

I felt like vomiting.

I could have given up and told Albert that his papers had gone missing; but, I'm not sure why, it seemed vital to persevere. I tried to get help from two other colleagues, one of whom refused, wringing his hands and looking scared sick, while the other threw me out on the street before I even got a chance to explain the aim of my visit.

So I turned to the Network – whose first reaction was lukewarm. Albert's reputation was wobbly, and as for me, I'd only just joined them. They did appreciate that Albert hadn't lent support to the new regime, and wouldn't have dreamed of doing so, but at the same time they were scathing about him being so bound up in his research rather than taking an active stand against the political developments which the Emperor was condoning.

I first mentioned the matter of Albert's papers at a meeting following Hitler's speech in Salzburg, where he made his intentions crystal clear: to rid the Austro-Hungarian Empire of all resident Jews and restrict the Slavs to menial occupations. "It goes without saying," he'd thundered, "that Aryans aren't savages," and he'd specified that he personally would oversee the emigration of the Jews with full respect for rights and justice and especially "with no violence". As if exile from one's homeland wasn't the worst sort of violence.

Isaac Levinsky, the co-ordinator for our sector, adopted a defensive stance and my request was rejected. But as I was heading away from the meeting, I heard the quick patter of footsteps behind me. A young woman, whom I'd noticed earlier, though barely so, was trying to catch up. I stopped to wait for her.

"What are those papers you want to recover for Mr Einstein? You seem to think they're very important for our cause." She was short of breath and hadn't even bothered to introduce herself. Once I pointed this out, she said, "Pardon me. I'm Countess Ester Egerhazy."

"Are you Jewish?"

"Does one have to be Jewish to fight injustice?"

I couldn't help but smile at this reply, which seemed a bit theatrical. She smiled too. What a superb woman this Ester was: in her thirties, with skin like milk, big almond eyes under-lined with a touch of make-up, hair black as jet tied back in a bun on the nape of her neck, revealing single-pearl earrings dimpling her lobes.

"I can help you."

"I beg your pardon?" For a moment I'd forgotten all about my quest, but her offer yanked me back firmly to reality. What a sad contrast between this elegant, perfumed young aristocrat and the filthy vagabond I'd become.

"I can help you," she said again. "I attended your final course."

"At high school, you mean?"

"No, at the university. I'm older than I look. I can always get into places. If you'll tell me exactly what you're looking for, I can get it and give it to you."

I felt hesitant. The imperial secret police were well known for their efficiency. There was a high chance that Ester was one of their agents, now on a mission to gull me into revealing what sort of papers Albert was so keen to get back. What the hell. I'd have given anything for the chance of another tête-à-tête with Ester. So I described precisely what the papers were and where they ought to be.

A week went by. Anxiety and impatience gnawed at me. Emma willingly believed this was only due to the mission with which Albert had entrusted me.

On the appointed day, Ester was there. Discreetly she slipped me a package neatly wrapped in brown paper, and we strolled along together.

"Are you going to meet Mr Einstein?" she asked innocently, and I failed to answer yes because I remembered of a sudden that my trip ought to be kept secret.

"No, no," I mumbled, "I'll just have this sent to him."

"Maybe I might dare suggest . . . ?"

"Suggest what?"

"No, never mind. I was merely thinking that my husband has just been appointed Second Secretary at the Imperial Embassy in Paris. I could take charge of . . . "

"Thanks so much, but that's too much trouble to go to."

I'd hated her mentioning her husband. But equally, it came to me that I'd have a chance to see her again in France. I'd heard that President Pergaud loved to hold big receptions with a mixed guest list of intellectuals, diplomats, artists and politicians . . . I took Ester's hand and was about to kiss her fingers, but she stopped me and instead she hugged me and kissed me swiftly on both cheeks.

She blushed in embarrassment. "I really loved your style of teaching . . ."

Then she turned on her heel and vanished away into the night.

Two months later, I reached Paris at last, for mine had been a tough journey. If I'd left Austria officially, no one would have hindered me; I'd even have been given an emigration allowance so long as I gave up forever the right to return. I wasn't prepared to do so.

Some nights, while I was shivering in the mountains, I imagined high in the sky the huge airships which could make the journey in a couple of days, airships such as Ester and her husband must have taken. Sometimes I heard trains rumbling through the night.

That was just a nasty memory by now. I was safe, enjoying the comfort of the sofa in the lounge of the posh apartment on the Avenue du Maine where Albert lived with his family. While the maid served me a glass of port, Albert hastened to check the contents of the package which I'd had with me all that while.

"What's in there has something to do with the clock experiment, right? One of the clocks sent into the future . . ."

"Ah, you haven't forgotten . . . So many things have happened in the meantime . . ."

Of course I knew what was in those papers. I wasn't so daft as to transport that package halfway across Europe without the least idea what this was all about. I must admit that, apart from some pages referring to the experiment carried out on 6 February 1934, I couldn't understand much – except that this surely wasn't a hoax, and that Albert was one of the most brilliant minds in human history, so therefore there was a chance that travel through time was possible. I waited until the maid had left the room before asking what I was dying to know:

"Albert? Time travel? Do you believe it can happen?"

"Of course, since I sent this clock into the future, even if like everyone else that day you thought I was *cinglé*."

Albert had said the word for crazy in French. He seemed to have mastered the language marvelously. Now that he'd obtained French citizenship and been admitted to the Academy of Sciences, I wondered if one day he'd be a member of the Légion d'honneur. But that wasn't my main concern.

"And the *past*, Albert, do you think it's possible to travel back into the past too . . . and return?"

"In theory, that's no great problem. But in practical terms . . ."

My heart skipped a beat.

"What's the practical problem?"

"Well actually, what you're describing would take more energy because you'd need to send a second machine to accompany whatever you sent into the past, in order to allow retrieval. A second machine, with enough stored energy to power it. So frankly I don't think time tourism is on the cards any time soon."

I felt shattered. During those long nights spent under the stars or in some risky refuge, I'd gone over my notion again and again, considering every angle. But it would only work if travel into the past was doable. Now Albert had flat out squashed the idea. I decided to level with him.

He listened to me attentively, as was his way, and needless to say brilliance sparkled in his eyes, but I couldn't say that the basic idea enthused him. That his discovery could be used to shed blood didn't please him one bit. And yet he had to agree that what I was suggesting might be the best solution. But the problem of the energy source remained. In Vienna he'd used the energy produced by the prototype pile, and that only sent a clock weighing a few hundred grams three minutes into the future. As for what I envisaged . . .

Of a sudden he exclaimed, "We shan't be able to transport a person any time soon, Otto – but, short-term, there's an option you're neglecting! You don't need to go there yourself. All we need to do is open a window – quite a small one will do – and exchange the two objects, B for A. As for returning object A, I believe we could handle this with, well, let's call it an auto-glider."

"Meaning—?"

"Meaning it moves with its load and its own power unit, like an automobile."

"Can such a thing be made quickly?"

"Alas, it'll take several months since I'll have to go about this discreetly. You do understand that from now on we'll need to observe the utmost discretion?"

The following months dragged. I kept in touch with Albert through Ester when she returned to Vienna with her husband – I too had gone back there as clandestinely as I'd left. Emma had thrown me out and the situation was getting worse by the day. Pogroms were reported in the regions of Salzburg, Timifloara, Lake Balaton and Carinthia. In Turkey, the progressive government of Mustapha Kemal's successors, which had massacred the Armenians and forced the survivors into exile, were rattling sabres, seeing a chance to grab territory from the Empire in disarray.

The situation was growing tense everywhere. Csar Michael had appointed old social democrat leader Kerensky as Prime Minister; so a united front was on the go from Saint Petersburg to Madrid, including Berlin where a revolutionary government had kicked out the old Kaiser and proclaimed a republic – which promptly went on to establish a long-term alliance with France in exchange for partial return of the areas confiscated in 1871 along with the breaking off of diplomatic and commercial relations with Franz-Ferdinand. Prince Otto, whom I liked not merely because we shared the same name, had publicly broken with his father and quit the country. All of this intensified my determination.

Through the Network, with the help of the Slav Resistance Front, I was able to get photos and detailed notes about the room in Sarajevo which Albert would need to carry out the plan; fortunately it seemed the room was just as it had been.

Things were getting urgent. It was already April 1943, and Franz-Ferdinand had surprised everyone by declaring his support for the Pact of Ceuta, and in this very same month the two other signatories to the pact, Franco and Gamelin, rebelled against their respective governments.

This didn't suit the business we had in hand, not one little bit. Albert let me know, via Ester, that he'd been registered as a suspect person and suspended from teaching because he hadn't spoken out clearly enough against the rebellions. Of course this delayed his work on our project.

I must confess I felt so discouraged that I thought of throwing in the towel even though I was well aware that our plan was the only thing that could stop our twentieth century from becoming known to history as the era of a world war, which I could see fast approaching.

With the shock of the Japanese landing in California in July, and the occupation of Provence by Gamelin a month later, matters became even more pressing. If we did nothing, the world was rushing towards doom. We absolutely had to succeed and there was no time to waste.

Another problem was that Fermi was supporting Mussolini's national fascist government in Italy. But Albert let me know, always by way of Ester, that he hoped he still had enough contact with the scientific community to be sure of access to the necessary energy when the moment came. Nevertheless, he had to decamp, this time to Germany, which meant more delay.

Thus far, war was raging in Spain and in the French colonial empire as well as in the USA; the Americans were hard put to block the Japanese advance at the Rocky Mountains. Meanwhile, my own life was getting harder. We were totally at the mercy of Hitler's gangs of thugs, abusing and assaulting us freely. I'd started attending the synagogue and became friends with the rabbi, Eliazar Ben Rahhem, with whom I studied the Torah twice a week. The rest of the time I spent struggling to survive, mostly by giving lessons to the kids of our community, who weren't allowed into the state schools any more.

Ester's husband was now ambassador in Rio de Janeiro, at the cost of leaving his wife behind – there was some Jewish blood in her ancestry. She let me know that she was now under surveillance; contact between us was increasingly difficult.

By the start of 1945 I was seriously thinking of giving up and going to join our people's settlements in Palestine. Then the Emperor suddenly banned all emigration and decided to gather all the Jews into special camps. Happily for me, the Network helped me get out of Austria so that I could finally meet Albert and hand over the object which Ester had managed to get to me the day before her arrest. Namely, the very gun which the Crime Department of the Ministry of the Interior had kept stored in the capital. In Berlin a gunmaker friend, to whom I couldn't of course spill the beans, quickly worked out why the pistol had jammed and supplied me with an identical, but functioning, twin.

In September Albert and I both took up residence in Munich where we could now work together. At last Comrade Albert (as one needed to call oneself under Rosa Luxemburg's regime) and I had almost reached our goal. Munich was the right place to be because of its close proximity to the German Energy Commissariat, which now had a Fermi-style pile in operation. Albert managed to get me a post as a secretary in the Physics department of the university, and in any spare time I worked on the necessary geographical co-ordinates while he was busy perfecting the autoglider. A wit once said that history is geography in practice, yet I had to be so exact with the maps and large-scale street plans.

Even though I can't go into too much detail, I think that I can safely say that with the help of the Network I managed to have a beacon sent to Sarajevo to be installed inside the wall just above the table, in the drawer of which the man had confessed during his pre-trial interrogation to having kept his pistol. Whereupon Albert installed the geographic co-ordinates, then proceeded to adjust the device "bite by bite", as he put it, to the date that concerned us.

I received news of Ester from a woman writer who'd been interned with her before being expelled, because of some quibblings about her national origin. This woman, Milena Jesenska, made no secret of how much worse conditions were in those special camps than anyone imagined. There'd been typhus epidemics. My poor Ester! I couldn't help thinking that I was partly to blame for what had happened to her. We absolutely had to succeed!

I can hardly believe it: the moment has come! Today, we did it. We met up at the nuclear lab at Dachau. The countryside was glorious in the May sunshine. In the morning I'd thought about Emma. Her birthday was on the 8 May . . . May the Lord (bless His name!) help me forget what she did to me. But in a few minutes that won't matter and even the sheets of paper I'm writing on probably won't have existed. Our task will be accomplished: Franz-Ferdinand will never have been the Emperor of Austria, never will he have called Hitler to power, and the twentieth century will be known to history as the century which brought happiness and prosperity to humanity.

I'm content. The involvement of a historian was essential to settle on the crucial moment as being the failed assassination attempt in Sarajevo, on the 28 June 1914. How often have we thought during the past years: "If only Prinzip's pistol *hadn't* jammed . . ."

Well, in ten minutes, that'll be it. Gavril Prinzip will be known as the one who assassinated Franz-Ferdinand, the world will be at peace and I, here in Dachau, will enjoy the happy tranquillity of a nice spring day, not even knowing what I've escaped.

Translated from the French by Sissy Pantelis and Ian Watson

Tales From the Venia Woods

Robert Silverberg

This all happened a long time ago, in the early decades of the Second Republic, when I was a boy growing up in Upper Pannonia.

Life was very simple then, at least for us. We lived in a forest village on the right bank of the Danubius, my parents, my grandmother, my sister Friya, and I. My father Tyr, for whom I am named, was a blacksmith, my mother Julia taught school in our house, and my grandmother was the priestess at the little Temple of Juno Teutonica nearby.

It was a very quiet life. The automobile hadn't yet been invented then – all this was around the year 2650, and we still used horse-drawn carriages or wagons – and we hardly ever left the village. Once a year, on Augustus Day – back then we still celebrated Augustus Day – we would all dress in our finest clothes and my father would get our big iron-bound carriage out of the shed, the one he had built with his own hands, and we'd drive to the great municipium of Venia, a two-hour journey away, to hear the imperial band playing waltzes in the Plaza of Vespasian. Afterwards there'd be cakes and whipped cream at the big hotel nearby, and tankards of cherry beer for the grown-ups, and then we'd begin the long trip home. Today, of course, the forest is gone and our little village has been swallowed up by the ever-growing municipium, and it's a twenty-minute ride by car to the center of the city from where we used to live. But at that time it was a grand excursion, the event of the year for us. I know now that Venia is only a minor provincial city, that compared with Londin or Parisi or Roma itself it's nothing at all. But to me it was the capital of the world. Its splendors stunned me and dazed me. We would climb to the top of the great column of Basileus Andronicus, which the Greeks put up 800 years ago to commemorate their victory over Caesar Maximilianus during the Civil War in the days when the Empire was divided, and we'd stare out at the whole city; and my mother, who had grown up in Venia, would point everything out to us, the senate building, the opera house, the aqueduct, the university, the ten bridges, the Temple of Jupiter Teutonicus, the proconsul's palace, the much greater palace that Trajan VII built for himself during that dizzying period when Venia was essentially the second capital of the Empire, and so forth. For days afterwards my dreams would glitter with memories of what I had seen in Venia, and my sister and I would hum waltzes as we whirled along the quiet forest paths.

There was one exciting year when we made the Venia trip twice. That was 2647, when I was ten years old, and I can remember it so exactly because that was the year when the First Consul died – C. Junius Scaevola, I mean, the Founder of the Second Republic. My father was very agitated when the news of his death came. "It'll be touch and go now, touch and go, mark my words," he said over and over. I asked my grandmother what he meant by that, and she said, "Your father's afraid that they'll bring back the Empire, now that the old man's dead." I didn't see what was so upsetting about that – it was all the same to me, Republic or Empire, Consul or Imperator – but to my father it was a big issue, and when the new First Consul came to Venia later that year, touring the entire vast Imperium province by province for the sake of reassuring everyone that the Republic was stable and intact, my father got out the carriage and we went to attend his Triumph and Processional. So I had a second visit to the capital that year.

Half a million people, so they say, turned out in downtown Venia to applaud the new First Consul. This was N. Marcellus Turritus, of course. You probably think of him as the fat, bald old man on the coinage of the late twenty-seventh century that still shows up in pocket change now and then, but the man I saw that day – I had just a glimpse of him, a fraction of a second as the consular chariot rode past, but the memory still blazes in my mind seventy years later – was lean and virile, with a jutting jaw and fiery eyes and dark, thick curling hair. We threw up our arms in the old Roman salute and at the top of our lungs we shouted out to him, "Hail, Marcellus! Long live the Consul!" (We shouted it, by the way, not in Latin but in Germanisch. I was very surprised at that. My father explained afterwards that it was by the First Consul's own orders. He wanted to show his love for the people by encouraging all the regional languages, even at a public celebration like this one. The Gallians had hailed him in Gallian, the Britannians in Britannic, the Japanese in whatever it is they speak there, and as he travelled through the Teutonic provinces he wanted us to yell his praises in Germanisch. I realize that there are some people today, very conservative Republicans, who will tell you that this was a terrible idea, because it has led to the resurgence of all kinds of separatist regional activities in the Imperium. It was the same sort of regionalist fervor, they remind us, that brought about the crumbling of the Empire two hundred years earlier. To men like my father, though, it was a brilliant political stroke, and he cheered the new First Consul with tremendous Germanische exuberance and vigor. But my father managed to be a staunch regionalist and a staunch Republican at the same time. Bear in mind that over my mother's fierce objections he had insisted on naming his children for ancient Teutonic gods instead of giving them the standard Roman names that everybody else in Pannonia favored then.) Other than going to Venia once a year, or on this one occasion twice, I never went anywhere. I hunted, I fished, I swam, I helped my father in the smithy, I helped my grandmother in the Temple, I studied reading and writing in my mother's school. Sometimes Friya and I would go wandering in the forest, which in those days was dark and lush and mysterious. And that was how I happened to meet the last of the Caesars.

There was supposed to be a haunted house deep in the woods. Marcus Aurelius Schwarzchild it was who got me interested in it, the tailor's son, a sly and unlikable boy with a cast in one eye.

He said it had been a hunting lodge in the time of the Caesars, and that the bloody ghost of an Emperor who had been killed in a hunting accident could be seen at noontime, the hour of his death, pursuing the ghost of a wolf around and around the building. "I've seen it myself," he said. "The ghost, I mean. He had a laurel wreath on, and everything, and his rifle was polished so it shined like gold."

I didn't believe him. I didn't think he'd had the courage to go anywhere near the haunted house and certainly not that he'd seen the ghost. Marcus Aurelius Schwarzchild was the sort of boy you wouldn't believe if he said it was raining, even if you were getting soaked to the skin right as he was saying it. For one thing, I didn't believe in ghosts, not very much. My father had told me it was foolish to think that the dead still lurked around in the world of the living. For another, I asked my grandmother if there had ever been an Emperor killed in a hunting accident in our forest, and she laughed and said no, not ever: the Imperial Guard would have razed the village to the ground and burned down the woods, if that had ever happened.

But nobody doubted that the house itself, haunted or not, was really there. Everyone in the village knew that. It was said to be in a certain dark part of the woods where the trees were so old that their branches were tightly woven together. Hardly anyone ever went there. The house was just a ruin, they said, and haunted besides, definitely haunted, so it was best to leave it alone.

It occurred to me that the place might just actually have been an imperial hunting lodge, and that if it had been abandoned hastily after some unhappy incident and never visited since, it might still have some trinkets of the Caesars in it, little statuettes of the gods, or cameos of the royal family, things like that. My grandmother collected small ancient objects of that sort. Her birthday was coming, and I wanted a nice gift for her. My fellow villagers might be timid about poking around in the haunted house, but why should I be? I didn't believe in ghosts, after all. But on second thought I didn't particularly want to go there alone. This wasn't cowardice so much as sheer common sense, which even then I possessed in full measure. The woods were full of exposed roots hidden under fallen leaves; if you tripped on one and hurt your leg, you would lie there a long time before anyone who might help you came by. You were also less likely to lose your way if you had someone else with you who could remember trail marks.

And there was some occasional talk of wolves. I figured the probability of my meeting one wasn't much better than the likelihood of ghosts, but all the same it seemed like a sensible idea to have a companion with me in that part of the forest. So I took my sister along.

I have to confess that I didn't tell her that the house was supposed to be haunted. Friya, who was about nine then, was very brave for a girl, but I thought she might find the possibility of ghosts a little discouraging. What I did tell her was that the old house might still have imperial treasures in it, and if it did she could have her pick of any jewelry we found. Just to be on the safe side we slipped a couple of holy images into our pockets – Apollo for her, to cast light on us as we went through the dark woods, and Woden for me, since he was my father's special god. (My grandmother always wanted him to pray to Jupiter Teutonicus, but he never would, saying that Jupiter Teutonicus was a god that the Romans invented to pacify our ancestors. This made my grandmother angry, naturally. "But 'we' are Romans," she would say. "Yes, we are," my father would tell her, "but we're Teutons also, or at least I am, and I don't intend to forget it.")

It was a fine Saturday morning in spring when we set out, Friya and I, right after breakfast, saying nothing to anybody about where we were going. The first part of the forest path was a familiar one: we had traveled it often. We went past Agrippina's Spring, which in medieval times was thought to have magical powers, and then the three battered and weather-beaten statues of the pretty young boy who was supposed to be the first Emperor Hadrianus's lover 2,000 years ago, and after that we came to Baldur's Tree, which my father said was sacred, though he died before I was old enough to attend the midnight rituals that he and some of his friends used to hold there. (I think my father's generation was the last one that took the old Teutonic religion seriously.)

Then we got into deeper, darker territory. The paths were nothing more than sketchy trails here. Marcus Aurelius had told me that we were supposed to turn left at a huge old oak tree with unusual glossy leaves. I was still looking for it when Friya said, "We turn here," and there was the shiny-leaved oak. I hadn't mentioned it to her. So perhaps the girls of our village told each other tales about the haunted house too; but I never found out how she knew which way to go. Onward and onward we went, until even the trails gave out, and we were wandering through sheer wilderness. The trees were ancient here, all right, and their boughs were interlaced high above us so that almost no sunlight reached the forest floor. But we didn't see any houses, haunted or otherwise, or anything else that indicated human beings had ever been here. We'd been hiking for hours, now. I kept one hand on the idol of Woden in my pocket and I stared hard at every unusual-looking tree or rock we saw, trying to engrave it on my brain for use as a trail marker on the way back. It seemed pointless to continue, and dangerous besides. I would have turned back long before, if Friya hadn't been with me; but I didn't want to look like a coward in front of her. And she was forging on in a tireless way, inflamed, I guess, by the prospect of finding a fine brooch or necklace for herself in the old house, and showing not the slightest trace of fear or uneasiness. But finally I had had enough.

"If we don't come across anything in the next five minutes . . . I said.

"There," said Friya. "Look."

I followed her pointing hand. At first all I saw was more forest. But then I noticed, barely visible behind a curtain of leafy branches, what could have been the sloping wooden roof of a rustic hunting lodge. Yes! Yes, it was! I saw the scalloped gables, I saw the boldly carved roof-posts. So it was really there, the secret forest lodge, the old haunted house. In frantic excitement I began to run towards it, Friya chugging valiantly along behind me, struggling to catch up. And then I saw the ghost. He was old – ancient – a frail, gaunt figure, white-bearded, his long white hair a tangle of knots and snarls. His clothing hung in rags. He was walking slowly towards the house, shuffling, really, a bent and stooped and trembling figure clutching a huge stack of kindling to his breast. I was practically on top of him before I knew he was there.

For a long moment we stared at each other, and I can't say which of us was the more terrified. Then he made a little sighing sound and let his bundle of firewood fall to the ground, and fell down beside it, and lay there like one dead. "Marcus Aurelius was right!" I murmured. "There really is a ghost here!" Friya shot me a glance that must have been a mixture of scorn and derision and real anger besides, for this was the first she had heard of the ghost story that I had obviously taken pains to conceal from her. But all she said was, "Ghosts don't fall down and faint, silly. He's nothing but a scared old man." And went to him unhesitatingly.

Somehow we got him inside the house, though he tottered and lurched all the way and nearly fell half a dozen times. The place wasn't quite a ruin, but close: dust everywhere, furniture that looked as if it'd collapse into splinters if you touched it, draperies hanging in shreds. Behind all the filth we could see how beautiful it all once had been, though. There were faded paintings on the walls, some sculptures, a collection of arms and armor worth a fortune.

He was terrified of us. "Are you from the quaestors?" he kept asking. Latin was what he spoke. "Are you here to arrest me? I'm only the caretaker, you know. I'm not any kind of a danger. I'm only the caretaker." His lips quavered. "Long live the First Consul!" he cried, in a thin, hoarse, ragged croak of a voice.

"We were just wandering in the woods," I told him. "You don't have to be afraid of us."

"I'm only the caretaker," he said again and again.

We laid him out on a couch. There was a spring just outside the house, and Friya brought water from it and sponged his cheeks and brow. He looked half starved, so we prowled around for something to feed him, but there was hardly anything: some nuts and berries in a bowl, a few scraps of smoked meat that looked like they were a hundred years old, a piece of fish that was in better shape, but not much. We fixed a meal for him, and he ate slowly, very slowly, as if he were unused to food. Then he closed his eyes without a word. I thought for a moment that he had died, but no, no, he had simply dozed off. We stared at each other, not knowing what to do.

"Let him be," Friya whispered, and we wandered around the house while we waited for him to awaken. Cautiously we touched the sculptures, we blew dust away from the paintings. No doubt of it, there had been imperial grandeur here. In one of the upstairs cupboards I found some coins, old ones, the kind with the Emperor's head on them that weren't allowed to be used any more. I saw trinkets, too, a couple of necklaces and a jewel-handled dagger. Friya's eyes gleamed at the sight of the necklaces, and mine at the dagger, but we let everything stay where it was. Stealing from a ghost is one thing, stealing from a live old man is another. And we hadn't been raised to be thieves.

When we went back downstairs to see how he was doing, we found him sitting up, looking weak and dazed, but not quite so frightened. Friya offered him some more of the smoked meat, but he smiled and shook his head.

"From the village, are you? How old are you? What are your names?"

"This is Friya," I said. "I'm Tyr. She's nine and I'm twelve."

"Friya. Tyr." He laughed. "Time was when such names wouldn't have been permitted, eh? But times have changed." There was a flash of sudden vitality in his eyes, though only for an instant. He gave us a confidential, intimate smile. "Do you know whose place this was, you two? The Emperor Maxentius, that's who! This was his hunting lodge. Caesar himself! He'd stay here when the stags were running, and hunt his fill, and then he'd go on into Venia, to Trajan's palace, and there'd be such feasts as you can't imagine, rivers of wine, and the haunches of venison turning on the spit – ah, what a time that was, what a time!"

He began to cough and sputter. Friya put her arm around his thin shoulders.

"You shouldn't talk so much, sir. You don't have the strength."

"You're right. You're right." He patted her hand. His was like a skeleton's. "How long ago it all was. But here I stay, trying to keep the place up – in case Caesar ever wanted to hunt here again – in case – in case—" A look of torment, of sorrow. "There isn't any Caesar, is there? First Consul! Hail! Hail Junius Scaevola!" His voice cracked as he raised it.

"The Consul Junius is dead, sir," I told him. "Marcus Turritus is First Consul now."

"Dead? Scaevola? Is it so?" He shrugged. "I hear so little news. I'm only the caretaker, you know. I never leave the place. Keeping it up, in case – in case—"

But of course he wasn't the caretaker. Friya never thought he was: she had seen, right away, the resemblance between that shriveled old man and the magnificent figure of Caesar Maxentius in the painting behind him on the wall. You had to ignore the difference in age – the Emperor couldn't have been much more than thirty when his portrait was painted – and the fact that the Emperor was in resplendent bemedalled formal uniform and the old man was wearing rags. But they had the same long chin, the same sharp, hawklike nose, the same penetrating icy-blue eyes. It was the royal face, all right. I hadn't noticed; but girls have a quicker eye for such things. The Emperor Maxentius' youngest brother was who this gaunt old man was, Quintus Fabius Caesar, the last survivor of the old imperial house, and, therefore, the true Emperor himself. Who had been living in hiding ever since the downfall of the Empire at the end of the Second War of Reunification.

He didn't tell us any of that, though, until our third or fourth visit. He went on pretending he was nothing but a simple old man who had happened to be stranded here when the old regime was overthrown, and was simply trying to do his job, despite the difficulties of age, on the chance that the royal family might some day be restored and would want to use its hunting lodge again. But he began to give us little gifts, and that eventually led to his admitting his true identity.

For Friya he had a delicate necklace made of long slender

bluish beads. "It comes from Aiguptos," he said. "It's thousands of years old. You've studied Aiguptos in school, haven't you? You know that it was a great empire long before Roma ever was?" And with his own trembling hands he put it around her neck.

That same day he gave me a leather pouch in which I found four or five triangular arrowheads made of a pink stone that had been carefully chipped sharp around the edges. I looked at them, mystified. "From Nova Roma," he explained. "Where the redskinned people live. The Emperor Maxentius loved Nova Roma, especially the far west, where the bison herds are. He went there almost every year to hunt. Do you see the trophies?" And, indeed, the dark musty room was lined with animal heads, great massive bison with thick curling brown wool, glowering down out of the gallery high above.

We brought him food, sausages and black bread that we brought from home, and fresh fruit, and beer. He didn't care for the beer, and asked rather timidly if we could bring him wine instead. "I am Roman, you know," he reminded us. Getting wine for him wasn't so easy, since we never used it at home, and a twelve-year-old boy could hardly go around to the wineshop to buy some without starting tongues wagging. In the end I stole some from the Temple while I was helping out my grandmother. It was thick sweet wine, the kind used for offerings, and I don't know how much he liked it. But he was grateful. Apparently an old couple who lived on the far side of the woods had looked after him for some years, bringing him food and wine, but in recent weeks they hadn't been around and he had had to forage for himself, with little luck: that was why he was so gaunt. He was afraid they were ill or dead, but when I asked where they lived, so I could find out whether they were all right, he grew uneasy and refused to tell me. I wondered about that. If I had realized then who he was, and that the old couple must have been Empire loyalists, I'd have understood. But I still hadn't figured out the truth.

Friya broke it to me that afternoon, as we were on our way home. "Do you think he's the Emperor's brother, Tyr? Or the Emperor himself?"

"What?"

"He's got to be one or the other. It's the same face."

"I don't know what you're talking about, sister."

"The big portrait on the wall, silly. Of the Emperor. Haven't you noticed that it looks just like him?"

I thought she was out of her mind. But when we went back the following week, I gave the painting a long close look, and looked at him, and then at the painting again, and I thought, yes, yes, it might just be so.

What clinched it were the coins he gave us that day. "I can't pay you in money of the Republic for all you've brought me," he said. "But you can have these. You can't spend them, but they're still valuable to some people, I understand. As relics of history." His voice was bitter. From a worn old velvet pouch he drew out half a dozen coins, some copper, some silver. "These are coins of Maxentius," he said. They were like the ones we had seen while snooping in the upstairs cupboards on our first visit, showing the same face as on the painting, that of a young, vigorous bearded man. "And these are older ones, coins of Emperor Laureolus, who was Caesar when I was a boy."

"Why, he looks just like you!" I blurted.

Indeed he did. Not nearly so gaunt, and his hair and beard were better trimmed; but otherwise the face of the regal old man on those coins might easily have been that of our friend the caretaker. I stared at him, and at the coins in my hand, and again at him. He began to tremble. I looked at the painting on the wall behind us again. "No," he said faintly. "No, no, you're mistaken – I'm nothing like him, nothing at all—" And his shoulders shook and he began to cry. Friya brought him some wine, which steadied him a little. He took the coins from me and looked at them in silence a long while, shaking his head sadly, and finally handed them back. "Can I trust you with a secret?" he asked. And his tale came pouring out of him.

A glittering boyhood, almost sixty years earlier, in that wondrous time between the two Wars of Reunification: a magical life, endlessly traveling from palace to palace, from Roma to Venia, from Venia to Constantinopolis, from Constantinopolis to Nishapur. He was the youngest and most pampered of five royal princes; his father had died young, drowned in a foolish swimming exploit, and when his grand-father Laureolus Caesar died the imperial throne would go to his brother Maxentius. He himself, Quintus Fabius, would be a provincial governor somewhere when he grew up, perhaps in India or Nova Roma, but for now there was nothing for him to do but enjoy his gilded existence.

Then death came at last to old Emperor Laureolus, and Maxentius succeeded him; and almost at once there began the six-year horror of the Second War of Reunification, when somber and harsh colonels who despised the lazy old Empire smashed it to pieces, rebuilt it as a Republic, and drove the Caesars from power. We knew the story, of course; but to us it was a tale of the triumph of virtue and honor over corruption and tyranny. To Quintus Fabius, weeping as he told it to us from his own point of view, the fall of the Empire had been not only a harrowing personal tragedy but a terrible disaster for the entire world.

Good little Republicans though we were, our hearts were wrung by the things he told us, the scenes of his family's agony: the young Emperor Maxentius trapped in his own palace, gunned down with his wife and children at the entrance to the imperial baths. Camillus, the second brother, who had been Prince of Constantinopolis, pursued through the streets of Roma at dawn and slaughtered by revolutionaries on the steps of the Temple of Castor and Pollux.

Prince Flavius, the third brother, escaping from the capital in a peasant's wagon, hidden under huge bunches of grapes, and setting up a government-in-exile in Neapolis, only to be taken and executed before he had been Emperor a full week. Which brought the succession down to sixteen-year-old Prince Augustus, who had been at the university in Parisi. Well named, he was: for the first of all the Emperors was an Augustus, and another one 2,000 years later was the last, reigning all of three days before the men of the Second Republic found him and put him before the firing squad.

Of the royal princes, only Quintus Fabius remained. But in the confusion he was overlooked. He was hardly more than a boy; and, although technically he was now Caesar, it never occurred to him to claim the throne. Loyalist supporters dressed him in peasant clothes and smuggled him out of Roma while the capital was still in flames, and he set out on what was to become a lifetime of exile.

"There were always places for me to stay," he told us. "In out-of-the-way towns where the Republic had never really taken hold, in backwater provinces, in places you've never heard of. The Republic searched for me for a time, but never very well, and then the story began to circulate that I was dead. The skeleton of some boy found in the ruins of the palace in Roma was said to be mine.

"After that I could move around more or less freely, though always in poverty, always in secrecy."

"And when did you come here?" I asked.

"Almost twenty years ago. Friends told me that this hunting lodge was here, still more or less intact as it had been at the time of the Revolution, and that no one ever went near it, that I could live here undisturbed. And so I have. And so I will, for however much time is left." He reached for the wine, but his hands were shaking so badly that Friya took it from him and poured him a glass. He drank it in a single gulp. "Ah, children, children, what a world you've lost! What madness it was, to destroy the Empire! What greatness existed then!"

"Our father says things have never been so good for ordinary folk as they are under the Republic," Friya said.

I kicked her ankle. She gave me a sour look.

Quintus Fabius said sadly, "I mean no disrespect, but your father sees only his own village. We were trained to see the entire world in a glance. The Imperium, the whole globe-spanning Empire. Do you think the gods meant to give the Imperium just to anyone at all? Anyone who could grab power and proclaim himself First Consul? Ah, no, no, the Caesars were uniquely chosen to sustain the Pax Romana, the universal peace that has enfolded this whole planet for so long. Under us there was nothing but peace, peace eternal and unshakeable, once the Empire had reached its complete form. But with the Caesars now gone, how much longer do you think the peace will last? If one man can take power, so can another, or another. There will be five First Consuls at once, mark my words. Or fifty. And every province will want to be an Empire in itself. Mark my words, children. Mark my words."

I had never heard such treason in my life. Or anything so wrongheaded. The Pax Romana? What Pax Romana? Old Quintus Fabius would have had us believe that the Empire had brought unbroken and unshakeable peace to the entire world, and had kept it that way for twenty centuries. But what about the Civil War, when the Greek half of the Empire fought for fifty years against the Latin half? Or the two Wars of Unification? And hadn't there been minor rebellions constantly, all over the Empire, hardly a century without one, in Persia, in India, in Britannica, in Africa Aethiopica? No, I thought, what he's telling us simply isn't true. The long life of the Empire had been a time of constant brutal oppression, with people's spirits held in check everywhere by military force. The real Pax Romana was something that existed only in modern times, under the Second Republic. So my father had taught me.

But Quintus Fabius was an old man, wrapped in dreams of his own wondrous lost childhood. Far be it from me to argue with him about such matters as these. I simply smiled and nodded, and poured more wine for him when his glass was empty. And Friya and I sat there spellbound as he told us, hour after hour, of what it had been like to be a prince of the royal family in the dying days of the Empire, before true grandeur had departed forever from the world.

When we left him that day, he had still more gifts for us. "My brother was a great collector," he said. "He had whole houses stuffed full of treasure. All gone now, all but what you see here, which no one remembered. When I'm gone, who knows what'll become of them? But I want you to have these. Because you've been so kind to me. To remember me by. And to remind you always of what once was, and now is lost."

For Friya there was a small bronze ring, dented and scratched, with a serpent's head on it, that he said had belonged to the Emperor Claudius of the earliest days of the Empire. For me a dagger, not the jewel-handled one I had seen upstairs, but a fine one all the same, with a strange undulating blade, from a savage kingdom on an island in the Oceanus Magnus. And for us both, a beautiful little figurine in smooth white alabaster of Pan playing on his pipes, carved by some master craftsman of the ancient days.

The figurine was the perfect birthday gift for grandmother. We gave it to her the next day. We thought she would be pleased, since all of the old gods of Roma are very dear to her; but to our surprise and dismay she seemed startled and upset by it. She stared at it, eyes bright and fierce, as if we had given her a venomous toad.

"Where did you get this thing? Where?"

I looked at Friya, to warn her not to say too much. But as usual she was ahead of me.

"We found it, grandmother. We dug it up."

"You dug it up?"

"In the forest," I put in. "We go there every Saturday, you know, just wandering around. There was this old mound of dirt – we were poking in it, and we saw something gleaming—"

She turned it over and over in her hands. I had never seen her look so troubled. "Swear to me that that's how you found it! Come, now, at the altar of Juno! I want you to swear to me before the Goddess. And then I want you to take me to see this mound of dirt of yours."

Friya gave me a panic-stricken glance.

Hesitantly I said, "We may not be able to find it again, grandmother. I told you, we were just wandering around – we didn't really pay attention to where we were—"

I grew red in the face, and I was stammering, too. It isn't easy to lie convincingly to your own grandmother.

She held the figurine out, its base towards me. "Do you see these marks here? This little crest stamped down here? It's the Imperial crest, Tyr. That's the mark of Caesar. This carving once belonged to the Emperor. Do you expect me to believe that there's Imperial treasure simply lying around in mounds of dirt in the forest? Come, both of you! To the altar, and swear!"

"We only wanted to bring you a pretty birthday gift, grandmother," Friya said softly. "We didn't mean to do any harm."

"Of course not, child. Tell me, now: where'd this thing come from?"

"The haunted house in the woods," she said. And I nodded my confirmation. What could I do? She would have taken us to the altar to swear.

Strictly speaking, Friya and I were traitors to the Republic. We even knew that ourselves, from the moment we realized who the old man really was. The Caesars were proscribed when the Empire fell; everyone within a certain level of blood kinship to the Emperor was condemned to death, so that no one could rise up and claim the throne in years hereafter.

Some minor members of the royal family did manage to escape, so it was said; but giving aid and comfort to them was a serious offense. And this was no mere second cousin or great-grandnephew that we had discovered deep in the forest: this was the Emperor's own brother. He was, in fact, the legitimate Emperor himself, in the eyes of those for whom the Empire had never ended. And it was our responsibility to turn him in to the quaestors. But he was so old, so gentle, so feeble. We didn't see how he could be much of a threat to the Republic. Even if he did believe that the Revolution had been an evil thing, and that only under a divinely chosen Caesar could the world enjoy real peace.

We were children. We didn't understand what risks we were taking, or what perils we were exposing our family to. Things were tense at our house during the next few days: whispered conferences between our grandmother and our mother, out of our earshot, and then an evening when the two of them spoke with father while Friya and I were confined to our room, and there were sharp words and even some shouting. Afterwards there was a long cold silence, followed by more mysterious discussions. Then things returned to normal. My grandmother never put the figurine of Pan in her collection of little artefacts of the old days, nor did she ever speak of it again.

That it had the imperial crest on it was, we realized, the cause of all the uproar. Even so, we weren't clear about what the problem was. I had thought all along that grandmother was secretly an Empire loyalist herself. A lot of people her age were; and she was, after all, a traditionalist, a priestess of Juno

Teutonica, who disliked the revived worship of the old Germanic gods that had sprung up in recent times – "pagan" gods, she called them – and had argued with father about his insistence on naming us as he had.

So she should have been pleased to have something that had belonged to the Caesars. But, as I say, we were children then. We didn't take into account the fact that the Republic dealt harshly with anyone who practiced Caesarism. Or that whatever my grandmother's private political beliefs might have been, father was the unquestioned master of our household, and he was a devout Republican.

"I understand you've been poking around that old ruined house in the woods," my father said, a week or so later. "Stay away from it. Do you hear me? Stay away."

And so we would have, because it was plainly an order. We didn't disobey our father's orders.

But then, a few days afterwards, I overheard some of the older boys of the village talking about making a foray out to the haunted house. Evidently Marcus Aurelius Schwarzchild had been talking about the ghost with the polished rifle to others beside me, and they wanted the rifle. "It's five of us against one of him," I heard someone say. "We ought to be able to take care of him, ghost or not."

"What if it's a ghost rifle, though?" one of them asked. "A ghost rifle won't be any good to us."

"There's no such thing as a ghost rifle," the first speaker said. "Rifles don't have ghosts. It's a real rifle. And it won't be hard for us to get it away from a ghost."

I repeated all this to Friya.

"What should we do?" I asked her.

"Go out there and warn him. They'll hurt him, Tyr."

"But father said—"

"Even so. The old man's got to go somewhere and hide. Other wise his blood will be on our heads."

There was no arguing with her. Either I went with her to the house in the woods that moment, or she'd go by herself. That left me with no choice. I prayed to Woden that my father wouldn't find out, or that he'd forgive me if he did; and off we went into the woods, past Agrippina's spring, past the statues of the pretty boy, past Baldur's Tree, and down the now familiar path beyond the glossy-leaved oak.

"Something's wrong," Friya said, as we approached the hunting lodge. "I can tell."

Friya always had a strange way of knowing things. I saw the fear in her eyes and felt frightened myself.

We crept forward warily. There was no sign of Quintus Fabius. And when we came to the door of the lodge we saw that it was a little way ajar, and off its hinges, as if it had been forced.

Friya put her hand on my arm and we stared at each other. I took a deep breath.

"You wait here," I said, and went in.

It was frightful in there. The place had been ransacked – the furniture smashed, the cupboards overturned, the sculptures in fragments. Someone had slashed every painting to shreds. The collection of arms and armor was gone.

I went from room to room, looking for Quintus Fabius. He wasn't there. But there were bloodstains on the floor of the main hall, still fresh, still sticky.

Friya was waiting on the porch, trembling, fighting back tears.

"We're too late," I told her.

It hadn't been the boys from the village, of course. They couldn't possibly have done such a thorough job. I realized – and surely so did Friya, though we were both too sickened by the realization to discuss it with each other – that grandmother must have told father we had found a cache of Imperial treasure in the old house, and he, good citizen that he was, had told the quaestors.

Who had gone out to investigate, come upon Quintus Fabius, and recognized him for a Caesar, just as Friya had. So my eagerness to bring back a pretty gift for grandmother had been the old man's downfall. I suppose he wouldn't have lived much longer in any case, as frail as he was; but the guilt for what I unknowingly brought upon him is something that I've borne ever since.

Some years later, when the forest was mostly gone, the old

house accidentally burned down. I was a young man then, and I helped out on the firefighting line. During a lull in the work I said to the captain of the fire brigade, a retired quaestor named Lucentius, "It was an Imperial hunting lodge once, wasn't it?"

"A long time ago, yes."

I studied him cautiously by the light of the flickering blaze.

He was an older man, of my father's generation.

Carefully I said, "When I was a boy, there was a story going around that one of the last Emperor's brothers had hidden himself away in it. And that eventually the quaestors caught him and killed him."

He seemed taken off guard by that. He looked surprised and, or a moment, troubled. "So you heard about that, did you?"

"I wondered if there was any truth to it. That he was a Caesar, I mean."

Lucentius glanced away. "He was only an old tramp, is all," he said, in a muffled tone. "An old lying tramp. Maybe he told fantastic stories to some of the gullible kids, but a tramp is all he was, an old filthy lying tramp." He gave me a peculiar look.

And then he stamped away to shout at someone who was uncoiling a hose the wrong way.

A filthy old tramp, yes. But not, I think, a liar.

He remains alive in my mind to this day, that poor old relic of the Empire. And now that I am old myself, as old, perhaps, as he was then, I understand something of what he was saying. Not his belief that there necessarily had to be a Caesar in order for there to be peace, for the Caesars were only men themselves, in no way different from the Consuls who have replaced them. But when he argued that the time of the Empire had been basically a time of peace, he may not have been really wrong, even if war had been far from unknown in Imperial days.

For I see now that war can sometimes be a kind of peace also: that the Civil Wars and the Wars of Reunification were the struggles of a sundered Empire trying to reassemble itself so peace might resume. These matters are not so simple. The Second Republic is not as virtuous as my father thought, nor was the old Empire, apparently, quite as corrupt. The only thing that seems true without dispute is that the worldwide hegemony of Roma these past 2,000 years under the Empire and then under the Republic, troubled though it has occasionally been, has kept us from even worse turmoil. What if there had been no Roma? What if every region had been free to make war against its neighbors in the hope of creating the sort of Empire that the Romans were able to build?

Imagine the madness of it! But the gods gave us the Romans, and the Romans gave us peace: not a perfect peace, but the best peace, perhaps, that an imperfect world could manage. Or so I think now.

In any case the Caesars are dead, and so is everyone else I have written about here, even my little sister Friya; and here I am, an old man of the Second Republic, thinking back over the past and trying to bring some sense out of it. I still have the strange dagger that Quintus Fabius gave me, the barbaric-looking one with the curious wavy blade, that came from some savage island in the Oceanus Magnus. Now and then I take it out and look at it. It shines with a kind of antique splendor in the lamplight. My eyes are too dim now to see the tiny imperial crest that someone engraved on its haft when the merchant captain who brought it back from the South Seas gave it to the Caesar of his time, four or five hundred years ago. Nor can I see the little letters, S P Q R, that are inscribed on the blade. For all I know, they were put there by the frizzy-haired tribesman who fashioned that odd, fierce weapon: for he, too, was a citizen of the Roman Empire. As in a manner of speaking are we all, even now in the days of the Second Republic.

As are we all.

Manassas, Again

Gregory Benford

There were worse things than getting swept up in the first battle of the first war in over a century, but Bradley could not right away think of any.

They had been out on a lark, really. Bradley got his buddy Paul to go along, flying low over the hills to watch the grand formations of men and machines. Bradley knew how to keep below the radar screens, sometimes skimming along so close to the treetops that branches snapped on their understruts. They had come in before dawn, using Bradley's Dad's luxury, ultra-quiet cruiser – over the broad fields, using the sunrise to blind the optical sensors below.

It had been enormously exciting. The gleaming columns, the acrid smoke of ruin, the distant muffled coughs of combat.

Then somebody shot them down.

Not a full, square hit, luckily. Bradley had got them over two ranges of hills, lurching through shot-wracked air. Then they came down heavily, air bags saving the two boys.

They had no choice but to go along with the team which picked them out of their wreckage. Dexter, a big swarthy man, seemed to be in charge. He said, "We got word a bunch of mechs are comin along this road. You stick with us, you can help out."

Bradley said irritably, "Why should we? I want to—"

"Cause it's not safe round here, kid," Dexter said. "You

joyriding rich kids, maybe you'll learn something about that today."

Dexter grinned, showing two missing teeth, and waved the rest of his company to keep moving into the slanting early morning glow.

Nobody had any food and Bradley was pretty sure they would not have shared it out if they had. The fighting over the ridge to the west had disrupted whatever supply lines there were into this open, once agricultural land.

They reached the crossroads by mid-morning and right away knocked out a servant mech by mistake. It saw them come hiking over the hill through the thick oaks and started chuffing away, moving as fast as it could. It was an R class, shiny and chromed.

A woman who carried one of the long rods over her shoulder whipped the rod down and sighted along it and a loud boom startled Bradley. The R mech went down. "First one of the day," the woman named Angel said.

"Musta been a scout," Dexter said.

"For what?" Bradley asked, shocked as they walked down the slope towards the mech in air still cool and moist from the dawn.

Paul said tentatively, "The mech withdrawal?"

Dexter nodded. "Mechs're on their way through here. Bet they're scared plenty."

They saw the R mech had a small hole punched through it right in the servo controls near the back. "Not bad shootin," a man said to Angel.

"I *tole* you these'd work," Angel said proudly. "I sighted mine in fresh this mornin. It helps."

Bradley realized suddenly that the various machined rods these dozen people carried were all weapons, fabrications turned out of factories exclusively human-run. *Killing tools*, he thought in blank surprise. *Like the old days. You see them in dramas and stuff, but they've been illegal for a century.*

"Maybe this mech was just plain scared," Bradley said. "It's got software for that."

"We sent out a beeper warning," Dexter said, slapping the pack on his back. "Goes out of this li'l rig here. Any mech wants no trouble, all they got to do is come up on us slow and then lie down so we can have a look at their programming cubes."

"Disable it?"

"Sure. How else we going to be sure?"

"This one ran, clear as anything," Angel said, reloading her rifle.

"Maybe it didn't understand," Bradley said. The R models were deft, subtle, terrific at social graces.

"It knew, all right," Angel said, popping the mech's central port open and pulling out its ID cube. "Look, it's from Sanfran."

"What's it doing all the way out here, then, if it's not a rebel?" a black man named Nelson asked.

"Yeah," Dexter said. "Enter it as reb." He handed Bradley a wrist comm. "We're keepin' track careful now. You'll be busy just takin' down score today, kid."

"Rebel, uh, I see," Bradley said, tapping into the comm. It was reassuring to do something simple while he straightened out his feelings.

"You bet," Nelson said, excitement lacing his voice. "Look at it. Fancy mech, smarter than most of them, tryin' to save itself. It's been runnin away from our people. They just broke up a big mech force west of here."

"I never could afford one of these chrome jobs," Angel said. "They knew that, too. I had one of these classy R numbers mean-mouth me in the market, try to grab a can of soya bean stew." She laughed sarcastically. "That was when there was a few scraps left on the shelves."

"Elegant thing, wasn't it?" Nelson kicked the mech, which rolled further downhill.

"You messed it up pretty well," Bradley said.

Dexter said, "Roll it down into that hollow so nobody can see it from the road." He gestured at Paul. "You go with the other party. Hey, Mercer!"

A tall man ambled over from where he had been trying to carefully pick the spines off a prickly pear growing in a gully. Everybody was hungry. Dexter said to him, "Go down across the road and set up shop. Take this kid – Paul's your name, right? – he'll help with the grunt work. We'll catch 'em in a crossfire here."

Mercer went off with Paul. Bradley helped get the dead mech going and with Angel rolled it into the gully. Its flailing arms dug fresh wet gouges in the spring grass. The exposed mud exhaled moist scents. They threw manzanita brush over the shiny carcass to be sure and by that time Dexter had deployed his people.

They were setting up what looked like traps of some kind well away from the blacktop crossroads. Bradley saw that this was to keep the crossroads from looking damaged or clogged. They wanted the mechs to come in fast and keep going.

As he worked he heard rolling bass notes, like the mumbles of a giant, come from the horizon. He could see that both the roads leading to the crossroads could carry mechs away from the distant battles. Dexter was everywhere, barking orders, Bradley noted with respect.

The adults talked excitedly to each other about what the mechs would make of it, how easy they were to fool about real-world stuff, and even threw in some insider mech slang – codes and acronyms that meant very little to mechs, really, but had got into the pop culture as hip new stuff. Bradley smiled at this. It gave him a moment of feeling superior to cover his uneasiness.

It was a crisp spring morning now that the sun had beamed up over the far hill at their backs. The perfect time for fresh growth, but the fields beyond had no plowing or signs of cultivation. Mechs should be there, laying in crops. Instead they were off over the rumpled ridgeline, clashing with the main body of humans and, Bradley hoped secretly, getting their asses kicked. Though mechs had no asses, he reminded himself.

Dexter and Bradley laid down behind a hummock halfway up the hill. Dexter was talking into his hushmike headset, face jumping with anticipation and concern. Bradley savored the rich scents of the sweet new grass and thought idly about eating some of it. Dexter looked out over the setup his team was building and said, "Y'know maybe we're too close but I figure you can't be in too close as long as you have the fire power.

These weapons, we need close, real close. Easier to hit them when they're moving fast but then it's easier for them to hit you, too."

Bradley saw that the man was more edgy here than he had been with his team. Nobody had done anything like this within living memory. Not in the civilized world, anyway.

"Got to be sure we can back out of this if it gets too hot," Dexter went on.

Bradley liked Dexter's no-nonsense scowl. "How did you learn how to fight?"

Dexter looked surprised. "Hobby of mine. Studied the great Roman campaigns in Africa, in Asia, then here against the Indians."

"They used ambushes a lot?"

"Sometimes. Of course, after Sygnius of Albion invented the steam-driven machine gun, well sir, then the Romans could dictate terms to any tribes that gave them trouble." Dexter squinted at him. "You study history, kid?"

"I'm Bradley, sir. My parents don't let me read about battles very much. They're always saying we've got beyond that."

"Yeah, that Universal Peace Church, right?"

"Yessir. They say—"

"That stuff's fine for people. Mechs, they're different."

"Different how?"

Dexter sucked on his teeth, peering down the road. "Not human. Fair game."

"Think they'll be hard to beat?"

Dexter grinned. "We're programmed for this by a couple of million years of evolution. They been around over half a century."

"Since 1800? I thought we'd always had mechs."

"Geez, kids never know any history."

"Well sir, I know all the big things, like the dates of American Succession from the Empire, and the Imperial ban on weapons like the ones you've got here, and how—"

"Dates aren't history, son. They're just numbers. What's it matter when we finally got out from under the Romans? Bunch of lily-livers, they were. 'Peace Empire' – contradiction in terms, kid. Though the way the 3D pumps you kids full of crap, not even allowin' any war shows or anything, except for prettified pussy historicals, no wonder you don't know which end of a gun does the business."

This seemed unfair to Bradley but he could see Dexter wasn't the kind of man he had known, so he shut up. *Fair game?* What did that mean? A fair game was where everybody enjoyed it and had a chance to win.

Maybe the world wasn't as simple as he had thought. There was something funny and tingly about the air here, a crackling that made his skin jump, his nerves strum.

Angel came back and lay beside them, wheezing, lugging a heavy contraption with tripod legs they had just assembled.

Nelson was down slope, cradling his rifle. He arranged the tripod and lifted onto it a big array of cylinders and dark, brushed-steel sliding parts unlike anything Bradley had ever seen. Sweating, Nelson stuck a long curved clip into all this freshly made metal and worked the clacking mechanism. Nelson smiled, looking pleased at the way the parts slid easily.

Bradley was trying to figure out what all the various weapons did when he heard something coming fast down the road. He looked back along the snaky black line that came around the far hills and saw a big shape flitting among the ash trees.

It was an open-topped hauler filled with copper-jacketed mechs. They looked like factory hands, packed like gleaming eggs in a carton.

Dexter talked into his hushmike and pointed towards three chalk-white stones set up by the road as aiming markers. The hauler came racing through the crossroads and plunged up the straight section of the road in front of Bradley. The grade increased here so they would slow as they passed the stones.

Bradley realized they had no way of knowing what the mechs were doing there, not for sure, and then he forgot that as a pulse-quickening sensation coursed through him. Dexter beside him looked like a cat that knows he has a canary stashed somewhere and can go sink his teeth into it any time he likes.

When the hauler reached the marker stones Angel opened

fire. The sound was louder than anything Bradley had ever heard and his first reaction was to bury his face in the grass. When he looked up the hauler was slewing across the road and then it hit the ditch and rolled.

The coppery mechs in the back flew out in slow motion. Most just smacked into the grass and lay still. The hauler thumped solidly and stopped rolling. A few of the factory mechs got up and tried to get behind the hauler, maybe thinking that the rifle fire was only from Angel, but then the party from across the road opened up and the mechs pitched forward into the ditch and did not move. Then there was quiet in the little valley. Bradley could hear the hauler's engine still humming with electric energy and then some internal override cut in and it whined into silence.

"I hit that hauler square in the command dome, you see that?" Angel said loudly.

Bradley hadn't seen it but he said, "Yes Ma'm, right."

Dexter said, "Try for that every time. Saves ammo if we don't have to shoot every one of them."

Nelson called up the slope, "Those're factory mechs, they look like Es and Fs, they're pretty heavy built."

Angel nodded, grinning. "Easier to just slam 'em into that ditch."

Dexter didn't hear this as he spoke into his hush mike next to Bradley. "Myron, you guys get them off the road. Use those power override keys and make them walk themselves into that place where the gully runs down into the stream. Tell 'em to jump right in the water."

"What about the hauler?" Bradley asked, and then was surprised at his own boldness.

Dexter frowned a moment. "The next batch, they'll think we hit it from the air. There was plenty of that yesterday to the west."

"I didn't see any of our planes today," Bradley said.

"We lost some. Rest are grounded because some mechs started to catch on, just about sunset. They knocked three of our guys right out of the sky. Mechs won't know that, though. They'll figure it's like yesterday and that hauler was just unlucky." Dexter smiled and checked his own rifle, which he had not fired.

"I'll go help them," Bradley said, starting to get up.

"No, we only got so many of those keys. The guys know how to use 'em. You watch the road."

"But I'd like to—"

"Shut up," Dexter said in a way that was casual and yet was not.

Bradley used his pocket binoculars to study the road. The morning heat sent ripples climbing up from the valley floor and he was not sure at first that he saw true movement several kilometers away and then he was. Dexter alerted the others and there was a mad scramble to get the mechs out of sight.

They were dead, really, but the humans could access their power reserves and make them roll down the road on their wheels and treads and then jounce down the gully and pitch into the stream. Bradley could hear laughter as the team across the road watched the mechs splash into the brown water. Some shorted out and started flailing their arms and rotors around, comic imitations of humans swimming. That lasted only a few seconds and then they sank like the rest.

Nelson came running back up the hill carrying on his back a long tube. "Here's that launcher you wanted. Rensink, he didn't look too happy to let go of it."

Dexter stood and looked down the road with his own binoculars. "Leave it here. We got higher elevation than Rensink."

Dexter took the steel tube, which looked to Bradley exactly like the telescopes he and his friends used to study the sky. Tentatively he said, "If you're not going to use that rifle, uh, sir, I'd . . ."

Dexter grinned. "You want in, right?"

"Well, yes, I thought that since you're—"

"Sure. Here. Clip goes like this," he demonstrated, "you hold it so, sight along that notch. I machined that so I know it's good. We had to learn a whole lot of old-timey craft to make these things."

Bradley felt the heft and import of the piece and tentatively practiced sighting down at the road. He touched the trigger with the caution of a virgin lover. If he simply pulled on the cool bit of metal a hole would – well, might – appear in the carapace of fleeing mech. A mech they would not have to deal with again in the chaos to come. It was a simple way to think about the whole complex issue. Something in Bradley liked that simplicity.

The mechs still had not arrived but Bradley could see them well enough through the binoculars now to know why. They were riding on self-powered inventions of their own, modified forms of the getarounds mechs sometimes used on streets. These were three-wheeled and made of shiny brass.

They were going slowly, probably running out of energy. As he watched one deployed a solar panel on its back to catch the rising sun and then the others did but this did not speed them up any. They did not look like the elegant social mechs he usually saw zipping on the bike paths, bound on some errand. They were just N- or P-class mechs who had rigged up some wheels.

They came pedaling into the crossroads, using their arms. The one in front saw the hauler on its side and knew something was wrong right away and started pumping hard. Nelson shot at him then even though Dexter had said nothing. He hit the lead mech and it went end over end, arms caught up in its own drive chain. Angel could not resist and she took out the next three with a burst. Then the others came in with a chorus of rattling shots and loud bangs, no weapon sounding like the other, and in the noise Bradley squeezed and felt the butt of the rifle kick him.

He had been aiming at one of the mechs at the rear of the little column and when he looked next the mech was down, sliding across the road with sparks jetting behind it, metal ripping across asphalt.

"Stop! Stop shooting!" Dexter called and in the sudden silence Bradley could hear the mechs clattering to a halt, clanging and squealing and thumping into the ditch.

"Get them off the road quick!" Dexter called. He waved Bradley down the hill and the boy ran to see the damage. As he dashed towards them the mechs seemed to be undamaged except for some dents but then up close each showed a few holes. He had time to glance at Paul, who was red-faced, breathing hard, his eyes veiled. There was no time to talk.

The men and women from across the road got most of the mechs started up again on override keys but one had suffered some sort of internal explosion and the back was blown off. Bradley helped three men tilt it up enough to roll off the gentle rounded asphalt and once they got it going it rolled and slid into a copse of eucalyptus. They threw branches over it. Bradley looked for the one he had shot at but it was impossible to tell which that was now.

He felt a prickly anticipation, a thickening of the air. The fragrances of trees and grass cut into his nostrils, vivid and sharp. They ran back up the slope. Bradley found the rifle he now thought of as his and sprawled down with it in the grass, getting down behind a hummock near Dexter.

He lay there just breathing and looking at the rifle, which seemed to be made of a lot of complicated parts. Dexter tossed him three clips and a box of copper-sheathed ammunition. The box promised that they were armor-piercing. Bradley fumbled a little learning how to load the clips but then he moved quickly, sliding the rounds in with a secure click as he heard the distant growl of a tracked vehicle.

It was coming closer along the other road. The crossroads looked pretty clear, no obvious signs of the ambush.

The Mercer team had laid two mines in the road. They had a chameleon surface and within a minute were indistinguishable from the asphalt. Bradley could tell where they were because they were lined up with the white marker stones and were smoother than the asphalt.

He wondered if the mechs could sense that. Their sensorium was better than human in some ways, worse than others. He realized that he had never thought very much about the interior life of a mech, any more than he could truly delve into the inner world of animals. But in principle mechs *were* knowable. Their entire perspective could be digitized and examined minutely.

The clatter and roar of the approach blotted this from his mind. "Activate!" Dexter shouted, his tight voice giving away some of his own excitement.

A big tracked vehicle came flitting through the trees that lined the black road, flickering like a video-game target. There were mechs perched all over it, hitching rides, and many more of them packed its rear platform. When Bradley looked back at the road nearby the mines jumped out at him like a spider on a lace tablecloth. The entire valley vibrated and sparkled with intense, sensory light. Smells coiled up his nostrils, the cool sheen of the rifle spoke to him through his hands.

The mech driver would surely see the mines, stop and back away, he thought. And the mechs aboard would jump off and some of them would attack the humans, rolling down the road and shooting the lasers which they had adapted from industrial purposes. Bradley had heard about the mechs which could override their safety commands and fight. He tightened his grip on his rifle. He was dimly aware of Dexter sighting along his tube-shaped weapon, and of Angel muttering to herself as she waited.

"If they were like us they'd stop, first sign of trouble they see," Dexter muttered, probably to himself but Bradley could hear. "Then they'd deploy fighter mechs on both sides of the road and they'd sweep us, outflank."

"Think they will?" Bradley asked wonderingly.

"Naw. They don't have what we do."

"What . . . what's that?" Bradley knew the wide range of special abilities mechs possessed.

"Balls."

The mechs perched atop the tracked vehicle were looking forward down the road and holding on tight against the rough swerves as they rounded curves.

Then one of them saw the mines and jerked a servo arm towards them. Some mechs sitting near the front began sending warning wails and the track car slammed on its brakes and slewed across the road. It stopped at the lip of the ditch and made a heavy grinding noise and began backing up.

Three mechs jumped off its front. Bradley brought his sights down onto one of them and the air splintered with a huge rolling blast that made him flinch and forget about everything else.

The gunmetal hood of the transport seemed to dissolve into a blue cloud. The tailgate of the tracker flew backward with a sharp *whap*.

The air became a fine array of tumbling dots as debris spewed up like a dark fountain and then showered down all across the hillside. Thunks and whacks told of big mech parts hitting nearby and Bradley tucked his head into the grass. He yelped as something nicked his knee and something else tumbled over him and was gone. Pebbles thumped his back.

When Bradley looked up he expected to see nothing but small scraps left on the road. His ears roared with the memory of the sound and he wondered if he would be deaf. But through the smoke he saw several mechs lurching away from the disemboweled transport. There were five of them bunched closely together.

He brought his rifle up and shot very swiftly at the lead mech. It went down and he shot the next object and the next, seeing only the moving forms and the swirling blur of action.

Angel was firing and Nelson too, sharp bangs so regular and fast Bradley thought of the clack of a stick held by a boy as he ran by a picket fence – and in a few seconds there were no more mechs standing on the road.

But there were two in the ditch. Grey smoke billowed everywhere.

Bradley saw a mech moving just as a quick rod of light leaped from it, cutting through the smoke. He heard Angel yelp and swear. She held up her hand and it was bloody.

Another instantaneous rod of light stood for a second in the air and missed her and then a third struck her weapon. It flew to pieces with a loud bang. Bradley aimed at the mech and kept firing until he saw it and the second one sprawl across the ditch and stop moving.

A compressed silence returned to the valley. The transport was burning but beyond its snaps and pops he could see nothing moving on the road.

Angel was moaning with her wound and Nelson took care of

her, pulling out a first aid kit as he ran over. When they saw that she was all right Dexter and Bradley walked slowly down to the road. Dexter said, "Bet that's the last big party. We'll get strays now, no problems."

Bradley's legs felt like logs thudding into the earth as he walked. He waved to Paul who was already on the road but he did not feel like talking to anybody. The air was crisp and layered with so many scents, he felt them sliding in and out of his lungs like separate flavors in an ice cream sundae.

"Hey," Mercer called from the transport cab. "They got food in here."

Everyone riveted attention on the cab. Mercer pitched out cartons of dry food, some cans, a case of soft drinks.

"Somethin', huh? – mechs carryin food," Angel said wonderingly. For several minutes they ate and drank and then Paul called, "There's a boy here."

They found Paul standing over a boy who was half concealed by a fallen mech. Bradley saw that the group of mechs had been shielding this boy when they were cut down. "Still alive," Paul said, "barely."

"The food was for him," Mercer said.

Bradley bent down. Paul cradled the boy but it was clear from the drawn, white face and masses of blood down the front, some fresh red and most brown, drying, that there was not much hope. They had no way to get him to cryopreservation. Thin lips opened, trembled, and the boy said, "Bad . . . mommy . . . hurt . . ."

Dexter said, "This ID says he's under mech care."

"How come?" Angel asked.

"Says he's mentally deficient. These're medical care mechs." Dexter pushed one of the mech carcasses and it rolled, showing H-caste insignia.

"Damn, how'd they get mixed in with these reb mechs?" Nelson asked irritably, the way people do when they are looking for something or someone to blame.

"Accident," Dexter said simply. "Confusion. Prob'ly thought they were doing the best thing, getting their charge away from the fighting."

"Damn," Nelson said again. Then his lips moved but nothing came out.

Bradley knelt down and brushed some flies away from the boy's face. He gave the boy some water but the eyes were far away and the lips just spat the water out. Angel was trying to find the wound and stop the bleeding but she had a drawn, waxy look.

"Damn war," Nelson said. "Mechs, they're to blame for this."

Bradley took a self-heating cup of broth from Paul and gave a little to the boy. The face was no more than fifteen and the eyes gazed abstractly up into a cloudless sky. Bradley watched a butterfly land on the boy's arm. It fluttered its wings in the slanting yellow-gold sunlight and tasted the drying brown blood. Bradley wondered distantly if butterflies ate blood. Then the boy choked and the butterfly flapped away on a breeze and when Bradley looked back the boy was dead.

They stood for a long moment around the body. The road was a chaos of ripped mech carapaces and tangled innards and the wreck of the exploded transport. Nobody was going to run into an ambush here any more today and nobody made a move to clear the road.

"Y'know, these med-care mechs, they're pretty smart," Paul said. "They just made the wrong decision."

"Smarter than the boy, probably," Bradley said. The boy was not much younger than Bradley but in the eyes there had been just an emptiness. "He was human, though."

The grand opening elation he had felt all morning slowly began to seep out of Bradley. "Hell of a note, huh?" he said to no one in particular. Others were doing that, just saying things to the breeze as they slowly dispersed and started to make order out of the shambles.

The snap and sparkle of the air was still with him, though. He had never felt so alive in his life. Suddenly he saw the soft, encased, abstract world he had inhabited since birth as an enclave, a preserve – a trap. The whole of human society had been in a cocoon, a velvet wrapping tended by mechs.

They had found an alternative to war: wealth. And simple human kindness. *Human* kindness.

Maybe that was all gone, now.

And it was no tragedy, either. Not if it gave them back the world as it could be, a life of tangs and zests and the gritty rub of real things. He had dwelled in the crystal spaces of the mind while beneath such cool antiseptic entertainments his body yearned for the hot raw earth and its moist mysteries.

Nelson and Mercer were collecting mech insignia. "Want an AB? We found one over here. Musta got caught up and brought along by these worker mechs?" Nelson asked Bradley.

"I'll just take down the serial numbers," Bradley said automatically, not wanting to talk to Nelson more than necessary. Or to anyone. There had been so much talk.

He spent time getting the numbers logged into his comm and then with shoving mech carcasses off the road.

Dexter came over to him and said, "Sure you don't want one of these?" It was a laser one of the reb mechs had used. Black, ribbed, with a glossy sheen. "Angel's keeping one. She'll be telling the story of her wound and showing the laser that maybe did it, prob'ly for rest of her life."

Bradley looked at the sleek, sensuous thing. It gleamed in the raw sunlight like a promise. "No."

"Sure?"

"Take the damned stuff away."

Dexter looked at him funny and walked off. Bradley stared at the mechs he was shoving off the road and tried to think how they were different from the boy, who probably was indeed less intelligent than they were, but it was all clouded over with the memory of how much he liked the rifle and the sweet grass and shooting at the targets when they came up to the crossfire point in the bright sun. It was hard to think at all as the day got its full heat and after a while he did not try. It was easier that way.

The Sleeping Serpent

Pamela Sargent

1

Yesuntai Noyan arrived in Yeke Geren in early winter, stumbling from his ship with the unsteady gait and the pallor of a man who had recently crossed the ocean. Because Yesuntai was a son of our Khan, our commander Michel Bahadur welcomed the young prince with speeches and feasts. Words of gratitude for our hospitality fell from Yesuntai's lips during these ceremonies, but his restless gaze betrayed his impatience. Yesuntai's mother, I had heard, was Frankish, and he had a Frank's height, but his sharp-boned face, dark slits of eyes, and sturdy frame were a Mongol's.

At the last of the feasts, Michel Bahadur seated me next to the Khan's son, an honor I had not expected. The commander, I supposed, had told Yesuntai a little about me, and would expect me to divert the young man with tales of my earlier life in the northern woods. As the men around us sang and shouted to servants for more wine, Yesuntai leaned towards me.

"I hear," he murmured, "that I can learn much from you, Jirandai Bahadur. Michel tells me that no man knows this land better than you."

"I am flattered by such praise." I made the sign of the cross over my wine, as I had grown used to doing in Yeke Geren.

Yesuntai dipped his fingers into his cup, then sprinkled a blessing to the spirits. Apparently he followed our old faith, and not the cross; I found myself thinking a little more of him.

"I am also told," Yesuntai went on, "that you can tell many tales of a northern people called the Hiroquois."

"That is only the name our Franks use for all the nations of the Long House." I gulped down more wine. "Once, I saw my knowledge of that people as something that might guide us in our dealings with them. Now it is only fodder on which men seeking a night's entertainment feed."

The Noyan lifted his brows. "I will not ask you to share your stories with me here."

I nodded, relieved. "Perhaps we might hunt together sometime, Noyan. Two peregrines I have trained need testing, and you might enjoy a day with them."

He smiled. "Tomorrow," he said, "and preferably by ourselves, Bahadur. There is much I wish to ask you."

Yesuntai was soon speaking more freely with the other men, and even joined them in their songs. Michel would be pleased that I had lifted the Noyan's spirits, but by then I cared little for what that Bahadur thought. I drank and thought of other feasts shared inside long houses with my brothers in the northern forests.

Yesuntai came to my dwelling before dawn. I had expected an entourage, despite his words about hunting by ourselves, but the Khan's son was alone. He gulped down the broth my wife Elgigetei offered, clearly impatient to ride out from the settlement.

We saddled our horses quickly. The sky was almost as grey as the slate-colored wings of the falcons we carried on our wrists, but the clouds told me that snow would not fall before dusk. I could forget Yeke Geren and the life I had chosen for one day, until the shadows of evening fell.

We rode east, skirting the horses grazing in the land our settlers had cleared, then moved north. A small bird was flying towards a grove of trees; Yesuntai loosed his falcon. The peregrine soared, a streak against the grey sky, her dark wings scimitars, then suddenly plummeted towards her prey. The Noyan laughed as her yellow talons caught the bird.

Yesuntai galloped after the peregrine. I spied a rabbit darting across the frost-covered ground, and slipped the tether from my falcon; he streaked towards his game. I followed, pondering what I knew about Yesuntai. He had grown up in the ordus and great cities of our Frankish Khanate, been tutored by the learned men of Paris, and would have passed the rest of his time in drinking, dicing, card-playing, and claiming those women who struck his fancy. His father, Sukegei Khan, numbered two grandsons of Genghis Khan among his ancestors, but I did not expect Yesuntai to show the vigor of those great forefathers. He was the Khan's son by one of his minor wives, and I had seen such men before in Yeke Geren, minor sons of Ejens or generals who came to this new land for loot and glory, but who settled for hunting along the great river to the north, trading with the nearer tribes, and occasionally raiding an Inglistani farm. Yesuntai would be no different; so I thought then.

He was intent on his sport that day. By afternoon, the carcasses of several birds and rabbits hung from our saddles. He had said little to me, and was silent as we tethered our birds, but I had felt him watching me. Perhaps he would ask me to guide him and some of his men on a hunt beyond this small island, before the worst of the winter weather came. The people living in the regions nearby would not trouble hunters. Our treaty with the Ganeagaono, the Eastern Gatekeepers of the Long House, protected us, and they had long since subdued the tribes to the south of their lands.

We trotted south. Some of the men watching the horse herds were squatting around fires near their shelters of tree branches and hides. They greeted us as we passed, and congratulated us on our game. In the distance, the rounded bark houses of Yeke Geren were visible in the evening light, wooden bowls crowned by plumes of smoke rising from their roofs.

The Great Camp – the first of our people who had come to this land had given Yeke Geren its name. "We will build a great camp," Cheren Noyan had said when he stepped from his ship, and now circles of round wooden houses covered the southern part of the island the Long House people called Ganono, while our horses had pasturage in the north. Our dwellings were much like those of the Manhatan people who had lived here, who had greeted our ships, fed us, sheltered us, and then lost their island to us.

Yesuntai reined in his horse as we neared Yeke Geren; he seemed reluctant to return to the Great Camp. "This has been the most pleasant day I have passed here," he said.

"I have also enjoyed myself, Noyan." My horse halted at his side. "You would of course find better hunting away from this island. Perhaps—"

"I did not come here only to hunt, Bahadur. I have another purpose in mind. When I told Michel Bahadur of what I wish to do, he said that you were the man to advise me." He paused. "My father the Khan grows even more displeased with his enemies the Inglistanis. He fears that, weak as they are, they may grow stronger here. His spies in Inglistan tell him that more of them intend to cross the water and settle here."

I glanced at him. All of the Inglistani settlements, except for the port they called Plymouth, sat along the coast north of the long island that lay to the east of Yeke Geren. A few small towns, and some outlying farms – I could not see why our Khan would be so concerned with them. It was unfortunate that they were there, but our raids on their westernmost farms had kept them from encroaching on our territory, and if they tried to settle farther north, they would have to contend with the native peoples there.

"If more come," I said, "then more of the wretches will die during the winter. They would not have survived this long without the aid of the tribes around them." Some of those people had paid dearly for aiding the settlers, succumbing to the pestilences the Inglistanis had brought with them.

"They will come with more soldiers and muskets. They will pollute this land with their presence. The Khan my father will conquer their wretched island, and the people of Eire will aid us to rid themselves of the Inglistani yoke. My father's victory will be tarnished if too many of the island dogs find refuge here. They must be rooted out."

"So you wish to be rid of the Inglistani settlements." I fingered the tether hanging from my falcon. "We do not have the men for such a task."

"We do not," he admitted, "but the peoples of these lands do."

He interested me. Perhaps there was some iron in his soul after all. "Only the Hodenosaunee, the Long House nations, can help you," I said, "and I do not know if they will. The Inglistanis pose no threat to the power of the Long House."

"Michel told me we have a treaty with that people."

"We have an agreement with the Ganeagaono, who are one of their five nations. Once the Long House People fought among themselves, until their great chiefs Deganawida and Hayawatha united them. They are powerful enough now to ignore the Inglistanis."

Yesuntai gazed at the bird that clutched his gauntleted wrist. "What if they believed the Inglistanis might move against them?"

"They might act," I replied. "The Hodenosaunee have no treaties with that people. But they might think they have something to gain from the Inglistani presence. We have never given firearms to the people here, but the Inglistanis do so when they think it's to their advantage. By making war on the Inglistani settlements, you might only drive them into an alliance with the Long House and its subject tribes, one that might threaten us."

"We must strike hard and exterminate the lot," Yesuntai muttered. "Then we must make certain that no more of the wretches ever set foot on these shores."

"You will need the Long House People to do it."

"I must do it, one way or another. The Khan my father has made his will known. I have his orders, marked with his seal. He will take Inglistan, and we will destroy its outposts here. There can be no peace with those who have not submitted to us – the Yasa commands it. Inglistan has not submitted, so it will be forced to bow."

I was thinking that Sukegei Khan worried too much over that pack of island-dwellers. Surely Hispania, even with a brother Khan ruling there, was more of a threat to him than Inglistan. I had heard many tales of the splendor of Suleiman Khan's court, of slaves and gold that streamed to Granada and Cordoba from the continent to our south, of lands taken by the Hispanic Khan's conquistadors. The Hispanians were as fervent in spreading their faith as in seizing loot. In little more than sixty years, it was said that as many mosques stood in the Aztec capital of Tenochtítlan as in Cordoba itself. Suleiman Khan, with African kings as vassals and conquests in this new world, dreamed of being the greatest of the European Khans. How easy it had been for him to allow us settlements in the north while he claimed the richer lands to the south.

But I was a Bahadur of Yeke Geren, who knew only what others told me of Europe. My Khanate was a land I barely remembered, and our ancient Mongol homeland no more than a setting for legends and tales told by travelers. The Ejens of the Altan Uruk, the descendants of Genghis Khan, still sent their tribute to Karakorum, but the bonds of our Yasa, the laws the greatest of men had given us, rested more lightly on their shoulders. They might bow to the Kha-Khan of our homeland, but many of the Khans ruled lands greater than his. A time might come when the Khans of the west would break their remaining ties to the east.

"Europe!" I cleared my throat. "Sometimes I wonder what our Khans will do when all their enemies are vanquished."

Yesuntai shook his head. "I will say this – my ancestor Genghis Khan would have wondered at what we are now. I have known Noyans who go no farther to hunt than the parks around their dwellings, and others who prefer brocades and perfumed lace to a sheepskin coat and felt boots. Europe has weakened us. Some think as I do, that we should become what we were, but there is little chance of that there."

Snow was sifting from the sky. I urged my horse on; Yesuntai kept near me.

By the time we reached my circle of houses, the falling snow had become a curtain veiling all but the nearest dwellings from our sight. Courtesy required that I offer Yesuntai a meal, and a place to sleep if the snow continued to fall. He accepted my hospitality readily; I suspected there was more he wanted to ask me.

We halted at the dwelling next to mine. Except for a horse-drawn wagon carrying a wine merchant's barrels, the winding roads were empty. I shouted to my servants; two boys hurried outside to take the peregrines and our game from us. A shadowy form stirred near the dwelling. I squinted, then recognized one of my Manhatan servants. He lay in the snow, his hands around a bottle.

Anger welled inside me. I told one of the boys to get the Manhatan to his house, then went after the wagon. The driver slowed to a stop as I reached him. I seized his collar and dragged him from his seat.

He cursed as he sprawled in the snow. "I warned you before," I said. "You are not to bring your wine here."

He struggled to his feet, clutching his hat. "To your Manhatans, Bahadur – that's what you said. I was passing by, and thought others among your households might have need of some refreshment. Is it my fault if your natives entreat me for—"

I raised my whip. "You had one warning," I said. "This is the last I shall give you."

"You have no reason—"

"Come back to my circle, Gérard, and I will take this whip to you. If you are fortunate enough to survive that beating—"

"You cannot stop their cravings, Bahadur." He glared up at me with his pale eyes. "You cannot keep them from seeking me out elsewhere."

"I will not make it easier for them to poison themselves." I flourished the whip; he backed away from me. "Leave."

He waded through the snow to his wagon. I rode back to my dwelling. Yesuntai had tied his horse to a post; he was silent as I unsaddled my mount.

I led him inside. Elgigetei greeted us; she was alone, and my wife's glazed eyes and slurred speech told me that she had been drinking. Yesuntai and I sat on a bench in the back of the house, just beyond the hearth fire. Elgigetei brought us wine and fish soup. I waited for her to take food for herself and to join us, but she settled on the floor near our son's cradle to work at a hide.

Her mother had been a Manhatan woman, and Elgigetei's brown face and thick black braids had reminded me of Dasiyu, the wife I had left among the Ganeagaono. I had thought her beautiful once, but Elgigetei had the weaknesses of the Manhatan people, the laziness, the craving for drink that had wasted so many of them. She scraped at her hide listlessly, then leaned over Ajiragha's cradle to murmur to our son in the Manhatan tongue. I had never bothered to learn the language. It was useless to master the speech of a people who would soon not exist.

"You are welcome to stay here tonight," I said to the Noyan.

"I am grateful for this snowstorm," he murmured. "It will give us more time to talk. I have much to ask you still about the Hiroquois." He leaned back against the wall. "In Khanbalik, there are scholars in the Khitan Khan's court who believe that the forefathers of the people in these lands came here long ago from the regions north of Khitai, perhaps even from our ancestral grounds. These scholars claim that once a land bridge far to the north linked this land to Sibir. So I was told by travelers who spoke to those learned men in Khitai."

"It is an intriguing notion, Noyan."

"If such people carry the seed of our ancestors, there may be greatness in them."

I sipped my wine. "But of course there can be no people as great as we Mongols."

"Greatness may slip from our grasp. Koko Mongke Tengri meant for us to rule the world, yet we may lose the strength to hold it."

I made a sign as he invoked the name of our ancient God, then bowed my head. Yesuntai lifted his brows. "I thought you were a Christian."

"I was baptized," I said. "I have prayed in other ways since then. The Long House People call God Hawenneyu, the Great Spirit, but He is Tengri by another name. It matters not how a man prays."

"That is true, but many who follow the cross or the crescent believe otherwise." Yesuntai sighed. "Long ago, my ancestor Genghis Khan thought of making the world our pasturage, but then learned that he could not rule it without mastering the ways of the lands he had won. Now those ways are mastering us." He gazed at me with his restless dark eyes. "When we have slaughtered the Inglistanis here, more of our people will come to settle these lands. In time, we may have to subdue those we call our friends. More will be claimed here for our Khanate and, if all goes well, my father's sons and grandsons will have more of the wealth this land offers. Our priests will come, itching to spread the word of Christ among the natives, and traders will bargain for what we do not take outright. Do you find this a pleasing prospect?"

"I must serve my Khan," I replied. His eyes narrowed, and I sensed that he saw my true thoughts. There were still times when I dreamed of abandoning what I had here and vanishing into the northern forests.

He said, "An ocean lies between us and Europe. It may become easier for those who are here to forget the Khanate."

"Perhaps."

"I am told," Yesuntai said then, "that you lived for some time among the Long House People."

My throat tightened. "I dwelled with the Ganeagaono, the Owners of the Flint. Perhaps Michel Bahadur told you the story."

"Only that you lived among them."

"It is a long tale, but I will try to make it shorter. My father and I came to these shores soon after we found this island – we were in one of the ships that followed the first expedition. Cheren Noyan had secured Yeke Geren by then. I was nine when we arrived, my father's youngest son. We came alone, without my mother or his second wife – he was hoping to return to Calais a richer man." I recalled little of that journey, only that the sight of the vast white-capped sea terrified me whenever I was well enough to go up on deck to help the men watch for Inglistani pirates. Perhaps Yesuntai had also trembled at being adrift on that watery plain, but I did not wish to speak of my fear to him.

"A year after we got here," I went on, "Cheren Noyan sent an expedition upriver. Hendrick, one of our Dutch sailors, captained the ship. He was to map the river and see how far it ran, whether it might offer us a passageway west. My father was ordered to join the expedition, and brought me along. I was grateful for the chance to be with the men."

Yesuntai nodded. "As any boy would be."

"We went north until we came to the region the Ganeagaono call Skanechtade – Beyond the Openings – and anchored there. We knew that the Flint People were fierce warriors. The people to the south of their lands lived in terror of them, and have given them the name of Mohawk, the Eaters of Men's Flesh, but we had been told the Owners of the Flint would welcome strangers who came to them in peace. Hendrick thought it wise to secure a treaty with them before going farther, and having an agreement with the Ganeagaono would also give us a bond with the other four nations of the Long House."

I swallowed more wine. Yesuntai was still, but his eyes kept searching me. He would want to know what sort of man I was before entrusting himself to me, but I still knew little about him. I felt somehow that he wanted more than allies in a campaign against the Inglistanis, but pushed that notion aside.

"Some of us," I said, "rowed to shore in our longboats. A few Ganeagaono warriors had spied us, and we made ourselves understood with hand gestures. They took us to their village. Everyone there greeted us warmly, and opened their houses to us. All might have gone well, but after we ate their food, our men offered them wine. We should have known better, after seeing what strong drink could do to the Manhatan. The Flint People have no head for wine, and our men would have done well to stay sober."

I stared at the earthen floor and was silent for a time. "I am not certain how it happened," I continued at last, "but our meeting ended in violence. A few of our men died with tomahawks in their heads. Most of the others fled to the boats. You may call them cowards for that, but to see a man of the Flint People in the throes of drunkenness would terrify the bravest of soldiers. They were wild – the wine is poison to them. They were not like the Manhatan, who grow sleepy and calmly trade even their own children for strong drink."

"Go on," Yesuntai said.

"My father and I were among those who did not escape. The Ganeagaono had lost men during the brawl, and now saw us as enemies. They began their tortures. They assailed my father and his comrades with fire and whips – they cut pieces of flesh from them, dining on them while their captives still lived, and tore the nails from their hands with hot pincers. My father bore his torment bravely, but the others did not behave as Mongols should, and their deaths were not glorious." I closed my eyes for a moment, remembering the sound of their shrieks when the children had thrown burning coals on their staked bodies. I had not known then whom I hated more, the men for losing their courage or the children for their cruelty.

"I am sorry to hear it," Yesuntai said.

"Only my father and I were left alive. They forced us to run through the village while rows of people struck at us with whips and heavy sticks. The men went at us first, then the women, and after them the children. I did not understand then that they were honoring us by doing this. My father's wounds robbed him of life, but I survived the beatings, and it was then that the Ganeagaono made me one of them. I was taken to a house, given to a woman who admired the courage my father had shown during the torture, and was made a member of their Deer Clan. My foster mother gave me the name of Senadondo."

"And after that?" he asked.

"Another ship came upriver not long after. We expected a war party, but Cheren Noyan was wise enough to send envoys out from the ship to seek peace. Because I knew the Ganeagaono tongue by then, I was useful as an interpreter. The envoys begged forgiveness, saying that their men were to blame for violating the hospitality of the Flint People, so all went well. In the years to follow, I often dealt with the traders who came to us offering cloth and iron for furs and beaver pelts – they did not make the mistake of bringing wine again. After a time, I saw that I might be of more use to both my own people and my adoptive brothers if I returned to Yeke Geren. The Ganeagaono said farewell to me and sent me back with many gifts."

Speaking of the past made me long for the northern woods,

for the spirits that sang in the mountain pines, for the sight of long houses and fields of corn, for Dasiyu, who had refused to come with me or to let our son depart with me. The boy belonged to her Wolf Clan, not to mine; his destiny was linked to hers. It had always been that way among the Long House People. I had promised to return, and she had called my promise a lie. Her last words to me were a curse.

"I might almost think," Yesuntai said, "that you wish you were among those people now."

"Is that so strange, Noyan?"

"They killed your father, and brought you much suffering."

"We brought that fate upon ourselves. If my father's spirit had not flown from him, they would have let him live, and honored him as one of their own. I lost everything I knew, but from the time the Ganeagaono adopted me, they treated me only with kindness and respect. Do you understand?"

"I think I do. The children of many who fought against us now serve us. Yet you chose to return here, Jirandai."

"We had a treaty. The Flint People do not forget their treaties – they are marked with the strings of beads they call wampum, which their wise men always have in their keeping." Even as I spoke, I wondered if, in the end, my exile would prove useless.

How full of pride and hope I had been, thinking that my efforts would preserve the peace between this outpost of the Khanate and the people I had come to love. I would be, so I believed, the voice of the Ganeagaono in the Mongol councils. But my voice was often ignored, and I had finally seen what lay behind Cheren Noyan's offer of peace. A treaty would give his men time to learn more about the Long House, and any weaknesses that could later be exploited. Eventually, more soldiers would come to wrest more of these lands from the natives. Our Khan's minions might eventually settle the lands to the north, and make the Long House People as wretched as the Manhatans.

"I came back," I continued, "so that our Noyans and Bahadurs would remember the promises recorded on the belts we exchanged with the Owners of the Flint. We swore peace, and I am the pledge of that peace, for the Ganeagaono promised that they would be bound to us in friendship for as long as I remained both their brother and the Khan's servant. That promise lives here." I struck my chest. "But some of our people are not so mindful of our promises."

Yesuntai nodded. "It is the European influence, Bahadur. Our ancestors kept the oaths they swore, and despised liars, but the Europeans twist words and often call lies the truth." He took a breath. "I will speak freely to you, Jirandai Bahadur. I have not come here only to rid this land of Inglistanis. Europe is filled with people who bow to the Khans and yet dream of escaping our yoke. I would hate to see them slip from their bonds on these shores. Destroying the Inglistani settlements will show others that they will find no refuge here."

"I can agree with such a mission," I said.

"And your forest brothers will be rid of a potential enemy."

"Yes."

"Will you lead me to them? Will you speak my words to them and ask them to join us in this war?"

"You may command me to do so, Noyan," I said.

He shifted his weight on the bench. "I would rather have your assent. I have always found that those who freely offer me their oaths serve me better than those pressed into service, and I imagine you have your own reasons for wishing to go north."

"I shall go with you, and willingly. You will need other men, Noyan. Some in Yeke Geren have lost their discipline and might not do well in the northern forests. They wallow in the few pleasures this place offers, and mutter that their Khan has forgotten them."

"Then I will leave it to you to find good men who lust for battle. I can trust those whom I brought with me."

I took out my pipe, tapped tobacco into it from my pouch, lit it, and held it out to Yesuntai. "Will you smoke a pipe with me? We should mark our coming expedition with some ceremony."

He accepted the pipe, drew in some smoke, then choked and gasped for air before composing himself. Outside, I heard a man, a sailor perhaps, and drunk from the sound of him, call out to another man in Frankish. What purpose could a man find here, waiting for yet another ship to arrive with news from the

Khanate and baubles to trade with the natives for the pelts, birds, animals, and plants the Khan's court craved? I was not the only man who thought of deserting Yeke Geren.

"I look forward to our journey," Yesuntai said, "and to seeing what lies beyond this encampment." He smiled as he passed the pipe to me.

That spring, with forty of Yesuntai's soldiers and twenty more men I had chosen, we sailed upriver.

2

The Ganeagaono of Skanechtade welcomed us with food. They crowded around us as we went from house to house, never leaving us alone even when we went to relieve ourselves. Several men of my Deer Clan came to meet me, urging more of the game and dried fish their women had prepared upon me and my comrades. By the time we finished our feast, more people had arrived from the outlying houses of the village to listen to our words.

Yesuntai left it to me to urge the war we wanted. After I was empty of eloquence, we waited in the long house set aside for our men. If the men of Skanechtade chose the warpath, they would gather war parties and send runners to the other villages of the Ganeagaono to persuade more warriors to join us.

I had spoken the truth to the people of Skanechtade. Deceit was not possible with the Ganeagaono, and especially not for me. I was still their brother, even after all the years I thought of as my exile. The Ganeagaono would know I could not lie to them; this war would serve them as well as us. Whoever was not at peace with them was their enemy. In that, they were much like us. A people who might threaten their domain as well as ours would be banished from the shores of this land.

Yet my doubts had grown, not about our mission, but of what might come afterwards. More of our people would cross the ocean, and the Bahadurs who followed us to Yeke Geren might dream of subduing the nations we now called our friends. There could be no peace with those who did not submit to us in the end, and I did not believe the Ganeagaono and the other nations of the Long House would ever swear an oath to our Khan.

I had dwelled on such thoughts as we sailed north, following the great river that led to Skanechtade. By the time we rowed away from the ship in our longboats, I had made my decision. I would do what I could to aid Yesuntai, but whatever the outcome of our mission, I would not return to Yeke Geren. My place was with the Ganeagaono who had granted me my life.

"Jirandai," Yesuntai Noyan said softly. He sat in the back of the long house, his back against the wall, his face hidden in shadows; I had thought he was asleep. "What do you think they will do?"

"A few of the young chiefs want to join us. That I saw when I finished my speech." Some of our men glanced towards me; most were sleeping on the benches that lined the walls. "We will have a few bands, at least."

"A few bands are useless to me," Yesuntai muttered. "A raid would only provoke our enemies. I must have enough men to destroy them."

"I have done what I can," I replied. "We can only hope my words have moved them."

Among the Ganeagaono, those who wanted war had to convince others to follow them. The sachems who ruled their councils had no power to lead in war; I had explained that to Yesuntai. It was up to the chiefs and other warriors seeking glory to assemble war parties, but a sign that a sachem favored our enterprise might persuade many to join us. I had watched the sachems during my speech; my son was among them. His dark eyes had not betrayed any of his thoughts.

"I saw how you spoke, Jirandai," Yesuntai said, "and felt the power in your words, even if I did not understand them. I do not believe we will fail."

"May it be so, Noyan." I thought then of the time I had traveled west with my adoptive father along the great trail that runs to the lands of the Nundawaono. There, among the Western Gatekeepers of the Long House nations, I had first heard the tale of the great serpent brought down by the thunderbolts of Heno, spirit of storms and rain. In his death throes, the serpent had torn the land asunder and created the mighty falls into which the rapids of the Neahga River flowed. My foster father had doubts about the story's ending, although he did not say so to our hosts. He had stood on a cliff near the falls and seen a rainbow arching above the tumultuous waters; he had heard the steady sound of the torrent and felt the force of the wind that never died. He believed that the serpent was not dead, but only sleeping, and might rise to ravage the land again.

Something in Yesuntai made me think of that serpent. When he was still, his eyes darted restlessly, and when he slept, his body was tense, ready to rouse itself at the slightest disturbance. Something was coiled inside him, sleeping but ready to wake.

Voices murmured beyond the doorway to my right. Some of the Ganeagaono were still outside. A young man in a deerskin kilt and beaded belt entered, then gestured at me.

"You," he said, "he who is called Senadondo." I lifted my head at the sound of the name his people had given to me. "I ask you to come with me," he continued in his own tongue.

I got to my feet and turned to Yesuntai. "It seems someone wishes to speak to me."

He waved a hand. "Then you must go."

"Perhaps some of the men want to hear more of our plans."

"Or perhaps a family you left behind wishes to welcome you home."

I narrowed my eyes as I left. The Noyan had heard nothing from me about my wife and son, but he knew I had returned to Yeke Geren as a man. He might have guessed I had left a woman here.

The man who had come for me led me past clusters of houses. Although it was nearly midnight, with only a sliver of moon to light our way, people were still awake; I heard them murmuring beyond the open doors. A band of children trailed us. Whenever I slowed, they crowded around me to touch my long coat or to pull at my silk tunic.

We halted in front of a long house large enough for three families. The sign of the Wolf Clan was painted on the door.

The man motioned to me to go inside, then led the children away.

At first, I thought the house was empty, then heard a whisper near the back. Three banked fires glowed in the central space between the house's bark partitions. I called out a greeting; as I passed the last partition, I turned to my right and saw who was waiting for me.

My son wore his headdress, a woven cap from which a single large eagle feather jutted from a cluster of smaller feathers. Braided bands with beads adorned his bare arms; rattles hung from his belt. My wife wore a deerskin cloak over a dress decorated with beads. Even in the shadows beyond the fire, I saw the strands of silver in her dark hair.

"Dasiyu," I whispered, then turned to my son. "Teyendanaga."

He shook his head slightly. "You forget – I am the sachem Sohaewahah now." He gestured at one of the blankets that covered the floor; I sat down.

"I hoped you would come back," Dasiyu said. "I wished for it, yet prayed that you would not."

"Mother," our son murmured. She pushed a bowl of hommony towards me, then sat back on her heels.

"I wanted to come to you right away," I said. "I did not know if you were here. When the men of my own clan greeted me, I feared what they might say if I asked about you, so kept silent. I searched the crowd for you when I was speaking."

"I was there," Dasiyu said, "sitting behind the sachems among the women. Your eyes are failing you."

I suspected that she had concealed herself behind others. "I thought you might have another husband by now."

"I have never divorced you." Her face was much the same, only lightly marked with lines. I thought of how I must look to her, leather-faced and broader in the belly, softened by the years in Yeke Geren. "I have never placed the few belongings you left with me outside my door. You are still my husband, Senadondo, but it is Sohaewahah who asked you to come to this house, not I."

My son held up his hand. "I knew you would return to us, my

father. I saw it in my vision. It is of that vision that I wish to speak now."

That a vision might have come to him, I did not doubt. Many spirits lived in these lands, and the Ganeagaono, as do all wise men, trust their dreams. But evil spirits can deceive men, and even the wise can fail to understand what the spirits tell them.

"I would hear of your vision," I said.

"Two summers past, not long after I became Sohaewahah, I fell ill with a fever. My body fought it, but even after it passed, I could not rise from my bed. It was then, after the fever was gone, that I had my vision and knew it to be truth." He gazed directly at me, his eyes steady. "Beyond my doorway, I saw a great light, and then three men entered my dwelling. One carried a branch, another a red tomahawk, and the third bore the shorter bow and the firestick that are your people's weapons. The man holding the branch spoke, and I knew that Hawenneyu was speaking to me through him. He told me of a storm gathering in the east, over the Ojikhadagega, the great ocean your people crossed, and said that it threatened all the nations of the Long House. He told me that some of those who might offer us peace would bring only the peace of death. Yet his words did not frighten me, for he went on to say that my father would return to me, and bring a brother to my side."

He glanced at his mother, then looked back at me. "My father and the brother he brought to me," he continued, "would help us stand against the coming storm – this was the Great Spirit's promise. When my vision passed, I was able to rise. I left my house and went through the village, telling everyone of what I had been shown. Now you are here, and the people remember what my vision foretold, and yet I see no brother."

"You have a brother," I said, thinking of Ajiragha. "I left him in Yeke Geren."

"But he is not here at my side, as my vision promised."

"He is only an infant, and the Inglistanis are the storm that threatens you. More of them will cross the Great Salt Water."

"A war against them would cost us many men. We might trade with them, as we do with you. Peace is what we have always desired – war is only our way to prove our courage and to bring that peace about. You should know that, having been one of us."

"The Inglistanis will make false promises, and when more of them come, even the Long House may fall before their soldiers. You have no treaties with the Inglistanis, so you are in a state of war with them now. Two of the spirits who came to you bore weapons – the Great Spirit means for you to make war."

"But against whom?" Dasiyu asked. She leaned forward and shook her fist. "Perhaps those who are on your island of Ganono are the storm that will come upon us, after we are weakened by battle with the pale-faced people you hate."

"Foolish woman," I muttered, "I am one of you. Would I come here to betray you?" Despite my words, she reminded me of my own doubts.

"You should not have come back," she said. "Whenever I dreamed of your return, I saw you alone, not with others seeking to use us for their own purposes. Look at you – there is nothing of the Ganeagaono left in you. You speak our words, but your garments and your companions show where your true loyalty lies."

"You are wrong." I stared at her; she did not look away. "I have never forgotten my brothers here."

"You come to spy on us. When you have fought with our warriors in this battle, you will see our weaknesses more clearly, the ways in which we might be defeated, and we will not be able to use your pale-faced enemies against you."

"Is this what you have been saying to the other women? Have you gone before the men to speak against this war?"

Dasiyu drew in her breath; our son clutched her wrist. "You have said enough, Mother," he whispered. "I believe what he says. My vision told me he would come, and the spirits held the weapons of war. Perhaps my brother is meant to join me later." He got to his feet. "I go now to add my voice to the councils. It may be that I can persuade those who waver. If we are to follow the warpath now, I will set aside my office to fight with you."

He left us before I could speak. "You will have your war," Dasiyu said. "The other sachems will listen to my son, and ask him to speak for them to the people. The wise old women will heed his words, because they chose him for his position."

"This war will serve you."

She scowled, then pushed the bowl of hommony towards me. "You insult me by leaving my food untouched."

I ate some of the dried corn, then set the bowl down. "Dasiyu, I did not come here only to speak of war. I swore an oath to myself that, when this campaign ends, I will live among you again."

"And am I to rejoice over that?"

"Cursed woman, anything I do would stoke your rage. I went back to speak for the Long House in our councils. I asked you to come with me, and you refused."

"I would have had to abandon my clan. My son would never have been chosen as a sachem then. You would not be promising to stay with us unless you believed you have failed as our voice."

Even after the years apart, she saw what lay inside me. "Whatever comes," I said, "my place is here."

She said nothing for a long time. The warmth inside the long house was growing oppressive. I opened my coat, then took off my headband to mop my brow.

"Look at you," she said, leaning towards me to touch the braids coiled behind my ears. Her hand brushed the top of my shaven head lightly. "You had such a fine scalplock – how could you have given it up?" She poked at my mustache. "I do not understand why a man would want hair over his lip." She fingered the fabric of my tunic. "And this – a woman might wear such a garment. I used to admire you so when I watched you dance. You were the shortest of the men, but no man here had such strong arms and broad shoulders, and now you hide them under these clothes."

I drew her to me. She was not as she had been, nor was I; once, every moment in her arms had only fed the flames inside me. Our fires were banked now, the fever gone, but her welcoming warmth remained.

"You have changed in another way, Senadondo," she said afterwards. "You are not so hasty as you were."

"I am no longer a young man, Dasiyu. I must make the most of what moments I am given."

She pulled a blanket over us. I held her until she was asleep; she nestled against me as she once had, her cheek against my shoulder, a leg looped around mine. I did not know how to keep my promise to stay with her. Yesuntai might want a spy among the Flint People when this campaign was concluded; he might believe I was his man for the task.

I slept uneasily. A war whoop awakened me at dawn. I slipped away from my wife, pulled on my trousers, and went to the door.

A young chief was running through the village. Rattles were bound to his knees with leather bands, and he held a red tomahawk; beads of black wampum dangled from his weapon. He halted in front of the war post, lifted his arm, and embedded the tomahawk in the painted wood. He began to dance, and other men raced towards him, until it seemed most of the village's warriors had enlisted in the war.

They danced, bodies bent from the waist, arms lifting as if to strike enemies, hands out to ward off attack. Their feet beat against the ground as drums throbbed. I saw Yesuntai then; he walked towards them, his head thrown back, a bow in one hand. I stepped from the doorway, felt my heels drumming against the earth, and joined the dancers.

3

Yesuntai, a Khan's son, was used to absolute obedience. The Ganeagaono, following the custom of all the Long House people, would obey any war chiefs in whom they had confidence. I had warned Yesuntai that no chief could command the Flint People to join in this war, and that even the women were free to offer their opinions of the venture.

"So be it," the young Noyan had said to that. "Our own women were fierce and brave before they were softened by other ways, and my ancestor Bortai Khatun often advised her husband Genghis Khan, although even that great lady would not have dared to address a war kuriltai. If these women are as formidable as you say, then they must have bred brave sons." I was grateful for his tolerance.

But the people of Skanechtade had agreed to join us, and soon their messengers returned from other villages with word that chiefs in every Ganeagaono settlement had agreed to go on the warpath. My son had advised us to follow the custom of the Hodenosaunee when all of their nations fought in a common war, and to choose two supreme commanders so that there would be unanimity in all decisions. Yesuntai, it was agreed, would command, since he had proposed this war, and Aroniateka, a cousin of my son's, would be Yesuntai's equal. Aroniateka, happily, was a man avid to learn a new way of warfare.

This was essential to our purpose, since to have any chance against the Inglistanis, the Ganeagaono could not fight in their usual fashion. The Long House people were still new to organized campaigns with many warriors, and most of their battles had been little more than raids by small parties. Their men were used to war, which, along with the hunt, was their favorite pursuit, but this war would be more than a ritual test of valor.

The Flint People had acquired horses from us in trade, but had never used them in warfare. Their warriors moved so rapidly on foot through the forests that mounts would only slow their progress. We would have to travel on foot, and take any horses we might need later from the Inglistanis. The men I had chosen in Yeke Geren had hunted and traded with the Hodenosaunee, and were used to their ways. Those Yesuntai had brought were veterans of European campaigns, but willing to adapt.

The whoops of Skanechtade's warriors echoed through the village as they danced. The women busied themselves making moccasins and preparing provisions for their men. Runners moved between villages with the orders of our two commanders and returned with promises that the other war parties would follow them. Yesuntai would have preferred more time for planning, to send out more scouts before we left Ganeagaono territory, but we had little time. War had been declared, and our

allies were impatient to fight. We needed a swift victory over our
enemy. If we did not defeat the Inglistanis by late autumn, the
Ganeagaono, their honor satisfied by whatever they had won by
then, might abandon us.

A chill remained in the early spring air, but most of the
Ganeagaono men had shed the cloaks and blankets that covered
their upper bodies in winter. Our Mongols followed their
example and stripped to the waist, and I advised Yesuntai's
men to trade their felt boots for moccasins. Dasiyu gave me a
kilt and a pair of deerskin moccasins; I easily gave up my
Mongol tunic and trousers for the garb I had once worn.

Eight days after we had come to Skanechtade, the warriors
performed their last war dance. Men streamed from the village
towards the river; Dasiyu followed me to the high wall that
surrounded the long houses and handed me dried meat and a
pouch of corn flour mixed with maple sugar.

"I will come back," I said, "when this war is over."

"If you have victory, I shall welcome you." She gripped my
arms for a moment, then let go. "If you suffer defeat, if you and
your chief lead our men only to ruin, your belongings will be
outside my door."

"We will win," I said.

The lines around her lids deepened as she narrowed her eyes.
"See that you do, Senadondo."

We crossed to the eastern side of the great river, then moved
south. Some of our scouts had explored these oak-covered hills,
and Yesuntai had planned his campaign with the aid of
Inglistani maps our soldiers had taken during a raid the year
before. We would travel south, then move east through the
Mahican lands, keeping to the north of the enemy settlements.
Our forces would remain divided during the journey, so as not
to alert the Inglistanis. Plymouth, the easternmost enemy settlement, overlooked an ocean bay. When Plymouth was taken, we
would move south towards another great bay and the town
called Newport. This settlement lay on an island at the mouth
of the bay, and we would advance on it from the east. Any who
escaped us would be forced to flee west towards Charlestown.

A wise commander always allows his enemy a retreat, since desperate defenders can cost a general many men, while a sweep by one wing of his force can pick off retreating soldiers. We would drive the Inglistanis west. When Charlestown fell, the survivors would have to run to the settlement they called New Haven. When New Haven was crushed, only New London, their westernmost town, would remain, and from there the Inglistanis could flee only to territory controlled by us.

At some point, the enemy was likely to sue for peace, but there could be no peace with the Inglistanis. Our allies and we were agreed; this would be a war of extermination.

These were our plans, but obstacles lay ahead. The Mahicans would present no problem; as payers of tribute to the Long House, they would allow us safe passage through their lands. But the Wampanoag people dwelled in the east, and the Pequots controlled the trails that would lead us south to Newport. Both groups feared the Flint People and had treaties with the Inglistanis. Our men would be more than a match for theirs if the Wampanoags and Pequots fought in defense of their pale-faced friends. But such a battle would cost us warriors, and a prolonged battle for Plymouth would endanger our entire strategy.

Our forces remained divided as we moved. Speed is one of a soldier's greatest allies, so we satisfied our hunger with our meager provisions and did not stop to hunt. At night, when we rested, Ganeagaono warriors marked the trees with a record of our numbers and movements, and we halted along the way to read the markings others had left for us. Yesuntai kept me at his side. I was teaching him the Ganeagaono tongue, but he still needed me to speak his words to his fellow commander Aroniateka.

In three days, we came to a Mahican settlement, and alerted the people there with war cries. Their chiefs welcomed us outside their stockade, met with us, and complained bitterly about the Inglistanis, who they believed had designs on their lands. They had refrained from raids, not wanting to provoke the settlers, but younger Mahicans had chided the chiefs for their caution. After we spoke of our intentions, several of their men offered to join us. We had expected safe passage, but to have warriors from among them lifted our spirits even higher.

We turned east, and markings on tree trunks told us of other Mahicans that had joined our forces. Yesuntai, with his bowcase, quiver, and sword hanging from his belt, and his musket over his shoulder, moved as easily through the woods as my son in his kilt and moccasins. A bond was forming between them, and often they communicated silently with looks and gestures, not needing my words. Wampanoag territory lay ahead, yet Yesuntai's confidence was not dampened, nor was my son's. The Great Spirit our Ganeagaono brethren called Hawenneyu, and that Yesuntai knew under the name of Tengri, would guide them; I saw their faith in their dark eyes when they lifted their heads to gaze through the arching tree limbs at the sky. God would give them victory.

4

God was with us. Our scouts went out, and returned with a Wampanoag boy, a wretched creature with a pinched face and tattered kilt. A Mahican with us knew the boy's tongue, and we soon heard of the grief that had come to his village. Inglistani soldiers had attacked without warning only a few days ago, striking in the night while his people slept. The boy guessed that nearly two hundred of his Wampanoag people had died, cut down by swords and firesticks. He did not know how many others had managed to escape.

We mourned with him. Inwardly, I rejoiced. Perhaps the Inglistanis would not have raided their allies if they had known we were coming against them, but their rash act served our purpose. The deed was proof of their evil intentions; they would slaughter even their friends to claim what they wanted. Wampanoags who might have fought against us now welcomed us as their deliverers. Yesuntai consulted with Aroniateka, then gave his orders. The left wing of our force would strike at Plymouth, using the Wampanoags as a shield as they advanced.

The Wampanoags had acquired muskets from the Inglistanis,

and now turned those weapons against their false friends. By the time my companions and I heard the cries of gulls above Plymouth's rocky shore, the flames of the dying town lighted our way. Charred hulls and blackened masts were sinking beneath the grey waters; warriors had struck at the harbor first, approaching it during the night in canoes to burn the ships and cut off any escape to the sea. Women leaped from rocks and were swallowed by waves; other Inglistanis fled from the town's burning walls, only to be cut down by our forces. There was no need to issue a command to take no prisoners, for the betrayed Wampanoags were in no mood to show mercy. They drove their captives into houses, and set the dwellings ablaze; children became targets for their arrows.

The Flint People do not leave the spirits of their dead to wander. We painted the bodies of our dead comrades, then buried them with their weapons and the food they would need for the long journey ahead. Above the burial mound, the Ganeagaono freed birds they had captured to help bear the spirits of the fallen to Heaven, and set a fire to light their way.

From the ruins of Plymouth, we salvaged provisions, bolts of cloth, and cannons. Much of the booty was given to the Wampanoags, since they had suffered most of the casualties. Having achieved the swift victory we needed, we loaded the cannons onto ox-drawn wagons, then moved south.

5

The center and left wings of our forces came together as we entered Pequot territory. The right wing would move towards Charlestown while we struck at Newport.

Parties of warriors fanned out to strike at the farms that lay in our path. We met little resistance from the Pequots, and they soon understood that our battle was with the Inglistanis, not with them. After hearing of how Inglistani soldiers had massacred helpless Wampanoags, many of their warriors joined us, and led us to the farms of those they had once called friends. The night was brightened by the fires of burning houses and crops, and the silence shattered by the screams of the dying. We took what we needed, and burned the rest.

A few farmers escaped us. The tracks of their horses ran south; Newport would be warned. The enemy was likely to think that only enraged Wampanoags and Pequots were moving against them, but would surely send a force to meet us. We were still four days' distance from the lowlands that surrounded Newport's great bay when we caught sight of Inglistani soldiers.

They were massed together along the trail that led through the forest, marching stiffly in rows, their muskets ready. The Wampanoags fired upon them from the trees, then swept towards them as the air was filled with the sharp cracks of muskets and the whistling of arrows. Volleys of our metal-tipped arrows and the flint-headed arrows of the Ganeagaono flew towards the Inglistanis; enemy soldiers fell, opening up breaks in their line. Men knelt to load their weapons as others fired at us from behind them, and soon the ground was covered with the bodies of Wampanoag and Pequot warriors.

The people of these lands had never faced such carnage in battle, but their courage did not fail them. They climbed over the bodies of dead and wounded comrades to fight the enemy hand to hand. The soldiers, unable to fire at such close range, used their muskets as clubs and slashed at our allies with swords; men drenched in blood shrieked as they swung their tomahawks. I expected the Inglistanis to retreat, but they held their ground until the last of their men had fallen.

We mourned our dead. The Wampanoags and the Pequots, who had lost so many men, might have withdrawn and let us fight on alone. Aroniateka consulted with their war chiefs, then gave us their answer. They would march with us against Newport, and share in that victory.

6

Swift, early successes hearten any warrior for the efforts that lie ahead. We advanced on Newport fueled by the victories we had already won. Summer was upon us as we approached the southeast end of the great bay. The island on which Newport stood lay to the west, across a narrow channel; the enemy had retreated behind the wooden walls of the town's stockade.

By day, we concealed ourselves amid the trees bordering the shore's wetlands. At night, the Ganeagaono cut down trees and collected rope we had gathered from Inglistani farms. Several of Yesuntai's older officers had experience in siege warfare; under their guidance, our allies quickly erected five catapults. In the early days of our greatness, we had possessed as little knowledge of sieges as the Flint People, but they seemed more than willing to master this new art. We did not want a long siege, but would be prepared for one if necessary. If Newport held out, we would leave a force behind and move on to our next objective.

When the moon showed her dark side to the earth, we brought out our catapults under cover of darkness and launched cannonballs at the five ships anchored in Newport's harbor, following them with missiles of rock packed with burning dried grass. The sails of the ships became torches, and more missiles caught enemy sailors as they leaped from the decks. The ships were sinking by the time we turned the catapults against the town's walls. The Inglistanis would have no escape by sea, and had lost the ships they might have used to bombard us.

We assaulted Newport for three days, until the Inglistani cannons fell silent. From the western side of the island, Inglistanis were soon fleeing in longboats towards Charlestown. There were many breaches in the stockade's walls, and few defenders left in the doomed town when we began to cross the channel in our canoes, but those who remained fought to the last man. Even after our men were inside the walls, Inglistanis shot at us from windows and roofs, and for every enemy we took there, two or three of our warriors were lost. We stripped enemy bodies, looted the buildings, then burned the town. Those hiding on the western side of the bay in Charlestown would see the great bonfire that would warn them of their fate.

The Wampanoags returned to their lands in the north. We left the Pequots to guard the bay and to see that no more Inglistani ships landed there. Our right wing would be advancing on Charlestown. We returned to the bay's eastern shore and went north, then turned west. A party of men bearing the weapons of war met us along one woodland trail, and led us to their chiefs. By then, the Narragansett people of the region had decided to throw in their lot with us.

7

Terror has always been a powerful weapon against enemies. Put enough fear into an enemy's heart, and victories can be won even before one meets him in the field. Thus it was during that summer of war. Charlestown fell, ten days after Newport. In spite of the surrender, we expected some of the survivors to hide in their houses and take their revenge when we entered the town. Instead, they gave up their weapons and waited passively for execution. Those I beheaded whispered prayers as they knelt and stretched their necks, unable to rouse themselves even to curse me. A few gathered enough courage to beg for their children's lives.

Yesuntai was merciful. He spared some women and children, those who looked most fearful, led them and a few old men to a longboat, and gave them a message in Frankish to deliver to those in New Haven. The message was much like the traditional one sent by Mongol Khans to their enemies: God has annihilated many of you for daring to stand against us. Submit to us, and serve us. When you see us massed against you, surrender and open your gates to us, for if you do not, God alone knows what will happen to you.

It was easy to imagine the effect this message would have on New Haven's defenders, if the Inglistanis we had spared survived their journey along the coast to deliver it. I did not believe that the Inglistanis would surrender immediately, but some among them would want to submit, and dissension would sap their spirit.

Most of our forces moved west, towards New Haven, followed by Inglistanis we had spared to carry canoes and haul cannons. Yesuntai had mastered enough of the Flint People's language to speak with Aroniateka, and left me with the rear guard. We would travel to the north of the main force, paralleling its path, and take the outlying farms.

Most of the farms we found were abandoned. We salvaged what we could and burned the rest. Days of searching empty farmhouses gave me time to reflect on how this campaign would affect my Ganeagaono brothers.

Their past battles had been for glory, to show their courage, to bring enemies to submission and to capture prisoners who might, in the end, become brothers of the Long House. They had seen that unity among their Five Nations would make them stronger. Now we were teaching them that a victory over certain enemies was not enough, that sometimes only the extermination of that enemy would end the conflict, that total war might be necessary. Perhaps they would have learned that lesson without us, but their knowledge of this new art would change them, as surely as the serpent who beguiled the first man and woman changed man's nature. They might turn what they had learned against us.

Victories can hearten any soldier, but a respite from battle can also cause him to let down his guard. With a small party led by my son, I followed a rutted road towards one farm. From the trees beyond the field, where the corn was still only tall enough to reach to a man's waist, we spied a log dwelling, with smoke rising from its chimney. A white flag attached to a stick stood outside the door.

"They wish to surrender," I murmured to my son.

He shook his head. "The corn will hide us. We can get close enough to—"

"They are willing to give themselves up. Your men will have captives when they return to their homes. The Inglistanis have lost. Yesuntai will not object if we spare people willing to surrender without a fight."

My son said, "You are only weary of killing. My people say that a man weary of war is also weary of life."

"The people whose seed I carry have the same saying." He had spoken the truth. I was tiring of the war I had helped to bring about, thinking of what might follow it. "I shall speak to them."

"And we will guard your back," my son replied.

I left the trees and circled the field as the others crept through the corn. When I was several paces from the door, I held out my hands, palms up. "Come outside," I shouted in Frankish, hoping my words would be understood. "Show yourselves." I tensed, ready to fling myself to the ground if my son and his men suddenly attacked.

The door opened. A man with a greying beard left the house, followed by a young girl. A white cap hid her hair, but bright golden strands curled over her forehead. She gazed at me steadily with her blue eyes; I saw sorrow in her look, but no fear. A brave spirit, I thought, and felt a heaviness over my heart that might have been pity.

The man's Frankish was broken, but I was able to grasp his words. Whatever his people had done, he had always dealt fairly with the natives. He asked only to be left on his farm, to have his life and his family's spared.

"It cannot be," I told him. "You must leave this place. My brothers will decide your fate. That is all I can offer you, a chance for life away from here."

The man threw up an arm. The girl was darting towards the doorway when I saw a glint of metal beyond a window. A blow knocked the wind from me and threw me onto my back. I clutched at my ribs and felt blood seep from me as the air was filled with the sound of war whoops.

They had been lying in wait for us. Perhaps they would not have fired at me if I had granted the man his request; perhaps they had intended an ambush all along. I cursed myself for my weakness and pity. I would have another scar to remind me of Inglistani treachery and the cost of a moment's lack of vigilance, if I lived.

When I came to myself, the cabin was burning. A man knelt beside me, tending my wounds. Pain stabbed at me along my right side as I struggled to breathe. Two bodies in the grey clothes of Inglistani farmers lay outside the door. The Ganeagaono warriors danced as the flames leaped before them.

My son strode towards me, a scalp of long, golden hair dangling from his belt. "You cost me two men," he said. I moved my head from side to side, unable to speak. "I am sorry, Father. I think this war will be your last."

"I will live," I said.

"Yes, you will live, but I do not think you will fight again." He sighed. "Yet I must forgive you, for leading us to what your people call greatness." He lifted his head and cried out, echoing the war whoops of his men.

8

I was carried west on a wagon, my ribs covered with healing herbs and bound tightly with Inglistani cloth. A few men remained with me while the rest moved on towards New Haven. Every morning, I woke expecting to find that they had abandoned me, only to find them seated around the fire.

A man's pride can be good medicine, and the disdain of others a goad. I was able to walk when Yesuntai sent a Bahadur to me with news of New Haven's surrender. Few soldiers were left in New Haven; most had fled to make a stand in New London. The young Noyan expected a fierce battle there, where the valor of the Inglistanis would be fired by desperation. He wanted me at his side as soon as possible.

The Bahadur had brought a spare horse for me. As we rode, he muttered of the difficulties Yesuntai now faced. Our Narragansett allies had remained behind in their territory, as we had expected, but the Mahicans, sated by glory, were already talking of returning to their lands. They thought they could wait until spring to continue the war; they did not understand. I wondered if the Ganeagaono had the stomach for a siege that might last the winter. They would be thinking of the coming Green Corn festival, of the need to lay in game for the colder weather and of the families that waited for them.

The oaks and maples gave way to more fields the Inglistanis had cleared and then abandoned. I smelled the salt of the ocean when we caught sight of Mongol and Mahican sentries outside a makeshift stockade. Yesuntai was camped to the east of New London, amid rows of Ganeagaono bark shelters. In the distance, behind a fog rolling in from the sea, I glimpsed the walls of the town.

Yesuntai and Aroniateka were outside one shelter, sitting at a fire with four other men. I heaved myself from my horse and walked towards them.

"Greetings, Jirandai," Yesuntai said in Mongol. "I am pleased to see you have recovered enough to take part in our final triumph."

I squatted by the fire and stretched out my hands. My ribs still pained me; I suspected they always would. "This is likely to be our hardest battle," I said.

"Then our glory will be all the greater when we win it." Yesuntai accepted a pipe from Aroniateka and drew in the smoke. "We will take New London before the leaves begin to turn."

"You plan to take it by storm?" I asked. "That will cost us."

"I must have it, whatever it costs. My fellow commander Aroniateka is equally impatient for this campaign to end, as I suspect you are, Bahadur." His eyes held the same look I had seen in my son's outside the burning farmhouse, that expression of pity mingled with contempt for an old man tired of war.

I slept uneasily that night, plagued by aching muscles strained by my ride and the pain of my wounds. The sound of intermittent thunder over the ocean woke me before dawn. I crept from my shelter to find other men outside, shadows in the mists, and then knew what we were hearing. The sound was that of cannons being fired from ships. The Inglistanis would turn the weapons of their ships against us, whatever the risk to the town. They would drive us back from the shore and force us to withdraw.

Yesuntai had left his shelter. He paced, his arms swinging as if he longed to sweep the fog away. I went to him, knowing how difficult it would be to persuade him to give up now. A man shouted in the distance, and another answered him with a whoop. Yesuntai would have to order a retreat, or see men slaughtered to no purpose. I could still hear the sound of cannons over the water, and wondered why the Inglistanis had sailed no closer to us.

A Mongol and a Ganeagaono warrior were pushing their way through knots of men. "Noyan!" the Mongol called out to Yesuntai. "From the shore, I saw three ships – they fly the blue and white banners of your father! They have turned their weapons against the Inglistanis!"

The men near us cheered. Yesuntai's face was taut, his eyes slits. He turned to me; his hands trembled as he clasped my shoulders.

"It seems," he said softly, "that we will have to share our triumph."

The ships had sailed to New London from Yeke Geren. They bombarded the town as we advanced from the north and east, driving our remaining Inglistani captives before us against the outer stockade. The sight of these wretches, crying out in Inglistani to their comrades and dying under the assault of their own people's weapons, soon brought New London's commander to send up white flags.

Michel Bahadur left his ship to accept the surrender. We learned from him that our Khan had at last begun his war against Inglistan that spring; a ship had brought Michel the news only recently. By now, he was certain, the Khanate's armies would be marching on London itself. Michel had quickly seen that his duty lay in aiding us, now that we were openly at war with the Inglistanis.

Michel Bahadur praised Yesuntai lavishly as they embraced in the square of the defeated town. He spoke of our courage, but in words that made it seem that only Michel could have given us this final triumph. I listened in silence, my mind filled with harsh thoughts about men who claimed the victories of others for their own.

We celebrated the fall of New London with a feast in the town hall. Several Inglistani women who had survived the ravages of Michel's men stood behind them to fill their cups. There were few beauties among those wan and narrow-faced creatures, but Michel had claimed a pretty dark-haired girl for himself.

He sat among his men, Yesuntai at his side, drinking to our victory. He offered only a grudging tribute to the Ganeagaono and the Mahicans, and said that they would be given their share of captives with the air of a man granting a great favor. I had chosen to sit with the Ganeagaono chiefs, as did most of the Mongols who had fought with us. Michel's men laughed when three of the Mahican chiefs slid under tables, overcome by the wine and whiskey. My son, watching them, refused to drink from his cup.

"Comrades!" Michel bellowed in Frankish. I brooded over my wine, wondering what sort of speech he would make now. "Our enemies have been crushed! I say now that in this place, where we defeated the last of the Inglistani settlers, we will make a new outpost of our Khanate! New London will become another great camp!"

I stiffened in shock. The men around Michel fell silent as they watched us. Yesuntai glanced in my direction; his fingers tightened around his cup.

"New London was to burn," Yesuntai said at last. "It was to suffer the fate of the other settlements."

"It will stand," Michel said, "to serve your father our Khan. Surely you cannot object to that, Noyan."

Yesuntai seemed about to speak, then sank back in his seat. Our Narragansett and Wampanoag allies would feel betrayed when they learned of Michel's intentions. The Bahadur's round, crafty face reminded me of everything I despised in Europeans, their greed, their treachery, their lies.

My son motioned to me, obviously expecting me to translate Michel's words. I leaned towards him. "Listen to me," I said softly in the tongue of the Flint People, "and do nothing rash when you hear what I must say now. The war chief who sailed here to aid us means to camp in this place. His people will live in this town we have won."

His hand darted towards his tomahawk, then fell. "So this is why we fought. I should have listened to Mother when she first spoke against you."

"I did not know what Michel Bahadur meant to do, but what happens here will not trouble the Long House."

"Until your people choose to forget another promise."

"I am one of you," I said.

"You are only an old man who allowed himself to be deceived." He looked away from me. "I know where honor lies, even if your people do not. I will not shame you before your chief by showing what I think of him. I will not break our treaty in this place." He turned to Aroniateka and whispered to him. The chiefs near them were still; only their eyes revealed their rage.

I had fulfilled my duty to my Khan. All that remained was to keep my promise to myself, and to Dasiyu.

9

I walked along New London's main street, searching for Yesuntai. Warriors stumbled along the cobblestones, intoxicated by drink, blind to the contemptuous stares of our Frankish and Dutch sailors. The whiskey Michel's men had given them from the looted stores had made them forget their villages and the tasks that awaited them there.

I found Yesuntai with a party of Ganeagaono warriors and a few Inglistani captives. "These comrades are leaving us," Yesuntai said. "You must say an eloquent farewell for me – I still lack the words to do it properly."

One of the men pulled at his scalplock. "It is time for us to go," he said in his language. Five Mahicans clutching bottles of whiskey staggered past us. "To see brave men in such a state sickens me."

I nodded in agreement. "My chief Yesuntai will forever remember your valor. May Grandfather Heno water your fields, the Three Sisters give you a great harvest, and the winter be filled with tales of your victories."

The warriors led their captives away; two of the smaller children wept as they clung to their mothers' hands. They would forget their tears and learn to love the People of the Long House, as I had.

"The rest should go home as well," I said to Yesuntai. "There is nothing for them here now."

"Perhaps not."

"They will have stories to tell of this war for many generations. Perhaps the tales of their exploits can make them forget how they were treated here. I wish to speak to you, Noyan."

"Good. I have been hoping for a chance to speak to you."

I led him along a side street to the house where Aroniateka and my son were quartered with some of their men. All of them were inside, sitting on blankets near the fireplace. At least these men had resisted the lure of drink, and had refused the bright baubles Michel's men had thrown to our warriors while claiming the greater share of the booty for themselves. They greeted us with restraint, and did not ask us to join them.

We seated ourselves at a table in the back of the room. "I swore an oath to you, Yesuntai Noyan," I said, "and ask you to free me from it now." I rested my elbows on the table. "I wish to return to Skanechtade, to my Ganeagaono brothers."

He leaned forward. "I expected you to ask for that."

"As for my wife Elgigetei and my son Ajiragha, I ask only that you accept them into your household. My wife will not miss me greatly, and perhaps you can see that Ajiragha does not forget his father. You were my comrade-in-arms, and I will not sneak away from your side in the night. You do not need me now. Even my son will tell you that I am a man who has outlived his taste for battle. You will lose nothing by letting me go."

"And what will you do," he said, "if my people forsake their treaties?"

"I think you know the answer to that."

"You told me of the treaty's words, that we and the Flint People would be at peace for as long as you were both their brother and the Khan's servant. You will no longer be our servant if you go back to Skanechtade."

"So you are ready to seize on that. If the men of Yeke Geren fail to renew their promises, that will show their true intentions. I had hoped that you—"

"Listen to me." Yesuntai's fingers closed around my wrist. "I have found my brothers in your son and Aroniateka, and among the brave men who fought with us. They are my brothers, not the rabble who came here under Michel's command."

"Those men serve your father the Khan."

"They serve themselves," he whispered, "and forget what we once were."

I shook my arm free of his grasp. He was silent for a while, then said, "Koko Mongke Tengri, the Eternal Blue Sky that covers all the world, promised us dominion over Etugen, the Earth. I told you of the wise men in Khitai who believe that the ancestors of the peoples in these lands once roamed our ancient homeland. I know now that what those scholars say is true. The people here are our long-lost brothers – they are more truly Mongol than men whose blood has been thinned by the ways of Europe. For them to rule here is in keeping with our destiny. They could make an ulus here, a nation as great as any we have known, one that might someday be a match for our Khanates."

I said, "You are speaking treason."

"I am speaking the truth. I have had a vision, Jirandai. The spirits have spoken to me and shown me two arcs closing in a great circle, joining those who have been so long separated. When the peoples of this land are one ulus, when they achieve the unity our ancestors found under Genghis Khan, then perhaps they will be the ones to bring the rest of the world under their sway. If the Khans in our domains cannot accept them as brothers, they may be forced to bow to them as conquerors." Yesuntai paused. "Are we to sweep the Inglistanis from these lands only so that more of those we rule can flood these shores? They will forget the Khanate, as our people are forgetting their old homeland. They will use the peoples of this land against one another in their own disputes, when they have forgotten their Khan and fall to fighting among themselves. I see what must be done to prevent that. You see it, too. We have one more battle to fight before you go back to Skanechtade."

I knew what he wanted. "How do you plan to take Yeke Geren?" I asked.

"We must have Michel's ships. My Mongols can man them. We also need the Ganeagaono." He gazed past me at the men seated by the fire. "You will speak my words to your son and

Aroniateka, and then we will act – and soon. Your brothers will
be free of all their enemies."

Yesuntai spoke of warring tribes on the other side of the world,
tribes that had wasted themselves in battles with one another
until the greatest of men had united them under his standard.
He talked of a time long before that, when other tribes had left
the mountains, forests, and steppes of their ancient homeland
to seek new herds and territories, and of the northern land
bridge they had followed to a new world. He spoke of a great
people's destiny, of how God meant them to rule the world, and
of those who, in the aftermath of their glory, were forgetting
their purpose. In the lands they had conquered, they would
eventually fall out among themselves; the great ulus of the
Mongols would fracture into warring states. God would forsake
them. Their brothers in this new world could reach for the
realm that rightly belonged to them.

Aroniateka was the first to speak after I translated the
Noyan's speech. "We have a treaty with your people," he said.
"Do you ask us to break it?"

"We ask that you serve the son of our Khan, who is our
rightful leader here," I replied. "Those who came here to claim
our victory will take the lands we freed for themselves, and their
greed will drive them north to yours. Michel Bahadur and the
men of Yeke Geren have already broken the treaty in their
hearts."

"I am a sachem," my son said, "and will take up my duties
again when I am home. I know what is recorded on the belts of
wampum our wise men have in their keeping. Our treaty binds
us as long as my father Senadondo is our brother and the
servant of his former people, as long as he is our voice among
them."

"I found that many grew deaf to my voice," I said. "I will not
go back to live in Yeke Geren. I have told my chief Yesuntai that
I will live among the Owners of the Flint until the end of my
days."

My son met Yesuntai's gaze. How alike their eyes were, as
cold and dark as those of a serpent. "My dream told me that my

father would bring me a brother," my son said. "I see my brother now, sitting before me." I knew then that he would bring the other chiefs to agree to our plans.

We secured the ships easily. Yesuntai's soldiers rowed out to the vessels; the few sailors left on board, suspecting nothing, were quickly overcome. Most of Michel's men were quartered in the Inglistani commander's house and the three nearest it; they were sleepy with drink when we struck. Michel and his officers were given an honorable death by strangulation, and some of the Dutch and Frankish sailors hastily offered their oaths to Yesuntai. The others were given to the Ganeagaono, to be tortured and then burned at the stake as we set New London ablaze.

I sailed with Yesuntai and his men. The Ganeagaono and the Mahicans who had remained with us went west on foot with their Inglistani captives. When we reached the narrow strait that separated Yeke Geren from the long island of Gawanasegeh, people gathered along the cliffs and the shore to watch us sail south towards the harbor. The ships anchored there had no chance to mount a resistance, and we lost only one of our vessels in the battle. By then, the Ganeagaono and Mahicans had crossed to the northern end of Yeke Geren in canoes, under cover of night, and secured the pastures there.

They might have withstood our assault. They might have waited us out, until our allies tired of the siege and the icy winds of winter forced us to withdraw to provision our ships. But too many in Yeke Geren had lost their fighting spirit, and others thought it better to throw in their lot with Yesuntai. They surrendered fourteen days later.

About half of the Mongol officers offered their oaths to Yesuntai; the rest were beheaded. Some of the Mahicans would remain in what was left of Yeke Geren, secure treaties with the tribes of Gawanasegeh and the smaller island to our southwest, and see that no more ships landed there. The people of the settlement were herded into roped enclosures. They would be distributed among the Ganeagaono and taken north, where the

Flint People would decide which of them were worthy of adoption.

I searched among the captives for Elgigetei and Ajiragha. At last an old man told me that they had been taken by a fever only a few days before we attacked the harbor. I mourned for them, but perhaps it was just as well. My son might not have survived the journey north, and Dasiyu would never have accepted a second wife. I had the consolation of knowing that my deeds had not carried their deaths to them.

Clouds of migrating birds were darkening the skies when I went with Yesuntai to our two remaining ships. A mound of heads, those of the officers we had executed, sat on the slope leading down to the harbor, a monument to our victory and a warning to any who tried to land there.

The Noyan's men were waiting by the shore with the surviving Frankish and Dutch sailors. The ships were provisioned with what we could spare, the sailors ready to board. Men of the sea would be useless in the northern forests, and men of uncertain loyalties who scorned the ways of the Flint People would not be welcome there.

Yesuntai beckoned to a grey-haired captain. "This is my decree," he said. "You will sail east, and carry this message to my father." He gestured with a scroll. "I shall recite the message for you now. I will make a Khanate of this land, but it will not be sullied by those who would bring the sins of Europe to its shores. When an ulus has risen here, it will be the mighty nation of our long-lost brothers. Only then will the circle close, and all our brothers be joined, and only if all the Khans accept the men of this land as their equals. It is then that we will truly rule the world, and if my brother Khans do not join this ulus of the world to come willingly, only God knows what will befall them."

"We cannot go back with such a message," the captain said. "Those words will cost us our heads."

"You dishonor my father by saying that. You are my emissaries, and no Khan would stain his hands with the blood of ambassadors." Yesuntai handed the scroll to the old man.

"These are my words, marked with my seal. My father the Khan will know that I have carried out his orders, that the people of Inglistan will not set foot here again. He will also know that there is no need for his men to come here, since it is I who will secure this new Khanate." He narrowed his eyes. "If you do not wish to claim the Khan's reward for this message, then sail where you will and find what refuge you can. The Khan my father, and those who follow him to his throne, will learn of my destiny in time."

We watched as the sailors boarded the longboats and rowed towards the ships. Yesuntai threw an arm over my shoulders as we turned away from the sea and climbed towards Yeke Geren. "Jirandai," he murmured, "or perhaps I should call you Senadondo now, as your Long House brothers do. You must guide me in my new life. You will show me what I must do to become a Khan among these people."

He would not be my Khan. I had served him for the sake of the Flint People, not to make him a Khan, but would allow him his dream for a little while. Part of his vision would come to pass; the Long House People would have a great realm, and Yesuntai might inspire them to even greater valor. But I did not believe that the Hodenosaunee, a people who allowed all to raise their voices in their councils, would ever bow to a Khan and offer him total obedience. My son would honor Yesuntai as a brother, but would never kneel to him. Yesuntai's sons would be Ganeagaono warriors, bound to their mother's clan, not a Mongol prince's heirs.

I did not say this to Yesuntai. He would learn it in time, or be forced to surrender his dream to other leaders who would make it their own. The serpent that had wakened to disturb the lands of the Long House would grow, and slip westward to meet his tail.

Waiting for the Olympians

Frederik Pohl

Chapter 1

The Day of the Two Rejections

If I had been writing it as a romance, I would have called the chapter about that last day in London something like "The Day of the Two Rejections". It was a nasty day in late December just before the holidays. The weather was cold, wet, and miserable – well, I said it was London, didn't I? – but everybody was in a sort of expectant holiday mood; it had just been announced that the Olympians would be arriving no later than the following August, and everybody was excited about that. All the taxi drivers were busy, and so I was late for my lunch with Lidia. "How was Manahattan?" I asked, sliding into the booth beside her and giving her a quick kiss.

"Manahattan was very nice," she said, pouring me a drink. Lidia was a writer, too – well they *call* themselves writers, the ones who follow famous people around and write down all their gossip and jokes and put them out as books for the amusement of the idle. That's not really *writing*, of course. There's nothing creative about it. But it pays well, and the research (Lidia always told me) was a lot of fun. She spent a lot of time travelling around the celebrity circuit, which was not very good for our romance. She watched me drink the first glass before she remembered to ask politely, "Did you finish the book?"

"Don't call it 'the book'," I said. "Call it by its name, *An Ass' Olympiad.* I'm going to see Marcus about it this afternoon."

"That's not what I'd call a great title," she commented – Lidia was always willing to give me her opinion on anything, when she didn't like it. "Really, don't you think it's too late to be writing another sci-rom about the Olympians?" And then she smiled brightly and said, "I've got something to say to you, Julie. Have another drink first."

So I knew what was coming right away, and that was the first rejection.

I'd seen this scene building up. Even before she left on that last "research" trip to the West I had begun to suspect that some of that early ardour had cooled, so I wasn't really surprised when she told me, without any further foreplay, "I've met somebody else, Julie."

I said, "I see." I really did see, and so I poured myself a third drink while she told me about it.

"He's a former space pilot, Julius. He's been to Mars and the Moon and everywhere, and oh, he's such a sweet man. And he's a champion wrestler, too, would you believe it? Of course, he's still married, as it happens. But he's going to talk to his wife about a divorce as soon as the kids are just a little older."

She looked at me challengingly, waiting for me to tell her she was an idiot. I had no intention of saying anything at all, as a matter of fact, but just in case I had, she added, "Don't say what you're thinking."

"I wasn't thinking anything," I protested.

She sighed. "You're taking this very well," she told me. She sounded as though that were a great disappointment to her. "Listen, Julius, I didn't plan this. Truly, you'll always be dear to me in a special way. I hope we can always be friends—" I stopped listening around then.

There was plenty more in the same vein, but only the details were a surprise. When she told me our little affair was over I took it calmly enough. I always knew that Lidia had a weakness for the more athletic type. Worse than that, she never respected the kind of writing I do, anyway. She had the usual establishment contempt for science-adventure romances about the future and adventures on alien planets, and what sort of relationship could that lead to, in the long run?

So I left her with a kiss and a smile, neither of them very sincere, and headed for my editor's office. That was where I got the second rejection. The one that really hurt.

Mark's office was in the old part of London, down by the river. It's an old company, in an old building, and most of the staff are old, too. When the company needs clerks or copy-editors it has a habit of picking up tutors whose students have grown up and don't need them any more, and retraining them. Of course, that's just for the people in the lower echelons. The higher-ups, like Mark himself, are free, salaried executives, with the executive privilege of interminable, winey author-and-editor lunches that don't end until the afternoon.

I had to wait half an hour to see him; obviously he had been having one of them that day. I didn't mind. I had every confidence that our interview was going to be short, pleasant, and remunerative. I knew very well that *An Ass' Olympiad* was one of the best sci-roms I had ever done. Even the title was clever. The book was a satire, with classical overtones – from *The Golden Ass* of the ancient writer, Lucius Apuleius, two thousand years ago or so; I had played off the classic in a comic, adventurous little story about the coming of the real Olympians. I can always tell when a book is going really well and I knew the fans would eat this one up . . .

When I finally got in to see Marcus he had a glassy, after-lunch look in his eye, and I could see my manuscript on his desk.

I also saw that clipped to it was a red-bordered certificate, and that was the first warning of bad news. The certificate was the censor's verdict, and the red border meant it was an obstat.

Mark didn't keep me in suspense. "We can't publish," he said, pressing his palm on the manuscript. "The censors have turned it down."

"They can't!" I cried, making his old secretary lift his head from his desk in the corner of the room to stare at me.

"They did," Mark said. "I'll read you what the obstat says: ' – of a nature which may give offence to the delegation from the Galactic Consortium, usually referred to as the Olympians – ' and ' – thus endangering the security and tranquillity of the Empire – ' and, well, basically it just says no. No revisions suggested. Just a complete veto; it's waste paper now, Julie. Forget it."

"But *everybody* is writing about the Olympians!" I yelped.

"Everybody *was*," he corrected. "Now they're getting close, and the censors don't want to take any more chances." He leaned back to rub his eyes, obviously wishing he could be taking a nice nap instead of breaking my heart. Then he added tiredly, "So what do you want to do, Julie? Write us a replacement? It would have to be fast, you understand; the front office doesn't like having contracts outstanding for more than thirty days after due date. And it would have to be good. You're not going to get away with pulling some old reject out of your trunk – I've seen all those already, anyway."

"How the hells do you expect me to write a whole new book in thirty days?" I demanded.

He shrugged, looking sleepier and less interested in my problem than ever. "If you can't, you can't. Then you'll just have to give back the advance," he told me.

I calmed down fast. "Well, no," I said, "there's no question of having to do that. I don't know about finishing it in thirty days, though—"

"I do," he said flatly. He watched me shrug. "Have you got an idea for the new one?"

"Mark," I said patiently, "I've *always* got ideas for new ones. That's what a professional writer is. He's a machine for thinking up ideas. I always have more ideas than I can ever write—"

"Do you?" he insisted.

I surrendered, because if I'd said yes the next thing would have been that he'd want me to tell him what it was. "Not exactly," I admitted.

"Then," he said, "you'd better go wherever you do to get ideas, because, give us the new book or give us back the advance, thirty days is all you've got."

There's an editor for you.

They're all the same. At first they're all honey and sweet talk, with those long alcoholic lunches and blue-sky conversation about million-copy printings while they wheedle you into signing the contract. Then they turn nasty. They want the actual book delivered. When they don't get it, or when the censors say they can't print it, then there isn't any more sweet talk and all the conversation is about how the aediles will escort you to debtors' prison.

So I took his advice. I knew where to go for ideas, and it wasn't in London. No sensible man stays in London in the winter anyway, because of the weather and because it's too full of foreigners. I still can't get used to seeing all those huge rustic Northmen and dark Hindian and Arabian women in the heart of town. I admit I can be turned on by that red caste mark or by a pair of flashing dark eyes shining through all the robes and veils – suppose what you imagine is always more exciting than what you can see, especially when what you see is the short, dumpy Britain women like Lidia.

So I made a reservation on the overnight train to Rome, to transfer there to a hydrofoil for Alexandria. I packed with a good heart, not neglecting to take along a floppy sun hat, a flask of insect repellent, and – oh, of course – stylus and blank tablets enough to last me for the whole trip just in case a book idea emerged for me to write. Egypt! Where the world conference on the Olympians was starting its winter session . . . where I would be among the scientists and astronauts who always sparked ideas for new science-adventure romances for me to write . . . where it would be warm . . .

Where my publisher's aediles would have trouble finding me, in the event that no idea for a new novel came along.

Chapter 2

On the Way to the Idea Place

No idea did.

That was disappointing. I do some of my best writing on trains, aircraft, and ships, because there aren't any interruptions and you can't decide to go out for a walk because there isn't any place to walk to. It didn't work this time. All the while the train was slithering across the wet, bare English winter countryside towards,the Channel, I sat with my tablet in front of me and the stylus poised to write, but by the time we dipped into the tunnel the tablet was still virgin.

I couldn't fool myself. I was stuck. I mean, *stuck*. Nothing happened in my head that could transform itself into an opening scene for a new sci-rom novel.

It wasn't the first time in my writing career that I'd been stuck with the writer's block. That's a sort of occupational disease for any writer. But this time was the worst. I'd really counted on *An Ass' Olympiad*. I had even calculated that the publication date could be made to coincide with that wonderful day when the Olympians themselves arrived in our solar system, with all sorts of wonderful publicity for my book flowing out of that great event, so the sales should be *immense* . . . and, worse than that, I'd already spent the on-signing advance. All I had left was credit, and not much of that.

Not for the first time, I wondered what it would have been like if I had followed some other career. If I'd stayed in the civil service, for instance, as my father had wanted.

Really, I hadn't had much choice. I was born during the Space Tricentennial Year, and my mother told me the first word I said was "Mars". She said there was a little misunderstanding there, because at first she thought I was talking about the god, not the planet, and she and my father had long talks about whether to train me for the priesthood, but by the time I could read she knew I was a space nut. Like a lot of my generation (the ones that read my books), I grew up on spaceflight. I was a teenager when the first pictures came back from the space probe to the Alpha Centauri planet Julia, with its crystal grasses and silver-leafed trees. As a boy I corresponded with another youth who lived in the cavern colonies on the Moon, and I read with delight the shoot-'em-ups about outlaws and aediles chasing each other around the satellites of Jupiter. I wasn't the only kid who grew up space-happy, but I never got over it.

Naturally I became a science-adventure romance writer; what else did I know anything about? As soon as I began to get actual money for my fantasies I quit my job as secretary to one of the imperial legates on the Western continents and went full-time pro.

I prospered at it, too – prospered reasonably, at least – well, to be more exact, I earned a liveable, if irregular, income out of the two sci-roms a year I could manage to write, and enough of a surplus to support the habit of dating pretty women like Lidia out of the occasional bonus when one of the books was made into a broadcast drama or a play.

Then along came the message from the Olympians, and the whole face of science-adventure romans was changed forever.

It was the most exciting news in the history of the world, of course. There really *were* other intelligent races out there among the stars of the Galaxy! It had never occurred to me that it would affect me personally, except with joy.

Joy it was, at first. I managed to talk my way into the Alpine radio observatory that had recorded that first message, and I heard it recorded with my own ears:

Dit *squab* dit.
Dit *squee* dit *squab* dit dit.
Dit *squee* dit *squee* dit *squab* dit dit dit.
Dit *squee* dit *squee* dit *squee* dit *squab* wooooo.
Dit *squee* dit *squee* dit *squee* dit *squee* dit *squab* dit dit dit dit dit.

It all looks so simple now, but it took a while before anyone figured out just what this first message from the Olympians was. (Of course, we didn't call them Olympians then. We wouldn't call them that now if the priests had anything to say about it, because they think it's almost sacrilegious, but what else are you going to call godlike beings from the heavens? The name caught on right away, and the priests just had to learn to live with it.) It was, in fact, my good friend Flavius Samuelus ben Samuelus who first deciphered it and produced the right answer to transmit back to the senders – the one that, four years later, let the Olympians know we had heard them.

Meanwhile, we all knew this wonderful new truth: we weren't alone in the universe! Excitement exploded. The market for sci-roms boomed. My very next book was *The Radio Gods*, and it sold its head off.

I thought it would go on forever.

It might have, too . . . if it hadn't been for the timorous censors.

I slept through the tunnel – all the tunnels, even the ones through the Alps – and by the time I woke up we were halfway down to Rome.

In spite of the fact that the tablets remained obstinately blank, I felt more cheerful. Lidia was just a fading memory, I still had twenty-nine days to turn in a new sci-rom and Rome, after all, is still Rome! The centre of the universe – well, not counting what new lessons in astronomical geography the Olympians might teach us. At least, it's the greatest city in the world. It's the place where all the action is.

By the time I'd sent the porter for breakfast and changed into a clean robe we were there, and I alighted into the great, noisy train shed.

I hadn't been in the city for several years, but Rome doesn't change much. The Tiber still stank. The big new apartment buildings still hid the old ruins until you were almost on top of them, the flies were still awful, and the Roman youths still clustered around the train station to sell you guided tours to the Golden House (as though any of them could ever get past the Legion guards!), or sacred amulets, or their sisters.

Because I used to be a secretary on the staff of the proconsul to the Cherokee Nation, I have friends in Rome. Because I hadn't had the good sense to call ahead, none of them were home. I had no choice. I had to take a room in a high-rise inn on the Palatine.

It was ferociously expensive, of course. Everything in Rome is – that's why people like to live in dreary outposts like London – but I figured that by the time the bills came in I would either have found something to satisfy Marcus and get the rest of the advance, or I'd be in so much trouble a few extra debts wouldn't matter.

Having reached that decision, I decided to treat myself to a servant. I picked out a grinning, muscular Sicilian at the rental desk in the lobby, gave him the keys for my luggage, and instructed him to take it to my room – and to make me a reservation for the next day's hover-flight to Alexandria.

That's when my luck began to get better.

When the Sicilian came to the wine shop to ask me for further orders, he reported, "There's another citizen who's booked on the same flight, Citizen Julius. Would you like to share a compartment with him?"

It's nice when you rent a servant who tries to save you money. I said approvingly, "What kind of a person is he? I don't want to get stuck with some real bore."

"You can see for yourself, Julius. He's in the baths right now. He's a Judaean. His name is Flavius Samuelus."

Five minutes later I had my clothes off and a sheet wrapped around me, and I was in the tepidarium, peering around at everybody there.

I picked Sam out at once. He was stretched out with his eyes closed while a masseur pummelled his fat old flesh. I climbed onto the slab next to his without speaking. When he groaned and rolled over, opening his eyes, I said, "Hello, Sam."

It took him a moment to recognize me; he didn't have his glasses in. But when he squinted hard enough his face broke out into a grin. "Julie!" he cried. "Small world! It's good to see you again!"

And he reached out to clasp fists-over-elbows, really welcoming, just as I had expected; because one of the things I like best about Flavius Samuelus is that he likes me.

One of the other things I like best about Sam is that, although he is a competitor, he is also an undepletable natural resource. He writes sci-roms himself. He does more than that. He has helped me with the science part of my own sci-roms any number of times, and it had crossed my mind as soon as I heard the Sicilian say his name that he might be just what I wanted in the present emergency.

Sam is at least seventy years old. His head is hairless. There's a huge brown age spot on the top of his scalp. His throat hangs in a pouch of flesh, and his eyelids sag. But you'd never guess any of that if you were simply talking to him on the phone. He has the quick, chirpy voice of a twenty-year-old, and the mind of one, too – of an extraordinarily *bright* twenty-year-old. He gets enthusiastic.

That complicates things, because Sam's brain works faster than it ought to. Sometimes that makes him hard to talk to, because he's usually three or four exchanges ahead of most people. So the next thing he says to you is as likely as not to be the response to some question that you are inevitably going to ask, but haven't yet thought of.

It is an unpleasant fact of life that Sam's sci-roms sell better than mine do. It is a tribute to Sam's personality that I don't hate him. He has an unfair advantage over the rest of us, since he is a professional astronomer himself. He only writes sci-roms for fun, in his spare time, of which he doesn't have a whole lot. Most of his working hours are spent running a space probe of his own, the one that circles the Epsilon Eridani planet, Dione. I can stand his success (and, admit it! his talent) because he is generous with his ideas. As soon as we had agreed to share the hoverflight compartment, I put it to him directly. Well, almost directly. I said, "Sam, I've been wondering about something. When the Olympians get here, what is it going to mean to us?"

He was the right person to ask, of course; Sam knew more about the Olympians than anyone alive. But he was the wrong person to expect a direct answer from. He rose up, clutching his robe around him. He waved away the masseur and looked at me in friendly amusement, out of those bright black eyes under the flyaway eyebrows and the drooping lids. "Why do you need a new sci-rom plot right now he?" asked.

"Hells," I said ruefully, and decided to come clean. "It wouldn't be the first time I asked you, Sam. Only this time I *really* need it." And I told him the story of the novel the censors obstatted and the editor who was after a quick replacement – or my blood, choice of one.

He nibbled thoughtfully at the knuckle of his thumb. "What was this novel of yours about?" he asked curiously.

"It was a satire, Sam. *An Ass' Olympiad.* About the Olympians coming down to Earth in a matter transporter, only there's a mix-up in the transmission and one of them accidentally gets turned into an ass. It's got some funny bits in it."

"It sure has, Julie. Has had for a couple dozen centuries."

"Well, I didn't say it was altogether *original* only—"

He was shaking his head. "I thought you were smarter than that, Julie. What did you expect the censors to do, jeopardize the most important event in human history for the sake of a dumb sci-rom?"

"It's not a dumb—"

"It's dumb to risk offending them," he said, overruling me firmly. "Best to be safe and not write about them at all."

"But everybody's been doing it!"

"Nobody's been turning them into asses," he pointed out. "Julie, there's a limit to sci-rom speculation. When you write about the Olympians you're right up at that limit. Any speculation about them can be enough reason for them to pull out of the meeting entirely, and we might never get a chance like this again."

"They wouldn't—"

"Ah, Julie," he said, disgusted, "you don't have any idea what they would or wouldn't do. The censors made the right decision. Who knows what the Olympians are going to be like?"

"You do," I told him.

He laughed. There was an uneasy sound to it, though. "I wish I did. About the only thing we do know is that they don't appear to be just any old intelligent race; they have moral standards. We don't have any idea what those standards are, really. I don't know what your book says, but maybe you speculated that the Olympians were bringing us all kinds of new things – a cure for cancer, new psychedelic drugs, even eternal life—"

"What kind of psychedelic drugs might they bring, exactly?" I asked.

"Down, boy! I'm telling you *not* to think about that kind of idea. The point is that whatever you imagined might easily turn out to be the most repulsive and immoral thing the Olympians can think of. The stakes are too high. This is a once-only chance. We can't let it go sour."

"But I need a *story*," I wailed.

"Well, yes," he admitted, "I suppose you do. Let me think about it. Let's get cleaned up and get out of here."

While we were in the hot drench, while we were dressing, while eating a light lunch, Sam chattered on about the forthcoming conference in Alexandria. I was pleased to listen. Apart from the fact that everything he said was interesting, I began to feel hopeful about actually producing a book for Mark. If anybody could help me, Sam could, and he was a problem addict. He couldn't resist a challenge.

That was undoubtedly why he was the first to puzzle out the Olympians' interminably repeated *squees* and *squabs*. If you simply took the dit to be numeral one, and the *squee* to be plus sign, and the *squab* to be an equals sign, then "Dit *squee* dit *squab* dit dit" simply came out as "One plus one equals two."

That was easy enough. It didn't take a super brain like Sam's to substitute our terms for theirs and reveal the message to be simple arithmetic – except for the mysterious "wooooo":

Dit *squee* dit *squee* dit *squee* dit *squab* wooooo.

What was the "wooooo" supposed to mean? A special convention to represent the numeral four?

Sam knew right away, of course. As soon as he heard the message he telegraphed the solution from his library in Padua:

"The message calls for an answer. 'Wooooo' means question mark. The answer is four."

And so the reply to the stars was transmitted on its way:

Dit *squee* dit *squee* dit *squee* dit *squab* dit dit dit dit.

The human race had turned in its test paper in the entrance

examination, and the slow process of establishing communication had begun.

It took four years before the Olympians responded. Obviously, they weren't nearby. Also obviously, they weren't simple folk like ourselves, sending out radio messages from a planet of a star two light-years away, because there wasn't any star there; the reply came from a point in space where none of our telescopes or probes had found anything at all.

By then Sam was deeply involved. He was the first to point out that the star folk had undoubtedly chosen to send a weak signal, because they wanted to be sure our technology was reasonably well developed before we tried to answer. He was one of the impatient ones who talked the collegium authorities into beginning transmission of all sorts of mathematical formulae, and then simple word relationships to start sending *something* to the Olympians while we waited for radio waves to creep to wherever they were and back with an answer.

Sam wasn't the only one, of course. He wasn't even the principal investigator when they got into the hard work of developing a common vocabulary. There were better specialists than Sam at linguistics and cryptanalysis.

But it was Sam who first noticed, early on, that the response time to our messages was getting shorter. Meaning that the Olympians were on their way towards us.

By then they'd begun sending picture mosaics. They came in as strings of dits and dahs, 550,564 bits long. Someone quickly figured out that that was the square of 742, and when they displayed the string as a square matrix, black cells for the dits and white ones for the dahs, the image of the first Olympian leaped out.

Everybody remembers that picture. Everyone on Earth saw it, except for the totally blind – it was on every broadcast screen and news journal in the world – and even the blind listened to the atomical descriptions every commentator supplied. Two tails. A fleshy, beard-like thing that hung down from its chin. Four legs. A ruff of spikes down what seemed to be the backbone. Eyes set wide apart on bulges from the cheekbones.

That first Olympian was not at all pretty, but it was definitely *alien*.

When the next string turned out very similar to the first, it was Sam who saw at once that it was simply a slightly rotated view of the same being. The Olympians took forty-one pictures to give us the complete likeness of that first one in the round . . .

Then they began sending pictures of the others.

It had never occurred to anyone, not even Sam, that we would be dealing not with one super race, but with at least twenty-two of them. There were that many separate forms of alien beings, and each one uglier and more strange than the one before.

That was one of the reasons the priests didn't like calling them Olympians. We're pretty ecumenical about our gods, but none of them looked anything like any of *those*, and some of the older priests never stopped muttering about blasphemy.

Halfway through the third course of our lunch and the second flask of wine, Sam broke off his description of the latest communique from the Olympians – they'd been acknowledging receipt of our transmissions about Earthly history – to lift his head and grin at me.

"Got it," he said.

I turned and blinked at him. Actually, I hadn't been paying a lot of attention to his monologue because I had been keeping my eye on the pretty Kievan waitress. She had attracted my attention because – well, I mean, *after* attracting my attention because of her extremely well-developed figure and the sparsity of clothing to conceal it – because she was wearing a gold citizen's amulet around her neck. She wasn't a slave. That made her more intriguing. I can't ever get really interested in slave women, because it isn't sporting, but I had got quite interested in this woman.

"Are you listening to me?" Sam demanded testily.

"Of course I am. What have you got?"

"I've got the answer to your problem." He beamed. "Not just a sci-rom novel plot. A whole new *kind* of sci-rom! Why don't you write a book about what it will be like if the Olympians *don't* come?"

I love the way half of Sam's brain works at questions while the other half is doing something completely different, but I can't always follow what comes out of it. "I don't see what you mean. If I write about the Olympians not coming, isn't that just as bad as if I write about them doing it?"

"No, no," he snapped. "Listen to what I say! Leave the Olympians out entirely. Just write about a future that might happen, but won't."

The waitress was hovering over us, picking up used plates. I was conscious of her listening as I responded with dignity, "Sam, that's not my style. My sci-roms may not sell as well as yours do, but I've got just as much integrity. I never write anything that I don't believe is at least possible."

"Julie, get your mind off your gonads" – so he hadn't missed the attention I was giving the girl – "and use that pitifully tiny brain of yours. I'm talking about something that *could* be possible, in some alternative future, if you see what I mean."

I didn't see at all. "What's an alternative future?"

"It's a future that *might* happen, but *won't*," he explained. "Like if the Olympians don't come to see us."

I shook my head, puzzled. "But we already know they're coming," I pointed out.

"But suppose they weren't! Suppose they hadn't contacted us years ago."

"But they did," I said, trying to straighten out his thinking on the subject. He only sighed.

"I see I'm not getting through to you," he said, pulling his robe around him and getting to his feet. "Get on with your waitress. I've got some messages to send. I'll see you on the ship."

Well, for one reason or another I didn't get anywhere with the waitress. She said she was married, happily and monogamously. Well, I couldn't see why any lawful, free husband would have his wife out working at a job like that, but I was surprised she didn't show more interest in one of my lineage –

I'd better explain about that.

You see, my family has a claim to fame. Genealogists say we are descended from the line of Julius Caesar himself.

I mention that claim myself, sometimes, though usually only when I've been drinking – I suppose it is one of the reasons that Lidia, always a snob, took up with me in the first place. It isn't a serious matter. After all, Julius Caesar died more than two thousand years ago. There have been sixty or seventy generations since then, not to mention the fact that, although Ancestor Julius certainly left a lot of children behind him, none of them happened to be born to a woman he happened to be married to. I don't even look very Roman. There must have been a Northman or two in the line, because I'm tall and fair-haired, which no respectable Roman ever was.

Still, even if I'm not exactly the lawful heir to the divine Julius, I at least come of a pretty ancient and distinguished line. You would have thought a mere waitress would have taken that into account before turning me down.

She hadn't, though. When I woke up the next morning – alone – Sam was gone from the inn, although the skipship for Alexandria wasn't due to sail until late evening.

I didn't see him all day. I didn't look for him very hard, because I woke up feeling a little ashamed of myself. Why should a grown man, a celebrated author of more than forty bestselling (well, reasonably *well*-selling) sci-roms, depend on somebody else for his ideas?

So I turned my baggage over to the servant, checked out of the inn, and took the underground to the Library of Rome.

Rome isn't only the imperial capital of the world, it's the scientific capital, too. The big old telescopes out on the hills aren't much use any more, because the lights from the city spoil their night viewing, and anyway the big optical telescopes are all out in space now. Still, they were where Galileus detected the first extrasolar planet and Tychus made his famous spectrographs of the last great supernova in our own galaxy, only a couple of dozen years after the first space-flight. The scientific tradition survives. Rome is still the headquarters of the Collegium of Sciences.

That's why the Library of Rome is so great for someone like me. They have direct access to the the Collegium data base, and you don't even have to pay transmission tolls. I signed myself in, laid out my tablets and stylus on the desk they assigned me, and began calling up files.

Somewhere there had to be an idea for a science-adventure romance no one had written yet . . .

Somewhere there no doubt was, but I couldn't find it. Usually you can get a lot of help from a smart research librarian, but it seemed they'd put on a lot of new people in the Library of Rome – Iberians, mostly; reduced to slave status because they'd taken part last year's Lusitanian uprising. There were so many Iberians on the market for a while that they depressed the price. I would have bought some as a speculation, knowing that the price would go up – after all, there aren't that many uprisings and the demand for slaves never stops. But I was temporarily short of capital, and besides you have to feed them. If the ones at the Library of Rome were a fair sample, they were no bargains anyway.

I gave up. The weather had improved enough to make a stroll around town attractive, and so I wandered towards the Ostia mono-rail.

Rome was busy, as always. There was a bullfight going on in the Coliseum and racing at the Circus Maximus. Tourist buses were jamming narrow streets. A long religious procession was circling the Pantheon, but I didn't get close enough to see which particular gods were being honoured today. I don't like crowds. Especially Roman crowds, because there are even more foreigners in Rome than in London, Africs and Hinds, Hans and Northmen – every race on the face of the Earth sends its tourists to visit the Imperial City. And Rome obliges with spectacles. I paused at one of them, for the changing of the guard at the Golden House. Of course, the Caesar and his wife were nowhere to be seen – off on one of their endless ceremonial tours of the dominions, no doubt, or at least opening a new supermarket somewhere. But the Algonkian family standing in front of me were thrilled as the honour Legions marched and counter-marched their standards around the palace. I remembered enough Cherokee to ask the Algonkians where they were from, but the languages aren't really very close and the man's Cherokee was even worse than mine. We just smiled at each other.

As soon as the Legions were out of the way I headed for the train.

I knew in the back of my mind that I should have been worrying about my financial position. The clock was running on my thirty days of grace. I didn't, though. I was buoyed up by a feeling of confidence. Confidence in my good friend Flavius Samuelus, who, I knew, no matter what he was doing with most of his brain, was still cogitating an idea for me with some part of it.

It did not occur to me that even Sam had limitations. Or that something so much more important than my own problems was taking up his attention that he didn't have much left for me.

I didn't see Sam come onto the skip-ship, and I didn't see him in our compartment. Even when the ship's fans began to rumble and we slid down the ways into the Tyrrhenian Sea he wasn't there. I dozed off, beginning to worry that he might have missed the boat; but late that night, already asleep, I half woke, just long enough to hear him stumbling in. "I've been on the bridge," he said when I muttered something. "Go back to sleep. I'll see you in the morning."

When I woke, I thought it might have been a dream, because he was up and gone before me. But his bed had been slept in, however briefly, and the cabin steward reassured me when he brought my morning wine. Yes, Citizen Flavius Samuelus was certainly on the hover. He was in the captain's own quarters, as a matter of fact, although what he was doing there the steward could not say.

I spent the morning relaxing on the deck of the hover, soaking in the sun. The ship wasn't exactly a hover any more. We had transited the Sicilian Straits during the night and now, out in the open Mediterranean, the captain had lowered the stilts, pulled up the hover skirts, and extended the screws. We were hydrofoiling across the sea at easily a hundred miles an hour. It was a smooth, relaxing ride; the vanes that supported us were twenty feet under the surface of the water, and so there was no wave action to bounce us around.

Lying on my back and squinting up at the warm southern

sky, I could see a three-winged airliner rise up from the horizon behind us and gradually overtake us, to disappear ahead of our bows. The plane wasn't going much faster than we were – and we had all the comfort, while they were paying twice as much for passage.

I opened my eyes all the way when I caught a glimpse of someone standing beside me. In fact, I sat up quickly, because it was Sam. He looked as though he hadn't had much sleep, and he was holding a floppy sun hat with one hand against the wind of our passage. "Where've you been?" I asked.

"Haven't you been watching the news?" he asked. I shook my head. "The transmissions from the Olympians have stopped," he told me.

I opened my eyes really wide at that, because it was an unpleasant surprise. Still, Sam didn't seem that upset. Displeased, yes. Maybe even a little concerned, but not as shaken up as I was prepared to feel. "It's probably nothing," he said. "It could be just interference from the sun. It's in Sagittarius now, so it's pretty much between us and them. There's been trouble with static for a couple of days now."

I ventured, "So the transmissions will start up again pretty soon?"

He shrugged and waved to the deck steward for one of those hot decoctions Judaeans like. When he spoke it was on a different topic. "I don't think I made you understand what I meant yesterday," he said. "Let me see if I can explain what I meant by an alternate world. You remember your history? How Fornius Vello conquered the Mayans and Romanized the Western Continents six or seven hundred years ago? Well, suppose he hadn't."

"But he did, Sam."

"I know he did," Sam said patiently. "I'm saying *suppose*. Suppose the Legions had been defeated at the Battle of Tehultapec."

I laughed. I was sure he was joking. "The Legions? Defeated? But the Legions have never been defeated."

"That's not true," Sam said in reproof. He hates it when people don't get their facts straight. "Remember Varus."

"Oh, hells, Sam, that was ancient history! When was it, two thousand years ago? In the time of Augustus Caesar? And it was only a temporary defeat, anyway. The Emperor Drusus got the eagles back." And got all of Gaul for the Empire, too. That was one of the first big trans-Alpine conquests. The Gauls are about as Roman as you can get these days, especially when it comes to drinking wine.

He shook his head. "Suppose Fornius Vello had had a temporary defeat, then."

I tried to follow his argument, but it wasn't easy. "What difference would that have made? Sooner or later the Legions would have conquered. They always have, you know."

"That's true," he said reasonably, "but if that particular conquest hadn't happened *then*, the whole course of history would have been different. We wouldn't have had the great westward migrations to fill up those empty continents. The Hans and the Hinds wouldn't have been surrounded on both sides, so they might still be independent nations. It would have been a different world. Do you see what I'm driving at? That's what I mean by an alternate world – one that might have happened, but didn't."

I tried to be polite to him. "Sam," I said, "you've just described the difference between a sci-rom and a fantasy. I don't do fantasy. Besides," I went on, not wanting to hurt his feelings, "I don't see how different things would have been, really. I can't believe the world would be changed enough to build a sci-rom plot on."

He gazed blankly at me for a moment, then turned and looked out to sea. Then, without transition, he said, "There's one funny thing. The Martian colonies aren't getting a transmission, either. And they aren't occluded by the sun."

I frowned. "What does that mean, Sam?"

He shook his head. "I wish I knew," he said.

Chapter 3

In Old Alexandria

The Pharos was bright in the sunset light as we came into the port of Alexandria. We were on hover again, at slow speeds, and the chop at the breakwater bumped us around. But once we got to the inner harbour the water was calm.

Sam had spent the afternoon back in the captain's quarters, keeping in contact with the Collegium of Sciences, but he showed up as we moored. He saw me gazing towards the rental desk on the dock but shook his head. "Don't bother with a rental, Julie," he ordered. "Let my niece's servants take your baggage. We're staying with her."

That was good news. Inn rooms in Alexandria are almost as pricey as Rome's. I thanked him, but he didn't even listen. He turned our bags over to a porter from his niece's domicile, a little Arabian who was a lot stronger than he looked, and disappeared towards the Hall of the Egyptian Senate-Inferior, where the conference was going to be held.

I hailed a three-wheeler and gave the driver the address of Sam's niece.

No matter what the Egyptians think, Alexandria is a dirty little town. The Choctaws have a bigger capital, and the Kievans have a cleaner one. Also Alexandria's famous library is a joke. After my (one would like to believe) ancestor Julius Caesar let it burn to the ground, the Egyptians did build it up again But it is so old-fashioned that there's nothing in it but books.

The home of Sam's niece was in a particularly run-down section of that run-down town, only a few streets from the harbourside. You could hear the noise of the cargo winches from the docks, but you couldn't hear them very well because of the noise of the streets themselves, thick with goods vans and drivers cursing each other as they jockeyed around the narrow corners. The house itself was bigger than I had expected. But, at least from the outside, that was all you could say for it. It was faced with cheap Egyptian stucco rather than marble, and right next door to it was a slave-rental barracks.

At least, I reminded myself, it was free. I kicked at the door and shouted for the butler.

It wasn't the butler who opened it for me. It was Sam's niece herself, and she was a nice surprise. She was almost as tall as I was and just as fair. Besides, she was young and very good-looking. "You must be Julius," she said. "I am Rachel, niece of Citizen Flavius Samuelus ben Samuelus, and I welcome you to my home."

I kissed her hand. It's a Kievan custom that I like, especially with pretty girls I don't yet know well, but hope to. "You don't look Judaean," I told her.

"You don't look like a sci-rom hack," she replied. Her voice was less chilling than her words, but not much. "Uncle Sam isn't here, and I'm afraid I've got work I must do. Basilius will show you to your rooms and offer you some refreshment."

I usually make a better first impression on young women. I usually work at it more carefully, but she had taken me by surprise. I had more or less expected that Sam's niece would look more or less like Sam, except probably for the baldness and the wrinkled face. I could not have been more wrong.

I had been wrong about the house, too. It was a big one. There had to be well over a dozen rooms, not counting servants' quarters, and the atrium was covered with one of those partly reflecting films that keep the worst of the heat out.

The famous Egyptian sun was directly overhead when Basilius, Rachel's butler, showed me my rooms. They were pleasingly bright and airy, but Basilius suggested I might enjoy being outside. He was right. He brought me wine and fruits in the atrium, a pleasant bench by a fountain. Through the film the sun looked only pale and pleasant instead of deadly hot. The fruit was fresh, too – pineapples from Lebanon, oranges from Judaea, apples that must have come all the way from somewhere in Gaul. The only thing wrong that I could see was that Rachel herself stayed in her rooms, so I didn't have a chance to try to put myself in a better light with her.

She had left instructions for my comfort, though. Basilius clapped his hands and another servant appeared, bearing stylus and tablets in case I should decide to work. I was surprised to see that both Basilius and the other one were Africs; they don't usually get into political trouble, or trouble with the aediles of any kind, so not many of them are slaves.

The fountain was a Cupid statue. In some circumstances I would have thought of that as a good sign, but here it didn't seem to mean anything. Cupid's nose was chipped, and the fountain was obviously older than Rachel was. I thought of just staying there until Rachel came out, but when I asked Basilius when that would be he gave me a look of delicate patronizing. "Citizeness Rachel works through the afternoon, Citizen Julius," he informed me.

"Oh? And what does she work at?"

"Citizeness Rachel is a famous historian," he said. "She often works straight through until bedtime. But for you and her uncle, of course, dinner will be served at your convenience."

He was quite an obliging fellow. "Thank you, Basilius," I said. "I believe I'll go out for a few hours myself." And then, as he turned politely to go, I said curiously, "You don't look like a very dangerous criminal. If you don't mind my asking, what were you enslaved for?"

"Oh, not for anything violent, Citizen Julius," he assured me. "Just for debts."

* * *

I found my way to the Hall of the Egyptian Senate-Inferior easily enough. There was a lot of traffic going that way, because it is, after all, one of the sights of Alexandria.

The Senate-Inferior wasn't in session at the time. There was no reason it should have been, of course, because what did the Egyptians need a Senate of any kind for? The time when they'd made any significant decisions for themselves was many centuries past.

They'd spread themselves for the conference, though. The Senate Temple had niches for at least half a hundred gods. There were the customary figures of Amon-Ra and Jupiter and all the other main figures of the pantheon, of course, but for the sake of the visitors they had installed Ahura-Mazda, Yahweh, Freya, Quetzalcoatl, and at least a dozen I didn't recognize at all. They were all decorated with fresh sacrifices of flowers and fruits, showing that the tourists, if not the astronomers – and probably the astronomers as well – were taking no chances in getting communications with the Olympians restored. Scientists are an agnostic lot, of course – well, most educated people are, aren't they? But even an agnostic will risk a piece of fruit to placate a god, just on the chance he's wrong.

Outside the hall, hucksters were already putting up their stands, although the first sessions wouldn't begin for another day. I bought some dates from one of them and wandered around, eating dates and studying the marble frieze on the wall of the Senate. It showed the rippling fields of corn, wheat, and potatoes that had made Egypt the breadbasket of the Empire for two thousand years. It didn't show anything about the Olympians, of course. Space is not a subject that interests the Egyptians a lot. They prefer to look back on their glorious (they *say* it's glorious) past; and there would have been no point in having the conference on the Olympians there at all, except who wants to go to some northern city in December?

Inside, the great hall was empty, except for slaves arranging seat cushions and cuspidors for the participants. The exhibit halls were noisy with workers setting up displays, but they didn't want people dropping in to bother them, and the participants' lounges were dark.

I was lucky enough to find the media room open. It was always good for a free glass of wine, and besides, I wanted to know where everyone was. The slave in charge couldn't tell me. "There's supposed to be a private executive meeting some-where, that's all I know – and there's all these journalists looking for someone to interview." And then, peering over my shoulder as I signed in: "Oh, you're the fellow that writes the sci-roms, aren't you? Well, maybe one of the journalists would settle for you."

It wasn't the most flattering invitation I'd ever had. Still, I didn't say no. Marcus is always after me to do publicity gigs whenever I get the chance, because he thinks it sells books, and it was worthwhile trying to please Marcus just then.

The journalist wasn't much pleased, though. They'd set up a couple of studios in the basement of the Senate, and when I found the one I was directed to, the interviewer was fussing over his hairdo in front of a mirror. A couple of technicians were lounging in front of the tube, watching a broadcast comedy series. When I introduced myself the interviewer took his eyes off his own image long enough to cast a doubtful look in my direction.

"You're not a real astronomer," he told me.

I shrugged. I couldn't deny it.

"Still," he grumbled, "I'd better get *some* kind of a spot for the late news. All right. Sit over there, and try to sound as if you know what you're talking about." Then he began telling the technical crew what to do.

That was a strange thing. I'd already noticed that the technicians wore citizens' gold. The interviewer didn't. But he was the one who was giving *them* orders.

I didn't approve of that at all. I don't like big commercial outfits that put slaves in positions of authority over free citizens. It's a bad practice. Jobs like tutors, college professors, doctors, and so on are fine; slaves can do them as well as a citizen, and usually a lot cheaper. But there's a moral issue involved here. A slave must have a master. Otherwise, how can you call him a slave? And when you let the slave *be* the master, even in something as trivial as a broadcasting studio, you strike at the foundations of society.

The other thing is that it isn't fair competition. There are free citizens who need those jobs. We had some of that in my own line of work a few years ago. There were two or three slave authors turning out adventure novels, but the rest of us got together and put a stop to it – especially after Marcus bought one of them to use as a sub-editor. Not one citizen writer would work with her. Mark finally had to put her into the publicity department, where she couldn't do any harm.

So I started the interview with a chip on my shoulder, and his first question made it worse. He plunged right in. "When you're pounding out those sci-roms of yours, do you make any effort to keep in touch with scientific reality? Do you know, for instance, that the Olympians have stopped transmitting?"

I scowled at him, regardless of the cameras. "Science-adventure romances are *about* scientific reality. And the Olympians haven't 'stopped' as you put it. There's just been a technical hitch of some kind, probably caused by radio interference from our own sun. As I said in my earlier romance, *The Radio Gods*, electromagnetic impulses are susceptible to—"

He cut me off. "It's been—" he glanced at his watch – "twenty-nine hours since they stopped. That doesn't sound like just a technical hitch."

"Of course it is. There's no reason for them to stop. We've already demonstrated to them that we're truly civilized, first because we're technological, second because we don't fight wars any more – that was cleared up in the first year. As I said in my roman, *The Radio Gods*—"

He gave me a pained look, then turned and winked into the camera. "You can't keep a hack from plugging his books, can you?" he remarked humorously. "But it looks like he doesn't want to use that wild imagination unless he gets paid for it. All I'm asking him for is a guess at why the Olympians don't want to talk to us any more, and all he gives me is commercials."

As though there were any other reason to do interviews! "Look here," I said sharply, "if you can't be courteous when you speak to a citizen, I'm not prepared to go on with this conversation at all."

"So be it, pal," he said, icy cold. He turned to the technical crew. "Stop the cameras," he ordered. "We're going back to the studio. This is a waste of time." We parted on terms of mutual dislike, and once again I had done something that my editor would have been glad to kill me for.

That night at dinner, Sam was no comfort. "He's an unpleasant man, sure," he told me. "But the trouble is, I'm afraid he's right."

"They've really *stopped*?"

Sam shrugged. "We're not in line with the sun any more, so that's definitely not the reason. Damn. I was hoping it would be."

"I'm sorry about that, Uncle Sam," Rachel said gently. She was wearing a simple white robe, Hannish silk by the look of it, with no decorations at all. It really looked good on her. I didn't think there was anything under it except for some very well-formed female flesh.

"I'm sorry, too," he grumbled. His concerns didn't affect his appetite, though. He was ladling in the first course – a sort of chicken soup, with bits of a kind of pastry floating in it – and, for that matter, so was I. Whatever Rachel's faults might be, she had a good cook. It was plain home cooking, none of your partridge-in-a-rabbit-inside-a-boar kind of thing, but well prepared and expertly served by her butler, Basilius. "Anyway," Sam said, mopping up the last of the broth, "I've figured it out."

"Why the Olympians stopped?" I asked, to encourage him to go on with the revelation.

"No, no! I mean about your romance, Julie. My alternate world idea. If you don't want to write about a different *future*, how about a different *now*?"

I didn't get a chance to ask him about what he was talking about, because Rachel beat me to it. "There's only one *now*, Sam, dear," she pointed out. I couldn't have said it better myself.

Sam groaned. "Not you, too, honey," he complained. "I'm talking about a new kind of sci-rom."

"I don't read many sci-roms," she apologized, in the tone that isn't an apology at all.

He ignored that. "You're a historian, aren't you?" She didn't bother to confirm it; obviously, it was the thing she was that shaped her life. "So what if history had gone a different way?"

He beamed at us as happily as though he had said something that made sense. Neither of us beamed back. Rachel pointed out the flaw in his remark. "It didn't, though," she told him.

"I said *suppose*! This isn't the only possible now, it's just the one that happened to occur! There could have been a million different ones. Look at all the events in the past that could have gone a different way. Suppose Annius Publius hadn't discovered the Western Continents in City Year 1820. Suppose

Caesar Publius Terminus hadn't decreed the development of a space program in 2122. Don't you see what I'm driving at? What kind of a world would we be living in now if those things hadn't happened?"

Rachel opened her mouth to speak, but she was saved by the butler. He appeared in the doorway with a look of silent appeal. When she excused herself to see what was needed in the kitchen, that left it up to me. "I never wrote anything like that, Sam," I told him. "I don't know anybody else who did, either."

"That's exactly what I'm driving at! It would be something completely *new* in sci-roms. Don't you want to pioneer a whole new kind of story?"

Out of the wisdom of experience, I told him, "Pioneers don't make any money, Sam." He scowled at me. "You could write it yourself," I suggested.

That just changed the annoyance to gloom. "I wish I could. But until this business with the Olympians is cleared up, I'm not going to have much time for sci-roms. No, it's up to you, Julie."

Then Rachel came back in, looking pleased with herself, followed by Basilius bearing a huge silver platter containing the main course.

Sam cheered up at once. So did I. The main dish was a whole roasted baby kid, and I realized that the reason Rachel had been called into the kitchen was so that she could weave a garland of flowers around its tiny baby horn buds herself. The maid servant followed with a pitcher of wine, replenishing all our goblets. All in all, we were busy enough eating to stop any conversation but compliments on the food.

Then Sam looked at his watch. "Great dinner, Rachel," he told his niece, "but I've got to get back. What about it?"

"What about what?" she asked.

"About helping poor Julie with some historical turning points he can use in the story?"

He hadn't listened to a word I'd said. I didn't have to say so, because Rachel was looking concerned. She said apologetically, "I don't know anything about those periods you were talking about – Publius Terminus, and so on. My speciality is the immediate post-Augustan period, when the Senate came back to power."

"Fine," he said, pleased with himself and showing it. "That's as good a period as any. Think how different things might be now if some little event then had gone in a different way. Say, if Augustus hadn't married Lady Livia and adopted her son Drusus to succeed him." He turned to me, encouraging me to take fire from his spark of inspiration. "I'm sure you see the possibilities, Julie! Tell you what you should do. The night's young yet; take Rachel out dancing or something; have a few drinks; listen to her talk. What's wrong with that? You two young people ought to be having fun, anyway!"

That was definitely the most intelligent thing intelligent Sam had said in days.

So I thought, anyway, and Rachel was a good enough niece to heed her uncle's advice. Because I was a stranger in town, I had to let her pick the place. After the first couple she mentioned I realized that she was tactfully trying to spare my pocketbook. I couldn't allow that. After all, a night on the town with Rachel was probably cheaper, and anyway a whole lot more interesting, than the cost of an inn and meals.

We settled on a place right on the harbour-side, out towards the breakwater. It was a revolving nightclub on top of an inn built along the style of one of the old Pyramids. As the room slowly turned we saw the lights of the city of Alexandria, the shipping in the harbour then the wide sea itself, its gentle waves reflecting starlight.

I was prepared to forget the whole idea of alternate worlds, but Rachel was more dutiful than that. After the first dance, she said, "I think I can help you. There was something that happened in Drusus' reign—"

"Do we have to talk about that?" I asked, refilling her glass.

"But Uncle Sam said we should. I thought you wanted to try a new kind of sci-rom."

"No, that's your uncle who wants that. See, there's a bit of a problem here. It's true that editors are always begging for something new and different, but if you're dumb enough to try to

give it to them they don't recognize it. When they ask for
different, what they mean is something right down the good old
'different' groove."

"I think," she informed me, with the certainty of an oracle
and a lot less confusion of style, "that when my uncle has an
idea, it's usually a good one." I didn't want to argue with her; I
didn't even disagree: at least usually. I let her talk. "You see,"
she said, "my speciality is the transfer of power throughout
early Roman history. What I'm studying right now is the
Judaean Diaspora, after Drusus' reign. You know what
happened then, I suppose?"

Actually, I did – hazily. "That was the year of the Judaean
rebellion, wasn't it?"

She nodded. She looked very pretty when she nodded, her
fair hair moving gracefully and her eyes sparkling. "You see,
that was a great tragedy for the Judaeans, and, just as my uncle
said, it needn't have happened. If Procurator Tiberius had
lived, it wouldn't have."

I coughed. "I'm not sure I know who Tiberius was," I said
apologetically.

"He was the Procurator of Judaea, and a very good one. He
was just and fair. He was the brother of the Emperor Drusus –
the one my uncle was talking about, Livia's son, the adopted
heir of Caesar Augustus. The one who restored the power of the
Senate after Augustus had appropriated most of it for himself.
Anyway, Tiberius was the best governor the Judaeans ever had,
just as Drusus was the best emperor. Tiberius died just a year
before the rebellion – ate some spoiled figs, they say, although
it might have been his wife who did it – she was Julia, the
daughter of Augustus by his first wife—"

I signalled distress. "I'm getting a little confused by all these
names," I admitted.

"Well, the important one to remember is Tiberius, and you
know who he was. If he had lived, the rebellion probably
wouldn't have happened. Then there wouldn't have been a
Diaspora."

"I see," I said. "Would you like another dance?"

She frowned at me, then smiled. "Maybe that's not such an

interesting subject – unless you're a Judaean, anyway," she said. "All right, let's dance."

That was the best idea yet. It gave me a chance to confirm with my fingers what my eyes, ears, and nose had already told me; this was a very attractive young woman. She had insisted on changing, but fortunately the new gown was as soft and clinging as the old, and the palms of my hands rejoined in the tactile pleasure of her back and arm. I whispered, "I'm sorry if I sound stupid. I really don't know a whole lot about early history – you know, the first thousand years or so after the Founding of the City."

She didn't bother to point out that she did. She moved with me to the music, very enjoyable, then she straightened up. "I've got a different idea," she announced. "Let's go back to the booth." And she was already telling it to me as we left the dance floor. "Let's talk about your own ancestor, Julius Caesar. He conquered Egypt, right here in Alexandria. But suppose the Egyptians had defeated him instead, as they very nearly did?"

I was paying close attention now – obviously she had been interested enough in me to ask Sam some questions! "They couldn't have," I told her. "Julius never lost a war. Anyway" – I discovered to my surprise that I was beginning to take Sam's nutty idea seriously – "that would be a really hard one to write, wouldn't it? If the Legions had been defeated, it would have changed the whole world. Can you imagine a world that isn't Roman?"

She said sweetly, "No, but that's more your job than mine, isn't it?"

I shook my head. "It's too bizarre," I complained. "I couldn't make the readers believe it."

"You could try, Julius," she told me. "You see, there's an interesting possibility there. Drusus almost didn't live to become Emperor. He was severely wounded in a war in Gaul, while Augustus was still alive. Tiberius – you remember Tiberius—"

"Yes, yes, his brother. The one you like. The one he made Procurator of Judaea."

"That's the one. Well, Tiberius rode day and night to bring

Drusus the best doctors in Rome. He almost didn't make it. They barely pulled Drusus through."

"Yes?" I said encouragingly. "And what then?"

She looked uncertain. "Well, I don't know what then."

I poured some more wine. "I guess I could figure out some kind of speculative idea," I said, ruminating. "Especially if you would help me with some of the details. I suppose Tiberius would have become Emperor instead of Drusus. You say he was a good man; so probably he would have done more or less what Drusus did – restore the power of the Senate, after Augustus and my revered great-great Julius between them had pretty nearly put it out of business—"

I stopped there, startled at my own words. It almost seemed that I was beginning to take Sam's crazy idea seriously!

On the other hand, that wasn't all bad. It almost seemed that Rachel was beginning to take *me* seriously.

That was a good thought. It kept me cheerful through half a dozen more dances and at least another hour of history lessons from her pretty lips . . . right up until the time when, after we had gone back to her house, I tiptoed out of my room towards hers, and found her butler, Basilius, asleep on a rug across her doorway, with a great, thick club by his side.

I didn't sleep well that night.

Partly it was glandular. My head knew that Rachel didn't want me creeping into her bedroom, or else she wouldn't have put the butler there in the way. But my glands weren't happy with that news. They had soaked up the smell and sight and feel of her, and they were complaining about being thwarted.

The worst part was waking up every hour or so to contemplate financial ruin.

Being poor wasn't so bad. Every writer has to learn how to be poor from time to time, between cheques. It's an annoyance, but not a catastrophe. You don't get enslaved just for poverty.

But I had been running up some pretty big bills. And you do get enslaved for debt.

Chapter 4

The End of the Dream

The next morning I woke up late and grouchy and had to take a three-wheeler to the Hall of the Senate-Inferior.

It was slow going. As we approached, the traffic thickened even more. I could see the Legion forming for the ceremonial guard as the Pharaoh's procession approached to open the ceremonies. The driver wouldn't take me any closer than the outer square, and I had to wait there with all the tourists, while the Pharaoh dismounted from her royal litter.

There was a soft, pleasured noise from the crowd, halfway between a giggle and a sigh. That was the spectacle the tourists had come to see. They pressed against the sheathed swords of the Legionaries while the Pharaoh, head bare, robe trailing on the ground, advanced on the shrines outside the Senate building. She sacrificed reverently and unhurriedly to them, while the tourists flashed their cameras at her, and I began to worry about the time. What if she ecumenically decided to visit all fifty shrines? But after doing Isis, Amon-Ra, and Mother Nile, she went inside to declare the Congress open. The Legionaries relaxed. The tourists began to flow back to their buses, snapping pictures of themselves now, and I followed the Pharaoh inside.

She made a good – by which I mean short – opening address. The only thing wrong with it was that she was talking to mostly empty seats.

The Hall of the Alexandrian Senate-Inferior holds two thousand people. There weren't more than a hundred and fifty in it. Most of those were huddled in small groups in the aisles and at the back of the hall, and they were paying no attention at all to the Pharaoh. I think she saw that and shortened her speech. At one moment she was telling us how the scientific investigation of the outside universe was completely in accord with the ancient traditions of Egypt – with hardly anyone listening – and at the next her voice had stopped without warning and she was handing her orb and sceptre to her attendants. She proceeded regally across the stage and out the wings.

The buzz of conversation hardly slackened. What they were talking about, of course, was the Olympians. Even when the Collegium-Presidor stepped forward and called for the first session to begin, the hall didn't fill. At least most of the scattered groups of people in the room sat down – though still in clumps, and still doing a lot of whispering to each other.

Even the speakers didn't seem very interested in what they were saying. The first one was an honorary Presidor-Emeritus from the southern highlands of Egypt, and he gave us a review of everything we knew about the Olympians.

He read it as hurriedly as though he were dictating it to a scribe. It wasn't very interesting. The trouble, of course, was that his paper had been prepared days earlier, while the Olympian transmissions were still flooding in and no one had any thought they might be interrupted. It just didn't seem relevant any more.

What I like about going to science congresses isn't so much the actual papers the speakers deliver – I can get that sort of information better from the journals in the library. It isn't even the back-and-forth discussion that follows each paper, although that sometimes produces useful background bits. What I get the most out of is what I call "the sound of science" – the kind of shorthand language scientists use when they're talking to each other about their own specialities. So I usually sit somewhere at the back of the hall, with as much space around me as I can manage, my tablet in my lap and my stylus in my hand, writing down bits of dialogue and figuring how to put them into my next sci-rom.

There wasn't much of that today. There wasn't much discussion at all. One by one the speakers got up and read their papers, answered a couple of cursory questions with cursory replies, and hurried off; and when each one finished he left, and the audience got smaller because, as I finally figured out, no one was there who wasn't obligated to be.

When boredom made me decide that I needed a glass of wine and a quick snack more than I needed to sit there with my still-blank tablet, I found out there was hardly anyone even in the lounges. There was no familiar face. No one seemed to know where Sam was. And in the afternoon, the Collegium-Presidor, bowing to the inevitable, announced that the remaining sessions would be postponed indefinitely.

The day was a total waste.

I had a lot more hopes for the night.

Rachel greeted me with the news that Sam had sent a message to say he was detained and wouldn't make dinner.

"Did he say where he was?" She shook her head. "He's off with some of the other top people," I guessed. I told her about the collapse of the convention. Then I brightened. "At least let's go out for dinner, then."

Rachel firmly vetoed the idea. She was tactful enough not to mention money, although I was sure Sam had filled her in on my precarious financial state. "I like my own cook's food better than any restaurant," she told me. "We'll eat here. There won't be anything fancy tonight – just a simple meal for the two of us."

The best part of that was "the two of us". Basilius had arranged the couches in a sort of V, so that our heads were quite close together, with the low serving tables in easy reach between us. As soon as she lay down, Rachel confessed, "I didn't get a lot of work done today. I couldn't get that idea of yours out of my head."

The idea was Sam's, actually, but I didn't see any reason to correct her. "I'm flattered," I told her. "I'm sorry I spoiled your work."

She shrugged and went on. "I did a little reading on the period, especially about an interesting minor figure who lived around then, a Judaean preacher named Jeshua of Nazareth. Did you ever hear of him? Well, most people haven't, but he had a lot of followers at one time. They called themselves Chrestians, and they were a very unruly bunch."

"I'm afraid I don't know much about Judaean history," I said. Which was true; but then I added, "But I'd really like to learn more." Which wasn't – or at least hadn't been until just then.

"Of course, Rachel said. No doubt to her it seemed quite

natural that everyone in the world would wish to know more about the post-Augustan period. "Anyway, this Jeshua was on trial for sedition. He was condemned to death.'

I blinked at her. "Not just to slavery?"

She shook her head. "They didn't just enslave criminals back then, they did physical things to them. Even executed them, sometimes in very barbarous ways. But Tiberius, as Proconsul, decided that the penalty was too extreme. So he commuted Jeshua's death sentence. He just had him whipped and let him go. A very good decision, I think. Otherwise he would have made him a martyr, and gods know what would have happened after that. As it was, the Chrestians just gradually waned away. . . . Basilius? You can bring the next course in now."

I watched with interest as Basilius complied. It turned out to be larks and olives! I approved, not simply for the fact that I liked the dish. The "simple meal" was actually a lot more elaborate than she had provided for the three of us the night before.

Things were looking up. I said, "Can you tell me something, Rachel? I think you're Judaean yourself, aren't you?"

"Of course."

"Well, I'm a little confused," I said. "I thought the Judaeans believed in the god Yahveh."

"Of course, Julie. We do."

"Yes but—" I hesitated. I didn't want to mess up the way things were going, but I was curious. "But you say 'gods'. Isn't that, well, a contradiction?"

"Not at all," she told me civilly enough. "Yahveh's commandments were brought down from a mountaintop by our great prophet, Moses, and they were very clear on the subject. One of them says, 'Thou shalt have no other gods before me.' Well, we don't, you see? Yahveh is our *first* god. There aren't any *before* him. It's all explained in the rabbinical writings."

"And that's what you go by, the rabbinical writings?"

She looked thoughtful. "In a way. We're a very traditional people, Julie. Tradition is what we follow, the rabbinical writings simply explain the traditions."

She had stopped eating. I stopped, too. Dreamily I reached out to caress her cheek.

She didn't pull away. She didn't respond, either. After a moment, she said, not looking at me, "For instance, there is a Judaean tradition that a woman is to be a virgin at the time of her marriage."

My hand came away from her face by itself, without any conscious command from me. "Oh?"

"And the rabbinical writings more or less define the tradition, you see. They say that the head of the household is to stand guard at an unmarried daughter's bedroom for the first hour of each night; if there is no male head of the household, a trusted slave is to be appointed to the job."

"I see," I said. "You've never been married, have you?"

"Not yet," said Rachel, beginning to eat again.

I hadn't ever been married, either, although, to be sure, I wasn't exactly a virgin. It wasn't that I had anything against marriage. It was only that the life of a sci-rom hack wasn't what you would call exactly financially stable, and also the fact that I hadn't ever come across the woman I wanted to spend my life with . . . or, to quote Rachel, "Not yet."

I tried to keep my mind off that subject. I was sure that if my finances had been precarious before, they were now close to catastrophic.

The next morning I wondered what to do with my day, but Rachel settled it for me. She was waiting for me in the atrium. "Sit down with me, Julie," she commanded, patting the bench beside me. "I was up late, thinking, and I think I've got something for you. Suppose this man Jeshua had been executed, after all."

It wasn't exactly the greeting I had been hoping for, nor was it something I had given a moment's thought to, either. But I was glad enough to sit next to her in that pleasant little garden, with the gentled early sun shining down on us through the translucent shades. "Yes?" I said noncommittally, kissing her hand in greeting.

She waited a moment before she took her hand back. "That

idea opened some interesting possibilities, Julie. Jeshua would have been a martyr, you see. I can easily imagine that under those circumstances his Chrestian followers would have had a lot more staying power. They might even have grown to be really important. Judaea was always in one kind of turmoil or another around that time, anyway – there were all sorts of prophecies and rumours about messiahs and changes in society. The Chrestians might even have come to dominate all of Judaea."

I tried to be tactful. "There's nothing wrong with being proud of your ancestors, Rachel. But, really, what difference would that have made?" I obviously hadn't been tactful enough. She had turned to look at me with what looked like the beginning of a frown. I thought fast, and tried to cover myself. "On the other hand," I went on quickly, "suppose you expanded that idea beyond Judaea."

It turned into a real frown, but puzzled rather than angry. "What do you mean, beyond Judaea?"

"Well, suppose Jeshua's Chrestian-Judaean kind of – what would you call it? Philosophy? Religion?"

"A little of both, I'd say."

"Religious philosophy, then. Suppose it spread over most of the world, not just Judaea. That could be interesting."

"But, really, no such thing hap—"

"Rachel, Rachel," I said, covering her mouth with a fingertip affectionately. "We're saying *what if*, remember? Every sci-rom writer is entitled to one big lie. Let's say this is mine. Let's say that Chrestian-Judaeanism became a world religion. Even Rome itself succumbs. Maybe the City becomes the – what do you call it – the place for the Sanhedrin of the Chrestian-Judaeans. And then what happens?"

"You tell me," she said, half-amused, half-suspicious.

"Why, then," I said, flexing the imagination of the trained sci-rom writer, "it might develop like the kind of conditions you've been talking about in the old days in Judaea. Maybe the whole world would be splintering into factions and sects, and then they fight."

"Fight *wars*?" she asked incredulously.

"Fight *big* wars. Why not? It happened in Judaea, didn't it? And then they might keep right on fighting them, all through historical times. After all, the only thing that's kept the world united for the past two thousand years has been the Pax Romana. Without that – why, without that," I went on, talking faster and making mental notes to myself as I went along, "let's say that all the tribes of Europe turned into independent city-states. Like the Greeks, only bigger. And more powerful. And they fight, the Franks against the Vik Northmen against the Belgiae against the Kelts."

She was shaking her head. "People wouldn't be so silly, Julie," she complained.

"How do you know that? Anyway, this is a sci-rom, dear." I didn't pause to see if she reacted to the "dear". I went right on, but not failing to notice that she hadn't objected. "The people will be as silly as I want them to be – as long as I can make it plausible enough for the fans. But you haven't heard the best part of it. Let's say the Chrestian-Judaeans take their religion seriously. They don't do anything to go against the will of their god. What Yahveh said still goes, no matter what. Do you follow? That means they aren't at all interested in scientific discovery, for instance."

"No, stop right there!" she ordered, suddenly indignant. "Are you trying to say that we Judaeans aren't interested in science? That I'm not? Or my Uncle Sam? And we're certainly Judaeans."

"But you're not *Chrestian*-Judaeans, sweet. There's a big difference. Why? Because I say there is, Rachel, and I'm the one writing the story. So, let's see – " I paused for thought – "all right, let's say the Chrestians go through a long period of intellectual stagnation, and then – " I paused, not because I didn't know what was coming next but to build the effect – "and then along come the Olympians!"

She gazed at me blankly. "Yes?" she asked, encouraging but vague.

"Don't you see it? And then this Chrestian-Judaean world, drowsing along in the middle of a pre-scientific dark age – no aircraft, no electronic broadcast, not even a printing press or a hovermachine – is suddenly thrown into contact with a super-technological civilization from outer space!" She was wrinkling her forehead at me, trying to understand what I was driving at. "It's terrible culture shock," I explained. "And not just for the people on Earth. Maybe the Olympians come to look us over, and they see that we're technologically backward and divided into warring nations and all that . . . and what do they do? Why, they turn right around and leave us! And . . . and that's the end of the book!"

She pursed her lips. "But maybe that's what they're doing now," she said cautiously.

"But not for that reason, certainly. See, this isn't *our* world I'm talking about. It's a *what if* world."

"It sounds a little far-fetched," she said.

I said happily, "That's where my skills come in. You don't understand sci-rom, sweetheart. It's the sci-rom writer's job to push an idea as far as it will go – to the absolute limit of credibility – to the point where if he took just one step more the whole thing would collapse into absurdity. Trust me, Rachel. I'll make them believe it."

She was still pursing her pretty lips, but this time I didn't wait for her to speak. I seized the bird of opportunity on the wing. I leaned towards her and kissed those lips, as I had been wanting to do for some time. Then I said, "I've got to get to a scribe; I want to get all this down before I forget it. I'll be back when I can be, and – and until then – well, here."

And I kissed her again, gently, firmly and long; and it was quite clear early in the process that she was kissing me back.

Being next to a rental barracks had its advantages. I found a scribe to rent at a decent price, and the rental manager even let me borrow one of their conference rooms that night to dictate in. By daybreak I had down the first two chapters and an outline of *Sidewise to a Chrestian World*.

Once I get that far in a book, the rest is just work. The general idea is set, the characters have announced themselves to me, it's just a matter of closing my eyes for a moment to see what's going to be happening and then opening them to dictate to the scribe. In this case, the scribes, plural, because the first one wore out in a few more hours and I had to employ a second, and then a third.

I didn't sleep at all until it was all down. I think it was fifty-two straight hours, the longest I'd worked in one stretch in years. When it was all done I left it to be fair-copied. The rental agent agreed to get it down to the shipping offices by the harbour and dispatch it by fast air to Marcus in London.

Then at last I stumbled back to Rachel's house to sleep. I was surprised to find that it was still dark, an hour or more before sunrise.

Basilius let me in, looking startled as he studied my sunken eyes and unshaved face. "Let me sleep until I wake up," I ordered. There was a journal neatly folded beside my bed, but I didn't look at it. I lay down, turned over once, and was gone.

When I woke up, at least twelve hours had passed. I had Basilius bring me something to eat and shave me, and when I finally got out to the atrium it was nearly sundown and Rachel was waiting for me. I told her what I'd done, and she told me about the last message from the Olympians. "Last?" I objected. "How can you be sure it's the last?"

"Because they said so," she told me sadly. "They said they were breaking off communications."

"Oh," I said, thinking about that. "Poor Sam." And she looked so doleful that I couldn't help myself, I took her in my arms.

Consolation turned to kissing, and when we had done quite a lot of that she leaned back, smiling at me.

I couldn't help what I said then, either. It startled me to hear the words come out of my mouth as I said, "Rachel, I wish we could get married."

She pulled back, looking at me with affection and a little surprised amusement. "Are you proposing to me?"

I was careful of my grammar. "That was a subjunctive, sweet. I said I *wished* we could get married."

"I understood that. What I want to know is whether you're asking me to grant your wish."

"No – well, hells, yes! But what I wish first is that I had the

right to ask you. Sci-rom writers don't have the most solid
financial situation, you know. The way you live here—"

"The way I live here," she said, "is paid for by the estate I
inherited from my father. Getting married won't take it away."

"But that's your estate, my darling. I've been poor, but I've
never been a parasite."

"You won't be a parasite," she said softly, and I realized that
she was being careful about her grammar, too.

Which took a lot of willpower on my part. "Rachel," I said, "I
should be hearing from my editor any time now. If this new
kind of sci-rom catches on – if it's as popular as it might be—"

"Yes?" she prompted.

"Why," I said, "then maybe I can actually ask you. But I
don't know that. Marcus probably has it by now, but I don't
know if he's read it. And then I won't know his decision till I
hear from him. And now, with all the confusion about the
Olympians, that might take weeks—"

"Julie," she said, putting her finger over her lips, "call him
up."

The circuits were all busy, but I finally got through – and,
because it was well after lunch, Marcus was in his office. More
than that, he was quite sober. "Julie, you bastard," he cried,
sounding really furious, "where the hells have you been hiding?
I ought to have you whipped."

But he hadn't said anything about getting the aediles after
me. "Did you have a chance to read *Sidewise to a Chrestian
World*?" I asked.

"The what? Oh, *that* thing. Nah. I haven't even looked at it.
I'll buy it, naturally," he said. "But what I'm talking about is *An
Ass' Olympiad*. The censors won't stop it now, you know. In
fact, all I want you to do now is make the Olympians a little
dumber, a little nastier – you've got a biggie here, Julie! I think
we can get a broadcast out of it, even. So when can you get back
here to fix it up?"

"Why – well, pretty soon, I guess, only I haven't checked the
hover timetable—"

"Hover, hell! You're coming back by fast plane – we'll pick

up the tab. And, oh, by the way, we're doubling your advance. The payment will be in your account this afternoon."

And ten minutes later, when I unsubjunctively proposed to Rachel, she quickly and unsubjunctively accepted; and the high-speed flight to London takes nine hours, but I was grinning all the way.

Chapter 5

The Way It Is When You've Got It Made

To be a freelance writer is to live in a certain kind of ease. Not very easeful financially, maybe, but in a lot of other ways. You don't have to go to an office every day, you get a lot of satisfaction out of seeing your very own words being read on hovers and trains by total strangers. To be a potentially *bestselling* writer is a whole order of magnitude different. Marcus put me up in an inn right next to the publishing company's offices and stood over me while I turned my poor imaginary Olympian into the most doltish, feckless, unlikeable being the universe had ever seen. The more I made the Olympian contemptibly comic, the more Marcus loved it. So did everyone else in the office; so did their affiliates in Kiev and Manahattan and Kalkut and half a dozen other cities all around the world, and he informed me proudly that they were publishing my book simultaneously in all of them. "We'll be the first ones out, Julie," he exulted. "It's going to be a mint! Money? Well, of course you can have more money – you're in the big-time now!" And, yes, the broadcast studios were interested – interested enough to sign a contract even before I'd finished the revisions; and so were the journals, who came for interviews every minute that Marcus would let me off from correcting the proofs and posing for jacket photographs and speaking to their sales staff; and, all in all, I hardly had a chance to breathe until I was back on the high-speed aircraft to Alexandria and my bride.

Sam had agreed to give the bride away, and he met me at the airpad. He looked older and more tired, but resigned. As we drove to Rachel's house, where the wedding guests were already beginning to gather, I tried to cheer him up. I had plenty of joy myself; I wanted to share it. So I offered, "At least, now you can get back to your real work."

He looked at me strangely. "Writing sci-roms?" he asked.

"No, of course not! That's good enough for me, but you've still got your extrasolar probe to keep you busy."

"Julie," he said sadly, "where have you been lately? Didn't you see the last Olympian message?"

"Well, sure," I said, offended. "Everybody did, didn't they?" And then I thought for a moment, and, actually, it had been Rachel who had told me about it. I'd never actually looked at a journal or a broadcast. "I guess I was pretty busy," I said lamely.

He looked sadder than ever. "Then maybe you don't know that they said they weren't only terminating all their own transmissions to us, they were terminating even our own probes."

"Oh, no, Sam! I would have heard if the probes had stopped transmitting!"

He said patiently, "No, you wouldn't, because the data they were sending is still on its way to us. We've still got a few years coming in from our probes. But that's it. We're out of interstellar space, Julie. They don't want us there."

He broke off, peering out the window. "And that's the way it is," he said. "We're here, though, and you better get inside. Rachel's going to be tired of sitting under that canopy without you around."

The greatest thing of all about being a bestselling author, if you like travelling, is that when you fly around the world somebody else pays for the tickets. Marcus's publicity department fixed up the whole thing. Personal appearances, bookstore autographings, college lectures, broadcasts, publishers' meetings, receptions – we were kept busy for a solid month, and it made a hell of a fine honeymoon.

Of course any honeymoon would have been wonderful as long as Rachel was the bride, but without the publishers bankrolling us we might not have visited six of the seven continents on the way. (We didn't bother with Polaris Australis – nobody there but penguins.) And we took time for ourselves along the way, on beaches in Hindia and the islands of Han, in the wonderful shops of Manahattan and a dozen other cities of the Western Continents – we did it all.

When we got back to Alexandria the contractors had finished the remodeling of Rachel's villa – which, we had decided, would now be our winter home, though our next priority was going to be to find a place where we could spend the busy part of the year in London. Sam had moved back in and, with Basilius, greeted us formally as we came to the door.

"I thought you'd be in Rome," I told him, once we were settled and Rachel had gone to inspect what had been done with her baths.

"Not while I'm still trying to understand what went wrong," he said "The research is going on right here; this is where we transmitted from."

I shrugged and took a sip of the Falernian wine Basilius had left for us. I held the goblet up critically: a little cloudy, I thought, and in the vat too long. And then I grinned at myself, because a few weeks earlier I would have been delighted at anything so costly. "But we know what went wrong," I told him reasonably. "They decided against us."

"Of course they did," he said. "But why? I've been trying to work out just what messages were being received when they broke off communications."

"Do you think we said something to offend them?"

He scratched the age spot on his bald head, staring at me. Then he sighed. "What would *you* think, Julius?"

"Well, maybe so," I admitted. "What messages were they?"

"I'm not sure. It took a lot of digging. The Olympians, you know, acknowledged receipt of each message by repeating the last hundred and forty groups—"

"I didn't know."

"Well, they did. The last message they acknowledged was a history of Rome. Unfortunately, it was 650,000 words long."

"So you have to read the whole history?"

"Not just *read* it, Julie; we have to try to figure out what might have been in it that wasn't in any previous message. We've had two or three hundred researchers collating every previous message, and the only thing that was new was some of the social data from the last census—"

I interrupted him. "I thought you said it was a history."

"It was at the *end* of the history. We were giving pretty current data – so many of equestrian rank, so many citizens, so many freedmen, so many slaves." He hesitated, and then said thoughtfully, "Paulus Magnus – I don't know if you know him, he's an Algonkan – pointed out that that was the first time we'd ever mentioned slavery."

I waited for him to go on. "Yes?" I said encouragingly.

He shrugged. "Nothing. Paulus is a slave himself, so naturally he's got it on his mind a lot."

"I don't quite see what that has to do with anything," I said. "Isn't there anything else?"

"Oh," he said, "there are a thousand theories. There were some health data, too, and some people think the Olympians might have suddenly got worried about some new microorganism killing them off. Or we weren't polite enough. Or maybe – who knows – there was some sort of power struggle among them, and the side that came out on top just didn't want any more new races in their community."

"And we don't know yet which it was?"

"It's worse than that, Julie," he told me sombrely. "I don't think we ever will find out what it was that made them decide they didn't want to have anything to do with us." And in that, too, Flavius Samuelus ben Samuelus was a very intelligent man. Because we never have.

Darwin Anathema

Stephen Baxter

Trailed by a porter with her luggage, Mary Mason climbed down the steamer's ramp to the dock at Folkestone, and waited in line with the rest of the passengers to clear security.

Folkestone, her first glimpse of England, was unprepossessing, a small harbour in the lee of cliffs fronting a dismal, smoke-stained townscape from which the slender spires of churches protruded. People crowded around the harbour, the passengers disembarking, stevedores labouring to unload the hold. There was a line of horse-drawn vehicles waiting, and one smoky-looking steam carriage. The ocean-going steamship, its rusting flank a wall, looked too big and vigorous for the port.

Mary, forty-five years old, felt weary, stiff, faintly disoriented to be standing on a surface that wasn't rolling back and forth. She had come to England all the way from Terra Australis to participate in the Inquisition's trial of Charles Darwin, a man more than a century dead. Back home in Cooktown it had seemed a good idea. Now she was here it seemed utterly insane.

At last the port inspectors stared at her passepartout, cross-examined her about her reasons for coming to England – they didn't seem to know what a "natural philosopher" was – and then opened every case. One of the officials finally handed back her passepartout. She checked it was stamped with the correct date: 9 February 2009. "Welcome to England," he grunted.

She walked forward, trailed by the porter.

"Lector Mason? Not quite the harbour at Cooktown, is it? Nevertheless I hope you've had a satisfactory voyage."

She turned. "Father Brazel?"

Xavier Brazel was the Jesuit who had coordinated her invitation and passage. He was tall, slim, elegant; he wore a modest black suit with a white clerical collar. He was a good bit younger than she was, maybe thirty. He smiled, blessed her with two fingers making a cross sign in the air, and shook her hand. "Call me Xavier. I'm delighted to meet you, truly. We're privileged you've agreed to participate in the trial, and I'm particularly looking forward to hearing you speak at St Paul's. Come, I have a carriage to the rail station . . ." Nodding at the porter, he led her away. "The trial of Alicia Darwin and her many-times-great-uncle starts tomorrow."

"Yes. The ship was delayed a couple of days."

"I'm sorry there's so little time to prepare, or recover."

"I'll be fine."

The carriage was small but sturdy, pulled by a pair of patient horses. It clattered away through crowded, cobbled streets.

"And I apologise for the security measures," Xavier said. "A tiresome welcome to the country. It's been like this since the 29 May attacks."

"That was six years ago. They caught the Vatican bombers, didn't they?" Pinprick attacks by Muslim zealots who had struck to commemorate the 550th anniversary of the Islamic conquest of Constantinople – and more than 120 years after a Christian coalition had taken the city back from the Ottomans.

He just smiled. "Once you have surrounded yourself with a ring of steel, it's hard to tear it down."

They reached the station where the daily train to London was, fortuitously, waiting. Xavier already had tickets. Xavier helped load Mary's luggage, and led her to an upper-class carriage. Aside from Mary everybody in here seemed to be a cleric of some kind, the men in black suits, the few women in nuns' wimples.

The train pulled away. Clouds of sooty steam billowed past the window.

A waiter brought coffees. Xavier sipped his with relish. "Please, enjoy."

Mary tasted her coffee. "That's good."

"French, from their American colonies. The French do know how to make good coffee. Speaking of the French – have you visited Britain before? As it happens this rail line follows the track of the advance of Napoleon's Grande Armee in 1807, through Maidstone to London. You may see the monuments in the towns we pass through . . . Are you all right, Lector? You don't seem quite comfortable."

"I'm not used to having so many clerics around me. Terra Australis is a Christian country, even if it followed the Marxist Reformation. But I feel like the only sinner on the train."

He smiled and spoke confidentially. "If you think this is a high density of dog-collars you should try visiting Rome."

She found herself liking him for his humour and candour. But, she had learned from previous experience, Jesuits were always charming and manipulative. "I don't need to go to Rome to see the Inquisition at work, however, do I?"

"We prefer not to use that word," he said evenly. "The Sacred Congregation for the Doctrine of Faith, newly empowered under Cardinal Ratzinger since the 29 May attacks, has done sterling work in the battle against Ottoman extremists."

"Who just want the freedom of faith they enjoyed up until the 1870s Crusade."

He smiled. "You know your history. But of course that's why you're here. The presence of unbiased observers is important; the Congregation wants to be seen to give Darwin a fair hearing. I have to admit we had refusals to participate from philosophers with specialities in natural selection—"

"So you had to settle for a historian of natural philosophy?"

"We are grateful for your help. The Church as a whole is keen to avoid unfortunate misunderstandings. The purpose of the Congregation's hearings is to clarify the relationship between theology and natural philosophy, not to condemn. You'll see. And frankly," he said, "I hope you'll think better of us after you've seen us at work."

She shrugged. "I guess I'm here for my own purposes too." As a historian she'd hope to gather some good material on the centuries-long tension between Church and natural philosophy, and maybe she could achieve more at the trial itself than contribute to some kind of Inquisition propaganda stunt. But now she was here, in the heart of the theocracy, she wasn't so sure.

She'd fallen silent. Xavier studied her with polite concern. "Are you comfortable? Would you like more coffee?"

"I think I'm a little over-tired," she said. "Sorry if I snapped." She dug her book out of her bag. "Maybe I'll read a bit and leave you in peace."

He glanced at the spine. "H. G. Wells. *The War of the Celestial Spheres.*"

"I'm trying to immerse myself in all things English."

"It's a fine read, and only marginally heretical." He actually winked at her.

She had to laugh, but she felt a frisson of unease.

So she read, and dozed a little, as the train clattered through the towns of Kent, Ashford and Charing and others. The towns and villages were cramped, the buildings uniformly stained black with soot. The rolling country was cluttered with small farms where people in mud-coloured clothes laboured over winter crops. The churches were squat buildings like stone studs pinning down the ancient green of the countryside. She'd heard there was a monument to Wellington at Maidstone, where he'd fallen as he failed to stop Napoleon crossing the Medway river. But if it existed at all it wasn't visible from the train.

By the time the train approached London, the light of the short English day was already fading.

As a guest of the Church she was lodged in one of London's best hotels. But her room was lit by smoky oil lamps. There seemed to be electricity only in the lobby and dining room – why, even the front porch of her own home outside Cooktown had an electric bulb. And she noticed that the telegraph they used to send a message home to her husband and son was an Australian Maxwell design.

Still, in the morning she found she had a terrific view of the Place de Louis XVI, and of Whitehall and the Mall beyond. The

day was bright, and pigeons fluttered around the statue of
Bonaparte set atop the huge Christian cross that dominated the
square. For a historian this was a reminder of the Church's slow
but crushing reconquest of Protestant England. In the eighteenth
century a Catholic league had cooperated with the French to
defeat Britain's imperial ambitions in America and India, and
then in 1807 the French King's Corsican attack-dog had been
unleashed on the homeland. By the time Napoleon withdrew,
England was once more a Catholic country under a new Bourbon
king. Looking up at Napoleon's brooding face, she was suddenly
glad her own home was 12,000 miles away from all this history.

Father Xavier called for her at nine. They travelled by horse-
drawn carriage to St Paul's Cathedral, where the trial of Charles
Darwin was to be staged.

St Paul's was magnificent. Xavier had sweetened her trip
around the world by promising her she would be allowed to give
a guest sermon to senior figures in London's theological and
philosophical community from the cathedral's pulpit. Now she
was here she started to feel intimidated at the prospect.

But she had no time to look around. Xavier, accompanied by
an armed Inquisition guard, led her straight through to the
stairs down to the crypt, which had been extended to a warren
of dark corridors with rows of hefty locked doors. In utter
contrast to the glorious building above, this was like a prison, or
a dungeon.

Xavier seemed to sense her mood. "You're doing fine,
Lector."

"Yeah. I'm just memorizing the way out."

They arrived at a room that was surprisingly small and bare,
for such a high-profile event, with plain plastered walls
illuminated by dangling electrical bulbs. The centrepiece was a
wooden table behind which sat a row of Inquisition examiners,
Mary presumed, stern men all of late middle age wearing
funereal black and clerical collars. Their chairman sat in an
elaborate throne-like seat, elevated above the rest.

A woman stood before them – stood because she had no seat
to sit on, Mary saw. The girl, presumably Alicia, Darwin's
grand-niece several times removed, wore a sober charcoal-grey

dress. She was very pale, with blue eyes and strawberry hair; she could have been no older than twenty, twenty-one.

On one side of her sat a young man, soberly dressed, good-looking, his features alive with interest. And on the other side, Mary was astounded to see, a coffin rested on trestles.

Xavier led Mary to a bench set along one wall. Here various other clerics sat, most of them men. On the far side were men and women in civilian clothes. Some were writing in notebooks, others sketching the faces of the principals.

"Just in time," Xavier murmured as they sat. "I do apologise. Did you see the look Father Boniface gave me?"

"Not *the* Boniface!"

"The Reverend Father Boniface Jones, Commissary General. Learned his trade at the feet of Commissary Hitler himself, in the old man's retirement years after all his good work during the Missionary Wars in Orthodox Russia . . ."

"Who's that lot on the far side?"

"From the chronicles. Interest in this case is world-wide."

"Don't tell me who's in that box."

"Respectfully disinterred from his tomb in Edinburgh and removed here. He could hardly not show up for his own trial, could he? Today we'll hear the deposition. The verdict is due to be given in a couple of days – on the twelfth, Darwin's 200th anniversary."

Xavier said that the young man sitting beside Alicia was called Anselm Fairweather; a friend of Alicia, he was the theological lawyer she had chosen to assist her in presenting her case.

"But he's not a defence lawyer," Xavier murmured. "You must remember this isn't a civil courtroom. In this case the defendant happens to have a general idea of the charges she's to face, as a living representative of Darwin's family – the only one who would come forward, incidentally; I think her presence was an initiative of young Fairweather. But she's not entitled to know those charges or the evidence, nor to know who brought them."

"That doesn't seem just."

"But this is not justice in that sense. This is the working-out of God's will, as focused through the infallibility of the Holy Father and the wisdom of his officers."

The proceedings opened with a rap of Jones's gavel. A clerk on the examiners' bench began to scribble a verbatim record. Jones instructed the principals present to identify themselves. Alongside him on the bench were other Commissaries, and a Prosecutor of the Holy Office.

When it was her turn, Mary stood to introduce herself as a Lector of Cooktown University, here to observe and advise in her expert capacity. Boniface actually smiled at her. He had a face as long and grey as the Reverend Darwin's coffin, and the skin under his eyes was velvet black.

A Bible was brought to Alicia, and she read Latin phrases from a card.

"I have no Latin," Mary whispered to Xavier. "She's swearing an oath to tell the truth, right?"

"Yes. I'll translate . . ."

Boniface picked up a paper, and began to work his way through his questions, in Latin that sounded like gravel falling into a bucket. Xavier whispered his translation: "*By what means and how long ago she came to London.*"

Mercifully the girl answered in English, with a crisp Scottish accent. "By train and carriage from my mother's home in Edinburgh. Which has been the family home since the Reverend Charles Darwin's time."

"*Whether she knows or can guess the reason she was ordered to present herself to the Holy Office.*"

"Well, I think I know." She glanced at the coffin. "To stand behind the remains of my uncle, while a book he published 150 years ago is considered for its heresy."

"*That she name this book.*"

"It was called *A Dialogue on the Origin of Species by Natural Selection.*"

"*That she explain the character of this book.*"

"Well, I've never read it. I don't know anybody who has. It was put on the Index even before it was published. I've only read second-hand accounts of its contents . . . It concerns an hypothesis concerning the variety of animal and vegetable forms we see around us. Why are some so alike, such as varieties of cat or bird? My uncle drew analogies with the well-known modification of forms of dogs, pigeons, peas and beans and other domesticated creatures under the pressure of selection for various desirable properties by mankind. He proposed – no, he proposed an *hypothesis* – that natural variations in living things could be caused by another kind of selection, unconsciously applied by nature as species competed for limited resources, for water and food. This selection, given time, would shape living things as surely as the conscious manipulation of human trainers."

"*Whether she believes this hypothesis to hold truth.*"

"I'm no natural philosopher. I want to be an artist. A painter, actually—"

"*Whether she believes this hypothesis to hold truth.*"

The girl bowed her head. "It is contrary to the teachings of Scripture."

"*Whether the Reverend Charles Darwin believed the hypothesis to hold truth.*"

She seemed rattled. "Maybe you should open the box and ask him yersel' . . ." Her lawyer, Anselm Fairweather, touched her arm. "I apologise, Father. He stated it as an hypothesis, an organizing principle, much as Galileo Galilei set out the motion of the Earth around the sun as an hypothesis only. Natural selection would explain certain observed patterns in nature. No doubt the truth of God's holy design lies beneath these observed patterns, but is not yet apprehended by our poor minds. Charles set this out clearly in his book, which he presented as a dialogue between a proponent of the hypothesis and a sceptic."

"*Whether she feels the heresy is properly denied in the course of this dialogue.*"

"That's for you to judge. I mean, his intention was balance, and if that was not achieved, it is only through the poor artistry of my uncle, who was a philosopher before he was a writer, and—"

"*Whether she is aware of the injunction placed on Charles Darwin on first publication of this book.*"

"That he destroy the published edition, and replace it with a revision more clearly emphasizing the hypothetical nature of his argument."

"*Whether she is aware of his compliance with this injunction.*"

"I'm not aware of any second edition. He fled to Edinburgh, whose Royal Society heard him state his hypothesis, and received his further work in the form of transactions in its journal."

Xavier murmured to Mary, "Those Scottish Presbyterians. Nothing but trouble."

"*Whether she approves of his departure from England, as assisted by the heretical criminals known as the Lyncean Academy.*"

"I don't know anything about that."

"*Whether she approves of his refusal to appear before a properly appointed court of the Holy Office.*"

"I don't know about that either."

"*Whether she approves of his non-compliance with the holy injunction.*"

"As I understand it he felt his book was balanced, therefore it wasn't heretical as it stood, and therefore the injunction was not applicable . . ."

So the hearing went on. The questioning seemed to have nothing to do with Darwin's philosophical case, which after all was the reason for Mary's presence here, but was more a relentless badgering of Alicia Darwin over the intentions and beliefs of her remote uncle – questions she couldn't possibly answer save in terms of her own interpretation, a line Alicia bravely stuck to.

To Mary, the trial began to seem a shabby epilogue to Darwin's own story. He had been a bright young cleric, with vague plans to become a Jesuit, who had signed on to a ship of discovery, the *Beagle*, in the year 1831: the English never assembled an empire, but they remained explorers. On board he had come under the influence of the work of some of the bright, radical thinkers from Presbyterian Edinburgh – the "Scottish Enlightenment", as the historians called it. And in the course of his travels Darwin saw for himself islands being created and destroyed, and island-bound species of cormorants and iguanas that seemed obviously in flux between one form and another . . . Far from the anchoring certainties of the Church, it was no wonder he had come home with a head full of a vision that had obsessed him for the rest of his life – but it was a vision fraught with danger.

All this was a long time ago, the voyage of the *Beagle* nearly 200 years past. But the Church thought in centuries, and was now exacting its revenge.

Alicia had volunteered to participate in this trial as an honour to her uncle, just as Mary had. Mary had imagined it would all be something of a formality. Yet the girl seemed slim, frail, defenceless standing there before the threatening row of theocrats before her – men who, Mary reminded herself uneasily, literally had the power of life and death over Alicia. Once, during the course of the questioning, Alicia glanced over at Mary, one of the few women in the room. Mary deliberately smiled back. *No, I don't know what the hell we've got ourselves into here either, kid.*

At last it ended for the day. Alicia had to glance over and sign the clerk's handwritten transcript of the session. She was ordered not to leave without special permission, and sworn to silence. She looked shocked when she was led away to a cell, somewhere in the crypt warren.

Mary stood. "She wasn't expecting that."

Xavier murmured, "Don't worry. It's just routine. She's not a prisoner."

"It looked like it to me."

"Darwin will be found guilty of defying that long-ago injunction, of course. But Alicia will be asked only to abjure her uncle's actions, and to condemn the book. A slap on the wrist—"

"I don't care right now. I just want to get out of this place. Can we go?"

"Once the Reverend Fathers have progressed . . ." He bowed as Boniface Jones and the others walked past, stately as sailing ships in their black robes.

Mary got a good turn-out for her sermon in the cathedral the next day.

She'd titled it "Galileo, Einstein and the Mystery of Transubstantiation" – a provocative theme that had seemed a good idea from the other side of the world. Now, standing at the pulpit of St Paul's itself, dwarfed by the stonework around her and facing rows of calm, black-robed, supremely powerful men, she wasn't so sure.

There in the front row, however, was Anselm Fairweather, Alicia Darwin's lawyer. He looked bright, with an engaging, youthful sort of curiosity that she felt she'd seen too little of in England. Xavier Brazel sat beside him, faintly sinister as usual, but relatively sane, and relatively reassuring.

For better or worse, she was stuck with her prepared text. "I'm well aware that to most churchmen and perhaps the lay public the philosophical career of Galileo, in astronomy, dynamics and other subjects, is of most interest for the period leading up to his summons to Rome in 1633 to face charges of heresy concerning his work regarding the hypothetical motion of the Earth – charges which, of course, were never in the end brought. But to a historian of natural philosophy such as myself it is the legacy of the man's work *after* Rome that is the most compelling . . ."

Nobody was quite sure what had been said to Galileo, by Pope Urban himself among others, in the theocratic snake-pit that was seventeenth-century Rome. Some said the Tuscan ambassador, who was hosting Galileo in Rome, had somehow intervened to soothe ruffled papal feathers. Galileo had not faced the humiliation of an Inquisition trial over his Copernican views, or, worse, sanctions afterwards. Instead, the increasingly frail, increasingly lonely old man had returned home to Tuscany. In his final years he turned away from the astronomical studies that had caused him so much trouble, and concentrated instead on "hypotheses" about dynamics, the physics of moving objects. This had been an obsession since, as a young man, he had noticed patterns in the pendulum-like swinging of church chandeliers.

"And in doing so, even so late in life, Galileo came to some remarkable and far-reaching conclusions."

Galileo's later work had run ahead of the mathematical techniques of the time, and to be fully appreciated had had to be reinterpreted by later generations of mathematicians, notably

Leibniz. Essentially Galileo had built on common-sense observations of everyday motion to build a theory that was now known as "relativity", in which objects moved so that their combined velocities never exceeded a certain "speed of finality". All this properly required framing in a four-dimensional spacetime. And buried in Galileo's work was the remarkable implication – or, as she carefully said, an "hypothesis" – that the whole of the universe was expanding into four-dimensional space.

These "hypotheses" had received confirmation in later centuries. James Clerk Maxwell, developing his ideas about electromagnetism in the comparatively intellectually free environment of Presbyterian Edinburgh, had proved that Galileo's "speed of finality" was in fact the speed of light.

"And later in the nineteenth century, astronomers in our Terra Australis observatories, measuring the Doppler shift of light from distant nebulae, were able to show that the universe does indeed appear to be expanding all around us, just as predicted from Galileo's work." She didn't add that the southern observatories, mostly manned by Aboriginal astronomers, had also long before proved from the parallax of the stars that the motion of the Earth around the sun was real, just as Galileo had clearly believed.

Finally she came to transubstantiation. "In the thirteenth century Thomas Aquinas justified the mystery of the Eucharist – how a communion host can simultaneously be a piece of bread and the flesh of Christ – using Aristotle's physics. The host has the outer form of bread but the inner substance of Christ. It's now more than a century since the Blessed Albert Einstein, then a mere clerk, showed that the transformation of bread to flesh could be described by means of a four-dimensional Galilean rotation, invisible to our senses. And I believe that a Vatican committee is considering accepting this interpretation as orthodoxy, a second Scholasticism. But all this stems from Galileo's insights . . ."

She had often wondered, she concluded, if Galileo's attention had not been focused on his dynamics work by his brush with the authorities – or, worse, if he had been left exhausted or had his life curtailed by their trial and sentencing – perhaps the discovery of relativity might have been delayed centuries.

She was greeted by nods and smiles, from churchmen accepting as justification for their central mystery the wisdom of a man they had come close to persecuting, four centuries dead.

At the end of the Mass Xavier and Anselm Fairweather approached her. "We could hardly clap," Xavier said. "Not in church. But your sermon was much appreciated, Lector Mason."

"Well, thank you."

Anselm said, "Points in your talk sparked my interest, Lector. Have you ever heard of the Lyncean Academy? Named for the lynx, the sharpest-eyed big cat. It was a group of free-thinking scholars, founded in Galileo's time to combat the Church's authority in philosophy. It published Galileo's later books. After Galileo it went underground, but supported later thinkers. It defended Newton at his excommunication trial, and protected Fontenelle, and later helped Darwin flee to Scotland . . ."

She glanced at the churchmen filing out ahead of her. Xavier's impassive face carried an unstated warning. "Is there something you want to tell me, Mr Fairweather?"

"Look, could we speak privately?"

Once out of the cathedral, she let Anselm lead her away. Xavier clearly did not want to hear whatever conversation Anselm proposed to have.

They walked down Blackfriars to the river, and then west along the Embankment. Under grimy iron bridges the Thames was crowded with small steam-driven vessels. The London skyline, where she could see it, was low and flat, a lumpy blanket of poor housing spread like a blanket over the city's low hills, pierced here and there by the slim spire of a Wren church. The city far dwarfed Cooktown, but it lay as if rotting under a blanket of smoky fog. In the streets there seemed to be children everywhere, swarming in this Catholic country, bare-footed, soot-streaked and ragged. She wondered how many of them got any schooling – and how many of them had access to the medicines shipped over from the Pasteur clinics in Terra Australis to the disease-ridden cities of Europe.

As they walked along the Embankment she addressed the issue directly. "So, Anselm, are you a member of this Lyncean Academy?"

He laughed. "You saw through me."

"You're not exactly subtle."

"No. Well, I apologise. But there's no time left for subtlety."

"What's so urgent?"

"The Darwin trial must have the right outcome. I want to make sure I have you on my side. For we intend to use the trial to reverse a mistake the Church never made."

She shook her head. "A mistake never made . . . You've lost me. And I'm not on anybody's side."

"Look – the Academy doesn't question the Church about morality and ethics, the domain of God. It's the Church's meddling in free thought that we object to. Human minds have been locked in systems of thought imposed by the Church for two millennia. Christianity was imposed across the Roman empire. Then Aquinas imposed the philosophy of Aristotle, his four elements, his cosmologies of crystal spheres – which is still the official doctrine, no matter how much the observations of our own eyes, of the instruments you've developed in Terra Australis, disprove every word he wrote! We take our motto from a saying of Galileo himself. 'I do not feel obliged to believe that the same God who has endowed us with sense, reason and intellect –' "

" ' – has intended us to forgo their use.' I don't see what this has to do with the trial."

"It is an echo of the trial of Galileo – which the Church abandoned! Galileo was taken to a prison, given a good fright about torture and the stake, he agreed to say whatever they wanted him to say – but he was *not* put on trial."

She started to see. "But what if he had been?"

He nodded eagerly. "You get the point. A few decades earlier the Church persecuted Giordano Bruno, another philosopher, for his supposed heresies. They *burned* him. But nobody knew who Bruno was. Galileo was famous across Europe! If they had burned *him* – even if they had put him through the public humiliation of a trial – it would have caused outrage, especially in the Protestant countries, England, the Netherlands, the German states. The Church's moral authority would have been rejected there, and weakened even in the Catholic countries.

"And the Church would not have been able to cow those thinkers who followed Galileo. You're a historian of natural philosophy; you must see the pattern. Before Galileo you had thinkers like Bacon, Leonardo, Copernicus, Kepler . . . It was a grand explosion of ideas. Galileo's work drew together and clarified all these threads – he wrote on atomism, you know. His work could have been the foundation of a revolution in thinking. But after him, comparatively speaking – nothing! Do you know that Isaac Newton the alchemist was working on a new mechanics, building on Galileo? If the Church had had not been able to impeach Newton, who knows what he might have achieved?"

"And all this because the Church *spared* Galileo."

"Yes! I know it's a paradox. We suspect the Church made the wise choice by accident . . ."

Mary had a basic sympathy for his position. But she had a gut feeling that history was more complex than this young man imagined. If Galileo's trial had gone ahead, would the work the old man completed later in life have been curtailed? It might have taken centuries more to discover relativity . . .

Anselm clearly had no room in his head for such subtleties. "It would have been better if Galileo had been a martyr! Then all men would have seen the Church for what it is."

Saying this, he seemed very young to Mary. "And now," she said carefully, "you want to use this Darwin trial to create a new martyr. Hmm. How old is Alicia Darwin?"

"Just twenty."

"Does she *know* she's to become some kind of token martyr for your cause?" When he hesitated, she pressed, "You produced her as the family representative for this trial, didn't you? What's your relationship with her?"

"We are lovers," he said defiantly. "Oh, it is chaste, Lector, don't worry about that. But she would do anything for me – and I for her."

"Would she be your lover if she weren't Darwin's grand-niece? And I ask you again: does she *know* what she's letting herself in for?"

He held her gaze, defiant. "The Lyncean Academy is ancient and determined. If the Church has a long memory, so do we. And I hope, I pray, that you, Lector, if the need arises, will use your considerable authority in that courtroom tomorrow to ensure that the *right* verdict is reached." He glanced around. "It's nearly noon. Care for some lunch?"

"No thanks," she said, and she walked sharply away.

On Thursday 12 February, Darwin's 200th anniversary, the final session of the hearing was held in another subterranean room, burrowed out of the London clay beneath St Paul's.

At least this was a grander chamber, Mary thought, its walls panelled with wood, its floor carpeted, and a decent light cast by a bank of electric bulbs. But this was evidently for the benefit of the eight cardinals who had come here to witness the final act of the trial. Sitting in their bright vestments on a curved bench at the head of the room, they looked oddly like gaudy Australasian birds, Mary thought irreverently.

Before them sat the court officials, led by Boniface Jones and completed by the earnest clerk with the rapidly scratching pen. The scribes from the chronicles scribbled and sketched. Anselm Fairweather, sitting away from his client-lover, looked excited, like a spectator at some sports event. Mary could see no guards, but she was sure they were present, ready to act if Alicia dared defy the will of this court. That ghastly coffin stood on its trestles.

And before them all, dressed in a penitent's white robe and with her wrists and ankles bound in chains, stood Alicia Darwin.

"I can't believe I volunteered for this farce," Mary muttered to Xavier Brazel. "I haven't contributed a damn word. And look at that wretched child."

"It is merely a formality," Xavier said. "The robe is part of an ancient tradition which—"

"Does the authority of a 2,000-year-old Church really rely on humiliating a poor bewildered kid?"

He seemed faintly alarmed. "You must not be seen to be

disrespecting the court, Mary." He leaned closer and whispered, "And whatever Anselm said to you I'd advise you to disregard it."

She tried to read his handsome, impassive face. "You choose what to hear, don't you? You have a striking ability to compartmentalize. Maybe that's what it takes to survive in your world."

"I only want what is best for the Church – and for my friends, among whom I would hope to count you."

"We'll see about that at the end of this charade, shall we?"

As before Jones began proceedings with a rap of a gavel; the murmuring in the room died down. Jones faced Alicia. "Alicia Darwin, daughter of James Paul Darwin of Edinburgh. Kneel to hear the clerical condemnation, and the sentence of the Holy See."

Alicia knelt submissively.

Jones picked up a sheet of paper and began to read in his sonorous Latin. Xavier murmured a translation for Mary.

"*Whereas he, the deceased Charles Robert, son of Robert Waring Darwin of London, was in the year 1859 denounced by the Holy Office for holding as true the false doctrine taught by some that the species of living things that populate the Earth are mutable one into the other, in accordance with a law of chance and selection, and in defiance of the teaching of the divine and Holy Scripture that all species were created by the Lord God for His purpose, and having published a book entitled* A Dialogue on the Origin of Species by Natural Selection. *Whereas he the said Darwin did fail to respect an injunction issued by the Holy Congregation held before his eminence the Lord Cardinal Joseph McInnery on 14 December 1859 to amend the said work to ensure an appropriate balance be given to argument and counter-argument concerning the false doctrine . . .*"

The Commissary's pronouncements went on and on, seeming to Mary to meld into a kind of repetition of the details of the previous session. It struck her how little thought had been applied to the material presented to this court, how little analysis had actually been done on the charges and the evidence, such as they were. The sheer anti-intellectual nature of the whole proceedings offended her.

And Alicia, kneeling, was rocking slightly, her face blanched, as if she might faint. The reality of the situation seemed to be dawning on her, Mary thought. But with a sinking heart she thought she saw a kind of stubborn determination on Alicia's face.

At last Boniface seemed to be reaching the end of his peroration. *"Therefore, involving the most Holy name of Our Lord Jesus Christ and His most glorious Mother, ever Virgin Mary, and sitting as a tribunal with the advice and counsel of the Reverend Masters of Sacred Theology and Doctors of both laws, we say, pronounce, sentence and declare that he, Charles Darwin, had rendered himself according to this Holy Office vehemently suspect of heresy, having held and believed a doctrine that is false and contrary to the divine and Holy Scripture, namely the doctrine known as "natural selection". Consequently, he has incurred all the censures and penalties enjoined and promulgated by the sacred Canons and all particular and general laws against such delinquents.*

"For adhering to the doctrine of the Origin of Species, let Darwin be anathema."

The chroniclers scribbled, excited; Mary imagined the telegraph wires buzzing the next day to bring the world the news that Charles Darwin had been formally, if posthumously, excommunicated.

But Alicia still knelt before the panel. The clerk came forward, and handed her a document. "A prepared statement," Xavier whispered to Mary. "She's not on trial herself, not under any suspicion. She's here to represent Darwin's legacy. All she has to do is read that out and she'll be free to go."

Alicia, kneeling, her voice small in the room before the rows of churchmen, began to read: "I, Alicia Rosemary Darwin, daughter of James Paul Darwin of Edinburgh, arraigned personally at this tribunal and kneeling before you, most Eminent and Reverend Lord Cardinals, Inquisitors General against heretical depravity throughout the whole Christian Republic . . ." She fell silent and read on rapidly. "You want me to say the *Origin of Species* was heretical. And to say my uncle deliberately defied the order to modify it to remove the heresy. And to say I and all my family abjure his memory and all his words for all time."

Boniface Jones' gravel-like voice sounded almost kind. "Just read it out, child."

She put the papers down on the floor. "I will not."

And this was the moment, Mary saw. The moment of defiance Anselm had coached into her.

There was uproar.

The chroniclers leaned forward, trying to hear, to be sure what Alicia had said. Anselm Fairweather was standing, the triumph barely disguised on his face. Even the cardinals were agitated, muttering to one another.

Only Boniface Jones sat silent and still, a rock in the storm of noise. Alicia continued to kneel, facing him.

When the noise subsided Boniface gestured at the clerk. "Don't record this. Child – Alicia. You must understand. *You* have not been on trial here. The heresy was your distant uncle's. But if you defy the will of the tribunal, if you refuse to read what has been given to you, then the crime becomes yours. By defending your uncle's work you would become heretical yourself."

"I don't care." She poked at the paper on the floor, pushing it away. "I won't read this. My family doesn't "abjure" Charles Darwin. We honour him. We're not alone. Why, the Reverend Dawkins said only recently that natural selection is the best hypothesis anybody ever framed . . ."

Mary whispered to Xavier, "And I wonder who put that in her mouth?"

"You mean Anselm Fairweather."

"You know about him?"

"He's hardly delicate in his operations."

"This is exactly what Anselm and his spooky friends want, isn't it? To have this beautiful kid throw herself to the flames. Smart move. I can just imagine how this will play back home."

Xavier frowned. "I can hear how angry you are. But there's nothing you can do."

"Isn't there?"

"Mary, *this is the Inquisition.* You can't defy it. We can only see how this is going to play out."

His words decided her. "Like hell." She stood up.

"What are you doing?"

"Injecting a little common sense from Terra Australis, that's what." Before Xavier could stop her she strode forward. She tried to look fearless, but it was physically difficult to walk past the angry faces of the cardinals, as if she was the focus of God's wrath.

She reached the bench. Boniface Jones towered over her, his face like thunder. Alicia knelt on the floor, the pages of the statement scattered before her.

Anselm was hovering, desperate to approach. Mary pointed at him. "You – stay away." She reached out a hand to Alicia. "Stand up, child. Enough's enough."

Bewildered, Alicia complied.

Mary glared up at Boniface. "May I address the bench?"

"Do I have a choice?" Boniface asked dryly.

Mary felt a flicker of hope at that hint of humour. Maybe Boniface would prove to be a realist. "I hope we all still have choices, Father. Look, I know I'm from the outside here. But maybe we can find a way to get out of this ridiculous situation with the minimum harm done to anybody – to this girl, to the Church."

Alicia said, " I don't want your help. I don't care what's done to me—"

Mary faced her. "I know you never spoke to me before in your life. But just listen, if you don't want to die in prison, serving the dreams of your so-called lover."

Alicia frowned, and glanced at Anselm.

Mary turned to Boniface. "This is a spectacle. A stunt, so the Church can show its muscles. Even death doesn't put an enemy out of your reach, right? So you dug up poor Darwin here and excommunicated him posthumously. But in your wisdom, and I use the word loosely, you decided even that wasn't enough. You wanted more. But it's all unravelling. Can't you see, Commissary, if you prosecute this innocent kid for being loyal to her family, how much harm you will do to the Church's image – even in your home territories, and certainly outside? You should come visit Cooktown some time. Imagine how this

580 *Stephen Baxter*

would play out there. If you punish this girl, you'll be doing precisely what your enemies want you to do."

"What would *you* have me do, Lector?"

"Your problem is with Darwin, not his remote grand-niece. If excommunication's not enough, punish *him* further. There are precedents in history. In the year 1600 Giordano Bruno was burned at the stake for his various heresies. But the punishment didn't end there. His bones were ground to dust! That showed him. So take Darwin's mouldering corpse out of that box and hang it from Tower Bridge. Grind his bones and scatter them on the wind. Whatever — I'm sure your imagination can do better than mine in coming up with ways to debase a dead man. Then you'll have the public spectacle you want, without the cruelty."

Boniface considered, his eyes hooded over those flaps of blackness. "But the holy court heard the girl defy me."

Xavier approached now. "I for one heard nothing, Holy Father. A cough, perhaps. I'm sure there is no reliable transcript."

Boniface nodded. "Hmm. You should consider a career in politics, Lector Mason. Or the Church."

"I don't think so," she said vehemently.

"I must consult my colleagues. You may withdraw." He turned away, dismissing her.

Mary grabbed Alicia by the arm and walked her away from the bench. "Let's get you out of here, kid."

Anselm followed, agitated. "What did you do? Alicia, you need to go back – Lector, let her go—" He reached for Alicia.

Xavier said, "I wouldn't advise it, Mr Fairweather."

Mary hissed, "Back off, kid. You'll get your martyr. Darwin's as much an intellectual hero as Galileo ever was. How do you think it's going to reflect on the Church to have his very bones abused in this grotesque way? You'll get the reaction you want, the anger, the disgust – with any luck, the mockery. And, look – you heard me speak about what the Aboriginal astronomers have discovered, back home. The expansion of the universe, building on Galileo's own work. The truth has a way of working its way out into the open. The Church has clung on for centuries, but its hold is weakening. You don't need to sacrifice Alicia to the Inquisition."

The blood had drained from Alicia's face. Perhaps she saw it all for the first time.

But Anselm still faced her. "Come with me, please, Alicia."

Alicia looked from Mary to Anselm. "Lector Mason – if I could stay with you – just until I get my thoughts sorted out—"

"Of course."

Xavier leaned forward. "Go, Lyncean. And I'd advise you, boy, never to come to the attention of the Inquisition again."

Anselm stared at the three of them. Then he turned and ran.

Mary looked at Xavier. "So how long have you known he was with this Academy?"

"A while."

"You're lenient."

"He's harmless. You know me by now, I prefer to avoid a fuss. The Church survived the fall of Rome, and Galileo and Darwin. It will survive a pipsqueak like Anselm Fairweather."

"So will you help us get out of here?"

He glanced back at Boniface. "I suspect the court will find a way to close this hearing gracefully. Nothing more will be asked of Miss Darwin. Umm, her clothes—"

"I don't care about my clothes," Alicia said quickly. "I just want to get out of this place."

"You and me both," Mary said. "You can borrow my coat." She started walking Alicia towards the door.

"Anselm set me up, didn't he?"

"I'm afraid so, dear."

"He said no harm would come to me if I refused to say anything bad about Charles Darwin. I believed him. Of course I did. He was my lawyer, and my, my—"

"Don't think about it now. Come see my hotel room. It's got a great view of the Place de Louis XVI. You can see right up Napoleon's nose. You know, I'm thinking of a trip up to Edinburgh. You have family there? I hear the air is cleaner. Why don't you come? And I'm thinking of booking an early berth back home. Maybe you can come visit."

"Are you serious?"

"Why not? After all, your uncle Charles was a traveller, wasn't he? Maybe it's in the blood. I think you'd like Terra Australis . . ."

Talking quietly, following Xavier through the warren under St Paul's, Mary led Alicia steadily towards the light of day.

About the Authors

A. A. Attanasio is the author of twenty-three novels and two short story collections. Alfred Angelo Attanasio lives by his imagination in a volcanic rift valley on the world's most remote island chain. With a background in biochemistry and linguistics, he burst upon the world with *Radix* in 1981 and has continued to astonish since with his complex, poetic, transformational works.

Stephen Baxter originally trained as an engineer, obtaining degrees in both mathematics and engineering at Cambridge and Southampton universities respectively. His first short fiction began to appear in the late 1980s and his first novel, *Raft*, was published in 1991. It has been followed by more than thirty subsequent novels, which have seen Stephen established as one of the UK's most significant SF authors. Renowned for its advanced theories and groundbreaking ideas, his work has earned him such honours as the Philip K. Dick, the Campbell, the BSFA, the Sidewise and Locus awards.

Gregory Benford is a physicist and identical twin (who better to study the Einstein twin paradox?). He's famous for "hard" SF with a poetic edge, notably featuring a cosmic struggle between biological and machine life. His breakthrough novel *Timescape*, about an urgent message sent into the past, shows what real scientists do. As well as researching stellar plasma jets, he co-founded Genescient to pursue longevity therapeutics which might enable people to live till 150. He has also co-edited a number of alternative history anthologies.

Eugene Byrne is a freelance journalist and fictioneer; he met Kim Newman at school, leading subsequently to several collaborations as well as to solo pieces such as "HMS Habakkuk" which was shortlisted for the Sidewise Award for Alternative History. Besides, he has written books about the city of Bristol and the engineer Isambard Kingdom Brunel.

Pat Cadigan is the author of fifteen books, including two short story collections, two non-fiction movie books and one young adult novel. In 1981 Pat and her then-husband Arnie Fenner won the World Fantasy Award for *Shayol*, though it was not until 1987 that she chose to pursue writing full-time. Dubbed "The Queen of Cyberpunk", she has since won a brace of both Arthur C. Clarke Awards and Locus Awards. Pat was born in Schenectady, New York, and educated at the universities of Massachusetts and Kansas before moving to England in 1996. She currently lives in North London with her husband, the original Chris Fowler, her son, and Miss Kitty Calgary: Queen of the Cats and Everything Else in the Universe!

Suzette Haden Elgin's SF writing is now focused on a future US that has a US Corps of Linguists (USCOL) analogous to the US Corps of Engineers, with linguists who must deal not only with Terran languages but with extraterrestrial ones. She has published two short stories in that fictional universe – "Honor Is Golden" and "We Have Always Spoken Panglish". As well, she has published two books on science fiction poetry – *The Science Fiction Poetry Handbook*, for which all royalties go to the Science Fiction Poetry Association, and *Twenty-One Novel Poems*, both with Sam's Dot Publishing; a number of the poems in the latter are set in the USCOL universe. You'll find homepages for her books at www.sfwa.org/members/elgin; just click on the "site map" link. And those books include the remarkable

Native Tongue about the creation of a "womanlanguage" which she has pioneered.

Esther Friesner is the Nebula Award-winning author of thirty-five novels and over 150 short stories. She has also edited seven popular anthologies and is a published poet and a produced playwright. Educated at Vassar College, gaining a BA degree in both Spanish and Drama, she went on to receive her MA and PhD in Spanish from Yale University, where she taught for a number of years. She is married, the mother of two, and lives in Connecticut. Currently she's working on two books for Random House about young Nefertiti, *Sphinx's Princess* and *Sphinx's Queen*, as well as *Burning Roses* for Penguin.

Pierre Gévart is currently editor-in-chief of France's outstanding SF magazine *Galaxies*. Starting out as an industrial designer, he then studied geology and taught natural sciences in Morocco before joining the École nationale d'administration, the French equivalent of Harvard. A senior civil servant and university professor and director, he developed a parallel literary career in theatre (with regular performances of his plays) and in SF, producing dozens of short stories and several novels. "The Einstein Gun" received the Prix Infini in 2001 in its original French version "Comment les choses se sont vraiment passées" ("How Things Really Happened").

Harry Harrison was born in Stamford, Connecticut in 1925 and was drafted into the army on his eighteenth birthday. His experiences during the Second World War left him less than enamoured with the military, sentiments which were made manifest in his satirical novel *Bill, the Galactic Hero*. In a career that has spanned more than fifty years he has produced a canon of highly respected stories, often reflecting his interest in environmental issues and non-violent resolutions to conflict. He will perhaps always be most associated with *The Stainless Steel Rat* and the novel *Make Room! Make Room!*, which formed the basis for the film *Soylent Green*. In 2009 he was awarded Grand Master status by the Science Fiction Writers of America.

Marc Laidlaw is the author of six novels, including the International Horror Guild Award winner, *The 37th Mandala*. His short stories have appeared in numerous magazines and anthologies since the 1970s. In 1997 he joined Valve Software as a writer and creator of Half-Life, which has become one of the most popular videogame series of all time. He lives in Washington State with his wife and two daughters, and continues to write occasional short fiction between playing too many video games.

Fritz Leiber was an expert chess player and a champion fencer, who might have followed his parents' example by becoming an actor or even trained to be a priest, but instead became a highly respected writer. Born in 1910, Leiber's earliest writings were inspired by H. P. Lovecraft, but he went on to encompass science fiction, fantasy and horror with equal success. In Fafhrd and the Gray Mouser he produced two of the most enduring and scurrilously endearing characters in fantasy. He won his first Hugo Award in 1958 with *The Big Time* (originally written as a one-act play) and followed this with six more. "Catch that Zeppelin" was one of three stories to win both the Hugo and Nebula, while his novel *Our Lady of Darkness* won the World Fantasy Award and another, *Conjure Wife*, has been made into a movie on three separate occasions. Reflecting his cross-genre dexterity, Leiber was awarded Grand Master of Fantasy status in 1975, Nebula Grand Master in 1980, and received the Bram Stoker Award for Life Achievement in 1987. He passed away in September 1992.

Paul McAuley worked as a research biologist in various universities, including Oxford and UCLA, and for six years was a lecturer in botany at St Andrews University, before he became a full-time writer. He has published more than seventy short stories, and his novels have won the Philip K. Dick Memorial Award, the Arthur C. Clarke Award, the John W. Campbell Memorial Award, and the Sidewise Award. The latest are *The Quiet War* and *Gardens of the Sun*. He lives in North London.

Ian R. MacLeod wrote this story after reading the excellent *White Mughals* by William Dalrymple about the British in the court of Hyderabad in the late 1700s, and began pondering the strange circumstance of an island as tiny as Britain gaining power over a civilization as great as India's. Then, the SF writer in him started wondering what things would have been like if it had been the other way around. He has a new short story collection due out soon from Subterranean Press, and has recently finished a novel set in an alternate version of Hollywood's Golden Age called *Wake Up and Dream*. He's been writing in and around the genre for many years, has published five novels to date and three short story collections. He lives in the riverside town of Bewdley, Worcestershire.

Ken MacLeod was born in Stornoway, Isle of Lewis, Scotland, on 2 August, 1954. He has an Honours and Masters degree in biological subjects and worked for some years in the IT industry. Since 1997 he has been a full-time writer, and is currently Writer in Residence at the ESRC Genomics Policy and Research Forum at Edinburgh University. He is the author of twelve novels, from *The Star Fraction* (1995) to *The Restoration Game* (2009), and many articles and short stories. His novels have received two BSFA Awards and three Prometheus Awards, and several have been short-listed for the Clarke and Hugo Awards. He is married with two children and lives in West Lothian.

James Morrow worked variously as an English teacher, a cartoonist and an independent filmmaker before succumbing to the fiction writing bug. Born in Philadelphia in 1947, he graduated from the University of Pennsylvania with a BA and then Harvard with a Masters. His first novel, *The Wine of Violence*, was published in 1981 and has since been followed by ten more, several of which have been shortlisted for Hugo, Nebula and Arthur C. Clarke Awards. Indeed, his short story "Bible Stories for Adults, No. 17: The Deluge" and novella "City of Truth" have both been awarded Nebulas, while his novel *Only Begotten Daughter* won the World Fantasy Award in 1991. Dubbing himself a "scientific humanist", his work frequently satirizes organized religion, humanism and atheism alike.

Kim Newman is a versatile author who specializes in giving a new spin to figures from history, frequently from the world of showbiz, although not neglecting a vampiric Queen Victoria and her court, since he also relocates other author's characters, such as Dracula, to new settings. His vampiresse Geneviève Dieudonné is so remarkable that she features as three different avatars in his works. Besides, he's a formidable genre film critic, a living encyclopaedia of Horror, SF and Gothic movies. Needless to say, at one time he also moonlighted as a kazoo player.

Frederik Pohl is one of the Olympians of SF, consequently the title of his story reprinted here seems rather appropriate. Amazingly, he has flourished since the late 1930s, editing award-winning SF magazines (and anthologies), acting as agent for many famous names in the field, but above all writing, often ironically and thrillingly, as in his famous collaboration with Cyril Kornbluth, *The Space Merchants*, and also in visionary vein as in his Hechee novels, the first of which, *Gateway*, won the hat trick of the Hugo, Nebula and John W. Campbell Memorial Awards.

Chris Roberson is a Texan whom Michael Moorcock has hailed as "one of that bold band of young writers who are taking the stuff of genre fiction and turning it into a whole new literary form". Particularly noted for his alternative history novels and stories, he won the 2003 Sidewise Award for Best Alternate History in the short form category, with "O One", reprinted here. After various occupations, including seven years as a product support engineer for Dell computers, he quit the world of wages to found with his spouse Allison Baker the independent publisher MonkeyBrain Books.

Keith Roberts wrote at the end of the 1960s one of the most famous and elegant alternative histories, *Pavane*, about an England dominated by the Church of Rome 400 years after

Elizabeth I was assassinated and the Spanish Armada triumphed; although he also wrote a splendid non-alternative historical novel about the dying of the Roman Empire, *The Boat of Fate*; and much else besides of high merit, which alas gained him little in life. According to an obituary published in 2000, he grew to hate the story reprinted here because it dominated public perception of him, simply by being so good, at the expense of his other stories. We plead guilty to reprinting it.

Kim Stanley Robinson was born in Illinois in 1952 but grew up in southern California. He holds a BA in literature and an MA and PhD in English, is a keen mountain climber and a frequent victim of scientific fascinations, which subsequently surface in his writing. The fifteen years of research he invested in his best-known work, the Martian trilogy, were rewarded when the three books received great acclaim both within the genre and beyond. Between them, they garnered two Hugo, one Nebula, two Locus and one BSFA Award. His wider work has received many other accolades, including a World Fantasy Award, a Campbell, and several Locus Awards.

Rudy Rucker has the distinction of being the great-great-great-grandson of the philosopher Hegel. Rudolph von Bitter Rucker (to grant him his full glory) has specialized mathematically in such matters as multiple dimensions and infinity, the latter being the subject of his first novel *White Light*. Numerous gonzo bravura novels followed, in the transrealist vein which he pioneered, one of the loveliest recently being *Mathematicians in Love*. He edits the avant-garde webzine *Flurb*. During a very brief sojourn in jail in Lynchburg, VA, he shared a cell with a black guy with the name of Other Rucker – that's transrealism for you!

Tom Shippey is currently Professor of Literature at St Louis University, Missouri. He went to the same school as Tolkien and later occupied Tolkien's chair at the University of Leeds, UK. Can it be a coincidence that he has written several highly regarded books about Tolkien? Besides, he edited *The Oxford Book of SF Stories* and *The Oxford Book of Fantasy Stories*, as well as being co-author with Harry Harrison (writing as John Holm) of *The Hammer and The Crown* trilogy of alternative history fantasy novels.

Pamela Sargent studied philosophy, ancient history and Greek in college, after which she continued to live in New York State, creating an awesome oeuvre ranging from big novels about the terraforming of the planet Venus ("a new high point in humanistic science fiction," said Gregory Benford) to *Ruler of the Sky*, a truly epic novel of Genghis Khan, told largely from the viewpoint of women, prefiguring the no less ambitious *Climb the Wind*, an alternative history novel in which the Plains Indians, akin to the Mongols under Genghis Khan, unite behind a strong leader to defeat an America weakened by the Civil War. Besides, she edited the landmark *Women of Wonder* anthologies of SF written by women about women, and authored several Young Adult novels, of which *Earthseed* was chosen as a Best Book by the American Library Association. Along the way, she picked up the Nebula and Locus Awards.

Robert Silverberg is elegant both in style and demeanour. Thoroughly Californian for many years, he is somewhat the Clint Eastwood of SF, perhaps. From being a prodigious word-smith in the Spaghetti Western fiction factory of New York (as it were), he upgraded and transcended to the passionate and anguished artistry of such novels of human and transhuman destiny as *Dying Inside*, *The Book of Skulls*, *Downward to the Earth*, *The Stochastic Man*, and various other masterpieces, before taking a four-year break to cultivate his cactus garden, emerging as epic science fantasy author of the Lord Valentine novels set on the giant world of Majipoor. His polished and perceptive short stories occupy many volumes. History fascinates him, as witness his novel *Gilgamesh the King* and his tales of a Roman Empire that never fell.

Judith Tarr is the author of numerous volumes of historical fiction, historical fantasy and alternate history. Other works in the Matière de France include the novels *His Majesty's Elephant*

(1993) and *Kingdom of the Grail* (2000). She has most recently published a pair of historical fantasies set in the world and time of Alexander the Great, *Queen of the Amazons* and *Bring Down the Sun*, and as Kathleen Bryan has published the War of the Rose fantasy series, most recently *The Last Paladin* (2009). She lives in Arizona, USA, where she breeds and trains Lipizzaner horses.

Harry Turtledove was born in Los Angeles in 1949 and holds a PhD in Byzantine History from UCLA, where he subsequently returned to teach ancient and medieval history. An acknowledged master of "alternate history", he saw his first novels published in 1979 and has been a full-time writer since 1991. A prolific writer, he has produced several epic series, stories and novels, the majority set in alternative timelines, and has been credited with bringing alternate history to the attention of mainstream readers. His work has been recognized with numerous awards including a Hugo and two Sidewise Awards. He is married to novelist Laura Frankos.

George Zebrowski is the son of Poles who were taken as slave labour into the Nazi Reich. He came to America in 1951 and is much respected for the measured eloquence and philosophical themes of his numerous novels and stories, as well as an authority on the future of humanity, most famously in his *Macrolife* which portrays with grandeur and keen intelligence that future as dependent upon mobile habitats in space rather than upon the vulnerable surfaces of planets. Indeed, Sir Arthur Clarke hailed *Macrolife* as "altogether a worthy successor to Olaf Stapledon's *Star Maker*". Zebrowski's *Brute Orbits*, about penal colonies in space, won the 1999 John W. Campbell Memorial Award for best novel of the year. In his "Cliometricon" stories Zebrowski experimented with alternative histories, as he does in the tale included here, which incidentally pulls off the remarkable literary coup of presenting two points of view within a first-person narrative.